Alexander Dyce, John Webster

The Works of John Webster

With Some Account of the Author, and Notes

Alexander Dyce, John Webster

The Works of John Webster
With Some Account of the Author, and Notes

ISBN/EAN: 9783337279349

Printed in Europe, USA, Canada, Australia, Japan

Cover: Foto ©Andreas Hilbeck / pixelio.de

More available books at **www.hansebooks.com**

THE WORKS

OF

JOHN WEBSTER:

WITH

SOME ACCOUNT OF THE AUTHOR, AND NOTES.

BY THE

REV. ALEXANDER DYCE.

A NEW EDITION, REVISED AND CORRECTED.

LONDON:
GEORGE ROUTLEDGE AND SONS,
THE BROADWAY, LUDGATE.
NEW YORK: 416, BROOME STREET.
1877.

NOTICE.

IN this re-impression of Webster's Works (which were first collected and edited by me in 1830) I have considerably altered both
the Text and Notes throughout, and made some slight additions to
the Memoir of the poet. I have also excluded from the present
edition a worthless drama, which I too hastily admitted into the
former one,—*The Thracian Wonder*; for though it was published by
Kirkman as "written by John Webster and William Rowley," internal
evidence decides that Webster could no more have had a hand in it
than in another play called *The Weakest goeth to the Wall*, a portion
of which is ignorantly ascribed to him by Phillips: see p. xv., note.

A. DYCE.

DECEMBER, 1857.

CONTENTS.

SOME ACCOUNT

OF

JOHN WEBSTER AND HIS WRITINGS.

SELDOM has the biographer greater cause to lament a deficiency of materials than when engaged on the life of any of our early dramatists. Among that illustrious band JOHN WEBSTER occupies a distinguished place; and yet so scanty is our information concerning him, that in the present essay I can do little more than enumerate his different productions, and adduce proof that he was not the author of certain prose-pieces which have been attributed to him.

On the title-page of his *Monuments of Honour, &c.*, 1624, Webster is styled "Merchant-Tailor;" and in the Dedication to that pageant he describes himself as "one born free of the Merchant-Tailors' Company." * Hence Mr. Collier conjectures

---

* "Which favours done to *one born free of your company*, and your servant," &c. See p. 364. That "*your company*" means the Merchant-Tailors' Company, is certain,—John Gore, whom Webster addresses, being "a right worthy brother" of that "fraternity."

It was, of course, desirable that the Court-Books of the Merchant-Tailors' Company should be examined for the present work: and the important information, illustrative of personal history, which is afforded by wills, was too obvious not to cause a search to be made in Doctors'-Commons. But we cannot identify our poet with any of the Websters of whom notices have been there discovered.

The following extracts from the Court-Book of Merchant-Tailors'-Company were made for me by the Clerk, 26th Dec. 1828, strangers, by a new regulation of the Company, not being allowed to inspect their documents :—

From Court-Book, vol. i. fol. 557 ;
"Lune Xº die decembris 1571.
"Item   Anne Sylver, Widdowe, pñted and made free John Webster her late Apprentise."

From Court-Book, vol. ii. fol. 48 ;
"Lune XXº die Januarij Aº dm 1576.
"Item   John Palmer pñted John Webster his Apprtize and also made the snide Webster free."

From Court-Book, vol. vi. fol. 633 ;
"Lune Decimo Septimo die Novemb
"Anno Dm 1617.
"John Webster made free by Henry Clinckard his Mr."

b

that he was the son of the John Webster, Merchant-Tailor, to whom John and Edward Alleyn acknowledge themselves debtors in the following terms :—

"All men shall know by these presents that we, John Allein, cytysen and Inholder, of London, and Edward Allein, of London, gentleman, do owe and ar indebted unto John Webster, cytysen and merchauntayler of London, the somme of fyftene shyllynges of lawfull money of England, to be payed to the sayd John Webster, or his

---

From Index-Book to Freemen ;

"Webster Johes—ℐ Annam Silver, wid. 10 decembr   1571
Webster Johes—ℐ Johem Palmer, ... 20 Januarij   1576
Webster Joshes—ℐ Henricum Clinckard, 17 Novembris 1617."

There are no other entries about any John Webster between the years 1571 and 1617.

The following memoranda are derived from the Prerogative Office :

JOHN WEBSTER, clothworker, of London, made his will on the 5th August, 1625. He bequeaths to his sister, Jane Cheney, dwelling within seven miles of Norwich, 10l., with remainder, if she died, to her children, and if they died, to his sister Elizabeth Pyssing ; to whom he also left 10l., with remainder to her children. To his sister, Anne Webster, of Holand, in Yorkshire, the same sum, with remainder to her children. To his father-in-law, William Hattfield, of Whittington, in Derbyshire, 15l., and to his four children 4l. each. To his cousin, Peter Webster, and his wife, dwelling in Doncaster, 40s. each. To his cousin, Peter Webster, of Whittington, in Derbyshire, he gives 10l., and if he died before it was paid, it was to be given to his brother, who was a protestant, "for I hear that one brother of my cousin Peter is a papist." To William Bradbury, of London, shoemaker, 5l. To Richard Matthew, his (the testator's) son-in-law, 16l. He mentions his father-in-law, Mr. Thomas Farman. He gives his cousin, Edward Curtice, 1l. 2s. To his cousin, Edward Curtis, son of Edward Curtis, senior, 3l. He leaves the residue of his property to his brothers and sisters in law, by his wife ; specially providing that Elizabeth Walker should be one. He constitutes Mr. Robert Aungel, and his cousin, Mr. Francis Asb, citizens, his executors ; and his cousins, Curtis and Tayler, overseers of his will,—which was proved by his executors on the 7th October, 1625.

JOHN WEBSTER, of St. Botolph's-without-Aldgate, citizen and tallow-chandler, of London, made his will on the 16th February, 1628, and orders by it, that his body should be buried in the churchyard of that parish, as near to his nephew, John Webster, as might be. To Katherine, his wife, he gives some freehold and copyhold lands in Clavering, in Essex, for life, with remainder to his nephew, James Webster ; together with some property in Houndsditch, she paying 50s. quarterly to Mary Lee, wife of James Lee, of London, Merchant-Tailor. To his nephew, James Webster, he bequeaths lands in Sabridgeworth, in Herts, with two-thirds of his printed books, sword, pike, and other arms, when of full age, with reversion, if he died without heirs, to William Webster, alias Wilkinson. To his three sisters, Dorothy Wilkinson, Susan Nettleton, and Alice Brookes, his lands at Clavering, after the decease of his wife ; they paying to Mary Wigge, Barbara Brend, Agnes Loveband, widow, and Clement Campe, his wife's four sisters, 4l., each yearly. He afterwards describes the beforementioned William Webster, alias Wilkinson, as "the eldest son of my eldest sister, Dorothy Wilkinson, late wife of Richard Wilkinson, of Yorkshire." If the said William died without issue, the property so given him was to go to the testator's nephews, Thomas, son of Thomas Nettleton, and Edmund, son of Robert Brookes. He also mentions his nephew, Henry Wilkinson ; his niece, Isabel Nettleton, then under age ; his apprentice, John Wigge ; his niece, Elizabeth Brend, and her father, George Brende : to the children of John Alderston, of Chelmsford, he gives 10l. each ; and to his cousin, Benjamin Crabtree, 2l. : and directs that the beforementioned James Webster, when of age, shall surrender to Michael Wilkinson a close in Cawood, in Yorkshire, which was the testator's father's, and fell, by descent, to his (the testator's) brother, James Webster, who sold it to Michael Wilkinson. He appoints Mr. Thomas Overman, alderman and leatherseller, of London, the aforesaid John Alderston, and Thomas Santy, citizen and merchant-tailor, of London, overseers, and his wife Katherine, executrix, of his will, who proved it on the 12th Nov., 1641.

It is evident that both these persons died without issue.

assygnes, on the last day of September next inscwinge the date hereof, wherto wee binde us, our heyres and assygnes, by these prescutes. Subscrybed this xxv[th] day of July, 1591, and in the xxxiii of her Ma[ties] raygne.

JOHN ALLEIN
ED. ALLEYN."[*]

We are told that our poet was clerk of St. Andrew's, Holborn; and it is possible that during some period of his career he may have filled that office: but the statement rests on a comparatively late and questionable authority.[†]

From the researches of Mr. Collier we learn (presuming the person mentioned to be the dramatist) that he "resided in Holywell Street, among the actors," and that "Alice Webster, his daughter, was baptized at St. Leonard's on the 9th May, 1606." Mr. Collier adds; "If the following, from the same registers, relate to his marriage, it must have occurred when he was very young:—

'*Married. John Webster and Isabell Sutton*, 25 July, 1590.'

Our principal reason for thinking that it may refer to him is, that elsewhere in the register he is sometimes called merchant-tailor, a designation himself assumed in his City Pageant of 1624." [‡]

Like several other of his contemporaries, he was perhaps an actor as well as a dramatist; but when, in a tract (hereafter to be mentioned) called *Histrio-mastix*, &c., Hall and his coadjutor speak of "Webster the quondam *player*," they appear to have used the word "player" as equivalent to "writer of plays."

The following notices of Webster as a dramatist occur in Henslowe's *Diary*:—

"Lent unto W[m] Jube, the 3 of novmbr 1601, to bye stamell clothe for a clocke for *the Gwisse—Webster* . . . . . . } iij[li]."

"Lent unto the company, to lend the littell tayller, to bye fusthen and lynynge for the clockes for *the masaker of France*, the some of . } xxx[s]."

"Lent unto the company, the 8 of novmbr 1601, to paye unto the littell tayller, upon his bell for mackyne of sewtes for *the gwesse*, the some of . . . . } xx[s]."

"Lent unto the companye, the 13 of novmbr 1601, to paye the litell tayllor, Radford, upon his bill for *the Gwisse*, the some of . . } xx[s]."

---

[*] *The Alleyn Papers*, &c., p. 14, ed. Shakespeare Soc.
[†] "This Author [John Webster] was Clerk of St. Andrew's Parish in Holbourne," &c. Gildon's *Lives and Characters of the English Dram. Poets*, 1698, p. 146.—I searched the registers of St. Andrew's Church, but the name of Webster did not occur in them; and I examined the MSS. belonging to the Parish-Clerks' Hall, in Wood-street, with as little success.
[‡] *Memoirs of the Principal Actors in the Plays of Shakespeare.—Introd.* p. xxxii., ed. Shakespeare Soc.

"I'd at the apoyntment of the companye, unto the littell tayllor, in fulle payment of his Bille for *the Gwisse*, the 26 of novmbr 1601, some   .   .   .   .   } **xxiiij^s 6^d."** *

The play which Henslowe in the above entries calls *The Guise* or *The Massacre of France*, is mentioned by Webster himself, under the first title, as one of his "works."† It has not come down to us ; and therefore we cannot determine whether it was a rifaccimento of Marlowe's *Massacre at Paris* or an original piece :—I am strongly inclined to believe that it was the latter.—Again :—

"Lent unto the companye, the 22 of maij 1602, to geve unto Antoney Monday and Mihell Drayton, *Webster*, Mydelton and the Rest, in earneste of a Boocke called *sesers Falle*, the some of   .   .   } **v^{li}."‡**

We are naturally curious to know how these combined poets treated a subject which employed the pen of Shakespeare ; but *Cæsar's Fall* has perished.—Again :—

"Lent unto Thomas Downton, the 29 of maye 1602, to paye Thomas Dickers, Drayton, Mydellton, and *Webester*, and Mondaye, in fulle paymente for ther playe called *too harpes* [?], the some of   .   } **iij^{li}."§**

The Two Harpies (if such be the correct title, which is far from certain) no longer exists.—Again :—

"Lent unto Thomas Hewode and *John Webster*, the 2 of novmbr 1602, in earneste of a playe called *Cyrssmas comes but once a yeare*, the some of.   .   .   .   .   } **iij^{li}."**

"Lent unto John Deweke, the 23 of novmbr 1602, to paye unto harye chettell and Thomas Deckers, in pte of paymente of a playe called *Crysmas comes but once a yeare*, the some of   .   .   .   } **xxxx^s."**

"Pd at the apoyntment of Thomas Hawode, the 26 of novmbr 1602, to harey chettell, in fulle paymente of a playe called *Cryssmas comes but once a yeare*, the some of   .   .   .   .   .   } **xxxx^s."**

"Layd owt for the companye, the 9 of novmbr [*December ?*] 1602, to bye ij calleco sowtes and ij buckram sowtes, for the playe of *Cryssmas comes but once a yeare*, the some of .   .   .   .   .   } **xxxviij^s 8^d."**

"Sowld unto the companye, the 9 of desembr 1602, ij peces of cangable taffetie, to macke a womones gowne and a robe, for the playe of *crysmas comes but once a year*, some of   .   .   .   .   } **iiij^{li} x^s."∥**

Christmas comes but once a year is also lost.—In the same *Diary*, under October

* Henslowe's *Diary*, pp. 202, 203, 204, ed. Shakespeare Soc.
† Dedication to *The Devil's Law-case,*—p. 105.
‡ Henslowe's *Diary*, p. 221.   § *Id.* p. 222.   ∥ *Id.* pp. 243, 244, 245.

1602, are three entries relating to a play in Two Parts, entitled *Lady Jane*, the First Part the joint-production of Chettle, Dekker, Heywood, Smith and Webster, the Second Part composed (it would seem) by Dekker alone. These entries will be found in the introductory remarks on *The Famous History of Sir Thomas Wyatt ;* * which drama, with its text miserably mutilated and corrupted, is evidently nothing more than an abridgement of the Two Parts of *Lady Jane*, for it embraces the story of Suffolk's unfortunate daughter from her forced accession to her death.

The second edition of Marston's *Malcontent* appeared in 1604, not only "augmented" by the original author, but "with additions" by Webster,—who was well qualified to supply them, resembling, as he did, Marston in the masculine character of his mind and style. How much he contributed to this vigorously written but unpleasing play, it is impossible to ascertain.†

In 1607 were given to the press *The Famous History of Sir Thomas Wyatt* (which has been noticed above), and *Westward Ho*, and *Northward Ho*,—two comedies composed by Webster in alliance with Dekker.

Westward Ho and *Northward Ho* (the former of which was on the stage in 1605) ‡ are full of life and bustle, and remarkable for the light they throw on the manners and customs of the time. Though by no means pure, they are comparatively little stained by that grossness from which none of our old comedies are entirely free. In them the worst things are always called by the worst names : the licentious and the debauched always speak most strictly in character ; and the rake, the bawd, and the courtezan, are as odious in representation as they would be if actually present. But the public taste has now reached the highest pitch of refinement, and such coarseness is tolerated in our theatres no more. Some will perhaps maintain, that the language of the stage is purified in proportion as our morals have deteriorated, and that we dread the mention of the vices which we are not ashamed to practise ; while our forefathers, under the sway of a less fastidious but a more energetic principle of virtue, were careless of words and only considerate of actions.

In 1612 *The White Devil* was printed; a play of extraordinary power. The story, though somewhat confused, is eminently interesting ; and, though abounding in,—if not a little overcharged with,—fearful incidents, it has nothing which we are disposed to reject as incredible. What genius was required to conceive, what skill to embody, so forcible, so various, and so consistent a character as Vittoria ! We shall not easily find, in the whole range of our ancient drama, a more effective scene than that in which she is arraigned for the murder of her husband. It is truth itself. Brachiano's flinging down his gown for his seat, and then, with impatient ostentation, leaving it behind him on his departure ; the pleader's Latin exordium ; the jesting interruption of the culprit ; the overbearing intemperance of the

---

* See p. 182.   † See p. 322.   ‡ See p. 206.

Cardinal ; the prompt and unconquerable spirit of Vittoria ;—all together unite in producing on us an impression as strong as could result from an event of real life. Lamb, in his *Specimens of English Dramatic Poets*, speaks of the " innocence-resembling boldness" of Vittoria.* For my own part, I admire the dexterity with which Webster has discriminated between that simple confidence in their own integrity which the innocent manifest under the imputation of a great crime, and that forced and practised presence of mind which the hardened offender exhibits when brought to trial. Vittoria stands before her judges, alive to all the terrors that surround her, relying on the quickness of her wit, conscious of the influence of her beauty, and not without a certain sense of protection, in case of extreme need, from the interposition of Brachiano. She surprises by the readiness of her replies ; but never, in a single instance, has the author assigned to her any words which were likely to have fallen from an innocent person under similar circumstances. Vittoria is undaunted, but it is by effort. Her intrepidity has none of the calmness which belongs to one who knows that a plain tale can put down his adversary ; it is a high-wrought and exaggerated boldness,—a determination to outface facts, to brave the evidence she cannot refute, and to act the martyr though convicted as a criminal. Scattered throughout the play are passages of exquisite poetic beauty, which, once read, can never be forgotten.

Three Elegies on the most lamented death of Prince Henry appeared in 1613 : the part of this tract written by Webster, entitled *A Monumental Column*, &c., contains some striking lines, but nothing characteristic of its author.

In 1623 were published *The Duchess of Malfi* (first produced about 1616 †) and *The Devil's Law-case*. Of the latter of these plays the plot is disagreeable and far from probable ; but portions of the serious scenes are not unworthy of Webster. Few dramas possess a deeper interest in their progress, or are more touching in their conclusion, than *The Duchess of Malfi*. The passion of the Duchess for Antonio, a subject most difficult to treat, is managed with infinite delicacy : in a situation of great peril for the author, she condescends without being degraded, declares to her dependant that he is the husband of her choice without losing anything of dignity and respect, and seems only to exercise the privilege of rank in raising merit from obscurity. We sympathize from the first moment in the loves of the Duchess and Antonio, as we would in a long-standing domestic affection ; and we mourn the more over the misery that attends them because we feel that happiness was the natural and legitimate fruit of so pure and rational an attachment. It is the wedded friendship of middle life transplanted to cheer the cold and glittering solitude of a court : it flourishes but a short time in that unaccustomed sphere, and then is blasted for ever. The sufferings and death of the imprisoned Duchess haunt the mind like painful realities ; but it is the less necessary to dwell on them here, as no part of our author's

---

* See the quotation in p. 24, note, of the present work.   † See p. 54.

writings is so well known to the generality of readers as the scenes where they
are depicted. In such scenes Webster was on his own ground. His imagination
had a fond familiarity with objects of awe and fear. The silence of the sepulchre,
the sculptures of marble monuments, the knolling of church-bells, the cerements
of the corpse, the yew that roots itself in dead men's graves, are the illustrations
that most readily present themselves to his imagination. If he speaks of the force
of love, his language is,—

> " This is flesh and blood, sir ;
> 'Tis not the figure cut in alabaster
> Kneels at my husband's tomb ; " [*]

and when he tells us that

> " Glories, like glow-worms, afar off shine bright,
> But look'd to near, have neither heat nor light," [†]

we are almost satisfied that the glow-worm which Webster saw, and which suggested
the reflection, was sparkling on the green sod of some lowly grave.

*Monuments of Honour, &c. Invented and written by John Webster, Merchant-
Tailor*, 1624, is the very rarest[‡] of all our old city-pageants :—it is not by any
means the best.

In September 1624 Sir Henry Herbert licensed " A new Tragedy, called *A late
Murther of the Sonn upon the Mother*, written by Forde and Webster[§] " ; of which,
when we consider how well the terrible subject was suited to the powers of the two
writers, we cannot fail to regret the loss.

Appius and Virginia was printed in 1654. This drama is so remarkable for its
simplicity, its deep pathos, its unobtrusive beauties, its singleness of plot, and the
easy unimpeded march of its story, that perhaps there are readers who will prefer it
to any other of our author's productions.

I need hardly observe that *Appius and Virginia* must have been brought on the
stage long before 1654 : indeed, at that date Webster was, in all probability, dead.

In 1661, Kirkman, the bookseller, published, from manuscripts in his possession,
A Cure for a Cuckold and *The Thracian Wonder*, both of them, according to the title-
pages, " *Written by John Webster and William Rowley.*" Webster's hand may, I
think, be traced in parts of the former play. Of any share in the concoction of the
latter he certainly was guiltless. [||]

---

[*] P. 65. [†] P. 36, and p. 88.

[‡] The only copy of this pageant known to exist, is in the possession of the Duke of Devonshire, who,
with his usual liberality, allowed me to transcribe it.

[§] Chalmers's *Supplemental Apology*, &c., p. 218.

[||] *The Thracian Wonder* (which I inconsiderately reprinted in the first edition of the present collection)
is partly founded on the story of Curan and Argentile in Warner's *Albion's England*. A poetical tract,
founded also on the same portion of Warner's work, appeared in 1617, written by a *William* Webster,

The following lines* concerning our author are found in Henry Fitzgeffrey's *Notes from Blackfryers*, 1620;

> " But h' st ! with him, crabbed *Websterio*,
> The *play-wright, cart-wright :* whether ! either ! *ho—*
> No further. Looke as yee'd bee look't into ;
> Sit as ye woo'd be *read : Lord !* who woo'd know him !
> Was euer man so mangl'd with a *poem !*
> See how he drawes his mouth awry of late,
> How he scrubs, wrings his wrests, scratches his pate !
> A *midwife !* helpe ! By his *braines coitus*
> Some *Centaure* strange, some huge *Bucephalus*,
> Or *Pallas*, sure, ingendred in his braine :—
> Strike, *Vulcan*, with thy hammer once againe.
>   This is the *crittick* that, of all the rest,
> I'de not haue view mee ; yet I feare him least :
> Heer 's not a word *cursiuely* I haue *writ*,
> But hee'l *industriously* examine it,
> And in some 12 monthes hence, or thereabout,
> Set in a shamefull sheete my errors *out*.
> But what care I ? it *will* be so obscure
> That none shall vnderstand him, I am sure." Sig. F. 6.

An inquiry now arises,—was John Webster, the dramatist, the same John Webster who was author of *The Saints' Guide*, of a celebrated tract called *Academiarum Examen or The Examination of Academies*, and of a volume of sermons entitled *The Judgment set and the Books opened ?* Our dramatist, as we have seen, was a writer for the stage in 1601 ; and the first of the pieces just mentioned was printed in 1653 : if he was only twenty-five when he composed *The Guise*, he must have been about seventy-seven when *The Saints' Guide* appeared. Those who are inclined to

---

and entitled *The most pleasant and delightfull Historie of Curan, Prince of Danske, and the fayre Princesse Argentile, Daughter and Heyre of Adelbright, sometime King of Northumberland :* and Mr. Collier plausibly conjectures (*Poet. Decam.*, vol. i. p. 268.) that Kirkman's recollection of the poem by *William* Webster induced him to attribute the play to *John* Webster.

Kirkman was not scrupulous in such matters. He published, in 1657, *Lusts Dominion, or The Lascivious Queen*, and put on the title-page " *Written by Christofer Marloe, Gent.*," though we have positive proof that it could not have been composed by that poet : see my *Account of Marlowe and his Writings,— Works*, i. lviii.

In the "Introduction" to his edition of *The Dramatic Works of John Webster*, 1857, Mr. Hazlitt announces his intention of including among them, not only *The Thracian Wonder* (which he justly describes as " a stream of dulness "), but *The Weakest goeth to the Wall*. The latter play he assigns to Webster " upon the authority of Winstanley " ; not being aware that when Winstanley wrote as follows in his *Lives of the most famous English Poets*, 1687, p. 137, he was merely transcribing the blunders of Phillips in the *Theatrum Poetarum*, 1675 : " He [Dekker] was also an associate with John Webster in several well entertain'd Plays, viz. *Northward, hoe ! The Noble Stranger ; New Trick to cheat the Devil ; Westward, hoe ! The Weakest goes to the Wall ; and A Woman will have her will.*" Here we have three plays confidently attributed to Dekker and Webster, of which we are certain that they did not write a word : *The Noble Stranger* is by Sharpe ; *A New Trick to cheat the Devil*, by Davenport ; and *A Woman will have her will*, by Haughton ! So much for the "authority" of Winstanley, or rather, of Phillips. As to *The Weakest goeth to the Wall*,—from beginning to end it is written in a style utterly unlike that of Webster.

* For verses by Sheppard on Webster's *White Devil*, see p. 2 ; for verses by Middleton, W. Rowley, and Ford, on his *Duchess of Malfi*, see p. 56.

suppose that he was the author of that tract will not, of course, allow his advanced age to be employed as an argument against the probability of their hypothesis ; and it must be confessed that some persons at as late a period of life have produced works indicating that they retained the full possession of their intellectual powers. I shall presently, however, show that he was neither the author of it, nor of the other two pieces noticed above : in the meantime it is necessary to describe them more particularly.

The Saints Guide, or, Christ the Rule and Ruler of Saints. Manifested by way of Positions, Consectaries, and Queries. Wherein is contayned the Efficacy of acquired Knowledge ; the Rule of Christians ; the Mission and Maintenance of Ministers ; and the power of Magistrates in Spiritual things. By John Webster, late Chaplain in the Army, a 4to. tract, was first printed in 1653 : it was reprinted in the same form the following year, and also in 12mo. in 1699*. No trace of the eloquence of Webster the poet is visible in this dull and fanatical production. In his prefatory address, "To all that love the Lord Jesus Christ in Truth and Sincerity," the author says ; "For after the Lord, about eighteen years ago, had in his wonderfull mercy brought me to the sad experience of mine own dead, sinfull, lost, and damnable condition in nature, and fully shewed me the nothingness and help-lessness of creaturely power, either without or within me," &c. : and Mr. Collier, who endeavours to prove that the writer of *The Saints' Guide* and the dramatist are the same person, thinks that the words "damnable condition," which have just been quoted, "can hardly mean anything but his 'damnable condition' as a player†." Surely, not : in "damnable condition" there is no allusion to any profession the author might have followed, but merely to what he conceived to be his reprobate condition before he became a Saint.

Academiarum Examen, or the Examination of Academies. Wherein is discussed and examined the Matter, Method, and Customes of Academick and Scholastick Learning, and the insufficiency thereof discovered and laid open ; As also some Expedients proposed for the Reforming of Schools, and the perfecting and promoting of all kind of Science. Offered to the judgements of all those that love the proficiencie of Arts and Sciences, and the advancement of Learning. By Jo. Webster. In moribus et institutis Academiarum, Collegiorum, et similium conventuum, quæ ad doctorum hominum sedes, & operas mutuas destinata sunt, omnia progressui scientiarum in ulterius adversa inveniri. Franc. Bacon. de Verulamio lib. de cogitat. & vis. pag. mihi 14., appeared in 4to. in 1654. That the John Webster who wrote *The Saints' Guide* wrote the *Acad. Examen*, there can be no doubt : both pieces were put forth by the same publisher, Giles Calvert‡,

---

* The dedication to this edition is dated "April 28, 1663," which is doubtless an error of the printer for 1653 ; the two earlier editions, of which it is an exact copy, having the dedication dated April 28, 1653. † *Poetical Decameron,* vol. i. p. 262.

‡ "To conclude, the world may here see what stuffe still comes from Lame Giles Calvers shop, that forge of the Devil, from whence so many blasphemous, lying, scandalous Pamphlets, for many yeers past,

and a second edition of the former was printed during the year in which the latter came from the press. In an *Epistle to the Reader*, prefixed to the *Acad. Examen*, the author says; "I am no Dean nor Master, President nor Provost, Fellow nor Pensioner, neither have I tyths appropriate nor impropriate, augmentation, nor State pay, nor all the levelling that hath been in these times hath not mounted nor raised me, nor can they make me fall lower, *Qui cadit in terram, non habet unde cadat.* And he that would raise himself by the ruins of others, or warm himself by the burning of schools, I wish him no greater plague than his own ignorance, nor that he may ever gain more knowledge than to live to repent." Though the *Acad. Examen* contains a good deal of nonsense about the language of nature, astrology, &c.; and though all the theological portion of it is as ridiculous and fanatical as *The Saints' Guide*, yet, taken as a whole, it manifests variety of learning and clearness of judgment.

To this tract, during the year of its publication, two answers were written. The first was by Seth Ward, afterwards Bishop of Salisbury, and Dr. John Wilkins of Wadham College*; it is entitled, *Vindiciæ Academiarum, containing Some briefe Animadversions upon Mr. Websters Book, stiled The Examination of Academies. Together with an Appendix concerning what M. Hobbs and M. Dell have published on this Argument.* The authors had evidently never dreamed of their adversary being the once-celebrated dramatist. "I have heard from very good hands," says Wilkins, "that he [Webster] is suspected to be a Friar, his conversation being much with men of that way; and the true designe of this Booke being very suitable to one of that profession, besides that his superficiall and confused knowledge of things is much about that elevation." p. 6. "In complyance therefore with your desire," says Ward, "I mean to runne over this reverend Authour." p. 9. "You know, Sir," he afterwards says, "and have observed in your Letter to mee, how vast a difference there is betwixt the Learning and Reputation of Mr. Hobbs and these two Gentlemen, and how scornefully he will take it to be ranked with a Friar [Webster] and an Enthusiast." p. 51. The second answer to the *Acad. Examen* is called† *Histrio-Mastix. A whip for Webster (as 'tis conceived) the Quondam Player: or, An examination of one John Websters delusive Examen of Academies, &c. In the end there is annexed an elaborate defence of Logick, by a very Learned Pen.* Mark how carefully the words "as 'tis conceived," are inserted here! One half of this answer is the production of Thomas Hall, the puritan, of whom an account may

have spread over the land, to the great dishonour of the Nation, in the sight of the Nations round about us, and to the provocation of God's wrath against us, which will certainly breake forth, both upon the actors and tolerators of such intollerable errours, without speedy reformation and amendment."
Histrio-mastix, a Whip for Webster, &c. 1654, p. 215.

* Wilkins wrote only the Epistle to the Author, signed N. S.; the remainder is by Ward, signed H. D.: the signatures are the final letters of their names.

† This piece forms part of a small duod. volume, the general title of which is *Vindiciæ Literarum, The Schools Guarded, &c. &c.* By Thomas Hall, B.D. and Pastour of Kings-Norton.

be found in Wood's *Athenæ Oxonienses*, vol. iii. p. 677, ed. Bliss; the other half (the defence of Logic) is from the pen of a "reverend acute Logician," whose name is not given. "We see *then*," says Hall, addressing Webster, "who you are, viz. an Herculean Leveller, a Famalisticall Lion, a dissembling Fryar, a Profane *Stage Player*, a professed friend to Judiciall Astrology and Astrologers," &c. p. 198. In this passage we must observe that Hall merely takes it for granted from what had been said before, that the author of the *Acad. Examen* was a player. The "reverend acute Logician" commences his defence of the Stagirite thus: "This Mr. Webster (*as I suppose*) is that Poet whose Glory was once to be the Author of Stage-plaies (as the Devils Law-case) but now the Tutor of Universities. But because his Stage-Players [Stage-Plays] have been discountenanced by one of the late Parliaments, does hee therefore addresse himselfe to the Army, for the like force, and as little favour in behalfe of all Humane Learning; for advancement whereof, the best way being already found, he that seeks for another, desires worse (and so none at all), though he pretend to a Reformation. For my own part, I could wish that his Poetry still had flourished upon Mr. Johnson's [Ben Jonson's] account, in his Epistle before one of his Playes (the Fox) to the two most equal Sisters, the Universities (a far better address then this here); but it is odious to be like the Fox in the Fable, who having lost his owne Ornament, envied his fellows theirs by pretending burthen or inconvenience." pp. 217-18. In those days there could have been no difficulty in ascertaining whether the author of the *Acad. Examen* was or was not the quondam dramatist; and we may be sure that the puritanical Hall and his coadjutor must have made particular inquiries into the matter. If they had been in possession of the fact that their adversary had ever been guilty of play-writing or play-acting, they would not have left their readers in any doubt on the subject; they would never have used the expressions "as 'tis conceived," or "as I suppose;" they would have charged Webster with his theatrical sins in the most direct terms, and they would have alluded to them over and over again, with many a coarse and bitter taunt. They were quite aware that their adversary was not the dramatist *; and they had recourse to the supposition of his being that same person, as a likely means of bringing reproach upon him in times of canting and hypocrisy †.

---

* Mr. Hazlitt, after citing what I say above, proceeds as follows: "This, however, is perfectly clear to the present Editor, that the writers of *Histrio-Mastix* would not, for the very sake of their sneer, have 'conceived' or 'supposed' any such identity as that malignantly suggested, *had not John Webster, the quondam player, been still alive, and had he not, also, been connected in some way with one of the universities—perhaps he had been a teacher of elocution there.*" Introd. to *The Dram. Works of John Webster*, 1857, p. viii. Mr. Hazlitt has previously remarked; "There remains to be mentioned *one other occupation which Webster is said to have filled—that of College Tutor.*" p. vi.

That the dramatist was alive in 1654, I greatly doubt; that he never was a teacher of elocution at one of the universities, or a college-tutor, I am as certain as that he never was Archbishop of Canterbury.

† Mr. Collier, in the work already quoted, compares two passages of the *Acad. Examen* with two from the plays of our author:

"On p. 3 of the *Examen* is this excellent sentence, 'So humane knowledge is good and excellent, and

In 1654 appeared also a quarto volume, entitled *The Judgement Set, and the Bookes Opened. Religion Tried whether it be of God or of men. The Lord cometh to visit his Own, For the time is come that Judgement must begin at the House of God.*

To separate
$$\begin{cases} \textit{The Sheep from the Goats,} \\ \textit{and} \\ \textit{The Precious from the Vile.} \end{cases}$$

---

is of manifold and transcendent use, while moving in its own orb; but when it will see further than its own light can lead it, it then becomes blind and destroys itself.' This sentiment, but more tersely and poetically expressed, is in 'The White Devil':

> ' While we looke vp to heauen we confound
> Knowledge with knowledge : O I am in a mist !'

There is a resemblance. But it is stronger in the next quotation and comparison I shall make. On p. 15 of the *Examen* is this simile : ' Like a curious spiders web cunningly interwoven with many various and subtill intertextures, and fit for nothing but the insnaring, manacling, and intricating of rash, forward, unwary, and incircumspect men :' in the tragedy of ' The Duchess of Malfy' are the following parallel lines :

> ' the law to him
> Is like a fowle black cobweb to a spider ;
> He makes it his dwelling, and a prison
> To entangle those shall feed him.' "
>
> *Poetical Decameron*, vol. i., pp. 262-3.

Between the first two passages which Mr. Collier compares, it must be allowed that there is some resemblance : but the similarity of the second two affords no grounds for inferring that they proceeded from the same pen, as the following quotations (and those in note †, p. 201) decidedly show ;

> " Others report, it [law] is a spider's web
> Made to entangle the poore helplesse flies,
> Whilst the great spiders that did make it first,
> And rule it, sit i' th' midst secure and laugh."
>
> Field' *A Woman's a Weathercock*, ed. 1612, Sig. E.

> " Laws are like spider-webs, small flies are tane,
> Whiles greater flies break in and out againe."
>
> Brathwait's *Honest Ghost*, 1658, p. 79.

> " Law 's as a spider's-web, and ever was,
> It takes the little flies, lets great ones passe."
>
> *Id.*, p. 170.

> " our Laws
> Must be no Spider-webs to take small Flyes,
> And let the great ones 'scape."
>
> *Lady Alimony*, 1659, Sig. I 3.

> " Your Laws, like Spiders webs are not a snare
> For little flyes, that them the bigge may breake."
>
> Lord Sterline's *Tragedy of Cræsus*, act iii., sc. 2.
> *Recreations with the Muses*, 1637, p. 24.

" It had been more for your credit and comfort to have imployed your time and talent in defence of Languages, Arts, and Sciences, (especially in such a season as this, when so many decry them) then thus to weave the Spiders Web, which may peradventure catch some feeble flies, when stronger ones break thorough." *Histrio-mastix, A Whip for Webster*, &c. 1654, p. 199.

And to discover the Blasphemy of those that say,

They are	*Apostles,* *Teachers,* *Alive,* *Rich,* *Jewes,*	*but are*	*Found Lyars,* *Deceivers,* *Dead,* *Poore, blind, naked,* *The Synagogue of Satan.*

In severall Sermons at Alhallows Lumbard-street, By John Webster, A servant of Christ and his Church. Micah 3. 5. &c. Thus saith the Lord, concerning the Prophets that make my people erre, that bite with their teeth, aud cry peace : and he that putteth not into their mouths, they prepare war against him: Therefore night shall be upon them, that they shall not have A vision, &c. The Sun shall goe down over the prophets, and the Day shall be dark. Their Seers shall be ashamed, and the Deviners confounded : yea, they shall All cover their lips, for there is no answer of God. Little information concerning the author is to be gathered from these tedious effusions, which in style resemble the *Saints' Guide,* and which were published at the desire of his hearers, who were greatly delighted with his preaching, "apprehending it," says an Address to the Reader, "to be the Bridegroomes voyce in him, and therefore savory to them*." Webster was absent from London when they were printed : "he being now," says the same Address, "at a great distance from the Presse." "Here," says a second Address to the Reader, "thou shalt not find Terms of Art, nor quirks of humane Learning and Fallen Wisdom (though the party through whom it was conveied excel in natural acquirements as much as the most) but naked truth." . . . . "And hereby thou mayest see (if thou be not blind in the carnal conceits of thy earthly wisdom, as most of the Earthen Saints of our times are) what self-denial is wrought in this Creature, through which the Eternal Spirit hath breathed forth these ensuing precious Truths, that he having and enjoying all those humane Excellencies of Learning and knowledge which are so in the worlds account," &c. To the volume is appended *A Responsion To certaine pretended Arguments against my Book called The Saints Guide.*

We have already seen that an answer to the *Academiarum Examen* was written by Seth Ward, afterwards Bishop of Salisbury : and Dr. Walter Pope, in his Life of that prelate, expressly states that the author of the *Examen* was "one Webster *of Cletherow†*." In all matters connected with the Bishop, Dr. Pope's authority is

---

* The Church of Allhallows Lombard Street, with all the documents belonging to it, was destroyed by the great fire of London in 1666 : John Weston, the Rector, "was for his Loyalty sequestred by the Rebels, about 1642. [*Merc. Rust.* p. 253]." Newcourt's *Repertorium Ecclesiasticum Parochiale Londinense,* vol. i. p. 255. "He [Weston] was sequesterd by the House about July, 1643; at which time J. Cordell was, by the same authority, thrust in to succeed him." Walker's *Account of the Sufferings of the Clergy,* p. 180.

† A monument was erected to the memory of Bishop Ward by his nephew, with a Latin inscription, which Dr. Pope characterises as long, erroneous, heavy, and tedious, but which he gives with what he calls a "sifted and garbled" translation : the following passage of it—"contra ingruentem Fanaticorum

unquestionable. " I am not," says he, "altogether unprovided for such a Work, having, during my long acquaintance with Him and his Friends, informed myself of most of the considerable Circumstances of his Life." *Life of Seth, Lord Bishop of Salisbury*, 1697, p. 2. "And now I have brought him to Oxford, where I first became acquainted with him, I can proceed upon more certain grounds ; I promise not to put any thing upon the Reader now, but what either I know or have heard attested by those whom I could trust." *Id.* p. 22.

The two works next to be mentioned were indisputably written by John Webster of Clitheroe. One is *Metallographia : or, An History of Metals. Wherein is declared the signs of Ores and Minerals both before and after digging, the causes and manner of their generations, their kinds, sorts, and differences ; with the description of sundry new Metals, or Semi-Metals, and many other things pertaining to Mineral knowledge. As also, the handling and shewing of their Vegetability, and the discussion of the most difficult Questions belonging to Mystical Chymistry, as of the Philosophers Gold, their Mercury, the Liquor Alkahest, Aurum potabile, and such like. Gathered forth of the most approved Authors that have written in Greek, Latine, or High-Dutch ; With some Observations and Discoveries of the Author himself. By John Webster Practitioner in Physick and Chirurgery. Qui principia naturalia in seipso ignoraverit, hic jam multum remotus est ab arte nostra, quoniam non habet radicem veram supra quam intentionem suam fundet. Geber. Sum. perfect. l. c. i. p. 21.*

Sed non ante datur telluris operta subire,
Auricomos quam quis discerpserit arbore fœtus.

Virg. Æneid. l. 6.

London, Printed by A. C. for Walter Kettilby at the Bishops-Head in Ducklane*, 1671, 4to. The other is *The Displaying of supposed Witchcraft. Wherein is affirmed that there are many sorts of Deceivers and Impostors. And Divers persons under a passive Delusion of Melancholy and Fancy. But that there is a Corporeal League made betwixt the Devil and the Witch, Or that he sucks on the Witches Body, has Carnal Copulation, or that Witches are turned into Cats, Dogs, raise Tempests, or the like, is utterly denied and disproved. Wherein also is handled, the Existence of Angels and Spirits, the truth of Apparitions, the Nature of Astral and Sydereal Spirits, the force of Charms and Philters ; with other abstruse matters. By John Webster, Practitioner in Physick. Falsæ etenim opiniones Hominum præoccupantes, non solum surdos, sed & cæcos faciunt, ita ut*

---

barbariem quid litteris ubique præsteterit, vindicatæ agnoscunt Academiæ," Pope renders thus ; "he wrote . . . . also a Vindication of the Universities, in reply to one *Webster of Cletherow,* who had writ a Pamflet to prove them useless." *Life of Seth, Lord Bishop of Salisbury,* 1697, pp. 185, 188. In an earlier part of the work just quoted we are told, " Whilst he [Ward] continued in that Chair, besides his Public Lectures, he wrote several Books . . . . one, in English and a jocose stile, against *one Webster,* asserting the Usefulness of the Universities." p. 27.

   * Instead of " *Ducklane* " some copies have " *St. Paul's Church-yard.*"

videre nequeant quæ aliis perspicua apparent. Galen. lib. 8. *de Comp. Med., London, Printed by J. M. and are to be sold by the Booksellers in London,* 1677, folio. Now, Dr. Henry More has attacked John Webster's *Displaying of supposed Witchcraft* in his *Opera Philosophica;* and in the *" Præfatio Generalissima "* prefixed to that collection, 1679, he alludes as follows, not only to it, but also to another production of the same writer, which is manifestly the *Academiarum Examen:* " De modo autem quo in Scholiis eos exceperim qui nostra impugnaverint ; est sano, festivus licet aliquando & jocosus, perpetuo tamen benignus. Nec certe severi offensique animi larvam contra quenquam indui præterquam unum Websterum. Quem non sic tractâsse præter decorum profecto futurum fuisset, & omnino præteriisse pigrum quid & ignavum. Quis enim ferre potuit hominem Fatuum virorum optimorum doctissimorumque memoriæ tanto cum supercilio ac fastu insultantem & tanta præterea cum inscitia & imperitia ? Quis summis Philosophis summisque Legislatoribus, Mose ipso non excepto, crassæ ignorantiæ Notam, etiam eis in rebus de quibus statuunt, turpiter impudenterque inurentem ? Quis Theologum si placet, & in sacris, ut gloriatur, a Reverendo Episcopo, D^{re} M.*, Ordinibus olim institutum, ad Castra quasi Atheorum omnes Angelos mere corporeos faciendo transfugientem, et Animam tamen humanam, ne nimis obvium & expositum censuris hominum se redderet, fucate subdoleque profitendo immaterialem ? fœdumque passim seculi hujus Somatistici Parasitum se gerentem et Gnathonem ? Ut taceam quam maligne & quam imperite interim ac imbecilliter nostra vellicaverit, beneque a me provisa diligenterque explorata Principia quam impotenter, sed irrito prorsus opere labefactare conatus sit ; et cum ne intelligeret quidem quæ scripsi (ut videre est ex ineptis illius Objectionibus), quo usum tamen honestissimorum meorum studiorum fructumque in publicum frustrari posset, non objicientis solum sed & vincentis speciem, ad vulgo imponendum, ausus sit dare. Talem, inquam, nactus Adversarium, Academiarum porro nostrarum, eis temporibus quibus spes aliqua suberat nocendi, importunum Calumniatorem & Sycophantam, nunc vero abjectissimum Somatistarum Parasitum, miserumque sed impudentem Lamiarum Patronum, parum profecto putabam Objectiones ejus diluere, quod facillimo fit negotio, argumentaque allata confutare, nisi insulsam pariter hominis temeritatem intolerandamque insolentiam castigarem. Sic enim fas est & sic oportet fieri in hoc genus hominum, qui sanctissimum Philosophiæ nomen usurpantes, omnes bonos Philosophiæ fines misera sua immiscendo commenta subvertunt." p. xvi.†

Nor is evidence wanting in the works themselves that the *Academiarum Examen, The Displaying of supposed Witchcraft,* and the *Metallographia* were written by the same individual.

---

* See the second quotation from the *Displaying of supposed Witchcraft* in p. xxiv.

† This passage was kindly pointed out to me by my learned friend, Mr. James Crossley of Manchester.

The author of the *Acad. Examen* was educated at Cambridge.* "On the 12th of October, 1653," says Antony Wood, "he [i. e. William Erbury] with John Webster, sometimes a Cambridge scholar, endeavoured to knock down learning and the ministry together, in a disputation that they then had against two ministers in a church in Lombard Street in London." *Athen. Oxon.* vol. iii. p. 361, ed. Bliss. We must bear in mind while we read the preceding extract that the Sermons of the author of the *Acad. Examen* were preached in All-Hallows, Lombard Street. "As for Dell [who also attacked the Universities, and to whom Seth Ward wrote an answer, published together with his reply to Webster], he had been educated in Cambridge; and Webster, who was then, or lately, a chaplain in the parliament army, had, as I conceive, been educated there also." *Id.* vol. iv. p. 250. Webster of Clitheroe, we may gather from the following passage, had been educated at the same seat of learning: "But I that then [i. e. in my youth] was much guilty of curiosity, and loth to be imposed upon in a thing of that nature, then also knowing the way and manner how all the common Jugglers about Cambridge and London (who make a Trade of it) did perform their Tricks," &c. *The Displaying of supposed Witchcraft*, p. 62.

The author of the *Acad. Examen* was a preacher. Webster of Clitheroe, "practitioner in physic," had also received holy orders: "Dr. Thomas Morton, then Bishop of Coventry and Lichfield: to whose memory I cannot but owe and make manifest all due respect, because he was well known unto me, and by the imposition of whose hands I was ordained Presbyter when he was Bishop of Durham." *The Displaying of supposed Witchcraft*, p. 275. "About the year 1634, ... it came to pass that this said Boy was brought into the Church of Kildwick, a large parish Church, where I (being then Curate there) was preaching in the afternoon." *Id.* p. 277.

The author of the *Acad. Examen* had been an army-chaplain. Webster of Clitheroe, it may be inferred from the following passage, had served in the same capacity; "And it will as far fail, that wounded bodies, that have been slain in the wars, after the natural heat be gone, will upon motion bleed any fresh or crimson blood at all; for we ourselves in the late times of Rebellion have seen some thousands of dead bodies, that have had divers wounds, and lying naked and being turned over and over, and by ten or twelve thrown into one pit, and yet not one of them have issued any fresh and pure blood." *The Displaying of supposed Witchcraft*, p. 306.

The author of the *Acad. Examen* was a believer in astrology; so was Webster of Clitheroe. The author of the *Acad. Examen* was a devoted admirer of the mystic chemistry of Paracelsus, Helmont, &c.; so was Webster of Clitheroe.

---

* I could find no mention of any John Webster in the Indices to Cole's voluminous MS. collections in the Brit. Museum.

I proceed to exhibit some striking parallel passages from the *Academiarum Examen, The Displaying of supposed Witchcraft,* and the *Metallographia.*

"And it is true that supposed difficulty, and impossibility, are great causes of determent from attempting or trying of new discoveries and enterprises, for the sloathful person usually cryeth, go not forth, there is a Lion or Bear in the way; and if *Columbus* had not had the spirit to have attempted, against all seeming impossibilities and discouragements, never had he gained that immortal honour, nor the Spaniards been Masters of the rich *Indies,* for we often admire why many things are attempted which appear to us as impossible, and yet when attained, we wonder they were no sooner set upon and tried ; so though the means here prescribed may seem weak and difficult to be put into use, yet being practised may be found easy and advantagious. And I hope *newness* need not be a brand to any indeavor or discovery, seeing *it is but a meer relative to our intellects,* for that of which we were ignorant being discovered to us, we call new, which ought rather to mind us of our imbecility and ignorance, than to be any stain or scandal to the thing discovered ; for doubtlessly he said well that accounted Philosophy to be that which taught us *nihil admirari,* and admiration is alwaies the daughter of ignorance." *Acad. Examen, Epistle to the Reader.*

"Antiquity and *Novelty* are but *relations quoad nostrum intellectum, non quoad naturam ;* for the truth, as it is fundamentally in things *extra intellectum,* cannot be accounted either old or new. And an opinion, when first found out and divulged, is as much a truth then, as when the current of hundreds or thousands of years have passed since its discovery. For it was no less a truth, when in the infancy of Philosophy it was holden, that there was generation and corruption in Nature in respect of Individuals, than it is now : so little doth Time, Antiquity, or Novelty alter, change, confirm, or overthrow truth ; for *veritas est temporis filia,* in regard of its discovery to us or by us, who must draw it forth *è puteo Democriti.* And the existence of the *West Indies* was as well before the discovery made by *Columbus* as since, and our ignorance of it did not impeach the truth of its being, neither did the novelty of its discovery make it less verity, nor the years since make it more : so that we ought simply to examine, whether an opinion be possible or impossible, probable or improbable, true or false ; and if it be false, we ought to reject it, though it seem never so venerable by the white hairs of Antiquity ; nor ought we to refuse it, though it seem never so young or near its birth. For, as St. Cyprian said : *Error vetustatis est vetustas erroris."* *The Displaying of supposed Witchcraft,* p. 15.

"What shall I say of the Science or art of Astrology ? Shall the blind fury of Misotechnists and malicious spirits deter me from giving it the commendations that it deserves ? shall the Academics who have not only slighted and neglected it, but also scoffed at it, terrifie me from expressing my thoughts of so noble and beneficial a Science? . . . . And therefore I cannot, without detracting from worth and vertue, pass without a due Elogy in the commendation of my learned and industrious Countrymen, Mr. Ashmole, Mr. William Lilly, Mr. Booker, Mr. Sanders, Mr. Culpepper, and others, who have taken unwearied pains for the resuscitation and promotion of this noble Science, and with much patience against many unworthy scandals have laboured to propagate it to posterity, and if it were not beyond the present scope I have in hand, I should have given sufficient reasons in the vindication of Astrology." *Acad. Examen,* p. 51.

"And that there is and may be a lawful use of Astrology, and many things may be foretold by it, few that are judicious are ignorant." *The Displaying of supposed Witchcraft,* p. 28. "And that there are great and hidden virtues both in Plants and Minerals, especially in Metals and Precious Stones, as they are by Nature produced, by Mystical Chymistry prepared and exalted, or commixed and insculped in their due and fit constellations, may not only be proved by the instances foregoing, but also by the reasons and authorities of persons of great judgment and experience in the secrets of nature, &c. . . . . Neither are those arguments of that learned person Galleotus Martius, for defending the natural and lawful effects of Planetary Sigills, when prepared forth of agreeable matter, and made in their due constellations, of such small weight as some insipid ignorants have pretended, but are convincing to any considerate and rational person." *Id.* p. 161.

"What shall I say of Staticks, Architecture, Pneumatithmie, Stratarithmetric, and the rest enumerated by that expert and *learned* man, *Dr. John Dee, in his Preface before Euclide?*" *Acad. Examen,* p. 52.

"Another of our Countrymen, *Dr. John Dee,* the greatest and ablest Philosopher, Mathematician, and Chymist that his Age (or it may be ever since) produced, could not evade the censure of the Monster-headed multitude, but even in his life time was accounted a Conjurer, of which he most sadly (and not without cause) complaineth *in his most learned Preface to Euclid.*" *The Displaying of supposed Witchcraft,* p. 7.

"Was not Magick amongst the Persians accepted for a sublime Sapience, and the science of the universal consent of things? And were not those men (supposed Kings) that came from the East styled by that honourable name Μαγοί, Magi, or Wisemen, which the Holy Ghost gives unto them, thereby to denote out that glorious mystery of which they were made partakers by the revelation of that spirit of life and light? Neither do I here Apologize for that impious and execrable Magick, that either is used for the hurt and destruction of mankind, or pretends to gain knowledge from him who is the grand enemy of all the sons of Adam; no, that I truly abominate. . . . . But that which I defend is that noble and laudable Science," &c. *Acad. Examen*, p. 69.

"It was not in vain superstitious Magick (wherewith, as Couringius laboureth to prove, they were much infected), but in the laudable Sciences of Arithmetick, Politicks, Geometry, Astronomy, and their Hieroglyphick learning, which doubtless contained natural and lawful Magick (such as those Magicians were partakers of, that came to worship Christ, whose learning all the Fathers and Interpreters do justifie to be good, natural, and lawful), the Art of Medicine, and knowledge of natural and artificial things, as in the next Branch we shall more at large make appear." *Metallographia*, p. 8.

"Paracelsus, that singular ornament of Germany." *Acad. Examen*, p. 70.

"That *totius Germaniæ decus, Paracelsus.*" *The Displaying of supposed Witchcraft*, p. 9.

"Now how false the Aristotelian Philosophy is in itself is in part made cleer, and more is to be said of it hereafter, and therfore truth and experience will declare the imperfection of that medicinal knowledge that stands upon no better a basis. For Galen, their great Coryphœus and Antesignanus, hath laid down no other principles to build medicinal skill upon, than the doctrine of Aristotle ; . . . . For this same author . . . . hath said enough sufficiently to confute and overthrow the whole Fabrick of the Galenical learning, which here I forbear to insert. And therefore it is very strange that the Schools, nay, in a manner, the whole world, should be inchanted and infatuated to admire and own this ignorant Pagan [Galen], who being ambitious of erecting his own fame," &c. *Acad. Examen*, pp. 72-3. "That neither antiquity nor novelty may take place above verity, lest it debarre us from a more diligent search after truth and Science. Neither that universality of opinion be any president or rule to sway our judgements from the investigation of knowledge ; for what matter is it whether we follow many or few, so the truth be our guide ? for we should not follow a multitude to do evil, and it is better to accompany verity single, than falsity and errour with never so great a number. Neither is it fit that Authority (whether of Aristotle or any other) should inchain us, but that there may be a general freedome to try all things, and to hold fast that which is good, that so there might be a Philosophical liberty to be bound to the authority of none but truth itself, then will men take pains, and arts will flourish." *Id.*, pp. 109-10.

"If the comparison I use be thought too large, and the rule be put only as to the greater part of the Learned that are in Europe, yet it will hold good that the greatest part of the Learned are not to be adhered to because of their numerousness ; nor that the rest are to be rejected because of their paucity . . . . did not the greatest number of the Physicians in Europe altogether adhere to the Doctrine of Galen, though now in Germany, France, England, and many other

Nations, tho most have exploded it ? And was not the Aristotelian Philosophy embraced by the greatest part of all the Learned in Europe ? And have not the Cartesians and others sufficiently now manifested the errours and imperfections of it ? . . . . So that multitude, as multitude, ought not to lead or sway us, but truth itself. . . . . It is not safe nor rational to receive or adhere to an opinion because of its Antiquity ; nor to reject one because of its Novelty." *The Displaying of supposed Witchcraft*, p. 14.

"Especially since our never-sufficiently honoured Countryman Doctor Harvey discovered that wonderful secret of the bloods circulary motion." *Acad. Examen*, p. 74.

"Our learned and most industrious Anatomist Dr. Harvey, who (notwithstanding the late cavils of some) first found forth and evidenced to the World that rare and profitable discovery of the Circulation of the blood." *The Displaying of supposed Witchcraft*, p. 3.

"Our learned Countryman Dr. Fludd." *Acad. Examen*, p. 74.

"Our Countryman Dr. Flud, a person of much learning." *The Displaying of supposed Witchcraft*, p. 319.

"Secondly, they are as ignorant in the most admirable and soul-ravishing knowledge of the three great Hypostatical principles of nature, Salt, Sulphur, and Mercury, first mentioned by Basilius Valentinus, and afterwards clearly and evidently manifested by that miracle of industry and pains Theophrastus Paracelsus. . . . . And though Helmont, with the experiments of his Gehennal fire and some other solid arguments, labour the labefactation of this truth, yet doth he not prove that they are not Hypostatical principles, but onely that they are not the ultimate reduction that the possibility of art can produce, which he truly proves to be water." *Acad. Examen*, p. 76.

"The ancient Chymical Philosophers held that the matter out of which the Metals were generated, were Sulphur and Mercury ; but Basilius Valentinus, Paracelsus, and the latter Chymists, have added Salt as a third." *Metallographia*, p. 72. "Sometimes (and perhaps not untruly) they affirm the Metals to be generated of the element of Water ; as Helmont, who proves not onely that metallick bodies, but also all other Concretes to have their rise from thence, and demonstrateth the immutability of elemental Water." *Id.*, p. 79. [78.]

"Another is no less faulty and hurtful than the precedent, and that is their too much admiring of, and adhering to antiquity, or the judgement of men that lived in ages far removed from us, as though they had known all things, and left nothing for the discovery of those that came after in subsequent ages. . . . . . And indeed we usually attribute knowledge and experience to men of the most years, and therefore these being the latter ages of the world should know more, for the grandævity of the world ought to be accounted for antiquity, and so to be ascribed to our times, and not to the Junior age of the world, wherein those that we call the antients did live, so that *antiquitas sæculi, juventus mundi."* *Acad. Examen*, pp. 93-4.

" In regard of Natural Philosophy and the knowledge [*sic*] of the properties of created things, and the knowledge of them, we preposterously reckon former Ages, and the men that lived in them, the Ancients ; which in regard of production and generation of the Individuals of their own Species are so ; but in respect of knowledge and experience this Age is to be accounted the most ancient. For as the learned Lord Bacon saith : Indeed to speak truly, *Antiquitas seculi, juventus mundi,* Antiquity of time is the youth of the World. Certainly our times are the ancient times, when the World is now ancient, and not those which we count ancient, *ordine retrogrado,* by a computation backward from our own times ; and yet so much credit hath been given to old Authors as to invest them with the power of Dictators, that their words should stand, rather than admit them as Consuls to give advice." *The Displaying of supposed Witchcraft,* p. 15.

It is certain, therefore, that John Webster the dramatist, and John Webster of Clitheroe, were different persons : the former was a writer for the stage as early as 1601 ; the latter was not born till 1610, and died in 1682 *.

---

* See Whitaker's *Hist. of Whalley and Clitheroe*, pp. 285, 493, ed. 1818. Dr. Whitaker seems never to have suspected that Webster of Clitheroe, on whose learning and talents he bestows just praise, was the author of the *Academiarum Examen*.

I may notice that *A Declaration of the Lords and Commons*, dated July 6th, 1644, was put forth against a *John Webster* and others as " Incendiaries between the United Provinces and the Kingdom and Parliament of England ;" and that all the said " Incendiaries" were *merchants*.

ADDENDUM.

In the prefatory remarks on *The White Devil* I have accidentally omitted to mention (what was obligingly communicated to me in a letter from Mr. Jourdain de Gatwick, June 19th, 1852) that "it is taken from the Life of Sixtus V[th]; the husband of Vittoria being the nephew of the Pope."—Vide *Biogr. Univ.* sub "Accoramboni (Virginie)" :—in the same work, sub "Sixte-Quint," is a reference to a publication, which I have not seen, entitled "*L'Histoire de Vittoria Accorambona,* 3.ᵉ edition, par M. Adry."

THE WHITE DEVIL;

OR,

VITTORIA COROMBONA.

The White Divel, or, the Tragedy of Paulo Giordano Ursini, Duke of Brachiano, With the Life and Death of Vittoria Corombona the famous Venetian Curtizan. Acted by the Queenes Maiesties Seruants. Written by John Webster. Non inferiora secutus. London, Printed by N. O. for Thomas Archer, and are to be sold at his Shop in Popes head Pallace, neere the Royall Exchange. 1612. 4to.

The White Devil, or, the Tragedy of Paulo Giordano Vrsini, Duke of Brachiano, With the Life, and Death, of Vittoria Corombona, the famous Venetian Curtizan. As it hath bin diuers times Acted, by the Queenes Maiesties seruants, at the Phœnix, in Drury-lane. Written by John Webster. Non inferiora secutus. London, Printed by I. N. for Hugh Perry, and are to be sold at his shop at the signe of the Harrow in Brittains-burse. 1631. 4to.

There were also editions in 1665, and 1672; and an alteration of it by N. Tate, called *Injured Love, or the Cruel Husband*, appeared in 1707. It has been reprinted in the different editions of Dodsley's *Collection of Old Plays*, and in the *Ancient British Drama*.

The reader who is familiar with original editions of our early poets will not be surprised to learn that some copies of the 4to. of 1612 differ slightly in several places from other copies of the *same edition*; a collation of my own copy with that in the Garrick collection (vol. II. 22.) has furnished some various readings, which I have given in the course of my notes. Such differences arose no doubt from alterations having been made in the text after a portion of the impression had been worked off.* I have not thought it necessary to set down every minute variation found in the 4tos. of 1665 and 1672, as, though they in several places rectify the errors of the two earliest 4tos., they are comparatively of little authority. The notes which have the names of Reed, Steevens, Gilchrist, and Collier attached to them, are taken from the second and third editions of Dodsley's *Collection of Old Plays*.

In a rare volume of poetry, *Epigrams theological, philosophical, and romantick, Six books, also the Socratick Session, or the Arraignment and Conviction of Julius Scaliger, with other Select Poems. By S. Sheppard*, 1651, 8vo, are the following lines:

" On Mr. Webster's most excellent Tragedy, called the White Devill.

" Wee will no more admire Euripides,
Nor praise the Tragick streines of Sophocles;
For why † thou in this Tragedie hast fram'd
All reall worth that can in them be nam'd.
How lively are thy persons fitted, and
How pretty are thy lines! thy Verses stand
Like unto pretious Jewels set in gold,
And grace thy fluent Prose. I once was told
By one well skil'd in Arts, he thought thy Play
Was onely worthy Fame to beare away
From all before it. Brachianos Ill,
Murthering his Dutchesse, hath by thy rare skill
Made him renown'd: Flamineo such another,
The Devils darling, Murtherer of his brother,
His part most strange (given him to Act by thee)
Doth gaine him Credit, and not Calumnie:
Vittoria Corombona, that fam'd Whore,
Desp'rato Lodovico weltring in his gore,
Subtile Francisco, all of them shall bee
Gaz'd at as Comets by Posteritie:
And thou meane time with never withering Bayes
Shalt Crowned bee by all that read thy Layes."

Lib. V. Epig. 27, pp. 133, 134.

From *A Funeral Elegy on the death of the famous actor, Richard Burbadge* (printed in Mr. Collier's *Memoirs of the principal actors in the plays of Shakespeare*, p. 52, ed. Shakes. Soc.) we learn that the part of Brachiano in *The White Devil* was performed by Durbadge.

---

* This is also the case with the old copies of some other of our author's plays. Gifford discovered similar variations in some of the early 4tos. of Massinger; vide his Introduction, p. ciii. ed. 1813: see too the prefatory remarks to Peele's *Honour of the Garter* in my ed. of his *Works*.

† *For why*] i. e. Because, for the reason that.

TO THE READER.

In publishing this tragedy, I do but challenge to myself that liberty which other men have ta'en before me : not that I affect praise by it, for *nos hæc novimus esse nihil ;*[*] only, since it was acted in so dull a time of winter, presented in so[†] open and black a theatre,[‡] that it wanted (that which is the only grace and setting-out of a tragedy) a full and understanding auditory ; and that, since that time, I have noted most of the people that come to that play-house resemble those ignorant asses, who, visiting stationers' shops, their use is not to inquire for good books, but new books ; I present it to the general view with this confidence,—

> Nec ronchos metues maligniorum,
> Nec scombris tunicas dabis molestas.[§]

If it be objected this is no true dramatic poem, I shall easily confess it ; *non potes in nugas dicere plura meas ipse ego quam dixi.*[||] Willingly, and not ignorantly, in this kind have I faulted : for, should a man present to such an auditory the most sententious tragedy that ever was written, observing all the critical laws, as height of style, and gravity of person, enrich it with the sententious Chorus, and, as it were, liven death in the passionate and weighty Nuntius ; yet, after all this divine rapture, *O dura messorum ilia,*[¶] the breath that comes from the uncapable multitude is able to poison it ; and, ere it be acted, let the author resolve to fix to every scene this of Horace,

> Hæc porcis hodie comedenda relinques.[**]

To those who report I was a long time in finishing this tragedy, I confess, I do not write with a goose quill winged with two feathers ; and if they will needs make it my fault, I must answer them with that of Euripides to Alcestides,[††] a tragic writer. Alcestides objecting that Euripides had only, in three days, composed three verses, whereas himself had written three hundred, "Thou tellest truth," quoth he, "but here's the difference,—thine shall only be read for three days, whereas mine shall continue three ages."

Detraction is the sworn friend to ignorance : for mine own part, I have ever truly cherished my good opinion of other men's worthy labours ; especially of that full and heightened style of Master Chapman ; the laboured and understanding works of Master Jonson ; the no less worthy composures of the both worthily excellent Master Beaumont and Master Fletcher ; and lastly (without wrong last to be named), the right happy and copious industry of Master Shakespeare, Master Dekker, and Master Heywood ; wishing what I write may be read by their light ; protesting that, in the strength of mine own judgment, I know them so worthy, that though I rest silent in my own work, yet to most of theirs I dare (without flattery) fix that of Martial,

> Non norunt hæc monumenta mori.[‡‡]

---

[*] *Nos hæc, &c.*] Martial, xiii. 2.
[†] *dull a time of winter, presented in so*] These words are ound only in the 4to. of 1612.
[‡] *black a theatre*] "I think we should read *blank*, i.e. vacant, unsupplied with articles necessary toward theatrical representation." STEEVENS.—"Qy. *bleak ?*" MS. note by MALONE.
[§] *Nec ronchos, &c.*] Martial, iv. 87.
[||] *non potes, &c*] Martial, xiii. 2.
[¶] *O dura, &c.*] Horace, *Epod.* iii.
[**] *Hæc porcis, &c.*] *Epist.* I. 7.
[††] *that of Euripides to Alcestides, &c.*] "Itaque etiam quod Alcestidi tragico poëtæ [Euripides] respondit, probabile: apud quem cum quereretur, quod eo triduo non ultra tres versus maximo impenso labore deducere potuisset, atque is se centum perfacile scripsisse gloriaretur : 'Sed hoc,' inquit, 'interest, quod tui in triduum tantummodo, mei vero in omne tempus sufficient.'" Valerius Maximus, Lib. iii. 7,—where the word "Alcestidi" is very questionable.
[‡‡] *Non norunt, &c.*] x. 2.

DRAMATIS PERSONÆ.

MONTICELSO, a cardinal, afterwards Pope.
FRANCISCO DE MEDICIS, Duke of Florence.
BRACHIANO, otherwise Paulo Giordano Ursini, Duke of Brachiano, husband to ISABELLA.
GIOVANNI, his son.
COUNT LODOVICO.
CAMILLO, husband to VITTORIA.
FLAMINEO, brother to VITTORIA, secretary to BRACHIANO.
MARCELLO, brother to VITTORIA, attendant on FRANCISCO DE MEDICIS.
HORTENSIO.
ANTONELLI.
GASPARO.
FARNESE.
CARLO.
PEDRO.
DOCTOR.
CONJURER.
LAWYER.
JAQUES.
JULIO.
CHRISTOPHERO.

ISABELLA, sister to FRANCISCO DE MEDICIS, wife to BRACHIANO.
VITTORIA COROMBONA, married first to CAMILLO, afterwards to BRACHIANO.
CORNELIA, mother to VITTORIA.
ZANCHE, a Moor, waiting-woman to VITTORIA.
Matron of the House of Convertites.

Ambassadors, Physicians, Officers, Attendants, &c.

In mentem auctoris.
Scire velis quid sit mulier? quo percitet astro?
En tibi, si sapias, cum sale, mille sales. *
J. WILSON

---

* These lines are not found in the two earliest 4tos. In the 4to. of 1665 they have the initials *J. W.* subjoined to them : in that of 1672 they are signed *J. Wilson.*

THE WHITE DEVIL;

OR,

VITTORIA COROMBONA.

Enter Count LODOVICO,[*] ANTONELLI, *and* GASPARO.

Lod. Banish'd!

Ant. It griev'd me much to hear the sentence.

Lod. Ha, ha! O Democritus, thy gods
That govern the whole world! courtly reward
And punishment. Fortune's a right whore:
If she give aught, she deals it in small parcels,
That she may take away all at one swoop †
This 'tis to have great enemies:—God quit‡ them!
Your wolf no longer seems to be a wolf
Than when she's hungry.

Gasp. You term those enemies
Are men of princely rank.

Lod. O, I pray for them:
The violent thunder is ador'd by those
Are pash'd § in pieces by it.

Ant. Come, my lord,
You are justly doom'd: look but a little back
Into your former life; you have in three years
Ruin'd the noblest earldom.

Gasp. Your followers
Have swallow'd you like mummia,|| and, being sick

With such unnatural and horrid physic,
Vomit you up i'the kennel.

Ant. All the damnable degrees
Of drinkings have you stagger'd through: one
    citizen
Is lord of two fair manors call'd you master
Only for caviare.

Gasp. Those noblemen
Which were invited to your prodigal feasts
(Wherein the phœnix scarce could scape your
    throats)
Laugh at your misery; as fore-deeming you
An idle meteor, which, drawn forth the earth,
Would be soon lost i'the air.

Ant. Jest upon you,
And say you were begotten in an earthquake,
You have ruin'd such fair lordships.

Lod. Very good.
This well goes with two buckets: I must tend
The pouring out of either.

Gasp. Worse than these; ·
You have acted certain murders here in Rome,
Bloody and full of horror.

Lod. 'Las, they were flea-bitings.
Why took they not my head, then!

Gasp. O, my lord,
The law doth sometimes mediate, thinks it good
Not ever to steep violent sins in blood:
This gentle penance may both end your crimes,
And in the example better these bad times.

Lod. So; but I wonder, then, some great men
    scape
This banishment: there's Paulo Giordano Ursini,

---

* *Enter Count Lodovico,* &c.] Scene. Rome. A street[?]
† *all at one swoop*] "So Shakespeare;
' What, *all* my pretty chickens and their dam,
    At one fell *swoop* ?' *Macbeth*, act IV. sc. 3." STEEVENS.
‡ *quit*] i.e. requite.
§ *pash'd*] The 4tos. of 1665 and 1672 "*dasht.*"—The
meaning of *pash* and *dash* are thus rightly distinguished
by Gifford: "the latter signifies to throw one thing
with violence against another: the former, to strike a
thing with such force as to crush it to pieces." Note on
Massinger's *Virgin Martyr*, act II. sc. 2.
|| *mummia*] The most satisfactory account of the
different kinds of mummy formerly used in medicine,
is to be found in a quotation from Hill's *Materia Medica*,
in Johnson's *Dictionary*, v. mummy, to which I refer the
reader.—"The Egyptian mummies," says Sir Thomas
Brown, " which Cambyses or time hath spared, avarice

now consumeth. Mummie is become merchandise, Miz-
raim cures wounds, and Pharaoh is sold for balsams."
Urn-Burial, p. 28. ed. 1658.

The Duke of Brachiano, now lives in Rome,
And by close panderism seeks to prostitute
The honour of Vittoria Corombona;
Vittoria, she that might have got my pardon
For one kiss to the duke.

Ant. Have a full man within you.
We see that trees bear no such * pleasant fruit
There where they grew first as where they are
    new set :
Perfumes, the more they are chaf'd, † the more
    they render
Their pleasing scents ; and so affliction
Expresseth virtue fully, whether true
Or else adulterate.

Lod. Leave your painted comforts :
I'll make Italian cut-works ‡ in their guts,
If ever I return.

Gasp. O, sir !

Lod. I am patient.
I have seen some ready to be executed
Give pleasant looks and money, and grown familiar
With the knave hangman : so do I : I thank
    them,
And would account them nobly merciful,
Would they despatch me quickly.

Ant. Fare you well :
We shall find time, I doubt not, to repeal
Your banishment.

Lod. I am ever bound to you :
This is the world's alms ; pray, make use of it.
Great men sell sheep thus to be cut in pieces,
When first they have shorn them bare and sold
    their fleeces.   [*Exeunt.*

Sennet.§ Enter BRACHIANO,‖ CAMILLO, FLAMINEO,
   VITTORIA COROMBONA, *and Attendants.*

Brach. Your best of rest !

Vit. Cor. Unto my lord, the duke,

---

* *such*] Some copies of the 4to. of 1612 " *sweet.*"

† *Perfumes, the more they are chaf'd, &c.*] Compare Lord
Bacon's *Essays* : "Certainly virtue is like precious odours,
most fragrant when they are incensed or crushed ; for
prosperity doth best discover vice, but adversity doth
best discover virtue." *Of Adversity.*
Our author in *The Duchess of Malfi* has—
  " Man, like to cassia, is prov'd best, being bruis'd."
             Act III. sc. 5.

‡ *cut-works*] Todd, in his additions to Johnson's *Dictionary,* wrongly explains *cutwork* to be " work in em-
broidery " : it is a kind of open-work, made by cutting
out or stamping.

§ *Sennet*] i. e. a particular sounding of trumpets or
cornets, not a flourish, as it has sometimes been explained. —In the 4tos. this portion of the stage-direction
is put on the margin opposite the preceding speech of
Lodovico, and given thus " *Enter Senate.*"

‖ *Enter Brachiano, &c.*] Scene. The Same. An outer
apartment in Camillo's house.

The best of welcome !—More lights ! attend the
    duke.
    [*Exeunt* CAMILLO *and* VITTORIA COROMBONA.

Brach. Flamineo,—

Flam. My lord ?

Brach. Quite lost, Flamineo.

Flam. Pursue your noble wishes, I am prompt
As lightning to your service. O, my lord,
The fair Vittoria, my happy sister,   [*Whisper.*
Shall give you present audience.—Gentlemen,
Let the caroche go on ; and 'tis his pleasure
You put out all your torches, and depart.
          [*Exeunt* Attendants.

Brach. Are we so happy ?

Flam. Can't be otherwise ?
Observ'd you not to-night, my honour'd lord,
Which way soe'er you went, she threw her eyes ?
I have dealt already with her chamber-maid,
Zanche the Moor ; and she is wondrous proud
To be the agent for so high a spirit.

Brach. We are happy above thought, because
    'bove merit.

Flam. 'Bove merit !—we may now talk freely
—'bove merit ! What is't you doubt ? her coyness ? that's but the superficies of lust most
women have : yet why should ladies blush to
hear that named which they do not fear to
handle ! O, they are politic : they know our desire
is increased by the difficulty of enjoying ; whereas
satiety is a blunt, weary, and drowsy passion.*
If the buttery-hatch at court stood continually
open, there would be nothing so passionate
crowding, nor hot suit after the beverage.

Brach. O, but her jealous husband.

Flam. Hang him ! a gilder that hath his brains
perished with quick-silver is not more cold in the
liver : the great barriers moulted not more
feathers † than he hath shed hairs, by the confession of his doctor : an Irish gamester that will
play himself naked,‡ and then wage all downwards
at hazard, is not more venturous : so unable to

---

* *whereas satiety is a blunt, weary, and drowsy passion*]
" Fie on this *satietie, 'tis a dul, blunt, weary, and drowsie
passion.*" Marston's *Parasitaster or the Fawne,* 1606,
Sig. F. 4.

† *the great barriers moulted not more feathers*] " i. e.
more feathers were not dislodged from the helmets of
the combatants at the great tilting-match." STEEVENS.

‡ *an Irish gamester that will play himself naked*] " Bar-
naby Rich in his *New Description of Ireland,* 1610, p. 38,
says ; 'There is (i. e. in Ireland) a certaine brotherhood,
called by the name of *Karrowes,* and these be common
gamsters, that do only exercise playing at cards, and
they will play away their mantels, and their shirts from
their backs, and when they have nothing left them, they
will trusse themselves in straw : this is the life they lead,
and from this they will not be reclaimed.'" REED.

please a woman, that, like a Dutch doublet, all his
back is shrunk into his breeches.
Shrowd you within this closet, good my lord:
Some trick now must be thought on to divide
My brother-in-law from his fair bed-fellow.

Brach. O, should she fail to come?

Flam. I must not have your lordship thus
unwisely amorous. I myself have loved a lady,
and pursued her with a great deal of under-age
protestation, whom some three or four gallants
that have enjoyed would with all their hearts
have been glad to have been rid of: 'tis just like
a summer bird-cage in a garden; the birds that
are without despair to get in, and the birds that
are within despair, and are in a consumption, for
fear they shall never get out. Away, away, my
lord! [*Exit* BRACHIANO.
See, here he comes. This fellow by his apparel
Some men would judge a politician;
But call his wit in question, you shall find it
Merely an ass in's foot-cloth.*

Re-enter CAMILLO.†
    How now, brother!
What, travelling to bed to your kind wife?

Cam. I assure you, brother, no; my voyage lies
More northerly, in a far colder clime:
I do not well remember, I protest,
When I last lay with her.

Flam. Strange you should lose your count.

Cam. We never lay together, but ere morning
There grew a flaw ‡ between us.

Flam. 'Thad been your part
To have made up that flaw.

Cam. True, but she loathes
I should be seen in't.

Flam. Why, sir, what's the matter?

Cam. The duke your master visits me, I thank
him;
And I perceive how, like an earnest bowler,
He very passionately leans that way
He should have his bowl run.

Flam. I hope you do not think—

Cam. That noblemen bowl booty? faith, his
cheek
Hath a most excellent bias;* it would fain
Jump with my mistress.

Flam. Will you be an ass,
Despite your† Aristotle? or a cuckold,
Contrary to your Ephemerides,
Which shows you under what a smiling planet
You were first swaddled?

Cam. Pew-wew, sir, tell not me
Of planets nor of Ephemerides:
A man may be made a cuckold in the day-time,
When the stars' eyes are out.

Flam. Sir, God b'wi'you;‡
I do commit you to your pitiful pillow
Stuff'd with horn-shavings.

Cam. Brother,—

Flam. God refuse me,§
Might I advise you now, your only course
Were to lock up your wife.

Cam. 'Twere very good.

Flam. Bar her the sight of revels.

Cam. Excellent.

Flam. Let her not go to church, but like a hound
In lyam ‖ at your heels.

Cam. 'Twere for her honour.

Flam. And so you should be certain in one
fortnight,
Despite her chastity or innocence,
To be cuckolded, which yet is in suspence:
This is my counsel, and I ask no fee for't.

Cam. Come, you know not where my night-cap
wrings me.

Flam. Wear it o' the old fashion; let your

---

* *faith, his cheek*
Hath a most excellent bias] "So in *Troilus and Cressida*,
a. iv. s. 5;
 ' Blow, villain, till thy sphered *bias cheek*
 Out-swell the colic of puff'd Aquilon.'" REED.
† *your*] Both the earliest 4tos. " *you.*"
‡ *God b'wi'you*] In the 4tos. (as it is frequently spelt in
old plays) "God boy you."
§ *God refuse me*] A fashionable imprecation at the time
this play was written: "would so many else," says
Taylor, the water-poet, "in their desperate madnes desire God to Damne them, to Renounce them, to Forsake
them, to Confound them, to Sinke them, to *Refuse
them?*" "*Against Cursing and Swearing,*" *Works*, 1630,
p 45. Compare also Middleton's *Family of Love*;
 "*Mis. P.* And what do they swear by, now their
money is gone?
 Club. Why, by } and *God refuse them.*"
       Works, ii. 122, ed. Dyce.
(In the passage just quoted the old copy has a break
between brackets as given here.)
‖ *lyam*] All the 4tos. have "*Leon*"; which Steevens
(as he well might) suspected to be an error of the press
for *leam* (or *lyam*), i. e. leash.

* *in's foot-cloth*] i. e. in his housings. See notes of the
commentators on Shakespeare's *Richard III.* Act III. sc 4.
† *Re-enter Camillo*] It is hardly possible to mark with
any certainty the stage-business of this play. Though
Brachiano, who has just withdrawn into a "closet," appears again at p. 9 when Flamineo calls him,—it would
seem that the audience were to *imagine* that a change of
scene took place here,—to another apartment of the house
(at p. 8 Flamineo says, "Sister, my lord attends you in the
banqueting-house"). In our author's days there was no
painted movable scenery; and consequently a great deal
was left to the imagination of the spectators.
‡ *flaw*] "*Flaw* anciently signified a *gust*, or *blast*; [—a
sense in which it is still used by seamen.—D.] it here
means a *quarrel.*" REED.

large ears come through, it will be more easy:—nay, I will be bitter:—bar your wife of her entertainment: women are more willingly and more gloriously chaste, when they are least restrained of their liberty. It seems you would be a fine capricious mathematically jealous coxcomb; take the height of your own horns with a Jacob's staff, afore they are up. These politic inclosures for paltry mutton make more rebellion in the flesh than all the provocative electuaries doctors have uttered * since last jubilee.

Cam. This doth not physic me.

Flam. It seems you are jealous: I'll show you the error of it by a familiar example. I have seen a pair of spectacles fashioned with such perspective art, that, lay down but one twelve pence o' the board, 'twill appear as if there were twenty: now, should you wear a pair of these spectacles, and see your wife tying her shoe, you would imagine twenty hands were taking up of your wife's clothes, and this would put you into a horrible causeless fury.

Cam. The fault there, sir, is not in the eye-sight.

Flam. True; but they that have the yellow jaundice think all objects they look on to be yellow.† Jealousy is worser: her fits present to a man, like so many bubbles in a bason of water, twenty several crabbed faces; many times makes his own shadow his cuckold-maker. See, she comes.

Re-enter VITTORIA COROMBONA.

What reason have you to be jealous of this creature? what an ignorant ass or flattering knave might he be counted, that should write sonnets to her eyes, or call her brow the snow of Ida or ivory of Corinth, or compare her hair to the black-bird's bill, when 'tis liker the black-bird's feather! This is all: be wise, I will make you friends; and you shall go to bed together. Marry, look you, it shall not be your seeking; do you stand upon that by any means: walk you aloof; I would not have you seen in't. [CAMILLO *retires.*] Sister, my lord attends you in the banquetting-house. Your husband is wondrous discontented.

Vit. Cor. I did nothing to displease him: I carved to him at supper-time.‡

Flam. You need not have carved him, in faith; they say he is a capon already. I must now seemingly fall out with you. Shall a gentleman so well descended as Camillo,—a lousy slave, that within this twenty years rode with the black guard * in the duke's carriage, 'mongst spits and dripping-pans,—

Cam. Now he begins to tickle her.

Flam. An excellent scholar,—one that hath a head filled with calves-brains without any sage in them,—come crouching in the hams to you for a night's lodging?—that hath an itch in's hams, which like the fire at the glass-house hath not gone out this seven years.—Is he not a courtly gentleman?—when he wears white satin, one would take him by his black muzzle to be no other creature than a maggot.—You are a goodly foil, I confess, well set out—but covered with a false stone, yon counterfeit diamond.†

Cam. He will make her know what is in me.

Flam. Come, my lord attends you: thou shalt go to bed to my lord—

Cam. Now he comes to't.

Flam. With a relish as curious as a vintner going to taste new wine.—I am opening your case hard.   [*To* CAMILLO

Cam. A virtuous brother, o' my credit!

Flam. He will give thee a ring with a philosopher's stone in it.

Cam. Indeed, I am studying alchymy.

Flam. Thou shalt lie in a bed stuffed with turtles' feathers; swoon in perfumed linen, like the fellow was smothered in roses. So perfect shall be thy happiness, that, as men at sea think

---

* *uttered*] i. e. vended.

† — *they that have the yellow jaundice think all objects they look on to be yellow*] "This thought is adopted by Pope:
'All seems infected that th' infected spy,
As all looks yellow to the jaundic'd eye.'" STEEVENS.
So also Flecknoe; "As *all things seem yellow to those infected with the Jaundies*, so all things seem of the colour of her suspicions." *Ænigmatical Characters*, 1665, p. 56.

‡ *I carved to him at supper-time*] Boswell, in a note on

Shakespeare's *Merry Wives of Windsor*, Act I. sc. 3 (where, I am confident, the word "*carves*" is not used in its common acceptation), quotes the present passage of Webster, and observes, "it seems to have been considered as a mark of kindness, when a lady carved to a gentleman." In *The Returne from Pernassus*, 1606, Sir Raderick says; "what do men marry for, but to stocke their ground, and to have one to looke to the linnen, sit at the upper end of the table, *and carve up a capon!*" Sig. F.2.

* *the black guard*] i. e. the meanest drudges in royal residences and great houses, who rode in the vehicles which carried the furniture and domestic utensils from mansion to mansion. See Gifford's note, *Ben Jonson's Works*, vol. ii. p. 169.

† *but covered with a false stone, yon counterfeit diamond*] So some copies of the 4to. of 1612; other copies "but cover with a false stone *your* counterfeit diamond:" the 4to. of 1631, "but covered with a false stone *you* counterfeit diamond:" the 4to. of 1665 has the reading of some of the copies of that of 1612, followed in my text: the 4to. of 1672 agrees with that of 1631.—The full meaning appears to be; "but [you, the goodly foil, are] covered with a false stone, [i. e your husband Camillo,] yon counterfeit diamond."

land and trees and ships go that way they go, so
both heaven and earth shall seem to go your
voyage. Shall't meet him; 'tis fixed with nails
of diamonds to inevitable necessity.

Vit. Cor. How shall's rid him hence?

Flam. I will put [the] breeze in's tail,—set him
gadding presently.—[*To* CAMILLO] I have almost
wrought her to it, I find her coming : but, might
I advise you now, for this night I would not lie
with her; I would cross her humour to make
her more humble.

Cam. Shall I, shall I?

Flam. It will show in you a supremacy of
judgment.

Cam. True, and a mind differing from the
tumultuary opinion ; for, *quæ negata, grata.*

Flam. Right : you are the adamant * shall
draw her to you, though you keep distance
off.

Cam. A philosophical reason.

Flam. Walk by her o'the nobleman's fashion,
and tell her you will lie with her at the end of
the progress.†

Cam. [*coming forward*]. Vittoria, I cannot be
induced, or, as a man would say, incited—

Vit. Cor. To do what, sir?

Cam. To lie with you to-night. Your silk-worm
useth to fast every third day, and the next
following spins the better. To-morrow at night
I am for you.

Vit. Cor. You'll spin a fair thread, trust
to't.

Flam. But, do you hear, I shall have you steal
to her chamber about midnight.

Cam. Do you think so? why, look you, brother,
because you shall not think I'll gull you, take the
key, lock me into the chamber, and say you shall
be sure of me.

Flam. In troth, I will ; I'll be your gaoler
once. But have you ne'er a false door?

Cam. A pox on't, as I am a Christian. Tell me
to-morrow how scurvily she takes my unkind
parting.

Flam. I will.

Cam. Didst thou not mark ‡ the jest of the
silk-worm? Good-night: in faith, I will use this
trick often.

Flam. Do, do, do. [*Exit* CAMILLO; *and* FLA-
MINEO *locks the door on him.*] So now you are
safe.—Ha, ha, ha! thou entanglest thyself in

thine own work like a silk-worm.*—Come, sister;
darkness hides your blush. Women are like
curst dogs: civility† keeps them tied all day-
time, but they are let loose at midnight; then
they do most good, or most mischief.—My lord,
my lord !

Re-enter BRACHIANO. ZANCHE *brings out a carpet, spreads
it, and lays on it two fair cushions.*

Brach. Give credit, I could wish time would
stand still,
And never end this interview, this hour :
But all delight doth itself soon'st devour.

Enter CORNELIA *behind, listening.*

Let me into your bosom, happy lady,
Pour out, instead of eloquence, my vows :
Loose me not, madam ; for, if you forgo me,
I am lost eternally.

Vit. Cor. Sir, in the way of pity,
I wish you heart-whole.

Brach. You are a sweet physician.

Vit. Cor. Sure, sir, a loathèd cruelty in ladies
Is as to doctors many funerals ;
It takes away their credit.

Brach. Excellent creature !
We call the cruel fair : what name for you
That are so merciful?

Zan. See, now they close.

Flam. Most happy union.

Cor. My fears are fall'n upon me : O, my heart !
My son the pander ! now I find our house
Sinking to ruin. Earthquakes leave behind,
Where they have tyranniz'd, iron, lead,‡ or stone;
But, woe to ruin, violent lust leaves none !

Brach. What value is this jewel?

Vit. Cor. 'Tis the ornament
Of a weak fortune.

Brach. In sooth, I'll have it; nay, I will but
change
My jewel for your jewel.

Flam. Excellent !
His jewel for her jewel :—well put in, duke.

Brach. Nay, let me see you wear it.

Vit. Cor. Here, sir?

Brach. Nay, lower, you shall wear my jewel
lower.

Flam. That's better; she must wear his jewel
lower.

---

* *adamant*] i. e. magnet.

† *the progress*] i. e. the travelling of the sovereign and
court to different parts of the kingdom.

‡ *mark*] So the 4to. of 1672.—The earlier 4tos. "make."

* *thou entanglest thyself in thine own work like a silk-
worm.*] "Thus Pope ;
'The silk-worm thus spins fine his little store,
And labours till he clouds himself all o'er.'" STEEVENS.

† *civility*] The 4to. of 1631, "cruelty."

‡ *lead*] The 4to. of 1612, "or lead."

Vit. Cor. To pass away the time, I'll tell your
  grace
A dream I had last night.
  Brach. Most wishedly.
  Vit. Cor. A foolish idle dream.
Methought I walk'd about the mid of night
Into a church-yard, where a goodly yew-tree
Spread her large root in ground. Under that yew,
As I sate sadly leaning on a grave
Chequer'd with cross sticks, there came stealing
  in
Your duchess and my husband: one of them
A pick-axe bore, the other a rusty spade ;
And in rough terms they gan to challenge me
About this yew.
  Brach. That tree ?
  Vit. Cor. This harmless yew :
They told me my intent was to root up
That well-grown yew, and plant i'the stead of it
A wither'd black-thorn ; and for that they vow'd
To bury me alive. My husband straight
With pick-axe gan to dig, and your fell duchess
With shovel, like a Fury, voided out
The earth, and scatter'd bones. Lord, how,
  methought,
I trembled ! and yet, for all this terror,
I could not pray.
  Flam. No; the devil was in your dream.
  Vit. Cor. When to my rescue there arose, me-
  thought,
A whirlwind, which let fall a massy arm
From that strong plant ;
And both were struck dead by that sacred yew,
In that base shallow grave that was their due.
  Flam. Excellent devil ! she hath taught him in
  a dream
To make away his duchess and her husband.
  Brach. Sweetly shall I interpret this your
  dream.
You are lodg'd within his arms who shall protect
  you
From all the fevers of a jealous husband ;
From the poor envy of our phlegmatic duchess.
I'll seat you above law, and above scandal ;
Give to your thoughts the invention of delight,
And the fruition ; nor shall government
Divide me from you longer than a care
To keep you great : you shall to me at once
Be dukedom, health, wife, children, friends, and
  all.
  Cor. [*coming forward*]. Woe to light hearts,
  they still fore-run our fall !
  Flam. What Fury rais'd thee up ?—Away,
  away !   [*Exit* ZANCHE.

Cor. What make you here, my lord, this dead
  of night ?
Never dropp'd mildew on a flower here
Till now.
  Flam. I pray, will you go to bed, then,
Lest you be blasted ?
  Cor. O, that this fair garden
Had with * all poison'd herbs of Thessaly
At first been planted ; made a nursery
For witchcraft, rather than † a burial plot
For both your honours !
  Vit. Cor. Dearest mother, hear me.
  Cor. O, thou dost make my brow bend to the
  earth,
Sooner than nature ! See, the curse of children !
In life they keep us frequently in tears ;
And in the cold grave leave us in pale fears.
  Brach. Come, come, I will not hear you.
  Vit. Cor. Dear, my lord,—
  Cor. Where is thy duchess now, adulterous
  duke ?
Thou little dreamd'st this night she is come to
  Rome.
  Flam. How ! come to Rome !
  Vit. Cor. The duchess !
  Brach. She had been better—
  Cor. The lives of princes should like dials move,
Whose regular example is so strong,
They make the times by them go right or wrong.
  Flam. So ; have you done ?
  Cor. Unfortunate Camillo !
  Vit. Cor. I do protest, if any chaste denial,
If any thing but blood could have allay'd
His long suit to me—
  Cor. I will join with thee,
To the most woeful end e'er mother kneel'd :
If thou dishonour thus thy husband's bed,
Be thy life short as are the funeral tears
In great men's—
  Brach. Fie, fie, the woman's mad.
  Cor. Be thy act, Judas-like,—betray in kissing :
Mayst thou be envied during his short breath,
And pitied like a wretch after his death !
  Vit. Cor. O me accurs'd !   [*Exit.*
  Flam. Are you out of your wits, my lord ?
I'll fetch her back again.
  Brach. No, I'll to bed :
Send Doctor Julio to me presently.—
Uncharitable woman ! thy rash tongue
Hath rais'd a fearful and prodigious storm :
Be thou the cause of all ensuing harm.   [*Exit.*

---

* *with*] Omitted in both the earliest 4tos.
† *than*] Omitted in both the earliest 4tos.

Flam. Now, you that stand so much upon your
honour,
Is this a fitting time o' night, think you,
To send a duke home without o'er a man?
I would fain know where lies the mass of wealth
Which you have hoarded for my maintenance,
That I may bear my beard out of the level
Of my lord's stirrup.
   Cor. What! because we are poor
Shall we be vicious?
   Flam. Pray, what means have you
To keep me from the galleys or the gallows?
My father prov'd himself a gentleman,
Sold all's land, and, like a fortunate fellow,
Died ere the money was spent. You brought
me up
At Padua, I confess, where, I protest,
For want of means (the university judge me)
I have been fain to heel my tutor's stockings,
At least seven years: conspiring with a beard,
Made me a graduate; then to this duke's service.
I visited the court, whence I return'd
More courteous, more lecherous by far,
But not a suit the richer: and shall I,
Having a path so open and so free
To my preferment, still retain your milk
In my pale forehead? no, this face of mine
I'll arm, and fortify with lusty wine,
'Gainst shame and blushing.
   Cor. O, that I ne'er had borne thee!
   Flam. So would I;
I would the common'st courtezan in Rome
Had been my mother, rather than thyself.
Nature is very pitiful to whores,
To give them but few children, yet those children
Plurality of fathers: they are sure
They shall not want. Go, go,
Complain unto my great lord cardinal;
Yet * may be he will justify the act.
Lycurgus wonder'd much men would provide
Good stallions for their mares, and yet would
suffer
Their fair wives to be barren.
   Cor. Misery of miseries!   [*Exit.*
   Flam. The duchess come to court! I like not
that.
We are engag'd to mischief, and must on:
As rivers to find out the ocean
Flow with crook bendings beneath forcèd banks;
Or as we see, to aspire some mountain's top,
The way ascends not straight, but imitates
The subtle foldings of a winter's † snake;

     * *Yet*] The 4to. of 1631 "*it.*"
     † *winter's*] The 4to. of 1631 "*winter.*"

So who knows policy and her true aspect,
Shall find her ways winding and indirect. [*Exit.*

Enter FRANCISCO DE MEDICIS,* *Cardinal* MONTICELSO,
  MARCELLO, ISABELLA, *young* GIOVANNI, *with little*
  JAQUES *the Moor*.
   Fran. de Med. Have you not seen your husband
since you arriv'd?
   Isab. Not yet, sir.
   Fran. de Med. Surely he is wondrous † kind:
If I had such a dove-house as Camillo's,
I would set fire on't, were't but to destroy
The pole-cats that haunt to it.—My sweet cousin!
   Giov. Lord uncle, you did promise me a horse
And armour.
   Fran. de Med. That I did, my pretty cousin.—
Marcello, see it fitted.
   Mar. My lord, the duke is here.
   Fran. de Med. Sister, away! you must not yet
be seen.
   Isab. I do beseech you,
Entreat him mildly; let not your rough tongue
Set us at louder variance: all my wrongs
Are freely pardon'd; and I do not doubt,
As men, to try the precious unicorn's horn,‡
Make of the powder a preservative circle,
And in it put a spider, so these arms
Shall charm his poison, force it to obeying,
And keep him chaste from an infected straying.
   Fran. de Med. I wish it may. Be gone, void
the chamber.
      [*Exeunt* ISABELLA, GIOVANNI, *and* JAQUES.

Enter BRACHIANO *and* FLAMINEO.
You are welcome: will you sit?—I pray, my lord,
Be you my orator, my heart's too full;
I'll second you anon.
   Mont. Ere I begin,
Let me entreat your grace forgo all passion,
Which may be raisèd by my free discourse.
   Brach. As silent as i'the church: you may
proceed.
   Mont. It is a wonder to your noble friends,
That you, having,§ as 'twere, enter'd the world
With a free sceptre in your able hand,

     * *Enter Francisco de Medicis, &c.*] Scene.—The same.
A room in Francisco's palace.
     † *wondrous*] The 4to. of 1631 "*wonderful.*"
     ‡ *unicorn's horn*] "The substance vended as such used
to be esteemed a counter-poison. 'Andrea Bacci a
physician of Florence, affirms the round of 16 ounces to
have been sold in the apothecaries' shops for 1536 crowns
when the same weight of gold was only worth 144
crowns.' Chambers's *Dict.* See also Sir Thomas Brown's
Vulgar Errors. B. 3. C. 23." REED.
     § *having*] So all the 4tos. except that of 1612, which has
"*have.*"

And to the use of nature * well applied
High gifts of learning, should in your prime age
Neglect your awful throne for the soft down
Of an insatiate bed. O, my lord,
The drunkard after all his lavish cups
Is dry, and then is sober: so at length,
When you awake from this lascivious dream,
Repentance then will follow, like the sting
Plac'd in the adder's tail. † Wretched are princes
When fortune blasteth but a petty flower
Of their unwieldy crowns, or ravisheth
But one pearl from their sceptres: ‡ but, alas,
When they to wilful shipwreck lose good fame,
All princely titles perish with their name !

   Brach. You have said, my lord.

   Mont. Enough to give you taste
How far I am from flattering your greatness.

   Brach. Now you that are his second, what say
you ?
Do not like young hawks fetch a course about :
Your game flies fair and for you.

   Fran. de Med. Do not fear it :
I'll answer you in your own hawking phrase.
Some eagles that should gaze upon the sun
Seldom soar high, but take their lustful ease ;
Since they from dunghill birds their prey can seize.
You know Vittoria ?

   Brach. Yes.

   Fran. de Med. You shift your shirt there,
When you retire from tennis ?

   Brach. Happily.§

   Fran. de Med. Her husband is lord of a poor
fortune ;
Yet she wears cloth of tissue.

   Brach. What of this ?—
Will you urge that, my good lord cardinal,
As part of her confession at next shrift,
And know from whence it sails ?

   Fran. de Med. She is your strumpet.

   Brach. Uncivil sir, there's hemlock in thy
breath,
And that black slander. Were she a whore of
mine,
All thy loud cannons, and thy borrow'd Switzers,‖

Thy galleys, nor thy sworn confederates,
Durst not supplant her.

   Fran. de Med. Let's not talk on thunder.
Thou hast a wife, our sister : would I had given
Both her white hands to death, bound and lock'd
fast
In her last winding-sheet, when I gave thee
But one !

   Brach. Thou hadst given a soul to God, then.

   Fran. de Med. True :
Thy ghostly father, with all's absolution,
Shall ne'er do so by thee.

   Brach. Spit thy poison.

   Fran. de Med. I shall not need ; lust carries
her sharp whip
At her own girdle. Look to't, for our anger
Is making thunder-bolts.

   Brach. Thunder ! in faith,
They are but crackers.

   Fran. de Med. We'll end this with the cannon.

   Brach. Thou'lt get naught by it but iron in
thy wounds,
And gunpowder in thy nostrils.

   Fran. de Med. Better that,
Than change perfumes for plasters.

   Brach. Pity on thee :
'Twere good you'd show your slaves or men con-
demn'd
Your new-plough'd * forehead-defiance ! and I'll
meet thee,
Even in a thicket of thy ablest men.

   Mont. My lords,† you shall not word it any
further
Without a milder limit.

   Fran. de Med. Willingly,

   Brach. Have you proclaim'd a triumph, that
you bait
A lion thus ?

   Mont. My lord !

   Brach. I am tame, I am tame, sir

   Fran. de Med. We send unto the duke for con-
ference
'Bout levies 'gainst the pirates ; my lord duke
Is not at home : we come ourself in person ;
Still my lord duke is busied. But we fear,

---

* *And to the use of nature,* &c.] All the 4tos. "And
have to the use of nature," &c. I have omitted "*have*"
as unnecessary, rather than alter it to "*having*," which
the sense requires.

† *Repentance then will follow, like the sting*
Plac'd in the adder's tail] So Thomson says ;
' *Amid the roses fierce repentance rears*
Her snaky crest.'   *Spring, l.* 992." REED.

‡ *sceptres*] The 4to. of 1612 "*sceptre.*"

§ *Happily*] Is frequently, as here, used for *haply* by
our old writers.

‖ *borrow'd Switzers*] "The early dramatists appear to
have delighted in making themselves merry with the
Swiss mercenaries, whose poverty, perhaps, rather than
their natural inclination, induced them to lend their
military services to their wealthier and contending neighbours ; till, as Osborne cleverly expresses it, 'they became the cudgels with which the rest of the world did,
upon all occasions, beat one another.' (431. Edit. 1682.)"
           O. GILCHRIST.

* *plough'd*] Spelt in all the 4tos. '*plow'd.*' Qy.
"*plum'd* ?"

† *lords*] The 4to. of 1631 "*lord.*"

When Tiber to each prowling passenger
Discovers flocks of wild ducks; then, my lord,
'Bout moulting time I mean, we shall be certain
To find you sure enough, and speak with you.

Brach. Ha!

Fran. de Med. A mere tale of a tub, my words
are idle;
But to express the sonnet by natural reason,—
When stags grow melancholic, you'll find the
season.

Mont. No more, my lord: here comes a
champion
Shall end the difference between you both,—

Re-enter GIOVANNI.

Your son, the prince Giovanni. See, my lords,
What hopes you store in him: this is a casket
For both your crowns, and should be held like
dear.
Now is he apt for knowledge; therefore know,
It is a more direct and even way
To train to virtue those of princely blood
By examples than by precepts: if by examples,
Whom should he rather strive to imitate
Than his own father? be his pattern, then;
Leave him a stock of virtue that may last,
Should fortune rend his sails and split his mast.

Brach. Your hand, boy: growing to a* soldier?

Giov. Give me a pike.

Fran. de Med. What, practising your pike so
young, fair cuz?

Giov. Suppose me one of Homer's frogs, my
lord,
Tossing my bull-rush thus. Pray, sir, tell me,
Might not a child of good discretion
Be leader to an army?

Fran. de Med. Yes, cousin, a young prince
Of good discretion might.

Giov. Say you so?
Indeed, I have heard, 'tis fit a general·
Should not endanger his own person oft;
So that he make a noise when he's o' horse-
back,
Like a Dansk † drummer,—O, 'tis excellent!—
He need not fight:—methinks his horse as well
Might lead an army for him. If I live,
I'll charge the French foe in the very front
Of all my troops, the foremost man.

Fran. de Med. What, what!

Giov. And will not bid my soldiers up and
follow,
But bid them follow me.

---

* a) Omitted in the 4to. of 1612.
† Dansk] i. e. Danish.

Brach. Forward lap-wing! *
He flies with the shell on's head.

Fran. de Med. Pretty cousin!

Giov. The first year, uncle, that I go to war,
All prisoners that I take I will set free
Without their ransom.

Fran. de Med. Ha, without their ransom!
How, then, will you reward your soldiers
That took those prisoners for you?

Giov. Thus, my lord;
I'll marry them to all the wealthy widows
That fall that year.

Fran. de Med. Why, then, the next year
following,
You'll have no men to go with you to war.

Giov. Why, then, I'll press the women to the war,
And then the men will follow.

Mont. Witty prince!

Fran. de Med. See, a good habit makes a child
a man,
Whereas a bad one makes a man a beast.
Come, you and I are friends.

Brach. Most wishedly;
Like bones which, broke in sunder, and well set,
Knit the more strongly.

Fran. de Med. Call Camillo hither.
[*Exit* MARCELLO.
You have receiv'd the rumour, how Count Lodo-
wick
Is turn'd a pirate?

Brach. Yes.

Fran. de Med. We are now preparing
Some ships to fetch him in. Behold your
duchess.
We now will leave you, and expect from you
Nothing but kind entreaty.

Brach. You have charm'd me.
[*Exeunt* FRANCISCO DE MEDICIS, MONTICELSO,
and GIOVANNI. FLAMINEO *retires.*

Re-enter ISABELLA.

You are in health, we see.

Isab. And above health,
To see my lord well.

Brach. So. I wonder much
What amorous whirlwind hurried you to Rome.

Isab. Devotion, my lord.

Brach. Devotion!
Is your soul charg'd with any grievous sin?

Isab. 'Tis burden'd with too many; and I think,

---

*   Forward lap-wing!
He flies with the shell on's head] "So Horatio says in
Hamlet, A. 5. S. 2. 'This lap-wing runs away with the
shell on his head.' See Mr. Steevens's note thereon."
REED.

The oftener that we cast our reckonings up,
Our sleeps will be the sounder.

Brach. Take your chamber.

Isab. Nay, my dear lord, I will not have you
angry:
Doth not my absence from you, now * two months,
Merit one kiss ?

Brach. I do not use to kiss :
If that will dispossess your jealousy,
I'll swear it to you.

Isab. O my lovèd lord,
I do not come to chide : my jealousy !
I am † to learn what that Italian means.
You are as welcome to these longing arms
As I to you a virgin.

Brach. O, your breath !
Out upon sweet-meats and continu'd physic,—
The plague is in them !

Isab. You have oft, for these two lips,
Neglected cassia or the natural sweets
Of the spring-violet: they are not yet much
wither'd.
My lord, I should be merry : these your frowns
Show in a helmet lovely ; but on me,
In such a peaceful interview, methinks
They are too-too roughly knit.

Brach. O, dissemblance !
Do you bandy factions 'gainst me ? have you learnt
The trick of impudent baseness, to complain
Unto your kindred ?

Isab. Never, my dear lord.

Brach. Must I be hunted ‡ out ? or was't your
trick
To meet some amorous gallant here in Rome,
That must supply our discontinuance ?

Isab. I pray, sir, burst§ my heart ; and in my
death
Turn to your ancient pity, though not love.

Brach. Because your brother is the corpulent
duke,
That is, the great duke, 'sdeath, I shall not shortly
Racket away five hundred crowns at tennis,
But it shall rest upon record ! I scorn him
Like a shav'd Polack : ‖ all his reverend wit
Lies in his wardrobe ; he's a discreet fellow.

When he is made up in his robes of state.
Your brother, the great duke, because h'as
galleys,
And now and then ransacks a Turkish fly-boat,
(Now all the hellish Furies take his soul !)
First made this match : accursèd be the priest
That sang the wedding-mass, and even my
issue !

Isab. O, too-too far you have curs'd !

Brach. Your hand I'll kiss ;
This is the latest ceremony of my love.
Henceforth I'll never lie with thee ; by this,
This wedding-ring, I'll ne'er more lie with thee :
And this divorce shall be as truly kept
As if the judge had doom'd it. Fare you well :
Our sleeps are sever'd.

Isab. Forbid it, the sweet union
Of all things blessèd ! why, the saints in heaven
Will knit their brows at that.

Brach. Let not thy love
Make thee an unbeliever ; this my vow
Shall never, on my soul, be satisfied
With my repentance ; let thy brother rage
Beyond a horrid tempest or sea-fight,
My vow is fixèd.

Isab. O my winding-sheet !
Now shall I need thee shortly.—Dear my lord,
Let me hear once more what I would not hear :
Never ?

Brach. Never.

Isab. O my unkind lord ! may your sins find
mercy,
As I upon a woful widow'd bed
Shall pray for you, if not to turn your eyes
Upon your wretched wife and hopeful son,
Yet that in time you'll fix them upon heaven !

Brach. No more : go, go complain to the great
duke.

Isab. No, my dear lord ; you shall have present
witness
How I'll work peace between you. I will make
Myself the author of your cursèd vow ;
I have some cause to do it, you have none.
Conceal it, I beseech you, for the weal
Of both your dukedoms, that you wrought the
means
Of such a separation : let the fault
Remain with my supposèd jealousy ;
And think with what a piteous and rent heart
I shall perform this sad ensuing part.

Re-enter FRANCISCO DE MEDICIS *and* MONTICELSO.

Brach. Well, take your course.—My honourable brother !

* *now*] Omitted in the two earliest 4tos.
am] The 4to. of 1612 "*come.*"
hunted] The three earliest 4tos. "*haunted.*"
§ *burst*] i. e. break.
‖ *shav'd Polack*] "i. e. Polander. See the Notes of
Mr. Pope, Dr. Johnson, Mr. Steevens, on *Hamlet*, A. 1.
S. 1. In Moryson's *Itinerary*, 1617, pt. 3. p. 170. it is
said, 'The Polonians *shave* all their heads close, excepting the hairs of the forehead, which they nourish very
long, and cast backe to the hinder part of the head.'"
REED.

Fran. de Med. Sister !—This is not well, my
lord.—Why, sister !—
She merits not this welcome.
    Brach. Welcome, say !
She hath given a sharp welcome.
    Fran. de Med. Are you foolish ?
Come, dry your tears : is this a modest course,
To better what is naught, to rail and weep ?
Grow to a reconcilement, or, by heaven,
I'll ne'er more deal between you.
    Isab. Sir, you shall not ;
No, though Vittoria, upon that condition,
Would become honest.
    Fran. de Med. Was your husband loud
Since we departed ?
    Isab. By my life, sir, no ;
I swear by that I do not care to lose.
Are all these ruins of my former beauty
Laid out for a whore's triumph ?
    Fran. de Med. Do you hear ?
Look upon other women, with what patience
They suffer these slight wrongs, with what justice
They study to requite them : take that course.
    Isab. O, that I were a man, or that I had power
To execute my apprehended wishes !
I would whip some with scorpions.
    Fran. de Med. What ! turn'd Fury !
    Isab. To dig the strumpet's eyes out ; let
her lie
Some twenty months a dying ; to cut off
Her nose and lips, pull out her rotten teeth ;
Preserve her flesh like mummia, for trophies
Of my just anger ! Hell to my affliction
Is mere snow-water. By your favour, sir ;—
Brother, draw near, and my lord cardinal ;—
Sir, let me borrow of you but one kiss :
Henceforth I'll never lie with you, by this,
This wedding-ring.
    Fran. de Med. How, ne'er more lie with him !
    Isab. And this divorce shall be as truly kept
As if in throngèd court a thousand ears
Had heard it, and a thousand lawyers' hands
Seal'd to the separation.
    Brach. Ne'er lie with me !
    Isab. Let not my former dotage
Make thee an unbeliever : this my vow
Shall never, on my soul, be satisfied
With my repentance ; *manet alta mente repostum.*[*]
    Fran. de Med. Now, by my birth, you are a
foolish, mad,
And jealous woman.
    Brach. You see 'tis not my seeking.

Fran. de Med. Was this your circle of pure
unicorn's horn
You said should charm your lord ? now, horns
upon thee,
For jealousy deserves them ! Keep your vow
And take your chamber.
    Isab. No, sir, I'll presently to Padua ;
I will not stay a minute.
    Mont. O good madam !
    Brach. 'Twere best to let her have her humour :
Some half day's journey will bring down her
stomach,
And then she'll turn in post.
    Fran. de Med. To see her come
To my lord cardinal for a dispensation
Of her rash vow, will beget excellent laughter.
    Isab. Unkindness, do thy office ; poor heart,
break :
Those are the killing griefs which dare not speak.[*]
                                [*Exit.*

Re-enter MARCELLO *with* CAMILLO.

    Mar. Camillo's come, my lord.
    Fran. de Med. Where's the commission ?
    Mar. 'Tis here.
    Fran. de Med. Give me the signet.
    [FRANCISCO DE MEDICIS, MONTICELSO, CAMILLO,
        and MARCELLO, *retire to the back of the stage.*

    Flam. My lord, do you mark their whispering ?
I will compound a medicine, out of their two
heads, stronger than garlic, deadlier than stibium ;†
the cantharides, which are scarce seen to stick
upon the flesh when they work to the heart,
shall not do it with more silence or invisible
cunning.
    Brach. About the murder ?
    Flam. They are sending him to Naples, but I'll
send him to Candy.

                Enter Doctor.

Here's another property too.
    Brach. O, the doctor !
    Flam. A poor quack-salving knave, my lord ;
one that should have been lashed for's lechery,
but that he confessed a judgment, had an execution laid upon him, and so put the whip to a
non plus.
    Doc. And was cozened, my lord, by an

---

* *Those are the killing griefs which dare not speak*]   "So
in *Macbeth*, A. 4. S. 3.
    'Give sorrow words : the grief that does not speak,
    Whispers the o'erfraught heart, and bids it break.'
Cura levei loquuntur, ingentes stupent. [Seneca, *Hippol.*
607.]" STEEVENS.
    † *stibium]* "An ancient name for antimony, now sel-
dom used." REED.

* *manet alta, &c.*] Virgil, Æn. i. 26.

arranter knave than myself, and made pay all
the colourable execution.

Flam. He will shoot pills into a man's guts
shall make them have more ventages than a cornet
or a lamprey; he will poison a kiss; and was
once minded, for his master-piece, because Ireland
breeds no poison,* to have prepared a deadly
vapour in a Spaniard's fart, that should have
poisoned all Dublin.

Brach. O, Saint Anthony's fire.

Doc. Your secretary is merry, my lord.

Flam. O thou cursed antipathy to nature!
—Look, his eye's bloodshed, like a needle a
chirurgeon stitcheth a wound with.—Let me
embrace thee, toad, and love thee, O thou
abominable loathsome† gargarism, that will fetch
up lungs, lights, heart, and liver, by scruples!

Brach. No more.—I must employ thee, honest
doctor:
You must to Padua, and by the way,
Use some of your skill for us.

Doc. Sir, I shall.‡

Brach. But, for Camillo?

Flam. He dies this night, by such a politic
strain,
Men shall suppose him by's own engine slain.
But, for your duchess' death—

Doc. I'll make her sure.

Brach. Small mischiefs are by greater made
secure.

Flam. Remember this, you slave; when knaves
come to preferment, they rise as gallowses are
raised i'the Low Countries, one upon another's
shoulders.
[*Exeunt* Brachiano, Flamineo, *and* Doctor.

Mont. Here is an emblem, nephew, peruse
it:
'Twas thrown in at your window.

Cam. At my window!
Here is a stag, my lord, hath shed his horns,
And, for the loss of them, the poor beast weeps:
The word,§ *Inopem me copia fecit.*‖

Mont. That is,
Plenty of horns hath made him poor of horns.

Cam. What should this mean?

Mont. I'll tell you: 'tis given out
You are a cuckold.

Cam. Is it* given out so?
I had rather such report as that, my lord,
Should keep within doors.

Fran. de Med. Have you any children?

Cam. None, my lord.

Fran. de Med. You are the happier:
I'll tell you a tale.

Cam. Pray, my lord.

Fran. de Med. An old tale.
Upon a time Phœbus, the god of light,
Or him we call the Sun, would needs† be married:
The gods gave their consent, and Mercury
Was sent to voice it to the general world.
But what a piteous cry there straight arose
Amongst smiths and felt-makers, brewers and
cooks,
Reapers and butter-women, amongst fishmongers,
And thousand other trades, which are annoy'd
By his excessive heat! 'twas lamentable.
They came‡ to Jupiter all in a sweat,
And do forbid the bans.§ A great fat cook
Was made their speaker, who entreats of Jove
That Phœbus might be gelded; for, if now,
When there was but one sun, so many men
Were like to perish by his violent heat,
What should they do if he were married,
And should beget more, and those children
Make fire-works like their father? So say I;
Only I will apply it to your wife:
Her issue, should not providence prevent it,
Would make both nature, time, and man repent
it.

Mont. Look you, cousin,
Go, change the air, for shame; see if your absence
Will blast your cornucopia. Marcello
Is chosen with you joint commissioner
For the relieving our Italian coast
From pirates.

Mar. I am much honour'd in't.

Cam. But, sir,
Ere I return, the stag's horns may be sprouted
Greater than those‖ are shed.

Mont. Do not fear it:
I'll be your ranger.

* *because Ireland breeds no poison*] Various old writers tell us that all venomous creatures were exterminated in Ireland by the prayers of St. Patrick.
† *loathsome*] Some copies of the 4to. of 1612 "*lothan.*"
‡ *Doc. Sir, I shall*] Omitted in some copies of the 4to. of 1612.
§ *The word*] i.e. the motto. So Middleton: "The device, a purse wide open, and the mouth downward; *the word, Alienis ecce crumenis.*" *Your Five Gallants, Works*, ii. 313, ed. Dyce.
‖ *Inopem, &c.*] Ovid, *Metam.* iii. 466.

* *Is it*] The 4to. of 1631 "*It is.*"
† *needs*] The 4to. of 1612 "*need.*"
‡ *came*] So, no doubt, our author wrote,—not "come." See before and after in this speech.
§ *bans*] The 4tos. have "banes"; and in the first edition of this work I allowed that spelling to stand: but I now think that it ought to be retained only in passages where the rhyme requires it.
‖ *those*] The 4to. of 1612, "*these.*"

Cam. You must watch i'the nights;
Theu's the most danger.

Fran. de Med. Farewell, good Marcello :
All the best fortunes of a soldier's wish
Bring you a-ship-board !

Cam. Were I not best, now I am turn'd soldier,
Ere that I leave my wife, sell all she hath,
And then take leave of her ?

Mont. I expect good from you,
Your parting is so merry.

Cam. Merry, my lord ! o' the captain's humour
right ;
I am resolvèd to be drunk this night.
      [*Exeunt* CAMILLO *and* MARCELLO.

Fran. de Med. So, 'twas well fitted : now shall
we discern
How his wish'd absence will give violent way
To Duke Brachiano's lust.

Mont. Why, that was it ;
To what scorn'd purpose else should we make
choice
Of him for a sea-captain ? and, besides,
Count Lodowick, which was rumour'd for a pirate,
Is now in Padua.

Fran. de Med. Is't true ?

Mont. Most certain.
I have letters from him, which are suppliant
To work his quick repeal from banishment :
He means to address himself for pension
Unto our sister duchess.

Fran. de Med. O, 'twas well :
We shall not want his absense past six days.
I fain would have the Duke Brachiano run
Into notorious scandal ; for there's naught
In such curs'd dotage to repair his name,
Only the deep sense of some deathless shame.

Mont. It may be objected, I am dishonourable
To play thus with my kinsman ; but I answer,
For my revenge I'd stake a brother's life,
That, being wrong'd, durst not avenge himself.

Fran. de Med. Come, to observe this strumpet.

Mont. Curse of greatness !
Sure he'll not leave her ?

Fran. de Med. There's small pity in't :
Like misletoo on sear elms spent by weather,
Let him cleave to her, and both rot together.
        [*Exeunt.*

Enter BRACHIANO,* *with a* Conjurer.

Brach. Now, sir, I claim your promise : 'tis
dead midnight,

The time prefix'd to show me, by your art,
How the intended murder of Camillo
And our loath'd duchess grow to action.

Con. You have won me by your bounty to a deed
I do not often practise. Some there are
Which by sophistic tricks aspire that name,
Which I would gladly lose, of necromancer ;
As some that use to juggle upon cards,
Seeming to conjure, when indeed they cheat ;
Others that raise up their confederate spirits
'Bout wind-mills, and endanger their own necks
For making of a squib ; and some there are
Will keep a curtal * to show juggling tricks,
And give out 'tis a spirit ; besides these,
Such a whole realm † of almanac-makers, figure-
flingers,
Follows, indeed, that only live by stealth,
Since they do merely lie about stol'n goods,
They'd make men think the devil were fast and
loose,
With speaking fustian Latin. Pray, sit down :
Put on this night-cap, sir, 'tis charm'd ; and now
I'll show you, by my strong commanding art,
The circumstance that breaks your duchess' heart.

A dumb show.

Enter suspiciously JULIO *and* CHRISTOPHERO : *they draw a curtain where* BRACHIANO'S *picture is ; they put on spectacles of glass, which cover their eyes and noses, and then burn perfumes afore the picture, and wash the lips of the picture ; that done, quenching the fire, and putting off their spectacles, they depart laughing.*

Enter ISABELLA *in her night-gown, as to bed-ward, with lights after her,* Count LODOVICO, GIOVANNI, GUID-ANTONIO, *and others waiting on her ; she kneels down as to prayers, then draws the curtain of the picture, does three reverences to it, and kisses it thrice ; she faints, and will not suffer them to come near it ; dies ; sorrow ex-pressed in* GIOVANNI *and in* Count LODOVICO : *she is conveyed out solemnly.*

Brach. Excellent ! then she's dead.

Con. She's poisonèd
By the fume'd picture. 'Twas her custom nightly,
Before she went to bed, to go and visit
Your picture, and to feed her eyes and lips
On the dead shadow. Doctor Julio,
Observing this, infects it with an oil
And other poison'd stuff, which presently
Did suffocate her spirits.

---

* *Enter Brachiano, &c.*] Scene. The Same. A room in the house o Camillo (In p. 13, the Conjurer, after exhibiting in dumb-show the murder of Camillo, says
    " We are now
  Beneath her [Vittoria's] roof.")

---

* *Will keep a curtol, &c.*] "This was said of Banks's celebrated horse so often mentioned in ancient writers."
          REED.

† *realm*]The 4 tos. have "reame,"—which was frequently the old spelling of "realm :" even when the latter spelling was given, the *l* was frequently not sounded :—see the note in my ed. of Marlowe's *Works* on "Give me a ream of paper : we'll have a kingdom of gold for't." *Jew of Malta*, act IV.

              C

Brach. Methought I saw
Count Lodowick there.

Con. He was: and by my art
I find he did most passionately dote
Upon your duchess. Now turn another way,
And view Camillo's far more politic fate.*—
Strike louder, music, from this charmèd
　　ground,
To yield, as fits the act, a tragic sound!

The second dumb show.

Enter FLAMINEO, MARCELLO, CAMILLO, *with four more, as
Captains: they drink healths, and dance: a vaulting-
horse is brought into the room: MARCELLO and two
more whispered out of the room, while FLAMINEO and
CAMILLO strip themselves into their shirts, as to vault;
they compliment who shall begin: as CAMILLO is about
to vault, FLAMINEO pitcheth him upon his neck, and,
with the help of the rest, writhes his neck about: seems to
see if it be broke, and lays him folded double, as 'twere,
under the horse: makes shows to call for help: MAR-
CELLO comes in, laments: sends for the Cardinal and
Duke, who come forth with armed men: wonder at the
act: command the body to be carried home: apprehend
FLAMINEO, MARCELLO, and the rest, and go, as 'twere,
to apprehend VITTORIA.*

Brach. 'Twas quaintly done; but yet each cir-
　　cumstance
I taste not fully.

Con. O, 'twas most apparent:
You saw them enter, charg'd with their deep
　　healths
To their boon voyage; and, to second that,
Flamineo calls to have a vaulting-horse
Maintain their sport; the virtuous Marcello
Is innocently plotted forth the room;
Whilst your eye saw the rest, and can inform you
The engine of all.

Brach. It seems Marcello and Flamineo
Are both committed.

Con. Yes, you saw them guarded;
And now they are come with purpose to appre-
　　hend
Your mistress, fair Vittoria. We are now
Beneath her roof: 'twere fit we instantly
Make out by some back-postern.

Brach. Noble friend,
You bind me ever to you: this shall stand
As the firm seal annexèd to my hand;
It shall enforce a payment.

Con. Sir, I thank you.　　[*Exit* BRACHIANO.
Both flowers and weeds spring when the sun is
　　warm,
And great men do great good or else great harm.
　　　　　　　　　　　　　[*Exit.*

---

* *fate*] So the 4to. of 1672: the earlier 4tos. have
"*face,*" which, though obviously a misprint, is followed
in all modern editions.

Enter FRANCISCO DE MEDICIS,* *and* MONTICELSO, *their
Chancellor and* Register.

Fran. de Med. You have dealt discreetly, to
　　obtain the presence
Of all the grave lieger ambassadors,†
To hear Vittoria's trial.

Mont. 'Twas not ill;
For, sir, you know we have naught but circum-
　　stances
To charge her with, about her husband's death:
Their approbation, therefore, to the proofs
Of her black lust shall make her infamous
To all our neighbouring kingdoms. I wonder
If Brachiano will be here.

Fran. de Med. O fie.
'Twere impudence too palpable.　　[*Exeunt.*

Enter FLAMINEO‡ *and* MARCELLO *guarded, and a
Lawyer.*

Lawyer. What, are you in by the week?§ so, I
will try now whether thy wit be close prisoner.
Methinks none should sit upon thy sister but
old whore-masters.

Flam. Or cuckolds; for your cuckold is your
most terrible tickler of lechery. Whore-masters
would serve; for none are judges at tilting but
those that have been old tilters.

Lawyer. My lord duke and she have been very
private.

Flam. You are a dull ass; 'tis threatened they
have been very public.

Lawyer. If it can be proved they have but
kissed one another—

Flam. What then?

Lawyer. My lord cardinal will ferret them.

Flam. A cardinal, I hope, will not catch conies.

Lawyer. For to sow kisses (mark what I say),
to sow kisses is to reap lechery; and, I am sure,
a woman that will endure kissing is half won.

Flam. True, her upper part, by that rule: if
you will win her nether part too, you know what
follows.

Lawyer. Hark! the ambassadors are lighted.

---

* *Enter Francisco de Medicis, &c.*] Scene. The Same.
Perhaps the court of the house where the trial of Vittoria
is to take place,—the mansion, it would seem, of Monticelso, for afterwards, p. 19, he says,
　　"This business by his holiness is left
　　　　To our examination:"
and compare Brachiano's speech, p. 22, "Thou liest, 'twas
my stool," &c.

† *lieger ambassadors*] i. e. resident ambassadors.

‡ *Enter Flamineo, &c.*] Perhaps this is not a new scene.

§ *What, are you in by the week?*] "This phrase appears
to signify an engagement for a time limited. It occurs
in *Love's Labour's Lost,* A. 5. S. 2. See note thereon."
　　　　　　　　　　　　　　　　STEEVENS.

Flam. [*aside*]. I do put on this feignèd garb of mirth
To gull suspicion.

Mar. O my unfortunate sister!
I would my dagger-point had cleft her heart
When she first saw Brachiano: you, 'tis said,
Were made his engine and his stalking-horse,
To undo my sister.

Flam. I am a kind of path
To her and mine own preferment.

Mar. Your ruin.

Flam. Hum! thou art a soldier,
Follow'st the great duke, feed'st his victories,
As witches do their serviceable spirits,
Even with thy prodigal blood: what hast got,
But, like the wealth of captains, a poor handful,
Which in thy palm thou bear'st as men hold water?
Seeking to gripe it fast, the frail reward
Steals through thy fingers.*

Mar. Sir!

Flam. Thou hast scarce maintenance
To keep thee in fresh shamois.†

Mar. Brother!

Flam. Hear me:—
And thus, when we have even pour'd ourselves
Into great fights, for their ambition
Or idle spleen, how shall we find reward?
But as we seldom find the misletoe
Sacred to physic, or the builder oak,‡
Without a mandrake by it; so in our quest of gain,
Alas, the poorest of their forc'd dislikes
At a limb proffers, but at heart it strikes!
This is lamented doctrine.

Mar. Come, come.

Flam. When age shall turn thee
White as a blooming hawthorn——

Mar. I'll interrupt you:—
For love of virtue bear an honest heart,
And stride o'er every politic respect,
Which, where they most advance, they most infect.
Were I your father, as I am your brother,

I should not be ambitious to leave you
A better patrimony.

Flam. I'll think on't.—
The lord ambassadors.

Here there is a passage of the lieger Ambassadors over the stage severally.

Lawyer. O my sprightly Frenchman!—Do you know him? he's an admirable tilter.

Flam. I saw him at last tilting: he showed like a pewter candlestick, fashioned † like a man in armour, holding a tilting-staff in his hand, little bigger than a candle of twelve i'the pound.

Lawyer. O, but he's an excellent horseman.

Flam. A lame one in his lofty tricks: he sleeps a-horseback, like a poulter.‡

Lawyer. Lo you, my Spaniard!

Flam. He carries his face in's ruff, as I have seen a serving-man carry glasses in a cipress hatband, monstrous steady, for fear of breaking: he looks like the claw of a black-bird, first salted, and then broiled in a candle. [*Exeunt.*

The Arraignment of VITTORIA.§

Enter FRANCISCO DE MEDICIS, MONTICELSO, *the six ‖ lieger* Ambassadors, BRACHIANO, VITTORIA COROMBONA, FLAMINEO, MARCELLO, Lawyer, *and a* Guard.

Mont. Forbear, my lord, here is no place assign'd you:
This business by his holiness is left
To our examination.

Brach. May it thrive with you!
[*Lays a rich gown under him.*

Fran. de Med. A chair there for his lordship!

Brach. Forbear your kindness: an unbidden guest
Should travel as Dutch women go to church,
Bear their stools with them.

Mont. At your pleasure, sir.—
Stand to the table, gentlewoman.¶—Now, signior,
Fall to your plea.

---

* I have here omitted, as superfluous, some notices, "*Enter French Ambassador,*" &c.

† *a pewter candlestick, fashioned, &c.*] See an engraving of such a candlestick in Malone's *Shakespeare* (by Boswell,) vol. xvii. p. 410.

‡ *poulter*] i. e. poulterer. "The Poulters send us in fowle." Heywood's *King Edward the Fourth, Part First,* Sig. B. ed. 1619.

§ *The Arraignment of Vittoria*] A new scene. See note*, p. 18.

‖ *six*] Was altered by Reed to "*four;*" but from a subsequent scene, where Lodovico enumerates their various orders of knighthood, it is evident that there were "*six*" ambassadors.—It is not a little extraordinary that all the editors should let the name of Isabella (whose death has been shown by the Conjurer) remain in this stage-direction.

¶ *gentlewoman*] Both the earliest 4tos. "*gentlewomen.*"

---

* *Which in thy palm thou bear'st as men hold water?*
Seeking to gripe it fast, the frail reward
Steals through thy fingers] "Dryden has borrowed this thought in *All for Love;* or, *The World well Lost,* A. 5:

  ' Oh, that I loss could fear to lose this being,
     Which, *like a snow-ball, in my coward hand*
       The more 'tis grasp'd, the faster melts away.'" REED.

† *shamois*] "i. e. shoes made of the wild goat's skin. *Chamois,* Fr." STEVENS.

‡ *the builder oak*] "The epithet of '*builder* oak' is originally Chaucer's;

  ' *The bilder oke,* and eke the hardy ashe,
     The piller elme,' &c.—*Assemble of Foules.*" COLLIER.

c 2

Lawyer. Domine judex, converte oculos in hanc pestem, mulierum corruptissimam.

Vit. Cor. What's he?

Fran. de Med. A lawyer that pleads against you.

Vit. Cor. Pray, my lord, let him speak his usual tongue;

I'll make no answer else.

Fran. de Med. Why, you understand Latin.

Vit. Cor. I do, sir; but amongst this auditory Which come to hear my cause, the half or more May be ignorant in't.

Mont. Go on, sir.

Vit. Cor. By your favour, I will not have my accusation clouded In a strange tongue: all this assembly Shall hear what you can charge me with.

Fran. de Med. Signior, You need not stand on't much; pray, change your language.

Mont. O, for God sake!—Gentlewoman, your credit Shall be more famous by it.

Lawyer. Well, then, have at you!

Vit. Cor. I am at the mark, sir: I'll give aim* to you, And tell you how near you shoot.

Lawyer. Most literated judges, please your lordships So to connive your judgments to the view Of this debauch'd and diversivolent woman; Who such a black † concatenation Of mischief hath effected, that to extirp The memory of't, must be the consummation Of her and her projections,—

Vit. Cor. What's all this?

Lawyer. Hold your peace: Exorbitant sins must have exulceration.

Vit. Cor. Surely, my lords, this lawyer here ‡ hath swallow'd Some pothecaries' § bills, or proclamations; And now the hard and undigestible words Come up, like stones we use give hawks for physic: Why, this is Welsh to Latin.

Lawyer. My lords, the woman Knows not her tropes nor figures,‖ nor is perfect

In the academic derivation Of grammatical elocution.

Fran. de Med. Sir, your pains Shall be well spar'd, and your deep eloquence Be worthily applauded amongst those Which understand you.

Lawyer. My good lord,—

Fran. de Med. Sir, Put up your papers in your fustian bag,—

[FRANCISCO *speaks this as in scorn.*

Cry mercy, sir, 'tis buckram,—and accept My notion of your learn'd verbosity.

Lawyer. I most graduatically thank your lordship: I shall have use for them elsewhere.

Mont. I shall be plainer with you, and paint out Your follies in more natural red and white Than that upon your cheek.

Vit. Cor. O, you mistake: You raise a blood as noble in this cheek As ever was your mother's.

Mont. I must spare you, till proof cry "whore" to that.— Observe this creature here, my honour'd lords, A woman of a most prodigious spirit, In her effected.

Vit. Cor. Honourable my lord,* It doth not suit a reverend cardinal To play the lawyer thus.

Mont. O, your trade instructs your language.— You see, my lords, what goodly fruit she seems; Yet, like those apples † travellers report To grow where Sodom and Gomorrah stood, I will but touch her, and you straight shall see She'll fall to soot and ashes.

Vit. Cor. Your envenom'd Pothecary ‡ should do't.

Mont. I am resolv'd,§

* *Honourable my lord]* The 4to. of 1631 "My honorable Lord:" but compare, in a later scene, " *Noble my lord,* most fortunately welcome," &c.

† *Yet, like those apples, &c.*] "This account is taken from Maundeville's *Travels.* See Edition, 1725, p. 122. 'And also the Cytees there woren lost, because of Synne. And there besyden growen trees, that beren fulle *faire Apples,* and *faire of colour to beholde; but whoso brekethe hen, or cuttethe hen in two, he schalle fynde within hem Coles and Cyndres;* in tokene that, be Wrathe of God, the Cytees and the Lond weren brento and sonken into Helle. Summon clepen that See, the Lake Dalfetidee; summe the Flom of Develes; and sume that Flom that is ever stynkynge. And in to that See sonken the 5 Cytees, be Wrathe of God; that is to seyne, *Sodom, Gomorre,* Aldama, Seboym, and Segor.'" REED.

‡ *Pothecary]* The 4to. of 1631 " *Apothecary.*

§ *resolv'd]* I. e. convinced.

* *I'll give aim]* "He who *gave aim* was stationed near the butts, and pointed out after every discharge, how wide, or how short, the arrow fell of the mark." See Gifford's note on the expressions *cry aim* and *give aim,* Massinger's *Bondman,* act 1. sc. 3.

† *black]* Omitted in the 4to. of 1631.

‡ *here]* Omitted in the 4to. of 1631.

§ *pothecaries']* The 4to. of 1631 " *apothecaries.'*

‖ *nor figures]* Omitted in the 4to. of 1631.

Were there a second Paradise to lose,
This devil would betray it.
Vit. Cor. O poor charity !
Thou art seldom found in scarlet.
Mont. Who knows not how, when several night
by night
Her gates were chok'd with coaches, and her rooms
Outbrav'd the stars with several kind of lights;
When she did counterfeit a prince's court
In music, banquets, and most riotous surfeits?
This whore, forsooth, was holy.
Vit. Cor. Ha ! whore! what's that?
Mont. Shall I expound whore to you? sure, I
shall;
I'll give their perfect character. They are first,
Sweet-meats which rot the eater ; * in man's
nostrils †
Poison'd perfumes: they are cozening alchymy;
Shipwrecks in calmest weather. What are whores!
Cold Russian winters, that appear so barren
As if that nature had forgot the spring :
They are the true material fire of hell : .
Worse than those tributes i'the Low Countries paid,
Exactions upon meat, drink, garments, sleep,
Ay, even on man's perdition, his sin :
They are those brittle evidences of law
Which forfeit all a wretched man's estate
For leaving out one syllable. What are whores !
They are those flattering bells none set one tune,
At weddings and at funerals. Your rich whores
Are only treasuries by extortion fill'd,
And emptied by curs'd riot. They are worse,
Worse than dead bodies which are begg'd at
gallows,‡
And wrought upon by surgeons, to teach man
Wherein he is imperfect. What's a whore !
She's like the guilty § counterfeited coin
Which, whosoe'er first stamps it, brings in trouble
All that receive it.
Vit. Cor. This character scapes me.
Mont. You, gentlewoman !
Take from all beasts and from all minerals
Their deadly poison—
Vit. Cor. Well, what then ?
Mont. I'll tell thee;
I'll find in thee a pothecary's ‖ shop,
To sample them all.

Fr. Am. She hath liv'd ill.
Eng. Am. True ; but the cardinal's too bitter.
Mont. You know what whore is. Next the
devil adultery,
Enters the devil murder.
Fran. de Med. Your unhappy
Husband is dead.
Vit. Cor. O, he's a happy husband :
Now he owes nature nothing.
Fran. de Med. And by a vaulting-engine.
Mont. An active plot; he jump'd into his grave.
Fran. de Med. What a prodigy was't
That from some two yards' height* a slender man
Should break his neck !
Mont. I'the rushes ! †
Fran. de Med. And what's more,
Upon the instant lose all use of speech,
All vital motion, like a man had lain
Wound up three days. Now mark each circum-
stance.
Mont. And look upon this creature was his
wife.
She comes not like a widow; she comes arm'd
With scorn and impudence : is this a mourning-
habit?
Vit. Cor. Had I foreknown his death, as you
suggest,
I would have bespoke my mourning.
Mont. O, you are cunning.
Vit. Cor. You shame your wit and judgment,
To call it so. What ! is my just defence
By him that is my judge call'd impudence ?
Let me appeal, then, from this Christian court‡
To the uncivil Tartar.
Mont. See, my lords,
She scandals our proceedings.
Vit. Cor. Humbly thus,
Thus low, to the most worthy and respected
Lieger ambassadors,§ my modesty
And woman-hood I tender ; but withal,
So entangled in a cursèd accusation,
That my defence, of force, like Perseus,‖

---

* *height*] The 4to. of 1631 "*high.*"
† *the rushes*] With which floors were formerly strewed,
before the introduction of carpets.
‡ *Christian court*] " We have here an instance of the
introduction of terms into one country, which peculiarly
belong to another. In England the Ecclesiastical Courts,
where causes of adultery are cognizable, are called *Courts
Christian.*" REED.
§ *Lieger ambassadors*] i. e. resident ambassadors.
‖ *Perseus*] A corruption, for which I know not what
to substitute. Can "Portia" be the right reading?
(" Portia, the wife of Brutus and daughter of Cato . . . .
she feared not with her womanish spirit to imitate
(if not exceed) the resolution of her father in his

---

* *Sweet-meats which rot the eater*] So Dekker;
    " What glues she me? good words,
    Sweet meates that rotte the eater."
        The Whore of Babylon, 1607, Sig. I. 2.
† *nostrils*] The 4to. of 1612 "*nostril.*"
‡ *gallows*] The 4to. of 1631 "*th'* gallows."
§ *guilty*] The 4to of 1631 "*gilt.*"
‖ *a pothecary's*] The 4to. of 1631 " *an apothecary's.*"

Must personate masculine virtue. To the point.
Find me but guilty, sever head from body,
We'll part good friends : I scorn to hold my life
At yours or any man's entreaty, sir.

Eng. Am. She hath a brave spirit.

Mont. Well, well, such counterfeit jewels
Make true ones oft suspected.

Vit. Cor. You are deceiv'd :
For know, that all your strict-combinèd heads,
Which strike against this mine of diamonds,
Shall prove but glassen hammers,— they shall
    break.
These are but feignèd shadows of my evils :
Terrify babes, my lord, with painted devils ; *
I am past such needless palsy. For your names
Of whore and murderess, they proceed from you,
As if a man should spit against the wind ;
The filth returns in's face.

Mont. Pray you, mistress, satisfy me one
    question :
Who lodg'd beneath your roof that fatal night
Your husband brake his neck ?

Brach. That question
Enforceth me break silence : I was there.

Mont. Your business ?

Brach. Why, I came to comfort her,
And take some course for settling her estate,
Because I heard her husband was in debt
To you, my lord.

Mont. He was.

Brach. And 'twas strangely fear'd
That you would cozen her.

Mont. Who made you overseer ?

Brach. Why, my charity, my charity, which
should flow
From every generous and noble spirit
To orphans and to widows.

Mont. Your lust.

Brach. Cowardly dogs bark loudest : sirrah
priest,
I'll talk with you hereafter. Do you hear ?
The sword you frame of such an excellent temper
I'll sheathe in your own bowels.
There are a number of thy coat resemble
Your common post-boys.

Mont. Ha !

Brach. Your mercenary post-boys :
Your letters carry truth, but 'tis your guise
To fill your mouths with gross and impudent lies.

death," &c.,—says Heywood, *Hist. of Women*, p. 136,
ed. 1624.)
   * *Terrify babes, my lord, with painted devils*] "So in
Macbeth, A. 2. S. 2.
      ' 'tis the eye of *childhood*
      That fears a *painted devil*.'" REED.

Serv. My lord, your gown.

Brach. Thou liest, 'twas my stool :
Bestow't upon thy master, that will challenge
The rest o' the household-stuff; for Brachiano
Was ne'er so beggarly to take a stool
Out of another's lodging : let him make
Vallance for his bed on't, or a demi-foot-cloth *
For his most reverend moil.† Monticelso,
Nemo me impune lacessit.   [*Exit.*

Mont. Your champion's gone.

Vit. Cor. The wolf may prey the better.

Fan. de Med. My lord, there's great auspicion
    of the murder,
But no sound proof who did it. For my part,
I do not think she hath a soul so black
To act a deed so bloody : if she have,
As in cold countries husbandmen plant vines,
And with warm blood manure them, even so
One summer she will bear unsavoury fruit,
And ere next spring wither both branch and root.
The act of blood let pass; only descend
To matter of incontinence.

Vit. Cor. I discern poison
Under your gilded pills.

Mont. Now the duke's gone, I will produce a
    letter,
Wherein 'twas plotted he and you should meet
At an apothecary's summer-house,
Down by the river Tiber,—view't, my lords,—
Where, after wanton bathing and the heat
Of a lascivious banquet,—I pray read it,
I shame to speak the rest.

Vit. Cor. Grant I was tempted ;
Temptation to lust proves not the act :
Casta est quam nemo rogavit.‡
You read his hot love to me, but you want
My frosty answer.

Mont. Frost i'the dog-days ! strange !

Vit. Cor. Condemn you me for that the duke
did love me ?
So may you blame some fair and crystal river
For that some melancholic distracted man
Hath drown'd himself in't.

Mont. Truly drown'd, indeed.

Vit. Cor. Sum up my faults, I pray, and you
shall find,
That beauty, and gay clothes, a merry heart,
And a good stomach to [a] feast, are all,
All the poor crimes that you can charge me with.
In faith, my lord, you might go pistol flies;
The sport would be more noble.

   * *demi-foot-cloth*] i. e. demi-housing.
   † *moil*] i. e. mule.
   ‡ *Casta est*, &c.] Ovid, *Amor.* I. 8.

Mont. Very good.

Vit. Cor. But take you your course : it seems
you have beggar'd me first,
And now would fain undo me.   I have houses,
Jewels, and a poor remnant of crusadoes : *
Would those would make you charitable !

Mont. If the devil
Did ever take good shape, behold his picture.

Vit. Cor. You have one virtue left,—
You will not flatter me.   -

Fran. de Med. Who brought this letter ?

Vit. Cor. I am not compell'd to tell you.

Mont. My lord duke sent to you a thousand
      ducats
The twelfth of August.

Vit. Cor. 'Twas to keep your cousin
From prison : I paid use for't.

Mont. I rather think,
'Twas interest for his lust.

Vit. Cor. Who says so
But yourself ? if you be my accuser,
Pray, cease to be my judge : come from the bench ;
Give in your evidence 'gainst me, and let these
Be moderators.   My lord cardinal,
Were your intelligencing ears as loving
As to my thoughts, had you an honest tongue,
I would not care though you proclaim'd them all.

Mont. Go to, go to.
After your goodly and vain-glorious banquet,
I'll give you a choke-pear.

Vit. Cor. O' your own grafting ?

Mont. You were born in Venice, honourably
      descended
From the Vittelli : 'twas my cousin's fate,—
Ill may I name the hour,—to marry you :
He bought you of your father.

Vit. Cor. Ha !

Mont. He spent there in six months
Twelve thousand ducats, and (to my acquaintance)
Receiv'd in dowry with you not one julio :†
'Twas a hard penny-worth, the ware being so light.
I yet but draw the curtain ; now to your picture :
You came from thence a most notorious strumpet,
And so you have continu'd.   -

Vit. Cor. My lord,—

Mont. Nay, hear me ;
You shall have time to prate. My Lord Brachiano—
Alas, I make but repetition
Of what is ordinary and Rialto talk,

And ballated, and would be play'd o' the stage,
But that vice many times finds such loud friends
That preachers are charm'd silent.—
You gentlemen, Flaminco and Marcello,
The court hath nothing now to charge you with
Only you must remain upon your sureties
For your appearance.

Fran. de Med. I stand for Marcello.

Flam. And my lord duke for me.

Mont. For you, Vittoria, your public fault,
Join'd to the condition of the present time,
Takes from you all the fruits of noble pity ;
Such a corrupted trial have you made
Both of your life and beauty, and been styl'd
No less an* ominous fate than blazing stars
To princes : hear† your sentence ; you are confin'd
Unto a house of convertites, and your bawd ‡—

Flam. [*aside.*] Who, I ?

Mont. The Moor.

Flam. [*aside.*] O, I am a sound man again.

Vit. Cor. A house of convertites ! what's that ?

Mont. A house
Of penitent whores.

Vit. Cor. Do the noblemen in Rome
Erect it for their wives, that I am sent
To lodge there ?

Fran. de Med. You must have patience.

Vit. Cor. I must first have vengeance.
I fain would know if you have your salvation
By patent, that you proceed thus.

Mont. Away with her !
Take her hence.

Vit. Cor. A rape ! a rape !

Mont. How !

Vit. Cor. Yes, you have ravish'd justice ;
Forc'd her to do your pleasure.

Mont. Fie, she's mad !

Vit. Cor. Die with these § pills in your most
      cursed maw ‖
Should bring you health ! or while you sit o' the
      bench,
Let your own spittle choke you !—

---

* *an*] The 4to. of 1612 "*in.*"

† *hear*] The 4to. of 1612 "*heares,*" i. e., perhaps,
"*here's.*"

‡ *Unto a house of convertites, &c.*] Both the earliest 4tos.
give this line to Vittoria. The 4to. of 1631 here, as
well as elsewhere, changes "*convertites*" into "*converts.*"
("*and your bawd the Moor,*" i. e., along with your bawd
the Moor [Zanche].)

§ *these*] So the two earliest 4tos. In a later 4to. "*those*"
was substituted : but our old writers very frequently use
"*these*" and "*those*" indiscriminately.

‖ *maw*] So the 4to. of 1631. The 4to. of 1612 "*mawes :*"
but she is speaking to Monticelso only ; see in her next
speech "leave you the same *devil*" &c.

---

* *crusadoes*] The Portuguese coin, called *Crusado* from
the cross on one side of it, has varied in value, at different
times, from 2*s.* 3*d.* to 10*s.*

† *julio*] "A coin of about six-pence value.   Moryson,
in the Table prefixed to his Itinerary, calls it a *Giulio* or
Paolo." REED.

Mont. She's turn'd Fury.

Vit. Cor. That the last day of judgment may
    so find you,
And leave you the same devil you were before !
Instruct me, some good horse-leech, to speak
    treason;
For since you cannot take my life for deeds,
Take it for words: O woman's poor revenge,
Which dwells but in the tongue ! I will not weep;
No, I do scorn to call up one poor tear
To fawn on your injustice: bear me hence
Unto this house of—what's your mitigating title ?

Mont. Of convertites.

Vit. Cor. It shall not be a house of convertites ;
My mind shall make it honester to me
Than the Pope's palace, and more peaceable
Than thy soul, though thou art a cardinal.
Know this, and let it somewhat raise your spite,
Through darkness diamonds spread their richest
    light.*
   [*Exeunt* VITTORIA COROMBONA, Lawyer, *and* Guards.

    Re-enter BRACHIANO.

Brach. Now you and I are friends, sir, we'll
    shake hands
In a friend's grave together; a fit place,
Being the emblem of soft peace, to atone† our
    hatred.

Fran. de Med. Sir, what's the matter ?

Brach. I will not chase more blood from that
    lov'd cheek ;
You have lost too much already : fare you well.
                    [*Exit.*

Fran. de Med. How strange those words sound !
    what's the interpretation ?

Flam. [*aside.*] Good ; this is a preface to the
discovery of the duchess' death : he carries it
well. Because now I cannot counterfeit a whining
passion for the death of my lady, I will feign a
mad humour for the disgrace of my sister ; and
that will keep off idle questions. Treason's

---

* "This White Devil of Italy sets off a bad cause so
speciously, and pleads with such an innocence-resembling
boldness, that we seem to see that matchless beauty of
her face which inspires such gay confidence into her ;
and are ready to expect, when she has done her plead-
ings, that her very judges, her accusers, the grave ambassadors who sit as spectators, and all the court, will
rise and make proffer to defend her in spite of the utmost
conviction of her guilt ; as the shepherds in Don Quixote
make proffer to follow the beautiful shepherdess Mar-
cela, 'without reaping any profit out of her manifest
resolution made there in their hearing.'
    ' So sweet and lovely does she make the shame,
    Which, like a canker in the fragrant rose,
    Does spot the beauty of her budding name. ' "
        C. Lamb. (*Spec. of Eng. Dram. Poets*, p. 229.)
† *atone*] "L e. reconcile." STEEVENS.

---

tongue hath* a villanous palsy in't : I will talk
to any man, hear no man, and for a time appear
a politic madman.   [*Exit.*

   Enter GIOVANNI, Count LODOVICO, *and* Attendant.

Fran. de Med. How now, my noble cousin !
    what, in black !

Giov. Yes, uncle, I was taught to imitate you
In virtue, and you must imitate me
In colours of your garments. My sweet mother
    Is—

Fran. de Med. How ! where ?

Giov. Is there ; no, yonder : indeed, sir, I'll
    not tell you,
For I shall make you weep.

Fran. de Med. Is dead ?

Giov. Do not blame me now,
I did not tell you so.

Lod. She's dead, my lord.

Fran. de Med. Dead !

Mont. Bless'd lady, thou art now above thy
    woes !—
Wilt please your lordships to withdraw a little ?
            [*Exeunt* Ambassadors.

Giov. What do the dead do, uncle ? do they
    eat,
Hear music, go a hunting, and be merry,
As we that live ?

Fran. de Med. No, coz ; they sleep.

Giov. Lord, Lord, that I were dead !
I have not slept these six nights.—When do
    they wake ?

Fran. de Med. When God shall please.

Giov. Good God, let her sleep ever !†
For I have known her wake an hundred nights,
When all the pillow where she laid her head
Was brine-wet with her tears. I am to complain
    to you, sir ;
I'll tell you how they have us'd her now she's
    dead :
They wrapp'd her in a cruel fold of lead,
And would not let me kiss her.

Fran. de Med. Thou didst love her.

Giov. I have often heard her say she gave me
    suck,
And it should seem by that she dearly lov'd me,
Since princes seldom do it.

Fran. de Med. O, all of my poor sister that
    remains !—
Take him away, for God's sake !
       [*Exeunt* GIOVANNI *and* Attendant.

Mont. How now, my lord !

---

* *hath*] The 4to. of 1631 "*with.*"
† Both the earliest 4tos. give this line to Francisco.

Fran. de Med. Believe me, I am nothing but
  her grave;
And I shall keep her blessèd memory
Longer than thousand epitaphs.
        [*Exeunt* FRANCISCO DE MEDICIS *and* MONTICELSO.

Re-enter FLAMINEO * *as distracted.*

Flam. We endure the strokes like anvils or
  hard steel,
Till pain itself make us no pain to feel.
Who shall do me right now? is this the end of
service? I'd rather go weed garlic; travel through
France, and be mine own ostler; wear sheep-skin
linings, or shoes that stink of blacking; be
entered into the list of the forty thousand ped-
lers in Poland.

Re-enter Ambassadors.

Would I had rotted in some surgeon's house at
Venice, built upon the pox as well as on piles,
ere I had served Brachiano!
Savoy Amb. You must have comfort.
Flam. Your comfortable words are like honey;
they relish well in your mouth that's whole, but
in mine that's wounded they go down as if the
sting of the bee were in them. O, they have
wrought their purpose cunningly, as if they
would not seem to do it of malice! In this a
politician imitates the devil, as the devil imitates
a cannon; wheresoever he comes to do mischief,
he comes with his backside towards you.
French Amb. The proofs are evident.
Flam. Proof! 'twas corruption. O gold, what
a god art thou! and O man, what a devil art
thou to be tempted by that cursed mineral!
Your† diversivolent lawyer, mark him: knaves
turn informers, as maggots turn to flies; you
may catch gudgeons with either. A cardinal!
I would he would hear me: there's nothing so
holy but money will corrupt and putrify it, like
victual‡ under the line. You are happy in
England, my lord: here they sell justice with
those weights they press men to death with. O
horrible salary!
Eng. Amb. Fie, fie, Flamineo! *
          [*Exeunt* Ambassadors.

Flam. Bells ne'er ring well, till they are at
their full pitch; and I hope yon cardinal shall
never have the grace to pray well, till he come
to the scaffold. If they were racked now to

know the confederacy,——but your noblemen are
privileged from the rack; and well may, for a
little thing would pull some of them a-pieces
afore they came to their arraignment. Religion,
O, how it is commedled* with policy! The first
bloodshed in the world happened about religion.
Would I were a Jew!
Mar. O, there are too many.
Flam. You are deceived: there are not Jews
enough, priests enough, nor gentlemen enough.
Mar. How?
Flam. I'll prove it; for if there were Jews
enough, so many Christians would not turn
usurers; if priests enough, one should not have
six benefices; and if gentlemen enough, so many
early mushrooms, whose best growth sprang
from a dunghill, should not aspire to gentility.
Farewell: let others live by begging; be thou
one of them practise the art of Wolner in
England,† to swallow all's given thee; and yet
let one purgation make thee as hungry again as
fellows that work in a ‡ saw-pit. I'll go hear the
screech-owl.   [*Exit.*
Lod. [*aside.*] This was Brachiano's pander;
          and 'tis strange
That, in such open and apparent guilt
Of his adulterous sister, he dare utter
So scandalous a passion. I must wind him.

---

* *commedled*] "i. e. *co-mingled.* To meddle anciently
signified to *mix,* or *mingle.*" STEEVENS.

† *the art of Wolner in England*] "The exploits of this
glutton, and the manner of his death, are mentioned by
Dr. *Moffit,* who wrote in Queen Elizabeth's time. See
his Treatise, entitled 'Health's Improvement: or, Rules
comprizing and discovering the nature, method, and
manner of preparing all sorts of foods used in this nation.'
Republished by Oldys and Dr. James, 12mo. 1746.
' Neither was our country always void of a *Woolman,* who,
living in my memory in the court seemed like another
Pandareus, of whom Antonius Liberalis writeth thus
much, that he had obtained this gift of the Goddess
Ceres, to eat iron, glass, oyster-shells, raw fish, raw
flesh, raw fruit, and whatsoever else he would put into
his stomach, without offence.' P. 376. 'Other fish being
eaten raw, is harder of digestion than raw beef; for
Diogenes died with eating of raw fish; and *Wolner* (our
English Pandareus) digesting iron, glass, and oyster-
shells, by eating a raw eel was over-mastered.' P. 123.
He is also mentioned by Taylor the Water Poet, in his
account of *The Great Eater of Kent,* p. 145. ' Milo the
Crotonian could hardly be his equall: and *Woolner* of
Windsor was not worthy to bee his footman.' In the
books of the Stationers' company, in the year 1587, is the
following entry: ' Rec. of Henry Denham, for his lycense
for the pryntinge of a booke intituled Pleasaunte Tales of
the lyf of *Rychard Wolner, &c.*'" REED.
The seventh chapter of *The Life of Long Meg of Westminster,* 1635, relates "how she used *Woolner the singing
man of Windsor, that was the great eater,* and how she
made him pay for his breakfast."

‡ *a*] Omitted in the 4to. of 1612.

---

* *Re-enter Flamineo, &c.*] This is not a new scene; for
Lodovico and Marcello are still on the stage, and speak
presently.

† *Your*] The three earliest 4tos " You."

‡ *victual*] The 4to. of 1631 "*victuals.*"

Re-enter FLAMINEO.

Flam. [*aside.*] How dares this banish'd count
     return to Rome,
His pardon not yet purchas'd! I have heard
The deceas'd duchess gave him pension,
And that he came along from Padua
I'the train of the young prince. There's some-
     what in't:
Physicians, that cure poisons, still do work
With counter-poisons.

Mar. Mark this strange encounter.

Flam. The god of melancholy turn thy gall to
     poison,
And let the stigmatic* wrinkles in thy face,
Like to the boisterous waves in a rough
     tide,
One still overtake another.

Lod. I do thank thee,
And I do wish ingeniously† for thy sake
The dog-days all year long.

Flam. How croaks the raven?
Is our good duchess dead?

Lod. Dead.

Flam. O fate!
Misfortune comes, like the coroner's business,
Huddle upon huddle.

Lod. Shalt thou and I join house-keeping?

Flam. Yes, content:
Let's be unsociably sociable.

Lod. Sit some three days together, and dis-
     course.

Flam. Only with making faces: lie in our
     clothes.

Lod. With faggots for our pillows.

Flam. And be lousy.

Lod. In taffata linings; that's genteel melan-
     choly:
Sleep all day.

Flam. Yes; and, like your melancholic‡ hare,
Feed after midnight.—
We are observ'd: see how yon couple grieve!§

Lod. What a strange creature is a laughing
     fool!

---

* *stigmatic*] "i. e. marked as with a brand of infamy."
                                         STEEVENS.

So Heywood;
          "Print in my face
     The most *stigmaticke* title of a villaine."
A Woman Kilde with Kindness, 1617, Sig. C. 4.
† *ingeniously*] By writers of Webster's time *ingenious*
and *ingenuous* are often confounded.
‡ *melancholic*] The 4to. of 1631 "*melancholy.*"—On the
melancholy of a hare see the notes of Shakespeare's commentators, *First Part of Henry IV.* act i. sc. 2.
§ *see how yon couple grieve*] Probably he alludes to
Francisco and Monticelso: but they certainly are not on
the stage at present.

As if man were created to no use
But only to show his teeth.

Flam. I'll tell thee what,—
It would do well, instead of looking-glasses,
To set one's face each morning by a* saucer
Of a witch's congealèd blood.

Lod. Precious gue!†
We'll never part.

Flam. Never, till the beggary of courtiers,
The discontent of churchmen, want of soldiers,
And all the creatures that hang manacled,
Worse than strappado'd, on the lowest felly
Of Fortune's wheel, be taught, in our two lives,
To scorn that world which life of means deprives.

Enter ANTONELLI *and* GASPARO.

Anto. My lord, I bring good news. The Pope,
     on's death-bed,
At the earnest suit of the Great Duke of Florence,
Hath sign'd your pardon, and restor'd unto
     you——

Lod. I thank you for your news.—Look up
     again,
Flamineo; see my pardon.

Flam. Why do you laugh?
There was no such condition in our covenant.

Lod. Why!

Flam. You shall not seem a happier man than I:
You know our vow, sir; if you will be merry,
Do it i'the like posture as if some great man
Sate while his enemy were executed;
Though it be very lechery unto thee,
Do't with a crabbed‡ politician's face.

Lod. Your sister is a damnable whore.

Flam. Ha!

Lod. Look you, I spake that laughing.

Flam. Dost ever think to speak again?

Lod. Do you hear?
Wilt sell me forty ounces of her blood
To water a mandrake?

Flam. Poor lord, you did vow
To live a lousy creature.

Lod. Yes.

Flam. Like one
That had for ever forfeited the day-light
By being in debt.

Lod. Ha, ha!

---

* *a*] The 4to. of 1631 "*the.*"
† *gue*] So some copies of the 4to. of 1612; other copies
"*grine rouge;*" the 4to. of 1631 "*gue;*" the 4tos. of 1665
and 1672 "*rogue.*"—*Gue* (from the Fr. *gueux*) means a rogue,
a sharper. Nares (*Gloss.* in v.), not aware of the present passage, when, after citing two examples of the
word from Brathwaite's *Honest Ghost*, he expressed a
suspicion that "*gue*" was "an affectation" of Brathwaite.
‡ *crabbed*] The 4to. of 1631 "*sabby.*"

Flam. I do not greatly wonder you do break;
Your lordship learn'd 't long since. But I'll tell
        you,—
Lod. What?
Flam. And 't shall stick by you,—
Lod. I long for it.
Flam. This laughter scurvily becomes your
        face :
If you will not be melancholy, be angry.
                                        [*Strikes him.*
See, now I laugh too.
Mar. You are to blame : I'll force you hence.
Lod. Unhand me.
                    [*Exeunt* MARCELLO *and* FLAMINEO.
That e'er I should be forc'd to right myself
Upon a pander !
Anto. My lord,—
Lod. H'ad been as good met with his fist a
        thunderbolt.
Gas. How this shows !
Lod. Uds'death, how did my sword miss him ?
These rogues that are most weary of their lives
Still scape the greatest dangers.
A pox upon him ! all his reputation,
Nay, all the goodness of his family,
Is not worth half this earthquake :
I learn'd it of no fencer to shake thus :
Come, I'll forget him, and go drink some wine.
                                        [*Exeunt.*

Enter FRANCISCO DE MEDICIS * *and* MONTICELSO.
Mont. Come, come, my lord, untie your folded
        thoughts,
And let them dangle loose as a bride's hair.†
Your sister's poison'd.
Fran. de Med. Far be it from my thoughts
To seek revenge.
Mont. What, are you turn'd all marble ?
Fran. de Med. Shall I defy him, and impose a
        war
Most burdensome on my poor subjects' necks,
Which at my will I have not power to end ?
You know, for all the murders, rapes, and thefts,
Committed in the horrid lust of war,
He that unjustly caus'd it first proceed
Shall find it in his grave and in his seed.
Mont. That's not the course I'd wish you ; pray,
        observe me.

We see that undermining more prevails
Than doth the cannon. Bear your wrongs
        conceal'd,
And, patient as the tortoise, let this camel
Stalk o'er your back unbruis'd : sleep with the lion,
And let this brood of secure foolish mice
Play with your nostrils, till the time be ripe
For the bloody audit and the fatal gripe :
Aim like a cunning fowler, close one eye,
That you the better may your game espy.
        Fran. de Med. Free me, my innocence, from
                treacherous acts !
I know there's thunder yonder ; and I'll stand
Like a safe valley, which low bends the knee
To some aspiring mountain ; since I know
Treason, like spiders weaving nets for flies,
By her foul work is found, and in it dies.
To pass away these thoughts, my honour'd lord,
It is reported you possess a book,
Wherein you have quoted,* by intelligence,
The names of all notorious offenders
Lurking about the city.
        Mont. Sir, I do ;
And some there are which call it my black book :
Well may the title hold ; for though it teach not
The art of conjuring, yet in it lurk
The names of many devils.
        Fran. de Med. Pray, let's see it.
        Mont. I'll fetch it to your lordship.   [*Exit.*
        Fran. de Med. Monticelso,
I will not trust thee ; but in all my plots
I'll rest as jealous as a town besieg'd.
Thou canst not reach what I intend to act :
Your flax soon kindles, soon is out again ;
But gold slow heats, and long will hot remain.

Re-enter MONTICELSO, *presents* FRANCISCO DE MEDICIS
        with a book.
Mont. 'Tis here, my lord.
Fran. de Med. First, your intelligencers, pray,
        let's see.
Mont. Their number rises strangely ; and some
        of them
You'd take for honest men. Next are panders,—
These are your pirates ; and these following leaves
For base rogues that undo young gentlemen
By taking up commodities ;† for politic bankrupts ;

---

* *Enter Francisco de Medicis, &c.*] Scene. The Same.
An apartment in the palace of Francisco.
† *—untie your folded thoughts,*
        And let them dangle loose, as a bride's hair] "Brides
formerly walked to church with their hair hanging loose
behind. Anne Bullen's was thus dishevelled when she
went to the altar with King Henry the Eighth."
                                        STEEVENS.

* *quoted*] "i. e. noted." REED.
† *—that undo young gentlemen*
        By taking up commodities] "It was the practice of
usurers formerly, and has been continued by their suc-
cessors even to the present times, to defraud the neces-
sitous who borrow money by furnishing them with
goods and wares, to be converted into cash at a great loss
to the borrower. This was done to avoid the penal
Statutes against Usury. It was called *taking up com-*

For fellows that are bawds to their own wives,
Only to put off horses, and slight jewels,
Clocks, defac'd plate, and such commodities,
At birth of their first children.

Fran. de Med. Are there such?

Mont. These are for impudent bawds
That go in men's apparel; for usurers
That share with scriveners for their good re-
portage;
For lawyers that will antedate their writs:
And some divines you might find folded there,
But that I slip them o'er for conscience' sake.
Here is a general catalogue of knaves:
A man might study all the prisons o'er,
Yet never attain this knowledge.

Fran. de Med. Murderers!
Fold down the leaf, I pray.
Good my lord, let me borrow this strange doctrine.

Mont. Pray, use't, my lord.

Fran. de Med. I do assure your lordship,
You are a worthy member of the state,
And have done infinite good in your discovery
Of these offenders.

Mont. Somewhat, sir.

Fran. de Med. O God!
Better than tribute of wolves paid in England:*
'Twill hang their skins o'the hedge.

Mont. I must make bold
To leave your lordship.

Fran. de Med. Dearly,† sir, I thank you:
If any ask for me at court, report
You have left me in the company of knaves.

         [*Exit* MONTICELSO.

I gather now by this, some cunning fellow
That's my lord's officer, one‡ that lately skipp'd
From a clerk's desk up to a justice'§ chair,
Hath made this knavish summons, and intends,
As the Irish rebels wont were ‖ to sell heads,
So to make prize of these. And thus it happens,

Your poor rogues pay for't which have not the *
     means
To present bribe in fist: the rest o'the band
Are raz'd out of the knaves' record; or else
My lord he winks at them with easy will;
His man grows rich, the knaves are the knaves still.
But to the use I'll make of it; it shall serve
To point me out a list† of murderers,
Agents for any villany. Did I want
Ten leash of courtezans, it would furnish me;
Nay, laundress three armies. That in so little
     paper
Should lie the undoing of so many men!‡
'Tis not so big as twenty declarations.
See the corrupted use some make of books:
Divinity, wrested by some factious blood,
Draws swords, swells battles, and o'erthrows all
     good.
To fashion my revenge more seriously,
Let me remember my dead sister's face:
Call § for her picture? no, I'll close mine eyes,
And in a melancholic thought I'll frame

          Enter ISABELLA's ghost.

Her figure 'fore me. Now I ha't:—how strong ‖
Imagination works! how she can frame
Things which are not! Methinks she stands
     afore me,
And by the quick idea of my mind,
Were my skill pregnant, I could draw her picture
Thought, as a subtle juggler, makes us deem
Things supernatural, which yet¶ have cause
Common as sickness. 'Tis my melancholy.—
How cam'st thou by thy death?—How idle am I
To question mine own idleness!—Did ever
Man dream awake till now?—Remove this object;
Out of my brain with't: what have I to do
With tombs, or death-beds, funerals, or tears,
That have to meditate upon revenge?

         [*Exit* Ghost.

So, now 'tis ended, like an old wife's story:
Statesmen think often they see stranger sights
Than madmen. Come, to this weighty business:

---

modities, and is often noticed in our ancient writers.
See several instances in the notes of Mr. Steevens and
Dr. Farmer to *Measure for Measure*, A. 4. S. 4." REED.

   * *Better than tribute*, &c.] "This tribute was imposed
on the Welsh by King Edgar, in order that the nation
might be freed from these ravenous and destructive
beasts. Drayton, in *Polyolbion*, Song 9th, says:

  'Thrice famous Saxon King, on whom time ne'er shall
     prey,
  O Edgar! who compeldst our Ludwal hence to pay
  Three hundred wolves a year for tribute unto thee:
  And for that tribute paid, as famous may'st thou be,
  O conquer'd British king, by whom was first destroy'd
  The multitude of wolves, that long this land annoy'd.'"
                          REED.

  † *Dearly*] The 4to. of 1631, "*dear*."
  ‡ *one*] Some copies of the 4to. of 1612, "*and*."
  § *justice'*] The 4to. of 1631, "*justice's*."
  ‖ *wont were*] The 4to. of 1631, "*were wont*."

---

  * *the*] Omitted in the 4to. of 1631.
  † *list*] Some copies of the 4to. of 1612, "*life*"—perhaps
a misprint for "*file*."
  ‡   — *That in so little paper*
Should lie the undoing of so many men] Some copies of
the 4to. of 1612;

       "That so little paper
     Should be th' undoing of so many men."
  § *Call*] Some copies of the 4to. of 1612, "*Look*."
  ‖ *Now I ha't:—how strong*] Some copies of the 4to. of 1612,
        "Now I—d'foot how strong,"
The 4to. of 1631, "*hav't*."
  ¶ *yet*] Omitted in the two earliest 4tos., and first in-
serted in that of 1665.

My tragedy must have some idle mirth in't,
Else it will never pass. I am in love,
In love with Corombona; and my suit
Thus halts to her in verse.—   [*Writes.*
I have done it rarely : O the fate of princes !
I am so us'd to frequent flattery,
That, being alone, I now flatter myself :
But it will serve; 'tis seal'd.

Enter Servant.*

Bear this
To the house of convertites,† and watch your
          leisure
To give it to the hands of Corombona,
Or to the matron, when some followers
Of Brachiano may be by. Away ! [*Exit* Servant.
He that deals all by strength, his wit is shallow :
When a man's head goes through, each limb will
          follow.
The engine for my business, bold Count Lodo-
          wick :
'Tis gold must such an instrument procure ;
With empty fist no man doth‡ falcons lure.
Brachiano, I am now fit for thy encounter :
Like the wild Irish, I'll ne'er think thee dead
Till I can play at football with thy head.
Flectere si nequeo superos, Acheronta movebo.§
                    [*Exit.*

Enter the Matron ‖ *and* FLAMINEO.

Matron. Should it be known the duke hath
          such recourse
To your imprison'd sister, I were like
To incur much damage by it.
Flam. Not a scruple :
The Pope lies on his death-bed, and their heads
Are troubled now with other business
Than guarding of a lady.

Enter Servant.

Servant. Yonder's Flamineo in conference
With the matrona.—Let me speak with you ;
I would entreat you to deliver for me
This letter to the fair Vittoria.
Matron. I shall, sir.
Servant. With all care and secrecy :
Hereafter you shall know me, and receive
Thanks for this courtesy.   [*Exit.*
Flam. How now ! what's that ?

---

* *Enter Servant*] I may observe that occasionally in
old plays *Servants* enter, as here, without being sum-
moned, just at the moment they happen to be wanted.
  † *convertites*] See note ‡, p. 23.
  ‡ *doth*] The 4to. of 1631, "*do.*"
  § *Flectere*, &c.] Virgil, *Æn.* vii. 312.
  ‖ *Enter the Matron*, &c.] Scene. The Same. A room
in the House of Convertites.

Matron. A letter.
Flam. To my sister ? I'll see't deliver'd.

Enter BRACHIANO.

Brach. What's that you read, Flamineo ?
Flam. Look.
Brach. Ha ! [*reads.*] "*To the most unfortunate,
his best respected Vittoria.*"—
Who was the messenger ?
Flam. I know not.
Brach. No ! who sent it ?
Flam. Ud'sfoot, you speak as if a man
Should know what fowl is coffin'd in a bak'd
          meat
Afore you cut it up.
Brach. I'll open't, were't her heart.—What's
          here subscrib'd !
"*Florence*" ! this juggling is gross and palpable :
I have found out the conveyance.—Read it,
          read it.
Flam. [*reads.*] "*Your tears I'll turn to triumphs,
be but mine :
Your prop is fall'n : I pity, that a vine,
Which princes heretofore have long'd to gather,
Wanting supporters, now should fade and wither.*"—
Wine, i'faith, my lord, with lees would serve
          his turn.—
"*Your sad imprisonment I'll soon uncharm,
And with a princely uncontrolled arm
Lead you to Florence, where my love and care
Shall hang your wishes in my silver hair.*"—
A halter on his strange equivocation !—
"*Nor for my years return me the sad willow :
Who prefer blossoms before fruit that's mellow ?*—
Rotten, on my knowledge, with lying too long
i'the bed-straw.—
"*And all the lines of age this line convinces,
The gods never wax old,' no more do princes.*"—
A pox on't, tear it ; let's have no more atheists,
for God's sake.
Brach. Ud'sdeath, I'll cut her into atomies,*
And let the irregular north-wind sweep her up,
And blow her into his nostrils ! Where's this
          whore ?
Flam. That what do you call her ?
Brach. O, I could be mad,
Prevent the curs'd disease† she'll bring me to,
And tear my hair off ! Where's this changeable
          stuff ?
Flam. O'er head and ears in water, I assure you :
She is not for your wearing.

---

* *atomies*] The 4to. of 1631 "*atomes.*"
  † *the curs'd disease*] One of the consequences of the
venereal disease is the coming off of the hair.

Brach. No,* you pander?

Flam. What, me, my lord? am I your dog?

Brach. A blood-hound: do you brave, do you stand me?

Flam. Stand you! let those that have diseases run?

I need no plasters.†

Brach. Would you be kick'd?

Flam. Would you have your neck broke?

I tell you, duke, I am not in Russia; ‡

My shins must be kept whole.

Brach. Do you know me?

Flam. O, my lord, methodically:

As in this world there are degrees of evils,

So in this world there are degrees of devils.

You're a great duke, I your poor secretary.

I do look now for a Spanish fig,§ or an Italian salad, daily.

Brach. Pander, ply your convoy, and leave your prating.

Flam. All your kindness to me is like that miserable courtesy of Polyphemus to Ulysses; you reserve me to be devoured last: you would

dig turfs out of my grave to feed your larks; that would be music to you. Come, I'll lead you to her.

Brach. Do you face me?

Flam. O,* sir, I would not go before a politic enemy with my back towards him, though there were behind me a whirlpool.

Enter VITTORIA COROMBONA.

Brach. Can you read, mistress? look upon that letter:

There are no characters nor hieroglyphics;

You need no comment: I am grown your receiver.

God's precious! you shall be a brave great lady,

A stately and advancèd whore.

Vit. Cor. Say, sir?

Brach. Come, come, let's see your cabinet, discover

Your treasury of love-letters. Death and Furies!

I'll see them all.

Vit. Cor. Sir, upon my soul,

I have not any. Whence was this directed?

Brach. Confusion on your politic ignorance!

You are reclaim'd,† are you? I'll give you the bells,

And let you fly to the devil.

Flam. Ware hawk, my lord.

Vit. Cor. "Florence"! this is some treacherous plot, my lord;

To me he ne'er was lovely,‡ I protest,

So much as in my sleep.

Brach. Right! they are plots.

Your beauty! O, ten thousand curses on't!

How long have I beheld the devil in crystal!§

Thou hast led me, like an heathen sacrifice,

With music and with fatal yokes of flowers,

To my eternal ruin. Woman to man

Is either a god or a wolf.

Vit. Cor. My lord,—

Brach. Away!

We'll be as differing as two adamants;

The one shall shun the other. What, dost weep?

Procure but ten of thy dissembling trade,

---

* *No*] Some copies of the 4to. of 1612 "*In ;*" the 4to. of 1631 "*i'en.*"

† *plasters*] The 4to. of 1631 "*plaster.*"

‡ *—I am not in Russia;*
My shins must be kept whole] "It appears from Giles Fletcher's *Russe Commonwealth*, 1591, p. 51, that on determining an action of debt in that country, 'the partie convicted is delivered to the Serjeant, who hath a writte for his warrant out of the Office, to carry him to the *Pravensh*, or Righter of Justice, if presently hee pay not the monie, or content not the partie. This *Pravensh*, or Righter, is a place neere to the office: where such as have sentence passed against them, and refuse to pay that which is adjudged, are beaten with great cudgels on *the shinnes* and calves of their legges. Every forenoone from eight to eleven they are set on the *Pravensh*, and beate in this sort till the monie be payd. The afternoones and night time they are kepts in chaines by the Serjeant: except they put in sufficient suerties for their appearance at the *Pravensh* at the hower appointed. You shall see fortie or fiftie stand together on the *Pravensh* all on a rowe, and their *shinnes* thvs bocudgelled and bebasted every morning with a piteous crie. If after a yeare's standing on the Pravensh, the partie will not, or lacke wherewithall to satisfie his creditour, it is lawfull for him to sell his wife and children, eyther outright, or for a certaine terme of yeares. And if the price of them doo not amount to the full payment, the creditour may take them to bee his bondslaves, for yeares or for ever, according as the value of the dubt requireth.'" REED.

So I. Daye;
  "Let him have Russian law for all his sins,
  Whats that? A 100 blowes on his bare shins."
      The Parliament of Bees, 1641, Sig. G. 2.

§ *a Spanish fig*] "Referring to the custom of giving poisoned figs to those who were the objects either of the Spanish or Italian revenge. See Mr. Steevens's note on *King Henry V.* A. 3. 8. 6." REED.

* *O*] Omitted in some copies of the 4to. of 1612.

† *reclaim'd*] Used here with a quibble: to *reclaim* a hawk is to make her gentle and familiar,—to tame her.

‡ *lovely*] Some copies of the 4to. of 1612, "*thought on.*"

§ *How long have I beheld the devil in crystal*] "The beril, which is a kind of crystal, hath a weak tincture of red in it. Among other tricks of astrologers, the discovery of past or future events was supposed to be the consequence of looking into it. See *Aubrey's Miscellanies*, p. 165. edit. 1721." REED.

S. Rowlands, describing a dabbler in magic, says;
  "He can transforme himselfe unto an asse,
  Shew you the *Divell in a Christall glasse.*"
The Letting of Humors Blood in the Head-Vaine, 1611, Sat. 3.

Ye'd* furnish all the Irish funerals
With howling past wild Irish.

Flam. Fie, my lord !

Brach. That hand, that cursèd hand, which I
have wearied
With doting kisses !—O my sweetest duchess,
How lovely art thou now !—My† loose thoughts
Scatter like quicksilver: I was bewitch'd;
For all the world speaks ill of thee.

Vit. Cor. No matter:
I'll live so now, I'll make that world recant,
And change her speeches. You did name your
duchess.

Brach. Whose death God pardon !

Vit. Cor. Whose death God revenge ‡
On thee, most godless duke !

Flam. Now for two § whirlwinds.

Vit. Cor. What have I gain'd by thee but
infamy !
Thou hast stain'd the spotless honour of my house,
And frighted thence noble society :
Like those, which, sick o'the palsy, and retain
Ill-scenting foxes 'bout them, are still shunn'd
By those of choicer nostrils. What do you call
this house ?
Is this your palace ? did not the judge style it
A house of penitent whores? who sent me to it?
Who hath the honour to advance Vittoria
To this incontinent college? is't not you?
Is't not your high preferment? Go, go, brag
How many ladies you have undone like me.
Fare you well, sir; let me hear no more of you :
I had a limb corrupted to an ulcer,
But I have cut it off; and now I'll go
Weeping to heaven on crutches. For your gifts,
I will return them all; and I do wish
That I could make you full executor
To all my sins. O, that I could toss myself
Into a grave as quickly ! for all thou art worth
I'll not shed one tear more,—I'll burst first.

[*She throws herself upon a bed.*

Brach. I have drunk Lethe.—Vittoria !
My dearest happiness ! Vittoria !
What do you ail, my love ? why do you weep ?

Vit. Cor. Yes, I now weep poniards, do you see?

Brach. Are not those matchless eyes mine ?

Vit. Cor. I had rather
They were not matchless.*

Brach. Is not this lip mine?

Vit. Cor. Yes; thus to bite it off, rather than
give it thee.

Flam. Turn to my lord, good sister.

Vit. Cor. Hence, you pander !

Flam. Pander! am I the author of your sin ?

Vit. Cor. Yes; he's a base thief that a thief
lets in.

Flam. We're blown up, my lord.

Brach. Wilt thou hear me?
Once to be jealous of thee, is to express
That I will love thee everlastingly,
And never more be jealous.

Vit. Cor. O thou fool,
Whose greatness hath by much o'ergrown thy wit !
What dar'st thou do that I not dare to suffer,
Excepting to be still thy whore? for that,
In the sea's bottom sooner thou shalt make
A bonfire.

Flam. O, no oaths, for God's sake !

Brach. Will you hear me?

Vit. Cor. Never.

Flam. What a damn'd imposthume is a woman's
will !
Can nothing break it ?—Fie, fie, my lord,
Women are caught as you take tortoises;
She must be turn'd on her back.—Sister, by this
hand,
I am on your side.—Come, come, you have wrong'd
her :
What a strange credulous man were you, my lord,
To think the Duke of Florence would† love her !
Will any mercer take another's ware
When once 'tis tous'd and sullied?—And yet, sister,
How scurvily this frowardness becomes you !
Young leverets stand not long; and women's anger
Should, like their fight, procure a little sport;
A full cry for a quarter of an hour,
And then be put to the dead quat.‡

Brach. Shall these eyes,
Which have so long time dwelt upon your face,
Be now put out?

Flam. No cruel landlady i'the world,
Which lends forth groats to broom-men, and takes
use for them,
Would do't.—
Hand her, my lord, and kiss her : be not like
A ferret, to let go your hold with blowing.

Brach. Let us renew right hands.

---

* *Ye'd*] The 4to. of 1631, " *We'll.*"

† *My*] The three earliest 4tos. " *Thy.*"

‡ *Brach. Whose death God pardon !*
Vit. Cor. Whose death God revenge, &c.] A recollection
of Shakespeare ;
  " *Glo.* Poor Clarence did forsake his father, Warwick ;
    Ay, and forswore himself,—*which Jesu pardon !*
Q. *Mar. Which God revenge !*" *Richard III.*, act i. sc. 3.

§ *two*] Some copies of the 4to. of 1612, " *ten ;*" the 4to.
of 1631, " *the.*"

* *matchless*] The 4to. of 1612, " *matches.*"

† *would*] Some copies of the 4to. of 1612, " *could.*"

‡ *quat*] A corrupt form of *squat*,—the sitting of a hare.

Vit. Cor. Hence!

Brach. Never shall rage or the forgetful wine
Make me commit like fault.

Flam. Now you are i'the way on't, follow't hard.

Brach. Be thou at peace with me, let all the
world
Threaten the cannon.

Flam. Mark his penitence:
Best natures do commit the grossest faults,
When they're given o'er to jealousy, as best wine,
Dying, makes strongest vinegar. I'll tell you,—
The sea's more rough and raging than calm rivers,
But not so sweet nor wholesome. A quiet woman
Is a still water under a great bridge;*
A man may shoot † her safely.

Vit. Cor. O ye dissembling men!—

Flam. We suck'd that, sister,
From women's breasts, in our first infancy.

Vit. Cor. To add misery to misery!

Brach. Sweetest,—

Vit. Cor. Am I not low enough?
Ay, ay, your good heart gathers like a snow-ball,
Now your affection's cold.

Flam. Ud'sfoot, it shall melt
To a heart again, or all the wine in Rome
Shall run o'the lees for't.

Vit. Cor. Your dog or hawk should be rewarded
better
Than I have been. I'll speak not one word more.

Flam. Stop her mouth with a sweet kiss, my
lord. So,
Now the tide's turn'd, the vessel's come about.
He's a sweet armful. O, we curl'd-hair'd men
Are still most kind to women! This is well.

Brach. That you should chide thus!

Flam. O, sir, your little chimneys
Do ever cast most smoke! I sweat for you.
Couple together with as deep a silence
As did the Grecians in their wooden horse.
My lord, supply your promises with deeds;
You know that painted meat no hunger feeds.

Brach. Stay, ingrateful Rome—‡

<hr>

* *Is a still water under a great bridge*] " 'Is *like* a still
water under *London* bridge' was the reading until now
[in the editions of Dodsley's *Old Plays*, 1744 and 1780]:
how or why the word *London* was foisted in, it is not
easy to guess, as both the old copies give the passage as
it is now printed." COLLIER.
Dodsley and Reed found the reading, which Mr. Collier
rightly rejected, in the 4tos. of 1665 and 1672.
† *shoot*] "To *shoot the bridge* was a term used by watermen, to signify going through London-bridge at the
turning of the tide. The vessel then went with great
velocity, and from thence it probably was called *shooting.*" REED.
‡ *Stay, ingrateful Rome*—] Qy. "Stay *in* ingrateful
Rome!"?

Flam. Rome! it deserves to be call'd Barbary
For our villanous usage.

Brach. Soft! the same project which the Duke
of Florence
(Whether in love or gullery I know not)
Laid down for her escape, will I pursue.

Flam. And no time fitter than this night, my
lord:
The Pope being dead, and all the cardinals
enter'd
The conclave for the electing a new Pope;
The city in a great confusion;
We may attire her in a page's suit,
Lay her post-horse, take shipping, and amain
For Padua.

Brach. I'll * instantly steal forth the Prince
Giovanni,
And make for Padua. You two with your old
mother,
And young Marcello that attends on Florence,
If you can work him to it, follow me:
I will advance you all:—for you, Vittoria,
Think of a duchess' title.

Flam. Lo you, sister!—
Stay, my lord; I'll tell you a tale. The crocodile,
which lives in the river Nilus, hath a worm breeds
i'the teeth of't, which puts it to extreme anguish:
a little bird, no bigger than a wren, is barber-
surgeon to this crocodile; flies into the jaws of't,
picks out the worm, and brings present remedy.
The fish, glad of ease, but ingrateful to her that
did it, that the bird may not talk largely of her
abroad for non-payment, closeth her chaps, intend-
ing to swallow her, and so put her to perpetual
silence. But nature, loathing such ingratitude,
hath armed this bird with a quill or prick on the
head, top o'the which wounds the crocodile i'the
mouth, forceth her open her bloody prison, and
away flies the pretty tooth-picker from her cruel
patient.†

Brach. Your application is, I have not rewarded
The service you have done me.

Flam. No, my lord.——
You, sister, are the crocodile: you are blemished
in your fame, my lord cures it; and though the
comparison hold not in every particle, yet observe,
remember what good the bird with the prick i'the
head hath done you, and scorn ingratitude.—

<hr>

* *I'll*] Omitted in the 4to. of 1631.
† This tale is an alteration of a fable told originally by
Herodotus, lib. ii. c. 68, that a bird, called trochilus,
enters the throat of the crocodile, and extracts the
leeches that gather there (or, according to some ancient
writers, picks particles of flesh from its teeth); and that
the grateful crocodile does the bird no injury.

It may appear to some ridiculous   [*Aside.*
Thus to talk knave and madman, and sometimes
Come in with a dried sentence, stuft with sage:
But this allows my varying of shapes;
Knaves do grow great by being great men's apes.
                      [*Exeunt.*

Enter FRANCISCO DE MEDICIS,* LODOVICO, GASPARO, *and*
six Ambassadors.

    Fran. de Med. So, my lord, I commend your
      diligence.
Guard well the conclave; and, as the order is,
Let none have conference with the cardinals.
    Lod. I shall, my lord.—Room for the ambas-
      sadors!
    Gasp. They're wondrous brave † to-day: why
      do they wear
These several habits?
    Lod. O, sir, they are knights
Of several orders:
That lord i'the black cloak, with the silver
    cross,
Is Knight of Rhodes;‡ the next, Knight of St.
    Michael;§
That, of the Golden Fleece;‖ the Frenchman,
    there,
Knight of the Holy Ghost;¶ my lord of Savoy,
Knight of the Annunciation;** the Englishman
Is Knight of the honour'd Garter,†† dedicated

---

* *Enter Francisco de Medicis,* &c.] Scene. The Same.
Before the building in which the cardinals are assembled
for the election of a Pope: from what presently follows
in our text it would seem that the conclave is held in a
church. (The Vatican, I believe, is the usual place of
conclave.)
    brave] "i. e. fine." REED.
  ‡ *That lord i'the black cloak, with the silver cross,*
  Is Knight of Rhodes] "A Knight of Rhodes was
formerly called a Knight of St. John Jerusalem, and now
a Knight of Malta. The Order was instituted some time
before the conquest of Jerusalem by the Christians in
1099. *Segar* says, that 's a governor, called *Gerardus*,
commanded that he and all others of that house should
wear a *white cross upon a blacke garment*, which was the
originall of the Order, and ever since hath been used.'—
Honor Military and Civill, fol. 1602, p. 97." REED.
  § *Knight of St. Michael*] "This Order was erected in
1469, by Lewis XI. King of France. See *Segar on Honor*,
p. 83." REED.
  ¶ *That, of the Golden Fleece*] "Instituted by Philip the
Good, Duke of Burgundy and Earl of Flanders, in 1429.
See *Segar,* p. 79." REED.
  ¶ *Knight of the Holy Ghost*] "Instituted by Henry III.
King of France and Poland, in the year 1579. See *Segar,*
p. 87." REED.
  ** *Knight of the Annunciation*] "An Order begun by
Amedes Count of Savoy, surnamed Il Verde, in memory
of Amedes the first Earl, who, having valorously de-
fended the Isle of Rhodes, did win those arms now borne
by the Dukes of Savoy. See *Segar,* p. 85." REED.
  †† *Knight of the honour'd Garter*] "Founded by King
Edward III." REED.

Unto their saint, St. George. I could describe to
    you
Their several institutions, with the laws
Annexed to their orders; but that time
Permits not such discovery.
    Fran. de Med. Where's Count Lodowick?
    Lod. Here, my lord.
    Fran. de Med. 'Tis o'the point of dinner time:
Marshal the cardinals' service.
    Lod. Sir, I shall.

Enter Servants, *with several dishes covered.*

Stand, let me search your dish: who's this for?
    Servant. For my lord cardinal Monticelso.
    Lod. Whose this?
    Servant. For my lord cardinal of Bourbon.
    Fr. Amb. Why doth he search the dishes? to
      observe
What meat is drest?
    Eng. Amb. No, sir, but to prevent
Lest any letters should be convey'd in,
To bribe or to solicit the advancement
Of any cardinal. When first they enter,
'Tis lawful for the ambassadors of princes
To enter with them, and to make their suit
For any man their prince affecteth best;
But after, till a general election,
No man may speak with them.
    Lod. You that attend on the lord cardinals,
Open the window, and receive their viands!
    A Cardinal [*at the window*]. You must return
      the service: the lord cardinals
Are busied 'bout electing of the Pope;
They have given over scrutiny, and are fall'n
To admiration.
    Lod. Away, away!
    Fran. de Med. I'll lay a thousand ducats you
      hear news
Of a Pope presently. Hark! sure, he's elected:
Behold, my lord of Arragon appears
On the church-battlements.
    Arragon [*on the church battlements*]. *Denuntio*
vobis *gaudium magnum. Reverendissimus cardi-*
nalis Lorenzo de Monticelso electus est in sedem
apostolicam, et elegit sibi nomen Paulum Quartum.

---

* *Denuntio vobis,* &c.] All the 4tos. except that of
1612, "*Annuntio.*"—This was nearly the form in which
the election of a pope was declared to the people. See
Roscoe's *Life of Leo the Tenth,* vol. ii. p. 166. ed. 1805.
Cartwright, perhaps, meant to parody this passage of
Webster, when he wrote the following:
  "*Moth.* Denuncio vobis gaudium magnum,
    Robertus de Tinea electus est in sedem Hospita-
    lem;
    Et assumit sibi nomen Galfridi."
          The Ordinary, Act 5. Sc. 4. (*Works,* 1651.)

Omnes. Vivat sanctus pater Paulus Quartus!*

Enter Servant.

Servant. Vittoria, my lord,—

Fran. de Med. Well, what of her?

Servant. Is fled the city,—

Fran. de Med. Ha!

Servant. With Duke Brachiano.

Fran. de Med. Fled! Where's the Prince Giovanni?

Servant. Gone with his father.

Fran. de Med. Let the matrona of the convertites

Be apprehended.—Fled! O, damnable!

　　　　　　　　　　　　　　[*Exit* Servant.

How fortunate are my wishes! why, 'twas this
I only labour'd: I did send the letter
To instruct him what to do. Thy fame, fond†
　　duke,
I first have poison'd; directed thee the way
To marry a whore: what can he worse? This
　　follows,—
The hand must act to drown the passionate
　　tongue:
I scorn to wear a sword and prate of wrong.

Enter MONTICELSO *in state.*

Mont. Concedimus vobis apostolicam benedictionem et remissionem peccatorum.‡
My lord reports Vittoria Corombona
Is stol'n from forth the house of convertites
By Brachiano, and they're fled the city.
Now, though this be the first day of our state,§
We cannot better please the divine power
Than to sequester from the holy church
These cursèd persons. Make it therefore known,
We do denounce excommunication
Against them both: all that are theirs in Rome
We likewise banish. Set on.

　　[*Exeunt* MONTICELSO, *his train,* Ambassadors, &c.

Fran. de Med. Come, dear Lodovico;
You have ta'en the sacrament to prosecute
The intended murder.

Lod. With all constancy.
But, sir, I wonder you'll engage yourself
In person, being a great prince.

Fran. de Med. Divert me not.
Most of his court are of my faction,

And some are of my council. Noble friend,
Our danger shall be like in this design:
Give leave, part of the glory may be mine.

　　[*Exeunt* FRAN. DE MED. *and* GASPARO.

Re-enter MONTICELSO.

Mont. Why did the Duke of Florence with
　　such care
Labour your pardon? say.*

Lod. Italian beggars will resolve you that,
Who, begging of an alms, bid those they beg of,
Do good for their own sakes; or it may be,
He spreads his bounty with a sowing hand,
Like kings, who many times give out of measure,
Not for desert so much, as for their pleasure.

Mont. I know you're cunning. Come, what
　　devil was that
That you were raising?

Lod. Devil, my lord!

Mont. I ask you †
How doth the duke employ you, that his bonnet
Fell with such compliment unto his knee,
When he departed from you?

Lod. Why, my lord,
He told me of a resty Barbary horse
Which he would fain have brought to the career,
The salt,‡ and the ring-galliard: now, my lord,
I have a rare French rider.§

Mont. Take you heed
Lest the jade break your neck. Do you put me off
With your wild horse-tricks? Sirrah, you do lie.
O, thou'rt a foul black cloud, and thou dost threat
A violent storm!

Lod. Storms are i'the air, my lord:
I am too low to storm.

Mont. Wretched creature!
I know that thou art fashion'd for all ill,
Like dogs that once get blood, they'll ever kill.
About some murder? was't not?

Lod. I'll not tell you:
And yet I care not greatly if I do;
Marry, with this preparation. Holy father,

---

* *Why did the Duke of Florence with such care*
Labour your pardon? say] In some copies of the 4to.
of 1612 this forms part of Francisco's speech, but in other
copies of that edition, and in the 4to. of 1631, it is rightly
given to Monticelso.

† *I ask you*] The two oldest 4tos. give this to Lodovico,
but the 4tos. of 1665 and 1672 assign it to Monticelso, to
whom it obviously belongs.

‡ *The salt*] The old eds. have "The *'sault,*" &c.: but a
particular kind of leaping or bounding is meant. "If
then you finde in him [your horse] a naturall inclination
of lightnesse, and a spirit both apt to apprehend and
execute any *Sault* above ground," &c. Markham's
Cavalarice, &c., p. 234, ed. 1617.

§ *French rider*] When this play was written, the French
excelled most nations in horsemanship.

---

* *Paulus Quartus*] Qy. did Webster, in making Monticelso Pope Paul IV., follow the work from which he took
the plot of this play? The person who was really raised
to that dignity was John Peter Caraffa.

† *fond*] i. e. simple, foolish.

‡ In some copies of the 4to. of 1612 this benediction is
not given.

§ *state*] Some copies of the 4to. of 1612, and the 4to. of
1631, "*seat.*"

I come not to you as an intelligencer,
But as a penitent sinner: what I utter
Is in confession merely; which you know
Must never be reveal'd.

Mont. You have o'erta'en me.

Lod. Sir, I did love Brachiano's duchess dearly,
Or rather I pursu'd her with hot lust,
Though she ne'er knew on't. She was poison'd;
Upon my soul, she was: for which I have sworn
To avenge her murder.

Mont. To the Duke of Florence?

Lod. To him I have.

Mont. Miserable creature!
If thou persist in this, 'tis damnable.
Dost thou imagine thou canst slide on blood,
And not be tainted with a shameful fall?
Or, like the black and melancholic yew-tree,
Dost think to root thyself in dead men's graves,
And yet to prosper? Instruction to thee
Comes like sweet showers to over-harden'd ground;
They wet, but pierce not deep. And so I leave
thee,
With all the Furies hanging 'bout thy neck,
Till by thy penitence thou remove this evil,
In conjuring from thy breast that cruel devil.
                                              [*Exit.*

Lod. I'll give it o'er; he says 'tis damnable:
Besides I did expect his suffrage,
By reason of Camillo's death.

Re-enter FRANCISCO DE MEDICIS *with a Servant.*

Fran. de Med. Do you know that count?

Servant. Yes, my lord.

Fran. de Med. Bear him these thousand ducats
to his lodging;
Tell him the Pope hath sent them. — [*Aside.*]
Happily
That will confirm [him] more than all the rest. [*Exit.*

Servant. Sir,—

Lod. To me, sir?

Servant. His Holiness hath sent you a thousand
crowns,
And wills you, if you travel, to make him
Your patron for intelligence.

Lod. His creature ever to be commanded.
                                    [*Exit* Servant.

Why, now 'tis come about. He rail'd upon me;
And yet these crowns were told out and laid ready
Before he knew my voyage. O the art,
The modest form of greatness! that do sit,
Like brides at wedding-dinners, with their looks
turn'd
From the least wanton jest, their puling stomach
Sick of the modesty, when their thoughts are loose,
Even acting of those hot and lustful sports

Are to ensue about midnight: such his cunning:
He sounds my depth thus with a golden plummet.
I am doubly arm'd now. Now to the act of blood.
There's but three Furies found in spacious hell,
But in a great man's breast three thousand dwell.
                                              [*Exit.*

A passage over the stage of BRACHIANO, FLAMINEO, MAR-
CELLO, HORTENSIO, VITTORIA COROMBONA, CORNELIA,
ZANCHE, *and others; exeunt omnes except* FLAMINEO
and HORTENSIO.*

Flam. In all the weary minutes of my life,
Day ne'er broke up till now. This marriage
Confirms me happy.

Hort. 'Tis a good assurance.
Saw you not yet the Moor that's come to court?

Flam. Yes, and confer'd with him i'the duke's
closet:
I have not seen a goodlier personage,
Nor ever talk'd with man better experienc'd
In state affairs or rudiments of war:
He hath, by report, serv'd the Venetian
In Candy these twice seven years, and been chief
In many a bold design.

Hort. What are those two
That bear him company?

Flam. Two noblemen of Hungary, that, living
in the emperor's service as commanders, eight
years since, contrary to the expectation of all the
court, entered into religion, into the strict order
of Capuchins: but, being not well settled in their
undertaking, they left their order, and returned
to court; for which, being after troubled in conscience, they vowed their service against the
enemies of Christ, went to Malta, were there
knighted, and in their return back, at this great
solemnity, they are resolved for ever to forsake
the world, and settle themselves here in a house
of Capuchins in Padua.

Hort. 'Tis strange.

Flam. One thing makes it so: they have vowed
for ever to wear, next their bare bodies, those
coats of mail they served in.

Hort. Hard penance! Is the Moor a Christian?

Flam. He is.

Hort. Why proffers he his service to our duke?

Flam. Because he understands there's like to
grow
Some wars† between us and the Duke of Florence,
In which he hopes employment.
I never saw one in a stern bold look
Wear more command, nor in a lofty phrase
Express more knowing or more deep contempt

---

* except *Flamineo and Hortensio*] Scene. Padua. An
apartment of a palace.

† wars] The 4to. of 1631, "war."

D 2

Of our slight airy courtiers. He talks
As if he had travell'd all the princes' courts
Of Christendom : in all things strives to express,
That all that should dispute with him may know,
Glories, like glow-worms,* afar off shine bright,
But look'd to near, have neither heat nor light.—
The duke !

Re-enter BRACHIANO; *with* FRANCISCO DE MEDICIS *disguised
like* MULINASSAR, LODOVICO, ANTONELLI, GASPARO,
FARNESE, CARLO, *and* PEDRO,† *bearing their swords
and helmets ; and* MARCELLO.

   Brach. You are nobly welcome. We have heard
     at full
Your honourable service 'gainst the Turk.
To you, brave Mulinassar, we assign
A competent pension : and are inly sorry,
The vows of those two worthy gentlemen
Make them incapable of our proffer'd bounty.
Your wish is, you may leave your warlike swords
For monuments in our chapel : I accept it
As a great honour done me, and must crave
Your leave to furnish out our duchess' revels.
Only one thing, as the last vanity
You e'er shall view, deny me not to stay
To see a barriers prepar'd to-night :
You shall have private standings. It hath pleas'd
The great ambassadors of several princes,
In their return from Rome to their own countries,
To grace our marriage, and to honour me
With such a kind of sport.
   Fran. de Med. I shall persuade them
To stay, my lord.
   Brach. Set on there to the presence ! ‡
    [*Exeunt* BRACHIANO, FLAMINEO, MARCELLO, *and*
    HORTENSIO.
   Car. Noble my lord, most fortunately welcome:
     [*The* Conspirators *here embrace.*
You have our vows, seal'd with the sacrament,
To second your attempts.
   Ped. And all things ready :
He could not have invented his own ruin
(Had he despair'd) with more propriety.§
   Lod. You would not take my way.
   Fran. de Med. 'Tis better order'd.

   Lod. To have poison'd his prayer-book, or a pair
    of beads,
The pummel of his saddle,* his looking-glass,
Or the handle of his racket,—O, that, that!
That while he had been bandying at tennis,
He might have sworn himself to hell, and strook
His soul into the hazard ! O, my lord,
I would have our plot be ingenious,
And have it hereafter recorded for example,
Rather than borrow example.
   Fran. de Med. There's no way
More speeding than this thought on.
   Lod. On,† then.
   Fran. de Med. And yet methinks that this
    revenge is poor,
Because it steals upon him like a thief.
To have ta'en him by the casque in a pitch'd
    field,
Led him to Florence !—
   Lod. It had been rare : and there
Have crown'd him with a wreath of stinking garlic,
To have shown the sharpness of his government
And rankness of his lust.‡—Flamineo comes.
    [*Exeunt* LODOVICO, ANTONELLI, GASPARO, FARNESE,
    CARLO, *and* PEDRO.

Re-enter FLAMINEO, MARCELLO, *and* ZANCHE.

   Mar. Why doth this devil haunt you, say ?
   Flam. I know not;
For, by this light, I do not conjure for her.
'Tis not so great a cunning as men think,
To raise the devil ; for here's one up already :
The greatest cunning were to lay him down.
   Mar. She is your shame.
   Flam. I prithee, pardon her.
In faith, you see, women are like to burs,
Where their affection throws them, there they'll
    stick.
   Zan. That is my countryman, a goodly person :
When he's at leisure, I'll discourse with him
In our own language.
   Flam. I beseech you do.   [*Exit* ZANCHE.
How is't, brave soldier ? O, that I had seen
Some of your iron days ! I pray, relate
Some of your service to us.
   Fran. de Med. 'Tis a ridiculous thing for a

---

  * *Glories, like glow-worms,* &c.] This fine simile occurs
again verbatim in the *Duchess of Malfi,* A. 4. S. 2.

  † *Carlo and Pedro*] In both the earliest 4tos. "*Car.*"
and "*Ped.*" are prefixed to the respective speeches of
these personages in this scene, though their entrance is
not marked ; and their names are found at full length
afterwards in stage directions. The 4tos. of 1665 and
1672 prefix to the two speeches in question, "*Lod.*" and
"*Gas.*"

  ‡ *Set on there to the presence*] This evidently belongs to
Brachiano, though all the 4tos. give it to Francisco.

  § *propriety*] The 4tos. of 1665 and 1672, "*dexterity.*"

  * *The pummel of his saddle*] "This was one of the
methods put in practice in order to destroy Queen
Elizabeth. In the year 1598, Edward Squire was convicted of anointing the pummel of the Queen's saddle
with poison, for which he was afterwards executed.
See *Camden's Elizabeth,* p. 726. Eliz. edit. 1639." REED.

  † *On*] The 4to. of 1631, "*Oh.*"

  ‡ *And rankness of his lust*] After these words, the 4tos.
of 1665 and 1672 insert "*But peace,*" not found in the two
earliest 4tos.

man to be his own chronicle: I did never wash my mouth with mine own praise for fear of getting a stinking breath.

Mar. You're too stoical. The duke will expect other discourse from you.

Fran. de Med. I shall never flatter him: I have studied man too much to do that. What difference is between the duke and I? no more than between two bricks, all made of one clay: only 't may be one is placed on the top of a turret, the other in the bottom of a well, by mere chance. If I were placed as high as the duke, I should stick as fast, make as fair a show, and bear out weather equally.

Flam. [*aside*] If this soldier had a patent to beg in churches, then he would tell them stories.

Mar. I have been a soldier too.

Fran. de Med. How have you thrived?

Mar. Faith, poorly.

Fran. de Med. That's the misery of peace: only outsides are then respected. As ships seem very great upon the river, which show very little upon the seas, so some men i'the court seem colossuses in a chamber, who, if they came into the field, would appear pitiful pigmies.

Flam. Give me a fair room yet hung with arras, and some great cardinal to lug me by 'the ears as his endeared minion.

Fran. de Med. And thou mayst do the devil knows what villany.

Flam. And safely.

Fran. de Med. Right: you shall see in the country, in harvest-time, pigeons, though they destroy never so much corn, the farmer dare not present the fowling-piece to them: why? because they belong to the lord of the manor; whilst your poor sparrows, that belong to the lord of heaven, they go to the pot for't.

Flam. I will now give you some politic instructions. The duke says he will give you a* pension: that's but bare promise; got it under his hand. For I have known men that have come from serving against the Turk, for three or four months they have had pension to buy them new wooden legs and fresh plasters; but, after, 'twas not to be had. And this miserable courtesy shows as if a tormentor should give hot cordial drinks to one three quarters dead o'the rack, only to fetch the miserable soul again to endure more dogdays.

[*Exit* FRANCISCO DE MEDICIA.†

Re-enter HORTENSIO *and* ZANCHE, *with a* Young Lord *and two more.*

How now, gallants! what, are they ready for the barriers?

Young Lord. Yes; the lords are putting on their armour.

Hort. What's he?

Flam. A new up-start; one that swears like a falconer, and will lie in the duke's ear day by day, like a maker of almanacs: and yet I knew him, since he came to the court, smell worse of sweat than an under-tennis-court-keeper.

Hort. Look you, yonder's your sweet mistress.

Flam. Thou art my sworn brother: I'll tell thee, I do love that Moor, that witch, very constrainedly. She knows some of my villany. I do love her just as a man holds a wolf by the ears: but for fear of turning upon me and pulling out my throat, I would let her go to the devil.

Hort. I hear she claims marriage of thee.

Flam. Faith, I made to her some such dark promise; and, in seeking to fly from't, I run on, like a frighted dog with a bottle at's tail, that fain would bite it off, and yet dares not look behind him.—Now, my precious gipsey.

Zanche. Ay, your love to me rather cools than heats.

Flam. Marry, I am the sounder lover: we have many wenches about the town heat too fast.

Hort. What do you think of these perfumed gallants, then?

Flam. Their satin cannot save them: I am confident
They have a certain spice of the disease;
For they that sleep with dogs shall rise with fleas.

Zanche. Believe it, a little painting and gay clothes make you love * me.

Flam. How! love a lady for painting or gay apparel? I'll unkennel one example more for thee. Æsop had a foolish dog that let go the flesh to catch the shadow: I would have courtiers be better divers.

Zanche. You remember your oaths?

Flam. Lovers' oaths are like mariners' prayers, uttered in extremity; but when the tempest is o'er, and that the vessel leaves tumbling, they fall from protesting to drinking. And yet, amongst gentlemen, protesting and drinking go together, and agree as well as shoe-makers and Westphalia bacon: they are both drawers on;

---

* a] Omitted in the 4to. of 1612.
† The 4tos. do not mark the Exit of Francisco; but it is necessary to get rid of him, as he *enters* towards the end of this scene.

* *love*] The three earliest 4tos. "*loath.*"

for drink draws on protestation, and protestation draws on more drink. Is not this discourse better now than the morality * of your sunburnt gentleman?

Re-enter CORNELIA.

Cor. Is this your perch, you haggard? fly to the stews.   [*Striking* ZANCHE.

Flam. You should be clapt by the heels now: strike i'the court!   [*Exit* CORNELIA.†

Zanche. She's good for nothing, but to make her maids
Catch cold a-nights: they dare not use a bed-staff
For fear of her light fingers.

Mar. You're a strumpet,
An impudent one.   [*Kicking* ZANCHE.

Flam. Why do you kick her, say?
Do you think that she is like a walnut tree?
Must she be cudgell'd ere she bear good fruit?

Mar. She brags that you shall marry her.

Flam. What, then?

Mar. I had rather she were pitch'd upon a stake
In some new-seeded garden, to affright
Her fellow crows thence.

Flam. You're a boy, a fool:
Be guardian to your hound; I am of age.

Mar. If I take her near you, I'll cut her throat.

Flam. With a fan of feathers?

Mar. And, for you, I'll whip
This folly from you.

Flam. Are you choleric?
I'll purge't with rhubarb.

Hort. O, your brother!

Flam. Hang him,
He wrongs me most that ought to offend me least.—
I do suspect my mother play'd foul play
When she conceiv'd thee.

Mar. Now, by all my hopes,
Like the two slaughter'd sons of Œdipus,
The very flames of our affection
Shall turn two‡ ways. Those words I'll make thee answer
With thy heart-blood.

---

* *morality*] The three earliest 4tos. "*mortality.*"
† The Exit of Cornelia is omitted in the 4tos.; but that she is not on the stage during the deadly quarrel of her sons, is evident from what she afterwards says;
    " I hear a whispering all about the court
    You are to fight: *who is your opposite?*
    What is the quarrel? "
‡ *two*] The 4to. of 1612, "10."
    "———— fiamma ————
Scinditur in partes, *geminoque* cacumine surgit,
Thebanos imitata rogos."   Lucan, *Phar.* i. 550.

Flam. Do, like the geese in the progress:*
You know where you shall find me.

Mar. Very good.   [*Exit* FLAMINEO.
An thou be'st a noble friend, bear him my sword,
And bid him fit the length on't.

Young Lord. Sir, I shall.
    [*Exeunt* Young Lord, MARCELLO, HORTENSIO, *and two more.*

Zanche. He comes. Hence petty thought of my disgrace!

Re-enter FRANCISCO DE MEDICIS.

I ne'er lov'd my complexion till now,
'Cause I may boldly say, without a blush,
I love you.

Fran. de Med. Your love is untimely sown;
there's a spring at Michaelmas, but 'tis but a faint one: I am sunk in years, and I have vowed never to marry.

Zanche. Alas! poor maids get more lovers than husbands: yet you may mistake my wealth. For, as when ambassadors are sent to congratulate princes, there's commonly sent along with them a rich present, so that, though the prince like not the ambassador's person nor words, yet he likes well of the presentment; so I may come to you in the same manner, and be better loved for my dowry than my virtue.

Fran. de Med. I'll think on the motion.

Zanche. Do: I'll now
Detain you no longer. At your better leisure
I'll tell you things shall startle your blood:
Nor blame me that this passion I reveal;
Lovers die inward that their flames conceal.
                    [*Exit.*

Fran. de Med. Of all intelligence this may prove the best:
Sure, I shall draw strange fowl from this foul nest.   [*Exit.*

Enter MARCELLO † *and* CORNELIA.

Cor. I hear a whispering all about the court
You are to fight: who is your opposite?
What is the quarrel?

Mar. 'Tis an idle rumour.

Cor. Will you dissemble? sure, you do not well
To fright me thus: you never look thus pale,
But when you are most angry. I do charge you
Upon my blessing,—nay, I'll call the duke,
And he shall school you.

Mar. Publish not a fear
Which would convert to laughter: 'tis not so.
Was not this crucifix my father's?

---

* *progress*] See note, p.   .
† *Enter Marcello,* &c.] Scene. Another apartment in the same.

Cor. Yes.

Mar. I have heard you say, giving my brother suck,
He took the crucifix between his hands,
And broke a limb off.

Cor. Yes; but 'tis mended.

Enter FLAMINEO.

Flam. I have brought your weapon back.
[*Runs* MARCELLO *through.*

Cor. Ha! O my horror!

Mar. You have brought it home, indeed.

Cor. Help! O, he's murder'd!

Flam. Do you turn your gall up? I'll to sanctuary,
And send a surgeon to you.   [*Exit.*

Enter CARLO, HORTENSIO, *and* PEDRO.

Hort. How! o' the ground!

Mar. O mother, now remember what I told
Of breaking of the crucifix! Farewell.
There are some sins which heaven doth duly punish
In a whole family. This it is to rise
By all dishonest means! Let all men know,
That tree shall long time keep a steady foot
Whose brancnes spread no wnder* than the root.
          [*Dies.*

Cor. O my perpetual sorrow!

Hort. Virtuous Marcello!
He's dead.—Pray, leave him, lady: come, you shall.

Cor. Alas, he is not dead;· he's in a trance.
Why, here's nobody shall get any thing by his death. Let me call him again, for God's sake!

Car. I would you were deceived.

Cor. O, you abuse me, you abuse me, you abuse me! How many have gone away thus, for lack of tendance! Rear up's head, rear up's head: his bleeding inward will kill him.

Hort. You see he is departed.

Cor. Let me come to him; give me him as he is: if he be turned to earth, let me but give him one hearty kiss, and you shall put us both into one coffin. Fetch a looking-glass;† see if his breath will not stain it: or pull out some feathers from my pillow, and lay them to Lis lips. Will you lose him for a little pains-taking?

* *wilder*] The 4to. of 1672, "*wider.*"

† *Fetch a looking-glass,* &c.] "So Shakespeare in *King Lear*, A. 5. S. 3:
  ' Lend me a *looking-glass;*
    If that *her breath* will *mist or stain* the stone,
    Why, then she lives. . . . . .
    This feather stirs; she lives! if it be so,
    It is a chance which does redeem all sorrows
    That ever I have felt.'" REED.

Hort. Your kindest office is to pray for him.

Cor. Alas, I would not pray for him yet. He may live to lay me i' the ground, and pray for me, if you'll let me come to him.

Enter BRACHIANO *all armed, save the beaver, with* FLAMINEO, FRANCISCO DE MEDICIS, LODOVICO, *and* Page.

Brach. Was this your handiwork?

Flam. It was my misfortune.

Cor. He lies, he lies; he did not kill him : these have killed him that would not let him be better looked to.

Brach. Have comfort, my griev'd mother.

Cor. O you* screech-owl!

Hort. Forbear, good madam.

Cor. Let me go, let me go.
[*She runs to* FLAMINEO *with her knife drawn, and, coming to him, lets it fall.*

The God of heaven forgive thee! Dost not wonder
I pray for thee? I'll tell thee what's the reason:
I have scarce breath to number twenty minutes;
I'd not spend that in cursing. Fare thee well:
Half of thyself lies there; and mayst thou live
To fill an hour-glass with his moulder'd ashes,
To tell how thou shouldst spend the time to come
In blest repentance!

Brach. Mother, pray tell me
How came he by his death? what was the quarrel?

Cor. Indeed, my younger boy presum'd too much
Upon his manhood, gave him bitter words,
Drew his sword first; and so, I know not how,
For I was out of my wits, he fell with's head
Just in my bosom.

Page. This is not true, madam.

Cor. I pray thee, peace.
One arrow's graz'd already: it were vain
To lose this for that will ne'er be found again.

Brach. Go, bear the body to Cornelia's lodging:
And we command that none acquaint our duchess
With this sad accident. For you, Flamineo,
Hark you, I will not grant your pardon.

Flam. No?

Brach. Only a lease of your life; and that shall last
But for one day: thou shalt be forc'd each evening
To renew it, or be hang'd.

Flam. At your pleasure.
[LODOVICO *sprinkles* BRACHIANO'S *beaver with a poison.*

Your will is law now, I'll not meddle with it.

* *you*] The 4tos. of 1665 and 1672, "*yon.*"

Brach. You once did brave me in your sister's lodging;
I'll now keep you in awe for't.—Where's our beaver?

Fran. de Med. [*aside.*] He calls for his destruction. Noble youth,
I pity thy sad fate! Now to the barriers.
This shall his passage to the black lake further;
The last good deed he did, he pardon'd murther.
                                    [*Exeunt.*
[*Charges and shouts.* They fight at barriers;† first single pairs, then three to three.*

Enter BRACHIANO, VITTORIA COROMBONA, GIOVANNI, FRANCISCO DE MEDICIS, FLAMINEO, *with others.*

Brach. An armorer! ud's death, an armorer!
Flam. Armorer! where's the armorer?
Brach. Tear off my beaver.
Flam. Are you hurt, my lord?
Brach. O, my brain's on fire!

                Enter Armorer.
The helmet is poison'd.
Armorer. My lord, upon my soul,—
Brach. Away with him to torture!
There are some great ones that have hand in this,
And near about me.
Vit. Cor. O my lov'd lord! poison'd!
Flam. Remove the bar. Here's unfortunate revels!
Call the physicians,

          Enter two Physicians.
                A plague upon you!
We have too much of your cunning here already:
I fear the ambassadors are likewise poison'd.
Brach. O, I am gone already! the infection
Flies to the brain and heart. O thou strong heart!
There's such a covenant 'tween the world and it,
They're loth to break.
Giov. O my most loved father!
Brach. Remove the boy away.—
Where's this good woman?—Had I infinite worlds,
They were too little for thee: must I leave thee?—
What say you, screech-owls, is the venom mortal?
First Phys. Most deadly.
Brach. Most corrupted politic hangman,
You kill without book; but your art to save
Fails you as oft as great men's needy friends.
I that have given life to offending slaves

---

* *Charges and shouts, &c.*] Scene. The lists at Padua.
† *barriers*] "Barriers cometh of the French word *Barres*, and signifieth with us that which the Frenchmen call *Jeu de Barres*, a martial sport or exercise of men armed, and fighting together with short swords within certain Barres or lists, whereby they are separated from the spectators." Cowell's *Interpreter*, ed. 1701.

And wretched murderers, have I not power
To lengthen mine own a twelve-month?—
Do not kiss me, for I shall poison thee.
This unction's sent from the great Duke of Florence.
Fran. de Med. Sir, be of comfort.
Brach. O thou soft natural death, that art* joint-twin
To sweetest slumber! no rough-bearded comet
Stares on thy mild departure; the dull owl
Beats not against thy casement; the hoarse wolf
Scents not thy carrion: pity winds thy corse,
Whilst horror waits on princes.
Vit. Cor. I am lost for ever.
Brach. How miserable a thing it is to die
'Mongst women howling!

Enter LODOVICO *and* GASPARO, *in the habit of Capuchins.*

                What are those?
Flam.   Franciscans:
They have brought the extreme unction.
Brach. On pain of death, let no man name death to me:
It is a word infinitely terrible.
Withdraw into our cabinet.
[*Exeunt all except* FRANCISCO DE MEDICIS *and* FLAMINEO.

Flam. To see what solitariness is about dying princes! as heretofore they have unpeopled towns, divorced friends, and made great houses unhospitable, so now, O justice! where are their flatterers now? Flatterers are but the shadows of princes' bodies; the least thick cloud makes them invisible.
Fran. de Med. There's great moan made for him.
Flam. Faith, for some few hours salt-water will run most plentifully in every office o'the court: but, believe it, most of them do but weep over their stepmothers' graves.†
Fran. de Med. How mean you?
Flam. Why, they dissemble; as some men do that live within compass o'the verge.
Fran. de Med. Come, you have thrived well under him.
Flam. Faith, like a wolf in a woman's breast;‡ I have been fed with poultry: but, for money, understand me, I had as good a will to cozen him as e'er an officer of them all; but I had not cunning enough to do it.
Fran. de Med. What didst thou think of him? faith, speak freely.

---

* *art*] The 4to. of 1631, "are."
† *graves*] The 4to. of 1631, "grave."
‡ *like a wolf in a woman's breast*] "The extraordinary cravings of women during their pregnancy were anciently accounted for, by supposing some voracious animal to be within them." STEEVENS.

Flam. He was a kind of statesman that would sooner have reckoned how many cannon-bullets he had discharged against a town, to count his expence that way, than how many of his valiant and deserving subjects he lost before it.

Fran. de Med. O, speak well of the duke.

Flam. I have done. Wilt hear some of my court-wisdom? To reprehend princes is dangerous; and to over-commend some of them is palpable lying.

Re-enter LODOVICO.

Fran. de Med. How is it with the duke?

Lod. Most deadly ill.
He's fall'n into a strange distraction:
He talks of battles and monopolies,
Levying of taxes; and from that descends
To the most brain-sick language. His mind fastens
On twenty several objects, which confound
Deep sense with folly. Such a fearful end
May teach some men that bear too lofty crest,
Though they live happiest, yet they die not best.
He hath conferr'd the whole state of the dukedom
Upon your sister, till the prince arrive
At mature age.

Flam. There's some good luck in that yet.

Fran. de Med. See, here he comes.

Enter BRACHIANO, *presented in a bed,* [*] VITTORIA COROM-
BONA, GASPARO, *and* Attendants.

        There's death in's face already.

Vit. Cor. O my good lord!

Brach. Away! you have abus'd me:
    [*These speeches are several kinds of distractions, and
       in the action should appear so.*†]

You have convey'd coin forth our territories,
Bought and sold offices, oppress'd the poor,
And I ne'er dreamt on't. Make up your accounts:
I'll now be mine own steward.

Flam. Sir, have patience.

Brach. Indeed, I am to blame:
For did you ever hear the dusky raven
Chide blackness? or was't ever known the devil
Rail'd against cloven creatures?

Vit. Cor. O my lord!

Brach. Let me have some quails to supper.

Flam. Sir, you shall.

Brach. No, some fried dog-fish; your quails
feed on poison.
That old dog-fox, that politician, Florence!

I'll forswear hunting, and turn dog-killer:
Rare! I'll be friends with him; for, mark you,
sir, one dog
Still sets another a-barking. Peace, peace!
Yonder's a fine slave come in now.

Flam. Where?

Brach. Why, there,
In a blue bonnet, and a pair of breeches
With a great cod-piece: ha, ha, ha!
Look you, his cod-piece is stuck full of pins,
With pearls o'the head of them. Do not you
    know him?

Flam. No, my lord.

Brach. Why, 'tis the devil;
I know him by a great rose [*] he wears on's shoe,
To hide his cloven foot. I'll dispute with him;
He's a rare linguist.

Vit. Cor. My lord, here's nothing.

Brach. Nothing! rare! nothing! when I want
    money,
Our treasury is empty, there is nothing:
I'll not be us'd thus.

Vit. Cor. O, lie still, my lord!

Brach. See, see Flamineo, that kill'd his brother,
Is dancing on the ropes there, and he carries
A money-bag in each hand, to keep him even,
For fear of breaking's neck: and there's a
    lawyer,
In a gown whipt with velvet, stares and gapes
When the money will fall. How the rogue cuts
    capers!
It should have been in a halter. 'Tis there:
what's she?

Flam. Vittoria, my lord.

Brach. Ha, ha, ha! her hair is sprinkled with
arras-powder,†
That makes her look as if she had sinn'd in the
pastry.—
What's he?

Flam. A divine, my lord.

    [BRACHIANO *seems here near his end;* LODOVICO
    and GASPARO, *in the habit of* Capuchins, *pre-
    sent him in his bed with a crucifix and hal-
    lowed candle.*

Brach. He will be drunk; avoid him: the
argument
Is fearful, when churchmen stagger in't.

---

* *rose*] i. e. knot of ribands.
† *arras-powder*] So our author again in the *Duchess of
Malfi;*
  "When I wax gray, I shall have all the court
Powder their hair with *arras*, to be like me."
                  A. III. S. 2.
Arras-powder means, we can hardly doubt, *orris-powder,*
—powder made of the root of the orris. (See Halliwell's
Dict. of Arch. and Prov. Words, sub *Arras.*)

* *Enter Brachiano, presented in a bed,* &c.] Here the
audience were to suppose that a change of scene had
taken place,—that the stage now represented Brachiano's
chamber: in p. 42 Gasparo says, "For Christian charity,
avoid the chamber."
† The 4to. of 1631 omits this stage-direction.

Look you, six grey rats,* that have lost their tails,
Crawl up the pillow : send for a rat-catcher :
I'll do a miracle, I'll free the court
From all foul vermin.   Where's Flamineo?

Flam. I do not like that he names me so often,
Especially on's death-bed : 'tis a sign   [*Aside.*
I shall not live long.—See, he's near his end.

  Lod. Pray, give us leave.—*Attende, domine
    Brachiane.*

Flam. See, see how firmly he doth fix his eye
Upon the crucifix.

  Vit. Cor. O, hold it constant !
It settles his wild spirits ; and so his eyes
Melt into tears.

  *Lod. Domine Brachiane, solebas in bello tutus
esse tuo clypeo ; nunc hunc clypeum hosti tuo op-
ponas infernali.*   [*By the crucifix.*

  *Gas. Olim hastâ valuisti in bello ; nunc hanc
sacram hastam vibrabis contra hostem animarum.*
        [*By the hallowed taper.*

  *Lod. Attende, domine Brachiane ; si nunc quoque
probas ea quæ acta sunt inter nos, flecte caput in
dextrum.*

  *Gas. Esto securus, domine Brachiane ; cogita
quantum habeas meritorum ; denique memineris
meam animam pro tuâ oppignoratam si quid esset
periculi.*

  *Lod. Si nunc quoque probas ea quæ acta sunt
inter nos, flecte caput in lævum.*—
He is departing : pray, stand all apart,
And let us only whisper in his ears
Some private meditations, which our order
Permits you not to hear.
    [*Here, the rest being departed, LODOVICO and GAS-
    PARO discover themselves.*

  Gas. Brachiano,—
  Lod. Devil Brachiano, thou art damn'd.
  Gas. Perpetually.
  Lod. A slave condemn'd and given up to the
      gallows
Is thy great lord and master.
  Gas. True ; for thou
Art given up to the devil.
  Lod. O you slave !
You that were held the famous politician,
Whose art was poison !
  Gas. And whose conscience, murder !
  Lod. That would have broke your wife's neck
      down the stairs,
Ere she was poison'd !
  Gas. That had your villanous salads !
  Lod. And fine embroider'd bottles and perfumes,
Equally mortal with a winter-plague !

  Gas. Now there's mercury—
  Lod. And copperas—
  Gas. And quicksilver—
  Lod. With other devilish pothecary * stuff,
A-melting in your politic brains : dost hear ?
  Gas. This is Count Lodovico.
  Lod. This, Gasparo :
And thou shalt die like a poor rogue.
  Gas. And stink
Like a dead fly-blown dog.
  Lod. And be forgotten
Before thy funeral sermon.
  Brach. Vittoria !
Vittoria !
  Lod. O, the cursèd devil
Comes † to himself again ! we are undone.
  Gas. Strangle him in private.

  Enter VITTORIA COROMBONA, FRANCISCO DE MEDICIS,
      FLAMINEO, *and Attendants.*

          What, will you call him again
To live in treble torments ? for charity,
For Christian charity, avoid the chamber.
    [*Exeunt* VITTORIA COROMBONA, FRANCISCO DE
      MEDICIS, FLAMINEO, *and Attendants.*

  Lod. You would prate, sir ? This is a true-love-
      knot
Sent from the Duke of Florence.
              [*BRACHIANO is strangled.*
  Gas. What, is it done ?
  Lod. The snuff is out. No woman-keeper i'
      the world,
Though she had practis'd seven year at the pest-
      house,
Could have done't quaintlier.

  Re-enter VITTORIA COROMBONA, FRANCISCO DE MEDICIS,
      FLAMINEO, *and Attendants.*

              My lords, he's dead.
  Omnes. Rest to his soul !
  Vit. Cor. O me ! this place is hell.   [*Exit.*
  Fran. de Med. How heavily she takes it !
  Flam. O, yes, yes ;
Had women navigable rivers in their eyes,
They would dispend them all : surely, I wonder
Why we should wish more rivers to the city,
When they sell water so good cheap.‡ I'll tell thee,
These are but moonish shades of griefs or fears ;
There's nothing sooner dry than women's tears.
Why, here's an end of all my harvest ; he has
      given me nothing.

---

* pothecary] The 4to. of 1631, "apothecary."
† comes] The 4to. of 1612, " come "
‡ good cheap] Answers to the French à bo marché :
cheap is an old word for market.

* rats] The 4to. of 1631, "cats."

Court promises! let wise men count them curs'd,
For while you live, he that scores best pays
  worst.

Fran. de Med. Sure, this was Florence' doing.

Flam. Very likely.

Those are found weighty strokes which come
  from the hand,
But those are killing strokes which come from the
  head.

O, the rare tricks of a Machiavelian!
He doth not come, like a gross plodding slave,
And buffet you to death; no, my quaint knave,
He tickles you to death, makes you die laughing,
As if you had swallow'd down a pound of saffron.
You see the feat, 'tis practis'd in a trice;
To teach court honesty, it jumps on ice.

  Fran. de Med. Now have the people liberty to
    talk,
And descant on his vices.

  Flam. Misery of princes,
That must of force be censur'd by their slaves!
Not only blam'd for doing things are ill,
But for not doing all that all men will:
One were better be a thresher.
Ud's death, I would fain speak with this duke yet.

  Fran. de Med. Now he's dead?

  Flam. I cannot conjure; but if prayers or oaths
Will get to the speech of him, though forty devils
Wait on him in his livery of flames,
I'll speak to him, and shake him by the hand,
Though I be blasted.   [*Exit.*

  Fran. de Med. Excellent Lodovico!
What, did you terrify him at the last gasp?

  Lod. Yes, and so idly, that the duke had like
To have terrified us.

  Fran. de Med. How?

  Lod. You shall hear that hereafter.

Enter ZANCHE.

See, yon's the infernal that would make up sport.
Now to the revelation of that secret
She promis'd when she fell in love with you.

  Fran. de Med. You're passionately met in this
    sad world.

  Zanche. I would have you look up, sir; these
    court-tears
Claim not your tribute to them: let those weep
That guiltily partake in the sad cause.
I knew last night, by a sad dream I had,
Some mischief would ensue; yet, to say truth,
My dream most concern'd you.

  Lod. Shall's fall a-dreaming?

  Fran. de Med. Yes; and for fashion sake I'll
    dream with her.

  Zanche. Methought, sir, you came stealing to
    my bed.

  Fran. de Med. Wilt thou believe me, sweeting?
    by this light,
I was a-dreamt on thee too; for methought
I saw thee naked.

  Zanche. Fie, sir! As I told you,
Methought you lay down by me.

  Fran. de Med. So dreamt I;
And lest thou shouldst take cold, I cover'd thee
With this Irish mantle.

  Zanche. Verily, I did dream
You were somewhat bold with me: but to come
    to't—

  Lod. How, how! I hope you will not go to't *
    here.

  Fran. de Med. Nay, you must hear my dream
    out.

  Zanche. Well, sir, forth.

  Fran. de Med. When I threw the mantle o'er
    thee, thou didst laugh
Exceedingly, methought.

  Zanche. Laugh!

  Fran. de Med. And cried'st out,
The hair did tickle thee.

  Zanche. There was a dream indeed!

  Lod. Mark her, I prithee; she simpers like the
    suds
A collier hath been wash'd in.

  Zanche. Come, sir, good fortune tends you. I
    did tell you
I would reveal a secret: Isabella,
The Duke of Florence' sister, was impoison'd
By a fum'd picture; and Camillo's neck
Was broke by damn'd Flamineo, the mischance
Laid on a vaulting-horse.

  Fran. de Med. Most strange!

  Zanche. Most true.

  Lod. The bed of snakes is broke.

  Zanche. I sadly do confess I had a hand
In the black deed.

  Fran. de Med. Thou kept'st their counsel?

  Zanche. Right;
For which, urg'd with contrition, I intend
This night to rob Vittoria.

  Lod. Excellent penitence!
Usurers dream on't while they sleep out sermons.

  Zanche. To further our escape, I have entreated
Leave to retire me, till the funeral,
Unto a friend i'the country: that excuse
Will further our escape. In coin and jewels
I shall at least make good unto your use
An hundred thousand crowns.

---

* *to't*] Some copies of the 4to. of 1612, "*to it.*"

Fran. de Med. O noble wench!

Lod. Those crowns we'll share.

Zanche. It is a dowry,

Methinks, should make that sun-burnt proverb false,

And wash the Æthiop white.

Fran. de Med. It shall. Away!

Zanche. Be ready for our flight.

Fran. de Med. An hour 'fore day.

[*Exit* Zanche.

O strange discovery! why, till now we knew not

The circumstance of either of their deaths.

Re-enter Zanche.

Zanche. You'll wait about midnight in the chapel?

Fran. de Med. There.   [*Exit* Zanche.

Lod. Why, now our action's justified.

Fran. de Med. Tush for justice!

What harms it justice? we now, like the partridge,

Purge the disease with laurel;* for the fame

Shall crown the enterprize, and quit the shame.

[*Exeunt.*

Enter Flamineo† *and* Gasparo, *at one door; another way,* Giovanni, *attended.*

Gas. The young duke: did you e'er see a sweeter prince?

Flam. I have known a poor woman's bastard better favoured: this is behind him; now, to his face, all comparisons were hateful. Wise was the courtly peacock that, being a great minion, and being compared for beauty by some dottrels that stood by to the kingly eagle, said the eagle was a far fairer bird than herself, not in respect of her feathers, but in respect of her long talons:‡ his will grow out in time.—My gracious lord!

Gio. I pray, leave me, sir.

Flam. Your grace must be merry: 'tis I have cause to mourn; for, wot you, what said the little boy that rode behind his father on horseback?

Gio. Why, what said he?

---

* *—we now, like the partridge,*

Purge the disease with laurel] "So Pliny, 'Palumbes, graccull, merulæ, perdices lauri folio annuum fastidium purgant.' Nat. Hist. lib. viii. c. 27." Reed.

† *Enter Flamineo, &c.*] Scene. An apartment in a palace.—Since in a later scene, p. 47, Flamineo speaks of Brachiano as *not yet having been four hours dead*, and since Brachiano certainly appears to have died at *Padua*, we cannot but wonder to find in the present scene the words "committed to *Castle Angelo*, to the tower yonder." Qy. ought we to read "committed to Castle Angelo, or to the tower yonder"? Or does all this confusion arise from the author's carelessness in determining the localities?

‡ *talons*] The earliest 4to. "Tallants,"—the word being formerly often so spelt.

Flam. "When you are dead, father," said he, "I hope that I shall ride in the saddle." O, 'tis a brave thing for a man to sit by himself! he may stretch himself in the stirrups, look about, and see the whole compass of the hemisphere. You're now, my lord, i'the saddle.

Gio. Study your prayers, sir, and be penitent: 'Twere fit you'd think on what hath former bin; I have heard grief nam'd the eldest child of sin.*

[*Exit.*

Flam. Study my prayers! he threatens me divinely:

I am falling to pieces already. I care not though, like Anacharsis, I were pounded to death in a mortar: and yet that death were fitter for usurers, gold and themselves to be beaten together, to make a most cordial cullis† for the devil.

He hath his uncle's villanous look already,

In decimo sexto.

Enter Courtier.

Now, sir, what are you?

Cour. It is the pleasure, sir, of the young duke,

That you forbear the presence, and all rooms

That owe him reverence.

Flam. So, the wolf and the raven

Are very pretty fools when they are young.

Is it your office, sir, to keep me out?

Cour. So the duke wills.

Flam. Verily, master courtier, extremity is not to be used in all offices: say that a gentlewoman were taken out of her bed about midnight, and committed to Castle Angelo, to the tower yonder, with nothing about her but her smock, would it not show a cruel part in the gentleman-porter to lay claim to her upper garment, pull it o'er her head and ears, and put her in naked?

Cour. Very good: you are merry.   [*Exit.*

Flam. Doth he make a court-ejectment of me? a flaming fire-brand casts more smoke without a chimney than within't. I'll smoor‡ some of them.

Enter Francisco de Medicis.

How now! thou art sad.

Fran. de Med. I met even now with the most piteous sight.

Flam. Thou meet'st§ another here, a pitiful Degraded courtier.

---

* *'Twere fit you'd think, &c.*] In the *Duchess of Malfi*, Act V. S. 5. this couplet, slightly altered, is given to the Cardinal.

† *cullis*] See note on the *Duchess of Malfi*, A. II. S. 4.

‡ *smoor*] i. e. smother.

§ *meet'st*] So the 4to. of 1672: the three earliest 4tos. "met'st."

Fran. de Med. Your reverend mother
Is grown a very old woman in two hours.
I found them winding of Marcello's corse;
And there is such a solemn melody,
'Tween doleful songs, tears, and sad elegies,—
Such as old grandams watching by the dead
Were wont to outwear the nights with,—that,
    believe me,
I had no eyes to guide me forth the room,
They were so o'ercharg'd with water.

   Flam. I will see them.

   Fran. de Med. 'Twere much uncharity in you;
    for your sight
Will add unto their tears.

   Flam. I will see them:
They are behind the traverse;* I'll discover
Their superstitious howling.

                [Draws the curtain.

CORNELIA, ZANCHE, *and three other Ladies discovered
   winding* MARCELLO'S *corse. A Song.*†

   Cor. This rosemary is wither'd; pray, get
    fresh.
I would have these herbs grow up in his grave,
When I am dead and rotten. Reach the bays,
I'll tie a garland here about his head;
'Twill keep my boy from lightning. This
    sheet
I have kept this twenty year,‡ and every day
Hallow'd it with my prayers: I did not think
He should have wore it.

   Zanche. Look you who are yonder.

   Cor. O, reach me the flowers.

   Zanche. Her ladyship's foolish.

   Lady. Alas, her grief
Hath turn'd her child again!

   Cor. You're very welcome:
There's rosemary § for you;—and rue for you;—
                [To FLAMINEO.
Heart's-ease for you; I pray make much of it:
I have left more for myself.

   Fran. de Med. Lady, who's this?

   Cor. You are, I take it, the grave-maker.

   Flam. So.

   Zanche. 'Tis Flamineo.

   Cor. Will you make me such a fool? here's a
white hand:

Can blood so soon be wash'd out?* let me see;
When screech-owls croak upon the chimney-tops,
And the strange cricket i' the oven sings and hops,
When yellow spots do on your hands appear,
Be certain then you of a corse shall hear.
Out upon't, how 'tis speckled! h'as handled a
    toad, sure.
Cowslip-water is good for the memory:
Pray, buy me three ounces of't.

   Flam. I would I were from hence.

   Cor. Do you hear, sir?
I'll give you a saying which my grand-mother
Was wont, when she heard the bell toll, to sing o'er
Unto her lute.

   Flam. Do, an you will, do.

   Cor. "*Call for the robin-red-breast and the wren,*†
     *[*CORNELIA *doth this in several forms of distraction.*
Since o'er shady groves they hover,
And with leaves and flowers do cover
The friendless bodies of unburied men.
Call unto his funeral dole
The ant, the field-mouse, and the mole,
To rear him hillocks that shall keep him warm,
And (when gay tombs are robb'd) sustain no harm:
But keep the wolf far thence, that's foe to men,
For with his nails he'll dig them up again."
They would not bury him 'cause he died in a
    quarrel;
But I have an answer for them:
"*Let holy church receive him duly,*
Since he paid the church-tithes truly."
His wealth is summ'd, and this is all his store,
This poor men get, and great men get no more.
Now the wares are gone, we may shut up shop.
Bless you all, good people.

      [Exeunt CORNELIA, ZANCHE, *and Ladies.*

   Flam. I have a strange thing in me, to the
    which
I cannot give a name, without it be
Compassion. I pray, leave me.

        [Exit FRANCISCO DE MEDICIS.
This night I'll know the utmost of my fate;
I'll be resolv'd what my rich sister means

---

* *the traverse*] "Beside the principal curtains that hung
in the front of the stage, they used others as substitutes
for scenes, which were denominated *traverses.*" Malone's
Hist. Acc. of the English Stage, p. 88. ed. Boswell.

† *A Song*] In the printed copies of old plays the
"songs" are frequently omitted.

‡ *year*] The 4to. of 1631, "*years.*"

§ *There's rosemary, &c.*] "See note on *Hamlet,* A. IV.
S. 5." STEEVENS.

* —*here's a white hand:
Can blood so soon be wash'd out?*] Reed calls this "An
imitation of Lady Macbeth's sleeping soliloquy."

† "I never saw any thing like this dirge, except the
ditty which reminds Ferdinand of his drowned father in
the Tempest. As that is of the water, watery; so this is
of the earth, earthy. Both have that intenseness of feel-
ing, which seems to resolve itself into the elements
which it contemplates." C. LAMB. (*Spec. of Eng. Dram.
Poets,* p. 233.) Reed charges Webster with imitating part
of this dirge from the well-known passage in Shakespeare's *Cymbeline,* A. IV. S. 2.
        "The ruddock would
   With charitable bill," &c.

To assign me for my service. I have liv'd
Riotously ill, like some that live in court,
And sometimes when my * face was full of smiles,
Have felt the maze of conscience in my breast.
Oft gay and honour'd robes those tortures try :
We think cag'd birds sing, when indeed they cry.

Enter BRACHIANO's *ghost, in his leather cassock and breeches,
and boots; with a cowl; in his hand a pot of lily-
flowers, with a skull in't.*

Ha ! I can stand thee : nearer, nearer yet.
What a mockery hath death made thee ! thou
    look'st sad.
In what place art thou ? in yon starry gallery ?
Or in the cursèd dungeon ?—No ! not speak ?
Pray, sir, resolve me, what religion's best
For a man to die in ? or is it in your knowledge
To answer me how long I have to live ?
That's the most necessary question.
Not answer ? are you still like some great men
That only walk like shadows up and down,
And to no purpose ? say :—
    [*The Ghost throws earth upon him, and shows him the
    skull.*

What's that ? O, fatal ! he throws earth upon me !
A dead man's skull beneath the roots of flowers !—
I pray, speak, sir : our Italian church-men
Make us believe dead men hold conference
With their familiars, and many times
Will come to bed to them, and eat with them.
    [*Exit Ghost.*

He's gone ; and see, the skull and earth are vanish'd.
This is beyond melancholy. I do dare my fate
To do its worst. Now to my sister's lodging,
And sum up all these horrors : the disgrace
The prince threw on me ; next the piteous sight
Of my dead brother ; and my mother's dotage ;
And last this terrible vision : all these
Shall with Vittoria's bounty turn to good,
Or I will drown this weapon in her blood. [*Exit.*

Enter FRANCISCO DE MEDICIS,† LODOVICO, *and* HORTENSIO.

    Lod. My lord, upon my soul, you shall no
    further ;
You have most ridiculously engag'd yourself
Too far already. For my part, I have paid
All my debts : so, if I should chance to fall,
My creditors fall not with me ; and I vow
To quit all in this bold assembly
To the meanest follower. My lord, leave the city,
Or I'll forswear the murder.   [*Exit.*
    Fran. de Med. Farewell, Lodovico :

If thou dost perish in this glorious act,
I'll rear unto thy memory that fame
Shall in the ashes keep alive thy name.   [*Exit.*
    Hor. There's some black deed on foot. I'll
    presently
Down to the citadel, and raise some force.
These strong court-factions, that do brook no
    checks,
In the career oft break the riders' necks.   [*Exit.*

Enter VITTORIA COROMBONA* *with a book in her hand, and*
ZANCHE ; FLAMINEO *following them.*

    Flam. What, are you at your prayers ? give o'er.
    Vit. Cor. How, ruffian !
    Flam. I come to you 'bout worldly business :
Sit down, sit down :—nay, stay, blouze, you may
    hear it :—
The doors are fast enough.
    Vit. Cor. Ha, are you drunk ?
    Flam. Yes, yes, with wormwood-water : you
    shall taste
Some of it presently.
    Vit. Cor. What intends the Fury ?
    Flam. You are my lord's executrix ; and I claim
Reward for my long service.
    Vit. Cor. For your service !
    Flam. Come, therefore, here is pen and ink ;
    set down
What you will give me.
    Vit. Cor. There.   [*Writes.*
    Flam. Ha ! have you done already ?
'Tis a most short conveyance.
    Vit. Cor. I will read it :   [*Reads.*
" *I give that portion to thee, and no other,
Which Cain groan'd under, having slain his
    brother.*"
    Flam. A most courtly patent to beg by !
    Vit. Cor. You are a villain.
    Flam. Is't come to this ? They say, affrights
    cure agues :
Thou hast a devil in thee ; I will try
If I can scare him from thee. Nay, sit still :
My lord hath left me yet two cases† of jewels
Shall make me scorn your bounty ; you shall see
    them.   [*Exit.*
    Vit. Cor. Sure, he's distracted.
    Zanche. O, he's desperate :
For your own safety give him gentle language.

    Re-enter FLAMINEO *with two case of pistols.*

    Flam. Look, these are better far at a dead lift
Than all your jewel-house.

---

* my] The 4to. of 1631, "his,"—a misprint perhaps for
"this."
    † *Enter Francisco de Medicis,* &c.] Scene. A street :
see note†, p. 44.

* *Enter Vittoria Corombona,* &c.] Scene. An apartment in the residence of Vittoria : see note†, p. 44.
    † *case*] i. e. pair.

Vit. Cor. And yet, methinks,
These stones have no fair lustre, they are ill set.
Flam. I'll turn the right side towards you: you
    shall see
How they will sparkle.
Vit. Cor. Turn this horror from me !
What do you want ? what would you have me do ?
Is not all mine yours ? have I any children ?
Flam. Pray thee, good woman, do not trouble me
With this vain worldly business; say your
    prayers :
I made a vow to my deceasèd lord,
Neither yourself nor I should outlive him
The numbering of four hours.
Vit. Cor. Did he enjoin it ?
Flam. He did; and 'twas a deadly jealousy,
Lest any should enjoy thee after him,
That urg'd him vow me to it.   For my death,
I did propound it voluntarily, knowing,
If he could not be safe in his own court,
Being a great duke, what hope, then, for us ?
Vit. Cor. This is your melancholy and despair.
Flam. Away !
Fool thou art to think that politicians
Do use to kill the effects of injuries
And let the cause live.   Shall we groan in irons,
Or be a shameful and a weighty burden
To a public scaffold ?   This is my resolve ;
I would not live at any man's entreaty,
Nor die at any's bidding.
Vit. Cor. Will you hear me ?
Flam. My life hath done service to other men ;
My death shall serve mine own turn.   Make you
    ready.
Vit. Cor. Do you mean to die indeed ?
Flam. With as much pleasure
As e'er my father gat me.
Vit. Cor. Are the doors lock'd ?
Zanche. Yes, madam.
Vit. Cor. Are you grown an atheist ? . will you
    turn your body,
Which is the goodly palace of the soul,
To the soul's slaughter-house ? O, the cursèd devil,
Which doth present us with all other sins
Thrice-candied o'er ; despair with gall and
    stibium ;
Yet we carouse it off ;—Cry out for help !—
              [*Aside to* ZANCHE.
Makes us forsake that which was made for man,
The world, to sink to that was made for devils,
Eternal darkness !
Zanche. Help, help !
Flam. I'll stop your throat
With winter-plums.

Vit. Cor. I prithee, yet remember,
Millions are now in graves, which at last day
Like mandrakes shall rise shrieking.
Flam. Leave your prating,
For these are but grammatical laments,
Feminine arguments : and they move me,
As some in pulpits move their auditory,
More with their exclamation than sense
Of reason or sound doctrine.
Zanche [*aside to* VIT.]. Gentle madam,
Seem to consent, only persuade him teach
The way to death ; let him die first.
Vit. Cor. 'Tis good.   I apprehend it,
To kill one's self is meat that we must take
Like pills, not chew't, but quickly swallow it ;
The smart o'the wound, or weakness of the
    hand,
May else bring treble torments.
Flam. I have held it
A wretched and most miserable life
Which is not able to die.
Vit. Cor. O, but frailty !
Yet I am now resolv'd : farewell, affliction !
Behold, Brachiano, I that while you liv'd
Did make a flaming altar of my heart
To sacrifice unto you, now am ready
To sacrifice heart and all.—Farewell, Zanche !
Zanche. How, madam ! do you think that I'll
    outlive you ;
Especially when my best self, Flamineo,
Goes the same voyage ?
Flam. O, most lovèd Moor !
Zanche. Only by all my love let me entreat
    you,—
Since it is most necessary one * of us
Do violence on ourselves,—let you or I
Be her sad taster, teach her how to die.
Flam. Thou dost instruct me nobly : take
    these pistols,
Because my hand is stain'd with blood already :
Two of these you shall level at my breast,
The other 'gainst your own, and so we'll die
Most equally contented : but first swear
Not to outlive me.
Vit. Cor. and Zanche. Most religiously.
Flam. Then here's an end of me ; farewell,
    daylight !
And, O contemptible physic, that dost take
So long a study, only to preserve
So short a life, I take my leave of thee !—
These are two cupping-glasses that shall draw
              [*Showing the pistols.*
All my infected blood out.   Are you ready ?

    * *one*] The 4to. of 1612, "*none.*"

Vit. Cor. and *Zanche.* Ready.

Flam. Whither shall I go now? O Lucian, thy
ridiculous purgatory! to find Alexander the
Great cobbling shoes, Pompey tagging points,
and Julius Cæsar making hair-buttons! Hannibal
selling blacking, and Augustus crying garlic!
Charlemagne selling lists by the dozen, and King
Popin crying apples in a cart drawn with one
horse!
Whether I resolve to fire, earth, water, air,
Or all the elements by scruples, I know not,
Nor greatly care.—Shoot, shoot:
Of all deaths the violent death is best;
For from ourselves it steals ourselves so fast,
The pain, once apprehended, is quite past.

[*They shoot; he falls; and they run to him, and tread
upon him.*

Vit. Cor. What, are you dropt?

Flam. I am mix'd with earth already: as you
are noble,
Perform your vows, and bravely follow me.

Vit. Cor. Whither? to hell?

Zanche. To most assur'd damnation?

Vit. Cor. O thou most cursèd devil!

Zanche. Thou art caught—

Vit. Cor. In thine own engine. I tread the
fire out
That would have been my ruin.

Flam. Will you be perjured? what a religious
oath was Styx, that the gods never durst swear
by, and violate! O, that we had such an oath to
minister, and to be so well kept in our courts of
justice!

Vit. Cor. Think whither thou art going.

Zanche. And remember
What villanies thou hast acted.

Vit. Cor. This thy death
Shall make me like a blazing ominous star:
Look up and tremble.

Flam. O, I am caught with a springe!

Vit. Cor. You see the fox comes many times
short home;
'Tis here prov'd true.

Flam. Kill'd with a couple of braches!*

Vit. Cor. No fitter offering for the infernal
Furies
Than one in whom they reign'd while he was
living.

Flam. O, the way's dark and horrid! I cannot
see:
Shall I have no company?

Vit. Cor. O, yes, thy sins

* *braches*] i. e. bitch-hounds.

Do run before thee to fetch fire from hell,
To light thee thither.

Flam. O, I smell soot,
Most stinking soot! the chimney is a-fire:
My liver's parboil'd, like Scotch holly-bread;
There's a plumber laying pipes in my guts, it
scalds.—
Wilt thou outlive me?

Zanche. Yes, and drive a stake
Thorough thy body; for we'll give it out
Thou didst this violence upon thyself.

Flam. O cunning devils! now I have tried
your love,
And doubled all your reaches.—I am not
wounded;   [*Rises.*
The pistols held no bullets: 'twas a plot
To prove your kindness to me: and I live
To punish your ingratitude. I knew,
One time or other, you would find a way
To give me a strong potion.—O men
That lie upon your death-beds, and are haunted
With howling wives, ne'er trust them! they'll
re-marry
Ere the worm pierce your winding-sheet, ere the
spider
Make a thin curtain for your epitaphs.—
How cunning you were to discharge! do you
practise at the Artillery-yard?—Trust a woman!
never, never! Brachiano be my precedent. We
lay our souls to pawn to the devil for a little
pleasure, and a woman makes the bill of sale.
That ever man should marry! For one Hypermnestra * that saved her lord and husband, forty-
nine of her sisters cut their husbands' throats all
in one night: there was a shoal of virtuous
horse-leeches!—Here are two other instruments.

Vit. Cor. Help, help!

Enter LODOVICO, GASPARO, PEDRO, *and* CARLO.

Flam. What noise is that? ha! false keys i'the
court!

Lod. We have brought you a mask.

Flam. A matachin,† it seems by your drawn
swords.
Church-men turn'd revellers!

* *one Hypermnestra*] "Hypermnestra, one of the fifty
daughters of Danaus, the son of Belus, brother of
Ægyptus. Her father, being warned by an oracle that
he should be killed by one of his nephews, persuaded his
daughters, who were compelled to marry the sons of
their uncle, to murder them on the first night. This
was executed by every one except Hypermnestra. She
preserved her husband Lynceus, who afterwards slew
Danaus." REED.

† *A matachin it seems by your drawn swords*] "Such a

Carlo.* Isabella! Isabella!

Lod. Do you know us now?

Flam. Lodovico! and Gasparo!

Lod. Yes; and that Moor the duke gave pension to

Was the great Duke of Florence.

Vit. Cor. O, we are lost!

Flam. You shall not take justice from forth my hands,—

O, let me kill her!—I'll cut my safety

Through your coats of steel. Fate's a spaniel,

We cannot beat it from us. What remains now?

Let all that do ill, take this precedent,—

Man may his fate foresee, but not prevent:

And of all axioms this shall win the prize,—

'Tis better to be fortunate than wise.

Gas. Bind him to the pillar.

Vit. Cor. O, your gentle pity!

I have seen a black-bird that would sooner fly

To a man's bosom, than to stay the gripe

Of the fierce sparrow-hawk.

Gas. Your hope deceives you.

Vit. Cor. If Florence be i'the court, would he would kill me! †

Gas. Fool! princes give rewards with their own hands,

But death or punishment by the hands of others.

Lod. Sirrah, you once did strike me: I'll strike you

Into ‡ the centre.

---

dance was that well known in France and Italy by the name of the dance of fools or *Matachins,* who were habited in short jackets, with gilt paper helmets, long streamers tied to their shoulders, and bells to their legs. *They carried in their hands a sword* and buckler, with which they made a clashing noise, and performed various quick and sprightly evolutions." Douce's *Illust. of Shakespeare,* vol. ii. p. 435.

Compare the following passage of a curious old drama; "*Avar.* What's this, a *Masque?*

Hind. A *Matachin,* you'l find it.

[*Hind stamps with his foot; then enters Turbo, Latro, &c. in vizards: gag dvaritio and his men."*

An excellent Comedy, called the Prince of Priggs Revels, or the Practises of that grand thief Captain James Hind, &c. 1658, Sig. A 3.

To some dance like a matachin Middleton alludes when he says;

"two or three varlets came

Into the house with all their rapiers drawn,

As if they'd dance the sword-dance on the stage."

A Chaste Maid in Cheapside,—*Works,* iv. 75, ed. Dyce.

* *Carlo*] The two earliest 4tos. "*Con.*"; those of 1665 and 1672, "*Gas.*"

† *would he would kill me*] The 4tos. of 1665 and 1672, "*he would not kill me!*"

‡ *Into*] The 4to. of 1631 "*Vnto:*" but our early writers frequently use "*into*" for "*unto*" (in proof of which more than one passage of Shakespeare might be adduced).

Flam. Thou'lt do it like a hangman, a base hangman,

Not like a noble fellow; for thou see'st

I cannot strike again.

Lod. Dost laugh?

Flam. Would'st have me die, as I was born, in whining?

Gas. Recommend yourself to heaven.

Flam. No, I will carry mine own commendations thither.

Lod. O, could I kill you forty times a day,

And use't four year together, 'twere too little!

Naught grieves but that you are too few to feed

The famine of our vengeance. What dost think on?

Flam. Nothing; of nothing: leave thy idle questions.

I am i'the way to study a long silence:

To prate were idle. I remember nothing.

There's nothing of so infinite vexation

As man's own thoughts.

Lod. O thou glorious strumpet!

Could I divide thy breath from this pure air

When't leaves thy body, I would suck it up,

And breathe't upon some dunghill.

Vit. Cor. You, my death's-man!

Methinks thou dost not look horrid enough,

Thou hast too good a face to be a hangman:

If thou be, do thy office in right form;

Fall down upon thy knees, and ask forgiveness.

Lod. O, thou hast been a most prodigious comet!

But I'll cut off your train,—kill the Moor first.

Vit. Cor. You shall not kill her first; behold my breast:

I will be waited on in death; my servant

Shall never go before me.

Gas. Are you so brave?

Vit. Cor. Yes, I shall welcome death

As princes do some great ambassadors;

I'll meet thy weapon half way.

Lod. Thou dost tremble:

Methinks fear should dissolve thee into air.

Vit. Cor. O, thou art deceiv'd, I am too true a woman:

Conceit can never kill me. I'll tell thee what,

I will not in my death shed one base tear;

Or if look pale, for want of blood, not fear.

Carlo. Thou art my task, black Fury.

Zanche. I have blood

As red as either of theirs: wilt drink some?

'Tis good for the falling-sickness. I am proud

Death cannot alter my complexion,

For I shall ne'er look pale.

E

Lod. Strike, strike,
With a joint motion.

     [*They stab* VITTORIA, ZANCHE, *and* FLAMINEO.

    Vit. Cor. 'Twas a manly blow:
The next thou giv'st, murder some sucking infant;
And then thou wilt be famous.

    Flam. O, what blade is't?
A Toledo, or an English fox?*
I ever thought a cutler should distinguish
The cause of my death, rather than a doctor.
Search my wound deeper; tent it with the steel
That made it.

    Vit. Cor. O, my greatest sin lay in my blood!
Now my blood pays for't.

    Flam. Thou'rt a noble sister!
I love thee now: if woman do breed man,
She ought to teach him manhood: fare thee well.
Know, many glorious women that are fam'd
For masculine virtue have been vicious,
Only a happier silence did betide them:
She hath no faults who hath the art to hide them.

    Vit. Cor. My soul, like to a ship in a black
      storm,
Is driven, I know not whither.

    Flam. Then cast anchor.
Prosperity doth bewitch men, seeming clear;
But seas do laugh, show white, when rocks are
    near.
We cease to grieve, cease to be fortune's slaves,
Nay, cease to die, by dying. Art thou gone?
And thou so near the bottom? false report,
Which says that women vie with the nine Muses
For nine tough durable lives! I do not look
Who went before, nor who shall follow me;
No, at myself I will begin and end.
While we look up to heaven, we confound
Knowledge with knowledge. O, I am in a mist!

    Vit. Cor. O, happy they that never saw the court,
Nor ever knew great men† but by report! [*Dies.*

    Flam. I recover like a spent taper, for a flash,
And instantly go out.
Let all that belong to great men remember the
old wives' tradition, to be like the lions i'the
Tower on Candlemas-day; to mourn if the sun
shine, for fear of the pitiful remainder of winter
to come.

---

* *A Toledo, or an English fox*] "*Toledo*, the capital city of New-Castile, was formerly much famed for making of sword-blades. *Fox*; a cant term for a sword." REED.

† *men*] The 4to. of 1612, "*man.*"

'Tis well yet there's some goodness in my death;
My life was a black charnel. I have caught
An everlasting cold; I have lost my voice
Most irrecoverably. Farewell, glorious villains!
This busy trade of life appears most vain,
Since rest breeds rest, where all seek pain by pain.
Let no harsh flattering bells resound my knell;
Strike, thunder, and strike loud, to my farewell!
                          [*Dies.*

    Eng. Amb. [*within.*] This way, this way! break
      ope the doors! this way!

    Lod. Ha! are we betray'd?
Why, then let's constantly die all together;
And having finish'd this most noble deed,
Defy the worst of fate, not fear to bleed.

      Enter Ambassadors *and* GIOVANNI.

    Eng. Amb. Keep back the prince: shoot, shoot.
      [*They shoot, and* LODOVICO *falls.*

    Lod. O, I am wounded!
I fear I shall be ta'en.

    Gio. You bloody villains,
By what authority have you committed
This massacre?

    Lod. By thine.

    Gio. Mine!

    Lod. Yes; thy uncle,
Which is a part of thee, enjoin'd us to't:
Thou know'st me, I am sure; I am Count Lodo-
    wick;
And thy most noble uncle in disguise
Was last night in thy court.

    Gio. Ha!

    Carlo. Yes, that Moor
Thy father chose his pensioner.

    Gio. He turn'd murderer!—
Away with them to prison and to torture!
All that have hands in this shall taste our justice,
As I hope heaven.

    Lod. I do glory yet
That I can call this act mine own. For my part,
The rack, the gallows, and the torturing wheel,
Shall be but sound sleeps to me: here's my rest;
I limn'd this night-piece, and it was my best.

    Gio. Remove the bodies.—See, my honour'd
    lords,*
What use you ought make of their punishment:
Let guilty men remember, their black deeds
Do lean on crutches made of slender reeds.
                        [*Exeunt.*

---

* *lords*] The old eds. "*Lord.*"

Instead of an EPILOGUE, only this of Martial supplies me :

*Hæc fuerint nobis præmia, si placui.**

For the action of the play, 'twas generally well, and I dare affirm, with the joint-testimony of some of their own quality, for the true imitation of life, without striving to make nature a monster, the best that ever became them : whereof as I make a general acknowledgment, so in particular I must remember the well-approved industry of my friend Master Perkins,† and confess the worth of his action did crown both the beginning and end.

---

the names of the chiefe players at the Red Bull, called the players of the Revelles, Robert Lee, *Richard Perkings,*" &c. *Hist. Ac. of the English Stage,* p. 59. ed. Boswell; again, "[about 1637,] I disposed of *Perkins,* Sumner, Sherlock and Turner, to Salisbury Court, and joynd them with the best of that company." Ib. p. 240. He was the original performer of Captain Goodlack in Heywood's *Fair Maid of the West,* of Sir John Belfare in Shirley's *Wedding,* and of Hanno in Nabbes's *Hannibal and Scipio :* the last piece, as we learn from the title-page, was played in 1635. When Marlowe's *Jew of Malta* was revived about 1633 (in which year it was first given to the press), Perkins acted Barabas ; see Heywood's Prologue at the Cock-pit on the occasion. According to Wright's *Historia Histrionica,* after the suppression of the theatres, Perkins and Sumner (who belonged to the same company) "kept house together at Clerkenwell, and were there buried :" they "died some years before the restoration." A copy of verses by Perkins is prefixed to Heywood's *Apology for Actors.*

---

* *Hæc fuerint, &*c.] ii. 91.

† *Master Perkins*] Richard Perkins was an actor of considerable eminence. As the old 4tos. of *The White Devil* do not give the names of the performers, we cannot determine what part he had in it. If, before this postscript was written, Burbadge had performed Brachiano (which we know was one of his characters, see p. 2), we cannot but wonder that no mention should be made of him here. Perhaps Perkins originally played that part.—Perkins continued to act for many years, chiefly, it appears, at the Cock-pit or Phœnix, where this play was produced. I find the following notices of him in Herbert's MSS. apud Malone ; "[about 1622-3

THE DUCHESS OF MALFI.

The Tragedy of the Dutchesse of Malfy. As it was Presented priuatly, at the Black-Friers; and publiquely at the Globe, By the Kings Maiesties Seruants. The perfect and exact Coppy, with diuerse things Printed, that the length of the Play would not beare in the Presentment. Written by John Webster. Hora.—Si quid——Candidus Imperti si non his utere mecum. London: Printed by Nicholas Okes, for Iohn Waterson, and are to be sold at the signe of the Crowne, in Paules Church-yard, 1623. 4to.

The Dvtchesse of Malfy. A Tragedy. As it was approvedly well acted at the Black-Friers, By his Majesties Servants. the perfect and exact Copy, with divers things Printed, that the length of the Play would not beare in the Presentment. Written by John Webster. Horat.—Si quid——Candidus Imperti si non his utere mecum. London; Printed by I. Raworth, for I. Benson, And are to be sold at his shop in St. Dunstans Churchyard in Fleetstreet. 1640. 4to.

The Duchess of Malfi was reprinted in 1678, and (newly adapted for representation) in 1708. Theobald's alteration of it, called *The Fatal Secret*, appeared in 1735. A reprint of the 4to. of 1640, "with all its imperfections on its head," is given in the *Ancient British Drama*.

The edition of 1623 is by far the most correct of the 4tos.: lines are found in it, which have dropt out from subsequent editions, leaving the different passages where they ought to stand, unintelligible. On collating several copies of this 4to., I have met with one or two various readings of no great importance: see prefatory remarks to *The White Devil*, p. 2.

Malone (note on Shakespeare's *Timon of Athens*, act iii. sc. 3.) is of opinion that the *Duchess of Malfi* had appeared before 1616, supposing that it is the play alluded to in the Prologue (first printed in that year) to Ben Jonson's *Every Man in his Humour :*

> "To make a child now-swaddled to proceed
> Man," &c.

but Malone ought to have been aware that in all probability the Prologue in question was written when *Every Man in his Humour* was first acted, in 1595 or 1596. Among the MSS. notes of the same commentator in the Bodleian Library, I find the following: "I think it is probable that the *Dutchess of Malfy* was produced about the year 1612, when the *White Devil* was printed." But enough of such conjectures. We are certain that the *Duchess of Malfi* was performed before March, 1618-19, when Burbadge, who originally played Ferdinand, died; and we may conclude that it was first produced about 1616.

The story of this play is in the *Novelle* of Bandello, Part I. N. 26; in Belleforest's translation of Bandello, N. 19; in Painter's *Palace of Pleasure*, vol. ii. N. 23, ed. Haslewood; in Beard's *Theatre of God's Judgments*, B. ii. ch. 22. p. 322, ed. 1597; and in Goulart's *Histoires Admirables*, vol. i. p. 319, ed. 1620.

Lope de Vega wrote *El Mayordomo de la Duquesa de Amalfi*, 1618: see his *Life* by Lord Holland, vol. ii. p. 147, ed. 1817.

DRAMATIS PERSONÆ.

Ferdinand, Duke of Calabria . . . . . $\begin{cases} 1.\text{* R. Burbadge,} \\ 2.\text{ J. Taylor.} \end{cases}$

Cardinal, his brother . . . . $\begin{cases} 1.\text{ H. Condell,} \\ 2.\text{ R. Robinson.} \end{cases}$

Antonio Bologna, steward of the household to the Duchess . . $\begin{cases} 1.\text{ W. Ostlar,} \\ 2.\text{ R. Benfield.} \end{cases}$

Delio, his friend . . . . J. Underwood

Daniel de Bosola, gentleman of the horse to the Duchess . . . . J. Lowin.

Castruccio.

Marquis of Pescara   J. Rice.

Count Malatesti.

Roderigo.

Silvio . .   T. Pollard.

Grisolan.

Doctor . . . . R. Pallant.

The Several Madmen . . . . $\begin{cases} \text{N. Tooley,} \\ \text{J. Underwood, &c.} \end{cases}$

Duchess of Malfi . . . . R. Sharpe.

Cariola, her woman . . . . R. Pallant.†

Julia, Castruccio's wife, and the Cardinal's mistress . . . . . J. Thomson.

Old Lady.

Ladies, Children, Pilgrims, Executioners, Officers, and Attendants &c.

---

* The names of the actors are given from the 4tos. of 1623 and 1640 Where two names are placed opposite to the same part, the first name is that of the actor who performed the part when the play was originally produced about 1616; the second name is that of his successor to the part on the revival of the play not long before 1623.

Whoever is desirous of learning all that is known concerning these worthies will find it in Malone's *Hist. Ac. of the English Stage* and Chalmers's *Farther Ac.*, &c. (Malone's *Shakespeare* by Boswell).—The preceding sentence was written in 1830. I have now also to refer the reader to Mr. Collier's *Memoirs of the principal actors in the plays of Shakespeare*, printed for the Shakespeare Society.

† Pallant, it appears from the two earliest 4tos., played not only the Doctor and Cariola, but also one of the Officers;

> "The Doctor,
> Cariola,   } R. Pallant.
> Court Officers."

From the same authority we learn that N, Tooley performed "Forobosco"; but no portion of the dialogue of the play, as it now stands, is given to such a character, though he is mentioned in act ii. sc. 2;

> "*Ant.* Who keeps the key o' the park-gate?
> *Rod.* Forobosco.
> *Ant.* Let him bring't presently."

This passage shows that he was one of the attendants.

TO THE

RIGHT HONOURABLE GEORGE HARDING, BARON BERKELEY,* OF BERKELEY CASTLE, AND KNIGHT OF THE ORDER OF THE BATH TO THE ILLUSTRIOUS PRINCE CHARLES.

My noble lord,

That I may present my excuse why, being a stranger to your lordship, I offer this poem to your patronage, I plead this warrant :—men who never saw the sea yet desire to behold that regiment of waters, choose some eminent river to guide them thither, and make that, as it were, their conduct or postilion : by the like ingenious means has your fame arrived at my knowledge, receiving it from some of worth, who both in contemplation and practice owe to your honour their clearest service. I do not altogether look up at your title ; the ancientest nobility being but a relic of time past, and the truest honour indeed being for a man to confer honour on himself, which your learning strives to propagate, and shall make you arrive at the dignity of a great example. I am confident this work is not unworthy your honour's perusal ; for by such poems as this poets have kissed the hands of great princes, and drawn their gentle eyes to look down upon their sheets of paper when the poets themselves were bound up in their winding-sheets. The like courtesy from your lordship shall make you live in your grave, and laurel spring out of it, when the ignorant scorners of the Muses, that like worms in libraries seem to live only to destroy learning, shall wither neglected and forgotten. This work and myself I humbly present to your approved censure, it being the utmost of my wishes to have your honourable self my weighty and perspicuous comment ; which grace so done me shall ever be acknowledged

By your lordship's

in all duty and observance,

JOHN WEBSTER.

---

* *George Harding, Baron Berkeley*] This nobleman, the twelfth Lord Berkeley, was the son of Sir Thomas Berkeley, and succeeded his grand-father, Henry, the eleventh Lord Berkeley. He was made Knight of the Bath at the creation of Charles Prince of Wales, November 4th, 1616. He married Elizabeth, second daughter and co-heir of Sir Michael Stanhope of Sudbury in Suffolk, and died 10th of August, 1658. According to the inscription on his monument in Cranford church, Middlesex, he "besides the nobility of his birth, and the experience he acquired by foreign travels, was very eminent for the great candour and ingenuity of his disposition, his singular bounty and affability towards his inferiors, and his readiness (had it been in his power) to have obliged all mankind."—" My good lord," says Massinger, inscribing *The Renegado* to him, "to be honoured for old nobility or hereditary titles, is not alone proper to yourself, but to some few of your rank, who may challenge the like privilege with you : but in our age to vouchsafe (as you have often done) a ready hand to raise the dejected spirits of the contemned sons of the Muses, such as would not suffer the glorious fire of poesy to be wholly extinguished, is so remarkable and peculiar to your lordship, that, with a full vote and suffrage, it is acknowledged that the patronage and protection of the dramatic poem is yours and almost without a rival."

The present dedication is found only in the 4to. of 1623.

IN THE JUST WORTH OF THAT WELL-DESERVER, MR. JOHN WEBSTER, AND UPON THIS MASTER-PIECE OF TRAGEDY.

In this thou imitat'st one rich and wise,
That sees his good deeds done before he dies :
As he by works, thou by this work of fame
Hast well provided for thy living name.
To trust to others' honourings is worth's crime,
Thy monument is rais'd in thy life-time ;
And 'tis most just ; for every worthy man
Is his own marble, and his merit can
Cut him to any figure, and express
More art than death's cathedral palaces
Where royal ashes keep their court.   Thy note
Be ever plainness ; 'tis the richest coat :
Thy epitaph only the title be,
Write *Duchess*, that will fetch a tear for thee ;
For who e'er saw this Duchess live and die,
That could get off under a bleeding eye ?
        In Tragœdiam.
Ut lux ex tenebris ictu percussa tonantis,
Illa, ruina malis, claris fit vita poetis.

                THOMAS MIDDLETONUS,*
                   Poeta et Chron. Londinensis.

TO HIS FRIEND MR. JOHN WEBSTER, UPON HIS "DUCHESS OF MALFI."

I never saw thy Duchess till the day
That she was lively bodied in thy play :
Howe'er she answer'd her low-rated love
Her brothers' anger did so fatal prove,
Yet my opinion is, she might speak more,
But never in her life so well before.

                WIL. ROWLEY.†

TO THE READER OF THE AUTHOR, AND HIS "DUCHESS OF MALFI."

Crown him a poet, whom nor Rome nor Greece
Transcend in all their's for a masterpiece ;
In which, whiles words and matter change, and men
Act one another, he, from whose clear pen
They all took life, to memory hath lent
A lasting fame to raise his monument.

                JOHN FORD.‡

---

* *Thomas Middletonus, Poeta et Chron. Londinensis*] Of Thomas Middleton, who holds no mean rank among our old dramatists, see some account prefixed to my edition of his *Works.—"Chron. Londinensis"* means Chronologer to the city of London.
† *Wil. Rowley*] See prefatory remarks to *A Cure for a Cuckold.*
‡ *John Ford*] Two modern editions of his plays have rendered the name of this poet familiar to most readers. These commendatory verses are found only in the 4to. of 1623.

THE DUCHESS OF MALFI.

ACT I.

SCENE I.*

Enter ANTONIO *and* DELIO.

Delio. You are welcome to your country, dear
    Antonio;
You have been long in France, and you return
A very formal Frenchman in your habit:
How do you like the French court?

  Ant. I admire it:
In seeking to reduce both state and people
To a fix'd order, their judicious king
Begins at home; quits first his royal palace
Of flattering sycophants, of dissolute
And infamous persons,—which he sweetly terms
His master's master-piece, the work of heaven;
Considering duly that a prince's court
Is like a common fountain, whence should flow
Pure silver drops in general, but if't chance
Some curs'd example poison't near the head,
Death and diseases through the whole land spread.
And what is't makes this blessèd government
But a most provident council, who dare freely
Inform him the corruption of the times?
Though some o'the court hold it presumption
To instruct princes what they ought to do,
It is a noble duty to inform them
What they ought to foresee.—Here comes Bosola,
The only court-gall; yet I observe his railing
Is not for simple love of piety:
Indeed, he rails at those things which he wants;
Would be as lecherous, covetous, or proud,
Bloody, or envious, as any man,
If he had means to be so.—Here's the cardinal.

Enter Cardinal *and* BOSOLA.

  Bos. I do haunt you still.
  Card. So.
  Bos. I have done you better service than to be
slighted thus. Miserable age, where only the
reward of doing well is the doing of it!

  Card. You enforce your merit too much.

  Bos. I fell into the galleys in your service;
where, for two years together, I wore two towels
instead of a shirt, with a knot on the shoulder,
after the fashion of a Roman mantle. Slighted
thus! I will thrive some way: black-birds fatten
best in hard weather; why not I in these dog-
days?

  Card. Would you could become honest!

  Bos. With all your divinity do but direct me
the way to it. I have known many travel far for
it, and yet return as arrant knaves as they went
forth, because they carried themselves always
along with them. [*Exit* Cardinal.] Are you
gone? Some fellows, they say, are possessed
with the devil, but this great fellow were able to
possess the greatest devil, and make him worse.

  Ant. He hath denied thee some suit?

  Bos. He and his brother are like plum-trees
that grow crooked over standing-pools; they are
rich and o'er-laden with fruit, but none but crows,
pies, and caterpillars feed on them. Could I be
one of their flattering panders, I would hang on
their ears like a horseleech, till I were full, and
then drop off. I pray, leave me. Who would
rely upon these miserable dependancies, in expectation to be advanced to-morrow? what creature ever fed worse than hoping Tantalus? nor
ever died any man more fearfully than he that
hoped for a pardon. There are rewards for hawks
and dogs when they have done us service;* but
for a soldier that hazards his limbs in a battle,
nothing but a kind of geometry is his last sup-
portation.

---

* *Scene I.*] Malfi. The presence-chamber in the palace
of the Duchess.

* *dogs when they have done us service*] The 4to. of 1623,
"dogges, and   when they haue done vs seruice,"
a word having dropt out, or having been purposely
omitted.

Delio. Geometry!

Bos. Ay, to hang in a fair pair of slings, take his latter swing in the world upon an honourable pair of crutches, from hospital to hospital. Fare ye well, sir: and yet do not you scorn us; for places in the court are but like beds in the hospital, where this man's head lies at that man's foot, and so lower and lower.   [*Exit.*

Del. I knew this fellow seven years in the galleys
For a notorious murder; and 'twas thought
The cardinal suborn'd it: he was releas'd
By the French general, Gaston de Foix,
When he recover'd Naples.

Ant. 'Tis great pity
He should be thus neglected: I have heard
He's very valiant. This foul melancholy
Will poison all his goodness; for, I'll tell you,
If too immoderate sleep be truly said
To be an inward rust unto the soul,
It then doth follow want of action
Breeds all black malcontents; and their close rearing,
Like moths in cloth, do hurt for want of wearing.

Delio. The presence gins to fill: you promis'd me
To make me the partaker of the natures
Of some of your great courtiers.

Ant. The lord cardinal's,
And other strangers' that are now in court?
I·shall.—Here comes the great Calabrian duke.

Enter FERDINAND, CASTRUCCIO, SILVIO, RODERIGO,
GRISOLAN, *and Attendants.*

Ferd. Who took the ring oftenest?*
Sil. Antonio Bologna, my lord.
Ferd. Our sister duchess' great-master of her household? give him the jewel.—When shall we leave this sportive action, and fall to action indeed?
Cast. Methinks, my lord, you should not desire to go to war in person.
Ferd. Now for some gravity:—why, my lord?
Cast. It is fitting a soldier arise to be a prince, but not necessary a prince descend to be a captain.
Ferd. No
Cast. No, my lord; he were far better do† it by a deputy.

Ferd. Why should he not as well sleep or eat by a deputy? this might take idle, offensive, and base office from him, whereas the other deprives him of honour.
Cast. Believe my experience, that realm is never long in quiet where the ruler is a soldier.
Ferd. Thou toldest me thy wife could not endure fighting.
Cast. True, my lord.
Ferd. And of a jest she broke of a captain she met full of wounds: I have forgot it. ᵢ
Cast. She told him, my lord, he was a pitiful fellow, to lie, like the children of Ismael, all in tents.*
Ferd. Why, there's a wit were able to undo all the chirurgeons o'the city; for although gallants should quarrel, and had drawn their weapons, and were ready to go to it, yet her persuasions would make them put up.
Cast. That she would, my lord.—How do you like my Spanish gennet?
Rod. He is all fire.
Ferd. I am of Pliny's opinion, I think he was begot by the wind;† he runs as if he were ballassed with quick-silver.
Silvio. True, my lord, he reels from the tilt often.
Rod. Gris. Ha, ha, ha!
Ferd. Why do you laugh? methinks you that are courtiers should be my touch-wood, take fire when I give fire; that is, laugh [but] when I laugh, were the subject never so witty.
Cast. True, my lord: I myself have heard a very good jest, and have scorned to seem to have so silly a wit as to understand it.
Ferd. But I can laugh at your fool, my lord.
Cast. He cannot speak, you know, but he makes faces: my lady cannot abide him.
Ferd. No?
Cast. Nor endure to be in merry company; for she says too much laughing, and too much company, fills her too full of the wrinkle.

---

* *Who took the ring oftenest*] The allusion is to the sport called Running at the Ring, when the tilter, riding at full speed, endeavoured to thrust the point of his lance through, and to bear away, the ring, which was suspended at a particular height.
† *do*] The 4to. of 1640, "to do."

---

* *to lie, like the children of Ismael, all in tents*] Middleton has the same precious pun;
  "All his discourse out of the Book of Surgery,
  Cere-cloth and salve, and *lies* you *all in tents,*
  Like your camp-vict'lers."
More Dissemblers besides Women.—Works, iii. 585, ed. Dyce. In surgery *tent* is a roll of lint, or other material, used in searching a wound.
† *I am of Pliny's opinion, I think he was begot by the wind*] "Constat in Lusitania circa Olisiponem oppidum et Tagum amnem equas Favonio flante obversas animalom concipere spiritum, idque partum fieri, et gigni pernicissimum ita: sed triennium vitæ non excedere." *Hist. Nat.* viii. 67, tom. ii. p. 212, ed. Delph.

Ferd. I would, then, have a mathematical instrument made for her face, that she might not laugh out of compass.—I shall shortly visit you at Milan, Lord Silvio.

Silvio. Your grace shall arrive most welcome.

Ferd. You are a good horseman, Antonio : you have excellent riders in France : what do you think of good horsemanship ?

Ant. Nobly, my lord : as out of the Grecian horse issued many famous princes, so out of brave horsemanship arise the first sparks of growing resolution, that raise the mind to noble action.

Ferd. You have bespoke it worthily.

Silvio. Your brother, the lord cardinal, and sister duchess.

Re-enter Cardinal, *with* Duchess, CARIOLA, *and* JULIA.

Card. Are the galleys come about ?

Gris. They are, my lord.

Ferd. Here's the Lord Silvio is come to take his leave.

Delio. Now, sir, your promise : what's that cardinal ?
I mean his temper ? they say he's a brave fellow,
Will play his five thousand crowns at tennis, dance,
Court ladies, and one that hath fought single combats.

Ant. Some such flashes superficially hang on him for form ; but observe his inward character : he is a melancholy churchman ; the spring in his face is nothing but the engendering of toads ; where he is jealous of any man, he lays worse plots for them than ever was imposed on Hercules, for he strews in his way flatterers, panders, intelligencers, atheists, and a thousand such political monsters. He should have been Pope ; but instead of coming to it by the primitive decency of the church, he did bestow bribes so largely and so impudently as if he would have carried it away without heaven's knowledge. Some good he hath done——

Delio. You have given too much of him. What's his brother ?

Ant. The duke there ? a most perverse and turbulent nature :
What appears in him mirth is merely outside ;
If he laugh heartily, it is to laugh
All honesty out of fashion.

Delio. Twins ?

Ant. In quality.
He speaks with others' tongues, and hears men's suits

With others' ears ; will seem to sleep o'the bench
Only to entrap offenders in their answers ;
Dooms men to death by information ;
Rewards by hearsay.

Delio. Then the law to him
Is like a foul black cob-web to a spider,—
He makes it his dwelling and a prison
To entangle those shall feed him.

Ant. Most true :
He never pays debts unless they be shrewd turns,
And those he will confess that he doth owe.
Last, for his brother there, the cardinal,
They that do flatter him most say oracles
Hang at his lips ; and verily I believe them,
For the devil speaks in them.
But for their sister, the right noble duchess,
You never fix'd your eye on three fair medals
Cast in one figure, of so different temper.
For her discourse, it is so full of rapture,
You only will begin then to be sorry
When she doth end her speech, and wish, in wonder,
She held it less vain-glory to talk much,
Than your penance to hear her : whilst she speaks,
She throws upon a man so sweet a look,
That it were able to raise one to a galliard
That lay in a dead palsy, and to dote
On that sweet countenance ; but in that look
There speaketh so divine a continence
As cuts off all lascivious and vain hope.
Her days are practis'd in such noble virtue,
That sure her nights, nay, more, her very sleeps,
Are more in heaven than other ladies' shrifts.
Let all sweet ladies break their flattering glasses,
And dress themselves in her.

Delio. Fie, Antonio,
You play the wire-drawer with her commendations.

Ant. I'll case the picture up : only thus much ;
All her particular worth grows to this sum,—
She stains the time past, lights the time to come.*

Cari. You must attend my lady in the gallery,
Some half an hour hence.

Ant. I shall. [*Exeunt* ANTONIO *and* DELIO.

Ferd. Sister, I have a suit to you.

Duch. To me, sir ?

Ferd. A gentleman here, Daniel de Bosola,
One that was in the galleys——

Duch. Yes, I know him.

* *She stains the time past, lights the time to come*] So again our author in his *Monumental Column, &c* :
   " *Stain the time past, and light the time to come.*"

Ferd. A worthy fellow he is: pray, let me entreat for
The provisorship of your horse.

Duch. Your knowledge of him
Commends him and prefers him.

Ferd. Call him hither. [*Exit* Attendant.
We [are] now upon parting. Good Lord Silvio,
Do us commend to all our noble friends
At the leaguer.

Silvio. Sir, I shall.

Ferd. You are for Milan?

Silvio. I am.

Duch. Bring the caroches.—We'll bring you
down to the haven.
[*Exeunt* Duchess, Silvio, Castruccio, Roderigo, Grisolan, Cariola, Julia, *and* Attendants.

Card. Be sure you entertain that Bosola
For your intelligence: I would not be seen in't;
And therefore many times I have slighted him
When he did court our furtherance, as this morning.

Ferd. Antonio, the great-master of her household,
Had been far fitter.

Card. You are deceiv'd in him:
His nature is too honest for such business.—
He comes: I'll leave you. [*Exit.*

Re-enter Bosola.

Bos. I was lur'd to you.

Ferd. My brother, here, the cardinal could never
Abide you.

Bos. Never since he was in my debt.

Ferd. May be some oblique character in your face
Made him suspect you.

Bos. Doth he study physiognomy?
There's no more credit to be given to the face
Than to a sick man's urine, which some call
The physician's whore because she cozens him.
He did suspect me wrongfully.

Ferd. For that
You must give great men leave to take their times.
Distrust doth cause us seldom be deceiv'd:
You see the oft shaking of the cedar-tree
Fastens it more at root.

Bos. Yet, take heed;
For to suspect a friend unworthily
Instructs him the next way to suspect you,
And prompts him to deceive you.

Ferd. There's gold.

Bos. So:

What follows? never rain'd such showers as these
Without thunderbolts i'the tail of them: whose throat must I cut?

Ferd. Your inclination to shed blood rides post
Before my occasion to use you. I give you that
To live i'the court here, and observe the duchess;
To note all the particulars of her haviour,*
What suitors do solicit her for marriage,
And whom she best affects. She's a young widow;
I would not have her marry again.

Bos. No, sir?

Ferd. Do not you ask the reason; but be satisfied
I say I would not.

Bos. It seems you would create me
One of your familiars.

Ferd. Familiar! what's that?

Bos. Why, a very quaint invisible devil in flesh,—
An intelligencer.

Ferd. Such a kind of thriving thing
I would wish thee; and ere long thou mayst arrive
At a higher place by't.

Bos. Take your devils,
Which hell calls angels: these curs'd gifts would make
You a corrupter, me an impudent traitor;
And should I take these, they'd take me [to] hell.

Ferd. Sir, I'll take nothing from you that I have given:
There is a place that I procur'd for you
This morning, the provisorship o'the horse;
Have you heard on't?

Bos. No.

Ferd. 'Tis yours: is't not worth thanks?

Bos. I would have you curse yourself now, that your bounty
(Which makes men truly noble) e'er should make me
A villain. O, that to avoid ingratitude
For the good deed you have done me, I must do
All the ill man can invent! Thus the devil
Candies all sins o'er; and what heaven terms vile,
That names he complimental.†

Ferd. Be yourself;
Keep your old garb of melancholy; 'twill express

---

* *haviour*] The 4to. of 1640, "*behaviour.*"
† *complimental*] Or "*complemental,*" i.e. ornamental, belonging to accomplishments.

You envy those that stand above your reach,
Yet strive not to come near 'em: this will
     gain
Access to private lodgings, where yourself
May, like a politic dormouse——
     Bos. As I have seen some
Feed in a lord's dish, half asleep, not seeming
To listen to any talk; and yet these rogues
Have cut his throat in a dream. What's my
     place?
The provisorship o'the horse? say, then, my
     corruption
Grew out of horse-dung: I am your creature.
     Ferd. Away!
     Bos. Let good men, for good deeds, covet good
     fame,
Since place and riches oft are bribes of shame:
Sometimes the devil doth preach.
                                        [*Exit.*

     Re-enter Duchess, Cardinal, *and* CARIOLA.

     Card. We are to part from you; and your own
     discretion
Must now be your director.
     Ferd. You are a widow:
You know already what man is; and therefore
Let not youth, high promotion, eloquence——
     Card. No,
Nor any thing without the addition, honour,
Sway your high blood.
     Ferd. Marry! they are most luxurious*
Will wed twice.
     Card. O, fie!
     Ferd. Their livers are more spotted
Than Laban's sheep.
     Duch. Diamonds are of most value,
They say, that have pass'd through most jewel-
     lers' hands.
     Ferd. Whores by that rule are precious.
     Duch. Will you hear me?
I'll never marry.
     Card.† So most widows say;
But commonly that motion lasts no longer
Than the turning of an hour-glass: the funeral
     sermon
And it end both together.
     Ferd. Now hear me:
You live in a rank pasture, here, i'the court;
There is a kind of honey-dew that's deadly;
'Twill poison your fame; look to't: be not
     cunning;
For they whose faces do belie their hearts

Are witches ere they arrive at twenty years,
Ay, and give the devil suck.
     Duch. This is terrible good counsel.
     Ferd. Hypocrisy is woven of a fine small
     thread,
Subtler than Vulcan's engine:* yet, believe't,
Your darkest actions, nay, your privat'st thoughts,
Will come to light.
     Card. You may flatter yourself,
And take your own choice; privately be married
Under the eaves of night—
     Ferd. Think't the best voyage
That e'er you made; like the irregular crab,
Which, though't goes backward, thinks that it
     goes right
Because it goes its own way: but observe,
Such weddings may more properly be said
To be executed than celebrated.
     Card. The marriage night
Is the entrance into some prison.
     Ferd. And those joys,
Those lustful pleasures, are like heavy sleeps
Which do fore-run man's mischief.
     Card. Fare you well.
Wisdom begins at the end: remember it. [*Exit.*
     Duch. I think this speech between you both
     was studied,
It came so roundly off.
     Ferd. You are my sister;
This was my father's poniard, do you see?
I'd be loth to see't look rusty, 'cause 'twas his.
I would have you give † o'er these chargeable
     revels:
A visor and a mask are whispering-rooms
That were never built for goodness;— fare ye
     well;—
And women like that part which, like the
     lamprey,
Hath never a bone in't.
     Duch. Fie, sir!
     Ferd. Nay,
I mean the tongue; variety of courtship:
What cannot a neat knave with a smooth tale
Make a woman believe? Farewell, lusty widow.
                                        [*Exit.*
     Duch. Shall this move me? If all my royal
     kindred
Lay in my way unto this marriage,
I'd make them my low footsteps: and even now,
Even in this hate, as men in some great battles,
By apprehending danger, have achiev'd

---

* *luxurious*] i. e. incontinent.
† *Card.*] The 4to. of 1640 gives, by mistake, this speech
to Ferdinand.

* *Vulcan's engine*] i. e. the net in which he caught Mars
and Venus.
† *give*] The 4to. of 1623, "*to glue.*"

Almost impossible actions (I have heard soldiers
  say so),
So I through frights and threatenings will assay*
This dangerous venture. Let old wives report
I wink'd and chose a husband.—Cariola,
To thy known secrecy I have given up
More than my life,—my fame.
 Cari. Both shall be safe;
For I'll conceal this secret from the world
As warily as those that trade in poison
Keep poison from their children.
 Duch. Thy protestation
Is ingenious † and hearty : I believe it.
Is Antonio come?
 Cari. He attends you.
 Duch. Good dear soul,
Leave me ; but place thyself behind the arras,
Where thou mayst overhear us. Wish me good
  speed;
For I am going into a wilderness
Where I shall find nor ‡ path nor friendly clew
To be my guide.
    [CARIOLA *goes behind the arras.*

   Enter ANTONIO §
   I sent for you : sit down ;
Take pen and ink, and write : are you ready?
 Ant. Yes.
 Duch. What did I say?
 Ant. That I should write somewhat.
 Duch. O, I remember.
After those‖ triumphs and this large expense
It's fit, like thrifty husbands, we inquire
What's laid up for to-morrow.
 Ant. So please your beauteous excellence.
 Duch. Beauteous !
Indeed, I thank you: I look young for your sake ;
You have ta'en my cares upon you.
 Ant. I'll fetch your grace
The particulars of your revenue and expense.
 Duch. O, you are
An upright treasurer : but you mistook ;
For when I said I meant to make inquiry
What's laid up for to-morrow, I did mean
What's laid up yonder for me.
 Ant. Where?
 Duch. In heaven.
I am making my will (as 'tis fit princes should,

In perfect memory), and, I pray, sir, tell me,
Were not one better make * it smiling, thus,
Than in deep groans and terrible ghastly looks,
As if the gifts we parted with procur'd
That violent distraction? †
 Ant. O, much better.
 Duch. If I had a husband now, this care were
  quit :
But I intend to make you overseer.
What good deed shall we first remember? say.
 Ant. Begin with that first good deed began
  i'the world‡
After man's creation, the sacrament of marriage:
I'd have you first § provide for a good husband ;
Give him all.
 Duch. All !
 Ant. Yes, your excellent self.
 Duch. In a winding-sheet?
 Ant. In a couple.
 Duch. Saint Winifred, that were a strange will !
 Ant. 'Twere stranger‖ if there were no will in
  you
To marry again.
 Duch. What do you think of marriage?
 Ant. I take't, as those that deny purgatory,
It locally contains or heaven or hell ;
There's no third place in't.
 Duch. How do you affect it?
 Ant. My banishment, feeding my melancholy,
Would often reason thus.
 Duch. Pray, let's hear it.
 Ant. Say a man never marry, nor have children,
What takes that from him? only the bare
  name
Of being a father, or the weak delight
To see the little wanton ride a-cock-horse
Upon a painted stick, or hear him chatter
Like a taught starling.
 Duch. Fie, fie, what's all this?
One of your eyes is blood-shot; use my ring to't,
They say 'tis very sovereign : 'twas my wedding-
  ring,
And I did vow never to part with it
But to my second husband.
 Ant. You have parted with it now.
 Duch. Yes, to help your eye-sight.
 Ant. You have made me stark blind.
 Duch. How?

---

* *assay*] The 4to. of 1640, "*affray.*"
† *ingenious*] I.e. *ingenuous.* See note †, p. 26.
‡ *nor*] The 4to of 1640, "*no.*"
§ *Enter Antonio*] As previously (p. 61) Antonio has been
told that he must attend the duchess "in the gallery."
It would seem that here the audience were to imagine
that a change of scene had taken place.
‖ *these*] Both the earliest 4tos. "*this.*"

---

* *make*] The 4to. of 1640, "*to make.*"
† *distraction*] Both the earliest 4tos. "*distruction.*"
‡ *that first good deed began i' the world*] The 4to. of 1640,
 "*That good deed that first began i' th' world.*"
§ *first*] Omitted in the 4to. of 1640.
‖ *stranger*] The old eds. "*strange.*"

Ant. There is a saucy and ambitious devil
Is dancing in this circle.

Duch. Remove him.

Ant. How?

Duch. There needs small conjuration, when your finger
May do it: thus; is it fit?

[*She puts the ring upon his finger: he kneels.*]

Ant. What said you?

Duch. Sir,
This goodly roof of yours is too low built;
I cannot stand upright in't nor discourse,
Without I raise it higher: raise yourself;
Or, if you please, my hand to help you: so.

[*Raises him.*]

Ant. Ambition, madam, is a great man's madness,
That is not kept in chains and close-pent-rooms,
But in fair lightsome lodgings, and is girt
With the wild noise of prattling visitants,
Which makes it lunatic beyond all cure.
Conceive not I am so stupid but I aim
Whereto your favours tend: but he's a fool
That, being a-cold, would thrust his hands i'the fire
To warm them.

Duch. So, now the ground's broke,
You may discover what a wealthy mine
I make you lord of.

Ant. O my unworthiness!

Duch. You were ill to sell yourself:
This darkening of your worth is not like that
Which tradesmen use i'the city; their false lights
Are to rid bad wares off: and I must tell you,
If you will* know where breathes a complete man
(I speak it without flattery), turn your eyes,
And progress through yourself.

Ant. Were there nor heaven nor hell,
I should be honest: I have long serv'd virtue,
And ne'er ta'en wages of her.

Duch. Now she pays it.
The misery of us that are born great!
We are forc'd to woo, because none dare woo us;
And as a tyrant doubles with his words,
And fearfully equivocates, so we
Are forc'd to express our violent passions
In riddles and in dreams, and leave the path
Of simple virtue, which was never made
To seem the thing it is not. Go, go brag
You have left me heartless; mine is in your bosom:

---

will] The 4to. of 1640, "*would.*"

I hope 'twill multiply love there. You do tremble:
Make not your heart so dead a piece of flesh,
To fear more than to love me. Sir, be confident:
What is't distracts you? This is flesh and blood, sir;
'Tis not the figure cut in alabaster
Kneels at my husband's tomb. Awake, awake, man!
I do here put off all vain ceremony,
And only do appear to you a young widow
That claims you for her husband, and, like a widow,
I use but half a blush in't.

Ant. Truth speak for me;
I will remain the constant sanctuary
Of your good name.

Duch. I thank you, gentle love:
And 'cause you shall not come to me in debt,
Being now my steward, here upon your lips
I sign your *Quietus est.* This you should have begg'd now:
I have seen children oft eat sweetmeats thus,
As fearful to devour them* too soon.

Ant. But for your brothers?

Duch. Do not think of them:
All discord without this circumference
Is only to be pitied, and not fear'd:
Yet, should they know it, time will easily
Scatter the tempest.

Ant. These words should be mine,
And all the parts you have spoke, if some part of it
Would not have savour'd flattery.

Duch. Kneel.

[*Cariola comes from behind the arras.*]

Ant. Ha!

Duch. Be not amaz'd; this woman's of my counsel:
I have heard lawyers say, a contract in a chamber
Per verba presenti is absolute marriage.

[*She and Antonio kneel.*]

Bless, heaven, this sacred gordian, which let violence
Never untwine!

Ant. And may our sweet affections, like the spheres,
Be still in motion!

Duch. Quickening, and make
The like soft music!

---

* *I have seen children oft eat sweetmeats thus,*
As fearful to devour them] Occurs again verbatim in
Appius and Virginia, A. I. S. 1.

F

Ant. That we may imitate the loving palms,*
Best emblem of a peaceful marriage,
That never bore fruit, divided !

Duch. What can the church force more ?

Ant. That fortune may not know an accident,
Either of joy or sorrow, to divide
Our fixèd wishes !

Duch. How can the church build faster ?
We now are man and wife, and 'tis the church
That must but echo this.—Maid, stand apart :
I now am blind.

Ant. What's your conceit in this ?

Duch. I would have you lead your fortune by
the hand

Unto your marriage-bed :
(You speak in me this, for we now are one :)
We'll only lie, and talk together, and plot
To appease my humorous kindred ; and if you
    please,
Like the old tale in Alexander and Lodowick,*
Lay a naked sword between us, keep us chaste.
O, let me shroud my blushes in your bosom,
Since 'tis the treasury of all my secrets !
                        [*Exeunt* DUCHESS *and* ANTONIO.

Cari. Whether the spirit of greatness or of
    woman
Reign most in her, I know not ; but it shows
A fearful madness : I owe her much of pity. [*Exit.*

ACT II.

SCENE I.†

Enter BOSOLA *and* CASTRUCCIO.

Bos. You say you would fain be taken for an
eminent courtier ?

Cast. 'Tis the very main of my ambition.

Bos. Let me see : you have a reasonable good
face for't already, and your night-cap expresses
your ears sufficient largely. I would have you
learn to twirl the strings of your band with a
good grace, and in a set speech, at the end of
every sentence, to hum three or four times, or
blow your nose till it smart again, to recover
your memory. When you come to be a president
in criminal causes, if you smile upon a prisoner,
hang him ; but if you frown upon him and
threaten him, let him be sure to scape the
gallows.

Cast. I would be a very merry president.

Bos. Do not sup o'nights ; 'twill beget you an
admirable wit.

Cast. Rather it would make me have a good
stomach to quarrel ; for they say, your roaring
boys† eat meat seldom, and that makes them so
valiant. But how shall I know whether the
people take me for an eminent fellow ?

Bos. I will teach a trick to know it : give out
you lie a-dying, and if you hear the common
people curse you, be sure you are taken for one
of the prime night-caps.‡

Enter an Old Lady.

You come from painting now.

Old Lady. From what ?

Bos. Why, from your scurvy face-physic. To
behold thee not painted inclines somewhat near
a miracle : these in thy face here were deep ruts

---

* *That we may imitate the loving palms, &c.*] Compare a
pretty passage of Glapthorne ;
            "O Argalus, I thought
We should have liv'd, and taught the erring world
Affection's primitive pureness ; grown like Palmes,
That do with amorous mixture twine their boughes
Into a league-union, and so florish
Old in each others armes."
            Argalus and Parthenia, 1639, Sig. F 4.
I may also cite here some lines entitled *The Dead Eagle*,
which were written by my friend Thomas Campbell
when he was at Oran ;
" And yet Numidia's landscape has its spots
Of pastoral pleasantness—though far between ;
The village planted near the Maraboot's
Round roof has aye its feathery palm trees
Pair'd, for in solitude they bear no fruits."
† *Scene I.*] Malfi. An apartment in the palace of the
Duchess.

* *Like the old tale in Alexander and Lodowick*] The
*Two Faithful Friends, the pleasant History of Alexander
and Lodowicke, who were so like one another, that none could
know them asunder ; wherein is declared how Lodowicke
married the Princesse of Hungaria, in Alexander's name,
and how each night he layd a naked sword betweene him and
the Princesse, because he would not wrong his friend,* is
reprinted (from the Pepys Collection) in Evans's *Old
Ballads*, vol. i. p. 77. ed. 1810. There was also a play
written by Martin Slaughter, called *Alexander and Lodowick*, the acting of which is several times mentioned in
Henslowe's *Diary :* but it never was printed.
† *roaring boys*] A cant term for the insolent bloods and
vapourers of the time, whose delight was to annoy the
well-behaved inhabitants of the capital, by quarrelling
and raising violent disturbances on all possible occasions.
‡ *night-caps*] Another cant term, used again by our
author in *The Devil's Law Case*, Act II. Sc. I.
    "Among a shoal or swarm of reeking *night-caps*."

aud foul sloughs the last progress.* There was a lady in France that, having had the small-pox, flayed the skin off her face to make it more level; and whereas before she looked like a nutmeg-grater, after she resembled an abortive hedge-hog.

Old Lady. Do you call this painting?

Bos. No, no, but you call [it] careening of an old morphewed lady, to make her disembogue again: there's rough-cast phrase to your plastic.

Old Lady. It seems you are well acquainted with my closet.

Bos. One would suspect it for a shop of witchcraft, to find in it the fat of serpents, spawn of snakes, Jews' spittle, and their young children's ordure; and all these for the face. I would sooner eat a dead pigeon taken from the soles of the feet of one sick of the plague, than kiss one of you fasting. Here are two of you, whose sin of your youth is the very patrimony of the physician; makes him renew his foot-cloth † with the spring, and change his high-priced courtezan with the fall of the leaf. I do wonder you do not loathe yourselves. Observe my meditation now.

What thing is in this outward form of man
To be belov'd? We account it ominous,
If nature do produce a colt, or lamb,
A fawn, or goat, in any limb resembling
A man, and fly from 't as a prodigy:
Man stands amaz'd to see his deformity
In any other creature but himself.
But in our own flesh though we bear diseases
Which have their true names only ta'en from beasts,—
As the most ulcerous wolf and swinish measle,—
Though we are eaten up of lice and worms,
And though continually we bear about us
A rotten and dead body, we delight
To hide it in rich tissue: all our fear,
Nay, all our terror, is, lest our physician
Should put us in the ground to be made sweet.—
Your wife's gone to Rome: you two couple, and get you to the wells at Lucca to recover your aches. I have other work on foot.

[*Exeunt* CASTRUCCIO *and* Old Lady.

I observe our duchess
Is sick a-days, she pukes, her stomach seethes,
The fins of her eye-lids look most teeming blue,‡

She wanes i'the cheek, and waxes fat i'the flank,
And, contrary to our Italian fashion,
Wears a loose-bodied gown: there's somewhat in't.
I have a trick may chance discover it,
A pretty one; I have bought some apricocks,
The first our spring yields.

Enter ANTONIO *and* DELIO.

Delio. And so long since married!
You amaze me.

Ant. Let me seal your lips for ever:
For, did I think that any thing but the air
Could carry these words from you, I should wish
You had no breath at all.—Now, sir, in your contemplation?
You are studying to become a great wise fellow.

Bos. O, sir, the opinion of wisdom is a foul tetter* that runs all over a man's body: if simplicity direct us to have no evil, it directs us to a happy being; for the subtlest folly proceeds from the subtlest wisdom: let me be simply honest.

Ant. I do understand your inside.

Bos. Do you so?

Ant. Because you would not seem to appear to the world
Puff'd up with your preferment, you continue
This out-of-fashion melancholy: leave it, leave it.

Bos. Give me leave to be honest in any phrase, in any compliment whatsoever. Shall I confess myself to you? I look no higher than I can reach: they are the gods that must ride on winged horses. A lawyer's mule of a slow pace will both suit my disposition and business; for, mark me, when a man's mind rides faster than his horse can gallop, they quickly both tire.

Ant. You would look up to heaven,† but I think
The devil, that rules i'the air, stands in your light.

Bos. O, sir, you are lord of the ascendant, chief man with the duchess; a duke was your cousin-german removed. Say you were lineally descended from King Pepin, or he himself, what of this? search the heads of the greatest rivers in the world, you shall find them but bubbles of water. Some would think the souls of princes were brought forth by some more weighty cause than those of meaner persons: they are deceived,

---

* *progress*] See note †, p. 9.
† *makes him renew his foot-cloth*] i. e. enables him to buy new housings for his horse (or mule).
The fins of her eye-lids look most teeming blue] So in *The Malcontent*, Act I. Sc. I.; "till *the fin of his eyes look as blue* as the welkin."

* *tetter*] The 4to. of 1640, "*terror*."
† *You would look up to heaven*, &c.] So our author again in *The Devil's Law-case*, Act V. S. 5:
"While they aspire to do themselves most right,
    The devil, that rules i' the air, hangs in their light."

F 2

there's the same hand to them ; the like passions
away them ; the same reason that makes a vicar
to go to law for a tithe-pig, and undo his neighbours, makes them spoil a whole province, and
batter down goodly cities with the cannon.

Enter DUCHESS *and Ladies.*

Duch. Your arm, Antonio : do I not grow fat?
I am exceeding short-winded.—Bosola,
I would have you, sir, provide for me a litter ;
Such a one as the Duchess of Florence rode in.

Bos. The duchess us'd one when she was great
with child.

Duch. I think she did.—Come hither, mend
my ruff :
Here, when?* thou art such a tedious lady ; and
Thy breath smells of lemon-pills : would thou
hadst done!
Shall I swoon under thy fingers? I am
So troubled with the mother!†

Bos. [*aside.*] I fear too much.

Duch. I have heard you say that the French
courtiers
Wear their hats on 'fore the king.

Ant. I have seen it.

Duch. In the presence?

Ant. Yes.

Duch.‡ Why should not we bring up that
fashion?
'Tis ceremony more than duty that consists
In the removing of a piece of felt :
Be you the example to the rest o' the court ;
Put on your hat first.

Ant. You must pardon me :
I have seen, in colder countries than in France,
Nobles stand bare to the prince ; and the dis-
tinction
Methought show'd reverently.

Bos. I have a present for your grace.

Duch. For me, sir?

Bos. Apricocks, madam.

Duch. O, sir, where are they?
I have heard of none to-year.

Bos. [*aside.*] Good ; her colour rises.

Duch. Indeed, I thank you : they are wondrous
fair ones.
What an unskilful fellow is our gardener!
We shall have none this month.

Bos. Will not your grace pare them?

Duch. No : they taste of musk, methinks ; indeed they do.

Bos. I know not : yet I wish your grace had
par'd 'em.

Duch. Why?

Bos. I forgot to tell you, the knave gardener,
Only to raise his profit by them the sooner,
Did ripen them in horse-dung.

Duch. O, you jest.—
You shall judge : pray, taste one.

Ant. Indeed, madam,
I do not love the fruit.

Duch. Sir, you are loth
To rob us of our dainties : 'tis a delicate fruit ;
They say they are restorative.

Bos. 'Tis a pretty art,
This grafting.

Duch. 'Tis so ; bettering of nature.

Bos. To make a pippin grow upon a crab,
A damson on a black-thorn.—[*Aside.*] How greedily
she eats them!
A whirlwind strike off these bawd farthingales!
For, but for that and the loose-bodied gown,
I should have discover'd apparently
The young springal cutting a caper in her
belly.

Duch. I thank you, Bosola : they were right
good ones,
If they do not make me sick.

Ant. How now, madam!

Duch. This green fruit and my stomach are
not friends :
How they swell me!

Bos. [*aside.*] Nay, you are too much swell'd
already.

Duch. O, I am in an extreme cold sweat!

Bos. I am very sorry.

Duch. Lights to my chamber!—O good Antonio,
I fear I am undone!

Delio. Lights there, lights!
[*Exeunt* DUCHESS *and Ladies.—Exit, on the other side,*
BOSOLA.

Ant. O my most * trusty Delio, we are lost!
I fear she's fall'n in labour ; and there's left
No time for her remove.

Delio. Have you prepar'd
Those ladies to attend her? and procur'd
That politic safe conveyance for the midwife
Your duchess plotted?

Ant. I have.

Delio. Make use, then, of this forc'd occasion :
Give out that Bosola hath poison'd her

---

* *when*] An exclamation of impatience (very common in
our old dramatists).
† *the mother*] i. e. hysterical passion.
‡ *Why, &c.*] This speech is given by mistake in the
three earliest 4tos. to Antonio.

* *most*] Omitted in the 4to. of 1640.

With these apricocks; that will give some colour
For her keeping close.

Ant. Fie, fie, the physicians
Will then flock to her.

Delio. For that you may pretend
She'll use some prepar'd antidote of her own,
Lest the physicians should re-poison her.

Ant. I am lost in amazement: I know not what
to think on't.   [*Exeunt.*

SCENE II.[*]

Enter BOSOLA.

Bos. So, so, there's no question but her techiness † and most vulturous eating of the apricocks
are apparent signs of breeding.

Now?

Enter an Old Lady.

Old Lady. I am in haste, sir.

Bos. There was a young waiting-woman had a
monstrous desire to see the glass-house—

Old Lady. Nay, pray, let me go.

Bos. And it was only to know what strange
instrument it was should swell up a glass to the
fashion of a woman's belly.

Old Lady. I will hear no more of the glass-
house. You are still abusing women?

Bos. Who, I? no; only, by the way now and
then, mention your frailties. The orange-tree
bears ripe and green fruit and blossoms all
together; and some of you give entertainment
for pure love, but more for more precious reward.
The lusty spring smells well; but drooping
autumn tastes well. If we have the same golden
showers that rained in the time of Jupiter the
thunderer, you have the same Danäes still, to
hold up their laps to receive them. Didst thou
never study the mathematics?

Old Lady. What's that, sir?

Bos. Why, to know the trick how to make a
many lines meet in one centre. Go, go, give your
foster-daughters good counsel: tell them, that
the devil takes delight to hang at a woman's
girdle, like a false rusty watch, that she cannot
discern how the time passes.   [*Exit* Old Lady.

Enter ANTONIO, RODERIGO, *and* GRISOLAN.

Ant. Shut up the court-gates.

Rod. Why, sir? what's the danger?

Ant. Shut up the posterns presently, and call
All the officers o'the court.

Gris. I shall instantly.   [*Exit.*

Ant. Who keeps the key o'the park-gate?

Rod. Forobosco.

Ant. Let him bring't presently.

Re-enter GRISOLAN *with* Servants.

First Serv. O, gentlemen o'the court, the foulest
treason!

Bos. [*aside.*] If that these apricocks should be
poison'd now,
Without my knowledge!

First Serv. There was taken even now a Switzer
in the duchess' bed-chamber—

Second Serv. A Switzer!

First Serv. With a pistol in his great cod-piece.

Bos. Ha, ha, ha!

First Serv. The cod-piece was the case for't.

Second Serv. There was a cunning traitor: who
would have searched his cod-piece?

First Serv. True, if he had kept out of the
ladies' chambers: and all the moulds of his
buttons were leaden bullets.

Second Serv. O wicked cannibal! a fire-lock
in's cod-piece!

First Serv. 'Twas a French plot, upon my life.

Second Serv. To see what the devil can do!

Ant. [Are] all the officers here?

Servants. We are.

Ant. Gentlemen,
We have lost much plate you know; and but
this evening
Jewels, to the value of four thousand ducats,
Are missing in the duchess' cabinet.
Are the gates shut?

Serv. Yes.

Ant. 'Tis the duchess' pleasure
Each officer be lock'd into his chamber
Till the sun-rising; and to send the keys
Of all their chests and of their outward doors
Into her bed-chamber. She is very sick.

Rod. At her pleasure.

Ant. She entreats you take't not ill: the
innocent
Shall be the more approv'd by it.

Bos. Gentleman o'the wood-yard, where's your
Switzer now?

First Serv. By this hand, 'twas credibly reported by one o'the black guard.[*]

     [*Exeunt all except* ANTONIO *and* DELIO

Delio. How fares it with the duchess?

Ant. She's expos'd
Unto the worst of torture, pain and fear.

Delio. Speak to her all happy comfort.

---

[*] *Scene II.*] A hall in the same palace.
† *techiness*] The 4tos. "*teatchiues,*" and "*teatchiues.*"

[*] *black guard*] See note [*], p. 8.

Ant. How I do play the fool with mine own
  danger !
You are this night, dear friend, to post to Rome:
My life lies in your service.
  Delio. Do not doubt me.
  Ant. O, 'tis far from me : and yet fear presents
    me
Somewhat that looks like danger.
  Delio. Believe it,
'Tis but the shadow of your fear, no more :
How superstitiously we mind our evils !
The throwing down salt, or crossing of a hare,
Bleeding at nose, the stumbling of a horse,
Or singing of a cricket, are of power
To daunt whole man in us. Sir, fare you well :
I wish you all the joys of a bless'd father ;
And, for my faith, lay this unto your breast,—
Old friends, like old swords, still are trusted best.
                                        [*Exit.*

    Enter CARIOLA.

  Cari. Sir, you are the happy father of a son :
Your wife commends him to you.
  Ant. Blessèd comfort !—
For heaven' sake tend her well : I'll presently
Go set a figure for's nativity.   [*Exeunt.*

———•———

    SCENE III.*

  Enter BOSOLA, *with a dark lantern.*

  Bos. Sure I did hear a woman shriek : list, ha !
And the sound came, if I receiv'd it right,
From the duchess' lodgings.   There's some
    stratagem
In the confining all our courtiers
To their several wards : I must have part of it ;
My intelligence will freeze else.   List, again !
It may be 'twas the melancholy bird,
Best friend of silence and of solitariness,
The owl, that scream'd so.—Ha ! Antonio !

    Enter ANTONIO.

  Ant. I heard some noise.—Who's there ? what
    art thou ? speak.
  Bos. Antonio, put not your face nor body
To such a forc'd expression of fear :
I am Bosola, your friend.
  Ant. Bosola !—
[*Aside.*] This mole does undermine me.—Heard
    you not
A noise even now ?
  Bos. From whence ?

———
  * *Scene III.*] The court of the same palace.

  Ant. From the duchess' lodging.
  Bos. Not I : did you ?
  Ant. I did, or else I dream'd.
  Bos. Let's walk towards it,
  Ant. No : it may be 'twas
But the rising of the wind.
  Bos. Very likely.
Methinks 'tis very cold, and yet you sweat :
You look wildly.
  Ant. I have been setting a figure
For the duchess' jewels.
  Bos. Ah, and how falls your question ?
Do you find it radical ?
  Ant. What's that to you ?
'Tis rather to be question'd what design,
When all men were commanded to their lodgings,
Makes you a night-walker.
  Bos. In sooth, I'll tell you :
Now all the court's asleep, I thought the devil
Had least to do here ; I came to say my prayers ;
And if it do offend you I do so,
You are a fine courtier.
  Ant. [*aside.*] This fellow will undo me.—
You gave the duchess apricocks to day :
Pray heaven they were not poison'd !
  Bos. Poison'd ! a Spanish fig
For the imputation.
  Ant. Traitors are ever confident
Till they are discover'd. There were jewels
    . stol'n too :
In my conceit, none are to be suspected
More than yourself.
  Bos. You are a false steward.
  Ant. Saucy slave, I'll pull thee up by the
    roots.
  Bos. May be the ruin will crush you to pieces.
  Ant. You are an impudent snake indeed, sir :
Are you scarce warm,. and do you show your
    sting ?
You libel well, sir.
  Bos. No, sir : copy it out,
And I will set my hand to't.
  Ant. [*aside.*] My nose bleeds.
One that were superstitious would count
This ominous, when it merely comes by chance :
Two letters, that are wrote here for my name,
Are drown'd in blood !
Mere accident.—For you, sir, I'll take order
I'the morn you shall be safe :—[*aside.*] 'tis that
    must colour
Her lying-in :—sir, this door you pass not :
I do not hold it fit that you come near
The duchess' lodgings, till you have quit your-
    self.—

[*Aside.*] The great are like the base, nay, they
　are the same,
When they seek shameful ways to avoid shame.
　　　　　　　　　　　　　　　　　　　　[*Exit.*
　Bos. Antonio hereabout did drop a paper :—
Some of your help, false friend :—O, here it is.
What's here ? a child's nativity calculated !
　　　　　　　　　　　　　　　　　　[*Reads.*
　" *The duchess was delivered of a son, 'tween the
hours twelve and one in the night, Anno Dom.
1504,*"—that's this year—" *decimo nono Decem-
bris,*"—that's this night,—" *taken according to the
meridian of Malfi,*"—that's our duchess : happy
discovery !—" *The lord of the first house being
combust in the ascendant, signifies short life ; and
Mars being in a human sign, joined to the tail of
the Dragon, in the eighth house, doth threaten a
violent death. Cætera non scrutantur.*"
Why, now 'tis most apparent : this precise fellow
Is the duchess' bawd :—I have it to my wish !
This is a parcel of intelligency
Our courtiers were cas'd up for : it needs must
　follow
That I must be committed on pretence
Of poisoning her ; which I'll endure, and laugh at.
If one could find the father now ! but that
Time will discover. Old Castruccio
I'the morning posts to Rome : by him I'll send
A letter that shall make her brothers' galls
O'erflow their livers. This was a thrifty way.
Though lust do mask in ne'er so strange disguise,
She's oft found witty, but is never wise. [*Exit.*

　　　　　　　————

　　　　　　SCENE IV.*
　　Enter Cardinal *and* Julia.
　Card. Sit : thou art my best of wishes. Prithee,
　　tell me
What trick didst thou invent to come to Rome
Without thy husband ?
　Julia. Why, my lord, I told him
I came to visit an old anchorite
Here for devotion.
　Card. Thou art a witty false one,—
I mean, to him.
　Julia. You have prevail'd with me
Beyond my strongest thoughts : I would not now
Find you inconstant.
　Card. Do not put thyself
To such a voluntary torture, which proceeds
Out of your own guilt,

　Julia. How, my lord !
　Card. You fear
My constancy, because you have approv'd
Those giddy and wild turnings * in yourself.
　Julia. Did you e'er find them ?
　Card. Sooth, generally for women,
A man might strive to make glass malleable,
Ere he should make them fixèd.
　Julia. So, my lord.
　Card. We had need go borrow that fantastic
　　glass
Invented by Galileo the Florentine
To view another spacious world i'the moon,　.
And look to find a constant woman there.
　Julia. This is very well, my lord.
　Card. Why do you weep ?
Are tears your justification ? the self-same tears
Will fall into your husband's bosom, lady,
With a loud protestation that you love him
Above the world. Come, I'll love you wisely,
That's jealously ; since I am very certain
You cannot make me † cuckold.
　Julia. I'll go home
To my husband.
　Card. You may thank me, lady,
I have taken you off your melancholy perch,
Bore you upon my fist, and show'd you game,
And let you fly at it.—I pray thee, kiss me.—
When thou wast with thy husband, thou wast
　watch'd
Like a tame elephant :—still you are to thank
　me :—
Thou hadst only kisses from him and high feeding ;
But what delight was that ? 'twas just like one
That hath a little fingering on the lute,
Yet cannot tune it :—still you are to thank me.
　Julia. You told me of a piteous wound i'the
　　heart
And a sick liver, when you woo'd me first,
And spake like one in physic.
　Card. Who's that ?—

　　　　　Enter Servant.
Rest firm, for my affection to thee,
Lightning moves slow to't.
　Serv. Madam, a gentleman,
That's come post from Malfi, desires to see you.
　Card. Let him enter : I'll withdraw. [*Exit.*
　Serv. He says
Your husband, old Castruccio, is come to Rome,
Most pitifully tir'd with riding post. [*Exit.*

---

* *turnings*] Both the earliest 4tos. "*turning.*"
† *make me*] The 4to. of 1623, "*me make.*"

Enter DELIO.

Julia [*aside*]. Signior Delio ! 'tis one of my old
suitors.

Delio. I was bold to come and see you.*

Julia. Sir, you are welcome.

Delio. Do you lie here ?

Julia. Sure, your own experience
Will satisfy you no :† our Roman prelates
Do not keep lodging for ladies.

Delio. Very well:
I have brought you no commendations from your
husband,
For I know none by him.‡

Julia. I hear he's come to Rome.

Delio. I never knew man and beast, of a horse
and a knight,
So weary of each other: if he had had a good back,
He would have undertook to have borne his horse,
His breech was so pitifully sore.

Julia. Your laughter
Is my pity.

Delio. Lady, I know not whether
You want money, but I have brought you some.

Julia. From my husband ?

Delio. No, from mine own allowance.

Julia. I must hear the condition, ere I be bound
to take it.

Delio. Look on't, 'tis gold : hath it not a fine
colour ?

Julia. I have a bird more beautiful.

Delio. Try the sound on't.

Julia. A lute string far exceeds it:
It hath no smell, like cassia or civet;
Nor is it physical, though some fond doctors
Persuade us seethe't § in cullises.‖   I'll tell you,
This is a creature bred by——

Re-enter Servant.

Serv. Your husband's come,
Hath deliver'd a letter to the Duke of Calabria
That, to my thinking, hath put him out of his wits.
[*Exit.*

Julia. Sir, you hear:
Pray, let me know your business and your suit
As briefly as can be.

---

* *to come and see you*] The 4to. of 1640, " and come to
see you."

† *no*] The 4to. of 1640, "*now.*"

‡ Here and subsequently in this scene, I have let the
lines stand as they are divided in the old copies, though
some of these speeches hardly read like verse. See
note †, p. 79.

§ *seethe't*] Both the earliest 4tos. "*seeth's.*"

‖ *cullises*] A cullis was a strong and savoury broth of
boiled meat strained, for debilitated persons: the old
receipt-books recommend "pieces of gold" among its
ingredients.

Delio. With good speed : I would wish you,
At such time as you are non-resident
With your husband, my mistress.

Julia. Sir, I'll go ask my husband if I shall,
And straight return your answer.   [*Exit.*

Delio. Very fine !
Is this her wit, or honesty, that speaks thus ?
I heard one say the duke was highly mov'd
With a letter sent from Malfi.   I do fear
Antonio is betray'd : how fearfully
Shows his ambition now ! unfortunate fortune !
They pass through whirl-pools, and deep woes do
shun,
Who the event weigh ere the action's done. [*Exit.*

SCENE V.*

Enter Cardinal, *and* FERDINAND *with a letter.*

Ferd. I have this night digg'd up a mandrake.

Card. Say you ?

Ferd. And I am grown mad with't.†

Card. What's the prodigy ?

Ferd. Read there,—a sister damn'd : she's loose
i'the hilts ;
Grown a notorious strumpet.

Card. Speak lower.

Ferd. Lower !
Rogues do not whisper't now, but seek to publish't
(As servants do the bounty of their lords)
Aloud ; and with a covetous searching eye,
To mark who note them. O, confusion seize her !
She hath had most cunning bawds to serve her
turn,
And more secure conveyances for lust
Than towns of garrison for service.

Card. Is't possible ?
Can this be certain ?

Ferd. Rhubarb, O, for rhubarb
To purge this choler ! here's the cursed day ‡
To prompt my memory ; and here't shall stick
Till of her bleeding heart I make a sponge
To wipe it out.

Card. Why do you make yourself
So wild a tempest ?

Ferd. Would I could be one,
That I might toss her palace 'bout her ears,

---

* *Scene V.*] Another apartment in the same palace.

† *I have this night digg'd up a mandrake.*] Compare Shakespeare ;
" And shrieks, like mandrakes torn out of the earth,
That living mortals hearing them run mad."
                        Romeo and Juliet, A. IV. S. 3.

‡ *the cursed day*] i. e. on which the Duchess had been
delivered of a son,—set down in the letter sent from
Bosola.

Root up her goodly forests, blast her meads,
And lay her general territory as waste
As she hath done her honours.

   Card. Shall our blood,
The royal blood of Arragon and Castile,
Be thus attainted ?

   Ferd. Apply desperate physic:
We must not now use balsamum, but fire,
The smarting cupping-glass, for that's the mean
To purge infected blood, such blood as hers.
There is a kind of pity in mine eye,—
I'll give it to my handkercher; and now 'tis here,
I'll bequeath this to her bastard.

   Card. What to do ?

   Ferd. Why, to make soft lint for his mother's
     wounds,
When I have hew'd her to pieces.

   Card. Cursèd creature !
Unequal nature, to place woman's hearts
So far upon the left side !

   Ferd. Foolish men,
That e'er will trust their honour in a bark
Made of so slight weak bulrush as is * woman,
Apt every minute to sink it !

   Card. Thus
Ignorance, when it hath purchas'd honour,
It cannot wield it.

   Ferd. Methinks I see her laughing,—
Excellent hyena ! Talk to me somewhat quickly,
Or my imagination will carry me
To see her in the shameful act of sin.

   Card. With whom ?

   Ferd. Happily with some strong-thigh'd barge-
     man,
Or one o'the wood-yard that can quoit the sledge
Or toss the bar, or else some lovely squire
That carries coals up to her privy † lodgings.

   Card. You fly beyond your reason.

   Ferd. Go to, mistress !
'Tis not your whore's milk that shall ‡ quench my
     wild-fire,
But your whore's blood.

   Card. How idly shows this rage, which carries
     you,

As men convey'd by witches through the air,
On violent whirlwinds ! this intemperate noise
Fitly resembles deaf men's shrill discourse,
Who talk aloud, thinking all other men
To have their imperfection.

   Ferd. Have not you
My palsy ?

   Card. Yes, [but] I can be angry
Without this rupture : * there is not in nature
A thing that makes man so deform'd, so beastly,
As doth intemperate anger. Chide yourself.
You have divers men who never yet express'd
Their strong desire of rest but by unrest,
By vexing of themselves. Come, put yourself
In tune.

   Ferd. So I will only study to seem
The thing I am not. I could kill her now,
In you, or in myself; for I do think
It is some sin in us heaven doth revenge
By her.

   Card. Are you stark mad ?

   Ferd. I would have their bodies
Burnt in a coal-pit with the ventage stopp'd,
That their curs'd smoke might not ascend to
     heaven ;
Or dip the sheets they lie in in pitch or
     sulphur,
Wrap them in't, and then light them like a match ;
Or else to-boil their bastard to a cullis,†
And give't his lecherous father to renew
The sin of his back.

   Card. I'll leave you.

   Ferd. Nay, I have done.
I am confident, had I been damn'd in hell,
And should have heard of this, it would have put
     me
Into a cold sweat. In, in; I'll go sleep.
Till I know who leaps my sister, I'll not stir :
That known, I'll find scorpions to string ‡ my
     whips,
And fix her in a general eclipse.   [*Exeunt.*

---

  * *is*] The 4to. of 1640, "*this.*"
  † *privy*] The 4to. of 1640, "*private.*"
  ‡ *shall*] The 4to. of 1640, "*can.*"

  * *rupture*] If right, means—breaking forth into passion : but qy. "rapture,"—transport, violent emotion ?
  † *cullis*] See note ||, p. 72.
  ‡ *string*] The 4to. of 1640, "*sting.*"
    "Last with *a whip of scorpions* I pursue
      Thy lingering." Milton's *Par. Lost*, ii. 701.

ACT III.

SCENE I.*

Enter ANTONIO *and* DELIO.

Ant. Our noble friend, my most belovèd Delio!
O, you have been a stranger long at court:
Came you along with the Lord Ferdinand?

Delio. I did, sir: and how fares your noble
duchess?

Ant. Right fortunately well: she's an excellent
Feeder of pedigrees; since you last saw her,
She hath had two children more, a son and
daughter.

Delio. Methinks 'twas yesterday: let me but
wink,
And not behold your face, which to mine eye
Is somewhat leaner, verily I should dream
It were within this half hour.

Ant. You have not been in law, friend Delio,
Nor in prison, nor a suitor at the court,
Nor begg'd the reversion of some great man's
place,
Nor troubled with an old wife, which doth make
Your time so insensibly hasten.

Delio. Pray, sir, tell me,
Hath not this news arriv'd yet to the ear
Of the lord cardinal?

Ant. I fear it hath:
The Lord Ferdinand, that's newly come to court,
Doth bear himself right dangerously.

Delio. Pray, why?

Ant. He is so quiet that he seems to sleep
The tempest out, as dormice do in winter:
Those houses that are haunted are most still
Till the devil be up.

Delio. What say the common people?

Ant. The common rabble do directly say
She is a strumpet.

Delio. And your graver heads
Which would be politic, what censure they?

Ant. They do observe I grow to infinite
purchase,†
The left hand way; and all suppose the duchess

Would amend it, if she could; for, say they,
Great princes, though they grudge their officers
Should have such large and unconfinèd means
To get wealth under them, will not complain,
Lest thereby they should make them odious
Unto the people: for other obligation
Of love or marriage between her and me
They never dream of.

Delio. The Lord Ferdinand
Is going to bed.

Enter DUCHESS, FERDINAND, *and* Attendants.

Ferd. I'll instantly to bed,
For I am weary.—I am to bespeak
A husband for you.

Duch. For me, sir! pray, who is't?

Ferd. The great Count Malatesti.

Duch. Fie upon him!
A count! he's a mere stick of sugar-candy; *
You may look quite thorough him. When I choose
A husband, I will marry for your honour.

Ferd. You shall do well in't.—How is't, worthy
Antonio?

Duch. But, sir, I am to have private conference
with you
About a scandalous report is spread
Touching mine honour.

Ferd. Let me be ever deaf to't:
One of Pasquil's paper-bullets, court-calumny,
A pestilent air, which princes' palaces
Are seldom purg'd of. Yet say that it were true,
I pour it in your bosom, my fix'd love
Would strongly excuse, extenuate, nay, deny
Faults, were they apparent in you. Go, be safe
In your own innocency.

Duch. [*aside*]. O bless'd comfort!
This deadly air is purg'd.

[*Exeunt* DUCHESS, ANTONIO, DELIO, *and* Attendants.

Ferd. Her guilt treads on
Hot-burning coulters.

Enter BOSOLA.
Now, Bosola,
How thrives our intelligence?

Bos. Sir, uncertainly:
'Tis rumour'd she hath had three bastards, but
By whom we may go read i' the stars.

---

* *Scene 1.*] Malfi. An apartment in the palace of the
Duchess.

† *purchase*] This word is generally used by old dramatists as a cant term for stolen goods, but here it means
riches, valuable property: our author in *The Devil's
Law Case* has;
"Tailors in France, they *grow to great abominable purchase*, and become great officers." Act II. Sc. 1.

* *he's a mere stick of sugar-candy*, &c.] Repeated almost
verbatim in *The Devil's Law Case*, Act II. Sc. 1.

Ferd. Why, some
Hold opinion all things are written there.

    Bos. Yes, if we could find spectacles to read
them.
I do suspect there hath been some sorcery
Us'd on the duchess.

    Ferd. Sorcery! to what purpose?

    Bos. To make her dote on some desertless fellow
She shames to acknowledge.

    Ferd. Can your faith give way
To think there's power in potions or in charms,
To make us love whether we will or no?

    Bos. Most certainly.

    Ferd. Away! these are mere gulleries, horrid
things,
Invented by some cheating mountebanks
To abuse us. Do you think that herbs or
charms
Can force the will? Some trials have been made
In this foolish practice, but the ingredients
Were lenitive poisons, such as are of force
To make the patient mad; and straight the
witch
Swears by equivocation they are in love.
The witch-craft lies in her rank blood. This
night
I will force confession from her. You told me
You had got, within these two days, a false key
Into her bed-chamber.

    Bos. I have.

    Ferd. As I would wish.

    Bos. What do you intend to do?

    Ferd. Can you guess?

    Bos. No.

    Ferd. Do not ask, then:
He that can compass me, and know my drifts,
May say he hath put a girdle 'bout the world,*
And sounded all her quick-sands.

    Bos. I do not
Think so.

    Ferd. What do you think, then, pray?

    Bos. That you are
Your own chronicle too much, and grossly
Flatter yourself.

    Ferd. Give me thy hand; I thank thee:
I never gave pension but to flatterers,
Till I entertainéd thee. Farewell.
That friend a great man's ruin strongly checks,
Who rails into his belief all his defects. [*Exeunt.*

---

* *May say he hath put a girdle 'bout the world*] So
Shakespeare ;
    " I'll *put a girdle* round *about the earth.*"
Midsummer-night's Dream, Act II. Sc. 2.; on which pas-
sage see Steevens's note.

SCENE II.*

Ente DUCHESS, ANTONIO, *and* CARIOLA.

    Duch. Bring me the casket hither, and the
glass.—
You get no lodging here to-night, my lord.

    Ant. Indeed, I must persuade one.

    Duch. Very good:
I hope in time 'twill grow into a custom,
That noblemen shall come with cap and knee
To purchase a night's lodging of their wives.

    Ant. I must lie here.

    Duch. Must! you are a lord of mis-rule.

    Ant. Indeed, my rule is only in the night.

    Duch. To what use will you put me?

    Ant. We'll sleep together.

    Duch. Alas,
What pleasure can two lovers find in sleep!

    Cari. My lord, I lie with her often; and I know
She'll much disquiet you.

    Ant. See, you are complain'd of.

    Cari. For she's the sprawling'st bedfellow.

    Ant. I shall like her the better for that.

    Cari. Sir, shall I ask you a question?

    Ant. Ay, pray thee, Cariola.

    Cari. Wherefore still, when you lie with my
lady,
Do you rise so early?

    Ant. Labouring men
Count the clock oftenest, Cariola,
Are glad when their task's ended.

    Duch. I'll stop your mouth. [*Kisses him.*

    Ant. Nay, that's but one; Venus had two soft
doves
To draw her chariot; I must have another.—
                  [*She kisses him again.*
When wilt thou marry, Cariola?

    Cari. Never, my lord.

    Ant. O, fie upon this single life! forgo it.
We read how Daphne, for her peevish † flight,
Became a fruitless bay-tree; Syrinx turn'd
To the pale empty reed; Anaxarete
Was frozen into marble: whereas those
Which married, or prov'd kind unto their friends,
Were by a gracious influence transhap'd
Into the olive, pomegranate, mulberry,
Became flowers, precious stones, or eminent stars.

    Cari. This is a vain poetry: but I pray you,
tell me,
If there were propos'd me, wisdom, riches, and
beauty,
In three several young men, which should I choose.

---

* *Scene II.*] The bed-chamber of the Duchess in the
same.
† *peevish*] i. e. foolish.

Ant. 'Tis a hard question: this was Paris' case,
And he was blind in't, and there was great cause;
For how was't possible he could * judge right,
Having three amorous goddesses in view,
And they stark naked? 'twas a motion
Were able to benight the apprehension
Of the severest counsellor of Europe.
Now I look on both your faces so well form'd,
It puts me in mind of a question I would ask.

Cari. What is't?

Ant. I do wonder why hard-favour'd ladies,
For the most part, keep worse-favour'd waiting-
    women
To attend them, and cannot endure fair ones.

Duch. O, that's soon answer'd.
Did you ever in your life know an ill painter
Desire to have his dwelling next door to the shop
Of an excellent picture-maker? 'twould disgrace
His face-making, and undo him. I prithee,
When were we so † merry?—My hair tangles.

Ant. Pray thee, Cariola, let's steal forth the
    room,
And let her talk to herself: I have divers times
Serv'd her the like, when she hath ‡ chaf'd
    extremely.
I love to see her angry. Softly, Cariola.
    [*Exeunt* ANTONIO *and* CARIOLA.

Duch. Doth not the colour of my hair gin to
    change?
When I wax gray, I shall have all the court
Powder their hair with arras,§ to be like me.
You have cause to love me; I enter'd you‖ into
    my heart
Before you would vouchsafe to call for the keys.

    Enter FERDINAND *behind.*

We shall one day have my brothers take you
    napping:
Methinks his presence, being now in court,
Should make you keep your own bed; but you'll
    say
Love mix'd with fear is sweetest. I'll assure you,
You shall get no more children till my brothers
Consent to be your gossips. Have you lost your
    tongue?
'Tis welcome:
For know, whether I am doom'd to live or die,
I can do both like a prince.

Ferd. Die, then, quickly!
    [*Giving her a poniard.*

Virtue, where art thou hid? what hideous thing
Is it that doth eclipse * thee?

Duch. Pray, sir, hear me.

Ferd. Or is it true thou art but a bare name,
And no essential thing?

Duch. Sir,—

Ferd. Do not speak.

Duch. No, sir:
I will plant my soul in mine ears, to hear you.

Ferd. O most imperfect light of human reason,
That mak'st us † so unhappy to foresee
What we can least prevent! Pursue thy wishes,
And glory in them: there's in shame no comfort
But to be past all bounds and sense of shame.

Duch. I pray, sir, hear me: I am married.

Ferd. So!

Duch. Happily, not to your liking: but for that,
Alas, your shears do come untimely now
To clip the bird's wings that's already flown!
Will you see my husband?

Ferd. Yes, if I could change
Eyes with a basilisk.

Duch. Sure, you came hither
By his confederacy.

Ferd. The howling of a wolf
Is music to thee, screech-owl: prithee, peace.—
Whate'er thou art that hast enjoy'd my sister,
For I am sure thou hear'st me, for thine own
    sake ‡
Let me not know thee. I came hither prepar'd
To work thy discovery; yet am now persuaded
It would beget such § violent effects
As would damn us both. I would not for ten
    millions
I had beheld thee: therefore use all means
I never may have knowledge of thy name;
Enjoy thy lust still, and a wretched life,
On that condition.—And for thee, vile woman,
If thou do wish thy lecher may grow old
In thy embracements, I would have thee build
Such a room for him as our anchorites
To holier use inhabit. Let not the sun
Shine on him till he's dead; let dogs and monkeys
Only converse with him, and such dumb things
To whom nature denies use to sound his name;
Do not keep a paraquito, lest she learn it;
If thou do love him, cut out thine own tongue,
Lest it bewray him.

---

* *could*] The 4to. of 1640, "*should.*"
† *so*) Omitted in the 4to. of 1640.
‡ *hath*) The 4to. of 1640, "*had.*"
§ *arras*) See note †. p. 41.
‖ *you*) Omitted in the 4to. of 1640.

* *eclipse*] The 4to. of 1640, "*clip.*"
† *us*) Not found in the three earliest 4tos.
‡ *For I am sure thou hear'st me, for thine own sake*] The
4to. of 1640:
    "For I am sure thou *heard'st* me, for *mine* own sake."
§ *such*) The 4to. of 1640, "*so.*"

Duch. Why might not I marry?
I have not gone about in this to create
Any new world or custom.
    Ferd. Thou art undone;
And thou hast ta'en that massy sheet of lead
That hid thy husband's bones, and folded it
About my heart.
    Duch. Mine bleeds for't.
    Ferd. Thine! thy heart!
What should I name't unless a hollow bullet
Fill'd with unquenchable wild-fire?
    Duch. You are in this
Too strict; and were you not my princely brother,
I would say, too wilful: my reputation
Is safe.
    Ferd. Dost thou know what reputation is?
I'll tell thee,—to small purpose, since the instruc-
    tion
Comes now too late.
Upon a time Reputation, Love, and Death
Would travel o'er the world; and it was concluded
That they should part, and take three several ways.
Death told them, they should find him in great
    battles,
Or cities plagu'd with plagues: Love gives them
    counsel
To inquire for him 'mongst unambitious shep-
    herds,
Where dowries were not talk'd of, and sometimes
'Mongst quiet kindred that had nothing left
By their dead parents: "Stay," quoth Reputation,
"Do not forsake me; for it is my nature,
If once I part from any man I meet,
I am never found again." And so for you:
You have shook * hands with Reputation,
And made him invisible. So, fare you well:
I will never see you more.
    Duch. Why should only I,
Of all the other princes of the world,
Be cas'd up, like a holy relic? I have 'youth
And a little beauty.
    Ferd. So you have some virgins
That are witches. I will never see thee more.
                          [*Exit.*

   Re-enter ANTONIO *with a pistol, and* CARIOLA.

    Duch. You saw this apparition?
    Ant. Yes: we are
Betray'd. How came he hither? I should turn
This to thee, for that.
    Cari. Pray, sir, do; and when
That you have cleft my heart, you shall read there
Mine innocence.

* *shook*] Some copies of the 4to. of 1623, "*shooked.*"

    Duch. That gallery gave him entrance.
    Ant. I would this terrible thing would come
    again,
That, standing on my guard, I might relate
My warrantable love.—
                   [*She shows the poniard.*
             Ha! what means this?
    Duch. He left this with me.
    Ant. And it seems did wish
You would use it on yourself.
    Duch. His action
Seem'd to intend so much.
    Ant. This hath a handle to't,
As well as a point: turn it towards him,
And so fasten the keen edge in his rank gall.
                 [*Knocking within.*
How now! who knocks? more earthquakes?
    Duch. I stand
As if a mine beneath my feet were ready
To be blown up.
    Cari. 'Tis Bosola.
    Duch. Away!
O misery! methinks unjust actions
Should wear these masks and curtains, and not we.
You must instantly part hence: I have fashion'd
    it already.   [*Exit* ANTONIO.

              Enter BOSOLA.

    Bos. The duke your brother is ta'en up in a
    whirlwind;
Hath took horse, and 's rid post to Rome.
    Duch. So late?
    Bos. He told me, as he mounted into the saddle,
You were undone.
    Duch. Indeed, I am very near it.
    Bos. What's the matter?
    Duch. Antonio, the master of our household,
Hath dealt so falsely with me in 's accounts:
My brother stood engag'd with me for money
Ta'en up of certain Neapolitan Jews,
And Antonio lets the bonds be forfeit.
    Bos. Strange!—[*Aside.*] This is cunning.
    Duch. And hereupon
My brother's bills at Naples are protested
Against.—Call up our * officers.
    Bos. I shall.   [*Exit.*

          Re-enter ANTONIO.

    Duch. The place that you must fly to is
Ancona:
Hire a house there; I'll send after you
My treasure and my jewels. Our weak safety

* *our*] The 4to. of 1640, "*the.*"

Runs upon enginous wheels:* short syllables
Must stand for periods. I must now accuse you
Of such a feignéd crime as Tasso calls
Magnanima menzogna,† a noble lie,
'Cause it must shield our honours.—Hark! they
    are coming.

Re-enter BOSOLA *and Officers*

Ant. Will your grace hear me?
Duch. I have got well by you; you have
    yielded me
A million of loss: I am like to inherit
The people's curses for your stewardship.
You had the trick in audit-time to be sick,
Till I had sign'd your quietus; and that cur'd
    you
Without help of a doctor.—Gentlemen,
I would have this man be an example to you all;
So shall you hold my favour; I pray, let him;
For h'as done that, alas, you would not think of,
And, because I intend to be rid of him,
I mean not to publish.—Use your fortune else-
    where.
Ant. I am strongly arm'd to brook my
    overthrow,
As commonly men bear with a hard year:
I will not blame the cause on't; but do think
The necessity of my malevolent star
Procures this, not her humour. O, the inconstant
And rotten ground of service! you may see,
'Tis even like him, that in a winter night,
Takes a long slumber o'er a dying fire,
A-loth‡ to part from't; yet parts thence as cold
As when he first sat down.
Duch. We do confiscate,
Towards the satisfying of your accounts,
All that you have.
Ant. I am all yours; and 'tis very fit
All mine should be so.
Duch. So, sir, you have your pass.
Ant. You may see, gentlemen, what 'tis to
    serve
A prince with body and soul.   [*Exit.*

---

* *enginous wheels*' The 4to. of 1640 substitutes "*in-genious.*" So Dekker;
   " For that one Acte giues like an *enginous wheele*
   Motion to all." *The Whore of Babylon*, 1607, Sig. C 2.
† —— *as Tasso calls*
   Magnanima menzogna] In *Gerus. Lib.* C. II. St. 22;
    " Così al pubblico fato il capo altero
    Offerse, o'l volse in sù sola raccorre,
    Magnanima menzogna, or quando è il vero
    Sì bello, che si possa a te preporre?"
Most readers must be aware that the great Italian imitates the "*splendide mendax*" of Horace.
‡ *A loth*] Some copies of the 4to. of 1623, and the 4to. of 1640, "*As loath.*"

Bos. Here's an example for extortion: what
moisture is drawn out of the sea, when foul
weather comes, pours down, and runs into the sea
again.
Duch. I would know what are your opinions
Of this Antonio.
Sec. Off. He could not abide to see a pig's head
gaping:* I thought your grace would find him a
Jew.
Third Off. I would you had been his† officer,
for your own sake.
Fourth Off. You would have had more money.
First Off. He stopped his ears with black wool,
and to those came to him for money said he was
thick of hearing.
Sec. Off. Some said he was an hermaphrodite,
for he could not abide a woman.
Fourth Off. How scurvy proud he would‡ look
when the treasury was full! Well, let him go.
First Off. Yes, and the chippings of the but-
tery fly after him, to scour his gold§ chain.
Duch. Leave us.   [*Exeunt* Officers.
What do you think of these?
Bos. That these are rogues that in's prosperity,
But to have waited on his‖ fortune, could have
    wish'd
His dirty stirrup rivetted through their noses,
And follow'd after's mule, like a bear in a ring;
Would have prostituted their daughters to his
    lust;
Made their first-born intelligencers;¶ thought
    none happy
But such as were born under his blest** planet,
And wore his livery: and do these lice drop off
    now?
Well, never look to have the like again:
He hath left a sort †† of flattering rogues behind
    him;
Their doom must follow. Princes pay flatterers

---

* *He could not abide to see a pig's head gaping*] So Shakespeare;
   " As there is no firm reason to be render'd
   Why he cannot *abide a gaping pig.*"
     Merchant of Venice, Act. IV. Sc. I.
Steevens, in a note on Shylock's speech cites the parallel passage from Webster, and in order to make it run like blank verse inserts a monosyllable. Shakespeare's commentators are too often incorrect their quotations from old poets.
† *his*] Omitted in the 4to. of 1640.
‡ *he would*] The 4to. of 1640, "*would he.*"
§ *gold*] The 4to. of 1640, "*golden.*" Our old dramatists frequently allude to *the gold chain* which was formerly worn (at least in this country) by stewards.
‖ *his*, The 4to. of 1640, "*this.*"
¶ *intelligencers*] Some of the copies of the 4to. of 1623, "*and* intelligencers."
** *bles*'] Omitted in the 4to. of 1640. †† *sort*] i.e. set.

In their own money: flatterers dissemble their
  vices,
And they dissemble their lies; that's justice.
Alas, poor gentleman !
  Duch. Poor ! he hath amply fill'd his coffers.
  Bos. Sure, he was too honest.   Pluto,* the
  god of riches,
When he's sent by Jupiter to any man,
He goes limping, to signify that wealth
That comes on God's name comes slowly ; but
  when he's sent
On the devil's errand, he rides post and comes in
  by scuttles.
Let me show you what a most unvalu'd jewel
You have in a wanton humour thrown away,
To bless the man shall find him.   He was an
  excellent
Courtier and most faithful; a soldier that
  thought it
As boastly to know his own value too little
As devilish to acknowledge it too much.
Both his virtue and form deserv'd a far better
  fortune:
His discourse rather delighted to judge itself
  than show itself:
His breast was fill'd with all perfection,
And yet it seem'd a private whispering-room,
It made so little noise of't.
  Duch. But he was basely descended.
  Bos. Will you make yourself a mercenary
  herald,
Rather to examine men's pedigrees than virtues?
You shall want him:
For know an honest statesman to a prince
Is like a cedar planted by a spring ;
The spring bathes the tree's root, the grateful
  tree

---

* *Pluto, the god of riches, &c.*] If Webster had elsewhere
used the name "Plutus," I should, for consistency's
sake, have substituted it here for "*Pluto.*" But the latter
name is not to be considered as wrong: even the Greeks
themselves confounded Πλούτων, the god of the lower
world, with Πλοῦτος, the god of riches (see Liddell and
Scott's *Greek Lex.* in v. Πλουτών). So, too, Marlowe, in his
Hero and Leander, towards the close of the Second
Sestiad ;
  "Whence his admiring eyes more pleasure took
    Than *Dis* on heaps of gold fixing his look."—
With the present passage of our author compare Bacon's
Essays: "The poets feign, that when Plutus (which is
riches,) is sent from Jupiter, he limps, and goes slowly;
but when he is sent from Pluto, he runs and is swift of
foot; meaning that riches gotten by good means and just
labour pace slowly . . . . . . it might be applied
likewise to Pluto taking him for the devil. For when
riches come from the devil, (as by fraud and oppression,
and unjust means), they come upon speed." *Of Riches.*

Rewards it with his shadow: you have not
  done so.
I would sooner swim to the Bermoothes * on
Two politicians' rotten bladders, tied
Together with an intelligencer's heart-string,
Than depend on so changeable a prince's favour.
Fare thee well, Antonio ! since the malice of the
  world
Would needs down with thee, it cannot be said
  yet
That any ill happen'd unto thee, considering thy
  fall
Was accompanied with virtue.†
  Duch. O, you render me excellent music !
  Bos. Say you?
  Duch. This good one that you speak of is my
  husband.
  Bos. Do I not dream ? can this ambitious age
Have so much goodness in't as to prefer
A man merely for worth, without these shadows‡
Of wealth and painted honours? possible?
  Duch. I have had three children by him.
  Bos. Fortunate lady !
For you have made your private nuptial bed
The humble and fair seminary of peace.
No question but many an unbenefic'd scholar
Shall pray for you for this deed, and rejoice
That some preferment in the world can yet
Arise from merit.   The virgins of your land
That have no dowries shall hope your example
Will raise them to rich husbands. Should you want
Soldiers, 'twould make the very Turks and
  Moors
Turn Christians, and serve you for this act.
Last, the neglected poets of your time,
In honour of this trophy of a man,
Rais'd by that curious engine, your white hand,
Shall thank you, in your grave, for't; and make
  that
More reverend than all the cabinets
Of living princes.   For Antonio,
His fame shall likewise flow from many a pen,
When heralds shall want coats to sell to men.
  Duch. As I taste comfort in this friendly
  speech,
So would I find concealment.

---

* *Bermoothes*] i. e. the Bermudas.
† This and the two preceding speeches of Bosola consist partly of lines which it would be difficult to read as
prose, and partly of sentences which will not admit of
any satisfactory metrical arrangement. In my uncer-
tainty how to deal with them, I have allowed them to
stand nearly as they are given in the old 4tos.
‡ *A man merely, &c.*] This line is found only in the
4to. of 1623.

Bos. O, the secret of my prince,
Which I will wear on the inside of my heart !*

Duch. You shall take charge of all my coin
and jewels,
And follow him; for he retires himself
To Ancona.

Bos. So.

Duch. Whither, within few days,
I mean to follow thee.

Bos. Let me think :
I would wish your grace to feign a pilgrimage
To our Lady of Loretto, scarce seven leagues
From fair Ancona; so may you depart
Your country with more honour, and your flight
Will seem a princely progress,† retaining
Your usual train about you.

Duch. Sir, your direction
Shall lead me by the hand.

Cari. In my opinion,
She were better progress to the baths at Lucca,
Or go visit the Spa
In Germany; for, if you will believe me,
I do not like this jesting with religion,
This feigned pilgrimage.

Duch. Thou art a superstitious fool :
Prepare us instantly for our departure.
Past sorrows, let us moderately lament them,
For those to come, seek wisely to prevent them.
  [*Exeunt* DUCHESS *and* CARIOLA.

Bos. A politician is the devil's quilted anvil;
He fashions all sins on him, and the blows
Are never heard: he may work in a lady's chamber,
As here for proof. What rests but I reveal
All to my lord? O, this base quality
Of intelligencer !‡ why, every quality i'the world
Prefers but gain or commendation :
Now, for this act I am certain to be rais'd,
And men that paint weeds to the life are prais'd.
  [*Exit.*

SCENE III.§

Enter Cardinal, FERDINAND, MALATESTI, PESCARA,
DELIO, *and* SILVIO.

Card.|| Must we turn soldier, then?

Mal. The emperor,

---

* *Which I will wear on the inside of my heart*] So
Shakespeare ;
  "I will wear him
  In my heart's core." *Hamlet,* A. III. S. 2.
† *progress*] See note †, p. 9.
‡ *intelligencer*] The 4to. of 1640, "*intelligencers*"
§ *Scene III.*] An apartment: qy. in the Cardinal's
palace at Rome?
|| Another scene that hovers between prose and verse.
See note †, p. 79.

Hearing your worth that way, ere you attain'd
This reverend garment, joins you in commission
With the right fortunate soldier the Marquis of
Pescara,
And the famous Lannoy.

Card. He that had the honour *
Of taking the French king prisoner?

Mal. The same.
Here's a plot † drawn for a new fortification
At Naples.

Ferd. This great Count Malatesti, I perceive,
Hath got employment?

Delio. No employment, my lord;
A marginal note in the muster-book, that he is
A voluntary lord.

Ferd. He's no soldier.

Delio. He has worn gun-powder in's hollow
tooth for the tooth-ache.

Sil. He comes to the leaguer‡ with a full intent
To eat fresh beef and garlic, means to stay
Till the scent be gone, and straight return to
court.

Delio. He hath read all the late service
As the City-Chronicle relates it;
And keeps two pewterers§ going, only to express
Battles in model.

Sil. Then he'll fight by the book.

Delio. By the almanac, I think,
To choose good days and shun the critical;
That's his mistress' scarf.

Sil. Yes, he protests
He would do much for that taffeta.

Delio. I think he would run away from a battle,
To save it from taking prisoner.

Sil. He is horribly afraid
Gun-powder will spoil the perfume on't.

Delio. I saw a Dutchman break his pate once
For calling him pot-gun; he made his head
Have a bore in't like a musket.

Sil. I would he had made a touch-hole to't.
He is indeed a guarded sumpter-cloth,||
Only for the remove of the court.

Enter BOSOLA.

Pes. Bosola arriv'd! what should be the
business?
Some falling-out amongst the cardinals.

---

* *He that had the honour,* &c.] Francis I. at the battle
of Pavia gave up his sword to Launoy.
† *plot*] i. e. plan.
‡ *leaguer*] i. e. camp.
§ *pewterers*] Some copies of the 4to. of 1623, 'and the
4to. of 1640, "*painters*"
|| *guarded sumpter-cloth*] i. e. a sumpter-cloth with
facings, trimmings.

These factions amongst great men, they are like
Foxes, when their heads are divided,
They carry fire in their tails, and all the country
About them goes to wreck for't.

Sil. What's that Bosola?

Delio. I knew him in Padua,—a fantastical scholar, like such who study to know how many knots was in Hercules' club, of what colour Achilles' beard was, or whether Hector were not troubled with the tooth-ache. He hath studied himself half blear-eyed to know the true symmetry of Cæsar's nose by a shoeing-horn; and this he did to gain the name of a speculative man.

Pes. Mark Prince Ferdinand:
A very salamander lives in's eye,
To mock the eager violence of fire.

Sil. That cardinal hath made more bad faces with his oppression than ever Michael Angelo made good ones: he lifts up's nose, like a foul porpoise before a storm.

Pes. The Lord Ferdinand laughs.

Delio. Like a deadly cannon
That lightens ere it smokes.

Pes. These are your true pangs of death,
The pangs of life, that struggle with great statesmen.

Delio. In such a deformed silence witches whisper their charms.

Card. Doth she make religion her riding-hood
To keep her from the sun and tempest?

Ferd. That,
That damns her. Methinks her fault and beauty,
Blended together, show like leprosy,
The whiter, the fouler. I make it a question
Whether her beggarly brats were ever christen'd.

Card. I will ·instantly solicit the ·state of Ancona .
To have them banish'd.

Ferd. You are for Loretto:
I shall not be at your ceremony ; fare you well.—
Write to the Duke of Malfi, my young nephew
She had by her first husband, and acquaint him
With's mother's honesty.

Bos. I will.

Ferd. Antonio !
A slave that only smell'd of ink and counters,
And never in's life look'd like a gentleman,
But in the audit-time.—Go, go presently,
Draw me out an hundred and fifty of our horse,
And meet me at the fort-bridge.   [*Exeunt.*

SCENE IV.

Enter Two Pilgrims to the Shrine of our Lady of Loretto.

First Pil. I have not seen a goodlier shrine than this ;
Yet I have visited many.

Second Pil. The Cardinal of Arragon
Is this day to resign his cardinal's hat:
His sister duchess likewise is arriv'd
To pay her vow of pilgrimage. I expect
A noble ceremony.

First Pil. No question.—They come.

Here the ceremony of the Cardinal's instalment, in the habit of a soldier, performed in delivering up his cross, hat, robes, and ring, at the shrine, and investing him with sword, helmet, shield, and spurs ; then ANTONIO, the DUCHESS, and their children, having presented themselves at the shrine, are, by a form of banishment in dumb-show expressed towards them by the Cardinal and the state of Ancona, banished : during all which ceremony, this ditty is sung, to very solemn music, by divers churchmen : and then exeunt all except the Two Pilgrims.

Arms and honours deck thy story, [*]
To thy fame's eternal glory !
Adverse fortune ever fly thee ;
No disastrous fate come nigh thee !
I alone will sing thy praises,
Whom to honour virtue raises,
And thy study, that divine is,
Bent to martial discipline is.
Lay aside all those robes lie by thee ;
Crown thy arts with arms, they'll beautify thee.
O worthy of worthiest name, adorn'd in this manner,
Lead bravely thy forces on under war's warlike banner !
O, mayst thou prove fortunate in all martial courses !
Guide thou still by skill in arts and forces !
Victory attend thee nigh, whilst fame sings loud thy powers ;
Triumphant conquest crown thy head, and blessings pour down showers !

First Pil. Here's a strange turn of state ! who would have thought
So great a lady would have match'd herself
Unto so mean a person ? yet the cardinal
Bears himself much† too cruel.

Sec. Pil. They are banish'd.

First Pil. But I would ask what power hath this state
Of Ancona to determine of a free prince ?

Sec. Pil. They are a free state, sir, and her brother show'd
How that the Pope, fore-hearing of her looseness,
Hath seiz'd into the protection of the church
The dukedom which she held as dowager.

First Pil. But by what justice ?

Sec. Pil. Sure, I think by none,
Only her brother's instigation.

---

* On this song, in the 4to. of 1623, is the following marginal note; "The Author disclaimes this Ditty to be his."
† *much*] Omitted in the 4to. of 1640.

G

First Pil. What was it with such violence he took
Off from her finger?
Sec. Pil. 'Twas her wedding-ring;
Which he vow'd shortly he would sacrifice
To his revenge.
First Pil. Alas, Antonio!
If that a man be thrust into a well,
No matter who sets hand to't, his own weight
Will bring him sooner to the bottom. Come,
let's hence.
Fortune makes this conclusion general,
All things do help the unhappy man to fall.
[*Exeunt.*

SCENE V.*

Enter DUCHESS, ANTONIO, Children, CARIOLA, *and*
Servants.

Duch. Banish'd Ancona!
Ant. Yes, you see what power
Lightens in great men's breath.
Duch. Is all our train
Shrunk to this poor remainder?
Ant. These poor men,†
Which have got little in your service, vow
To take your fortune: but your wiser buntings,
Now they are fledg'd, are gone.
Duch. They have done wisely.
This puts me in mind of death: physicians thus,
With their hands full of money, use to give o'er
Their patients.‡
Ant. Right the fashion of the world:
From decay'd fortunes every flatterer shrinka;
Men cease to build where the foundation sinks.
Duch. I had a very strange dream to-night.
Ant. What was't?§
Duch. Methought I wore my coronet of state,
And on a sudden all the diamonds
Were chang'd to pearls.
Ant. My interpretation
Is, you'll weep shortly; for to me the pearls
Do signify your tears.
Duch. The birds that live i'the field

On the wild benefit of nature * live
Happier than we; for they may choose their mates,
And carol their sweet pleasures to the spring.

Enter BOSOLA *with a letter.*

Bos. You are happily o'erta'en.
Duch. From my brother?
Bos. Yes, from the Lord Ferdinand your
brother
All love and safety.
Duch. Thou dost blanch mischief,
Wouldst make it white. See, see, like to calm
weather†
At sea before a tempest, false hearts speak fair
To those they intend most mischief. [*Reads.*
"*Send Antonio to me; I want his head in a
business.*"
A politic equivocation!
He doth not want your counsel, but your head;
That is, he cannot sleep till you be dead.
And here's another pitfull that's strew'd o'er
With roses; mark it, 'tis a cunning one: [*Reads.*
"*I stand engaged for your husband for several
debts at Naples: let not that trouble him; I had
rather have his heart than his money:*"—
And I believe so too.
Bos. What do you believe?
Duch. That he so much distrusts my husband's
love,
He will by no means believe his heart is with him
Until he see it: the devil is not cunning enough
To circumvent us in riddles.
Bos. Will you reject that noble and free league
Of amity and love which I present you?
Duch. Their league is like that of some politic
kings,
Only to make themselves of strength and power
To be our after-ruin: tell them so.
Bos. And what from you?
Ant. Thus tell him; I will not come.
Bos. And what of this?
Ant. My brothers have dispers'd
Blood-hounds abroad; which till I hear are
muzzled,
No truce, though hatch'd with ne'er such politic
skill,
Is safe, that hangs upon our enemies' will.
I'll not come at them.

---

* *Scene V.*] Near Loretto?
† *These poor men*] The 4to. of 1640, "these *are* poor
men."
‡ *physicians thus,*
With their hands full of money, use to give o'er
Their patients] Cited by the commentators on Shakespeare, to defend the reading "*thrive*" in the following
passage of *Timon of Athens,* under the idea that Webster
imitated it;
 "His friends, like physicians,
 Thrive, give him over." Act III. Sc. 3.
§ *was't*] The 4to. of 1640, "*is't?*"

* *The birds that live i'the field*
 On the wild benefit of nature] "Think how compassionate *the creatures of the field, that only live on the wild
benefits of nature,* are unto their young ones." Middleton's
Any thing for a quiet life.—Works, iv. 472, ed. Dyce.
† *like to calm weather*] The 4to. of 1640, "like to *the*
calm weather."

Bos. This proclaims your breeding:
Every small thing draws a base mind to fear,
As the adamant draws iron. Fare you well, sir:
You shall shortly hear from's.   [*Exit.*

Duch. I suspect some ambush:
Therefore by all my love I do conjure you
To take your eldest son, and fly towards Milan.
Let us not venture all this poor remainder
In one unlucky bottom.

Ant. You counsel safely.
Best of my life, farewell, since we must part:
Heaven hath a hand in't; but no otherwise
Than as some curious artist takes in sunder
A clock or watch, when it is out of frame,
To bring't in better order.

Duch. I know not which is best,
To see you dead, or part with you.—Farewell,
            boy:
Thou art happy that thou hast not understanding
To know thy misery; for all our wit
And reading brings us to a truer sense
Of sorrow.—In the eternal church, sir,
I do hope we shall not part thus.

Ant. O, be of comfort!
Make patience a noble fortitude,
And think not how unkindly we are us'd:
Man, like to cassia,* is prov'd best, being bruis'd.

Duch. Must I, like to a slave-born Russian,†
Account it praise to suffer tyranny?
And yet, O heaven, thy heavy hand is in't!
I have seen my litle boy oft scourge his top,
And compar'd myself to't: naught made me e'er
Go right but heaven's scourge-stick.

Ant. Do not weep:
Heaven fashion'd us of nothing; and we strive
To bring ourselves to nothing.—Farewell, Cariola,
And thy sweet armful.—If I do never see thee more,
Be a good mother to your little ones,
And save them from the tiger: fare you well.

Duch. Let me look upon you once more, for
            that speech
Came from a dying father: your kiss is colder
Than that I have seen an holy anchorite
Give to a dead man's skull.

Ant. My heart is turn'd to a heavy lump of lead,
With which I sound my danger: fare you well.
            [*Exeunt* ANTONIO *and his son.*

Duch. My laurel is all wither'd.

Cari. Look, madam, what a troop of armèd men
Make toward us.

Duch. O, they are very welcome:
When Fortune's wheel is over-charg'd with princes,

The weight makes it move swift: I would have
            my ruin
Be sudden.

            Re-enter BOSOLA *visarded, with a guard.*
            I am your adventure, am I not?

Bos. You are: you must see your husband no
            more.

Duch. What devil art thou that counterfeit'st
            heaven's thunder?

Bos. Is that terrible? I would have you tell
            me whether
Is that note worse that frights the silly birds
Out of the corn, or that which doth allure them
To the nets? you have hearken'd to the last too
            much.

Duch. O misery! like to a rusty o'er-charg'd
            cannon,
Shall I never fly in pieces?—Come, to what prison?

Bos. To none.

Duch. Whither, then?

Bos. To your palace.

Duch. I have heard
That Charon's boat serves to convey all o'er
The dismal lake, but brings none back again.

Bos. Your brothers mean you safety and pity.

Duch. Pity!
With such a pity men preserve alive
Pheasants and quails, when they are not fat enough
To be eaten.

Bos. These are your children?

Duch. Yes.

Bos. Can they prattle?

Duch. No:
But I intend, since they were born accurs'd,
Curses shall be their first language.

Bos. Fie, madam!
Forget this base, low fellow,—

Duch. Were I a man,
I'd beat that counterfeit face into thy other.

Bos. One of no birth.

Duch. Say that he was born mean,
Man is most happy when's own actions
Be arguments and examples of his virtue.

Bos. A barren, beggarly virtue.

Duch. I prithee, who is greatest? can you tell?
Sad tales befit my woe: I'll tell you one.
A salmon, as she swam unto the sea,
Met with a dog-fish, who encounters her
With this rough language; "Why art thou so bold
To mix thyself with our high state of floods,"

---

* Man, like to cassia, &c.] See note †, p. 6.
† *Russian*] The 4to. of 1640, "*ruffian.*"

* *To mix thyself with our high state of floods*] From
Shakespeare;
            "Where it shall *mingle with the state of floods.*"
                        Second Part of *Henry IV.* Act V. Sc. 2.
                                                o 2

Being no eminent courtier, but one
That for the calmest and fresh time o'the year
Dost live in shallow rivers, rank'st thyself
With silly smelts and shrimps? and darest
      thou
Pass by our dog-ship without reverence?"
"O," quoth the salmon, "sister, be at peace:
Thank Jupiter we both have pass'd the net!
Our value never can be truly known,
Till in the fisher's basket we be shown:

I'the market then my price may be the higher,
Even when I am nearest to the cook and fire."
So to great men the moral may be stretch'd;
Men oft are valu'd high, when they're most
      wretch'd.—
But come, whither you please. I am arm'd 'gainst
      misery;
Bent to all sways of the oppressor's will:
There's no deep valley but near some great hill.
                              [Exeunt.

ACT IV.

SCENE I.[*]
Enter FERDINAND and BOSOLA.

Ferd. How doth our sister duchess bear herself
In her imprisonment?
Bos. Nobly: I'll describe her
She's sad as one long † us'd to't, and she seems
Rather to welcome the end of misery
Than shun it; a behaviour so noble
As gives a majesty to adversity:
You may discern the shape of loveliness
More perfect in her tears than in her smiles:
She will muse four hours together; and her
      silence,
Methinks, expresseth more than if she spake.
Ferd. Her melancholy seems to be fortified
With a strange disdain.
Bos. 'Tis so; and this restraint,
Like English mastives that grow fierce with tying,
Makes her too passionately apprehend
Those pleasures she's kept from.
Ferd. Curse upon her!
I will no longer study in the book
Of another's heart. Inform her what I told you.
                              [Exit.

Enter DUCHESS.‡

Bos. All comfort to your grace!
Duch. I will have none.
Pray thee, why dost thou wrap thy poison'd pills
In gold and sugar?
Bos. Your elder brother, the Lord Ferdinand,
Is come to visit you, and sends you word,

'Cause once he rashly made a solemn vow
Never to see you more, he comes i'the night;
And prays you gently neither torch nor taper
Shine in your chamber: he will kiss your hand,
And reconcile himself; but for his vow
He dares not see you.
Duch. At his pleasure.—
Take hence the lights.—He's come.

Enter FERDINAND.

Ferd. Where are you?
Duch. Here, sir.
Ferd. This darkness suits you well.
Duch. I would ask you pardon.
Ferd. You have it;
For I account it the honorabl'st revenge,
Where I may kill, to pardon.—Where are your
      cubs?
Duch. Whom?
Ferd. Call them your children;
For though our national law * distinguish bastards
From true legitimate issue, compassionate nature
Makes them all equal.
Duch. Do you visit me for this?
You violate a sacrament o'the church
Shall make you howl in hell for't.
Ferd. It had been well,
Could you have liv'd thus always; for, indeed,
You were too much i'the light:—but no more;
I come to seal my peace with you. Here's a hand
                    [Gives her a dead man's hand.
To which you have vow'd much love; the ring
      upon't
You gave.

---

* *Scene I.*] Malfi. An apartment in the palace of the
Duchess.
   † *long*] Omitted in the 4to. of 1640.
   ‡   " *Exit.*
   Enter DUCHESS] Here the audience had to imagine
a change of scene,—to a chamber in "the lodging"
(p. 80) of the Duchess, who is now a prisoner, confined
to certain apartments of her own "palace:" see p. 83.

* *For though our national law, &c.*] So our author
again in *The Devil's Law-case*, Act IV. Sc. 2;
   " For though our civil law makes difference
   'Twen the base and the legitimate,
   Compassionate nature makes them equal."

Duch. I affectionately kiss it.

Ferd. Pray, do, and bury the print of it in your
heart.

I will leave this ring with you for a love-token;
And the hand as sure as the ring; and do not
doubt
But you shall have the heart too : when you need
a friend,
Send it to him that ow'd * it; you shall see
Whether he can aid you.

Duch. You are very cold :
I fear you are not well after your travel.—
Ha ! lights !——O, horrible !

Ferd. Let her have lights enough.   [*Exit.*

Duch. What witchcraft doth he practise, that
he hath left
A dead man's hand here
[*Here is discovered, behind a traverse,† the artificial
figures of* ANTONIO *and his children, appearing
as if they were dead.*

Bos. Look you, here's the piece from which
'twas ta'en.

He doth present you this sad spectacle,
That, now you know directly they are dead,
Hereafter you may wisely cease to grieve
For that which cannot be recovered.

Duch. There is not between heaven and earth‡
one wish
I stay for after this : it wastes me more
Than were't my picture, fashion'd out of wax,
Stuck with a magical needle, and then buried
In some foul dunghill; and yond's an excellent
property
For a tyrant, which I would account mercy.

Bos. What's that ?

Duch. If they would bind me to that lifeless
trunk,
And let me freeze to death.

Bos. Come, you must live.

Duch. That's the greatest torture souls feel in
hell,
In hell, that they must live, and cannot die.
Portia, I'll new kindle thy coals again,
And revive the rare and almost dead example
Of a loving wife.

Bos. O, fie ! despair ? remember
You are a Christian.

Duch. The church enjoins fasting :
I'll starve myself to death.

Bos. Leave this vain sorrow
Things being at the worst begin to mend: the bee

When he hath shot his sting into your hand,
May then play with your eye-lid.

Duch. Good comfortable fellow,
Persuade a wretch that's broke upon the wheel
To have all his bones new set; entreat him live
To be executed again.   Who must despatch me ?
I account this world a tedious theatre,
For I do play a part in't 'gainst my will.

Bos. Come, be of comfort; I will save your life.

Duch. Indeed, I have not leisure to tend
So small a business.

Bos. Now, by my life, I pity you.

Duch. Thou art a fool, then,
To waste thy pity on a thing so wretched
As cannot pity itself.*   I am full of daggers.
Puff, let me blow these vipers from me.

Enter Servant.

What are you ?

Serv. One that wishes you long life.

Duch. I would thou wert hang'd for the horrible
curse
Thou hast given me : I shall shortly grow one
Of the miracles of pity.   I'll go pray ;—
No, I'll go curse.

Bos. O, fie !

Duch. I could curse the stars.

Bos. O, fearful !

Duch. And those three smiling seasons of the
year
Into a Russian winter : nay, the world
To its first chaos.

Bos. Look you, the stars shine still.

Duch. O, but you must
Remember, my curse hath a great way to go.—
Plagues, that make lanes through largest families,
Consume them !—

Bos. Fie, lady !

Duch. Let them, like tyrants,
Never be remember'd but for the ill they have
done;
Let all the zealous prayers of mortified
Churchmen forget them !—

Bos. O, uncharitable !

Duch. Let heaven a little while cease crowning
martyrs,
To punish them !—
Go, howl them this, and say, I long to bleed :
It is some mercy when men kill with speed. [*Exit.*

Re-enter FERDINAND.

Ferd. Excellent, as I would wish ; she's plagu'd
in art:

---

* *ow'd*] i. e. owned.
† *traverse*] See note *, p. 45.
‡ *earth*] The 4to. of 1640, "*the* earth."

---

* *itself*] The three earliest 4tos. "*it.*"

These presentations are but fram'd in wax
By the curious master in that quality,
Vincentio Lauriola, and she takes them
For true substantial bodies.

Bos. Why do you do this?

Ferd. To bring her to despair.

Bos. Faith, end here,
And go no farther in your cruelty:
Send her a penitential garment to put on
Next to her delicate skin, and furnish her
With beads and prayer-books.

Ferd. Damn her! that body of hers,
While that my blood ran pure in't, was more worth
Than that which thou wouldst comfort, call'd a
soul.
I will send her masks of common courtezans,
Have her meat serv'd up by bawds and ruffians,
And, 'cause she'll needs be mad, I am resolv'd
To remove forth the common hospital
All the mad-folk, and place them near her lodging;
There let them practise together, sing and dance,
And act their gambols to the full o'the moon:
If she can sleep the better for it, let her.
Your work is almost ended.

Bos. Must I see her again?

Ferd. Yes.

Bos. Never.

Ferd. You must.

Bos. Never in mine own shape;
That's forfeited by my intelligence
And this last cruel lie: when you send me next,
The business shall be comfort.

Ferd. Very likely;
Thy pity is nothing of kin to thee. Antonio
Lurks about Milan: thou shalt shortly thither,
To feed a fire as great as my revenge,
Which never will slack till it have spent his fuel:
Intemperate agues make physicians cruel. [*Exeunt.*

SCENE II.[*]

Enter DUCHESS *and* CARIOLA.

Duch. What hideous noise was that?

Cari. 'Tis the wild consort [†]
Of madmen, lady, which your tyrant brother
Hath plac'd about your lodging: this tyranny,
I think, was never practis'd till this hour.

Duch. Indeed, I thank him: nothing but noise
and folly
Can keep me in my right wits; whereas reason

---

[*] Another room in "the lodging" of the Duchess: see note ‡, p. 84. This is properly "Scene III."

[†] *consort*] See note on *Northward Ho*, Act II. Sc. 1.

And silence make me stark mad. Sit down;
Discourse to me some dismal tragedy.

Cari. O, 'twill increase your melancholy.

Duch. Thou art deceiv'd:
To hear of greater grief would lessen mine.
This is a prison?

Cari. Yes, but you shall live
To shake this durance off.

Duch. Thou art a fool:
The robin-red-breast and the nightingale
Never live long in cages.

Cari. Pray, dry your eyes.
What think you of, madam?

Duch. Of nothing;
When I muse thus, I sleep.

Cari. Like a madman, with your eyes open?

Duch. Dost thou think we shall know one
another
In the other world?

Cari. Yes, out of question.

Duch. O, that it were possible we might
But hold some two days' conference with the
dead!
From them I should learn somewhat, I am sure,
I never shall know here. I'll tell thee a miracle;
I am not mad yet, to my cause of sorrow:
The heaven o'er my head seems made of molten
brass,
The earth of flaming sulphur, yet I am not mad.
I am acquainted with sad misery
As the tann'd galley-slave is with his oar;
Necessity makes me suffer constantly,
And custom makes it easy. Who do I look like
now?

Cari. Like to your picture in the gallery,
A deal of life in show, but none in practice;
Or rather like some reverend monument
Whose ruins are even pitied.

Duch. Very proper;
And Fortune seems only to have her eye-sight
To behold my tragedy.—How now!
What noise is that?

Enter Servant.

Serv. I am come to tell you
Your brother hath intended you some sport.
A great physician, when the Pope was sick
Of a deep melancholy, presented him
With several sorts of madmen, which wild object
Being full of change and sport, forc'd him to laugh,
And so the imposthume broke: the self-same cure
The duke intends on you.

Duch. Let them [*] come in.

---

[*] *them*] The 4to. of 1640, "*me*," a misprint for "*'em*."

Serv. There's a mad lawyer; and a secular
priest;
A doctor that hath forfeited his wits
By jealousy; an astrologian
That in his works said such a day o'the month
Should be the day of doom, and, failing o't,
Ran mad; an English tailor craz'd i'the brain
With the study of new fashions;* a gentleman-usher
Quite beside himself with care to keep in mind
The number of his lady's salutations
Or "How do you" she employ'd him in each
morning; †
A farmer, too, an excellent knave in grain,
Mad 'cause he was hinder'd transportation:
And let one broker that's mad loose to these,
You'd think the devil were among them.

Duch. Sit, Cariola.—Let them loose when you
please,
For I am chain'd to endure all your tyranny.

Enter Madmen.

*Here by a Madman this song is sung to a dismal
kind of music.*

> O, let us howl some heavy note,
> Some deadly dogged howl,
> Sounding as from the threatening throat
> Of beasts and fatal fowl!
> As ravens, screech-owls, bulls, and bears,
> We'll bell, and bawl our parts,
> Till irksome noise have cloy'd your ears
> And corrosiv'd your hearts.
> At last, whenas our quire wants breath,
> Our bodies being blest,
> We'll sing, like swans, to welcome death,
> And die in love and rest.

First Madman. Doom's-day not come yet! I'll
draw it nearer by a perspective, or make a glass
that shall set all the world on fire upon an instant.
I cannot sleep; my pillow is stuffed with a litter
of porcupines.

Second Madman. Hell is a mere glass-house,
where the devils are continually blowing up
women's ‡ souls on hollow irons, and the fire
never goes out.

Third Madman. I will lie with every woman
in my parish the tenth night; I will tythe them
over like hay-cocks.

Fourth Madman. Shall my pothecary out-go me
because I am a cuckold? I have found out his

roguery; he makes allum of his wife's urine, and
sells it to Puritans that have sore throats with
over-straining.

First Madman. I have skill in heraldry.

Second Madman. Hast?

First Madman. You do give for your crest a
woodcock's head with the brains picked out on't;
you are a very ancient gentleman.

Third Madman. Greek is turned Turk: we
are only to be saved by the Helvetian translation.

First Madman. Come on, sir, I will lay the
law to you.

Second Madman. O, rather lay a corrosive: the
law will eat to the bone.

Third Madman. He that drinks but to satisfy
nature is damned.

Fourth Madman. If I had my glass here, I would
show a sight should make all the women here call
me mad doctor.

First Madman. What's he? a rope-maker?

Second Madman. No, no, no, a snuffling knave
that, while he shows the tombs, will have his
hand in a wench's placket.

Third Madman. Woe to the caroche that
brought home my wife from the mask at three
o'clock in the morning! it had a large featherbed
in it.

Fourth Madman. I have pared the devil's nails
forty times, roasted them in raven's eggs, and
cured agues with them.

Third Madman. Get me three hundred milch-
bats, to make possets to procure sleep.

Fourth Madman. All the college may throw
their caps at me: I have made a soap-boiler
costive; it was my masterpiece.

[*Here the dance, consisting of Eight Madmen, with
music answerable thereunto; after which, Bo-
SOLA, like an old man, enters.*

Duch. Is he mad too?

Serv. Pray, question him. I'll leave you.
[*Exeunt Servant and Madmen.*

Bos. I am come to make thy tomb.

Duch. Ha! my tomb!
Thou speak'st as if I lay upon my death-bed,
Gasping for breath: dost thou perceive me sick?

Bos. Yes, and the more dangerously, since thy
sickness is insensible.

Duch. Thou art not mad, sure: dost know me?

Bos. Yes.

Duch. Who am I?

Bos. Thou art a box of worm-seed, at best but
a salvatory of green mummy.* What's this flesh?
a little crudded† milk, fantastical puff-paste.

---

* *fashions*] The 4to. of 1623, "*fashion.*"

† *Or "how do you" she employ'd him in each morning*]
In Brome's *Northern Lasse*, 1632, Mistress Fitchow's gentleman-usher is named *How-dee*; see, as illustrative of
our text, Act 1. Sc. 6. of that amusing comedy. So too
Nabbes; "and thou a Ladies Gentleman Usher, a bundle
of complemental follyes stitcht up with *how-dees.*" *Covent-
Garden*, 1638, Sig. D.

‡ *woman's*] The 4to. of 1640, "*men's.*"

* *mummy*] See note ||, p. 5.

† *crudded*] The 4to. of 1640, "*curded.*"

Our bodies are weaker than those paper-prisons
boys use to keep flies in; more contemptible,
since ours is to preserve earth-worms. Didst thou
ever * see a lark in a cage? Such is the soul in
the body: this world is like her little turf of
grass, and the heaven o'er our heads like her
looking-glass, only gives us a miserable knowledge
of the small compass of our prison.

Duch. Am not I thy duchess?

Bos. Thou art some great woman, sure, for riot
begins to sit on thy forehead (clad in gray hairs)
twenty years sooner than on a merry milk-maid's.
Thou sleepest worse than if a mouse should be
forced to take up her † lodging in a cat's ear:
a little infant that breeds its teeth, should it lie
with thee, would cry out, as if thou wert the
more unquiet bedfellow.

Duch. I am Duchess of Malfi still.

Bos. That makes thy sleeps so broken:
Glories, like glow-worms, afar off shine bright,
But, look'd to near, have neither heat nor light.‡

Duch. Thou art very plain.

Bos. My trade is to flatter the dead, not the
living; I am a tomb-maker.

Duch. And thou comest to make my tomb?

Bos. Yes.

Duch. Let me be a little merry:—of what stuff
wilt thou make it?

Bos. Nay, resolve me first, of what fashion?

Duch. Why, do we grow fantastical in our death-
bed? do we affect fashion in the grave?

Bos. Most ambitiously. Princes' images on
their tombs do not lie, as they were wont, seeming
to pray up to heaven; but with their hands under
their cheeks, as if they died of the tooth-ache:
they are not carved with their eyes fixed upon
the stars; but as their minds were wholly bent
upon the world, the self-same way they seem to
turn their faces.

Duch. Let me know fully therefore the effect
Of this thy dismal preparation,
This talk fit for a charnel.

Bos. Now I shall:—

Enter Executioners, with a coffin, cords, and a bell.

Here is a present from your princely brothers;
And may it arrive welcome, for it brings
Last benefit, last sorrow.

Duch. Let me see it:
I have so much obedience in my blood,
I wish it in their veins to do them good.

Bos. This is your last presence-chamber.*

Cari. O my sweet lady!

Duch. Peace; it affrights not me.

Bos. I am the common bellman,
That usually is sent to condemn'd persons
The night before they suffer.

Duch. Even now thou said'st
Thou wast a tomb-maker.

Bos. 'Twas to bring you
By degrees to mortification. Listen.

Hark, now every thing is still,
The screech-owl and the whistler shrill †
Call upon our dame aloud,
And bid her quickly don her shroud!
Much you had of land and rent;
Your length in clay's now competent:
A long war disturb'd your mind;
Here your perfect peace is sign'd.
Of what is't fools make such vain keeping?
Sin their conception, their birth weeping,
Their life a general mist of error,
Their death a hideous storm of terror.
Strew your hair with powders sweet,
Don clean linen, bathe your feet,
And (the foul fiend more to check)
A crucifix let bless your neck:
'Tis now full tide 'tween night and day;
End your groan, and come away.

Cari. Hence, villains, tyrants, murderers! alas!
What will you do with my lady?—Call for help.

Duch. To whom? to our next neighbours? they
are mad-folks.

Bos. Remove that noise.

Duch. Farewell, Cariola.
In my last will I have not much to give:
A many hungry guests have fed upon me;
Thine will be a poor reversion.

Cari. I will die with her.

Duch. I pray thee, look thou giv'st my little boy
Some syrup for his cold, and let the girl
Say her prayers ere she sleep.

CARIOLA is forced out by the Executioners.

Now what you please:
What death?

Bos. Strangling; here are your executioners.

Duch. I forgive them:
The apoplexy, catarrh, or cough o'the lungs,
Would do as much as they do.

---

* *ever*] The 4to. of 1640, "never."
† *her*] The 4to. of 1640, "his."
‡ *Glories, like glow-worms,* &c.] See note *, p. 86.

* *This is your last presence-chamber*] Walker (*Shakespeare's Versification*, &c., p. 90) would read here " *This*' [i. e. *This* is] your last," &c.
† *the whistler shrill*] So Spenser;
" *The whistler shrill,* that whoso heares doth dy."
The Faerie Queene, B. ii. C. xii. st. 36.

Bos. Doth not death fright you?

Duch. Who would be afraid on't, ·
Knowing to meet such excellent company
In the other world?

Bos. Yet, methinks,
The manner of your death should much afflict you:
This cord should terrify you.

Duch. Not a whit:
What would it pleasure me to have my throat cut
With diamonds? or to be smother'd
With cassia? or to be shot to death with pearls?
I know death hath ten thousand several doors
For men to take their exits; and 'tis found
They go on such strange geometrical hinges,
You may open them both ways: any way, for
    heaven-sake,
So I were out of your whispering. Tell my brothers
That I perceive death, now I am well awake,
Best gift is they can give or I can take.
I would fain put off my last woman's fault,
I'd not be tedious to you.

First Execut. We are ready.

Duch. Dispose my breath how please you; but
    my body
Bestow upon my women, will you?

First Execut. Yes.

Duch. Pull, and pull strongly, for your able
    strength
Must pull down heaven upon me:—
Yet stay; heaven-gates are not so highly arch'd*
As princes'† palaces; they that enter there
Must go upon their knees [*Kneels*].—Come, violent
    death,
Serve for mandragora to make me sleep!—
Go tell my brothers, when I am laid out,
They then may feed in quiet.

    [*The* Executioners *strangle the* DUCHESS.‡]

Bos. Where's the waiting-woman?
Fetch her: some other strangle the children.

    [CARIOLA *and* Children *are brought in by the* Exe-
    cutioners; *who presently strangle the* Children.

Look you; there sleeps your mistress.

Cari. O, you are* damn'd
Perpetually for this! My turn is next;
Is't not so order'd?

Bos. Yes, and† I am glad
You are so well prepar'd for't.

Cari. You are deceiv'd, sir,
I am not prepar'd for't, I will not die;
I will first‡ come to my answer, and know
How I have offended.

Bos. Come, despatch her.——
You kept her counsel; now you shall keep ours.

Cari. I will not die, I must not; I am contracted
To a young gentleman.

First Execut. Here's your wedding-ring.

Cari. Let me but speak with the duke · I'll
    discover
Treason to his person.

Bos. Delays:—throttle her.

First Execut. She bites and scratches.

Cari. If you kill me now,
I am damn'd; I have not been at confession
This two years.

Bos. [*to* Executioners]. When?§

Cari. I am quick with child.

Bos. Why, then,
Your credit's sav'd.

    [*The* Executioners *strangle* CARIOLA.
    Bear her into the next room;
Let these ∥ lie still.

    [*Exeunt the* Executioners *with the body of* CARIOLA.

    Enter FERDINAND.

Ferd. Is she dead?

---

* *Yet stay; heaven-gates are not so highly arch'd*
  As princes' palaces, &c.] When Webster wrote this
passage, the following charming lines of Shakespeare
were in his mind;

    "Stoop, boys: this gate
Instructs you how to adore the heavens, and bows you
To a morning's holy office: the gates of monarchs
Are arch'd so high, that giants may jet through
And keep their impious turbans on, without
Good morrow to the sun." *Cymbeline,* Act III. Sc. 3.

† *princes'*] The 4to. of 1640 "*princely.*"

‡ "All the several parts of the dreadful apparatus with
which the duchess's death is ushered in are not more remote from the conceptions of ordinary vengeance than
the strange character of suffering which they seem to
bring upon their victim is beyond the imagination of
ordinary poets. As they are not like inflictions *of this
life,* so her language seems *not of this world.* She has
lived among horrors till she is become 'native and endowed unto that element.' She speaks the dialect of
despair, her tongue has a smatch of Tartarus and the
souls in bale. What are 'Luke's iron crown,' the brazen
bull of Perillus, Procrustes' bed, to the waxen images
which counterfeit death, to the wild masque of madmen,
the tomb-maker, the bell-man, the living person's dirge,
the mortification by degrees! To move a horror skil-
fully, to touch a soul to the quick, to lay upon fear as
much as it can bear, to wean and weary a life till it is
ready to drop, and then step in with mortal instruments
to take its last forfeit; this only a Webster can do.
Writers of an inferior genius may 'upon horror's head
horrors accumulate,' but they cannot do this. They
mistake quantity for quality, they 'terrify babes with
painted devils,' but they know not how a soul is capable
of being moved; their terrors want dignity, their
affrightments are without decorum." C. Lamb, (*Spec. of
Eng. Dram. Poets,* p. 217.)

* *you are*] The 4to of 1640, "*thou art.*"
† *and*] Omitted in the 4to of 1640.
‡ *first*] Omitted in the 4to of 1640.
§ *When*] See note *, p. 68.
∥ *these*] Old eds. "this /

Bos. She is what
You'd have her. But here begin your pity :
                    [*Shows the* Children *strangled.*
Alas, how have these offended?
    Ferd. The death
Of young wolves is never to be pitied.
    Bos. Fix your eye here.
    Ferd. Constantly.
    Bos. Do you not weep?
Other sins only speak ; murder shrieks out :
The element of water moistens the earth,
But blood flies upwards and bedews the heavens.
    Ferd. Cover her face;* mine eyes dazzle: she
        died young.
    Bos. I think not so; her infelicity
Seem'd to have years too many.
    Ferd. She and I were twins ;
And should I die this instant, I had liv'd
Her time to a minute.
    Bos. It seems she was born first :
You have bloodily approv'd the ancient truth,
That kindred commonly do worse agree
Than remote strangers.
    Ferd. Let me see her face
Again. Why didst not thou pity her? what
An excellent honest man mightst thou have been,
If thou hadst borne her to some sanctuary !
Or, bold in a good cause, oppos'd thyself,
With thy advancèd sword above thy head,
Between her innocence † and my revenge !
I bade thee, when I was distracted of my wits,
Go kill my dearest friend, and thou hast done't.
For let me but examine well the cause :
What was the meanness of her match to me ?
Only I must confess I had a hope,
Had she continu'd widow, to have gain'd
An infinite mass of treasure by her death :
And what ‡ was the main cause? her marriage,
That drew a stream of gall quite through my heart.
For thee, as we observe in tragedies
That a good actor many times is curs'd
For playing a villain's part, I hate thee for't,
And, for my sake, say, thou hast done much ill
    well.
    Bos. Let me quicken your memory, for I
        perceive
You are falling into ingratitude : I challenge
The reward due to my service.
    Ferd. I'll tell thee

---

* *Cover her face*] So in Shakespeare's *King Lear*, act v.
sc. 3, when the dead bodies of Goneril and Regan are
brought in, Albany says, "Cover their faces."
† *innocence*] The 4to. of 1640, "*innocency*."
‡ *what*] The 4to. of 1623, "*that*."

What I'll give thee.
    Bos. Do.
    Ferd. I'll give thee a pardon
For this murder.
    Bos. Ha !
    Ferd. Yes, and 'tis
The largest bounty I can study to do thee.
By what authority didst thou execute
This bloody sentence? *
    Bos. By yours.
    Ferd. Mine ! was I her judge?
Did any ceremonial form of law
Doom her to not-being? did a complete jury
Deliver her conviction up i'the court?
Where shalt thou find this judgment register'd,
Unless in hell? See, like a bloody fool,
Thou'st forfeited thy life, and thou shalt die
    for't.
    Bos. The office of justice is perverted quite
When one thief hangs another. Who shall dare
To reveal this?
    Ferd. O, I'll tell thee;
The wolf shall find her grave, and scrape it up,
Not to devour the corpse, but to discover
The horrid murder.†
    Bos. You, not I, shall quake for't.
    Ferd. Leave me.
    Bos. I will first receive my pension.
    Ferd. You are a villain.
    Bos. When your ingratitude
Is judge, I am so.
    Ferd. O horror,
That not the fear of him which binds the devils
Can prescribe man obedience !—
Never look upon me more.
    Bos. Why, fare thee well.
Your brother and yourself are worthy men :
You have a pair of hearts are hollow graves,
Rotten, and rotting others ; and your vengeance,

---

* *sentence*] The 4to of 1640, "*service.*"
† *The wolf shall,* &c.] A common superstition: "For
the same moneth next after that Adrian and Justinian
had buried the dead body of De Laurier, behold a huge
and ravening Wolf (being lately aroused from the adja-
cent vast woods), seeking up and down for his prey, came
into Adrian's orchard next adjoyning to his house (purposely sent thither by God as a Minister of his sacred
justice and revenge); who senting some dead carrion
(which indeed was the dead Corps of De Laurier, that
was but shallowly buried there in the ground), he fiercely
with his paws and nose tears up the earth, and at last
pulls and draggs it up, and there till an hour after the
break of day remains devouring and eating up of the
flesh of his Arms, Legs, Thighs and Buttocks. But (as
God would have it) he never touched any part of his
face, but leaves it fully undisfigured." *God's Revenge
against Murther*, Book VI. Hist. 27, p. 407, ed. 1670.

Like two chain'd bullets,* still goes arm in arm :
You may be brothers; for treason, like the plague,
Doth take much in a blood. I stand like one
That long hath ta'en a sweet and golden dream :
I am angry with myself, now that I wake.

Ferd. Get thee into some unknown part o'the
world,
That I may never see thee.†

Bos. Let me know
Wherefore I should be thus neglected. Sir,
I serv'd your tyranny, and rather strove
To satisfy yourself than all the world :
And though I loath'd the evil, yet I lov'd
You that did counsel it; and rather sought
To appear a true servant than an honest man.

Ferd. I'll go hunt the badger by owl-light :
'Tis a deed of darkness.   [*Exit.*

Bos. He's much distracted. Off, my painted
honour !
While with vain hopes our faculties we tire,
We seem to sweat in ice and freeze in fire.
What would I do, were this to do again ?
I would not change my peace of conscience
For all the wealth of Europe.—She stirs ; here's
life :—
Return, fair soul, from darkness, and lead mine
Out of this sensible hell :—she's warm, she
breathes :—
Upon thy pale lips I will melt my heart,
To store them with fresh colour.—Who's there !
Some cordial drink !—Alas ! I dare not call :
So pity would destroy pity.—Her eye opes,

And heaven in it seems to ope, that late was shut,
To take me up to mercy.

Duch. Antonio !*

Bos. Yes, madam, he is living ;
The dead bodies you saw were but feign'd statues :
He's reconcil'd to your brothers ; the Pope hath
wrought
The atonement.†

Duch. Mercy !   [*Dies.*

Bos. O, she's gone again ! there the cords of
life broke.
O sacred innocence, that sweetly sleeps
On turtles' feathers, whilst a guilty conscience
Is a black register wherein is writ
All our good deeds and bad, a perspective
That shows us hell ! That we cannot be suffer'd
To do good when we have a mind to it !
This is manly sorrow ;
These tears, I am very certain, never grow
In my mother's milk : my estate is sunk
Below the degree of fear : where were
These penitent fountains while she was living ?
O, they were frozen up ! Here is a sight
As direful to my soul as is the sword
Unto a wretch hath slain his father. Come,
I'll bear thee hence,
And execute thy last‡ will; that's deliver
Thy body to the reverend dispose
Of some good women : that the cruel tyrant
Shall not deny me. Then I'll post to Milan,
Where somewhat I will speedily enact
Worth my dejection.   [*Exit.*

ACT V.

SCENE I.‡

Enter ANTONIO *and* DELIO.

Ant. What think you of my hope of reconcilement
To the Arragonian brethren ?

Delio. I misdoubt it ;

For though they have sent their letters of safe-con-
For your repair to Milan, they appear   [duct
But nets to entrap you. The Marquis of Pescara,
Under whom you hold certain land in cheat,
Much 'gainst his noble nature hath been mov'd
To seize those lands; and some of his dependants
Are at this instant making it their suit
To be invested in your revenues.
I cannot think they mean well to your life
That do deprive you of your means of life,
Your living.

---

* *Like two chain'd bullets*] So Heywood ;
    "My friend and I
    Like two chain-bullets, side by side, will fly
    Thorow the jawes of death."
                    A Challenge for Beautie, 1636, Sig. D.
† *That I may never see thee*] In composing this scene,
Webster seems to have had an eye to that between King
John and Hubert in Shakespeare's *King John*, Act IV.
Sc. 2.
‡ *Scene I.*] Milan. A public place (it would seem).

* The idea of making the Duchess speak after she has
been strangled, was doubtless taken from the death of
Desdemona in Shakespeare's *Othello*, Act V. last scene.
† *atonement*] i. e. reconciliation.
‡ *last*] Omitted in the 4to of 1640.

Ant. You are still an heretic
To any safety I can shape myself.

   Delio. Here comes the marquis: I will make
myself
Petitioner for some part of your land,
To know whither it is flying.

   Ant. I pray, do.

Enter PESCARA.

   Delio. Sir, I have a suit to you.

   Pes. To me?

   Delio. An easy one:
There is the Citadel of Saint Bennet,
With some demesnes, of late in the possession
Of Antonio Bologna,—please you bestow them on
me.

   Pes. You are my friend; but this is such a suit,
Nor fit for me to give, nor you to take.

   Delio. No, sir?

   Pes. I will give you ample reason for't
Soon in private :—here's the cardinal's mistress.

Enter JULIA.

   Julia. My lord, I am grown your poor peti-
tioner,
And should be an ill beggar, had I not
A great man's letter here, the cardinal's,
To court you in my favour.   [*Gives a letter.*

   Pes. He entreats for you
The Citadel of Saint Bennet, that belong'd
To the banish'd Bologna.

   Julia. Yes.

   Pes. I could not have thought of a friend I
could rather
Pleasure with it: 'tis yours.

   Julia. Sir, I thank you;
And he shall know how doubly I am engag'd
Both in your gift, and speediness of giving
Which makes your grant the greater.   [*Exit.*

   Ant. How they fortify
Themselves with my ruin!

   Delio. Sir, I am
Little bound to you.

   Pes. Why?

   Delio. Because you denied this suit to me, and
gave't
To such a creature.

   Pes. Do you know what it was?
It was Antonio's land; not forfeited
By course of law, but ravish'd from his throat
By the cardinal's entreaty: it were not fit
I should bestow so main a piece of wrong
Upon my friend; 'tis a gratification
Only due to a strumpet, for it is injustice.

Shall I sprinkle the pure blood of innocents
To make those followers I call my friends
Look ruddier upon me? I am glad
This land, ta'en from the owner by such wrong,
Returns again unto so foul an use
As salary for his lust. Learn, good Delio,
To ask noble things of me, and you shall find
I'll be a noble giver.

   Delio. You instruct me well.

   Ant. Why, here's a man now would fright impudence
From sauciest beggars.

   Pes. Prince Ferdinand's come to Milan,
Sick, as they give out, of an apoplexy;
But some say 'tis a frenzy: I am going
To visit him.   [*Exit.*

   Ant. 'Tis a noble old fellow.

   Delio. What course do you mean to take,
Antonio?

   Ant. This night I mean to venture all my
fortune,
Which is no more than a poor lingering life,
To the cardinal's worst of malice: I have got
Private access to his chamber; and intend
To visit him about the mid of night,
As once his brother did our noble duchess.
It may be that the sudden apprehension
Of danger,—for I'll go in mine own shape,—
When he shall see it fraight* with love and duty,
May draw the poison out of him, and work
A friendly reconcilement: if it fail,
Yet it shall rid me of this infamous calling;
For better fall once than be ever falling.

   Delio. I'll second you in all danger; and, howe'er,
My life keeps rank with yours.

   Ant. You are still my lov'd and best friend.
   [*Exeunt.*

SCENE II.†

Enter PESCARA *and* DOCTOR.

   Pes. Now, doctor, may I visit your patient?

   Doc. If't please your lordship: but he's instantly
To take the air here in the gallery
By my direction.

   Pes. Pray thee, what's his disease?

   Doc. A very pestilent disease, my lord,
They call lycanthropia.

   Pes. What's that?
I need a dictionary to't.

---

* *fraight*] i.e. fraught.
† *Scene II.*] The same. A gallery in the residence of
the Cardinal and Ferdinand (a palace, it appears: see
the speech of Pescara towards the close of the play,—
   " The noble Delio, as I came to *the palace*," &c.)

Doc. I'll tell you.*
In those † that are possess'd with't there o'erflows
Such melancholy humour they imagine
Themselves to be transformèd into wolves ;
Steal forth to church-yards in the dead of night,
And dig dead bodies up: as two nights since
One met the duke 'bout midnight in a lane
Behind Saint Mark's church, with the leg of a man
Upon his shoulder ; and he howl'd fearfully ;
Said he was a wolf, only the difference
Was, a wolf's skin was ‡ hairy on the outside,
His on the inside ; bade them take their swords,
Rip up his flesh, and try : straight I was sent for,
And, having minister'd to him, found his grace
Very well recover'd.

Pes. I am glad on't.

Doc. Yet not without some fear
Of a relapse. If he grow to his fit again,
I'll go a nearer way to work with him §
Than ever Paracelsus dream'd of ; if
They'll give me leave, I'll buffet his madness out
     of him.
Stand aside ; he comes.

Enter FERDINAND, *Cardinal,* MALATESTI, *and* BOSOLA.

Ferd. Leave me.

Mal. Why doth your lordship love ‖ this so-
     litariness ?

---

* *I'll tell you,* &c.] " Ceste Maladie, comme tesmoigne
Aetius au sixiesme liure chapitre II. & Paulus au 3. liu.
chap. 16. & autres modernes, est une espece de melan-
cholie, mais estrangement noire & vehemente. Car ceux
qui en sont atteints sortent de leurs maisons au mois de
Feurier, contrefont les loups presques en toute chose, &
toute nuict ne font que courir par les cœmitieres et
autour des sepulchres. . . . .
. . . . vn de ces melancholiques Lycanthropes, que
nous appelons Loups garoux . . . . . *il portoit
lors sur ses espaules la cuisse entiere & la jambe d'vn mort*
. . . . Il y eust aussi, comme recite
Job Fincel au 2. liu. des Miracles, vn villageois pres de
Panie, l'an mil cinq cens quarante & vn, lequel pensoit
estre Loup, & assaillit plusieurs hommes par les champes:
en tua quelques vns. En fin, prins & non sans grande
difficulté, *il assura fermement, qu'il estoit loup, & qu'il n'y
auoit autre difference, sinon que les loups ordinairement
estoyent velus dehors, et lui l'estoit entre cuir et chair.*
Quelques vns trop inhumains & loups par effect, voulans
experimenter la verite du faict, lui firent plusieurs
millades sur les bras & sur les jambes : puis connoissans
leur faute, & l' innocence de ce pauure melancholique, le
commirent aux chirurgiens pour le penser, entre les
mains desquels il mourut quelques iours apres." Goulart,—*Histoires admirables et memorables de nostre temps,
recueillies de plusieurs autheurs,* &c. tom. I. pp. 336-337.
ed. 1620.

† *those*] The 4to. of 1640, "*these.*"

‡ *was*] The 4to. of 1640, "*is.*"

§ *I'll go a nearer way to work with him*] This line is
found only in the 4to. of 1623.

‖ *love*] The 4to. of 1640 "*use.*"

Ferd. Eagles commonly fly alone : they are
crows, daws, and starlings that flock together.
Look, what's that follows me ?

Mal. Nothing, my lord.

Ferd. Yes.

Mal. 'Tis your shadow.

Ferd. Stay it ; let it not haunt me.

Mal. Impossible, if you move, and the sun shine.

Ferd. I will throttle it.
     [*Throws himself down on his shadow.*

Mal. O, my lord, you are angry with nothing.

Ferd. You are a fool : how is't possible I should
catch my shadow, unless I fall upon't ? When I go
to hell, I mean to carry a bribe ; for, look you, good
gifts evermore make way for the worst persons.

Pes. Rise, good my lord.

Ferd. I am studying the art of patience.

Pes. 'Tis a noble virtue.

Ferd. To drive six snails before me from this
town to Moscow ; neither use goad nor whip to
them, but let them take their own time ;—the
patient'st man i'the world match me for an experiment ;—and I'll crawl after like a sheep-biter.

Card. Force him up.   [*They raise him.*

Ferd. Use me well, you were best. What I
have done, I have done : I'll confess nothing.*

Doc. Now let me come to him.—Are you mad,
my lord ? are you out of your princely wits ?

Ferd. What's he ?

Pes. Your doctor.

Ferd. Let me have his beard sawed off, and his
eye-brows filed more civil.

Doc. I must do mad tricks with him, for that's
the only way on't.—I have brought your grace a salamander's skin to keep you from sun-burning.

Ferd. I have cruel sore eyes.

Doc. The white of a cockatrix's egg is present
remedy.

Ferd. Let it be a new-laid one, you were best.—
Hide me from him : physicians are like kings,—
They brook no contradiction.

Doc. Now he begins to fear me : now let me
alone with him.

Card. How now ! put off your gown ! †

---

* *What I have done, I have done : I'll confess nothing*]
Like Iago's ;
" Demand me nothing : what you know, you know :
    From this time forth I never will speak word."
          Othello, Act V. last scene.

† *put off your gown*] A piece of buffoonery, similar to
that with which the Grave-digger in Hamlet still amuses
the galleries, used to be practised here ; for in the 4to. of
1708, the Doctor, according to the stage-direction, "*puts
off his four cloaks, one after another.*"—What precedes was
written in 1830 : since that time, the managers have properly restricted the Grave-digger to a single waistcoat.

Doc. Let me have some forty urinals filled
with rose-water: he and I'll go pelt one another
with them.—Now he begins to fear me.—Can
you fetch a frisk, sir?—Let him go, let him go,
upon my peril: I find by his eye he stands in
awe of me; I'll make him as tame as a dormouse.

Ferd. Can you fetch your frisks, sir?—I will
stamp him into a cullis,* flay off his skin, to cover
one of the anatomies this rogue hath set i'the
cold yonder in Barber-Chirurgeon's-hall.—Hence,
hence! you are all of you like beasts for sacrifice:
there's nothing left of you but tongue and belly,
flattery and lechery.   [*Exit.*

Pes. Doctor, he did not fear you throughly.

Doc. True; I was somewhat too forward.

Bos. Mercy upon me, what a fatal judgment
Hath fall'n upon this Ferdinand!

Pes. Knows your grace
What accident hath brought unto the prince
This strange distraction?

Card. [*aside*]. I must feign somewhat.—Thus
  they say it grew.
You have heard it rumour'd, for these many years
None of our family dies but there is seen
The shape of an old woman, which is given
By tradition to us to have been murder'd
By her nephews for her riches.   Such a figure
One night, as the prince sat up late at's book,
Appear'd to him; when crying out for help,
The gentlemen of's chamber found his grace
All on a cold sweat, alter'd much in face
And language: since which apparition,
He hath grown worse and worse, and I much fear
He cannot live.

Bos. Sir, I would speak with you.

Pes. We'll leave your grace,
Wishing to the sick prince, our noble lord,
All health of mind and body.

Card. You are most welcome.
              [*Exeunt* PESCARA, MALATESTI, *and Doctor.*
Are you come? so.—[*Aside*] This fellow must
                     not know
By any means I had intelligence
In our duchess' death; for, though I counsell'd
     it,
The full of all the engagement† seem'd to grow
From Ferdinand.—Now, sir, how fares our sister?
I do not think but sorrow makes her look
Like to an oft-dy'd garment: she shall now
Taste comfort from me.   Why do you look so
     wildly?
O, the fortune of your master here the prince

Dejects you; but be you of happy comfort:
If you'll do one thing for me I'll entreat,
Though he had a cold tomb-stone o'er his bones,
I'd make you what you would* be.

Bos. Any thing;
Give it me† in a breath, and let me fly to't:
They that think long small expedition win,
For musing much o'the end cannot begin.

Enter JULIA.

Julia. Sir, will you come in to supper?

Card. I am busy; leave me.

Julia. [*aside*]. What an excellent shape hath
     that fellow!   [*Exit.*

Card. 'Tis thus.   Antonio lurks here in Milan:
Inquire him out, and kill him.   While he lives,
Our sister cannot marry; and I have thought
Of an excellent match for her.   Do this, and
     style me
Thy advancement.

Bos. But‡ by what means shall I find him out?

Card. There is a gentleman call'd Delio
Here in the camp, that hath been long approv'd
His loyal friend.   Set eye upon that fellow;
Follow him to mass; may be Antonio,
Although he do account religion
But a school-name, for fashion of the world
May accompany him; or else go inquire out
Delio's confessor, and see if you can bribe
Him to reveal it.   There are a thousand ways
A man might find to trace him; as to know
What fellows haunt the Jews for taking up
Great sums of money, for sure he's in want;
Or else to go to the picture-makers, and learn
Who bought§ her picture lately: some of these
Happily may take.

Bos. Well, I'll not freeze i'the business:
I would see that wretched thing, Antonio,
Above all sights i'the world.

Card. Do, and be happy.   [*Exit.*

Bos. This fellow doth breed basilisks in's
     eyes,
He's nothing else but murder; yet he seems
Not to have notice of the duchess' death.
'Tis his cunning: I must follow his example;
There cannot be a surer way to trace
Than that of an old fox.

Re-enter JULIA.

Julia. So, sir, you are well met.

Bos. How now!

---

* *a cullis*] See note ¶, p. 72.
† *engagement*] The 4to. of 1610, "*agreement*."

* *would*] The 4to. of 1640, "*should*."
† *it me*] The 4to. of 1640, "*me it*."
‡ *But*] Omitted in the 4to. of 1640.
§ *bought*] The 4tos. "*brought*."

Julia. Nay, the doors are fast enough:
Now, sir, I will make you confess your treachery.

Bos. Treachery!

Julia. Yes, confess to me
Which of my women 'twas you hir'd to put
Love-powder into my drink?

Bos. Love-powder!

Julia. Yes, when I was at Malfi.
Why should I fall in love with such a face else?
I have already suffer'd for thee so much pain,
The only remedy to do me good　　　-
Is to kill my longing.

Bos. Sure, your pistol holds
Nothing but perfumes or kissing-comfits.*
Excellent lady!
You have a pretty way on't to discover
Your longing. Come, come, I'll disarm you,
And arm you thus: yet this is wondrous strange.

Julia. Compare thy form and my eyes together,
You'll find my love no such great miracle.
Now you'll say
I am wanton: this nice modesty in ladies
Is but a troublesome familiar
That haunts them.

Bos. Know you me, I am a blunt soldier.

Julia. The better:
Sure, there wants fire where there are no lively
　　　sparks
Of roughness.

Bos. And I want compliment.

Julia. Why, ignorance
In courtship cannot make you do amiss,
If you have a heart to do well.

Bos. You are very fair.

Julia. Nay, if you lay beauty to my charge,
I must plead unguilty.

Bos. Your bright eyes
Carry a quiver of darts in them sharper
Than sun-beams.

Julia. You will mar me with commendation,
Put yourself to the charge of courting me,
Whereas now I woo you.

Bos. [*aside*] I have it, I will work upon this
　　　creature.—
Let us grow most amorously familiar:
If the great cardinal now should see me thus,
Would he not count me a villain?

Julia. No; he might count me a wanton,
Not lay a scruple of offence on you;
For if I see and steal a diamond,
The fault is not i'the stone, but in me the thief
That purloins it. I am sudden with you:

We that are great women of pleasure use to cut off
These uncertain wishes and unquiet longings,
And in an instant join the sweet delight
And the pretty excuse together. Had you been
　　　i'the street,
Under my chamber-window, even there *
I should have courted you.

Bos. O, you are an excellent lady!

Julia. Bid me do somewhat for you presently
To express I love you.

Bos. I will; and if you love me,
Fail not to effect it.
The cardinal is grown wondrous melancholy;
Demand the cause, let him not put you off
With feign'd excuse; discover the main ground on't.

Julia. Why would you know this?

Bos. I have depended on him,
And I hear that he is fall'n in some disgrace
With the emperor: if he be, like the mice
That forsake falling houses, I would shift
To other dependance.

Julia. You shall not need
Follow the wars: I'll be your maintenance.

Bos. And I your loyal servant: but I cannot
Leave my calling.

Julia. Not leave an ungrateful
General for the love of a sweet lady!
You are like some cannot sleep in feather-beds,
But must have blocks for their pillows.

Bos. Will you do this?

Julia. Cunningly.

Bos. To-morrow I'll expect the intelligence.

Julia. To-morrow! get you into my cabinet;
You shall have it with you. Do not delay me,
No more than I do you: I am like one
That is condemn'd; I have my pardon promis'd,
But I would see it seal'd. Go, get you in:
You shall see me wind my tongue about his heart
Like a skein of silk. 　　　[*Exit* BOSOLA.

Re-enter Cardinal.

Card. Where are you?

Enter Servants.

Servants. Here.

Card. Let none, upon your lives, have conference
With the Prince Ferdinand, unless I know it.—
[*Aside*] In this distraction he may reveal
The murder.　　　・　　　[*Exeunt* Servants.
　　　　　Youd's my lingering consumption:
I am weary of her, and by any means
Would be quit of.

---

* *kissing-comfits*] i. e. perfumed sugar-plums, to sweeten
the breath.

* *Under my chamber window, even there*] This line is
found only in the 4to. of 1623.

Julia. How now, my lord ! what ails you ?
Card. Nothing.
Julia. O, you are much alter'd :
Come, I must be your secretary, and remove
This lead from off your bosom : what's the matter?
Card. I may not tell you.
Julia. Are you so far in love with sorrow
You cannot part with part of it ? or think you
I cannot love your grace when you are sad
As well as merry ? or do you suspect
I, that have been a secret to your heart
These many winters, cannot be the same
Unto your tongue ?
Card. Satisfy thy longing,—
The only way to make thee keep my counsel
Is, not to tell thee.*
Julia. Tell your echo this,
Or flatterers, that like echoes still report
What they hear though most imperfect, and not
me ;
For if that you be true unto yourself,
I'll know.
Card. Will you rack me ?
Julia. No, judgment shall
Draw it from you : it is an equal fault,
To tell one's secrets unto all or none.
Card. The first argues folly.
Julia. But the last tyranny.
Card. Very well : why, imagine I have committed
Some secret deed which I desire the world
May never hear of.
Julia. Therefore may not I know it ?
You have conceal'd for me as great a sin
As adultery. Sir, never was occasion †
For perfect trial of my constancy
Till now : sir, I beseech you—
Card. You'll repent it.
Julia. Never.
Card. It hurries thee to ruin : I'll not tell thee.
Be well advis'd, and think what danger 'tis
To receive a prince's secrets : they that do,
Had need have their breasts hoop'd with adamant ‡

---

* *The only way to make thee keep my counsel*
Is, not to tell thee] So Shakespeare, whom our author
so frequently imitates ;
    "and for secrecy,
No lady closer ; for I well believe
Thou wilt not utter what thou dost not know."
            First Part of *Henry IV.* Act II. Sc. 3.
† *As adultery. Sir, never was occasion*] The 4to. of 1640 ;
    "As adultery. Sir, I beseech you."
‡ *Had need have their breasts hoop'd with adamant*] Resembles a line of Heywood ;
    "Or be his *breast hoop't* with *ribbes of brasse.*"
            The Silver Age, 1613, Sig. G.

To contain them. I pray thee, yet be satisfied ;
Examine thine own frailty ; 'tis more easy
To tie knots than unloose them : 'tis a secret
That, like a lingering poison, may chance lie
Spread in thy veins, and kill thee seven year hence.
Julia. Now you dally with me.
Card. No more ; thou shalt know it.
By my appointment the great Duchess of Malfi
And two of her young children, four nights since,
Were strangl'd.
Julia. O heaven ! sir, what have you done !
Card. How now ? how settles this ? think you
        your bosom
Will be a grave dark and obscure enough
For such a secret ?
Julia. You have undone yourself, sir.
Card. Why ?
Julia. It lies not in me to conceal it.
Card. No ?
Come, I will swear you to't upon this book.
Julia. Most religiously.
Card. Kiss it.   [*She kisses the book.*
Now you shall never utter it ; thy curiosity
Hath undone thee : thou'rt poison'd with that
        book ;
Because I knew thou couldst not keep my counsel,
I have bound thee to't by death.

Re-enter BOSOLA.

Bos. For pity-sake, hold !
Card. Ha, Bosola !
Julia. I forgive you
This equal piece of justice you have done ;
For I betray'd your counsel to that fellow :
He over-heard it ; that was the cause I said
It lay not in me to conceal it.
Bos. O foolish woman,
Couldst not thou have poison'd him ?
Julia. 'Tis weakness,
Too much to think what should have been done.
I go,
I know not whither.   [*Dies.*
Card. Wherefore com'st thou hither ?
Bos. That I might find a great man like yourself,
Not out of his wits as the Lord Ferdinand,
To remember my service.
Card. I'll have thee hew'd in pieces.
Bos. Make not yourself such a promise of that
        life
Which is not yours to dispose of.
Card. Who plac'd thee here !
Bos. Her lust, as she intended.
Card. Very well :
Now you know me for your fellow-murderer.

Bos. And wherefore should you lay fair marble
　colours
Upon your rotten purposes to me?
Unless you imitate some that do plot great
　treasons,
And when they have done, go hide themselves
　i'the graves
Of those were actors in't?
　Card. No more; there is
A fortune attends thee.
　Bos. Shall I go sue to * Fortune any longer?
'Tis the fool's pilgrimage.
　Card. I have honours in store for thee.
　Bos. There are many † ways that conduct to
　seeming honour,
And some of them very dirty ones.
　Card. Throw to the devil
Thy melancholy. The fire burns well;
What need we keep a stirring of't, and make
A greater ‡ smother? Thou wilt kill Antonio?
　Bos. Yes.
　Card. Take up that body.
　Bos. I think I shall
Shortly grow the common bier for church-yards.
　Card. I will allow thee some dozen of attendants
To aid thee in the murder.
　Bos. O, by no means. Physicians that apply
horse-leeches to any rank swelling use to cut off
their tails, that the blood may run through them
the faster: let me have no train when I go to
shed blood, lest it make me have a greater when
I ride to the gallows.
　Card. Come to me after midnight, to help to
　remove
That body to her own lodging:. I'll give out
She died o'the plague; 'twill breed the less
　inquiry
After her death.
　Bos. Where's Castruccio her husband?
　Card. He's rode to Naples, to take possession
Of Antonio's citadel.
　Bos. Believe me, you have done a very happy
　turn.
　Card. Fail not to come: there is the master-key
Of our lodgings; and by that you may conceive
What trust I plant in you.
　Bos. You shall find me ready. [*Exit* Cardinal.
O poor Antonio, though nothing be so needful
To thy estate as pity, yet I find
Nothing so dangerous! I must look to my footing:
In such slippery ice-pavements men had need

To be frost-nail'd well, they may break their necks
　else;
The precedent's here afore me. How this man
Bears up in blood! seems fearless! Why, 'tis well:
Security some men call the suburbs of hell,
Only a dead wall between. Well, good Antonio,
I'll seek thee out; and all my care shall be
To put thee into safety from the reach
Of these most cruel biters that have got
Some of thy blood already. It may be,
I'll join with thee in a most just revenge:
The weakest arm is strong enough that strikes
With the sword of justice. Still methinks the
　duchess
Haunts me: there, there!—'Tis nothing but my
　melancholy.
O Penitence, let me truly taste thy cup,
That throws men down only to raise * them up!
　　　　　　　　　　　　　　　　　　　[*Exit.*

SCENE III.†
Enter ANTONIO *and* DELIO.

　Delio. Yond's the cardinal's window. This for-
tification
Grew from the ruins of an ancient abbey;
And to yond side o'the river lies a wall,
Piece of a cloister, which in my opinion
Gives the best echo that you ever heard,
So hollow and so dismal, and withal
So plain in the distinction of our words,
That many have suppos'd it is a spirit
That answers.
　Ant. I do love these ancient ruins.
We never tread upon them but we set
Our foot upon some reverend history:
And, questionless, here in this open court,
Which now lies naked to the injuries
Of stormy weather, some men ‡ lie interr'd
Lov'd the church so well, and gave so largely to't,
They thought it should have canopied their
　bones
Till dooms-day; but all things have their end:
Churches and cities, which have diseases like to
　men,
Must have like death that we have.
　Echo. Like death that we have.
　Delio. Now the echo hath caught you.
　Ant. It groan'd, methought, and gave
A very deadly accent.
　Echo. Deadly accent.

---

* *to*] The 4to. of 1640, "*a.*"
† *many*] The 4to. of 1623, "*a many.*"
‡ *greater*] The 4to. of 1640, "*great.*"

* *raise*] The 4to. of 1640, "*rise.*"
† *Scene III.*] The same. A fortification.
‡ *men*] Omitted in the 4to. of 1640.

H

Delio. I told you 'twas a pretty one : you may
    make it
A huntsman, or a falconer, a musician,
Or a thing of sorrow.
  Echo. A thing of sorrow.
  Ant. Ay, sure, that suits it best.
  Echo. That suits it best.
  Ant. 'Tis very like my wife's voice.
  Echo. Ay, wife's voice.
  Delio. Come, let us walk further from't.
I would not have you go* to the cardinal's to-night:
Do not.
  Echo. Do not.
  Delio. Wisdom doth not more moderate wasting
    sorrow
Than time : take time for't; be mindful of thy
    safety.
  Echo. Be mindful of thy safety.
  Ant. Necessity compels me :
Make scrutiny throughout the passages †
Of your own life, you'll find it impossible
To fly your fate.
  Echo. O, fly your fate !
  Delio. Hark ! the dead stones seem to have
    pity on you,
And give you good counsel.
  Ant. Echo, I will not talk with thee,
For thou art a dead thing.
  Echo. Thou art a dead thing.
  Ant. My duchess is asleep now,
And her little ones, I hope sweetly : O heaven,
Shall I never see her more !
  Echo. Never see her more.
  Ant. I mark'd not one repetition of the echo
But that; and on the sudden a clear light
Presented me a face folded in sorrow.
  Delio. Your fancy merely.
  Ant. Come, I'll be out of this ague,
For to live thus is not indeed to live;
It is a mockery and abuse of life :
I will not henceforth save myself by halves ;
Lose all, or nothing.
  Delio. Your own virtue save you !
I'll fetch your eldest son, and second you :
It may be that the sight of his own blood
Spread in ‡ so sweet a figure may beget
The more compassion. However, fare you
    well.
Though in our miseries Fortune have a part,

Yet in our noble sufferings she hath none :
Contempt of pain, that we may call our own.
                    [*Exeunt.*

SCENE IV.*

Enter Cardinal, Pescara, Malatesti, Roderigo, *and*
    Grisolan.

  Card. You shall not watch to-night by the sick
    prince ;
His grace is very well recover'd.
  Mal. Good my lord, suffer us.
  Card. O, by no means ;
The noise, and change of object in his eye,
Doth more distract him : I pray, all to bed ;
And though you hear him in his violent fit,
Do not rise, I entreat you.
  Pes. So, sir; we shall not.
  Card. Nay, I must have you promise
Upon your honours, for I was enjoin'd to't
By himself; and he seem'd to urge it sensibly.
  Pes. Let our honours bind this trifle.
  Card. Nor any of your followers.
  Mal. Neither.
  Card. It may be, to make trial of your promise,
When he's asleep, myself will rise and feign
Some of his mad tricks, and cry out for help,
And feign myself in danger.
  Mal. If your throat were cutting,
I'd not come at you, now I have protested against it.
  Card. Why, I thank you.
  Gris. 'Twas a foul storm to-night.
  Rod. The Lord Ferdinand's chamber shook like
    an osier.
  Mal. 'Twas nothing but pure kindness in the
    devil,
To rock his own child.
         [*Exeunt all except the* Cardinal.
  Card. The reason why I would not suffer these
About my brother, is, because at midnight
I may with better privacy convey
Julia's body to her own lodging. O, my conscience !
I would pray now ; but the devil takes away my
    heart
For having any confidence in prayer.
About this hour I appointed Bosola
To fetch the body : when he hath serv'd my turn,
He dies.   . [*Exit.*

Enter Bosola.

  Bos. Ha ! 'twas the cardinal's voice ; I heard
    him name
Bosola and my death. Listen ; I hear one's footing.

---

  * *go*] Omitted in the 4to. of 1640.
  † *passages*] So the 4to. of 1708 (an alteration of the play,
and of no authority ; but evidently right here) The
earlier 4t*o.* "*passes.*"
  ‡ *in*] The 4to. of 1640, "*into.*"

  * *Scene IV.*] The same. An apartment in the residence of the Cardinal and Ferdinand : see note †, p. 92.

Enter FERDINAND.

Ferd. Strangling is a very quiet death.

Bos. [*aside*]. Nay, then, I see I must stand upon my guard.

Ferd. What say [you] to that? whisper softly; do you agree to't? So; it must be done i'the dark: the cardinal would not for a thousand pounds the doctor should see it.   [*Exit.*

Bos. My death is plotted; here's the consequence of murder.

We value not desert nor Christian breath,
When we know black deeds must be cur'd with death.

Enter ANTONIO *and* Servant.

Serv. Here stay, sir, and be confident, I pray:
I'll fetch you a dark lantern.   [*Exit.*

Ant. Could I take him at his prayers,
There were hope of pardon.

Bos. Fall right, my sword!—   [*Stabs him.*
I'll not give thee so much leisure as to pray.

Ant. O, I am gone! Thou hast ended a long suit
In a minute.

Bos. What art thou?

Ant. A most wretched thing,
That only have thy benefit in death,
To appear myself.

Re-enter Servant *with a lantern.*

Serv. Where are you, sir?

Ant. Very near my home.—Bosola!

Serv. O, misfortune!

Bos. Smother thy pity, thou art dead else.—Antonio!

The man I would have sav'd 'bove mine own life!
We are merely the stars' tennis-balls, struck and banded
Which way please them.—O good Antonio,
I'll whisper one thing in thy dying ear
Shall make thy heart break quickly! thy fair duchess
And two sweet children——

Ant. Their very names
Kindle a little life in me.

Bos. Are murder'd.

Ant. Some men have wish'd to die
At the hearing of sad tidings; I am glad
That I shall do't in sadness:* I would not now
Wish my wounds balm'd nor heal'd, for I have no use
To put my life to. In all our quest of greatness,
Like wanton boys, whose pastime is their care,

———

* *sadness*] i. e. seriousness, earnest.

We follow after bubbles blown in the air.
Pleasure of life, what is't? only the good hours
Of an ague; merely a preparative to rest,
To endure vexation. I do not ask
The process of my death; only commend me
To Delio.

Bos. Break, heart!

Ant. And let my son fly the courts of princes.
        [*Dies.*

Bos. Thou seem'st to have lov'd Antonio

Serv. I brought him hither,
To have reconcil'd him to * the cardinal.

Bos. I do not ask thee that.
Take him up, if thou tender thine own life,
And bear him where the lady Julia
Was wont to lodge.†—O, my fate moves swift!
I have this cardinal in the forge already;
Now I'll bring him to the hammer. O direful misprision!
I will not imitate things glorious,
No more than base; I'll be mine own example.—
On, on, and look thou represent, for silence,
The thing thou bear'st.   [*Exeunt.*

———

SCENE V.‡

Enter Cardinal, *with a book.*

Card. I am puzzled in a question about hell:
He says, in hell there's one material fire,
And yet it shall not burn all men alike.
Lay him by. How tedious is a guilty conscience!
When I look into the fish-ponds in my garden,
Methinks I see a thing arm'd with a rake,
That seems to strike at me.

Enter BOSOLA, *and* Servant *bearing* ANTONIO'S *body.*

        Now, art thou come?
Thou look'st ghastly:
There sits in thy face some great determination
Mix'd with some fear.

Bos. Thus it lightens into action:
I am come to kill thee.

Card. Ha!—Help! our guard!

Bos. Thou art deceiv'd;
They are out of thy howling.

Card. Hold; and § I will faithfully divide
Revenues with thee.

Bos. Thy prayers and proffers
Are both unseasonable.

———

* *to*] The 4to. of 1640, "*with.*"
†   *where the lady Julia*
    Was wont to lodge] i. e. in that part of the palace where, &c.: see note †, p. 92.
‡ *Scene V.*] Another apartment in the same.
§ *and*] Omitted in the 4to. of 1640.

                                      H 2

Card. Raise the watch ! we are betray'd !

Bos. I have confin'd your flight :
I'll suffer your retreat to Julia's chamber,
But no further.

Card. Help ! we are betray'd !

Enter, above, [*] PESCARA, MALATESTI, RODERIGO, *and*
GRISOLAN.

Mal. Listen.

Card. My dukedom for rescue !

Rod. Fie upon his counterfeiting !

Mal. Why, 'tis not the cardinal.

Rod. Yes, yes, 'tis he :
But I'll see him hang'd ere I'll go down to him.

Card. Here's a plot upon me ; I am assaulted !
I am lost,
Unless some rescue !

Gris. He doth this pretty well ;
But it will not serve to laugh me out of mine
honour.

Card. The sword's at my throat !

Rod. You would not bawl so loud then.

Mal. Come, come, let's go
To bed : he told us 'thus much aforehand.

Pes. He wish'd you should not come at him ;
but, believe't,
The accent of the voice sounds not in jest :
I'll down to him, howsoever, and with engines
Force ope the doors. [*Exit above.*

Rod. Let's follow him aloof,
And note how the cardinal will laugh at him.
[*Exeunt, above,* MALATESTI, RODERIGO, *and*
GRISOLAN.

Bos. There's for you first,
'Cause you shall not unbarricade the door
To let in rescue. [*Kills the* Servant.

Card. What cause hast thou to pursue my life ?

Bos. Look there.

Card. Antonio !

Bos. Slain by my hand unwittingly.
Pray, and be sudden : when thou kill'd'st thy
sister,
Thou took'st from Justice her most equal balance,
And left her naught but her † sword.

Card. O, mercy !

Bos. Now it seems thy greatness was only
outward ;
For thou fall'st faster of thyself than calamity
Can drive thee. I'll not waste longer time ; there !
[*Stabs him.*

Card. Thou hast hurt me.

Bos. Again ! [*Stabs him again.*

---

* *above*] i. e. on the upper stage ; the raised platform
towards the back of the stage.

† *her*] The 4to. of 1640, "*the.*"

Card. Shall I die like a leveret,
Without any resistance ?—Help, help, help !
I am slain !

Enter FERDINAND.

Ferd. The alarum ! give me a fresh horse ;
Rally the vaunt-guard, or the day is lost.
Yield, yield ! I give you the honour of arms,
Shake my sword over you ; will you yield ?

Card. Help me ; I am your brother !

Ferd. The devil !
My brother fight upon the adverse party !
[*He wounds the* Cardinal, *and, in the scuffle,
gives* BOSOLA *his death-wound.*

There flies your ransom.

Card. O justice !
I suffer now for what hath former bin :
Sorrow is held the eldest child of sin.*

Ferd. Now you're brave fellows. Cæsar's fortune was harder than Pompey's ; Cæsar died in
the arms of prosperity, Pompey at the feet of
disgrace. You both died in the field. The pain's
nothing : pain many times is taken away with the
apprehension of greater, as the tooth-ache with
the sight of a barber that comes to pull it out :
there's philosophy for you.

Bos. Now my revenge is perfect.—Sink, thou
main cause [*Kills* FERDINAND.
Of my undoing !—The last part of my life
Hath done me best service.

Ferd. Give me some wet hay ; I am broken-
winded.
I do account this world but a dog-kennel :
I will vault credit and affect high pleasures
Beyond death.†

Bos. He seems to come to himself,
Now he's so near the bottom.

Ferd. My sister, O my sister ! there's the cause
on't.
Whether we fall by ambition, blood, or lust,
Like diamonds, we are cut with our own dust.
[*Dies.*

Card. Thou hast thy payment too.

Bos. Yes, I hold my weary soul in my teeth ;
'Tis ready to part from me. I do glory
That thou, which stood'st like a huge pyramid
Begun upon a large and ample base,
Shalt end in a little point, a kind of nothing.

Enter, below, PESCARA, MALATESTI, RODERIGO, *and*
GRISOLAN.

Pes. How now, my lord !

Mal. O sad disaster !

Rod. How comes this ?

---

* *I suffer now, &c.*] See note *, p. 44.

† *Beyond death*] Found only in the 4to. of 1623.

Bos. Revenge for the Duchess of Malfi murder'd
By the Arragonian brethren; for Antonio
Slain by this * hand; for lustful Julia
Poison'd by this man; and lastly for myself,
That was an actor in the main of all
Much 'gainst mine own good nature, yet i'the end
Neglected.

Pes. How now, my lord!

Card. Look to my brother:
He gave us these large wounds, as we were
          struggling
Here i'the rushes.† And now, I pray, let me
Be laid by and never thought of.   [*Dies.*

Pes. How fatally, it seems, he did withstand
His own rescue!

Mal. Thou wretched thing of blood,‡
How came Antonio by his death?

Bos. In a mist; I know not how:
Such a mistake as I have often seen
In a play. O, I am gone!
We are only like dead walls or vaulted graves,
That, ruin'd, yield no echo. Fare you well.
It may be pain, but no harm, to me to die

---

* *this*] The three earliest 4tos. "*his.*"
† *the rushes*] See note †, p. 21.
‡ *thing of blood*] Shakespeare has
          "from face to foot
   " He was a *thing of blood.*"
                    Coriolanus, Act ii. Sc. 2.

In so good a quarrel. O, this gloomy world!
In what a shadow, or deep pit of darkness,
Doth womanish and fearful mankind live!
Let worthy minds ne'er stagger in distrust
To suffer death or shame for what is just.
Mine is another voyage.   [*Dies.*

Pes. The noble Delio, as I came to the palace,
Told me of Antonio's being here, and show'd me
A pretty gentleman, his son and heir.

Enter DELIO, *and* ANTONIO's Son.

Mal. O sir, you come too late!

Delio. I heard so, and
Was arm'd for't, ere I came. Let us make noble
          use
Of this great ruin; and join all our force
To establish this young hopeful gentleman
In's mother's right. These wretched eminent
          things
Leave no more fame behind 'em, than should one
Fall in a frost, and leave his print in snow;
As soon as the sun shines, it ever melts,
Both form and matter. I have ever thought
Nature doth nothing so great for great men
As when she's pleas'd to make them lords of truth:
Integrity of life is fame's best friend,
Which nobly, beyond death, shall crown the end.
                              [*Exeunt.*

THE DEVIL'S LAW-CASE.

The Devils Law-case. Or, When Women goe to Law, the Devill is full of Businesse. A new Tragecomoedy. The true and perfect Copie from the Originall. As it was approovedly well Acted by her Maiesties Seruants. Written by Iohn Webster. Non quam diu, sed quam bene. London, Printed by A. M. for John Grismand, and are to be sold at his Shop in Pauls Alley at the Signe of the Gunne. 1623. 4to.

That this play must have been written but a short time before it was given to the press is evident from the following allusion in it to the massacre of the English by the Dutch at Amboyna, which took place in February, 1622;

"How! go to the East Indies, and so many Hollanders gone to fetch sauce for their pickled herrings! some have been peppered there too lately." Act IV. Sc. 2.

Whence the author derived the story of *The Devil's Law Case* I know not. The following observations by Langbaine are hardly worth quoting: "An accident like that of Romelio's stabbing Contarino out of malice, which turned to his preservation, is (if I mistake not,) in Skenkius his Observations: At least I am sure, the like happened to Phereus Jason, as you may see in Q. Val. Maximus, lib. i. cap. 8. The like story is related in Goulart's *Histoires Admirables*, tome 1. p. 178." *Account of the Eng. Dram. Poets, &c.*

TO THE RIGHT WORTHY AND ALL-ACCOMPLISHED GENTLEMAN, SIR THOMAS FINCH, KNIGHT BARONET.[*]

SIR,

Let it not appear strange, that I do aspire to your patronage. Things that taste of any goodness love to be sheltered near goodness : nor do I flatter in this, which I hate, only touch at the original copy of your virtues. Some of my other works, as *The White Devil, The Duchess of Malfi, Guise,*[†] and others, you have formerly seen : I present this humbly to kiss your hands, and to find your allowance : nor do I much doubt it, knowing the greatest of the Cæsars have cheerfully entertained less poems than this ; and had I thought it unworthy, I had not inquired after so worthy a patronage. Yourself I understand to be all courtesy : I doubt not therefore of your acceptance, but resolve that my election is happy ; for which favour done me, I shall ever rest

Your worship's humbly devoted,

JOHN WEBSTER.

TO THE JUDICIOUS READER.

I HOLD it in these kind of poems with that of Horace, *Sapientia prima stultitiâ caruisse,*[‡] to be free from those vices which proceed from ignorance ; of which, I take it, this play will ingeniously acquit itself. I do chiefly therefore expose it to the judicious : *locus est et pluribus umbris,*[§] others have leave to sit down and read it, who come unbidden. But to these, should a man present them with the most excellent music, it would delight them no more than *auriculas citharæ collecta sorde dolentes*[||]. I will not further insist upon the approvement of it ; for I am so far from praising myself, that I have not given way to divers of my friends, whose unbegged commendatory verses offered themselves to do me service in the front of this poem. A great part of the grace of this, I confess, lay in action ; yet can no action ever be gracious, where the decency of the language, and ingenious structure of the scene, arrive not to make up a perfect harmony. What I have failed of this, you that have approved my other works, (when you have read this,) tax me of. For the rest, *Non ego ventosæ plebis suffragia venor.*[¶]

---

[*] *Sir Thomas Finch, Knight Baronet*] Was the second son of Sir Moyle Finch. His mother having been created Countess of Winchelsea, he, on her decease in 1633, succeeded to her honours as first Earl of Winchelsea. He married Cecille, daughter of Sir John Wentworth, Bart. ; and died in 1639. In the later editions of Collins's *Peerage* his death is fixed in 1634 ; but see Hasted's *Hist. of Kent,* vol. iii. p. 199, and the Corrigenda to it, p. 48.
[†] *Guise*] A lost play. See the Introductory Essay to this work.
[‡] *Sapientia prima, &c.*] *Epist.* i. 1.
[§] *locus est, &c.*] Horace, *Epist.* i. 5.
[||] *auriculas citharæ, &c.*] Horace, *Epist.* i. 2.
[¶] *Non ego, &c.*] Horace, *Epist.* i. 19.

DRAMATIS PERSONÆ.

ROMELIO, a merchant, son of LEONORA.
CONTARINO, a nobleman.
ERCOLE, a knight of Malta.
CRISPIANO, a Spanish lawyer.
JULIO, his son.
ARIOSTO, an advocate.
CONTILUPO, a lawyer.
SANITONELLA.
PROSPERO.
BAPTISTA.
A Capuchin.
Two Surgeons.
Judges, Lawyers, Bellmen, Register, Marshal, Herald, and Servants.

LEONORA.
JOLENTA, her daughter.
ANGIOLELLA, a nun.
WINIFRED.

THE DEVIL'S LAW-CASE.

ACT I.

SCENE I.*

Enter ROMELIO *and* PROSPERO.

Pros. You have shown a world of wealth: I
did not think
There had been a merchant liv'd in Italy
Of half your substance.

Rom. I'll give the King of Spain
Ten thousand ducats yearly, and discharge
My yearly custom. The Hollanders scarce trade
More generally than I: my factors' wives
Wear chaperons of velvet; and my scriveners,
Merely through my employment, grow so rich
They build their palaces and belvederes
With musical water-works. Never in my life
Had I a loss at sea: they call me on the Exchange
The Fortunate Young Man, and make great suit
To venture with me. Shall I tell you, sir,
Of a strange confidence in my way of trading?
I reckon it as certain as the gain
In erecting a lottery.

Pros. I pray, sir, what do you think
Of Signior Baptista's estate?

Rom. A mere beggar:
He's worth some fifty thousand ducats.

Pros. Is not that well?

Rom. How, well! for a man to be melted to
snow-water
With toiling in the world from three-and-twenty
Till three-score, for poor fifty thousand ducats!

Pros. To your estate 'tis little, I confess:
You have the spring-tide of gold.

Rom. Faith, and for silver,

---

* *Scene I.*] Naples. A room in the house of Leonora.
(I had originally marked this scene "in the house of
Romelio;" but compare act ii. sc. 3, where Leonora says,
"Why do they ring
Before *my gate* thus?")

Should I not send it packing to the East Indies,
We should have a glut on't.

Enter Servant.

Serv. Here's the great lord Contarino.

Pros. O, I know
His business; he's a suitor to your sister.

Rom. Yes, sir: but to you,
As my most trusted friend, I utter it,—
I will break the alliance.

Pros. You are ill advis'd, then:
There lives not a completer gentleman
In Italy, nor of a more ancient house.

Rom. What tell you me of gentry? 'tis naught
else
But a superstitious relic of time past:
And sift it to the true worth, it is nothing
But ancient riches; and in him, you know,
They are pitifully in the wane. He makes his
colour
Of visiting us so often, to sell land,
And thinks, if he can gain my sister's love,
To recover the treble value.

Pros. Sure, he loves her
Entirely, and she deserves it.

Rom. Faith, though she were
Crook'd-shoulder'd, having such a portion,
She would have noble suitors: but truth is,
I would wish my noble venturer take heed;
It may be, whiles he hopes to catch a gilt-head,
He may draw up a gudgeon.

Enter CONTARINO.

Pros. He's come. Sir, I will leave you.
[*Exeunt* PROSPERO *and* Servant.

Con. I sent you the evidence of the piece of
land

I motiou'd to you for the sale.

Rom. Yes.

Con. Has your counsel perus'd it?

Rom. Not yet, my lord. Do you intend to travel?

Con. No.

Rom. O, then you lose
That which makes man most absolute.

Con. Yet I have heard
Of divers that, in passing of the Alps,
Have but exchang'd their virtues at dear rate
For other vices.

Rom. O, my lord, lie not idle:
The chiefest action for a man of great spirit
Is, never to be out of action.* We should think
The soul was never put into the body,
Which has so many rare and curious pieces
Of mathematical motion, to stand still.
Virtue is ever sowing of her seeds;
In the trenches for the soldier; in the wakeful
    study
For the scholar; in the furrows of the sea
For men of our profession; of all which
Arise and spring up honour. Come, I know
You have some noble great design in hand,
That you levy so much money.

Con. Sir, I'll tell you:
The greatest part of it I mean to employ
In payment of my debts, and the remainder
Is like to bring me into greater bonds,
As I aim it.

Rom. How, sir?

Con. I intend it
For the charge of my wedding.

Rom. Are you to be married, my lord?

Con. Yes, sir; and I must now entreat your
    pardon,
That I have conceal'd from you a business
Wherein you had at first been call'd to counsel,
But that I thought it a less fault in friendship,
To engage myself thus far without your knowledge,
Than to do it against your will: another reason
Was, that I would not publish to the world,
Nor have it whisper'd scarce, what wealthy voyage
I went about, till I had got the mine
In mine own possession.

Rom. You are dark to me yet.

Con. I'll now remove the cloud. Sir, your
    sister and I
Are vow'd each other's, and there only wants
Her worthy mother's and your fair consents
To style it marriage: this is a way,
Not only to make a friendship, but confirm it
For our posterities. How do you look upon't?

Rom. Believe me, sir, as on the principal column
To advance our house: why, you bring honour
    with you,
Which is the soul of wealth. I shall be proud
To live to see my little nephews ride
O'the upper hand of their uncles; and the
    daughters
Be rank'd by heralds at solemnities
Before the mother; all this deriv'd
From your nobility. Do not blame me, sir,
If I be taken with't exceedingly;
For this same honour, with us citizens,
Is a thing we are mainly fond of, especially
When it comes without money, which is very
    seldom.
But as you do perceive my present temper,
Be sure I am yours,—[*aside*] fir'd with scorn and
    laughter
At your over-confident purpose,—and, no doubt,
My mother will be of your mind.

Con. 'Tis my hope, sir.   [*Exit* ROMELIO.
I do observe how this Romelio
Has very worthy parts, were they not blasted
By insolent vain-glory. There rests now
The mother's approbation to the match;
Who is a woman of that state and bearing,
Though she be city-born, both in her language
Her garments, and her table, she excels
Our ladies of the court: she goes not gaudy,
Yet have I seen her wear one diamond
Would have bought twenty gay ones out of their
    clothes,
And some of them, without the greater grace,
Out of their honesties. She comes: I will try
How she stands affected to me, without relating
My contract with her daughter.

Enter LEONORA.

Leon. Sir, you are nobly welcome, and presume
You are in a place that's wholly dedicated
To your service.

Con. I am ever bound to you
For many special favours.

Leon. Sir, your fame renders you
Most worthy of it.

Con. It could never have got

---

* *The chiefest action for a man of great spirit
Is, never to be out of action*] Mr. Collier (*Preface* to
Coleridge's Seven Lectures, &c., p. XCVI) maintains that
here the right reading is "The chiefest *axiom*," &c.,—
which I think very doubtful, considering how our old
dramatists (even Shakespeare himself) affect the repetition of words.

A sweeter air to fly in than your breath.*

Leon. You have been strange a long time; you
    are weary
Of our unseasonable time of feeding:
Indeed, the Exchange-bell makes us dine so late,
I think the ladies of the court from us
Learn to lie so long a-bed.

    Con. They have a kind of Exchange among them
    too :
Marry, unless it be to hear of news, I take it,
Their's is, like the New Burse,† thinly furnish'd
With tires and new fashions. I have a suit to you.

    Leon. I would not have you value it the loss,
If I say, 'tis granted already.

    Con. You are all bounty :
'Tis to bestow your picture on me.

    Leon. O, sir,
Shadows are coveted in summer, and with me
'Tis fall o'the leaf.

    Con. You enjoy the best of time :
This latter spring of yours shows in my eye
More fruitful, and more temperate withal,
Than that whose date is only limited
By the music of the cuckoo.

    Leon. Indeed, sir, I dare tell you,
My looking-glass is a true one, and as yet
It does not terrify me. Must you have my picture?

    Con. So please you, lady; and I shall preserve it
As a most choice object.

    Leon. You will enjoin me to a strange punish-
    ment.
With what a compell'd face a woman sits
While she is drawing! I have noted divers,
Either to feign smiles, or suck in the lips
To have a little mouth; ruffle the cheeks
To have the dimple seen; and so disorder
The face with affectation, at next sitting
It has not been the same: I have known others
Have lost the entire fashion of their face
In half an hour's sitting.

    Con. How!

Leon. In hot weather
The painting on their face has been so mellow,
They have left the poor man harder work by half,
To mend the copy he wrought by. But, indeed,
If ever I would have mine drawn to the life,
I would have a painter steal it at such a time
I were devoutly kneeling at my prayers :
There is then a heavenly beauty in't, the soul
Moves in the superficies.

    Con. Excellent lady,
Now you teach beauty a preservative
More than 'gainst fading colours, and your
    judgment
Is perfect in all things.

    Leon. Indeed, sir, I am a widow,
And want the addition to make it so;
For man's experience has still been held
Woman's best eyesight. I pray, sir, tell me :—
You are about to sell a piece of land
To my son, I hear.

    Con. 'Tis truth.

    Leon. Now I could rather wish
That noblemen would ever live i'the country,
Rather than make their visits up to the city
About such business. O, sir, noble houses
Have no such goodly prospects any way
As into their own land : the decay of that,
Next to their begging church-land, is a ruin
Worth all men's pity. Sir, I have forty thousand
    crowns
Sleep in my chest shall waken when you please,
And fly to your commands. Will you stay
    supper?

    Con. I cannot, worthy lady.

    Leon. I would not have you come hither, sir,
    to sell,
But to settle your estate. I hope you understand
Wherefore I make this proffer: so, I leave you.
                       [*Exit.*

    Con. [On] what a treasury have I perch'd! "I
    hope
You understand wherefore I make this proffer!"
She has got some intelligence how I intend to
    marry
Her daughter, and ingenuously* perceiv'd
That by her picture, which I begg'd of her,
I meant the fair Jolenta. Here's a letter
Which gives express charge not to visit her
Till midnight.   [*Reads.*
"*Fail not to come, for 'tis a business that concerns
both our honours.*
        Yours, in danger to be lost, Jolenta."

---

  * It could never have got
    A sweeter air to fly in than your breath] So again our
author in his *Monumental Column*, &c. ;
" Never found prayers, since they convers'd with death,
A sweeter air to fly in than his breath."
And so too Massinger;
          "My own praises *flying*
In such pure air as your sweet breath, fair lady,
Cannot but please me."
             The Picture, act v. sc. last.
  † *the New Burse*] I. e. the New Exchange in the Strand,
where were shops in which female finery and trinkets of
every description were sold. Our old dramatists do not
scruple to attribute to a foreign country the peculiarities
of their own.

  * *ingenuously*] See note †, p. 26.

'Tis a strange injunction: what should be the
   business?
She is not chang'd, I hope: I'll thither straight;
For women's resolutions in such deeds,
Like bees, light oft ou flowers, and oft on weeds.
                                        [*Exit.*

SCENE II.*

Enter ERCOLE, ROMELIO, *and* JOLENTA.

Rom. O, sister, come, the tailor must to work,
To make your wedding-clothes.
   Jol. The tomb-maker,
To take measure of my coffin.
   Rom. Tomb-maker!
Look you, the King of Spain greets you.
   Jol. What does this mean?
Do you serve process on me?
   Rom. Process! come,
You would be witty now.
   Jol. Why, what's this, I pray?
   Rom. Infinite grace to you: it is a letter
From his catholic majesty for the commends
Of this gentleman for your husband.
   Jol. In good season:
I hope he will not have my allegiance stretch'd
To the undoing of myself.
   Rom. Undo yourself! he does proclaim him
   here—
   Jol. Not for a traitor, does he?
   Rom. You are not mad:—
For one of the noblest gentlemen.
   Jol. Yet kings many times
Know merely but men's out-sides. Was this
   commendation
Voluntary, think you?
   Rom. Voluntary! what mean you by that?
   Jol. Why, I do not think but he begg'd it of
   the king,
And it may fortune to be out of's way:
Some better suit, that would have stood his lord-
   ship
In far more stead. Letters of commendations!
Why, 'tis reported that they are grown stale
When places fall i'the University.
I pray you, return his pass; for to a widow
That longs to be a courtier this paper
May do knight's service.
   Erco. Mistake not, excellent mistress: these
   commends
Express, his majesty of Spain has given me
Both addition of honour, as you may perceive

* *Scene II.*] Another room in the same.

By my habit, and a place here to command
O'er thirty galleys: this your brother shows,
As wishing that you would be partner
In my good fortune.
   Rom. I pray, come hither:
Have I any interest in you?
   Jol. You are my brother.
   Rom. I would have you, then, use me with that
   respect
You may still keep me so, and to be sway'd
In this main business of life, which wants
Greatest consideration, your marriage,
By my direction: here's a gentleman——
   Jol. Sir, I have often told you,
I am so little my own to dispose that way,
That I can never be his.
   Rom. Come, too much light
Makes you moon-ey'd: are you in love with
   title?
I will have a herald, whose continual practice
Is all in pedigree, come a wooing to you,
Or an antiquary in old buskins.
   Erco. Sir, you have done me
The mainest wrong that e'er was offer'd to
A gentleman of my breeding.
   Rom. Why, sir?
   Erco. You have led me
With a vain confidence that I should marry
Your sister; have proclaim'd it to my friends;
Employ'd the greatest lawyers of our state
To settle her a jointure; and the issue
Is, that I must become ridiculous
Both to my friends and enemies: I will leave you,
Till I call to you for a strict account
Of your unmanly dealing.
   Rom. Stay, my lord.—
Do you long to have my throat cut?—Good my
   lord,
Stay but a little, till I have remov'd
This court-mist from her eyes, till I wake her
From this dull sleep, wherein she'll dream herself
To a deformed beggar.—You would marry
The great lord Contarino—

Enter LEONORA.

   Leon. Contarino!
Were you talking of? he lost last night at dice
Five thousand ducats; and when that was gone,
Set at one throw a lordship that twice trebled
The former loss.
   Rom. And that flew after.
   Leon. And most carefully
Carried the gentleman in his caroche

To a lawyer's chamber, there most legally
To put him in possession : was this wisdom?

Rom. O, yes, their credit in the way of gaming
Is the main thing they stand on ; that must be paid,
Though the brewer bawl for's money: and this
    lord
Does she prefer, i'the way of marriage,
Before our choice here, noble Ercole.

Leon. You'll be advis'd, I hope. Know for
    your sakes
I married, that I might have children ;
And for your sakes, if you'll be rul'd by me,
I will never marry again. Here's a gentleman
Is noble, rich, well featur'd, but 'bove all,
He loves you entirely : his intents are aim'd
For an expedition 'gainst the Turk,
Which makes the contract cannot be delay'd.

Jol. Contract! you must do this without my
    knowledge!
Give me some potion to make me mad,
And happily not knowing what I speak,
I may then consent to't.

Rom. Come, you are mad already ;
And I shall never hear you speak good sense
Till you name him for husband.

Erco. Lady, I will do
A manly office for you ; I will leave you
To the freedom of your own soul: may it move
    whither
Heaven and you please!

Jol. Now you express yourself
Most nobly.

Rom. Stay, sir ; what do you mean to do?

Leon. Hear me: [*kneels*] if thou dost marry
    Contarino,
All the misfortune that did ever dwell
In a parent's curse light on thee !

Erco. O, rise, lady : certainly heaven never
Intended kneeling to this fearful purpose.

Jol. Your imprecation has undone me for ever.

Erco. Give me your hand.

Jol. No, sir.

Rom. Give't me, then.
O, what rare workmanship have I seen this
To finish with your needle ! what excellent music
Have these struck upon the viol ! Now I'll teach
A piece of art.

Jol. Rather, a damnable cunning,
To have me go about to give't away
Without consent of my soul.

Rom. Kiss her, my lord :
If crying had been regarded, maidenheads
Had ne'er been lost ; at least some appearance
Of crying, as an April shower i'the sunshine.

Leon. She is yours.

Rom. Nay, continue your station, and deal you
In dumb show : kiss this doggedness out of her.

Leon. To be contracted in tears is but fashion-
    able.

Rom. Yet suppose that they were hearty,—

Leon. Virgins must seem unwilling.

Rom. O, what else?
And you remember, we observe the like
In greater ceremonies than these contracts ;
At the consecration of prelates they use ever
Twice to say nay, and take it.

Jol. O brother !

Rom. Keep your possession, you have the door
    by the ring ;
That's livery and seisin in England :* but, my lord,
Kiss that tear from her lip ; you'll find the rose
The sweeter for the dew.

Jol. Bitter as gall.

Rom. Ay, ay, all you women,
Although you be of never so low stature,
Have gall in you most abundant ; it exceeds
Your brains by two ounces. I was saying some-
    what :—
O, do but observe i'the city, and you'll find
The thriftiest bargains that were ever made,
What a deal of wrangling ere they could be
    brought
To an upshot !

Leon. Great persons do not overcome together—

Rom. With revelling faces ; nor is it necessary
They should : the strangeness and unwillingness
Wears the greater state, and gives occasion that
The people may buzz and talk oft, though the
    bells
Be tongue-tied at the wedding.

Leon. And truly I have heard say,
To be a little strange to one another
Will keep your longing fresh.

Rom. Ay, and make you beget
More children when you're married: some doctors
Are of that opinion. You see, my lord, we are
    merry
At the contract : your sport is to come hereafter.

Erco. I will leave you, excellent lady, and
    withal
Leave a heart with you so entirely yours,
That, I protest, had I the least of hope

---

  *   you have the door by the ring ;*
  That's livery and seisin in England] The allusion here
is to a ceremony used in the common law, on conveyance
of lands, houses, &c. when the ring or latch of the door
is delivered to the feoffee : *livery* and *seisin* are delivery
and possession.

To enjoy you, though I were to wait the time
That scholars do in taking their degree
In the noble arts, 'twere nothing: howsoe'er,
He parts from you that will depart from life
To do you any service; and so, humbly
I take my leave.

　Jol. Sir, I will pray for you. 　[*Exit* ERCOLE.
　Rom. Why, that's well; 'twill make your
　　　prayer complete,
To pray for your husband.
　Jol. Husband!
　Leon. This is
The happiest hour that I ever arriv'd at. [*Exit.*
　Rom. Husband! ay, husband: come, you
　　peevish thing,
Smile me a thank for the pains I have ta'en.
　Jol. I hate myself for being thus euforc'd:
You may soon judge, then, what I think of you
Which are the cause of it.

　　　Enter WINIFRED, *passing over.*

　Rom. You, lady of the laundry, come hither.
　Win. Sir?
　Rom. Look,* as you love your life, you have an
　　eye
Upon your mistress: I do henceforth bar her
All visitants. I do hear there are bawds abroad
That bring cut-works† and mantoons,‡ and
　convey letters
To such young gentlewomen; and there are others
That deal in corn-cutting and fortune-telling:
Let none of these come at her, on your life;
Nor Deuce-ace, the wafer-woman, that prigs abroad
With musk-melons and malakatoons;§ nor

---

* *Look, as you love your life, you have an eye*
　Upon your mistress, &c.] Here Webster recollected
Ben Jonson:
　　"Be you sure, now,
You have all your eyes about you; and let in
No lace-woman, nor bawd, *that brings* French masks
And *cut-works;* see you? nor *old crones with wafers,*
To convey letters: nor no youths, disguis'd
Like country-wives, with cream and *marrow-puddings.*
Much knavery may be vented in a pudding,
Much bawdy intelligence: they are shrewd cyphers."
　　　　　　　The Devil is an ass, act ii. sc. 1.
† *cut-works*] See note ‡, p. 6.
‡ *mantoons*] Qy. if from "*mantone,* a great robe or
mantle"? Florio's *Ital. Dict.* ed. 1611.
§ *malakatoons*] The malakatoon, melicotton, male-
cotoon, malecotone, or maligatoon, (for so variously do
old writers spell the word,) was a sort of late peach.
Gerard in his *Herball,* enumerating different kinds of
peaches, mentions "the Blacke Peach; the *Melocotone;*
the White," &c. p. 1446. ed. 1633.
　"Pine are much after the Figure of a Scoth [Scotch?]
Thistle, and in my minde taste most like a Peach, or
Maligatoon." Note on a poem (p. 10) entitled *A Description of the Last Voyage to Bermudas, in the Ship Mary
Gold,* by J. H. [ardy]. 1671, 4to.

The Scotchwoman with the cittern, do you mark;
Nor a dancer by any means, though he ride on's
　foot-cloth; *
Nor a hackney-coachman, if he can speak French.
　Win. Why, sir,—
　Rom. By no means; no more words:—
Nor the woman with marrow-bone-puddings: I
　have heard
Strange juggling tricks have been convey'd to a
　woman
In a pudding: you are apprehensive?
　Win. O good sir, I have travell'd.
　Rom. When you had a bastard, you travell'd†
　　indeed:
But, my precious chaperoness,
I trust thee the better for that; for I have heard,
There is no warier keeper of a park,
To prevent stalkers or your night-walkers,
Than such a man as in his youth has been
A most notorious deer-stealer.
　Win. Very well, sir,
You may use me at your pleasure.
　Rom. By no means, Winifred; that were the way
To make thee travel again. Come, be not angry,
I do but jest; thou know'st, wit and a woman
Are two very frail things; and so, I leave you.
　　　　　　　　　　　　　　　　[*Exit.*
　Win. I could weep with you; but 'tis no matter,
I can do that at any time; I have now
A greater mind to rail a little: plague of these
Unsanctified matches! they make us loathe
The most natural desire our grandam Eve ever
　left us.
Force one to marry against their will! why, 'tis
A more ungodly work than enclosing the commons.
　Jol. Prithee, peace:
This is indeed an argument so common,
I cannot think of matter new enough
To express it bad enough.
　Win. Here's one, I hope,
Will put you out of 't.

　　　Enter CONTARINO.

　Con. How now, sweet mistress!
You have made sorrow look lovely of late;
You have wept.
　Win. She has done nothing else these three
days: had you stood behind the arras, to have
heard her shed so much salt water as I have
done, you would have thought she had been
turned fountain.

---

* *foot-cloth*] See note *, p. 7.
† *travell'd*] Here, in the first edition of this collection,
I printed "*travail'd*": but the pun is plain enough with
the old spelling.

Con. I would fain know the cause can be
  worthy
This thy sorrow.
Jol. [*to* WIN.] Reach me the caskanet.*—I am
  studying, sir,
To take an inventory of all that's mine.
  Con. What to do with it, lady?
  Jol. To make you a deed of gift.
  Con. That's done already; you are all mine.
  Win. Yes, but the devil would fain put in for's
    share,
In likeness of a separation.
  Jol. O, sir, I am bewitch'd.
  Con. Ha!
  Jol. Most certain; I am forospoken †
To be married to another: can you ever think
That I shall ever thrive in't? am I not, then,
  bewitch'd?
All comfort I can teach myself is this,—
There is a time left for me to die nobly,
When I cannot live so.
  Con. Give me, in a word, to whom, or by whose
    means,
Are you thus torn from me?
  Jol. By Lord Ercole, my mother, and my ‡
    brother.
  Con. I'll make his bravery § fitter for a
    grave
Than for a wedding.
  Jol. So you will beget
A far more dangerous and strange disease
Out of the cure: you must love him again
For my sake; for the noble Ercole
Had such a true compassion of my sorrow,—
Hark in your ear, I'll show you his right
  worthy
Demeanour to me.
  Win. O you pretty ones!
I have seen this lord many a time and oft
Set her in's lap, and talk to her of love·
So feelingly, I do protest it has made me
Run out of myself to think on't.

O sweet-breath'd monkeys,* how they grow
  together!
Well, 'tis my opinion,
He was no woman's friend that did invent
A punishment for kissing.
  Con. If he bear himself so nobly,
The manliest office I can do for him
Is to afford him my pity, since he's like
To fail of so dear a purchase: for your mother,
Your goodness quits her ill: for your brother,
He that vows friendship to a man, and proves
A traitor, deserves rather to be hang'd
Than he that counterfeits money; yet for your sake
I must sign his pardon too. Why do you tremble?
Be safe, you are now free from him.
  Jol. O, but, sir,
The intermission from a fit of an ague
Is grievous; for, indeed, it doth prepare us
To entertain torment next morning.
  Con. Why, he's gone to sea.
  Jol. But he may return too soon.
  Con. To avoid which, we will instantly be
    married.
  Win. To avoid which, get you instantly to bed
    together;
Do; and I think no civil lawyer for his fee
Can give you better counsel.
  Jol. Fie upon thee! prithee, leave us.
  Con. Be of comfort, sweet mistress.
  Jol. On one condition, we may have no quarrel
About this.
  Con. Upon my life, none.
  Jol. None, upon your honour?
  Con. With whom? with Ercole? †
You have delivered him guiltless.
With your brother? he's part of yourself.
With your complimental mother?
I use not fight with women.
To-morrow we'll be married:
Let those that would oppose this union
Grow ne'er so subtle, and entangle themselves
In their own work like spiders; while we two
Haste to our noble wishes, and presume,
The hindrance of it will breed more delight,
As black copartiments show ‡ gold more bright.
                                          [*Exeunt.*

---

* *caskanet*] A word not found in dictionaries. I meet
with it in a formidable list of articles necessary for a
lady's toilette in *Lingua*; "such stirre with Stickes and
Combes, *Caseanets*, Drossings, Purles, Falles, Squares,
Buskes, Bodies, Scarffes, Neck-laces, Carcanets," &c.
Sig. I. 2, ed. 1607.
† *forospoken*] Used here with a quibble,—one of its
meanings being "bewitched."
‡ *my*] The old copy "*by.*"
§ *bravery*] i. e. finery.

* *monkeys*] The old copy "monkey."
† *With whom? with Ercole?* &c.] I let the first six lines
of this speech stand as they do in the old copy:—they
seem to defy any tolerable metrical arrangement.
‡ *copartiments show*] The old copy "*copartaments
shewes.*"

I

ACT II.

SCENE I.*

Enter CRISPIANO *and* SANITONELLA.

Cris. Am I well habited?

San. Exceeding well; any man would take you
for a merchant. But, pray, sir, resolve me, what
should be the reason that you, being one of the
most eminent civil lawyers in Spain, and but
newly arrived from the East Indies, should take
this habit of a merchant upon you?

Cris. Why, my son lives here in Naples, and in's
riot doth far exceed the exhibition† I allowed him.

San. So, then, and in this disguise you mean
to trace him?

Cris. Partly for that; but there is other business
Of greater consequence.

San. Faith, for his expense, 'tis nothing to your
estate: what, to Don Crispiano, the famous corre-
gidor of Seville, who by his mere practice of the
law, in less time than half a jubilee, hath gotten
thirty thousand ducats a-year!

Cris. Well, I will give him line,
Let him run on in's course of spending.

San. Freely?

Cris. Freely:
For I protest, if that I could conceive
My son would take more pleasure or content,
By any course of riot, in the expense,
Than I took joy, nay, soul's felicity,
In the getting of it, should all the wealth I have
Waste to as small an atomy as flies
I'the sun, I do protest on that condition
It should not move me.

San. How's this? Cannot he take more pleasure
in spending it riotously than you have done by
scraping it together? O, ten thousand times more!
and I make no question, five hundred young
gallants will be of my opinion.
Why, all the time of your collectionship
Has been a perpetual calendar: begin first
With your melancholy study of the law
Before you came‡ to finger the ruddocks; after
that,
The tiring importunity of clients,
To rise so early, and sit up so late;

You made yourself half ready in a dream,*
And never pray'd but in your sleep. Can I think
That you have half your lungs left with crying out
For judgments and days of trial? Remember, sir,
How often have I borne you on my shoulder,
Among a shoal or swarm of reeking night-caps,†
When that your worship has bepiss'd yourself,
Either with vehemency of argument,
Or being out from the matter. I am merry.

Cris. Be so.

San. You could eat like a gentleman, at leisure;
But swallow['d] it like flap-dragons,‡ as if you had
liv'd
With chewing the cud after.

Cris. No pleasure in the world was comparable
to't.

San. Possible?

Cris. He shall never taste the like,
Unless he study law.

San. What, not in wenching, sir?
'Tis a court-game, believe it, as familiar
As gleek § or any other.

Cris. Wenching! O, fie! the disease follows it:
Beside, can the fingering taffetas or lawns,
Or a painted hand or a breast, be like the pleasure
In taking clients' fees, and piling them
In several goodly rows before my desk?
And according to the bigness of each heap,
Which I took by a leer (for lawyers do not tell
them),
I vail'd‖ my cap, and withal gave great hope
The cause should go on their sides.

San. What think you, then,
Of a good cry of hounds? it has been known
Dogs have hunted lordships to a fault.

---

* *Scene I.*] An apartment in some house of public
resort,—on the Quay or on the Exchange, perhaps.
† *exhibition*] i. e. pension, allowance
‡ *came*] The old copy "come."

* *You made yourself half ready in a dream*] To make
ones-self *ready* is the old expression for *dressing* ones-self.
† *night-caps*] See note ‡, p. 66.
‡ *flap-dragons*] Raisins, plums, *candles' ends!* &c made
to float in a dish of ardent spirits, from which, when set
on fire, they were to be snatched by the mouth and
swallowed. The amorous youths of olden time delighted
in drinking off flap-dragons to the health of their mistresses. This nasty sport, still common in Holland, I
have seen practised in our own country by boys during
Christmas holidays.
§ *gleek*] A fashionable game at cards in our author's
time. Full instructions how to play at "this noble and
delightful Game or Recreation" may be found in *The
Compleat Gamester*, p. 67, et seq. ed. 1709.
‖ *vail'd*] i. e. lowered.

Cris. Cry of curs!
The noise of clients at my chamber-door
Was sweeter music far, in my conceit,
Than all the hunting in Europe.
San. Pray, stay, sir:
Say he should spend it in good house-keeping.
Cris. Ay, marry, sir, to have him keep a good
house,
And not sell't away, I'd find no fault with that:
But his kitchen I'd have no bigger than a saw-pit;
For the smallness of a kitchen, without question,
Makes many noblemen in France and Spain
Build the rest of the house the bigger.
San. Yes, mock-beggars.
Cris. Some sevenscore chimneys,
But half of them have no tunnels.
San. A pox upon them, kickshaws, that beget
Such monsters without fundaments!
Cris. Come, come, leave citing other vanities;
For neither wine, nor lust, nor riotous feasts,
Rich clothes, nor all the pleasure that the devil
Has ever practis'd with to raise a man
To a devil's likeness, e'er brought man that
pleasure
I took in getting my wealth: so I conclude,
If he can out-vie me, let it fly to the devil.—
Yon's my son: what company keeps he?

Enter ROMELIO, JULIO, ARIOSTO, *and* BAPTISTA.

San. The gentleman he talks with is Romelio,
The merchant.
Cris. I never saw him till now:
'A has a brave sprightly look. I knew his father,
And sojourn'd in his house two years together
Before this young man's birth. I have news to
tell him
Of certain losses happen'd him at sea,
That will not please him.
San. What's* that dapper fellow
In the long stocking? I do think 'twas he
Came to your lodging this morning.
Cris. 'Tis the same:
There he stands but a little piece of flesh,
But he is the very miracle of a lawyer;
One that persuades men to peace, and compounds
quarrels
Among his neighbours, without going to law.
San. And is he a lawyer?
Cris. Yes, and will give counsel
In honest causes gratis; never in his life
Took fee but he came and spake for't; is a man
Of extreme practice; and yet all his longing
Is to become a judge.

* *What's*] The old copy "What."

San. Indeed, that's a rare longing with men of
his profession. I think he'll prove the miracle of
a lawyer indeed.
Rom. Here's the man brought word your father
died i'the Indies.
Jul. He died in perfect memory, I hope,
And made me his heir.
Cris. Yes, sir.
Jul. He's gone the right way, then, without
question. Friend, in time of mourning we must
not use any action that is but accessary to the
making men merry: I do therefore give you
nothing for your good tidings.
Cris. Nor do I look for it, sir.
Jul. Honest fellow, give me thy hand: I do
not think but thou hast carried new-year's-gifts
to the court in thy days, and learned'st there to
be so free of thy pains-taking.
Rom. Here's an old gentleman says he was
chamber-fellow to your father, when they studied
the law together at Barcelona.
Jul. Do you know him?
Rom. Not I; he's newly come to Naples.
Jul. And what's his business?
Rom. 'A says he's come to read you good counsel.
Cris. [*aside to* ARI.] To him, rate him soundly.
Jul. And what's your counsel?
Ari. Why, I would have you leave
Your whoring.
Jul. He comes hotly upon me at first.—
Whoring!
Ari. O young quat,* incontinence is plagu'd
In all the creatures of the world!
Jul. When did you ever hear that a cock-
sparrow
Had the French pox?
Ari. When did you ever know any of them fat
but in the nest? ask all your cantharide-mongers
that question: remember yourself, sir.
Jul. A very fine naturalist! a physician, I take
you, by your round slop,† for 'tis just of the
bigness, and no more, of the case for a urinal:
'tis concluded you are a physician. What do
you mean, sir? you'll take cold.
Ari. 'Tis concluded you are a fool, a precious
one: you are a mere stick of sugar-candy;‡ a
man may look quite thorough you.
Jul. You are a very bold gamester.

* *O young quat*] *Quat* means originally a pimple—
Compare Shakespeare;
"I have rubb'd this *young quat* almost to the sense."
Othello, Act V. Sc. I.
† *slop*] i. e. breeches (properly, large wide ones)
‡ *you are a mere stick of sugar-candy*, &c.] See note*,
p. 74.

I 2

Ari. I can play at chess, and know how to handle a rook.

Jul. Pray, preserve your velvet from the dust.

Ari. Keep your hat upon the block, sir; 'twill continue fashion the longer.

Jul. I was never so abus'd with the hat in the hand
In my life.

Ari. I will put on. Why, look you,
Those lands that were the client's are now become
The lawyer's; and those tenements that were
The country gentleman's are now grown
To be his tailor's.

Jul. Tailor's!

Ari. Yes, tailors in France, they grow to great abominable purchase,* and become great officers.
—How many ducats think you he has spent within a twelvemonth, besides his father's allowance?

Jul. Besides my father's allowance! Why, gentleman, do you think an auditor begat me? Would you have me make even at year's end?

Rom. A hundred ducats a month in breaking Venice glasses.

Ari. He learnt that of an English drunkard, and a knight too, as I take it.—This comes of your numerous wardrobe.

Rom. Ay, and wearing cut-work,† a pound a purl.

Ari. Your dainty embroidered stockings, with overblown roses,‡ to hide your gouty ankles.

Rom. And wearing more taffeta for a garter than would serve the galley dung-boat for streamers.

Ari. Your switching up at the horse-race, with the illustrissimi.

Rom. And studying a puzzling arithmetic at the cock-pit.

Ari. Shaking your elbow at the table-board.§

Rom. And resorting to your whore in hired velvet, with a spangled copper fringe at her Netherlands.

Ari. Whereas, if you had stayed at Padua, and fed upon cow-trotters and fresh beef to supper,—

Jul. How I am baited!

Ari. Nay, be not you so forward with him neither, for 'tis thought you'll prove a main part of his undoing.

---

* *purchase*] See note †, p. 74.
† *cut-work*] See note †, p. 6.
‡ *roses*] See note *, p. 41.
§ *table-board*] The old copy "*Taule-board.*"—Tables (Lat. *Tabularum lusus*, Fr. *Tables*,) is the old name for backgammon: but other games were played with the same board. On the back of the title-page of the old play of *Arden of Feversham*, ed. 1633, is a representation of a table-board.

Jul. I think this fellow is a witch.

Rom. Who I, sir?

Ari. You have certain rich city chuffs, that when they have no acres of their own, they will go and plough up fools, and turn them into excellent meadow; besides some enclosures for the first cherries in the spring, and apricocks, to pleasure a friend at court with. You have pothecaries deal in selling commodities* to young gallants, will put four or five coxcombs into a sieve, and so drum with them upon their counter, they'll searce them through like Guinea pepper: they cannot endure to find a man like a pair of terriers, they would undo him in a trice.

Rom. May be there are such.

Ari. O, terrible exactors, fellows with six hands and three heads!

Jul. Ay, those are hell-hounds.

Ari. Take heed of them; they'll rent thee like tenterhooks. Hark in your ear; there is intelligence upon you: the report goes, there has been gold conveyed beyond the sea in hollow anchors. Farewell; you shall know me better; I will do thee more good than thou art aware of.   [*Exit.*

Jul. He's a mad fellow.

San. He would have made an excellent barber, he does so curry it with his tongue.   [*Exit.*

Cris. Sir, I was directed to you.

Rom. From whence?

Cris. From the East Indies.

Rom. You are very welcome.

Cris. Please you walk apart,
I shall acquaint you with particulars
Touching your trading i'the East Indies.

Rom. Willingly: pray, walk, sir.
    [*Exeunt* CRISPIANO *and* ROMELIO.

Enter ERCOLE.

Erc. O my right worthy friends, you have stay'd me long:
One health, and then aboard; for all the galleys
Are come about.

Enter CONTARINO.

Con. Signior Ercole,
The wind has stood my friend, sir, to prevent
Your putting to sea.

Erc. Pray, why, sir!

Con. Only love, sir,
That I might take my leave, sir, and withal
Entreat from you a private recommends
To a friend in Malta: it would be deliver'd
To your bosom, for I had no time to write.

---

* *commodities*] See note †, p. 27.

Erc. Pray, leave us, gentlemen.

[*Exeunt* JULIO *and* BAPTISTA.

Wilt please you sit? [*They sit down.*

Con. Sir, my love to you has proclaim'd you
one
Whose word was still led by a noble thought,
And that thought follow'd by as fair a deed.
Deceive not that opinion: we were students
At Padua together, and have long
To the world's eye shown like friends: was it
hearty
On your part to me?

Erc. Unfeign'd.

Con. You are false
To the good thought I held of you, and now
Join the worst part of man to you, your malice,
To uphold that falsehood: sacred innocence
Is fled your bosom. Signior, I must tell you,
To draw the picture of unkindness truly,
Is to express two that have dearly lov'd,
And fall'n at variance. 'Tis a wonder to me,
Knowing my interest in the fair Jolenta,
That you should love her.

Erc. Compare her beauty and my youth together,
And you will find the fair effects of love
No miracle at all.

Con. Yes, it will prove
Prodigious to you: I must stay your voyage.

Erc. Your warrant must be mighty.

Con. 'T has a seal
From heaven to do it, since you would ravish
from me
What's there entitled mine: and yet I vow,
By the essential front of spotless virtue,
I have compassion of both our youths;
To approve which, I have not ta'en the way,
Like an Italian, to cut your throat
By practice,* that had given you now for dead,
And never frown'd upon you.

Erc. You deal fair, sir.

Con. Quit me of one doubt, pray, sir.

Erc. Move it.

Con. 'Tis this;
Whether her brother were a main instrument
In her design for marriage.

Erc. If I tell truth,
You will not credit me.

Con. Why?

Erc. I will tell you truth,
Yet show some reason you have not to believe me.
Her brother had no hand in't: is't not hard
For you to credit this? for you may think,

I count it baseness to engage another
Into my quarrel; and for that take leave
To dissemble the truth. Sir, if you will fight
With any but myself, fight with her mother;
She was the motive.

Con. I have no enemy in the world, then, but
yourself:
You must fight with me.

Erc. I will, sir.

Con. And instantly.

Erc. I will haste before you: point whither.

Con. Why, you speak nobly; and for this fair
dealing,
Were the rich jewel which we vary for
A thing to be divided, by my life,
I would be well content to give you half:
But since 'tis vain to think we can be friends,
'Tis needful one of us be ta'en away
From being the other's enemy.

Erc. Yet, methinks,
This looks not like a quarrel.

Con. Not a quarrel!

Erc. You have not apparelled your fury well;
It goes too plain, like a scholar.

Con. It is an ornament
Makes it more terrible, and you shall find it
A weighty injury, and attended on
By discreet valour: because I do not strike you,
Or give you the lie,—such foul preparatives
Would show like the stale injury of wine,—
I reserve my rage to sit on my sword's point,
Which a great quantity of your best blood
Cannot satisfy.

Erc. You promise well to yourself.
Shall's have no seconds?

Con. None, for fear of prevention.

Erc. The length of our weapons?

Con. We'll fit them by the way:
So whether our time calls us to live or die,
Let us do both like noble gentlemen
And true Italians.

Erc. For that let me embrace you.

Con. Methinks, being an Italian, I trust you
To come somewhat too near me:
But your jealousy gave that embrace to try
If I were arm'd, did it not?

Erc. No, believe me,
I take your heart to be sufficient proof,
Without a privy coat; and, for my part,
A taffeta is all the shirt of mail
I am arm'd with.

Con. You deal equally.* · [*Exeunt.*

---

* *practice*] i. e. artifice, treachery.

* Mr. Lamb calls this scene between Contarino and

Re-enter JULIO, *with a Servant.*

Jul. Where are these gallants, the brave Ercole
And noble Contarino?

Ser. They are newly gone, sir,
And bade me tell you that they will return
Within this half hour.

Re-enter ROMELIO.

Jul. Met you the Lord Ercole?

Rom. No, but I met the devil in villanous
tidings.

Jul. Why, what's the matter?

Rom. O, I am pour'd out
Like water! the greatest rivers i'the world
Are lost in the sea; and so am I: pray, leave me.
Where's Lord Ercole?

Jul. You were scarce gone hence,
But in came Contarino.

Rom. Contarino!

Jul. And entreated
Some private conference with Ercole;
And on the sudden they have given's the slip.

Rom. One mischief never comes alone: they
are gone
To fight.

Jul. To fight!

Rom. An you be gentlemen,
Do not talk, but make haste after them.

Jul. Let's take several ways, then;
And if 't be possible, for women's sakes,
For they are proper men, use our endeavours
That the prick do not spoil them.   [*Exeunt.*

SCENE II.[*]

Enter ERCOLE *and* CONTARINO

Con. You'll not forgo your interest in my
mistress?

Erc. My sword shall answer that: come, are
you ready?

Con. Before you fight, sir, think upon your
cause;
It is a wondrous foul one, and I wish
That all your exercise, these four days past,
Had been employ'd in a most fervent prayer,
And the foul sin for which you are to fight
Chiefly remember'd in't.

Erc. I'd as soon take
Your counsel in divinity at this present,
As I would take a kind direction from you

Ercole "the model of a well-managed and gentlemanlike
difference." *Spec. of Eng. Dram. Poets*, p. 199.

[*] *Scene II.*] A field near Naples.

For the managing my weapon; and, indeed,
Both would show much alike. Come, are you
ready?

Con. Bethink yourself
How fair the object is that we contend for.

Erc. O, I cannot forget it.   [*They fight.*

Con. You are hurt.

Erc. Did you come hither only to tell me so,
Or to do it? I mean well, but 'twill not thrive.

Con. Your cause, your cause, sir:
Will you yet be a man of conscience, and make
Restitution for your rage upon your death-bed?

Erc. Never, till the grave gather one of us.
                                [*They fight again.*

Con. That was fair, and home, I think.

Erc. You prate as if you were in a fence-school.

Con. Spare your youth, have compassion on
yourself.

Erc. When I am all in pieces! I am now unfit
For any lady's bed; take the rest with you.
        [CONTARINO, *wounded, falls upon* ERCOLE.

Con. I am lost in too much daring.—Yield
your sword.

Erc. To the pangs of death I shall, but not to
thee.

Con. You are now at my repairing or confusion:
Beg your life.

Erc. O, most foolishly demanded,—
To bid me beg that which thou canst not give!

Enter ROMELIO, PROSPERO, BAPTISTA, ARIOSTO, *and*
JULIO.

Pros. See, both of them are lost! we come too
late.

Rom. Take up the body, and convey it
To Saint Sebastian's monastery.

Con. I will not part with his sword, I have
won't.

Jul. You shall not.—
Take him up gently; so; and bow his body,
For fear of bleeding inward.
Well, these are perfect lovers.

Pros. Why, I pray?

Jul. It has been ever my opinion,
That there are none love perfectly indeed,
But those that hang or drown themselves for love:
Now these have chose a death next to beheading;
They have cut one another's throats, brave valiant
lads.

Pros. Come, you do ill, to set the name of
valour
Upon a violent and mad despair.
Hence may all learn, that count such actions well,
The roots of fury shoot themselves to hell.
                                        [*Exeunt.*

SCENE III.*

Enter ROMELIO *and* ARIOSTO.

Ario. Your losses, I confess, are infinite;
Yet, sir, you must have patience.

Rom. Sir, my losses
I know, but you I do not.

Ario. 'Tis most true
I am but a stranger to you; but am wish'd
By some of your best friends to visit you,
And, out of my experience in the world,
To instruct you patience.

Rom. Of what profession are you?

Ario. Sir, I am a lawyer.

Rom. Of all men living,
You lawyers I account the only men
To confirm patience in us: your delays
Would make three parts of this little Christian world
Run out of their wits else. Now I remember
You read lectures to Julio: are you such a leech
For patience?

Ario. Yes, sir, I have had some crosses.

Rom. You are married, then, I am certain.

Ario. That I am, sir.

Rom. And have you studied patience?

Ario. You shall find I have.

Rom. Did you ever see your wife make you cuckold?

Ario. Make me cuckold!

Rom. I ask it seriously: an you have not seen that,
Your patience has not ta'en the right degree
Of wearing scarlet; I should rather take you
For a bachelor in the art than for a doctor.

Ario. You are merry.

Rom. No, sir, with leave of your patience,
I am horrible angry.

Ario. What should move you
Put forth that harsh interrogatory, if these eyes
Ever saw my wife do the thing you wot of?

Rom. Why, I'll tell you,—
Most radically ▓▓▓▓ your patience;
And the mere ▓▓▓▓ shows you but a dunce in't,—
It has made you angry: there's another lawyer's beard
In your forehead; you do bristle.

Ario. You are very conceited.†

But, come, this is not the right way to cure you:
I must talk to you like a divine.

Rom. I have heard

Some talk of it very much, and many times
To their auditors' impatience: but, I pray,
What practice do they make of 't in their lives?
They are too full of choler with living honest,
And some of them not only impatient
Of their own slightest injuries, but stark mad
At one another's preferment. Now to you, sir:
I have lost three goodly caracks.*

Ario. So I hear.

Rom. The very spice in them,
Had they been shipwreck'd here upon our coast,
Would have made all our sea a drench.

Ario. All the sick horses in Italy
Would have been glad of your loss, then.

Rom. You are conceited too.

Ario. Come, come, come,
You gave those ships most strange, most dreadful,
And unfortunate names; I never look'd they'd prosper.

Rom. Is there any ill omen in giving names to ships?

Ario. Did you not call one *The storm's defiance*,
Another *The scourge of the sea*, and the third
The great leviathan?

Rom. Very right, sir.

Ario. Very devilish names
All three of them; and surely I think
They were curs'd in their very cradles,—I do mean,
When they were upon their stocks.

Rom. Come, you are superstitious:
I'll give you my opinion, and 'tis serious:
I am persuaded there came not cuckolds enow
To the first launching of them, and 'twas that made them
Thrive the worse for't. O, your cuckold's handsel
Is pray'd for i'the city!

Ario. I will hear no more.
Give me thy hand: my intent of coming hither
Was to persuade you to patience: as I live,
If ever I do visit you again,
It shall be to entreat you to be angry: sure, I will,
I'll be as good as my word, believe it.

Rom. So, sir. [*Exit* ARIOSTO.] How now!
Are the screech-owls abroad already?

Enter LEONORA.

Leon. What a dismal noise yon bell makes!
Sure, some great person's dead.

Rom. No such matter;
It is the common bell-man goes about
To publish the sale of goods.

Leon. Why do they ring

---

* *Scene III.*] The court of Leonora's house.
† *conceited*] i. e. disposed to jest, merry.

' *caracks*] i. e. large ships of burden.

Before my gate thus? Let them into the court:*
I cannot understand what they say.

Enter Two Bellmen and a Capuchin.

Cap. For pity's sake, you that have tears to shed,
Sigh a soft requiem, and let fall a bead
For two unfortunate nobles, whose sad fate
Leaves them both dead and excommunicate:
No churchman's prayer to comfort their last
    groans,
No sacred sod † of earth to hide their bones;
But as their fury wrought them out of breath,
The canon speaks them guilty of their own death.

Leon. What noblemen, I pray, sir?

Cap. The Lord Ercole
And the noble Contarino, both of them slain
In single combat.

Leon. O, I am lost for ever!

Rom. Denied Christian burial! I pray, what
    does that,
Or the dead lazy march in the funeral,
Or the flattery in the epitaphs, which shows
More sluttish far than all the spiders' webs
Shall ever grow upon it; what do these
Add to our well-being after death?

Cap. Not a scruple.

Rom. Very well, then:
I have a certain meditation,
If I can think of['t], somewhat to this purpose:
I'll say it to you, while my mother there
Numbers her beads.
    You that dwell near these graves and vaults,
Which oft do hide physicians' faults,
Note what a small room does suffice
To express men's good: their vanities
Would fill more volume in small hand
Than all the evidence of church-land.
Funerals hide men in civil wearing,
And are to the drapers a good hearing,
Make the heralds laugh in their black raiment,
And all die worthies die worth payment
To the altar offerings, though their fame,
And all the charity of their name,
'Tween heaven and this yield no more light
Than rotten trees which shine i'the night.
O, look the last act be the best i'the play,
And then rest, gentle bones: yet pray,
That when by the precise you are view'd,
A supersedeas be not su'd,
To remove you to a place more airy,

That, in your stead, they may keep chary
Stock-fish or sea-coal; for the abuses
Of sacrilege have turn'd graves to viler uses.
How, then, can any monument say,
Here rest these bones till the last day,
When Time, swift both of foot and feather,
May bear them the sexton kens not whither?
What care I, then,* though my last sleep
Be in the desert or in the deep,
No lamp nor taper, day and night,
To give my charnel chargeable light?
I have there like quantity of ground,
And at the last day I shall be found.—
Now, I pray, leave me.

Cap. I am sorry for your losses.

Rom. Um, sir, the more spacious that the
    tennis-court is,
The more large is the hazard.
I dare the spiteful Fortune do her worst;
I can now fear nothing.

Cap. O, sir, yet consider,
He that is without fear is without hope,
And sins from presumption: better thoughts
    attend you!   [*Exeunt* Capuchin *and* Bellmen.

Rom. Poor Jolenta! should she hear of this,
She would not, after the report, keep fresh
So long as flowers in graves.

Enter PROSPERO.

                    How now, Prospero!

Pros. Contarino has sent you here his will,
Wherein 'a has made your sister his sole heir.

Rom. Is he not dead?

Pros. He's yet living.

Rom. Living! the worse luck.

Leon. The worse! I do protest it is the best
That ever came to disturb my prayers.

Rom. How!

Leon. Yet I would have him live
To satisfy public justice for the death
Of Ercole. O, go visit him, for heaven's sake!
I have within my closet a choice relic,
Preservative 'gainst swooning, and some earth
Brought from the Holy Land, right sovereign
To stanch blood.—Has he skilful surgeons, think
    you?

Pros. The best in Naples.

Rom. How oft has he been dress'd?

Pros. But once.

---

* *Let them into the court*] Here we are to suppose that
the court-gate is opened either by Romelio or by an
attendant.

† *sod*] The old copy "seed."

* *What care I, then, &c.*] Compare the splendid conclusion of Sir Thomas Brown's *Urn-Burial;* "'Tis all'one to
lie in St. Innocent's Church-yard as in the sands of
Egypt; ready to be any thing in the ecstasie of being
ever; as content with six foot as the Moles of Adrianus."

Leon. I have some skill this way:
The second or third dressing will show clearly
Whether there be hope of life. I pray, be near him,
If there be any soul can bring me word,
That there is hope of life.
    Rom. Do you prize his life so?
    Leon. That he may live, I mean,
To come to his trial, to satisfy the law.
    Rom. O, is't nothing else?
    Leon. I shall be the happiest woman!
                [*Exeunt* LEONORA *and* PROSPERO.
    Rom. Here is cruelty apparell'd in kindness!
I am full of thoughts, strange ones, but they're no
    good ones.
I must visit Contarino; upon that
Depends an engine shall weigh up my losses,
Were they sunk as low as hell: yet let me think,
How I am impair'd in an hour, and the cause of't,
Lost in security: O, how this wicked world
    bewitches,
Especially made insolent with riches!
So sails with fore-winds stretch'd do soonest break,
And pyramids a'the top are still most weak. [*Exit.*

<hr/>

SCENE IV.*

Enter Capuchin, *and* ERCOLE *led between two.*

    Cap. Look up, sir:
You are preserv'd beyond natural reason;
You were brought dead out o'the field, the
    surgeons
Ready to have embalm'd you.
    Erc. I do look
On my action with a thought of terror:
To do ill and dwell in't is unmanly.
    Cap. You are divinely inform'd, sir.
    Erc. I fought for one in whom I have no more
    right
Than false executors have in orphans' goods
They cozen them of: yet though my cause were
    naught,
I rather chose the hazard of my soul,

    * *Scene IV.*] A room in the monastery of Saint Sebastian.

Than forgo the compliment of a choleric man.
I pray, continue the report of my death, and give
    out,
'Cause the church denied me Christian burial,
The vice-admiral of my galleys took my body,
With purpose to commit it to the earth,
Either in Sicil or Malta.
    Cap. What aim you at
By this rumour of your death?
    Erc. There is hope of life
In Contarino; and he has my prayers
That he may live to enjoy what is his own,
The fair Jolenta: where,* should it be thought
That I were breathing, happily her friends
Would oppose it still.
    Cap. But if you be suppos'd dead,
The law will strictly prosecute his life
For your murder.
    Erc. That's prevented thus.
There does belong a noble privilege
To all his family, ever since his father
Bore from the worthy emperor Charles the Fifth
An answer to the French king's challenge, at such
    time
The two noble princes were engag'd to fight
Upon a frontier arm o'the sea, in a flat-bottom'd
    boat,
That if any of his family should chance
To kill a man i'the field in a noble cause,
He should have his pardon: now, sir, for his cause,
The world may judge if it were not honest.
Pray, help me in speech; 'tis very painful to me.
    Cap. Sir, I shall.
    Erc. The guilt of this lies in Romelio;
And, as I hear, to second this good contract,
He has got a nun with child.
    Cap. These are crimes
That either must make work for speedy repentance
Or for the devil.
    Erc. I have much compassion on him;
For sin and shame are ever tied together
With gordian knots, of such a strong thread spun,
They cannot without violence be undone. [*Exeunt.*

    * *where*] i. e. whereas.

ACT III.

SCENE I.*

Enter ARIOSTO *and* CRISPIANO.

Ari. Well, sir, now I must claim
Your promise, to reveal to me the cause
Why you live thus clouded.
Cris. Sir, the King of Spain
Suspects that your Romelio here, the merchant,
Has discover'd some gold-mine to his own use,
In the West Indies, and for that employs me
To discover in what part of Christendom
He vents this treasure: besides, he is inform'd
What mad tricks have been play'd of late by
  ladies.
Ari. Most true; and I am glad the king has
  heard on't:
Why, they use their lords as if they were their
  wards;
And as your Dutchwomen in the Low-Countries
Take all and pay all, and do keep their husbands
So silly all their lives of their own estates,
That, when they are sick and come to make their
  will,
They know not precisely what to give away
From their wives, because they know not what
  they are worth;
So here should I repeat what factions,
What bat-fowling for offices,
As you must conceive their game is all i'the night,
What calling in question one another's honesties,
Withal what sway they bear i'the viceroy's court,
You'd wonder at it:
'Twill do well shortly, can we keep them off
From being of our council of war.
Cris. Well, I have vow'd
That I will never sit upon the bench more,
Unless it be to curb the insolencies
Of these women.
Ari. Well, take it on my word, then,
Your place will not long be empty.   [*Exeunt.*

SCENE II.†

Enter ROMELIO *in the habit of a Jew.*

Rom. Excellently well habited! why, methinks
That I could play with mine own shadow now,

And be a rare Italianated Jew;
To have as many several change of faces
As I have seen carv'd upon one cherry-stone;
To wind about a man like rotten ivy,
Eat into him like quicksilver; poison a friend
With pulling but a loose hair from's beard, or give
  a drench,
He should linger oft nine years, and ne'er
  complain
But in the spring and fall, and so the cause
Imputed to the disease natural: for slight villanies,
As to coin money, corrupt ladies' honours,
Betray a town to the Turk, or make a bonfire
O'the Christian navy, I could settle to't,
As if I had eat a politician,
And digested* him to nothing but pure blood.
But stay: I lose myself: this is the house.—
Within there!

Enter Two Surgeons

First Sur. Now, sir!
Rom. You are the men of art that, as I hear,
Have the Lord Contarino under cure.
Second Sur. Yes, sir, we are his surgeons;
But he is past all cure.
Rom. Why, is he dead?
First Sur. He is speechless, sir, and we do find
  his wound
So fester'd near the vitals, all our art,
By warm drinks, cannot clear th' imposthumation;
And he's so weak, to make [incision]†
By the orifix were present death to him.
Rom. He has made a will, I hear.
First Sur. Yes, sir.
Rom. And deputed Jolenta his heir.
Second Sur. He has; we are witness to't.
Rom. Has not Romelio been with you yet,
To give you thanks and ample recompense
For the pains you have ta'en?
First Sur. Not yet.
Rom. Listen to me, gentlemen, for I protest,
If you will seriously mind your own good,
I am come about a business shall convey
Large legacies from Contarino's will
To both of you.

---

* *Scene I.*] A room in the house of Ariosto.
† *Scene II.*] A street. Before the lodging of Contarino.

* *digested*] The old copy "disgested" (a spelling common in early writers).
† *incision*] A word has here dropt out from the old copy.

Second Sur. How, sir! why, Romelio has the
will,
And in that he has given us nothing.

Rom. I pray, attend me: I am a physician.

Second Sur. A physician! where do you
practise?

Rom. In Rome.

First Sur. O, then you have store of patients.

Rom. Store! why, look you, I can kill my
twenty a month
And work but i'the forenoons : you will give me
leave
To jest and be merry with you. But as I said,
All my study has been physic: I am sent
From a noble Roman that is near akin
To Contarino, and that ought indeed,
By the law of alliance, be his only heir,
To practise his good and yours.

Both Sur. How, I pray, sir?

Rom. I can by an extraction which I have,
Though he were speechless, his eyes set in's head,
His pulses without motion, restore to him,
For half an hour's space, the use of sense,
And perhaps a little speech : having done this,
If we can work him, as no doubt we shall,
To make another will, and therein assign
This gentleman his heir, I will assure you,
Fore I depart this house, ten thousand ducats ;
And then we'll pull the pillow from his head,
And let him e'en go whither the religion sends him
That he died in.

First Sur. Will you give's ten thousand ducats?

Rom. Upon my Jewism.

Second Sur. Tis a bargain, sir, we are yours.
[CONTARINO *in a bed.*

Here is the subject you must work on.

Rom. Well said, you are honest men,
And go to the business roundly : but, gentlemen,
I must use my art singly.

First Sur. O, sir, you shall have all privacy.

Rom. And the doors lock'd to me.

Second Sur. At your best pleasure.—
Yet for all this, I will not trust this Jew.

First Sur. Faith, to say truth,
I do not like him neither ; he looks like a rogue.
This is a fine toy, fetch a man to life,

To make a new will ! there is some trick in't.
I'll be near you, Jew. [*Exeunt* Surgeons.

Rom. Excellent, as I would wish : these credu-
lous fools
Have given me freely what I would have bought
With a great deal of money.—Softly ! here's
breath yet.
Now, Ercole, for part of the revenge
Which I have vow'd for thy untimely death !
Besides this politic working of my own,
That scorns precedent, why should this great man
live,
And not enjoy my sister, as I have vow'd
He never shall? O, he may alter's will
Every new moon, if he please : to prevent which,
I must put in a strong caveat. Come forth, then,
My desperate stiletto, that may be worn
In a woman's hair, and ne'er discover'd,
And either would be taken for a bodkin,
Or a curling-iron at most : why, 'tis an engine
That's only fit to put in execution
Barmotho pigs;* a most unmanly weapon,
That steals into a man's life he knows not how.
O, [that] great Cæsar, he that pass'd the shock
Of so many armèd pikes, and poison'd darts,
Swords, slings, and battleaxes, should at length,
Sitting at ease on a cushion, come to die
By such a shoe-maker's awl as this, his soul let
forth
At a hole no bigger than the incision
Made for a wheal ! Ud's foot, I am horribly angry
That he should die so scurvily : yet wherefore
Do I condemn thee thereof so cruelly,
Yet shake him by the hand? 'tis to express,
That I would never have such weapons us'd
But in a plot like this, that's treacherous.
Yet this shall prove most merciful to thee,
For it shall preserve thee
From dying on a public scaffold, and withal
Bring thee an absolute cure, thus. [*Stabs him.*
So, 'tis done :
And now for my escape.

Re-enter Surgeons.

First Sur. You rogue mountebank,

---

* *Contarino in a bed*] Here the audience were to
imagine a change of scene,—to the bed-chamber of the
wounded Contarino. Either, a traverse (or curtain)
being drawn back, Contarino was discovered lying on a
bed ; or else a bed, containing Contarino, was thrust
upon the stage.—In Heywood's *If you know not me, you
know nobody*, we find " *Enter Elizabeth in her bed*," Sig. A
4. ed. 1623 ; and similar stage-directions occur in various
other old plays.

* *Barmotho pigs*] i. e. pigs of the Bermudas, or (as the
word was also written,—see p. 79) Bermoothes.

    " 'Tis the land of peace,
Where *hogs* and tobacco yield fair increase.
.   .   .   .
    I am for the *Bermudas*."
Middleton's *Any Thing for a Quiet Life*, *Works*, iv. 499,
ed. Dyce. In *Odcomb's Complaint* by Taylor, the water-
poet, is an " Epitaph in the *Barmooda tongue, which must
be pronounced with the accent of the grunting of a hogge.*"

I will try whether your inwards can endure
To be wash'd in scalding lead.

Rom. Hold! I turn Christian.

Second Sur. Nay, prithee, be a Jew still;
I would not have a Christian be guilty
Of such a villanous act as this is.

Rom. I am Romelio the merchant.

First Sur. Romelio! you have prov'd yourself
A cunning merchant indeed.

Rom. You may read why I came hither.

Second Sur. Yes, in a bloody Roman letter.

Rom. I did hate this man; each minute of his
    breath
Was torture to me.

First Sur. Had you forborne this act, he had
    not liv'd
This two hours.

Rom. But he had died then,
And my revenge unsatisfied. Here's gold:
Never did wealthy man purchase the silence
Of a terrible scolding wife at a dearer rate
Than I will pay for yours: here's your earnest
In a bag of double ducats.

Second Sur. Why, look you, sir, as I do weigh
    this business,
This cannot be counted murder in you by no
    means.
Why, 'tis no more than should I go and choke
An Irishman, that were three quarters drown'd,
With pouring usquebaugh in's throat.

Rom. You will be secret?

First Sur. As your soul.

Rom. The West Indies shall sooner want gold
    than you, then.

Second Sur. That protestation has the music of
    the mint in't.

Rom. [*aside.*] How unfortunately was I surpris'd!
I have made myself a slave perpetually
To these two beggars.   [*Exit.*

First Sur. Excellent! by this act he has made
    his estate ours.

Second Sur. I'll presently grow a lazy surgeon,
and ride on my foot-cloth.* I'll fetch from him
every eight days a policy for a hundred double
ducats: if he grumble, I'll peach.

First Sur. But let's take heed he do not poison
    us.

Second Sur. O, I will never eat nor drink with
    him,
Without unicorn's horn in a hollow tooth.

Con. O!

First Sur. Did he not groan?

Second Sur. Is the wind in that door still?

First Sur. Ha! come hither, note a strange
    accident:
His stool has lighted in the former wound,
And made free passage for the congeal'd blood:
Observe in what abundance it delivers
The putrefaction.

Second Sur. Methinks he fetches
His breath very lively.

First Sur. The hand of heaven is in't,
That his intent to kill him should become
The very direct way to save his life.

Second Sur. Why, this is like one I have heard
    of in England,
Was cur'd o'the gout by being rack'd i'the Tower.
Well, if we can recover him, here's reward
On both sides: howsoever we must be secret.

First Sur. We are tied to't:
When we cure gentlemen of foul diseases,
They give us so much for the cure, and twice as
    much,
That we do not blab on't. Come, let's to work
    roundly;
Heat the lotion, and bring the searing. [*Exeunt.*

SCENE III.*—*A table set forth with two tapers,
    a death's-head, a book.* JOLENTA *in mourning.*
ROMELIO *sits by her.*

Rom. Why do you grieve thus? take a looking-
    glass,
And see if this sorrow become you: that pale face
Will make men think you us'd some art before,
Some odious painting. Contarino's dead.

Jol. O, that he should die so soon!

Rom. Why, I pray, tell me,
Is not the shortest fever the best? and are not
    bad plays
The worse for their length?

Jol. Add not to the ill you've done
An odious slander: he stuck i'the eyes o'the court
As the most choice jewel there.

Rom. O, be not angry:
Indeed, the court to well-composèd nature
Adds much to perfection; for it is, or should be,
As a bright crystal mirror to the world
To dress itself: but I must tell you, sister,
If the excellency of the place could have
Wrought salvation, the devil had ne'er fall'n
From heaven: he was proud.—Leave us, leave us!
Come, take your seat again: I have a plot,

---

* *foot-cloth*] See note *, p. 7.

* *Scene III.*] A room in the house of Leonora.

If you will listen to it seriously,
That goes beyond example; it shall breed,
Out of the death of these two noblemen,
The advancement of our house.
   Jol. O, take heed:
A grave is a rotten foundation.
   Rom. Nay, nay, hear me.
'Tis somewhat indirectly, I confess;
But there is much advancement in the world
That comes in indirectly. I pray, mind me.
You are already made by absolute will
Contarino's heir: now, if it can be prov'd
That you have issue by Lord Ercole,
I will make you inherit his land too.
   Jol. How's this?
Issue by him, he dead, and I a virgin!
   Rom. I knew* you would wonder how it could
     be done;
But I have laid the case so radically,
Not all the lawyers in Christendom
Shall find any the least flaw in't. I have a mistress
Of the order of Saint Clare, a beauteous nun,
Who, being cloister'd ere she knew the heat
Her blood would arrive to, had only time enough
To repent, and idleness sufficient
To fall in love with me; and to be short,
I have so much disorder'd the holy order,
I have got this nun with child.
   Jol. Excellent work
Made for a dumb mid-wife!
   Rom. I am glad you grow thus pleasant.
Now will I have you presently give out
That you are full two months quicken'd with child
By Ercole; which rumour can beget
No scandal to you, since we will affirm
The precontract was so exactly done
By the same words us'd in the form of marriage,
That with a little dispensation,
A money matter, it shall be register'd
Absolute matrimony.
   Jol. So, then, I conceive you;
My conceiv'd child must prove your bastard.
   Rom. Right;
For at such time my mistress falls in labour,
You must feign the like.
   Jol. 'Tis a pretty feat this;
But I am not capable of it.
   Rom. Not capable!
   Jol. No, for the thing you would have me
     counterfeit
Is most essentially put in practice, nay, 'tis done;
I am with child already.

---

knew] The old copies "know."

   Rom. Ha! by whom?
   Jol. By Contarino: do not knit the brow;
The precontract shall justify it, it shall;
Nay, I will get some singular fine churchman,
Or though he be a plural one, shall affirm
He coupled us together.
   Rom. O, misfortune!
Your child must, then, be reputed Ercole's.
   Jol. Your hopes are dash'd, then, since your
     votary's issue
Must not inherit the land.
   Rom. No matter for that,
So I preserve her fame. I am strangely puzzled.
Why, suppose that she be brought a-bed before you,
And we conceal her issue till the time
Of your delivery, and then give out
That you have two at a birth; ha, were't not
     excellent?
   Jol. And what resemblance think you would
     they have
To one another? twins are still alike:
But this is not your aim; you would have your
     child
Inherit Ercole's land. O my sad soul!
Have you not made me yet wretched enough,
But after all this frosty age in youth,
Which you have witch'd upon me, you will seek
To poison my fame?
   Rom. That's done already.
   Jol. No, sir, I did but feign it,
To a fatal purpose, as I thought.
   Rom. What purpose?
   Jol. If you had lov'd or tender'd my dear
     honour,
You would have lock'd your poniard in my heart,
When I nam'd I was with child: but I must live
To linger out till the consumption
Of my own sorrow kill me.
   Rom. [*aside*] This will not do.
The devil has on the sudden furnish'd me
With a rare charm, yet a most unnatural
Falsehood: no matter, so 'twill take.—
Stay, sister, I would utter to you a business,
But I am very loth; a thing, indeed,
Nature would have compassionately conceal'd
Till my mother's eyes be clos'd.
   Jol. Pray, what's that, sir?
   Rom. You did observe
With what a dear regard our mother tender'd
The Lord Contarino, yet how passionately
She sought to cross the match: why, this was
     merely
To blind the eye o'the world; for she did know
That you would marry him, and he was capable.

My mother doted upon him; and it was plotted
Cunningly between them, after you were married,
Living all three together in one house.—
A thing I cannot whisper without horror :
Why, the malice scarce of devils would suggest
Incontinence 'tween them two.

Jol. I remember, since his hurt,
She has been very passionately inquiring
After his health.

Rom. Upon my soul, this jewel,
With a piece of the holy cross in't, this relic,
Valu'd at many thousand crowns, she would have
　　　　　sent him
Lying upon his death-bed.

Jol. Professing, as you say,
Love to my mother, wherefore did he make
Me his heir ?

Rom. His will was made afore he went to fight,
When he was first a suitor to you.

Jol. To fight ! O, well remember'd :
If he lov'd my mother, wherefore did he lose
His life in my quarrel ?

Rom. For the affront sake ; a word you under-
　　　　　stand not ;
Because Ercole was pretended rival to him,
To clear your suspicion ; I was gull'd in't too :
Should he not have fought upon't, he had under-
　　　　　gone
The censure of a coward.

Jol. How came you by
This wretched knowledge ?

Rom. His surgeons* overheard it,
As he did sigh it out to his confessor,
Some half hour fore he died.

Jol. I would have the surgeons hang'd
For abusing confession, and for making me
So wretched by the report.　Can this be truth ?

Rom. No, but direct falsehood,
As ever was banish'd the court.　Did you ever hear
Of a mother that has kept her daughter's husband
For her own tooth ?　He fancied you in one kind,
For his lust, and he lov'd
Our mother in another kind, for her money,—
The gallant's fashion right.　But, come, ne'er
　　　　　think on't,
Throw the fowl to the devil that hatch'd it, and
　　　　　let this
Bury all ill that's in't,—she is our mother.

Jol. I never did find any thing i'the world

Turn my blood so much as this: here's such a
　　　　　conflict
Between apparent presumption and unbelief,
That I shall die in't.
O, if there be another world i'the moon,
As some fantastics dream,* I could wish all men,
The whole race of them, for their inconstancy,
Sent thither to people that !　Why, I protest,
I now affect the Lord Ercole's memory
Better than the other's.

Rom. But, were Contarino living ?—

Jol. I do call any thing to witness,
That the divine law prescrib'd us†
To strengthen an oath, were he living and in
　　　　　health,
I would never marry with him.　Nay, since I have
　　　　　found the world
So false to me, I'll be as false to it;
I will mother this child for you.

Rom. Ha !

Jol. Most certainly it will beguile part of my
　　　　　sorrow.

Rom. O, most assuredly; make you smile to
　　　　　think,
How many times i'the world lordships descend
To divers men, that might, an truth were known,
Be heir, for any thing belongs to the flesh,
As well to the Turk's richest eunuch.

Jol. But do you not think
I shall have a horrible strong breath now ?

Rom. Why ?

Jol. O, with keeping your counsel, 'tis so terrible
　　　　　foul.

Rom. Come, come, come, you must leave these
　　　　　bitter flashes.

Jol. Must I dissemble dishonesty ?　you have
　　　　　divers
Counterfeit honesty; but I hope here's none
Will take exceptions I now must practise
The art of a great-bellied woman, and go feign
Their qualms and swoonings.

Rom. Eat unripe fruit and oatmeal,
To take away your colour.

Jol. Dine in my bed
Some two hours after noon.

Rom. And when you are up,
Make to your petticoat a quilted preface,
To advance your belly.

---

* *surgeons*] Here, and the next speech, the old copy
has " Surgeon "; and further on in this scene it has,—
　　　" In the absence of his *Surgeon*,
　My charitie did that for him in a trice,
　They would haue done at leasure," &c.
(Compare the preceding scene.)

* *O, if there be another world i'the moon,*
　As some fantastic dream] Compare Milton ;
" Not in the neighbouring moon, as some have dream'd,"
　　　　　　　　　Par. Lost, Book iii. v. 459.
† *That the divine law prescrib'd us*] Qy. " That the
divine law *has* prescrib'd *to* us " (or "*has* prescribed us ")?

Jol. I have a strange conceit now.
I have known some women, when they were with
  child,
Have long'd to beat their husbands: what if I,
To keep decorum, exercise my longing
Upon my tailor that way, and noddle him soundly?
He'll make the larger bill for't.
  Rom. I'll get one
Shall be as tractable to't as stockfish.
  Jol. O my fantastical sorrow! cannot I now
Be miserable enough, unless I wear
A pied fool's coat? nay, worse; for when our
  passions
Such giddy and uncertain changes breed,
We are never well till we are mad indeed. [*Exit.*
  Rom. So, nothing in the world could have done
  this,
But to beget in her a strong distaste
Of the Lord Contarino. O jealousy,
How violent, especially in women!
How often has it rais'd the devil up
In form of a law-case! My especial care
Must be, to nourish craftily this fiend
'Tween the mother and the daughter, that the
  deceit
Be not perceiv'd. My next task, that my sister,
After this suppos'd child-birth, be persuaded
To enter into religion: 'tis concluded
She must never marry; so I am left guardian
To her estate. And lastly, that my two surgeons
Be wag'd to the East Indies: let them prate
When they are beyond the line; the calenture,
Or the scurvy, or the Indian pox, I hope,
Will take order for their coming back.—
O, here's my mother.

          Enter LEONORA.

                I ha' strange news for you;
My sister is with child.
  Leon. I do look now for some great misfortunes
To follow; for, indeed, mischiefs
Are like the visits of Franciscan friars,—
They never come to prey upon us single.
In what estate left you Contarino?
  Rom. Strange that you can skip
From the former sorrow to such a question!
I'll tell you: in the absence of his surgeons,*
My charity did that for him in a trice
They would have done at leisure and been paid
  for't;
I have kill'd him.
  Leon. I am twenty years elder
Since you last open'd your lips.

          * *surgeons*] The old copy "Surgeon."

  Rom. Ha!
  Leon. You have given him the wound you
  speak of
Quite thorough your mother's heart.
  Rom. I will heal it presently, mother; for this
  sorrow
Belongs to your error: you would have him live
Because you think he's father of the child;
But Jolenta vows by all the rights of truth,
'Tis Ercole's. It makes me smile to think
How cunningly my sister could be drawn
To the contract, and yet how familiarly
To his bed: doves never couple without
A kind of murmur.
  Leon. O, I am very sick!
  Rom. Your old disease; when you are griev'd,
You are troubled with the mother.*
  Leon. I am rapt with the mother indeed,
That I ever bore such a son.
  Rom. Pray, tend my sister;
I am infinitely full of business.
  Leon. Stay; you will mourn for Contarino?
  Rom. O, by all means: 'tis fit; my sister is his
  heir.   [*Exit.*
  Leon. I will make you chief mourner, believe it.
Never was woe like mine. O, that my care,
And absolute study to preserve his life,
Should be his absolute ruin! Is he gone, then?
There is no plague i'the world can be compar'd
To impossible desire; for they are plagu'd
In the desire itself. Never, O, never
Shall I behold him living, in whose life
I liv'd far sweetlier than in mine own!
A precise curiosity† has undone me: why did I not
Make my love known directly? 'thad not been
Beyond example, for a matron
To affect i'the honourable way of marriage
So youthful a person. O, I shall run mad!
For as we love our youngest children best,
So the last fruit of our affection,
Wherever we bestow it, is most strong,
Most violent, most unresistible,
Since 'tis indeed our latest harvest-home,
Last merriment fore winter; and we widows,
As men report of our best picture-makers,
We love the piece we are in hand with better
Than all the excellent work we have done before.
And my son has depriv'd me of all this! ha, my
  son!
I'll be a Fury to him: like an Amazon lady,
I'd cut off this right pap that gave him suck,

          * *the mother*] See note †, p. 68.
          † *curiosity*] i. e. niceness, scrupulousness.

To shoot him dead: I'll no more tender him
Than had a wolf stol'n to my teat i'the night,
And robb'd me of my milk; nay, such a creature
I should love better far.—Ha, ha! what say you?
I do talk to somewhat, methinks; it may be
My evil Genius. Do not the bells ring?
I have a strange noise in my head: O, fly in pieces!
Come, age, and wither me into the malice
Of those that have been happy! let me have
One property more than the devil of hell,
Let me envy the pleasure of youth heartily:
Let me in this life fear no kind of ill,
That have no good to hope for: let me die
In the distraction of that worthy princess
Who loathèd food,* and sleep, and ceremony,
For thought of losing that brave gentleman
She would fain have sav'd, had not a false convey-
ance
Express'd him stubborn-hearted: let me sink
Where neither man nor memory may e'er find me.
                                                    [*Falls down.*]

          Enter Capuchin *and* ERCOLE.

Cap. This is a private way which I command
As her confessor. I would not have you seen yet,
Till I prepare her [ERCOLE *retires*]—Peace to you,
          lady!
Leon. Ha!
Cap. You are well employ'd, I hope: the best
          pillow i'the world
For this your contemplation is the earth,
And the best object heaven.
Leon. I am whispering to a dead friend.
Cap. And I am come
To bring you tidings of a friend was dead
Restor'd to life again.
Leon. Say, sir.
Cap. One whom,
I dare presume, next to your children,
You tender'd above life.
Leon. Heaven will not suffer me
Utterly to be lost.
Cap. For he should have been
Your son-in-law,—miraculously sav'd
When surgery gave him o'er.
Leon. O, may you live
To win many souls to heaven, worthy sir,
That your crown may be the greater! Why, my son
Made me believe he stole into his chamber,

---

* *In the distraction of that worthy princess
Who loathèd food, &c.*] Here, I think, there is a
manifest allusion to the closing scene of Queen Elizabeth's life, and to what Mr. Lodge calls "the well-
known, but weakly authenticated tale of the Countess of
Nottingham and the ring."

And ended that which Ercole began
By a deadly stab in's heart.
Erco. [*aside*] Alas, she mistakes!
'Tis Contarino she wishes living: but I must fasten
On her last words, for my own safety.
Leon. Where, O, where shall I meet this comfort?
Erco. [*coming forward*] Here in the vowèd
          comfort of your daughter.
Leon. O, I am dead again! instead of the man,
You present me the grave swallow'd him.
Erco. Collect yourself, good lady.
Would you behold brave Contarino living,
There cannot be a nobler chronicle
Of his good than myself: if you would view him
          dead,
I will present him to you bleeding fresh
In my penitency.
Leon. Sir, you do only live
To redeem another ill you have committed,
That my poor innocent daughter perish not,
By your vile sin, whom you have got with child.
Erco. Here begin all my compassion. O poor
          soul!
She is with child by Contarino; and he dead,
By whom should she preserve her fame to the
          world
But by myself that lov'd her 'bove the world?
There never was a way more honourable
To exercise my virtue, than to father it,
And preserve her credit, and to marry her.
I'll suppose her Contarino's widow, bequeath'd
          to me
Upon his death; for, sure, she was his wife,
But that the ceremony o'the church was wanting.
Report this to her, madam, and withal,
That never father did conceive more joy
For the birth of an heir, than I to understand
She had such confidence in me. I will not now
Press a visit upon her, till you have prepar'd her;
For I do read in your distraction,
Should I be brought o'the sudden to her presence,
Either the hasty fright, or else the shame,
May blast the fruit within her. I will leave you
To commend as loyal faith and service to her
As e'er heart harbour'd: by my hope of bliss,
I never liv'd to do good act but this.
Cap. [*aside to* ERCO.] Withal, an you be wise,
Remember what the mother has reveal'd
Of Romelio's treachery.
                              [*Exeunt* ERCOLE *and* Capuchin.
Leon. A most noble fellow! in his loyalty
I read what worthy comforts I have lost
In my dear Contarino; and all adds
To my despair.—Within there!

Enter WINIFRED.

Fetch the picture
Hangs in my inner closet.   [*Exit* WINIFRED.]
I remember
I let a word slip of Romelio's practice *
At the surgeons'; no matter, I can salve it:
I have deeper vengeance that's preparing for him;
To let him live and kill him, that's revenge
I meditate upon.

Re-enter WINIFRED *with the Picture.*

So, hang it up.
I was enjoin'd by the party ought that picture,
Forty years since, ever when I was vex'd,
To look upon that: what was his meaning in't
I know not, but methinks upon the sudden
It has furnish'd me with mischief, such a plot
As never mother dream'd of.   Here begins
My part i'the play: my son's estate is sunk
By loss at sea, and he has nothing left
But the land his father left him. 'Tis concluded,
The law shall undo him.—Come hither:
I have a weighty secret to impart;
But I would have theo first confirm to me,
How I may trust that thou canst keep my counsel
Beyond death.

Win. Why, mistress, 'tis your only way,
To enjoin me first that I reveal to you
The worst act I e'er did in all my life;
So one secret shall bind one another.

Leon. Thou instruct'st me
Most ingenuously;† for, indeed, it is not fit,
Where any act is plotted that is naught,
Any of counsel to it should be good;
And in a thousand ills have happ'd i'the world,
The intelligence of one another's shame
Have wrought far more effectually than the tie
Of conscience or religion.

Win. But think not, mistress,
That any sin which ever I committed
Did concern you; for proving false in one thing,
You were a fool if ever you would trust me
In the least matter of weight.

Leon. Thou hast liv'd with me
These forty years, we have grown old together,
As many ladies and their women do,
With talking nothing and with doing less;
We have spent our life in that which least con-
cerns life,
Only in putting on our clothes: and now I think
on't,
I have been a very courtly mistress to thee,—
I have given thee good words, but no deeds:
now's the time
To requite all : my son has six lordships left him.

Win. 'Tis truth.

Leon. But he cannot live four days to enjoy them.

Win. Have you poison'd him ?

Leon. No, the poison is yet but brewing.

Win. You must minister it to him with all
privacy.

Leon. Privacy ! It shall be given him
In open court; I'll make him swallow it
Before the judge's face: if he be master
Of poor ten arpines * of land forty hours longer,
Let the world repute me an honest woman.

Win. So 'twill, I hope.

Leon. O, thou canst not conceive
My unimitable plot ! Let's to my ghostly father ;
Where first I will have thee make a promise
To keep my counsel, and then I will employ thee
In such a subtle combination,
Which will require, to make the practice fit,
Four devils, five advocates, to one woman's wit.

[*Exeunt*

ACT IV.

SCENE I.‡

Enter, at one door, LEONORA, SANITONELLA, WINIFRED,
and Register ; *at the other,* ARIOSTO.

San. Take her into your office, sir ; she has that
In her belly will dry up your ink, I can tell you.—

This is the man that is your learnèd counsel,
A fellow that will troll it off with tongue :
He never goes without restorative powder
Of the lungs of fox in's pocket, and Malaga raisins,
To make him long-winded.— Sir, this gentle-
woman
Entreats your counsel in an' honest cause,

---

* *practice*] See note *, p. 117.
† *ingenuously*] See note †, p. 26.
‡ *Scene I.*] A room, it would appear, in the house of
Ariosto : but, on his exit, p. 130, a change of scene
seems to be *supposed*,—to the house of Contilupo. (Qy,
might this scene be marked as taking place in one of the

halls surrounding the Hall of Justice in the ancient
palace of the Vicaria ? See *Naples, Political, Social, and
Religious, By Lord B* * * * *, 1856, vol. ii. 27—8).
* *arpines*] Fr. *arpent*, an acre.

K

Which, please you, sir, this brief, my own poor
   labour,
Will give you light of.   [*Gives the brief.*
   Ario. Do you call this a brief?
Here's, as I weigh them, some four-score sheets of
   paper:
What would they weigh, if there were cheese
   wrapt in them,
Or fig-dates?
   San. Joy come to you, you are merry:
We call this but a brief in our office:
The scope of the business lies i'the margent.
   Ario. Methinks you prate too much:
I never could endure an honest cause
With a long prologue to't.
   Leon. You trouble him.
   Ario. What's here? O strange! I have liv'd this
   sixty years,
Yet in all my practice never did shake hands
With a cause so odious.—Sirrah, are you her
   knave?
   San. No, sir, I am a clerk.
   Ario. Why, you whoreson fogging rascal,
Are there not whores enow for presentations
Of overseers wrong the will o'the dead,
Oppressions of widows or young orphans,
Wicked divorces, or your vicious cause
Of *Plus quam satis* to content a woman,
But you must find new stratagems, new purse-
   nets?—*
O women, as the ballad lives to tell you,
What will you shortly come to?
   San. Your fee is ready, sir.
   Ario. The devil take such fees,
And all such suits i'the tail of them!—See, the slave
Has writ false Latin!—Sirrah ignoramus,
Were you ever at the university?
   San. Never, sir:
But 'tis well known to divers I have commenc'd
In a pew of our office.
   Ario. Where? in a pew of your office!
   San. I have been dry-founder'd in't this four
   years,
Seldom found non-resident from my desk.
   Ario. Non-resident, sub-sumner!
I'll tear your libel for abusing that word,
By virtue of the clergy.   [*Tears the brief.*
   San. What do you mean, sir?
It cost me four nights' labour.
   Ario. Hadst thou been drunk so long,
Thou'dst done our court better service.

---

* *purse-nets*] i. e. nets, the mouths of which are drawn
together by a string.

   Leon. Sir, you do forget your gravity, methinks.
   Ario. Cry ye mercy, do I so?
And, as I take it, you do very little remember
Either womanhood or Christianity. Why do ye
   meddle
With that seducing knave, that's good for naught,
Unless't be to fill the office full of fleas,
Or a winter-itch; wears that spacious ink-horn
All a vacation only to cure tetters,
And his penknife to weed corns from the splay
   toes
Of the right worshipful of the office?
   Leon. You make bold with me, sir.
   Ario. Woman, you're mad, I'll swear't, and
   have more need
Of a physician than a lawyer.
The melancholy humour flows in your face;
Your painting cannot hide it. Such vile suits
Disgrace our courts, and these make honest
   lawyers
Stop their own ears whilst they plead; and that's
   the reason
Your younger men, that have good conscience,
Wear such large night-caps. Go, old woman,
   go pray
For lunacy, or else the devil himself
Has ta'en possession of thee. May like cause
In any Christian court never find name!
Bad suits, and not the law, bred the law's shame.
                        [*Exit.*
   Leon. Sure, the old man's frantic.
   San. Plague on's gouty fingers!
Were all of his mind, to entertain no suits
But such they thought were honest, sure our
   lawyers
Would not purchase * half so fast.

          Enter CONTILUPO, *a spruce lawyer.*
                 But here's the man,
Learn'd Signior Contilupo; here's a fellow
Of another piece, believe't. —I must make shift
With the foul copy.
   Contil. Business to me?
   San. To you, sir, from this lady.
   Contil. She is welcome.
   San. 'Tis a foul copy, sir, you'll hardly read it:
There's twenty double-ducats,—can you read, sir?
   Contil. Exceeding well, very, very exceed-
   ing well.
   San. [*aside*]. This man will be sav'd, he can
   read: Lord, Lord,
To see what money can do! be the hand ne'er so foul,
Somewhat will be pick'd out on't.

---

* *purchase*] i. e. acquire wealth: see note †, p. 74.

Contil. Is not this *vivere honeste?*

` *San.* No, that's struck out, sir;
And wherever you find *vivere honeste* in these
papers,
Give it a dash, sir.

Contil. I shall be mindful of it.
In troth, you write a pretty secretary:
Your secretary-hand ever takes best,
In mine opinion.

San. Sir, I have been in France,
And there, believe't, your court-hand generally
Takes beyond thought.

Contil. Even as a man is traded in't.

San. [*aside*]. That I could not think of this
    virtuous gentleman
Before I went to the other hog-rubber ! *
Why, this was wont to give young clerks half
    fees
To help him to clients. — Your opinion in the
    case, sir ?

Contil. I am struck with wonder, almost
    ecstasi'd,
With this most goodly suit.

Leo. It is the fruit
Of a most hearty penitence.

Contil. 'Tis a case
Shall leave a precedent to all the world,
In our succeeding annals, and deserves
Rather a spacious public theatre
Then a pent court for audience: it shall teach
All ladies the right path to rectify
Their issue.

San. Lo, you, here's a man of comfort !

Contil. And you shall go unto a peaceful
    grave,
Discharg'd of such a guilt as would have lain
Howling for ever at your wounded heart,
And rose with you to judgment.

San. O, give me such a lawyer as will think
Of the day of judgment !

Leon. You must urge the business
Against him as spitefully as may be.

Contil. Doubt not.—What, is he summon'd ?

San. Yes, and the court will sit within this
    half hour:
Peruse your notes; you have very short warning.

Contil. Never fear you that.—
Follow me, worthy lady, and make account
This suit is ended already.   [*Exeunt.*

---

* *hog-rubber*] Not a "dictionary word ;" but old Burton uses it ; "The very rusticks and *hog-rubbers*, Me-
nalcas and Coridon, &c." *Anat. of Melancholy*, p. 540,
ed. 1660.

SCENE II.*

Enter Officers, preparing seats for the Judges; to them
ERCOLE *muffled.*

First Off. You would have a private seat, sir ?

Erc. Yes, sir.

Second Off. Here's a closet belongs to the court
Where you may hear all unseen.

Erc. I thank you: there's money.

Second Off. I give you your thanks again, sir.
    [ERCOLE *goes into the closet.*

Enter CONTARINO *and the Two Surgeons, disguised.*

Con. Is't possible Romelio's persuaded
You are gone to the East Indies ?

First Sur. Most confidently.

Con. But do you mean to go ?

Second Sur. How ! go to the East Indies ! and
so many Hollanders gone to fetch sauce for their
pickled herrings ! some have been peppered there
too lately.† But, I pray, being thus well recovered
of your wounds, why do you not reveal yourself ?

Con. That my fair Jolenta should be rumour'd
To be with child by noble Ercole,
Makes me expect to what a violent issue
These passages will come. I hear her brother
Is marrying the infant she goes with,
Fore it be born ; as, if it be a daughter,
To the Duke of Austria's nephew,—if a son,
Into the noble ancient family
Of the Palavafini.‡ He's a subtle devil ;
And I do wonder what strange suit in law
Has happ'd between him and's mother.

First Sur. 'Tis whisper'd 'mong the lawyers,
'Twill undo him for ever.

Enter SANITONELLA *and* WINIFRED.

San. Do you hear, officers ?
You must take special care that you let in
No brachygraphy-men § to take notes.

First Off. No, sir ?

San. By no means:
We cannot have a cause of any fame,
But you must have scurvy pamphlets and lewd
    ballads

---

* *Scene II.*] A court of justice.

† *some have been peppered there too lately*] Webster alludes
to the massacre of the English by the Dutch at Amboyna, in February, 1622. The *True Relation* of the
atrocity has been several times reprinted. Dryden
wrote an execrable play on the subject.

‡ *Palavafini*] Qy. "*Pallavicini.*"

§ *brachygraphy-men*] i. e. short-hand writers :—no great
favourites of our old dramatists, who had sometimes to
complain of their plays being printed without their consent, in a mutilated state, from copies taken down by
brachygraphy during the representation.

    K 2

Engender'd of it presently.—Have you broke
   fast yet ?
Win. Not I, sir.
San. 'Twas very ill done of you,
For this cause will be long a-pleading; but no*
   matter,
I have a modicum in my buckram bag
To stop your stomach.
Win. What is't ? green ginger ?
San. Green ginger, nor pellitory of Spain
Neither; yet 'twill stop a hollow tooth better
Than either of them.
Win. Pray, what is't ?
San. Look you,
It is a very lovely pudding-pie,
Which we clerks find great relief in.
Win. I shall have no stomach.
San. No matter an you have not; I may plea-
   sure
Some of our learnèd counsel with't : I have done it
Many a time and often, when a cause
Has prov'd like an after-game at Irish.†

*Enter, at one bar, CRISPIANO like a Judge, with another
Judge, CONTILUPO, and another lawyer; at another
bar, ROMELIO, ARIOSTO, LEONORA with a black veil
over her, and JÚLIO.*

Cris. 'Tis a strange suit.—Is Leonora come ?
Contil. She's here, my lord.—Make way there
   for the lady !
Cris. Take off her veil: it seems she is asham'd
To look her cause i'the face.
Contil. She's sick, my lord.
Ario. She's mad, my lord, and would be kept
   more dark.—
[*To* ROM.] By your favour, sir, I have now occasion
To be at your elbow, and within this half-hour
Shall entreat you to be angry, very angry.
Cris. Is Romelio come ?
Rom. I am here, my lord, and call'd, I do
   protest,
To answer what I know not, for as yet
I am wholly ignorant of what the court
Will charge me with.
Cris. I assure you, the proceeding
Is most unequal then, for I perceive

---

* no] The old copy "not."
† an after-game at Irish] Irish, "a game within the
tables," differed very little from back-gammon. "Irish,"
says *The Compleat Gamester*, "is an ingenious game, and
requires a great deal of skill to play it well, *especially the
After-game* : . . . . for an *After-game* I know not
what instructions to give you : you must herein trust to
your own judgment and the chance of the dice, and if
they run low for some time, it will be so much the
better." pp. 111, 112, ed. 1709.

The counsel of the adverse party furnish'd
With full instruction.
Rom. Pray, my lord, who is my accuser ?
Cris. 'Tis your mother.
Rom. [*aside*]. She has discover'd Contarino's
   murder :
If she prove so unnatural to call
My life in question, I am arm'd to suffer
This to end all my losses.
Cris. Sir, we will do you
This favour, you shall hear the accusation ;
Which being known, we will adjourn the court
Till a fortnight hence : you may provide your
   counsel.
Ario. I advise you take their proffer,
Or else the lunacy runs in a blood ;
You are more mad than she.
Rom. What are you, sir ?
Ario. An angry fellow that would do thee good,
For goodness' sake itself, I do protest,
Neither for love nor money.
Rom. Prithee, stand further, I shall gall your
   gout else.
Ario. Come, come, I know you for an East
   Indy merchant ;
You have a spice of pride in you still.
Rom. My lord,
I am so strengthen'd in my innocence,
For any the least shadow of a crime
Committed 'gainst my mother or the world,
That she can charge me with, here do I make it
My humble suit, only this hour and place
May give it as full hearing, and as free
And unrestrain'd a sentence.
Cris. Be not too confident ;
You have cause to fear.
Rom. Let fear dwell with earthquakes,
Shipwrecks at sea, or prodigies in heaven :
I cannot set myself so many fathom
Beneath the height of my true heart as fear.
Ario. Very fine words, I assure you, if they were
To any purpose.
Cris. Well, have your entreaty :
And if your own credulity undo you,
Blame not the court hereafter.—Fall to your plea.
Contil. May it please your lordship and the
   reverend court
To give me leave to open to you a case
So rare, so altogether void of precedent,
That I do challenge all the spacious volumes
Of the whole civil law to show the like.
We are of counsel for this gentlewoman ;
We have receiv'd our fee : yet the whole course
Of what we are to speak is quite against her ;

Yet we'll deserve our fee too. There stands one,
Romelio the merchant: I will name him to you
Without either title or addition;
For those false beams of his supposèd honour,
As void of true heat as are painted * fires
Or glow-worms in the dark, suit him all basely,
As if he had bought his gentry from the herald
With money got by extortion: I will first
Produce this Æsop's crow, as he stands forfeit
For the long use of his gay borrow'd plumes,
And then let him hop naked. I come to the
        point.
T'as been a dream in Naples, very near
This eight-and-thirty years, that this Romelio
Was nobly descended; he has rank'd himself
With the nobility, shamefully usurp'd
Their place, and in a kind of saucy pride,
Which, like to mushrooms, ever grow most rank
When they do spring from dung-hills, sought to
        o'ersway
The Fliski,† the Grimaldi, Dorii,
And all the ancient pillars of our state:
View now what he is come to,—this poor thing
Without a name, this cuckoo hatch'd i'the nest
Of a hedge-sparrow !
    Rom. Speaks he all this to me?
    Ario. Only to you, sir.
    Rom. I do not ask thee; prithee, hold thy
        prating.
    Ario. Why, very good; you will be presently
As angry as I could wish.
    Contil. What title shall I set to this base coin?
He has no name; and for's aspect, he seems
A giant in a May-game, that within
Is nothing but a porter. I'll undertake,
He had as good have travell'd all his life
With gipsies: I will sell him to any man
For an hundred cecchins, and he that buys him
        of me
Shall lose by the hand too.
    Ario. Lo, what you are come to,
You that did scorn to trade in any thing
But gold, or spices, or your cochineal!
He rates you now at poor John.‡
    Rom. Out upon thee!
I would thou wert of his side.
    Ario. Would you so?
    Rom. The devil and thee together on each hand,

<hr/>

* *are painted*] The old copy "*are all painted*,"—the eye
of the transcriber or compositor having caught the
"*all*" in the next line.
† *Fliski*] Qy. "*Fieschi!*"
‡ *poor-John*] i. e. a coarse kind of fish (generally hake)
salted and dried.

To prompt the lawyer's memory when he
        founders.
    Cris. Signior Contilupo, the court holds it fit
You leave this stale declaiming 'gainst the person,
And come to the matter.
    Contil. Now I shall, my lord.
    Cris. It shows a poor malicious eloquence;
And it is strange men of your gravity
Will not forgo it: verily, I presume,
If you but heard yourself speaking with my ears,
Your phrase would be more modest.
    Contil. Good my lord, be assur'd
I will leave all circumstance, and come to the
        purpose:
This Romelio is a bastard.
    Rom. How, a bastard!
O mother, now the day begins grow hot
On your side!
    Contil. Why, she is your accuser.
    Rom. I had forgot that. Was my father married
To any other woman at the time
Of my begetting?
    Contil. That's not the business.
    Rom. I turn me, then, to you that were my
        mother;
But by what name I am to call you now,
You must instruct me: were you ever married
To my father?
    Leon. To my shame I speak it, never.
    Cris. Not to Francisco Romelio?
    Leon. May it please your lordships,
To him I was; but he was not his father.
    Contil. Good my lord, give us leave in a few
        words
To expound the riddle, and to make it plain
Without the least of scruple; for I take it
There cannot be more lawful proof i'the world
Than the oath of the mother.
    Cris. Well, then, to your proofs,
And be not tedious.
    Contil. I'll conclude in a word.
Some nine-and-thirty years since, which was the
        time
This woman was married, Francisco Romelio,
This gentleman's putative father and her husband,
Being not married to her past a fortnight,
Would needs go travel; did so, and continu'd
In France and the Low-Countries eleven months:
Take special note o'the time, I beseech your
        lordship,
For it makes much to the business. In his
        absence
He left behind to sojourn at his house
A Spanish gentleman, a fine spruce youth

By the lady's confession, and you may be sure
He was no eunuch neither : he was one
Romelio lov'd very dearly; as oft haps
No man alive more welcome to the husband
Than he that makes him cuckold. This gentle-
man, I say,
Breaking all laws of hospitality,
Got his friend's wife with child, a full two months
Fore the husband return'd.

San. Good sir, forget not the lamb-skin.

Contil. I warrant thee.

San. I will pinch by the buttock
To put you in mind of't.

Contil. Prithee, hold thy prating.—
What's to be practis'd now, my lord? marry,
this :
Romelio being a young novice, not acquainted
With this precedence, very innocently
Returning home from travel, finds his wife
Grown an excellent good huswife, for she had set
Her women to spin flax, and, to that use,
Had in a study which was built of stone
Stor'd up at least an hundred weight of flax :
Marry, such a thread as was to be spun from the
flax,
I think the like was never heard of.

Cris. What was that?

Contil. You may be certain she would lose no
time
In bragging that her husband had got up
Her belly : to be short, at seven mouths' end,
Which was the time of her delivery,
And when she felt herself to fall in travail,
She makes her waiting-woman, as by mischance,
Set fire to the flax; the fright * whereof,
As they pretend, causes this gentlewoman
To fall in pain, and be deliverèd
Eight weeks afore her reckoning.

San. Now, sir, remember the lamb-skin.

Contil. The midwife straight howls out, there
was no hope
Of the infant's life ; swaddles it in a flay'd lamb-
skin,
As a bird hatch'd too early ; makes it up
With three quarters of a face, that made it look
Like a changeling; cries out to Romelio
To have it christen'd, lest it should depart
Without that it came for: and thus are many
serv'd
That take care to get gossips for those children
To which they might be godfathers themselves,
And yet be no arch-puritans neither.

---

* *fright*] The old copy "*flight*."

Cris. No more !

Ario. Pray, my lord, give him way, you spoil
his oratory else :
Thus would they jest, were they fee'd to open
Their sisters' cases.

Cris. You have urg'd enough :
You first affirm her husband was away from her
Eleven months?

Contil. Yes, my lord.

Cris. And at seven months' end,
After his return, she was deliver'd
Of this Romelio, and had gone her full time ?

Contil. True, my lord.

Cris. So by this account this gentleman was
begot
In his suppos'd father's absence ?

Contil. You have it fully.

Cris. A most strange suit this : 'tis beyond
example,
Either time past or present, for a woman
To publish her own dishonour voluntarily,
Without being call'd in question, some forty years
After the sin committed, and her counsel
To enlarge the offence with as much oratory
As ever I did hear them in my life
Defend a guilty woman ; 'tis most strange:
Or why with such a poison'd violence
Should she labour her son's undoing : we observe
Obedience of creatures to the law of nature
Is the stay of the whole world ; here that law is
broke ;
For though our civil law makes difference
[Be]tween the base and the legitimate,
Compassionate nature makes them equal, nay,
She many times prefers them.—I pray, resolve
me, sir,
Have not you and your mother had some suit
In law together lately ?

Rom. None, my lord.

Cris. No ! no contention about parting your
goods ?

Rom. Not any.

Cris. No flaw, no unkindness ?

Rom. None that ever arriv'd at my knowledge.

Cris. Bethink yourself: this cannot choose but
savour
Of a woman's malice deeply ; and I fear
You're practis'd upon most devilishly.— How
happ'd,
Gentlewoman, you reveal'd this no sooner ?

Leon. While my husband liv'd, my lord, I durst
not.

Cris. I should rather ask you why you reveal
it now ?

Leon. Because, my lord, I loath'd that such
  a sin
Should lie smother'd with me in my grave: my
  penitence,
Though to my shame, prefers the revealing of it
'Bove worldly reputation.

Cris. Your penitence!
Might not your penitence have been as hearty,
Though it had never summon'd to the court
Such a conflux of people?

Leon. Indeed, I might have confess'd it
  privately
To the church, I grant; but you know repentance
Is nothing without satisfaction.

Cris. Satisfaction! why, your husband's dead:
What satisfaction can you make him?

Leon. The greatest satisfaction in the world,
  my lord;
To restore the land to the right heir, and that's
My daughter.

Cris. O, she's straight begot, then.

Ario. Very well: may it please this honourable
  court,
If he be a bastard, and must forfeit his land
  for't,
She has prov'd herself a strumpet, and must lose
Her dower: let them go a begging together.

San. Who shall pay us our fees, then?

Cris. Most just.

Ario. You may see now what an old house
You are like to pull over your head, dame.

Rom. Could I conceive this publication
Grew from a hearty penitence, I could bear
My undoing the more patiently: but, my lord,
There is no reason, as you said even now,
To satisfy me but this suit of hers
Springs from a devilish malice, and her pretence
Of a griev'd conscience and religion,
Like to the horrid powder-treason in England,
Has a most bloody unnatural revenge
Hid under it. O, the violences of women!
Why, they are creatures made up and compounded
Of all monsters, poison'd minerals,
And sorcerous herbs that grow.

Ario. Are you angry yet?

Rom. Would man* express a bad one, let him
  forsake
All natural example, and compare
One to another: they have no more mercy
Than ruinous fires in great tempests.

Ario. Take heed you do not crack your voice,
  sir.

---

* man] The old copy "*men.*"

Rom. Hard-hearted creatures, good for nothing
  else
But to wind dead bodies.

Ario. Yes, to weave seaming-lace
With the bones of their husbands that were long
  since buried,
And curse them when they tangle.

Rom. Yet why do I
Take bastardy so distastefully, when i'the world
A many things that are essential parts
Of greatness are but by-slips, and are father'd
On the wrong parties,
Preferment in the world a many times
Basely begotten? nay, I have observ'd
The immaculate justice of a poor man's cause,
In such a court as this, has not known whom
To call father, which way to direct itself
For compassion—but I forget my temper:
Only, that I may stop that lawyer's throat,
I do beseech the court, and the whole world,
They will not think the baselier of me
For the vice of a mother; for that woman's sin,
To which you all dare swear when it was done,
I would not give my consent.

Cris. Stay, here's an accusation,
But here's no proof. What was the Spaniard's name
You accuse of adultery?

Contil. Don Crispiano, my lord.

Cris. What part of Spain was he born in?

Contil. In Castile.

Jul. This may prove my father.

San. And my master: my client's spoil'd, then.

Cris. I knew that Spaniard well: if you be a
  bastard,
Such a man being your father, I dare vouch you
A gentleman:—and in that, Signior Contilupo,
Your oratory went a little too far.
When do we name Don John of Austria,
The emperor's son, but with reverence?
And I have known in divers families
The bastards the greater spirits. But to the
  purpose:
What time was this gentleman begot?
And be sure you lay your time right.

Ario. Now the metal comes to the touchstone.

Contil. In anno seventy-one, my lord.

Cris. Very well, seventy-one;
The battle of Lepanto was fought in't;
A most remarkable time, 'twill lie
For no man's pleasure: and what proof is there,
More than the affirmation of the mother,
Of this corporal dealing?

Contil. The deposition
Of a waiting-woman serv'd her the same time.

Cris. Where is she?

Contd. Where is our solicitor with the waiting-woman?

Ario. Room for the bag and baggage!

San. Here, my lord, *ore tenus.*

Cris. And what can you say, gentlewoman?

Win. Please your lordship, I was the party that dealt in the business, and brought them together.

Cris. Well.

Win. And conveyed letters between them.

Cris. What needed letters, when 'tis said he lodged in her house?

Win. A running ballad now and then to her viol, for he was never well but when he was fiddling.

Cris. Speak to the purpose: did you ever know them bed together?

Win. No, my lord; but I have brought him to the bed-side.

Cris. That was somewhat near to the business. And, what, did you help him off with his shoes?

Win. He wore no shoes, an't please you, my lord.

Cris. No! what, then,—pumps?

Win. Neither.

Cris. Boots were not fit for his journey.

Win. He wore tennis-court woollen slippers, for fear of creaking, sir, and making a noise, to wake the rest o'the house.

Cris. Well, and what did he there in his tennis-court woollen slippers?

Win. Please your lordship, question me in Latin, for the cause is very foul: the examiner o'the court was fain to get it out of me alone i'the counting-house, 'cause he would not spoil the youth o'the office.

Ario. Here's a latten spoon, and a long one, to feed with the devil! *

Win. I'd be loth to be ignorant that way, for I hope to marry a proctor, and take my pleasure abroad at the commencements with him.

Ario. Come closer to the business.

Win. I will come as close as modesty will give me leave. Truth is, every morning when he lay with her, I made a caudle for him, by the appointment of my mistress, which he would still refuse, and call for small drink.

Cris. Small drink!

Ario. For a julep?

Win. And said he was wondrous thirsty.

Cris. What's this to the purpose?

Win. Most effectual, my lord. I have heard them laugh together extremely, and the curtain-rods fall from the tester of the bed: and he ne'er came from her but he thrust money in my hand, —and once, in truth, he would have had some dealing with me,—which I took; he thought 'twould be the only way i'the world to make me keep counsel the better.

San. That's a stinger: 'tis a good wench; be not daunted.

Cris. Did you ever find the print of two in the bed?

Win. What a question's that to be asked! may it please your lordship, 'tis to be thought he lay nearer to her than so.

Cris. What age are you of, gentlewoman?

Win. About six-and-forty, my lord.

Cris. Anno seventy-one,
And Romelio is thirty-eight: by that reckoning,
You were a bawd at eight year old: now, verily,
You fell to the trade betimes.

San. There you're from the bias.

Win. I do not know my age directly; sure, I am elder: I can remember two great frosts, and three great plagues, and the loss of Calais, and the first coming up of the breeches with the great codpiece; and I pray what age do you take me of, then?

San. Well come off again.

Ario. An old hunted hare;
She has all her doubles.

Rom. For your own gravities,
And the reverence of the court, I do beseech you,
Rip up the cause no further, but proceed
To sentence.

---

* *Here's a latten spoon and a long one, to feed with the devil!* Latten means a kind of mixed metal, the composition of which has been variously explained by lexicographers. According to Mr. Halliwell (*Dict. of Arch. and Prov. Words*) it very much resembled brass in its nature and colour.—Webster alludes here to the proverb: "he had need of a long spoon, that eats with the devil." The following anecdote, which fathers upon Shakespeare a pun similar to that in the text, has been repeated in several books: I now transcribe it from the MS. volume where it was originally discovered,—a collection of *Merry Passages and Jests* by L'Estrange, Sir Roger's nephew, among the Harleian MSS. 6395, Plut. LIX. A. "Shakespeare was godfather to one of Ben Jonson's children, and after the christening being in a deep study Jonson came to cheer him up, and askt him why he was so melancholy? no faith Ben (sayes he) not I, but I have been considering a great while what should be the fittest gift for me to bestow upon my God-child, and I

have resolved at last; I pry'the what, sayes he? I faith Ben I'le e'en give him a dozen good Lattin spoones, and thou shall translate them." At the end of the vol. the writer gives a list of his authorities, from which we learn, that the story just quoted was told to him by "Dun" (Donne?).

Cris. One question more, and I have done :
Might not this Crispiano, this Spaniard,
Lie with your mistress at some other time,
Either afore or after, than i'the absence
Of her husband ?

Leon. Never.

Cris. Are you certain of that ?

Leon. On my soul, never.

Cris. That's well, he never lay with her
But in anno seventy-one ; let that be remember'd.—
Stand you aside awhile.—Mistress, the truth is,
I knew this Crispiano, liv'd in Naples
At the same time, and lov'd the gentleman
As my bosom friend ; and, as I do remember,
The gentleman did leave his picture with you,
If age or neglect have not in so long time
Ruin'd it.

Leon. I preserve it still, my lord.

Cris. I pray, let me see't ; let me see the face
I then lov'd so much to look on.

Leon. Fetch it.

Win. I shall, my lord.

Cris. No, no, gentlewoman,
I have other business for you.

                    [*Exit one for the picture.*

First Sur. Now were the time to cut Romelio's
            throat,
And accuse him for your murder.

Con. By no means.

Second Sur. Will you not let us be men of
            fashion,
And down with him now he's going ?

Con. Peace ; let's attend the sequel.

Cris. I commend you, lady ;
There was a main matter of conscience.
How many ills spring from adultery !
First, the supreme law that is violated,
Nobility oft stain'd with bastardy,
Inheritance of land falsely possess'd,
The husband scorn'd, wife sham'd, and babes
            unblest.   [*The picture is brought in.*
So, hang it up i'the court.—You have heard
What has been urg'd against Romelio :
Now my definitive sentence in this cause
Is, I will give no sentence at all.

Ario. No ?

Cris. No, I cannot, for I am made a party.

San. How, a party ! here are fine cross tricks.
What the devil will he do now !

Cris. Signior Ariosto, his majesty of Spain
Confers my place upon you by this patent,
Which till this urgent hour I have kept
From your knowledge : may you thrive in't, noble
            sir,

And do that which but few in our place do,—
Go to their grave uncurs'd.

Ario. This law-business
Will leave me so small leisure to serve God,
I shall serve the king the worse.

San. Is he a judge ?
We must, then, look for all conscience, and no law :
He'll beggar all his followers.

Cris. Sir,
I am of your counsel, for the cause in hand
Was begun at such a time 'fore you could speak ;
You had need therefore have one speak for you.

Ario. Stay ; I do here first make protestation,
I ne'er took fee of this Romelio
For being of his counsel ; which may free me,
Being now his judge, for the imputation
Of taking a bribe. Now, sir, speak your mind.

Cris. I do first entreat that the eyes of all here
            present
May be fix'd upon this.

Leon. O, I am confounded ! this is Crispiano.

Jul. This is my father : how the judges have
            bleated him !

Win. You may see truth will out in spite of the
            devil.

Cris. Behold, I am the shadow of this shadow ;
Age has made me so : take from me forty years,
And I was such a summer-fruit as this,
At least the painter feign'd so ; for, indeed,
Painting and epitaphs are both alike,—
They flatter us, and say we have been thus.
But I am the party here that stands accus'd
For adultery with this woman, in the year
Seventy-one : now I call you, my lord, to witness,
Four years before that time I went to the Indies,
And till this month did never set my foot since
In Europe ; and for any former incontinence,
She has vow'd there was never any : what remains,
            then,
But this is a mere practice * 'gainst her son ?
And I beseech the court it may be sifted,
And most severely punish'd.

San. Ud's foot, we are spoil'd :
Why, my client's prov'd an honest woman.

Win. What do you think will become of me
            now ?

San. You'll be made dance *Lacrymæ*,† I fear, at a
            cart's tail.

---

* *practice*] See note *, p. 117.

† *dance Lacrymæ*] One of the allusions, so frequent in
our old dramatists, to a musical work by John Dowland,
the famous lutanist, "the rarest musician" according to
A. Wood, (*Fasti Oxon.* Part I. p. 242, ed. Bliss,) "that his
age did behold :" it is dedicated to Anne, the Queen of
James I. and entitled *Lacrimæ, or seven Teares figured in*

Ario. You, mistress, where are you now?
Your tennis-court slippers * and your ta'en drink
In a morning for your hot liver? where's the man
Would have had some dealing with you, that you
     might
Keep counsel the better?

Win. May it please the court, I am but a young
thing, and was drawn arsy-varsy into the business.

Ario. How young? of five-and-forty?

Win. Five-and-forty! an shall please you, I am
not five-and-twenty: she made me colour my hair
with bean-flower, to seem elder than I was; and
then my rotten teeth, with eating sweet-meats,—
why, should a farrier look in my mouth, he might
mistake my age.—O mistress, mistress, you are
an honest woman; and you may be ashamed on't,
to abuse the court thus!

Leon. Whatso'er I have attempted
'Gainst my own fame or the reputation
Of that gentleman my son, the Lord Contarino
Was cause of it.

Con. [*aside*]. Who, I?

Ario. He that should have married your
     daughter?
It was a plot belike, then, to confer
The land on her that should have been his wife.

Leon. More than I have said already all the world
Shall ne'er extract from me:—I entreat from both
Your equal pardons.

Jul. And I from you, sir.

Cris. Sirrah, stand you aside;
I will talk with you hereafter.

Jul. I could never away with † after-reckonings.

Leon. And now, my lords, I do most voluntarily
Confine myself unto a stricter prison
And a severer penance than this court
Can impose; I am enter'd into religion.

Con. [*aside*]. I the cause of this practice! this
     ungodly woman
Has sold herself to falsehood: I will now
Reveal myself.

Erco. [*coming from the closet*]. Stay, my lord;
     here's a window
To let in more light to the court.

Con. [*aside*]. Mercy upon me! O, that thou art
     living,
Is mercy indeed!

First Sur. Stay; keep in your shell a little longer.

Erco. I am Ercole.

---

*scaven passionate Pauans, with divers other Pauans,
Galiards, and Almands, set forth for the Lute, Viols, or
Violons, in five parts.*

* *slippers*] The old copy "*slips*;" but see p. 136.

† *away with*] i. e. endure.

Ario. A guard upon him for the death of
     Contarino!

Erco. I obey the arrest o'the court.

Rom. O, sir, you are happily restor'd to life
And to us your friends!

Erco. Away! thou art the traitor
I only live to challenge: this former suit
Touch'd but thy fame; this accusation
Reaches to thy fame and life. The brave Contarino
Is generally suppos'd slain by this hand,—

Con. [*aside*]. How knows he the contrary?

Erco. But truth is,
Having receiv'd from me some certain wounds
Which were not mortal, this vile murderer,
Being by will deputed overseer
Of the nobleman's estate to his sister's use,
That he might make him sure from * surviving
To revoke that will, stole to him in his bed
And kill'd him.

Rom. Strange, unheard of! more practice yet!

Ario. What proof of this?

Erco. The report of his mother deliver'd to me,
In distraction for Contarino's death.

Con. [*aside*]. For my death! I begin to apprehend
That the violence of this woman's love to me
Might practise the disinheriting of her son.

Ario. What say you to this, Leonora?

Leon. Such a thing
I did utter out of my distraction:
But how the court will censure that report,
I leave to their wisdoms.

Ario. My opinion is,
That this late slander urg'd against her son
Takes from her all manner of credit: she
That would not stick to deprive him of his living
Will as little tender his life.

Leon. I beseech the court
I may retire myself to my place of penance
I have vow'd myself and my woman.

Ario. Go when you please.
     [*Exeunt* LEONORA, *and* WINIFRED.
         What should move you be
Thus forward in the accusation?

Erco. My love to Contarino.

Ario. O, it bore
Very bitter fruit at your last meeting.

Erco. 'Tis true: but I begun to love him when
I had most cause to hate him; when our bloods
Embrac'd each other, then I pitied
That so much valour should be hazarded
On the fortune of a single rapier,
And not spent against the Turk.

Ario. Stay, sir, be well advis'd;

---

* *from*] In some of the old copies this word is omitted.

There is no testimony but your own
To approve you slew him; therefore no other way
To decide it but by duel.

    Con. Yes, my lord, I dare affirm, 'gainst all the
      world,
This nobleman speaks truth.

    Ario. You will make yourself a party in the duel.

    Rom. Let him; I will fight with them both, six-
teen of them.

    Erco. Sir, I do not know you.

    Con. Yes, but you have forgot me; you and I
Have sweat in the breach together at Malta.

    Erco. Cry you mercy; I have known of your
nation
Brave soldiers.

    Jul. [*aside*]. Now, if my father
Have any true spirit in him, I'll recover
His good opinion.—Do you hear? do not swear, sir,
For I dare swear that you will swear a lie,
A very filthy, stinking, rotten lie;
And if the lawyers think not this sufficient,
I'll give the lie in the stomach,—
That's somewhat deeper than the throat,—
Both here, and all France over and over,
From Marseilles or Bayonne to Calais' sands,
And there draw my sword upon thee, and new
    scour it
In the gravel of thy kidneys.

    Ario. You the defendant
Charg'd with the murder, and you second there,

Must be committed to the custody
Of the Knight-Marshal;—and the court gives
    charge
They be to-morrow ready in the lists
Before the sun be risen.

    Rom. I do entreat the court there be a guard
Plac'd o'er my sister, that she enter not
Into religion : she's rich, my lords,
And the persuasions of friars, to gain
All her possessions to their monasteries,
May do much upon her.

    Ario. We'll take order for her.

    Cris. There is a nun too you have got with child :
How will you dispose of her?

    Rom. You question me as if I were grav'd
    already :
When I have quench'd this wild-fire in Ercole's
Tame blood, I'll tell you.   [*Exit.*

    Erco. You have judg'd to-day
A most confused practice, that takes end
In as bloody a trial; and we may observe
By these great persons, and their indirect
Proceedings, shadow'd in a veil of state,
Mountains are deform'd heaps, swell'd up aloft,
Vales wholesomer, though lower and trod on oft.

    San. Well, I will put up my papers,
And send them to France for a precedent,
That they may not say yet, but for one strange
    law-suit
We come somewhat near them.   [*Exeunt.*

ACT V.

SCENE I.*

Enter JOLENTA, *and* ANGIOLELLA *great-bellied.*

    Jol. How dost thou, friend? welcome: thou
    and I
Were play-fellows together, little children,
So small a while ago, that, I presume,
We are neither of us wise yet.

    Angio. A most sad truth on my part.

    Jol. Why do you pluck your veil
Over your face?

    Angio. If you will believe truth,
There's naught more terrible to a guilty heart
Than† the eye of a respected friend.

    Jol. Say, friend,
Are you quick with child?

    Angio. Too sure.

    Jol. How could you know first *
Of your child when you quicken'd?

    Angio. How could you know, friend!
'Tis reported you are in the same taking.

    Jol. Ha, ha, ha! so 'tis given out;
But Ercole's coming to life again has shrunk
And made invisible my great belly; yes, faith,
My being with child was merely in supposition,
Not practice.

    Angio. You are happy : what would I give
To be a maid again!

    Jol. Would you? to what purpose?
I would never give great purchase for that thing
Is in danger every hour to be lost. Pray thee,
    laugh :
A boy or a girl, for a wager?

---

   * *Scene I.*] A room in the house of Leonora.
   † *Than*] The old copy "*As.*"

               first
Of your] The old copy "*Of your first.*"

Angio. What heaven please.

Jol. Nay, nay, will you venture
A chain of pearl with me, whether?

Angio. I'll lay nothing;
I have ventur'd too much for't already, my fame.
I make no question, sister, you have heard
Of the intended combat.

Jol. O, what else?
I have a sweetheart in't against a brother.

Angio. And I a dead friend, I fear: what good
counsel
Can you minister unto me?

Jol. Faith, only this;
Since there's no means i'the world to hinder it,
Let thou and I, wench, get as far as we can
From the noise of it.

Angio. Whither?

Jol. No matter, any whither.

Angio. Any whither, so you go not by sea:
I cannot abide rough * water.

Jol. Not endure to be tumbled? say no more,
then;
We'll be land-soldiers for that trick: take heart,
Thy boy shall be born a brave Roman.

Angio. O, you mean
To go to Rome, then.

Jol. Within there!

     Enter a Servant.

         Bear this letter
To the Lord Ercole.   [*Exit Servant with letter.*]
         Now, wench, I am for thee,
All the world over.

Angio. I, like your shade, pursue you.
                        [*Exeunt.*]

SCENE II.†

Enter PROSPERO *and* SANITONELLA.

Pros. Well, I do not think but to see you as
pretty a piece of law-flesh!

San. In time I may: marry, I am resolved to
take a new way for't. You have lawyers take
their clients' fees, and their backs are no sooner
turned but they call them fools, and laugh at them.

Pros. That's ill done of them.

San. There's one thing too that has a vile abuse
in't.

Pros. What's that?

San. Marry, this,—that no proctor in the term-
time be tolerated to go to the tavern above six
times i'the forenoon.

Pros. Why, man?

San. O, sir, it makes their clients overtaken,
and become friends sooner than they would be.

Enter ERCOLE *with a letter, and* CONTARINO, *coming in
friars' habits, as having been at the Bathanites, a
ceremony used afore these combats.*

Erco. Leave the room, gentlemen.
                [*Exeunt* SANIT. *and* PROS.

Con. [*aside*]. Wherefore should I with such an
obstinacy
Conceal myself any longer? I am taught,
That all the blood which will be shed to-morrow
Must fall upon my head: one question
Shall fix it or untie it.—Noble brother,
I would fain know how it is possible,
When it appears you love the fair Jolenta
With such a height of fervor you were ready
To father another's child and marry her,
You would so suddenly engage yourself
To kill her brother, one that ever stood
Your loyal and firm friend?

Erco. Sir, I'll tell you;
My love, as I have formerly protested,
To Contarino, whose unfortunate end
The traitor wrought: and here is one thing more
Deads all good thoughts of him, which I now
receiv'd
From Jolenta.

Con. In a letter?

Erco. Yes, in this letter;
For, having sent to her to be resolv'd
Most truly who was father of the child,
She writes back that the shame she goes withal
Was begot by her brother.

Con. O most incestuous villain!

Erco. I protest,
Before I thought 'twas Contarino's issue,
And for that would have veil'd her dishonour.

Con. No more.
Has the armorer brought the weapons?

Erco. Yes, sir.

Con. I will no more think of her.

Erco. Of whom?

Con. Of my mother,—I was thinking of my
mother.
Call the armorer.   [*Exeunt.*

SCENE III.*

Enter First Surgeon, *and* WINIFRED.

Win. You do love me, sir, you say?

First Sur. O, most entirely!

---

* *salt*] Some of the old copies "*sault.*"
† *Scene II.*] An apartment in Castel Nuovo.

* *Scene III.*] A room in the house of Leonora.

Win. And you will marry me ?

First Sur. Nay, I'll do more than that :
The fashion of the world is many times
To make a woman naught, and afterwards
To marry her ; but I, o'the contrary,
Will make you honest first, and afterwards
Proceed to the wedlock.

Win. Honest ! what mean you by that ?

First Sur. I mean, that your suborning the
    late law-suit
Has got you a filthy report : now, there's no way,
But to do some excellent piece of honesty,
To recover your good name.

Win. How, sir ?

First Sur. You shall straight go and reveal to
    your old mistress,
For certain truth, Contarino is alive.

Win. How, living !

First Sur. Yes, he is living.

Win. No, I must not tell her of it.

First Sur. No ! why ?

Win. For she did bind me yesterday by oath
Never more to speak of him.

First Sur. You shall reveal it, then,
To Ariosto the judge.

Win. By no means ; he has heard me tell
So many lies i'the court, he'll ne'er believe me.
What if I told it to the Capuchin ?

First Sur. You cannot
Think of a better ; as for* your young mistress,
Who, as you told me, has persuaded you
To run away with her, let her have her humour.
I have a suit Romelio left i'the house,
The habit of a Jew, that I'll put on,
And pretending I am robb'd, by break of day,
Procure all passengers to be brought back,
And by the way reveal myself, and discover
The comical event. They say she's a little mad ;
This will help to cure her. Go, go presently,
And reveal it to the Capuchin.

Win. Sir, I shall.   [*Exeunt.*

———◆———

SCENE IV.†

Enter JULIO, PROSPERO, *and* SANITOGELLA.

Jul. A pox on't,
I have undertaken the challenge very foolishly :
What if I do not appear to answer it ?

Pro. It would be absolute conviction
Of cowardice and perjury ; and the Dane
May to your public shame reverse your arms,

     * *as for*] The old copy "*for as.*"
     † *Scene IV.*] An apartment in Castel Nuovo.

Or have them ignominiously fasten'd
Under his horse-tail.

Jul. I do not like that so well.
I see, then, I must fight, whether I will or no.

Pros. How does Romelio bear himself ? They say
He has almost brain'd one of our cunning'st
    fencers
That practis'd with him.

Jul. Very certain : and now you talk of fencing,
Do not you remember the Welsh gentleman
That was travelling to Rome upon return ?

Pros. No : what of him ?

Jul. There was a strange experiment of a fencer.

Pros. What was that ?

Jul. The Welshman in's play, do what the
    fencer could,
Hung still an arse ; he could not for his life
Make him come on bravely ; till one night at
    supper,
Observing what a deal of Parma-cheese
His scholar devour'd, goes ingeniously
The next morning and makes a spacious button
For his foil of toasted cheese ; and, as sure as
    you live,
That made him come on the braveliest.

Pros. Possible ?

Jul. Marry, it taught him an ill grace in's play,
It made him gape still, gape as he put in for't,
As I have seen some hungry usher.

San. The toasting of it belike
Was to make it more supple, had he chanc'd
To have hit him o'the chaps.

Jul. Not unlikely. Who can tell me
If we may breathe in the duel ?

Pros. By no means.

Jul. Nor drink ?

Pros. Neither.

Jul. That's scurvy ; anger will make me very
    dry.

Pros. You mistake, sir ; 'tis sorrow that is very
    dry.

San. Not always, sir ; I have known sorrow
    ·very wet.

Jul. In rainy weather ?

San. No ; when a woman has come dropping wet
Out of a cucking-stool.

Jul. Then 'twas wet indeed. sir.

Enter ROMELIO *very melancholy ; and then the* Capuchin.

Cap. [*aside*]. Having from Leonora's waiting-
    woman
Deliver'd a most strange intelligence
Of Contarino's recovery, I am come
To sound Romelio's penitence ; that perform'd,

To end these errors by discovering
What she related to me.—Peace to you, sir !
                                        [To ROMELIO.
Pray, gentlemen, let the freedom of this room
Be mine a little.—Nay, sir, you may stay.
                                        [To JULIO.
                [Exeunt PROSPERO and SANITONELLA.
Will you pray with me?
    Rom. No, no, the world and I
Have not made up our accounts yet.
    Cap. Shall I pray for you?
    Rom. Whether you do or no, I care not.
    Cap. O, you have a dangerous voyage to take !
    Rom. No matter, I will be mine own pilot:
Do not you trouble your head with the business.
    Cap. Pray, tell me, do not you meditate of death?
    Rom. Phew, I took out that lesson,
When I once lay sick of an ague : I do now
Labour for life, for life. Sir, can you tell me,
Whether your Toledo or your Milan blade
Be best temper'd?
    Cap. These things, you know,
Are out of my practice.
    Rom. But these are things, you know,
I must practise with to-morrow.
    Cap. Were I in your case,
I should present to myself strange shadows.
    Rom. Turn you,—were I in your case, I should
                                        laugh
At mine own shadow. Who has hirèd you
To make me coward?
    Cap. I would make you a good Christian.
    Rom. Withal let me continue
An honest man ; which I am very certain
A coward can never be. You take upon you
A physician's place, rather than a divine's :
You go about to bring my body so low,
I should fight i'the lists to-morrow like a dor-
And be made away in a slumber.   [mouse,
    Cap. Did you murder Contarino?
    Rom. That's a scurvy question now.
    Cap. Why, sir?
    Rom. Did you ask it as a confessor or as a spy?
    Cap. As one that fain would justle the devil
Out of your way.
    Rom. Um, you are but weakly made for't :
He's a cunning wrestler, I can tell you, and has
                                        broke
Many a man's neck.
    Cap. But to give him the foil
Goes not by strength.
    Rom. Let it go by what it will.
Get me some good victuals to breakfast, I am
    hungry.

    Cap. Here's food for you. [*Offering him a book.*
    Rom. Phew, I am not to commence doctor ;
For then the word,* "Devour that book," were
    proper.
I am to fight, to fight, sir ; and I'll do't,
As I would feed, with a good stomach.
    Cap. Can you feed,
And apprehend death?
    Rom. Why, sir, is not death
A hungry companion? say, is not the grave
Said to be a great devourer? Get me some victuals :
I know a man that was to lose his head
Feed with an excellent good appetite,
To strengthen his heart, scarce half an hour
    before ;
And if he did it that only was to speak,
What should I that am to do?
    Cap. This confidence,
If it be grounded upon truth, 'tis well.
    Rom. You must understand that resolution
Should ever wait upon a noble death,
As captains bring their soldiers out o'the field,
And come off last ; for, I pray, what is death?
The safest trench i'the world to keep man free
From fortune's gunshot : to be afraid of that,
Would prove me weaker than a teeming woman,
That does endure a thousand times more pain
In bearing of a child.
    Cap. O, I tremble for you !
For I do know you have a storm within you
More terrible than a sea-fight, and, your soul
Being heretofore drown'd in security,
You know not how to live nor how to die :
But I have an object that shall startle you,
And make you know whither you are going.
    Rom. I am arm'd for't.

*Enter LEONORA, with two coffins borne by her servants, and
    two winding-sheets stuck with flowers ; presents one to
    her son, and the other to Julio.*

'Tis very welcome ; this is a decent garment
Will never be out of fashion : I will kiss it.—
All the flowers of the spring
Meet to perfume our burying :
These have but their growing prime ;
And man does flourish but his time :
Survey our progress from our birth ;
We are set, we grow, we turn to earth.
Courts adieu, and all delights,   [*Soft music.*
All bewitching appetites !
Sweetest breath, and clearest eye,
Like perfumes, go out and die ;

                * *the word*] See note §, p. 16.

And consequently this is done
As shadows wait upon the sun.
Vain the ambition of kings,
Who seek by trophies and dead things
To leave a living name behind,
And weave but nets to catch the wind.—
O, you have wrought a miracle, and melted
A heart of adamant! you have compris'd
In this dumb pageant a right excellent form
Of penitence.

Cap. I am glad you so receive it.

Rom. This object does persuade me to forgive
The wrong she has done me, which I count the way
To be forgiven yonder; and this shrowd
Shows me how rankly we do smell of earth,
When we are in all our glory.—Will it please you
　　　　　　　　　　　　　　　[*To* LEONORA.

Enter that closet, where I shall confer
'Bout matters of most weighty consequence,
Before the duel? 　[*Exit* LEONORA *into the closet.*

Jul. Now I am right in the bandoleer for the
gallows.
What a scurvy fashion 'tis, to hang one's coffin in
a scarf!

Cap. Why, this is well:
And now that I have made you fit for death,
And brought you even as low as is the grave,
I will raise you up again, speak comforts to you
Beyond your hopes, turn this intended duel
To a triumph.

Rom. More divinity yet!
Good sir, do one thing first: there's in my closet
A prayer-book that is cover'd with gilt vellum;
Fetch it; and, pray you, certify my mother
I'll presently come to her.
　　　　　[*Exit the* Capuchin *into the closet, the door of
　　　　　which* RUMELIO *locks.*

　　　　　　　　　So now you are safe.

Jul. What have you done?

Rom. Why, I have lock'd them up
Into a turret of the castle, safe enough
For troubling us this four hours: an he please,
He may open a casement, and whistle out to
　　the sea
Like a boatswain; not any creature can hear him.
Was't not thou a-weary of his preaching?

Jul. Yes, if he had had an hour-glass by him,
I would have wish'd him he would have jogg'd
it a little.
But your mother, your mother's lock'd in too.

Rom. So much the better;
I am rid of her howling at parting.

Jul. Hark! he knocks to be let out, an he
were mad.

Rom. Let him knock till his sandals fly in pieces.

Jul. Ha! what says he? Contarino living!

Rom. Ay, ay,
He means he would have Contarino's living
Bestow'd upon his monastery; 'tis that
He only fishes for. So, 'tis break of day;
We shall be call'd to the combat presently.

Jul. I am sorry for one thing.

Rom. What's that?

Jul. That I made not mine own ballad: I do fear
I shall be roguishly abus'd in metre,
If I miscarry. Well, if the young Capuchin
Do not talk o'the flesh as fast now to your mother
As he did to us o'the spirit! If he do,
'Tis not the first time that the prison royal
Has been guilty of close committing.

Rom. Now to the combat.　　　　[*Exeunt.*

　　　　　　　　　———◆———

　　　　　　　　SCENE V.*

Enter CAPUCHIN *and* LEONORA, *above,† at a window.*

Leon. Contarino living!

Cap. Yes, madam, he is living, and Ercole's
second.

Leon. Why has he lock'd us up thus?

Cap. Some evil angel
Makes him deaf to his own safety: we are shut
Into a turret, the most desolate prison
Of all the castle; and his obstinacy,
Madness, or secret fate, has thus prevented
The saving of his life.

Leon. O, the saving Contarino's!
His is worth nothing. For heaven's sake, call
louder.

Cap. To little purpose.

Leon. I will leap these battlements;
And may I be found dead time‡ enough
To hinder the combat!

Cap. O, look upwards rather:
Their deliverance must come thence. To see how
heaven
Can invert man's firmest purpose! His intent
Of murdering Contarino was a mean
To work his safety; and my coming hither
To save him is his ruin: wretches turn
The tide of their good fortune, and being drench'd
In some presumptuous and hidden sins,
While they aspire to do themselves most right,
The devil, that rules i'the air§, hangs in their light.

---

* *Scene V.*" Before Castel Nuovo.
† *above*] See note *, p. 100.
‡ *time*] Qy. "*in time*"? But the versification of this
play is in many places wretched.
§ *The devil, that rules i' the air,* &c.] See note †, p. 67.

Leon. O, they must not be lost thus! Some good
 Christian
Come within our hearing! Ope the other case-
 ment
That looks into the city.
 Cap. Madam, I shall.   [*Exeunt.*

SCENE VI.

The lists set up. *Enter the* Marshal, CRISPIANO, *and*
ARIOSTO, *who take their seats as Judges; and*
SANITONELLA.

 Mar. Give the appellant his summons; do the
 like
To the defendant.

Two tuckets by several trumpets. Enter, at one door, ERCOLE
and CONTARINO; *at the other,* ROMELIO *and* JULIO.

Can any of you allege aught why the combat
Should not proceed?
 Combatants. Nothing.
 Ario. Have the knights weigh'd,
And measur'd their weapons?
 Mar. They have.
 Ario. Proceed, then, to the battle, and may
 heaven
Determine the right!
 Herald. Soit la battaile, et victoire à ceux qui
 ont droit!
 Rom. Stay! I do not well know whither I am
 going;
'Twere needful therefore, though at the last gasp,
To have some church-man's prayer.—Run, I pray
 thee,
To Castel Nuovo*: this key will release
A Capuchin and my mother, whom I shut
Into a turret; bid him† make haste and pray;
I may be dead ere he comes. [*Exit an* Attendant.
Now, *Victoire à ceux qui ont droit!*
All the Champ. Victoire à ceux qui ont droit!

The combat is continued to a good length, when enter
LEONORA *and the* CAPUCHIN.

 Leon. Hold, hold, for heaven's sake, hold!
 Ario. What are these that interrupt the combat?
Away to prison with them!
 Cap. We have been prisoners too long.—
O, sir, what mean you? Contarino's living.
 Erco. Living!
 Cap. Behold him living.

---

* *Castel Nuovo*] Concerning "the Castel Nuovo, an
ancient Spanish castle, of enormous dimensions," see
Naples, Political, Social, and Religious. By Lord B * * * * *,
1856, vol. i. 6.
† *him*] The old copy "*them.*"

 Erco. You were but now my second; now I
 make you
Myself for ever.
 Leon. O, here's one between
Claims to be nearer.
 Con. And to you, dear lady,
I have entirely vow'd my life.
 Rom. If I do not
Dream, I am happy too.
 Ario. How insolently
Has this high Court of Honour been abus'd!

Enter ANGIOLELLA *veiled, and* JOLENTA, *her face coloured
like a Moor; the two* Surgeons, *one of them like a Jew.*

How now! who are these?
 Sec. Sur. A couple of strange fowl, and I the
 falconer
That have sprung them: this is a white nun
Of the order of Saint Clare; and this a black one;
You'll take my word for't. [*Discovers* JOLENTA.
 Ario. She's a black one, indeed.
 Jol. Like or dislike me, choose you whether:
The down upon the raven's feather
Is as gentle and as sleek
As the mole on Venus' cheek.
Hence, vain show! I only care
To preserve my soul most fair
Never mind the outward skin,
But the jewel that's within;
And though I want the crimson blood,
Angels boast the sisterhood.
Which of us now judge you whiter?
Her whose credit proves the lighter,
Or this black and ebon hue,
That, unstain'd, keeps fresh and true?
For I proclaim't without control,
There's no true beauty but i'the soul.
 Erco. O, 'tis the fair Jolenta!—To what purpose
Are you thus eclips'd?
 Jol. Sir, I was running away
From the rumour of this combat; I fled likewise
From the untrue report my brother spread,
To his politic ends, that I was got with child.
 Leon. Cease here all further scrutiny; this paper
Shall give unto the court each circumstance
Of all these passages.
 Ario. No more: attend the sentence of the
 court.
Rareness and difficulty give estimation
To all things are i'the world: you have met both
In these several passages: now it does remain
That these so comical events be blasted
With no severity of sentence. You, Romelio,
Shall first deliver to that gentleman,
Who stood your second, all those obligations

Wherein he stands engag'd to you, receiving
Only the principal.

Rom. I shall, my lord.

Jul. I thank you:
I have an humour now to go to sea
Against the pirates; and my only ambition
Is to have my ship furnish'd with a rare consort *
Of music, and when I am pleas'd to be mad,
They shall play me *Orlando.*

San. You must lay wait for the fiddlers;
They'll fly away from the press like watermen.

Ario. Next, you shall marry that nun.

Rom. Most willingly.

Angio. O sir, you have been unkind;
But I do only wish that this my shame
May warn all honest virgins not to seek

* *consort*] See note on *Northward Ho*, act ii., scene 1.

The way to heaven, that is so wondrous steep,
Th[o]rough those vows they are too frail to keep.

Ario. Contarino, and Romelio, and yourself,
Shall for seven years maintain against the Turk
Six galleys.—Leonora, Jolenta,
And Angiolella there, the beauteous nun,
For their vows' breach unto the monastery,
Shall build a monastery. — Lastly, the two
    surgeons,
For concealing Contarino's recovery,
Shall exercise their art at their own charge
For a twelvemonth in the galleys.—So we leave
    you,
Wishing your future life may make good use
Of these events, since that these passages,
Which threaten'd ruin, built on rotten ground,
Are with success beyond our wishes crown'd.

                  [*Exeunt.*

APPIUS AND VIRGINIA.

Appius and Virginia, a Tragedy. By John Webster. Printed in the year 1654. 4to.

The above is the only old edition of this play: it was put forth in 1659, with a new title-page, professing to be *Printed for Humphrey Moseley;* and again, with a third title-page, in 1679, as *Acted at the Dukes Theater under the name of The Roman Virgin or Unjust Judge,* and as *Printed, and are to be sold by most Booksellers.* It has been reprinted in the fifth vol. of a *Continuation of Dodsley's Old Plays.*

From a MS. in the Lord Chamberlain's Office, (see Malone's *Hist. Acc. of the English Stage,* p. 159, ed. Boswell,) entitled on the margin *Cockpitt Playes Appropried,* and dated Aug. 10, 1639, it appears that William Biestou [or Beeston] gent. governor of the King's and Queen's young company of players at the Cockpit in Drury-lane, having represented unto his Majesty, that forty-five plays, of which the names are given, and of which the last mentioned is *Appius and Virginia,* "doe all and every of them properly and of right belong to the myd house, and consequently that they are all his propriety," his Majesty signified his royal pleasure to the Lord Chamberlain, requiring him to declare to all other companies of actors, "that they are not any ways to intermeddle with or act any of the above-mentioned playes."

DRAMATIS PERSONÆ.

Virginius.
Appius Claudius.
Minutius.
Spurius Oppius.
Marcus Claudius.
Numitorius.
Icilius.
Valerius.
Horatius.*
Sertorius.
Two Cousins of Applus.
An Advocate.
A Roman Officer.
Senators
Corbulo, the Clown.

Virginia.
Julia.
Calphurnia.
Nurse.

Lictors, Soldiers, Servants, &c.

---

* *Horatius*] In the old copy, this personage is, throughout the play, called "*Horatio*."

APPIUS AND VIRGINIA.

ACT I.

SCENE I.*

Enter MINUTIUS, OPPIUS, *and* Lictors.

Min. Is Appius sent for, that we may acquaint him
With the decree o' the senate?

First Lict. He is, my lord,
And will attend your lordships presently.

Opp. Lictor, did you tell him that our business
Was from the senate?

First Lict. I did, my lord; and here he is at hand.

Enter APPIUS CLAUDIUS, *his two* Cousins, *and* MARCUS CLAUDIUS.

App. Claud. My lords, your pleasure?

Min. Appius,† the senate greet you well, and by us do signify unto you that they have chosen you one of the Decemviri.

App. Claud. My lords, far be it from the thoughts of so poor a plebeian as your unworthy servant Appius to soar so high: the dignity of so eminent a place would require a person of the best parts and blood in Rome. My lords, he that must steer at the head of an empire ought to be the mirror of the times for wisdom and for policy; and therefore I would beseech the senate to elect one worthy of the place, and not to think of one so unfit as Appius.

Min. My lord, my lord, you dally with your wits.

---

* *Scene I.*] Rome. Before the Senate-house.

† *Appius*, &c.] Though this and the next speech are so arranged in the old copy as to look like blank-verse, they are undoubtedly prose (to which the editor of 1816 reduced only the latter one). Qy. is there any corruption here? Since throughout all the rest of the play Minutius and Appius speak in blank-verse, we may wonder that in this solitary instance Webster should have made them speak in prose.

I have seen children * oft eat sweetmeats thus,
As fearful to devour them:
You are wise, and play the modest courtier right,
To make so many bits of your delight.

Opp. But you must know, what we have once concluded
Cannot, for any private man's affection,
Be slighted. Take your choice, then, with best judgment
Of these two proffers; either to accept
The place propos'd you, or be banish'd Rome
Immediately.—Lictors, make way!—We expect
Your speedy resolution.

[*Exeunt* OPPIUS, MINUTIUS, *and* Lict

First Cous. Noble cousin,
You wrong yourself extremely to refuse
So eminent a place.

Sec. Cous. It is a means
To raise your kindred. Who shall dare t' oppose
Himself against our family, when yonder
Shall sit your power and frown?

App. Claud. Or banish'd Rome!—
I pray, forbear a little.—Marcus,—

Mar. Claud. Sir?

App. Claud. How dost thou like my cunning?

Mar. Claud. I protest
I was be-agu'd, fearing lest the senate
Should have accepted at your feign'd refusal.
See how your kindred and your friends are muster'd
To warm them at your sun-shine! Were you now
In prison, or arraign'd before the senate
For some suspect of treason, all these swallows
Would fly your stormy winter; not one sing:
Their music is the summer and the spring.

---

* *I have seen children*, &c.] See note *, p. 65.

App. Claud. Thou observ'st shrewdly. Well,
    I'll fit them for't.
I must be one of the Decemviri,
Or banish'd Rome! banish'd! laugh, my trusty
    Marcus;
I am enforc'd to my ambition.
I have heard of cunning footmen that have worn
Shoes made of lead some ten days fore a race,
To give them nimble and more active feet:
So great men should, that aspire eminent place,
Load themselves with excuse and faint denial,
That they with more speed may perform the trial.
" Mark his humility," says one : " How far
His dreams are from ambition !" says another;
" He would not show his eloquence, lest that
Should draw him into office :" and a third
Is meditating on some thrifty suit
To beg fore dinner. Had I as many hands
As had Briareus, I'd extend them all
To catch this office : 'twas my sleep's disturber,
My diet's ill digestion, my melancholy,
Past physic's cure.
    Mar. Claud. The senators return.

    Re-enter MINUTIUS, OPPIUS, *and* Lictors.

Min. My lord, your answer ?
App. Claud. To obey, my lord, and to know
    how to rule,
Do differ much : to obey, by nature comes ;
But to command, by long experience.
Never were great men in so eminent place
Without their shadows : envy will attend
On greatness till this general frame takes end.
'Twixt these extremes of state and banishment
My mind hath held long conflict, and at last
I thus return my answer :—noble friends,
We now must part ; necessity of state
Compels it so ;
I must inhabit now a place unknown ;
You see't compels me leave you. Fare you well.
    First Cous. To banishment, my lord ?
    App. Claud. I am given up
To a long travel full of fear and danger ;
To waste the day in sweat, and the cold night
In a most desolate contemplation ;
Banish'd from all my kindred and my friends ;
Yea, banish'd from myself ; for I accept
This honourable calling.
    Min. Worthy Appius,
The gods conduct you hither.— Lictors, his
    robes.
    Sec. Cous. We are made for ever, noble kins-
    man :
'Twas but to fright us

App. Claud. But, my loving kinsmen,
Mistake me not ; for what I spake was true,
Bear witness all the gods. I told you first,
I was to inhabit in a place unknown :
'Tis very certain, for this reverend seat
Receives me as a pupil ; rather gives
Ornament to the person, than our person
The least of grace to it. I show'd you next
I am to travel ; * 'tis a certain truth :
Look, by how much the labour of the mind
Exceeds the body's, so far am I bound
With pain and industry, beyond the toil
Of those that sweat in war ; beyond the toil
Of any artisan : pale cheeks, and sunk eyes,
A head with watching dizzied, and a hair
Turn'd white in youth,—all these at a dear rate
We purchase speedily that tend a state.
I told you I must leave you ; 'tis most true :
Henceforth the face of a barbarian
And yours shall be all one ; henceforth I'll know
    you
But only by your virtue : brother or father,
In [a] dishonest suit, shall be to me
As is the branded slave. Justice should have
No kindred, friends nor foes, nor hate nor love ;
As free from passion as the gods above.
I was your friend and kinsman, now your judge ;
And whilst I hold the scales, a downy feather
Shall as soon turn them as a mass of pearl
Or diamonds.
    Mar. Claud. [*aside*]. Excellent, excellent lap-
    wing !
There's other stuff clos'd in that subtle breast :
He sings and beats his wings far from his nest.
    App. Claud. So, gentlemen, I take it, here
    takes end
Your business, my acquaintance : fare you well.
    First Cous. Here's a quick change ! who did
    expect this cloud ?
Thus men when they grow great do straight
    grow proud.   [*Exeunt* Cousins.
    App. Claud. Now to our present business at the
    camp.
The army that doth winter before Algidum †
Is much distress'd we hear : Minutius,
You, with the levies and the little corn
This present dearth will yield, are speedily
To hasten thither ; so to appease the mind
Of the intemperate soldier.
    Min. I am ready ;
The levies do attend me : our lieutenant
Send on our troops.

---

* *travel*] See note †, p. 112.
† *before Algidum*] Old copy "'fore Agidon."

App. Claud. Farewell, Minutius:
The gods go with you, and be still at hand
To add a triumph to your bold command.
                                    [*Exeunt.*

SCENE II.*

Enter NUMITORIUS, ICILIUS, *and* VIRGINIA

Num. Noble Icilius, welcome: teach yourself
A bolder freedom here; for, by our love,
Your suit to my fair niece doth parallel
Her kindred's wishes. There's not in all Rome
A man that is by honour more approv'd,
Nor worthier, were you poor, to be belov'd.

Icil. You give me, noble lord, that character
Which I could never yet read in myself:
But from your censure † shall I take much care
To adorn it with the fairest ornaments
Of unambitious virtue. Here I hold
My honourable pattern; one whose mind
Appears more like a ceremonious chapel
Full of sweet music, than a thronging presence.
I am confirm'd the court doth make some show
Fairer than else they would do; but her port,
Being simple virtue, beautifies the court.

Virginia. It is a flattery, my lord,
You breathe upon me; and it shows much like
The borrow'd painting which some ladies use:
It is not to continue many days;
My wedding-garments will outwear this praise.

Num. Thus ladies still foretell the funeral
Of their lords' kindness.

Enter a Servant, who whispers ICILIUS *in the ear.*

                    But, my lord, what news?
Icil. Virginius, my lord, your noble brother,
Disguis'd in dust and sweat, is new arriv'd
Within the city: troops of artisans
Follow his panting horse, and with a strange
Confus'd noise, partly with joy to see him,
Partly with fear for what his haste portends;
They show as if a sudden mutiny
O'erspread the city.

Num. Cousin, take your chamber.
                    „ [*Exit* VIRGINIA.

What business from the camp?
Icil. Sure, sir, it bears
The form of some great danger; for his horse,
Bloody with spurring, shows as if he came
From forth a battle: never did you see
'Mongst quails or cocks in fight a bloodier heel
Than that your brother strikes with. In this form

Of o'erspent horseman, having, as it seems,
With the distracting of his news, forgot
House, friends, or change of raiment, he is gone
To the senate-house.

Num. Now the gods bring us safety!
The face of this is cloudy: let us haste
To the senate-house, and there inquire how near
The body moves of this our threaten'd fear.
                                    [*Exeunt.*

SCENE III.*

Enter APPIUS CLAUDIUS *melancholy; after,* MARCUS
CLAUDIUS.

Mar. Claud. My lord,—
App. Claud. Thou troublest me.
Mar. Claud. My hand's as ready arm'd to
        work your peace,
As my tongue bold to inquire your discontents:
Good my lord, hear me.

App. Claud. I am at much variance
Within myself; there's discord in my blood;
My powers are all in combat; I have nothing
Left but sedition in me.

Mar. Claud. Trust my bosom
To be the closet of your private griefs
Believe me, I am uncrannied.

App. Claud. May I trust thee?
Mar. Claud. As the firm centre to endure the
        burden
Of your light foot; as you would trust the poles
To bear on them this airy canopy,
And not to fear their shrinking. I am strong,
Fix'd, and unshaking.

App. Claud. Art thou? then thine ear: †
I love.

Mar. Claud. Ha! ha! he!
App. Claud. Can this my ponderous secrecy
Be in thine ear so light? seems my disturbance
Worthy such scorn that thou derid'st my griefs
Believe me, Claudius, I am not a twig
That every gust can shake, but 'tis a tempest
That must be able to use violence
On my grown branches. Wherefore laugh'st
        thou, then?

Mar. Claud. Not that you're mov'd: it makes
        me smile in scorn,
That wise men cannot understand themselves,
Nor know their own prov'd greatness. Claudius
        laughs not
To think you love; but that you are so hopeless
Not to presume to enjoy whom you affect.

What's she iu Rome your greatuess cannot awe,
Or your rich purse purchase?　Promises and
　　threats
Are statesmen's lictors to arrost such pleasures
As they would bring within their strict com-
　　mands:
Why should my lord droop, or deject his eye?
Can you command Rome, and not countermand
A woman's weakness?　Let your grace bestow
Your purse and power on me: I'll prostrate you.*
　　App. Claud. Ask both, and lavish them to
　　　　purchase me
The rich fee-simple of Virginia's heart.
　　Mar. Claud. Virginia's!
　　App. Claud. Hers.
　　Mar. Claud. I have already found
An easy path which you may safely tread,
Yet no man trace you.
　　App. Claud. Thou art my comforter.
　　Mar. Claud. Her father's busied iu our foreign
　　　　wars,
And there hath chief employment: all their pay
Must your discretion scantle; keep it back;
Restrain it in the common treasury:
Thus may a statesman 'gainst a soldier stand,
To keep his purse weak, whilst you arm his
　　hand.
Her father thus kept low, gifts and rewards
Will tempt the maid the sooner; nay, haply
　　draw
The father in to plead in your behalf.
But should these fail, then siege her virgin tower
With two prevailing engines, fear aud power.
　　App. Claud. Go, then, and prove a speeding ad-
　　　　vocate:
Arm thee with all our bounty, oratory,
Variety of promise.

Enter VALERIUS.

　　Val. Lord Appius, the Decemvirate entreat
Your voice in this day's senate.　Old Virginius
Craves audience from the camp, with earnest suit
For quick despatch.
　　App. Claud. We will attend the senate.—
Claudius, be gone.
　　　　　[*Exeunt* MARCUS CLAUDIUS *and* VALERIUS.

Enter OPPIUS *and* SENATORS.†

　　Opp. We sent to you to assist us in this council
Touching the expeditions of our war.

　　App. Claud. Ours is a willing presence to the
　　trouble
Of all state-cares.—Admit him from the camp.

Enter VIRGINIUS.

　　Opp. Speak the camp's will.
　　Virginius. The camp wants money; we have
　　store of knocks,
And wounds God's plenty, but we have no pay:
This three months did we never house our heads
But in yon great star-chamber; never bedded
But in the cold field-beds; our victual fails us,
Yet meet with no supply; we're fairly promis'd,
But soldiers cannot feed on promises;
All our provant apparel's* torn to rags,
And our munition fails us.　Will you send us
To fight for Rome like beggars?　Noble gentle-
　　men,
Are you the high state of Decemviri,
That have those things in manage?　Pity us,
For we have need on't.　Let not your delays
Be cold to us, whose bloods have oft been
　　heated
To gain you fame and riches.　Prove not to us
(Being our friends) worse foes than we fight with:
Let's not be starv'd in kindness.　Sleep you now
Upon the bench, when your deaf ears should
　　listen
Unto the wretchless clamours of the poor?
Then would I had my drums here, they might
　　rattle,
And rouse you to attendance!　Most grave fathers,
Show yourselves worthy stewards to our mother,
Fair Rome, to whom we are no bastard sons,
Though we be soldiers.　She hath in her store
Food to maintain life in the camp, as well
As surfeit for the city.　Do not save
The foe a labour: send us some supply,
Lest, ere they kill us, we by famine die.
　　App. Claud. Shall I, my lords, give answer to
　　this soldier?
　　Opp. Be you the city's voice.
　　App. Claud. Virginius, we would have you
　　thus possess'd:†
We sit not here to be prescrib'd and taught,
Nor to have any suitor give us limit,
Whose power admits no curb.　Next know,
　　Virginius,
The camp's our servant, and must be dispos'd,

Controll'd, and us'd by us, that have the strength
To knit it or dissolve it. When we please,
Out of our princely grace and clemency,
To look upon your wants, it may be then
We shall redress them: but till then, it fits not
That any petty fellow wag'd by us
Should have a tongue sound here, before a bench
Of such grave auditors. Further,—
  Virginius. Pray, give me leave.
Not here! Pray, Appius, is not this the judg-
    ment-seat?
Where should a poor man's cause be heard but
    here?
To you the statists of long-flourishing Rome,
To you I call,—if you have charity,
If you be human, and not quite given o'er
To furs and metal; if you be Romans;
If you have any soldier's blood at all
Flow in your veins; help with your able arms
To prop a sinking camp: an infinite
Of fair Rome's sons, cold, weak, hungry, and
    clotheless,
Would feed upon your surfeit: will you save
    them,
Or shall they perish?
  App. Claud. What we will, we will;
Be that your answer: perhaps at further leisure
We'll help you; not your merit, but our pleasure.
  Virginius. I will not curse thee, Appius; but I
    wish
Thou wert i'the camp amongst the mutineers
To tell my answers, not to trouble me.
Make you us dogs, yet not allow us bones?
O, what are soldiers come to! Shall your camp,
The strength of all your peace, and the iron wall
That rings this pomp in from invasive steel,
Shall that decay? Then let the foreign fires
Climb o'er those buildings; let the sword and
    slaughter
Chase the gown'd senate through the streets of
    Rome,
To double-dye their robes in scarlet; let
The enemy's stripp'd arm have his crimson'd
    brawns
Up to the elbows in your traitorous blood;
Let Janus' temple be devolv'd; your treasures
Ripp'd up to pay the common adversaries
With our due wages. Do you look for less?
The rottenness of this misgovern'd state
Must grow to some disease, incurable
Save with a sack or slaughter.
  App. Claud. You're too bold.
  Virginius. Know you our extremities?
  App. Claud. We do.

  Virginius. And will not help them?
  App. Claud. Yes.
  Virginius. When?
  App. Claud. Hereafter.
  Virginius. Hereafter! when so many gallant
    spirits,
That yet may stand betwixt you and destruction,
Are sunk in death? Hereafter! when disorder
Hath swallow'd all our forces?
  App. Claud. We'll hear no more.
  Opp. Peace, fellow, peace! know the Decemviri
And their authority: we shall commit you else.
  Virginius. Do so, and I shall thank you; be
    reliev'd,
And have a strong house o'er me; fear no alarms
Given in the night by any quick perdu.
Your guilty in the city feeds more dainty
Than doth your general: 'tis a better office
To be an under-keeper than a captain:—
The gods of Rome amend it!
  App. Claud. Break up the senate.
  Virginius. And shall I have no answer?
  App. Claud. So, farewell.
          [*Exeunt all except* VIRGINIUS.
  Virginius. What slave would be a soldier, to be
    censur'd
By such as ne'er saw danger? to have our pay,
Our worths, and merits, balanc'd in the scale
Of base moth-eaten peace? I have had wounds
Would have made all this bench faint and look
    pale
But to behold them scorch'd. They lay their heads
On their soft pillows, pore upon their bags,
Grow fat with laziness and resty ease;
And us that stand betwixt them and disaster
They will not spare a drachma. O my soldiers,
Before you want, I'll sell my small possessions
Even to my skin to help you; plate and jewels,
All shall be yours. Men that are men indeed,
The earth shall find, the sun and air must feed.

Enter NUMITORIUS, ICILIUS, VALERIUS, *and* VIRGINIA.

  Num. Your daughter, noble brother, hearing
    late
Of your arrival from the camp, most humbly
Prostrates her filial duty.
  Virginius. Daughter, rise:—
And, brother, I am only rich in her,
And in your love, link'd with the honour'd
    friendship
Of those fair Roman lords.—For you, Icilius,
I hear I must adopt you with the title
Of a new son: you are Virginia's chief;
And I am proud she hath built her fair election

Upon such store of virtues. May you grow,
Although a city's child, to know a soldier,
And rate him to his merit!

Icil. Noble father
(For henceforth I shall only use that name),
Our meeting was to urge you to the process
Of our fair contract.

Virginius. Witness, gentlemen,
Here I give up a father's interest,
But not a father's love; that I will ever
Wear next my heart, for it was born with her,
And grows still with my age.

Num. Icilius,
Receive her :—witness, noble gentlemen.

Val. With all my heart. I would Icilius
could
Do as much for me : but Rome affords not such
Another Virginia.

Virginia. I am my father's daughter, and by him
I must be sway'd in all things.

Num. Brother, this happy contract asks a feast,
As a thing due to such solemnities :
It shall be at my house, where we this night
Will sport away some hours.

Virginius. I must to horse.

Num. What, ride to-night!

Virginius. Must see the camp to-night:
'Tis full of trouble and distracted fears,
And may grow mutinous : I am bent to ride.

Val. To-night!

Virginius. I am engag'd: short farewells now
must serve;
The universal business calls me hence,
That toucheth a whole people. Rome, I fear,
Thou wilt pay use for what thou dost forbear.
[*Exeunt.*

ACT II.

ACT II.—SCENE I.*

Enter CORBULO, *the* Clown, *whispering* VIRGINIA.†

Virginia. Sirrah, go tell Calphurnia I am
walking
To take the air: entreat her company;
Say I attend her coming.

Corb. Madam, I shall: but if you could walk
abroad, and get an heir, it were better: for your
father hath a fair revenue, and never a son to
inherit.

Virginia. You are, sirrah,——

Corb. Yes, I am sirrah; but not the party that
is born to do that: though I have no lordships,
yet I have so much manners to give my betters
place.

Virginia. Whom mean you by your betters?

Corb. I hope I have learnt to know the three
degrees of comparison; for though I be *bonus,*
and you *melior* as well as *mulier,* yet my Lord
Icilius is *optimus.*

Virginia. I see there's nothing in such private
done
But you must inquire after.

Corb. And can you blame us, madam, to long
for the merry day, as you do for the merry night?

Virginia. Will you be gone, sir?

Corb. O yes, to my Lady Calphurnia's; I remember my errand.   [*Exit.*

Virginia. My father's wondrous pensive, and
withal
With a suppress'd rage left his house displeas'd,
And so in post is hurried to the camp:
It sads me much; to expel which melancholy,
I have sent for company.

Enter MARCUS CLAUDIUS *and* Musicians.

Mar. Claud. This opportunity was subtly
waited:
It is the best part of a politician,
When he would compass aught to fame his
industry,
Wisely to wait the advantage of the hours;
His happy minutes are not always present.——
Express your greatest art; Virginia hears you.
[*Song.*

Virginia. O, I conceive the occasion of this
harmony :
Icilius sent it; I must thank his kindness.

Mar. Claud. Let not Virginia rate† her
contemplation

---

* *Scene I.*] A street.
† To this stage-direction, the old copy adds, "*after
her M. Clodius with presents.*"

* *Song*] See note ‡, p. 45.
† *rate*] So the Editor of 1816.—The old copy "*wate.*"—
Mr. Collier (*Preface to Coleridge's Seven Lectures, &c.*, p.
lxxxv.), treating of various typographical errors in the
works of our old dramatists, writes as follows. "But
the most remarkable proof to the same effect occurs in

So high, to call this visit au intrusion;
For when she understands I took my message
From one that did compose it with affection,
I know she will not only extend pardon,
But grace it with her favour.

Virginia. You mediate excuse for courtesies,
As if I were so barren of civility,
Not to esteem it worthy of my thanks:
Assure yourself I could be longer patient
To hear my ears so feasted.

Mar. Claud. Join all your voices till you make
the air
Proud to usurp your notes, and to please her
With a sweet echo; serve Virginia's pleasure.
[*Song.*

As you have been so full of gentleness
To hear with patience what was brought to serve
you,
So hearken with your usual clemency
To the relation of a lover's sufferings.
Your figure still does revel in his dreams;
He banquets on your memory, yet finds
Not thoughts enough to satisfy his wishes;
As if Virginia had compos'd his heart,
And fills it with her beauty.

Virginia. I see he is a miser in his wishes,
And thinks he never has enough of that
Which only he possesses: but, to give
His wishes satisfaction, let him know
His heart and mine do dwell so near together,
That hourly they converse and guard each other.

Mar. Claud. Is fair Virginia confident she
knows
Her favour dwells with the same man I plead for?

Virginia. Unto Icilius.

Webster's 'Appius and Virginia' (edit. Dyce, II. 160),
where this passage is met with as it is printed in the old
copy:
     ' Let not Virginia wate her contemplation
        So high, to call this visit an intrusion.'
It is clear that 'wate' must be wrong, and the editor
suggests *wate* (i.e. weigh) as the fit emendation; when,
as in the two preceding cases, he did not see that it is
only a blunder of *w* for *r*, because the person who
delivered the line could not pronounce the letter *r*:
read *rate* for 'wate,' and the whole difficulty vanishes."
     Now, it was with something more than surprise that
I read what I have just quoted; for in the first edition
of the present work (vol. "II, 160."—to which Mr. Collier
so carefully refers), I gave the passage in question
literatim thus,
     "Let not Virginia *rate* her contemplation," &c.
and the note on it in that edition is,—
     "*rate*] So the Editor of 1816. The old copy, 'wate.'
Qy. If a misprint for '*waie*,' i.e. weigh."
     Why has Mr. Collier entirely suppressed the fact that
I inserted "*rate*" in the text of my former edition?
and why has he not mentioned that the emendation
"*rate*" was made by Mr. Dilke forty years ago?

Mar. Claud. Worthy fair one,
I would not wrong your worth so to employ
My language for a man so much beneath
The merit of your beauty: he I plead for
Has power to make your beauty populous;*
Your frown shall awe the world; and in your smile
Great Rome shall build her happiness;
Honour and wealth shall not be styl'd companions,
But servants to your pleasure.
Then shall Icilius (but a refin'd citizen)
Boast your affection, when Lord Appius loves
you?

Virginia. Bless his great lordship! I was much
mistaken.
Let thy lord know, thou advocate of lust,
All the intentions of that youth are honourable,
Whilst his are fill'd with sensuality:
And for a final resolution know,
Our hearts in love, like twins, alike shall grow.
[*Exit.*

Mar. Claud. Had I a wife or daughter that
could please him,
I would devote her to him: but I must
Shadow this scorn, and soothe him still in lust.
[*Exit.*

———◆———

SCENE II.†
Enter Six Soldiers.

First Soldier. What news yet of Virginius'
return?

Second Soldier. Not any.

First Sold. O, the misery of soldiers!
They doubly starve us with fair promises.
We spread the earth like hail or new-reap'd corn
In this fierce famine; and yet patiently
Make our obedience the confinèd gaol
That starves us.

Third Sold. Soldiers, let us draw our swords
While we have strength to use them.

First Sold. 'Tis a motion
Which nature and necessity commands.

————————

* *populous*] "*Populous*," says the Editor of 1816,
"must be used here in the same sense as *popular.*
Should we not substitute it?" The following quota-
tions show that the text requires no alteration :—
     " It should have bene some fine confection,
        That might have given the broth some daintie taste;
        This powder was to grosse and *populus.*"
          The Tragedie of Arden of Feversham, 1592, Sig. D 4.
The edition of *Arden*, 1633, has "*populous.*"
     " You wrong my health in thinking I love them:
        Do not I know their *populous* imperfections?"
Why, they cannot live till Easter," &c.
Middleton's *Your Five Gallants,—Works*, ii. 245, ed. Dyce.
     † *Scene II.*] The camp, before Algidum.

Enter MINUTIUS.

Min. Ye're of Virginius's regiment?

Omnes. We are.

Min. Why do you swarm in troops thus? To
    your quarter!
Is our command grown idle? To your trench!
Come, I'll divide you: this your conference
Is not without suspect of mutiny.

First Sold. Soldiers, shall I relate the grievances
Of the whole regiment?

Omnes. Boldly.

First Sold. Then thus, my lord,——

Min. Come, I will not hear thee.

First Sold. Sir, you shall.
Sound all the drums and trumpets in the camp
To drown my utterance, yet above them all
I'll rear our just complaint. Stir not, my lord:
I vow you are not safe, if you but move
A sinew till you hear us.

Min. Well, sir, command us;
You are the general.

First Sold. No, my lord, not I:
I am almost starv'd; I wake in the wet trench,
Loaded with more cold iron than a gaol
Would give a murderer, while the general
Sleeps in a field-bed, and to mock our hunger
Feeds us with scent of the most curious fare
That makes his tables crack; our pay detain'd
By those that are our leaders; and at once
We, in this sad and unprepared plight,
With the enemy and famine daily fight.

Min. Do you threaten us?

Omnes. Sir, you shall hear him out.

First Sold. You send us whips, and iron
    manacles,
And shackles plenty, but the devil a coin.
Would you would teach us that cannibal trick,
    my lord,
Which some rich men i'the city oft do use!
Shall's one devour another?

Min. Will you hear me?

First Sold. O Rome, thou'rt grown a most
    unnatural mother
To those have held thee by the golden locks
From sinking into ruin! Romulus
Was fed by a she-wolf; but now our wolves,
Instead of feeding us, devour our flesh,
Carouse our blood, yet are not drunk with it,
For three parts of't is water.

Min. Your captain,
Noble Virginius, is sent [to] Rome
For ease of all your grievances.

First Sold. 'Tis false.

Omnes. Ay, 'tis false.

First Sold. He's stol'n away from's, never to
    return:
And, now his age will suffer him no more
Deal on the enemy, belike he'll turn
An usurer, and in the city air
Cut poor men's throats at home, sitting in's
    chair.

Min. You wrong one of the honourablest com-
    manders.

Omnes. Honourable commander!

First Sold. Commander! ay, my lord, there goes
    the thrift:
In victories the general and commanders
Share all the honour, as they share the spoil:
But in our overthrows where lies the blame?
The common soldier's fault; ours is the shame.
What is the reason that, being so far distant
From the affrighted enemy, we lie
I'the open field, subject to the sick humours
Of heaven and earth, unless you could bestow
Two summers of* us? Shall I tell you truth?
You account the expense of engines and of swords,
Of horses and of armour, dearer far
Than soldiers' lives.

Omnes. Now, by the gods, you do.

First Sold. Observe you not the ravens and the
    crows
Have left the city-surfeit, and with us
They make full banquets? Come, you birds of
    death,
And fill your greedy crops with human flesh;
Then to the city fly, disgorge it there
Before the senate; and from thence arise
A plague to choke all Rome!

Omnes. And all the suburbs!

Min. Upon a soldier's word, bold gentlemen,
I expect every hour Virginius
To bring fresh comfort.

Omnes. Whom? Virginius?

First Sold. Now, by the gods, if ever he return,
We'll drag him to the slaughter by his locks
Turn'd white with riot and incontinence,
And leave a precedent to all the world
How captains use their soldiers!

Enter VIRGINIUS.

Min. See, he's return'd.—
Virginius, you are not safe; retire;
Your troops are mutinous: we are begirt
With enemies more daring and more fierce
Than is the common foe.

Virginius. My troops, my lord!

---

* *of*] l.c. on.

Min. Your life is threaten'd by those desperate men:
Betake you to your horse.

Virginius. My noble lord,
I never yet profess'd to teach the art
Of flying.—Ha! our troops grown mutinous!
He dares not look on me with half a face
That spread this wildfire.—Where is our lieutenant?

Enter VALERIUS.

Val. My lord?

Virginius. Sirrah, order our companies.

Min. What do you mean, my lord?

Virginius. Take air a little, they have heated me.—
Sirrah, is't you will mutiny?

Third Sold. Not I, sir.

Virginius. Is your gall burst, you traitor?

Fourth Sold. The gods defend,* sir!

Virginius. Or is your stomach sea-sick? doth it rise?
I'll make a passage for it.

Fifth Sold. Noble captain,
I'll die beneath your foot.

Virginius. You rough porcupine, ha!
Do you bristle, do you shoot your quills, you rogue?

First Sold. They have no points to hurt you, noble captain.

Virginius. Was't you, my nimble shaver, that would whet
Your sword 'gainst your commander's throat, you, sirrah?

Sixth Sold. My lord, I never dream'd on't.

Virginius. Slaves and cowards,
What, are you choleric now? By the gods,
The way to purge it were to let you blood!
I am i'the centre of you, and I'll make
The proudest of you teach the aspen-leaf
To tremble, when I breathe.

Min. A strange conversion.

Virginius. Advance your pikes! the word!

Omnes. Advance your pikes!

Virginius. See, noble lord, these are no mutineers;
These are obedient soldiers, civil men:
You shall command these, if your lordship please,
To fill a ditch up with their slaughter'd bodies,
That with more ease you may assault some town.—
So, now lay down your arms! Villains and traitors,
I here cashier you: hence from me, my poison,
Not worthy of our discipline! go beg,
Go beg, you mutinous rogues! brag of the service

You ne'er durst look on: it were charity
To hang you, for my mind gives ye're reserv'd
To rob poor market-women.

Min. O Virginius,—

Virginius. I do beseech you to confirm my sentence,
As you respect me. I will stand myself
For the whole regiment; and safer far
In mine own single valour, than begirt
With cowards and with traitors.

Min. O my lord,
You are too severe.

Virginius. Now, by the gods, my lord,
You know no discipline, to pity them.
Precious devils! no sooner my back turn'd
But presently to mutiny!

Omnes. Dear captain,—

Virginius. Refuse me,* if such traitorous rogues
Would not confound an army!—When do you march?
When do you march, gentlemen?

First Sold. My lord, we'll starve first;
We'll hang first; by the gods, do any thing,
Ere we'll forsake you.

Min. Good Virginius,
Limit your passion.

Virginius. Sir, you may take my place,
Not my just anger from me. These are they
Have bred a dearth i'the camp: I'll wish our foes
No greater plague than to have their company:
Show but among them all so many scars
As stick upon this flesh, I'll pardon them.

Min. How now, my lord, breathless?

Virginius. By your favour: I ha' said.
Mischiefs confound me, if I could not wish
My youth renew'd again, with all her follies,
Only to have breath enough to rail against
These——'Tis too short.

Min. See, gentlemen, what strange distraction
Your falling off from duty hath begot
In this most noble soldier: you may live,
The meanest of you, to command a troop,
And then in others you'll correct those faults
Which in yourselves you cherish'd: every captain
Bears in his private government that form
Which kings should o'er their subjects, and to them
Should be the like obedient. We confess
You have been distress'd; but can you justly challenge
Any commander that hath surfeited,
While that your food was limited? You cannot.

---

* *defend*] i.e. forbid.

* *Refuse me*] See note §, p. 7.

Virginius. My lord, I have shar'd with them an
    equal fortune,
Hunger and cold, march'd thorough watery fens,
Borne as great burdens as the pioneer,
When scarce the ground would bear me,—
    Min. Good my lord, give us leave to proceed.—
The punishment your captain hath inflicted
Is not sufficient; for it cannot bring   ·
Any example to succeeding times
Of penance worth your faulting: happily
It may in you beget a certain shame;
But it will [breed] in others a strong hope
Of the like lenity. Yet, gentlemen,
You have in one thing given me such a taste
Of your obedience,—when the fire was rais'd
Of fierce sedition, and the cheek was swoll'n
To sound the fatal trumpet, then the sight
Of this your worthy captain did disperse
All those unfruitful humours, and even then
Convert you from fierce tigers to staid men:
We therefore pardon you, and do restore
Your captain to you, you unto your captain.
    Omnes. The gods requite you, noble general!
    Min. My lord, my lord!
    Omnes. Your pardon, noble captain!
    Virginius. Well, you are the general, and the
    fault is quit:
A soldier's tears, an elder brother's wit,
Have little salt in them, nor do they season
Things worth observing, for their want of reason.—
Take up your arms and use them, do, I pray:
Ere long you'll take your legs to run away.
    Min. And what supply from Rome?
    Virginius. Good store of corn.
    Min. What entertainment there?
    Virginius. Most honourable,
Especially by the Lord Appius.
There is great hope that Appius will grow
The soldier's patron; with what vehemency
He urg'd our wants, and with what expedition
He hasted the supplies, it is almost
Incredible. There's promis'd to the soldier,
Besides their corn, a bounteous donative;
                                    [*A shout.*
But 'tis not certain yet when't shall be paid.
    Min. How for your own particular?
    Virginius. My lord,
I was not enter'd fully two pikes' length
Into the senate, but they all stood bare,
And each man offer'd me his seat. The business
For which I went despatch'd, what gifts, what fa-
    vours,
Were done me, your good lordship shall not hear,
For you would wonder at them; only this,—

'Twould make a man fight up to the neck in blood,
To think how nobly he shall be receiv'd
When he returns to the city.
    Min. 'Tis well.
Give order the provision be divided,
And sent to every quarter.
    Virginius. Sir, it shall.—
[*Aside.*] Thus men must slight their wrongs, or
    else conceal them,
When general safety wills us not reveal them.
                                    [*Exeunt.*

———◆———

SCENE III.*

Enter Two Petitioners *at one Door; at the other,* MARCUS
    CLAUDIUS.

    First Pet. Pray, is your lord at leisure?
    Mar. Claud. What is your suit?
    First Pet. To accept this poor petition, which
    makes known
My many wrongs, in which I crave his justice
And upright sentence to support my cause,
Which else is trod down by oppression.
    Mar. Claud. My lord's hand is the prop of
    innocence,
And if your cause be worthy his supportance,
It cannot fail.
    First. Pet. The gods of Rome protect him!
    Mar. Claud. What, is your paper, too, petition-
    ary?
    Sec. Pet. It leans upon the justice of the judge,
Your noble lord, the very stay of Rome.
    Mar. Claud. And surer basis for a poor man's
    cause
She cannot yield. Your papers I'll deliver;
And when my lord ascends the judgment-seat,
You shall find gracious comfort.

Enter ICILIUS *troubled.*

    Icil. Where's your lord?
    Mar. Claud. [*aside*]. Icilius! fair Virginia's late
    betroth'd!
    Icil. Your ears, I hope, you have not forfeited,
That you return no answer: where's your lord?
    Mar. Claud. At's study.
    Icil. I desire admittance to him.

———

* *Scene III.*] Rome. An outer-apartment, it would
seem, in the house of Appius. But presently, when
Appius is left alone with Icilius, a change of scene is
supposed; for, p. 160, Appius says to Claudius,
        " To send a ruffian hither,
        Even to *my closet*," &c.
(And yet, in the First Scene of the next Act, Icilius
speaks of this interview with Appius as having taken
place "*in the lobby*"!)

Mar. Claud. Please you attend: I'll know his
    lordship's pleasure.—
[*Aside.*] Icilius! I pray heaven she have not
    blabb'd.   [*Exit.*
Icil. "Attend!" A petty lawyer t'other day,
Glad of a fee, but call'd to eminent place,
Even to his betters now the word 's "Attend;"
This gownèd office, what a breadth it bears!
How many tempests wait upon his frown!

        Re-enter MARCUS CLAUDIUS.

Mar. Claud. All the petitioners withdraw.
                [*Exeunt* Petitioners.
        Lord Appius
Must have this place more private, as a favour
Reserv'd for you, Icilius.—Here's my lord.

  Enter APPIUS CLAUDIUS *with* Lictors *afore him.*

App. Claud. Be gone; this place is only spar'd
    for us,   [*Exeunt Lictors.*
And you, Icilius.   Now your business.
Icil. May I speak it freely?
App. Claud. We have suffering ears,
A heart the softest down may penetrate:
Proceed.
Icil. My lord,—
App. Claud. We are private; pray, your cour-
    tesy.
Icil. My duty—
App. Claud. Leave that to the public eye
Of Rome and of Rome's people.—Claudius, there!
Mar. Claud. My lord?
App. Claud. Place me a second chair; that done,
Remove yourself. So, now your absence, Claudius.
                [*Exit* MAR. CLAUDIUS.
Icilius, sit: this grace we make not common
Unto the noblest Roman, but to you
Our love affords it freely.   Now your suit?
Icil. It is, you would be kind unto the camp.
App. Claud. Wherein, Icilius, doth the camp
    touch thee?
Icil. Thus: old Virginius, now my father-in-law,
Kept from the public pay, consumes himself,
Sells his revenues, turns his plate to coin,
To wage his soldiers and supply the camp;
Wasting that useful substance which indeed
Should rise to me as my Virginia's dowry.
App. Claud. We meet that opposition thus, Ici-
    lius:
The camp's supplies do not consist in us,
But those that keep the common treasury;
Speak or entreat we may, but not command.
But, sir, I wonder you, so brave a youth,
Son to a thrifty Roman, should ally you
And knit your strong arms to such falling branches

Which rather in their ruin will bear down
Your strength, than you support their rottenness.
Be sway'd by me; fly from that ruinous house,
Whose fall may crush you, and contract with mine,
Whose bases are of marble, deeply fix'd
To maugre * all gusts and impending storms.
Cast off that beggar's daughter, poor Virginia,
Whose dowry and beauty I'll see trebled both
In one allied to me.   Smile you, Icilius?
Icil. My lord, my lord, think you I can imagine
Your close and sparing hand can be profuse
To give that man a palace whom you late
Denied a cottage? Will you from your own coffers
Grant me a treble dowry, yet interpose me
A poor third from the common treasury?
You must move me by possibilities,
For I have brains: give first your hand and seal,
That old Virginius shall receive his pay,
Both for himself and soldiers; and, that done,
I shall perhaps be soon induc'd to think
That you, who with such willingness did that,—
App. Claud. Is my love mispriz'd?
Icil. Not to Virginia.
App. Claud. Virginia!
Icil. Yes, Virginia, lustful lord.
I did but trace your cunning all this while:
You would bestow me on some Appian trull,
And for that dross to cheat me of my gold:
For this the camp pines, and the city smarts:
All Rome fares worse for thy incontinence.
App. Claud. Mine, boy!
Icil. Thine, judge. This hand hath intercepted
Thy letters, and perus'd thy tempting gifts †;
These ears have heard thy amorous passions,
    wretch!
These eyes beheld thy treacherous name subscrib'd.
A judge? a devil!
App. Claud. Come, I'll hear no more.
Icil. Sit still, or, by the powerful gods of Rome,
I'll nail thee to the chair: but suffer me,
I'll offend nothing but thine ears.
App. Claud. Our secretary!
Icil. Tempt not a lover's fury: if thou dost,

---

* *To maugre*] i.e. to defy. I know no other instance
of this word being used as a verb; as an adverb, with
the sense *in spite of*, it often occurs.
† *gifts*] The old copy "*guests.*"—The Rev. J. Mitford
(*Gent. Mag.* for June 1833, p. 491) would read "*guests.*"
But compare what Appius says a little after;
    "and for those letters,
    Tokens, and *presents*, we acknowledge none.'
I may add, that in Shakespeare's *Tempest*, act IV. sc. 1,
the first folio has the same misprint,—
    "Then, as my *guest*, and thine own acquisition
    Worthily purchas'd, take my daughter," &c.

Now, by my vow insculp'd in heaven, I'll send
    thee—
  App. Claud. You see I am patient.
  Icil. But withal revengeless.
  App. Claud. So, say on.
  Icil. Hope not of any grace or the least favour:
I am so covetous of Virginia's love,
I cannot spare thee the least look, glance, touch:
Divide one bare imaginary thought
Into a thousand thousand parts, and that
I'll not afford thee.
  App. Claud. Thou shalt not.
  Icil. Nay, I will not :
Hadst thou a judge's place above those judges
That judge all souls, having power to sentence me,
I would not bribe thee, no, not with one hair
From her fair temples.
  App. Claud. Thou shouldst not.
  Icil. Nay, I would not.
Think not her beauty shall have leave to crown
Thy lustful hopes with the least spark of bliss,
Or have thine ears charm'd with the ravishing
    sound
Even of her harshest phrase.
  App. Claud. I will not.
  Icil. Nay, thou shalt not.
She's mine; my soul is crown'd in her desire;
To her I'd travel through a land of fire.
  App. Claud. Now have you done?
  Icil. I have spoke my thoughts.
  App. Claud. Then will thy fury give me leave
    to speak ?
  Icil. I pray, say on.
  App. Claud. Icilius, I must chide you, and
    withal
Tell you your rashness hath made forfeiture
Even of your precious life, which we esteem
Too dear to call in question. If I wish'd you
Of my alliance, graff'd into my blood,
Condemn you me for that? O, see the rashness
And blind misprision of distemper'd youth !
As for the maid Virginia, we are far
Even in least thought from her; and for those
    letters,
Tokens, and presents, we acknowledge none.
Alas, though great in place, we are not gods :
If any false impostor hath usurp'd
Our hand or greatness in his own behoof,
Can we help that? Icilius, there's our hand ;
Your rashness we remit : let's have hereafter
Your love and best opinion. For your suit,
Repair to us at both our better leisures,
We'll breathe in it new life.
  Icil. I crave your pardon.

  App. Claud. Granted ere crav'd, my good
    Icilius.
  Icil. Morrow.
  App. Claud. It is no more, indeed. Morrow,
    Icilius.
If any of our servants wait without,
Command them in.
  Icil. I shall.
  App. Claud. Our secretary,—
We have use for him ; Icilius, send him hither :
Again, good-morrow.   [*Exit Icilius.*
Go to thy death ; thy life is doom'd and cast.
Appius, be circumspect, and be not rash
In blood, as thou'rt in lust: be murderous still ;
But when thou strik'st, with unseen weapons kill.

Re-enter MARCUS CLAUDIUS.

  Mar. Claud. My honourable lord,—
  App. Claud. Deride me, dog ?
  Mar. Claud. Who hath stirr'd up this tempest
    in your brow?
  App. Claud. Not you ! fie, you !
  Mar. Claud. All you Pantheon gods
Confound me, if my soul be accessary
To your distractions !
  App. Claud. To send a ruffian hither,
Even to my closet ; first, to brave my greatness,
Play with my beard, revile me, taunt me, hiss me ;
Nay, after all these deep disparagements,
Threat me with steel, and menace me unarm'd,
To nail me to my seat if I but mov'd :
All these are slight, slight toys.
  Mar. Claud. Icilius do this?
  App. Claud. Ruffian Icilius : he that, in the front
Of a smooth citizen, bears the rugged soul
Of a most base banditto.
  Mar. Claud. He shall die for't.
  App. Claud. Be not too rash.
  Mar. Claud. Were there no more men to sup-
    port great Rome,
Even falling Rome should perish ere he stand :
I'll after him, and kill him.
  App. Claud. Stay, I charge thee.
Lend me a patient ear: to right our wrongs,
We must not menace with a public hand ;
We stand in the world's eye, and shall be tax'd
Of the least violence where we revenge :
We should smile smoothest where our hate's
    most deep,
And when our spleen's broad waking, seem to sleep.
Let the young man play still upon the bit,
Till we have brought and train'd him to our lure
Great men should strike but once, and then strike
    sure.

Mar. Claud. Love you Virginia still ?
App. Claud. Do I still live?
Mar. Claud. Then she's your own. Virginia
is, you say,
Still in the camp?
App. Claud. True.
Mar. Claud. Now in his absence will I claim
Virginia
To be the daughter of a bondwoman,
And slave to me; to prove which, I'll produce
Firm proofs, notes probable, sound witnesses:
Then, having with your Lictors summon'd her,
I'll bring the cause before your judgment-seat;
Where, upon my infallid evidence,
You may pronounce the sentence on my side,
And she become your strumpet, not your bride.
App. Claud. Thou hast a copious brain: but
how in this
Shall we dispose Icilius?

Mar. Claud. If he spurn,
Clap him up close: there's ways to charm his
spleen.
By this no scandal can redound to you ;
The cause is mine ; you but the sentencer
Upon that evidence which I shall bring,
The business is, to have warrants by arrest,
To descant on the matter, Appius may
Examine, try, and doom Virginia.
But all this must be sudden.
App. Claud. Thou art born
To mount me high above Icilius' scorn.
I'll leave it to thy manage. [*Exeunt.*

The business is, to have warrants by arrest,
To answer such things at the judgment-bar
As can be laid against her: ere her friends
Can be assembled, ere herself can study
Her answer, or scarce know her cause of sum-
mons

ACT III.

SCENE I.*
Enter Nurse *and* CORBULO.

Corb. What was that you said, nurse?
Nurse. Why, I did say thou must bestir thyself.
Corb. I warrant you, I can bestir my stumps as
soon as another, if fit occasion be offered: but why
do you come upon me in such haste? is it because,
nurse, I should come over you at leisure?
Nurse. Come over me, thou knave! what dost
thou mean by that?
Corb. Only this; if you will come off, I will
come on.
Nurse. My lord hath strangers to-night: you
must make ready the parlour; a table and lights :
nay, when,† I say?
Corb. Methinks you should rather wish for a
bed than for a board, for darkness than for lights :
yet I must confess you have been a light woman
in your time; but now—
Nurse. But now! what now, you knave?
Corb. But now I'll go fetch the table and some
lights presently.

Enter NUMITORIUS, HORATIUS, VALERIUS, *and* ICILIUS.

Num. Some lights to usher in these gentlemen !

Clear all the rooms without there !—Sit, pray,
sit.—
None interrupt our conference.

Enter VIRGINIA.

Ha, who's that ?
Nurse. My most [dear *] child, if it please you.
Num. Fair Virginia, you are welcome.—
The rest forbear us till we call.
[*Exeunt* Nurse *and* CORBULO.
Sweet cousin,
Our business and the cause of our discourse
Admits you to this council: take your place.—
Icilius, we are private ; now proceed.
Icil. Then thus: Lord Appius doth intend me
wrong ;
And under his smooth calmness cloaks a tempest
That will ere long break out in violence
On me and on my fortunes.
Num. My good cousin,
You are young, and youth breeds rashness. Can I
think
Lord Appius will do wrong, who is all justice ;
The most austere and upright censurer
That ever sat upon the awful bench ?

---

* *Scene I.*] Rome. An apartment in the house of
Numitorius.
† *when*] See note *, p. 68.

* *My most [dear] child*] The old copy, "*My most* ——
child," the printer, it would seem, having been unable to
decipher the word which he has marked by a break.
M

Val. Icilius, you are near to me in blood,
And I esteem your safety as mine own :
If you will needs wage * eminence and state,
Choose out a weaker opposite, not one
That in his arm bears all the strength of Rome.

Num. Besides, Icilius,
Know you the danger what it is to scandal
One of his place and sway ?

Icil. I know it, kinsmen ; yet this popular
    greatness
Can be no bugbear to affright mine innocence.
No, his smooth crest hath cast a palpèd † film
Over Rome's eyes. He juggles, a plain juggler ;
Lord Appius is no less.

Num. Nay, then, cousin,
You are too harsh, and I must hear no more.
It ill becomes my place and gravity
To lend a face to such reproachful terms
'Gainst one of his high presence.

Icil. Sit, pray, sit,
To see me draw his picture fore your eyes,
To make this man seem monstrous, and this god
Rome so adores, a devil, a plain devil.
This lord, this judge, this Appius, that professeth
To all the world a vestal chastity,
Is an incontinent, loose lecher grown.

Num. Fie, cousin !

Icil. Nay, 'tis true. Daily and hourly
He tempts this blushing virgin with large promises,
With melting words, and presents of high rate,
To be the stale to his unchaste desires.

Omnes. Is't possible ?

Icil. Possible !
'Tis actual truth : I pray, but ask your niece.

Virginia. Most true, I am extremely tir'd and
    wearied
With messages and tokens of his love ;
No answer, no repulse will satisfy
The tediousness of his importunate suit.
And whilst I could with modesty and honour,
Without the danger of reproach and shame,
I kept it secret from Icilius ;
But when I saw their boldness found no limit,
And they from fair entreaty grew to threats,
I told him all.

Icil. True : understanding which,
To him I went.

Val. To Appius ?

Icil. To that giant,
The high Colossus that bestrides us all ; *
I went to him.

Hor. How did you bear yourself ?

Icil. Like Appius, at the first, dissemblingly ;
But when I saw the coast clear, all withdrawn,
And none but we two in the lobby, then
I drew my poniard, took him by the throat,
And, whon he would have clamour'd, threaten'd
    death,
Unless he would with patience hear me out.

Num. Did he, Icilius ?

Icil. I made him that he durst not squeak,
Not move an eye, not draw a breath too loud,
Nor stir a finger.

Hor. What succeeded then ?

Num. Keep fast the door there !—Sweet coz,
    not too loud.
What then succeeded ?

Icil. Why, I told him all ;
Gave him his due, call'd him lascivious judge,
(A thousand things which I have now forgot,)
Show'd him his hand a witness 'gainst himself,
And every thing with such known circumstance,
That he might well excuse, but not deny.

Num. How parted you ?

Icil. Why, friends in outward show ;
But I perceiv'd his heart : that hypocrite
Was born to gull Rome, and deceive us all.
He swore to me quite to abjure her lust ;
Yet, ere myself could reach Virginia's chamber,
One was before me with regrets † from him ;
I know his hand. The intent of this our meeting
Was to entreat your counsel and advice :
The good old man, her father, is from home ;
I think it good that she now in his absence
Should lodge in secret with some private friend,
Where Appius nor his Lictors, those blood-
    hounds,
Can hunt her out. You are her uncle, sir ;
I pray, counsel the best.

Num. To oppose ourselves,
Now in this heat, against so great a man,
Might, in my judgment, to ourselves bring danger,
And to my niece no safety. If we fall,
She cannot stand ; let's, then, preserve ourselves
Until her father be discharg'd the camp.

Val. And, good Icilius, for your private ends,

---

* *wage*] "Webster," says Nares in his Glossary, " has
used the singular expression of *waging.* ' eminence and
state,' meaning to contend in those points." Afterwards,
p. 165, we have, " My purse is too scant to *wage* law
with them."

  † *palpèd*] So Heywood ;
    " And bring a *palpèd* darkness ore the earth."
                  Brazen Age, 1613, Sig. F.

---

* *The high Colossus that bestrides us all*] From Shakespeare ;—
    "he doth bestride the narrow world
Like a Colossus."   *Julius Cæsar,* Act i. Sc. ii.
  † *regrets*] i. e. fresh greetings.

And the dear safety of your friends and kindred,
Against that statist spare to use your spleen.

Icil. I will be sway'd by you.—My lords, 'tis
late,
And time to break up conference.—Noble uncle,
I am your growing debtor.

Num. Lights without there !

Icil. I will conduct Virginia to her lodging.
Good night to all at once.

Num. The gods of Rome protect you all ! and
then
We need not fear the envious rage of men.
　　　　　　　　　　　　　　　[*Exeunt.*

SCENE II.*

Enter MARCUS CLAUDIUS, *with* Four Lictors.

Mar. Claud. Lictors, bestow yourselves in some
close shops,
About the Forum, till you have the sight
Of fair Virginia; for I understand
This present morning she'll come forth to buy
Some necessaries at the sempsters' shops:
Howe'er accompanied, be it your care
To seize her at our action.　Good my friends,
Disperse yourselves, and keep a careful watch.
　　　　　　　　　　　　　　　[*Exit.*

First Lict. 'Tis strange that ladies will not pay
their debts.

Sec. Lict. It were strange, indeed, if that our
Roman knights would give them good example
and pay theirs.

First Lict. The calendar that we Lictors go by
is all dog-days.

Sec. Lict. Right ; our common hunt is still to
dog unthrifts.

First Lict. And what's your book of common-
prayer ?

Sec. Lict. Faith, only for the increase of riotous
young gentlemen i' the country, and bankrupts i'
the city.

First Lict. I know no man more valiant than
we are, for we back knights and gentlemen daily.

Sec. Lict. Right, we have them by the back
hourly : your French fly applied to the nape of
the neck for the French rheum is not so sore a
drawer as a Lictor.

First Lict. Some say that, if a little-timbered
fellow would justle a great loggerhead, let him be
sure to lay him i' the kennel; but when we
shoulder a knight, or a knight's fellow, we make
him more sure, for we kennel him i' the counter.

Sec. Lict. Come, let's about our business.
　　　　　　　　　　　　　　　[*Exeunt.*

Enter VIRGINIA, Nurse, *and* CORBULO.

Virginia. You are grown wondrous amorous of
late :
Why do you look back so often ?

Corb. Madam, I go as a Frenchman rides, all
upon one buttock.

Virginia. And what's the reason ?

Corb. Your ladyship never saw a monkey in
all your lifetime have a clog at's tail, but he's
still looking back to see what the devil 'tis that
follows him.

Nurse. Very good; we are your clogs, then.

Virginia. Your crest is grown regardant :*
here's the beauty
That makes your eyes forgetful of their way.

Corb. Beauty ! O the gods! madam, I cannot
endure her complexion.

Nurse. Why, sir, what's my complexion ?

Corb. Thy complexion is just between a Moor
and a French-woman.

Virginia. But she hath a matchless eye, sir.

Corb. True, her eyes are not right matches :
besides, she is a widow.

Nurse. What then, I pray you ?

Corb. Of all waters I would not have my beef
powdered with a widow's tears.

Virginia. Why, I beseech you ?

Corb. O, they are too fresh, madam; assure
yourself they will not last for the death of fourteen
husbands above a day and a quarter : besides, if
a man come a wooing to a widow, and invite her
to a banquet, contrary to the old rule, she will
sooner fill her eye than her belly.　Besides that,
if he look into her estate, first—look you, here
are four fingers—first the charge of her husband's
funeral, next debts and legacies, and lastly the
reversion : now, take away debts and legacies, and
what remains for her second husband ?

Nurse. I would some of the tribe heard you.

Corb. There's a certain fish that, as the learned
divulge, is called a shark : now, this fish can
never feed while he swims upon 's belly; marry,
when he lies upon his back, O, he takes it at
pleasure.

Virginia. Well, sir, about your business; make
provision
Of those things I directed.

Corb. Sweet lady, these eyes shall be the clerks
of the kitchen for your belly; but I can assure

---

* *Scene II.*] The same.　The Forum.

* *regardant*] "A term in heraldry, and signifies *looking
behind.*"　*Editor of* 1818.

M 2

you, woodcocks will be hard to be spoke with, for
there's a great feast towards.

Virginia. You are very pleasant.

Corb. And fresh cod is taken down thick and
threefold; women without great bellies go together
by the ears for't; and such a number of sweet-
toothed caters* in the market, not a calf's head
to be got for love or money; mutton's mutton
now.

Virginia. Why, was it not so ever?

Corb. No, madam, the sinners i' the suburbs
had almost ta'en the name† quite away from't,
'twas so cheap and common: but now 'tis at a
sweet reckoning; the term-time is the mutton-
monger in the whole calendar.

Nurse. Do your lawyers eat any salads with
their mutton?

Corb. Yes, the younger revellers use capers to
their mutton so long till with their shuffling and
cutting some of them be out at heels again.—A
bountiful mind and a full purse ever attend your
ladyship!

Virginia. O, I thank you.

Re-enter MARCUS CLAUDIUS *and Lictors.*

Mar. Claud. See, yon's the lady.

Corb. I will buy up for your ladyship all the
young cuckoos in the market.

Virginia. What to do?

Corb. O, 'tis the most delicatest dish, I'll assure
you, and newest in fashion: not a great feast in
all Rome without a cuckoo.

Mar. Claud. Virginia,—

Virginia. Sir?

Mar. Claud. Mistress, you do not know me,
Yet we must be acquainted: follow me.

Virginia. You do salute me strangely. Follow
you!

Corb. Do you hear, sir? methinks you have
followers enough. Many gentlemen that I know
would not have so many tall followers as you have
for the price of ten hunting geldings, I'll assure
you.

Mar. Claud. Come, will you go?

Virginia. Whither? by what command?

Mar. Claud. By warrant of these men, and
privilege
I hold even on thy life. Come, ye proud dame,
You are not what you seem.

Virginia. Uncivil sir,

* *caters*] i.e. caterers.
† *the name*] *Mutton* was a very common cant term for
a prostitute.

What makes you thus familiar and thus bold?
Unhand me, villain!

Mar. Claud. What, mistress, to your lord?
He that can set the razor to your throat,
And punish you as freely as the gods,
No man to ask the cause? Thou art my slave,
And here I seize what's mine.

Virginia. Ignoble villain!
I am as free as the best king or consul
Since Romulus. What dost thou mean? Unhand
        me.—
Give notice to my uncle and Icilius
What violence is offer'd me.

Mar. Claud. Do, do.

Corb. Do you press women for soldiers, or do
you beg women, instead of other commodities, to
keep your hands in ure?* By this light, if thou
hast any ears on thy head, as it is a question, I'll
make my lord pull you out by the ears, though
you take a castle.   [*Exit.*

Mar. Claud. Come, will you go along?

Nurse. Whither should she go, sir? Here's
pulling and haling a poor gentlewoman!

Mar. Claud. Hold you your prating, reverence:
        the whip
Shall seize on you for your smooth cozenage.

Virginia. Are not you servant to Lord Appius?

Mar. Claud. Howe'er I am your lord, and will
        approve it
Fore all the senate.

Virginia. Thou wilt prove thyself
The cursèd pander for another's lust;
And this your plot shall burst about your ears
Like thunderbolts.

Mar. Claud. Hold you that confidence:
First I will seize you by the course of law,
And then I'll talk with you.

Enter ICILIUS *and* NUMITORIUS.

Num. How now, fair cousin!

Icil. How now, gentlemen!
What's the offence of fair Virginia,
You bend your weapons on us?

Lict. Sir, stand back;
We fear a rescue.

Icil. There's no need of fear,
Where there's no cause of rescue. What's the
        matter?

Virginia. O my Icilius, your incredulity
Hath quite undone me! I am now no more
Virginius's daughter, so this villain urges,
But publish'd for his bondwoman.

Num. How's this?

* *ure*] i.e. use.

Mar. Claud. 'Tis true, my lord, and I will take
   my right
By course of law.
   Icil. Villains, set her free,
Or, by the power of all our Roman gods,
I'll give that just revenge unto my rage
Which should be given to justice! Bondwoman!
   Mar. Claud. Sir, we do not come [here] to fight;
   we'll deal
By course of law.

   Enter APPIUS CLAUDIUS.
         My lord, we fear a rescue.
   App. Claud. A rescue! never fear't; here's
      none in presence
But civil men.—My lord, I am glad to see you.—
Noble Icilius, we shall ever love you.—
Now, gentlemen, reach your petitions.
   Icil. My lord, my lord,——
   App. Claud. Worthy Icilius,
If you have any business, defer't
Until to-morrow or the afternoon:
I shall be proud to pleasure you.
   Icil. The fox
Is earth'd, my lord, you cannot wind him yet.
   App. Claud. Stools for my noble friends!—I
   pray you, sit.
   Mar. Claud. May it please your lordship,——
   App. Claud. Why, uncivil sir,
Have I not begg'd forbearance of my best
And dearest friends, and must you trouble me?
   Mar. Claud. My lord, I must be heard, and will
      be heard:
Were all the gods in parliament, I'd burst
Their silence with my importunity,
But they should hear me.
   App. Claud. The fellow's mad.—
We have no leisure now to hear you, sir.
   Mar. Claud. Hast now no leisure to hear just
      complaints?
Resign thy place, O Appius, that some other
May do me justice, then!
   App. Claud. We'll hear't to-morrow.
   Mar. Claud. O my lord,
Deny me justice absolutely, rather
Than feed me with delays.
   Icil. Good my lord, hear him;
And wonder when you hear him, that a case
So full of vile imposture should desire
To be unfolded.
   Mar. Claud. Ay, my lord, 'tis true;
The imposture is on their parts.
   App. Claud. Hold your prating.—
Away with him to prison, clamorous fellow!—
Suspect you our uprightness?

   Mar. Claud. No, my lord;
But I have mighty enemies, my lord,
Will overflow my cause. See, here I hold
My bondwoman, that brags herself to be
Descended of a noble family.
My purse is too scant to wage law with them:
I am enforc'd be mine own advocate,
Not one will plead for me. Now, if your lordship
Will do me justice, so; if not, then know
High hills are safe, when seas poor dales o'erflow.
   App. Claud. Sirrah, I think it fit to let you know,
Ere you proceed in this your subtle suit,
What penalty and danger you accrue,
If you be found to double. Here's a virgin
Famous by birth, by education noble;
And she, forsooth, haply * but to draw
Some piece of money from her worthy father,
Must needs be challeng'd for a bondwoman.
Sirrah, take heed, and well bethink yourself:
I'll make you a precedent to all the world,
If I but find you tripping.
   Mar. Claud. Do it freely:
And view on that condition these just proofs.
      [*Gives papers to* APPIUS CLAUDIUS.
   App. Claud. Is that the virgin's nurse?
   Nurse. Her milch-nurse, my lord: I had a sore
hand with her for a year and a quarter: I have
had somewhat to do with her since, too, for the
poor gentlewoman hath been so troubled with
the green sickness.
   Icil. I pray thee, nurse, entreat Sertorius
To come and speak with me.   [*Exit Nurse.*
   App. Claud. Here is strange circumstance; view
it, my lord:
If he should prove this, it would make Virginius
Think he were wrong'd.
   Icil. There is a devilish cunning
Express'd in this black forgery.
   App. Claud. Icilius and Virginia, pray come near.
Compound with this base fellow: you were better
Disburse some trifle, than to undergo
The question of her freedom.
   Icil. O my lord,
She were not worth a handful of a bribe,
If she did need a bribe!
   App. Claud. Nay, take your course;
I only give you my opinion,
I ask no fee for't.—Do you know this fellow?
   Virginia. Yes, my lord; he's your servant.
   App. Claud. You're i'the right:
But will you truly know his character?
He was at first a petty notary;

---

* *haply*] Even if we substitute "happily" (as the word
was often written), the line still halts.

A fellow that, being trusted with large sums
Of honest citizens, to be employ'd
I' the trade of usury,—this gentleman,
Couching his credit like a tilting-staff
Most cunningly, it brake, and at one course
He ran away with thirty thousand pound :
Returning to the city seven year after,
Having compounded with his creditors
For the third moiety, he buys an office
Belonging to our place, depends on us ;
In which the oppression and vile injuries
He hath done poor suitors, they have cause to rue,
And I to pity : he hath sold his smiles
For silver, but his promises for gold ;
His delays have undone men.
The plague that in some folded cloud remains,
The bright sun soon disperseth ; but observe,
When black infection in some dunghill lies,
There's work for bells and graves, if it do rise.

   Num. He was an ill prop to your house, my lord.

   App. Claud. 'Tis true, my lord : but we that have
     such servants
Are like to cuckolds that have riotous wives ;
We are the last that know it : this is it
Makes noblemen suspected * to have done ill,
When the oppression lies in their proud followers.

   Mar. Claud. My lord, it was some soothing syco-
     phant,
Some base detracting rascal, that hath spread
This falsehood in your ears.

   App. Claud. Peace, impudence !
Did I not yesterday, no longer since,
Surprise thee in thy study counterfeiting
Our hand ?

   Mar. Claud. 'Tis true, my lord.

   App. Claud. Being subscrib'd
Unto a letter fill'd with amorous stuff
Unto this lady ?

   Mar. Claud. I have ask'd your pardon,
And gave you reason why I was so bold
To use that forgery.

   App. Claud. Did you receive it ?

   Virginia. I did, my lord, and I can show your
     lordship
A packet of such letters.

   App. Claud. Now, by the gods,
I'll make you rue it ! I beseech you, sir,
Show them the reason mov'd you counterfeit
Our letter.

       Enter SERTORIUS.†

   Mar. Claud. Sir, I had no other colour
To come to speak with her.

   App. Claud. A goodly reason !
Did you until this hour acquaint the lady
With your intended suit ?

   Mar. Claud. At several times ;
And would have drawn her by some private
     course
To have compounded for her liberty.

   Virginia. Now, by a virgin's honour and true
     birth,
'Tis false, my lord ! I never had a dream
So terrible as is this monstrous devil.

   App. Claud. Well, sir, referring my particular
     wrong
To a particular censure, I would know
What is your suit ?

   Mar. Claud. My lord, a speedy trial.

   App. Claud. You shall obtain't with all severity :
I will not give you longer time to dream
Upon new sleights to cloak your forgery.—
Observe you this chameleon, my lords,
I'll make him change his colour presently.

   Num. My lord, although the uprightness of our
     cause
Needs no delays, yet for the satisfaction
Of old Virginius, let him be present
When we shall crave a trial.

   App. Claud. Sir, it needs not :
Who stands for father of the innocent,
If not the judge ? I'll save the poor old man
That needless travel.

   Virginia. With your favour, sir,
We must entreat some respite in a business
So needful of his presence.

   App. Claud. I do protest
You wrong yourselves thus to importune it.
Well, let it be to-morrow : I'll not sleep
Till I have made this thicket a smooth plain,
And given you your true honour back again.

   Icil. My lord, the distance 'twixt the camp and
     us
Cannot be measur'd in so short a time ·
Let us have four days' respite.

   App. Claud. You are unwise ;
Rumour by that time will have fully spread
The scandal, which, being ended in one hour,
Will turn to air : to-morrow is the trial :
In the mean time let all contented thoughts
Attend you.

   Mar. Claud. My lord, you deal unjustly
Thus to dismiss her ; this is that they seek for :
Before to-morrow they'll convey her hence,
Where my claim shall not seize her.

---

* *suspected*] The author probably wrote " suspect."

† *Enter Sertorius*] The old copy, "*Enter Valerius ;*"

but *Sertorius* was the person sent for by Icilius ; and see
towards the close of this scene.

App. Claud. Cunning knave!
You would have bond for her appearance? say.
Mar. Claud. I think the motion's honest.
App. Claud. Very good.
Icilius shall engage his honour'd word
For her appearance.
Mar. Claud. As you please, my lord;
But it were fitting her old uncle there
Were jointly bound with him.
App. Claud. Well, sir, your pleasure
Shall have satiety. You'll take our word
For her appearance; will you not, sir, I pray?
Mar. Claud. Most willingly, my lord.
App. Claud. Then, sir, you have it:
And i'the mean time I'll take the honour'd lady
Into my guardianship; and, by my life,
I'll use her in all kindness as my wife.
Icil. Now, by the gods, you shall not!
App. Claud. Shall not, what?
Icil. Not use her as your wife, sir.
App. Claud. O my lord,
I spake it from my heart.
Icil. Ay, very likely.
She is a virgin, sir, and must not lie
Under a man's forthcoming; do you mark?
Not under your forthcoming, lecherous Appius.
App. Claud. Mistake me not, my lord.—Our
secretary
Take bonds for the appearance of this lady.—
And now to you, sir: you that were my servant,
I here cashier you; never shalt thou shroud
Thy villanies under our noble roof,
Nor scape the whip or the fell hangman's hook
By warrant of our favour.
Mar. Claud. So, my lord,
I am more free to serve the gods, I hope,
Now I have lost your service.
App. Claud. Hark you, sirrah,
Who shall give bonds for your appearance, ha,
To justify your claim?
Mar. Claud. I have none, my lord.
App. Claud. Away!—Commit him prisoner to
his chamber.—
I'll keep you safe from starting.
Mar. Claud. Why, my lord,—
App. Claud. Away! I will not hear you:
A judge's heart here in the midst must stand,
And move not a hair's breadth to either hand.
[*Exeunt* APPIUS CLAUDIUS, MARCUS CLAUDIUS,
and Lictors.
Num. O, were thy heart but of the self-same piece
Thy tongue is, Appius, how bless'd were Rome!
Icil. Post to the camp, Sertorius: thou hast heard
The effect of all; relate it to Virginius:

I pray thee, use thy ablest horsemanship,
For it concerns us near.
Sert. I go, my lord. [*Exit.*
Icil. Sure, all this is damn'd cunning.
Virginia. O my lord,
Seamen in tempests shun the flattering shore;
To bear full sails upon 't were danger more :
So men o'erborne with greatness still hold dread
False seeming friends that on their bosoms
spread;
For this is a safe truth which never varies,
He that strikes all his sails seldom miscarries.
Icil. Must we be slaves both to a tyrant's will,*
And [to] confounding ignorance at once?
Where are we? in a mist? or is this hell?
I have seen as great as the proud judge have fell :
The bending willow, yielding to each wind,
Shall keep his rooting firm, when the proud oak,
Braving the storm, presuming on his root,
Shall have his body rent from head to foot.
Let us expect the worst that may befal,
And with a noble confidence bear all. [*Exeunt.*

SCENE III.†

Enter APPIUS CLAUDIUS, MARCUS CLAUDIUS, *and a
Servant.*

App. Claud. Here, bear this packet to Minutius,
And privately deliver 't : make as much speed
As if thy father were deceas'd i'the camp,
And that thou went'st to take the administration
Of what he left thee. Fly!
Serv. I go, my lord. [*Exit.*
App. Claud. O my trusty Claudius!
Mar. Claud. My dear lord,
Let me adore your divine policy.
You have poison'd them with sweatmeats; you
have, my lord.
But what contain those letters?

---

* *Must we be slaves both to a tyrant's will, &c.*] The
Rev. J. Mitford (*Gent. Mag.* for June 1833, p. 491) thinks
that the whole of this speech ought to be in rhyme, and
accordingly would read,—
"Must we be slaves both to a tyrant's will,
And confounding ignorance at once *of ill?*
* * * * *
The bending willow yielding to each *stroke*," &c.
But I believe that the old copy gives here the very
words of the author, except that it omits "*to*" in the
second line; speeches partly blank verse and partly
prose being not uncommon in our early dramatists :
and the impropriety of the alteration "each *stroke*" is
evinced by what follows,—"Braving the *storm.*"
† *Scene III.*] The same A room in the house of
Appius.

App. Claud. Much importance.
Minutius is commanded by that packet
To hold Virginius prisoner in the camp
On some suspect of treason.'

Mar. Claud. But, my lord,
How will you answer this?

App. Claud. Tush, any fault
Or shadow of a crime will be sufficient
For his committing : thus, when he is absent,
We shall in a more calm and friendly sea
Sail to our purpose.

Mar. Claud. Mercury himself
Could not direct more safely.

App. Claud. O my Claudius,
Observe this rule,—one ill must cure another;
As aconitum,* a strong poison, brings
A present cure against all serpents' stings.
In high attempts the soul hath infinite eyes,
And 'tis necessity makes men most wise.
Should I miscarry in this desperate plot,
This of my fate in aftertimes be spoken,
I'll break that with my weight on which I am
          broken.   [*Exeunt.*

———

SCENE IV.†

Enter, from one side, Two Servingmen ; *from the other,*
Corbulo, *the Clown, melancholy.*

First Serv. Why, how now, Corbulo! thou
wast not wont to be of this sad temper. What's
the matter now?

Corb. Times change, and seasons alter,
Some men are born to the bench, and some to
          the halter.
What do you think now that I am?

First Serv. I think thee to be Virginia's man,
and Corbulo.

Corb. No, no such matter: guess again: tell
me but what I am, or what manner of fellow you
imagine me to be.

First Serv. I take thee to be an honest good
fellow.

Corb. Wide of the bow-hand ‡ still: Corbulo is
no such man.

Sec. Serv. What art thou, then?

Corb. Listen, and I'll describe myself to you :
I am something better than a knave, and yet come
short of being an honest man ; and though I can
sing a treble, yet am accounted but as one of the
base, being, indeed, and, as the case stands with
me at this present, inferior to a rogue, and three
degrees worse than a rascal.

First. Serv. How comes this to pass?

Corb. Only by my service's success. Take heed
whom you serve, O you serving creatures! for this
is all I have got by serving my lady Virginia.

Sec. Serv. Why, what of her?

Corb. She is not the woman you take her to
be ; for though she have borrowed no money, yet
she is entered into bonds; and though you may
think her a woman not sufficient, yet 'tis very
like her bond will be taken. The truth is, she
is challenged to be a bondwoman : now, if she be
a bondwoman and a slave, and I her servant and
vassal, what do* you take me to be? I am an
ant, a gnat, a worm ; a woodcock amongst birds;
a hodmondod amongst flies; amongst curs a
trindle-tale, and amongst fishes a poor iper ; but,
amongst serving-men, worse, worse than the man's
man to the under-yeoman-fewterer.†

First Serv. But is it possible thy lady is challenged to be a slave? What witness have they?

Corb. Witness these fountains, these flood-
gates, these well-springs: the poor gentlewoman
was arrested in the open market: I offered, I
offered to bail her; but (though she was) I could
not be taken. The grief hath gone so near my
heart that, until I be made free, I shall never
be mine own man. The Lord Appius hath committed her to ward, and it is thought she shall
neither lie on the Knight-side, nor in the Twopenny-ward ; ‡ for if he may have his will of her,
he means to put her in the Hole. His warrant
hath been out for her ; but how the case stands
with him, or how matters will be taken up with
her, 'tis yet uncertain.

Sec. Serv. When shall the trial be?

Corb. I take it to be as soon as the morning is
brought a-bed of a new son and heir.

Sec. Serv. And when is that?

Corb. Why, to-morrow ; for every morning,

---

* *As aconitum,* &c.] Compare Ben Jonson, who follows
Plin. *Nat. Hist.* xxvii. 2 ;
          "I have heard that aconite,
     Being timely taken, hath a healing might
     Against the scorpion's stroke ; the proof we'll give,
     That, while two poisons wrestle, we may live."
                                        Sejanus, act iii. sc. 3.
† *Scene IV.*] The same. A street.
‡ *wide of the bow-hand*] i. e. considerably to the left of
the mark ; a metaphor taken from archery.

* *do*] The old copy "did."
† *yeoman-fewterer*] Was the person immediately under
the huntsman, who led out and let loose the dogs in the
chase. *Fewterer* is from the French *vautrier* or *vaultrier.*
‡ *Twopenny-ward*] Old copy "*Troping Ward.*" The
Knight's Ward, the Master's Ward, the *Twopenny-Ward,*
and the Hole, were the four prison-divisions or sides.
See a curious description of them in Fenner's *Compter's
Commonwealth,* 1617.

you know, brings forth a new sun: but they are
all short-lived; for every night she drowns them
in the western sea. But to leave these enigmas
as too high for your dull apprehensions, shall I
see you at the trial to-morrow?

First. Serv. By Jove's help I'll be there.

Sec. Serv. And I, if I live.

Corb. And I, if I die for't: here's my hand,
I'll meet you. It is thought my old master
will be there at the bar; for though all the
timber of his house yet stand, yet my Lord
Numitorius hath sent one of his posts to the
camp to bid him spur, cut, and come to the sentence. O, we have a house at home as heavy as
if it were covered with lead! But you will
remember to be there.

First Serv. And not to fail.

Corb. If I chance to meet you there, and that
the case go against us, I will give you a quart,
not of wine, but of tears; for, instead of a new
roll, I purpose to break my fast with sops of
sorrow.   [*Exeunt.*

ACT IV.

SCENE I.*

Enter VIRGINIUS *like a slave,* NUMITORIUS, ICILIUS, VALE-
RIUS, HORATIUS, VIRGINIA *like a slave,* JULIA, CAL-
PHURNIA, *and* Nurse.

Virginius. Thanks to my noble friends; it now
appears
That you have rather lov'd me than my fortune,
For that's near shipwreck'd: chance, you see,
still ranges,
And this short dance of life is full of changes.
Appius—how hollow that name sounds, how
dreadful!
It is a question whether the proud lecher
Will view us to our merit; for they say
His memory to virtue and good men
Is still carousing Lethe. O the gods!
Not with more terror do the souls in hell
Appear before the seat of Rhadamant
Than the poor client yonder.
     [*Pointing to the tribunal.*

Num. O Virginius,
Why do you wear this habit? it ill fits
Your noble person or this reverend place.

Virginius. That's true, old man; but it well
fits the case
That's now in question. If with form and show
They prove her slav'd, all freedom I'll forego.

Icil. Noble Virginius,
Put out a bold and confident defence;
Search the imposture, like a cunning trier;
False metals bear the touch, but brook not
fire,—
Their brittleness betrays them: let your breath
Discover as much shame in them as death
Did e'er draw from offenders: let your truth
Nobly supported, void of fear or art,
Welcome whatever comes with a great heart.

Virginius. Now, by the gods, I thank thee,
noble youth!
I never fear'd in a besieged town
Mines or great engines like yon lawyer's gown.

Virginia. O my dear lord and father! once you
gave me
A noble freedom: do not see it lost
Without a forfeit; take the life you gave me,
And sacrifice it rather to the gods
Than to a villain's lust. Happy the wretch
Who, born in bondage, lives and dies a slave,
And sees no lustful projects bent upon her,
And neither knows the life nor death of
honour.

Icil. We have neither justice, no, nor violence,
Which should reform corruption, sufficient
To cross their black premeditated doom.
Appius will seize her: all the fire in hell
Is leap'd into his bosom.

Virginius. O you gods,
Extinguish it with your compassionate tears,
Although you make a second deluge spread,
And swell more high than Teneriff's high head!
Have not the wars heap'd snow sufficient
Upon this aged head, but they will still
Pile winter upon winter?

Enter APPIUS CLAUDIUS, OPPIUS, MARCUS CLAUDIUS, Six
Senators, Advocate, *and* Lictors.

App. Claud. Is he come, say?—
Now, by my life, I'll quit the general.

Num. Your reverence to the judge, good
brother.

Virginius. Yes, sir, I have learnt my compliment thus:

* *Scene I.*] Rome. Before the tribunal of Appius.

Bless'd mean estates who stand in fear of many,
And great are curs'd for that they fear not any.

App. Claud. What, is Virginius come?

Virginius. I am here, my lord.

App. Claud. Where is your daughter?

Num. Here, my reverend lord.—

[*To Virginia.*] Your habit shows you strangely.

Virginia. O, 'tis fit;

It suits both time and cause. Pray, pardon it.

App. Claud. Where is your advocate?

Virginius. I have none, my lord;

Truth needs no advocate: the unjust cause
Buys up the tongues that travel with applause
In those your throngèd courts: I want not any,
And count him the most wretched that needs
     many.

Adv. May it please your reverend lordships,—

App. Claud. What are you, sir?

Adv. Of counsel with my client, Marcus
     Claudius.

Virginius. My lord, I undertake a desperate
     combat
To cope with this most eloquent lawyer:
I have no skill i' the weapon, good my lord;
I mean I am not travell'd in your laws:
My suit is therefore, by your special goodness,
They be not wrested against me.

App. Claud. O Virginius,
The gods defend* they should!

Virginius. Your humble servant shall ever†
     pray for you.
Thus shall your glory be above your place,
Or those high titles which you hold in court;
For they die bless'd that die in good report.—
Now, sir, I stand you.

Adv. Then have at you, sir!—
May it please your lordships, here is such a case,
So full of subtlety, and, as it were,
So far benighted in an ignorant mist,
That though my reading be sufficient,
My practice more, I never was entangled
In the like purse-net.‡ Here is one that claims
This woman for his daughter: here's another
Affirms she is his bond-slave: now the question
(With favour of the bench) I shall make plain
In two words only without circumstance.

App. Claud. Fall to your proofs.

Adv. Where are our papers?

Mar. Claud. Here, sir.

Adv. Where, sir? I vow you're the most tedious
     client.——

---

* *defend*] i. e. forbid.
† *shall ever*] Qy. "*ever shall*" .
‡ *purse net*] See note *, p. 130.

Now we come to 't, my lord. Thus stands the case
The law is clear on our sides.—
          Hold your prating.
          [*To* MARCUS CLAUDIUS.

That honourable lord, Virginius,
Having been married about fifteen year,
And issueless, this virgin's politic mother,
Seeing the land was likely to descend
To Numitorius,—I pray, sir, listen;
You, my Lord Numitorius, attend;
We are on your side,—old Virginius
Employ'd in foreign wars, she sends him word
She was with child; observe it, I beseech you,
And note the trick of a deceitful woman:
She in the mean time feigns the passions
Of a great-bellied woman; counterfeits
Their passions and their qualms; and verily
All Rome held this for no imposturous stuff.
What's to be done now? Here's a rumour spread
Of a young heir, gods bless it! and [a] belly
Bombasted with a cushion: but there wants
(What wants there?) nothing but a pretty babe,
Bought with some piece of money, where it skills
     not,
To furnish this supposèd lying-in.

Nurse. I protest, my lord, the fellow i' the
     nightcap
Hath not spoke one true word yet.

App. Claud. Hold you your prating, woman,
     till you are call'd.

Adv. 'Tis purchas'd. Where? From this man's
     bondwoman;
The money paid:—[*To* MARCUS CLAUDIUS.] what
     was the sum of money?

Mar. Claud. A thousand drachmas.

Adv. Good; a thousand drachmas.

App. Claud. Where is that bondwoman?

Mar. Claud. She's dead, my lord.

App. Claud. O, dead; that makes your cause
     suspicious.

Adv. But here's her deposition on her death-bed,
With other testimony to confirm
What we have said is true. Will 't please your
     lordship
Take pains to view these writings? Here, my
     lord:—
We shall not need to hold your lordships long;
We'll make short work on't.

Virginius. My lord,——

App. Claud. By your favour.—
If that your claim be just, how happens it
That you have discontinu'd it the space
Of fourteen years?

Adv. I shall resolve your lordship.

Icil. I vow this is a practis'd dialogue:
Comes it not rarely off?

Virginius. Peace: give them leave.

Adv. 'Tis very true: this gentleman at first
Thought to conceal this accident, and did so;
Only reveal'd his knowledge to the mother
Of this fair bondwoman, who bought his silence,
During her lifetime, with great sums of coin.

App. Claud. Where are your proofs of that?

Adv. Here, my good lord,
With depositions likewise.

App. Claud. Well, go on.

Adv. For your question
Of discontinuance : put case my slave
Run away from me, dwell in some near city
The space of twenty years, and there grow rich,
It is in my discretion, by your favour,
To seize him when I please.

App. Claud. That's very true.

Virginia. Cast not your nobler beams, you
    reverend judges,
On such a putrefied dunghill.

App. Claud. By your favour; you shall be
    heard anon.

Virginius. My lords, believe not this spruce
    orator:
Had I but fee'd him first, he would have told
As smooth a tale on our side.

App. Claud. Give us leave.

Virginius. He deals in formal glosses, cunning
    shows,
And cares not greatly which way the case goes.
Examine, I beseech you, this old woman,
Who is the truest witness of her birth.

App. Claud. Soft, you! is she your only witness?

Virginius. She is, my lord.

App. Claud. Why, is it possible
Such a great lady, in her time of child-birth,
Should have no other witness but a nurse?

Virginius. For aught I know, the rest are dead,
    my lord.

App. Claud. Dead! no, my lord; belike they
    were of counsel
With your deceasèd lady, and so sham'd
'Twice to give colour to so vile an act.—
Thou, nurse, observe me : thy offence already
Doth merit punishment beyond our censure;
Pull not more whips upon thee.

Nurse. I defy your whips, my lord.

App. Claud. Command her silence, Lictors.

Virginius. O injustice !
You frown away my witness: is this law?
Is this uprightness?

App. Claud. Have you view'd the writings?

This is a trick to make our slaves our heirs
Beyond prevention.

Virginius. Appius, wilt thou hear me?
You have slander'd a sweet lady that now sleeps
In a most noble monument. Observe me,
I would have ta'en her simple word to gage
Before his soul or thine.

App. Claud. That makes thee wretched.
Old man, I am sorry for thee that thy love
By custom is grown natural, which by nature
Should be an absolute loathing: note the sparrow,
That having hatch'd a cuckoo, when it sees
Her brood a monster to her proper kind,
Forsakes it, and with more fear shuns the nest,
Than she had care i' the spring to have it dress'd.
Cast thy affection, then, behind thy back,
And think——

Adv. Be wise; take counsel of your friends.
You have many soldiers in their time of service
Father strange children.

Virginius. True; and pleaders too,
When they are sent to visit provinces.
You, my most neat and cunning orator,
Whose tongue is quicksilver, pray thee, good
    Janus,
Look not so many several ways at once,
But go to the point.

Adv. I will; and keep you out
At point's end, though I am no soldier.

App. Claud. First, the oath of the deceasèd
    bondwoman,—

Adv. A very virtuous matron.

App. Claud. Join'd with the testimony of
    Claudius,—

Adv. A most approvèd honest gentleman.

App. Claud. Besides, six other honest gentle-
    men,—

Adv. All knights; and there's no question but
    their oaths
Will go for current.

App. Claud. See, my reverend lords,
And wonder at a case so evident.

Virginius. My lord, I knew it.

Adv. Observe, my lord, how their own policy
Confounds them. Had your lordship yesterday
Proceeded, as 'twas fit, to a just sentence,
The apparel and the jewels that she wore,
More worth than all her tribe, *had then been due

---

* *The apparel and the jewels that she wore,*
  More worth than all her tribe] Reads like a recollection
of Shakespeare ;

      "Whose hand
  Like the base Indian, threw a pearl away,
  Richer than all his tribe."
          Othello, act v. sc. 2.

Unto our client: now, to cozen him
Of such a forfeit, see, they bring the maid
In her most proper habit, bondslave-like,
And they will save by the hand too.—Please your
     lordships,
I crave a sentence.
     Virginius. Appius,—
     Virginia. My lord,—
     Icil. Lord Appius,—
     Virginius. Now, by the gods, here's juggling !
     Num. Who cannot counterfeit a dead man's
          hand ?
     Virginius. Or hire some villains to swear
          forgeries ?
     Icil. Claudius was brought up in your house,
          my lord,
And that 's suspicious.
     Num. How is 't probable
That our wife being present at the child-birth,
Whom this did nearest concern, should ne'er
     reveal it ?
     Virginius. Or if ours dealt thus cunningly, how
          haps it
Her policy, as you term it, did not rather
Provide an issue male to cheer the father ?
     Adv. I'll answer each particular.
     App. Claud. It needs not;
Here's witness, most sufficient witness.—
Think you, my lord, our laws are writ in snow,
And that your breath can melt them ?
     Virginius. No, my lord,
We have not such hot livers * : mark you that.
     Virginia. Remember yet the gods, O Appius,
Who have no part in this ! Thy violent lust
Shall, like the biting of the envenom'd aspic,
Steal thee to hell. So subtle are thy evils,
In life they'll seem good angels, in death devils.
     App. Claud. Observe you not this scandal ?
     Icil. Sir, 'tis none:
I'll show thy letters full of violent lust
Sent to this lady.
     App. Claud. Wilt thou breathe a lie
Fore such a reverend audience
     Icil. That place
Is sanctuary to thee. Lie ! see, here they are.
     App. Claud. My lords, these are but dilatory
          shifts.—
Sirrah, I know you to the very heart,
And I'll observe you.
     Icil. Do, but do it with justice.
Clear thyself first, O Appius, ere thou judge

Our imperfections rashly ; for we wot
The office of justice is perverted quite,
When one thief hangs another. *
     First Sen. You are too bold.
     App. Claud. Lictors, take charge of him.
                              [*They seize* ICILIUS.
     Icil. 'Tis very good.
Will no man view these papers ? What, not one ?
Jove, thou hast found a rival upon earth :—
His nod strikes all men dumb.—My duty to you !
The ass that carried Isis on his back
Thought that the superstitious people kneel'd
To give his dulness humble reverence :
If thou think'st so, proud judge, I let thee see
I bend low to thy gown, but not to thee.
     Virginius. There's one in hold already.—Noble
          youth,
Fetters grace one, being worn for speaking truth :
I'll lie with thee, I swear, though in a dungeon.—
[*To* APP.] The injuries you do us we shall pardon ;
But it is just the wrongs which we forgive,
The gods are charg'd therewith to see reveng'd.
     App. Claud. Come, you're a proud plebeian.
     Virginius. True, my lord ;
Proud in the glory of my ancestors,
Who have continu'd these eight hundred years :
The heralds have not known you these eight
     months.
     App. Claud. Your madness wrongs you : by
          my soul, I love you.
     Virginius. Thy soul !—
O, thy opinion, old Pythagoras !—
Whither, O, whither should thy black soul fly ?
Into what ravenous bird or beast most vile ?
Only into a weeping crocodile.
Love me !
Thou lov'st me, Appius, as the earth loves rain ;
Thou fain wouldst swallow me.
     App. Claud. Know you the place you speak in ?
     Virginius. I'll speak freely.
Good men, too much trusting their innocence,
Do not betake them to that just defence
Which gods and nature gave them ; but even
          wink
In the black tempest, and so fondly † sink.
     App. Claud. Let us proceed to sentence.
     Virginius. Ere you speak,
One parting farewell let me borrow of you
To take of my Virginia.
     App. Claud. Now, my lords,

---

* *such hot livers*] "In allusion to the lustful motive by
which Appius was influenced : the liver being then supposed the seat of the amorous passions." *Editor of* 1816.

* *The office of justice is perverted quite,*
     When one thief hangs another] Has occurred before, in
The Duchess of Malfi, p. 90. Here the old copy has by
mistake "the Office of a Justice," &c.
† *fondly*] i. e. foolishly.

We shall have fair confession of the truth.—
Pray, take your course.

    Virginius. Farewell, my sweet Virginia : never,
      never
Shall I taste fruit of the most blessèd hope
I had in thee. Let me forget the thought
Of thy most pretty infancy ; when first
Returning from the wars, I took delight
To rock thee in my target ; when my girl
Would kiss her father in his burganet
Of glittering steel hung 'bout his armèd neck,
And, viewing the bright metal, smile to see
Another fair Virginia smile on thee ;
When I first taught thee how to go, to speak ;
And when my wounds have smarted, I have sung
With an unskilful, yet a willing voice,
To bring my girl asleep. O my Virginia,
When we begun to be, begun our woes,
Increasing still, as dying life still grows !

    App. Claud. This tediousness doth much offend
      the court.
Silence ! attend her sentence.

    Virginius. Hold ! without sentence I'll resign
      her freely,
Since you will prove her to be none of mine.

    App. Claud. See, see, how evidently truth
      appears.—
Receive her, Claudius.

    Virginius. Thus I surrender her into the court
                           [*Kills her.*
Of all the gods. And see, proud Appius, see,
Although not justly, I have made her free :
And if thy lust with this act be not fed,
Bury her in thy bowels, now she's dead.

    Omnes. O horrid act !

    App. Claud. Lay hand upon the murderer !

    Virginius. O for a ring of pikes to circle me !
What, have I stood the brunt of thousand
    enemies,
Here to be slain by hangmen ? No ; I'll fly
To safety in the camp.   [*Exit.*

    App. Claud. Some pursue the villain,
Others take up the body. Madness and rage
Are still the attendants of old doting age.
                             [*Exeunt.*

SCENE II.*

Enter Two Soldiers.

    First Sold. Is our hut swept clean ?

    Sec. Sold. As I can make it.

    First. Sold. 'Tis betwixt us two ;

* *Scene II.*] The camp before Algidum.

But how many, think'st thou, bred of Roman
    blood,
Did lodge with us last night ?

    Sec. Sold. More, I think, than the camp hath
      enemies ;
They are not to be number'd.

    First Sold. Comrague,* I fear
Appius will doom us to Acteon's death,
To be worried by the cattle that we feed.
How goes the day ?

    Sec. Sold. My stomach has struck twelve.

    First Sold. Come, see what provant our knap-
      sack yields.
This is our store, our garner.

    Sec. Sold. A small pittance.

    First Sold. Feeds Appius thus ? Is this a city
      feast ?
This crust doth taste like date-stones ; and this
    thing,
If I knew what to call it, ——

    Sec. Sold. I can tell you ;
Cheese struck in years.

    First Sold. I do not think but this same crust
      was bak'd,
And this cheese frighted out of milk and whey,
Before we two were soldiers : though it be old,
I see 't can crawl : what living things be these
That walk so freely 'tween the rind and pith ?
For here's no sap left.

    Sec. Sold. They call them gentles.

    First Sold. Therefore 'tis thought fit
That soldiers, by profession gentlemen,
Should thus be fed with gentles. I am stomach-
    sick ;
I must have some strong water.

    Sec. Sold. Where will you have 't ?

    First Sold. In yon green ditch, a place which
      none can pass
But he must stop his nose : thou know'st it well ;
There where the two dead dogs lie.

    Sec. Sold. Yes, I know 't.

    First Sold. And see the cat, that lies a distance off,

* *Comrague*] The Editor of 1816, and Nares (*Gloss.* in v. *Comrogue*), incline to think this word a misprint, neither of them having met with it, except in the present passage. I had, however, noted down more than one example of its use, but have mislaid them all except the following :—

    "Nay, rest by me,
Good Morglay, my *comrague* and bed-fellow."
Heywood and Brome's *Lancashire Witches*, 1634, Sig. K.
Comrogue has the same sense as, and perhaps is a corruption of, *comrade*, which used to be accented on the last syllable,—

    "And his *comrades*, that daff the world aside."
Shakespeare's *First Part of Henry IV.*, act IV. sc. I.

Be flay'd for supper: though we dine to-day
As Dutchmen feed their soldiers, we will sup
Bravely like Roman leaguerers.

Sec. Sold. Sir, the general.

First Sold. We'll give him place:
But tell none of our dainties, lest we have
Too many guests to supper.   [*Exeunt.*

Enter MINUTIUS *reading a letter, with* Officers
and Soldiers.

Min. Most sure 'tis so, it cannot otherwise be;
Either Virginius is degenerate
From the ancient virtues he was wont to boast,
Or in some strange displeasure with the senate:
Why should these letters else from Appius
Confine him a close prisoner to the camp?
And, which confirms his guilt, why should he fly?
Needs, then, must I incur some high displeasure
For negligence, to let him thus escape:
Which to excuse, and that it may appear
I have no hand with him, but am of faction
Oppos'd in all things to the least misdeed,
I will cashier him, and his tribuneship
Bestow upon some noble gentleman
Belonging to the camp.—Soldiers and friends,
You that beneath Virginius' colours march'd,
By strict command from the Decemvirate
We take you from the charge of him late fled,
And his authority, command, and honour
We give this worthy Roman. Know his colours,
And prove his faithful soldiers.

Roman. Warlike general,
My courage and my forwardness in battle
Shall plead how well I can deserve the title,
To be a Roman tribune.

Re-enter First Soldier *in haste.*

Min. Now, the news?

First Sold. Virginius, in a strange shape of
distraction,
Enters the camp, and at his heels a legion
Of all estates, growths, ages, and degrees,
With breathless paces dog his frighted steps.
It seems half Rome's unpeopled with a train
That, either for some mischief done, pursue him,
Or to attend some uncouth novelty.

Min. Some wonder our fear promises.—Worthy
soldiers,
Marshal yourselves, and entertain this novel
Within a ring of steel: wall in this portent
With men and harness*, be it ne'er so dreadful.
He's entered, by the clamour of the camp,
That entertains him with these echoing shouts.

---

* *harness*] i. e. armour.

Affection that in soldiers' hearts is bred
Survives the wounded, and outlives the dead.

Enter VIRGINIUS, *with his knife; that, and his arms stripped
up to the elbows, all bloody: coming into the midst of
the soldiers, he makes a stand.*

Virginius. Have I, in all this populous assembly
Of soldiers that have prov'd Virginius' valour,
One friend? Let him come thrill * his partisan
Against this breast, that through a large wide
wound
My mighty soul might rush out of this prison,
To fly more freely to yon crystal palace,
Where honour sits enthroniz'd. What, no friend?
Can this great multitude, then, yield an enemy
That hates my life? Here let him seize it freely.
What, no man strike? am I so well belov'd?—
Minutius, then to thee: if in this camp
There lives one man so just to punish sin,
So charitable to redeem from torments
A wretched soldier, at his worthy hand
I beg a death.

Min. What means Virginius?

Virginius. Or if the general's heart be so obdure
To an old begging soldier, have I here
No honest legionary of mine own troop,
At whose bold hand and sword, if not entreat,
I may command a death?

First. Sold. Alas, good captain!

Min. Virginius, you have no command at all:
Your companies are elsewhere now bestow'd.
Besides, we have a charge to stay you here,
And make you the camp's prisoner.

Virginius. General, thanks:
For thou hast done as much with one harsh word
As I begg'd from their weapons; thou hast kill'd
me,
But with a living death.

Min. Besides, I charge you
To speak what means this ugly face of blood
You put on your distractions? What's the reason
All Rome pursues you, covering those high hills,
As if they dogg'd you for some damnèd act?
What have you done?

Virginius. I have play'd the parricide;
Kill'd mine own child.

Min. Virginia?

Virginius. Yes, even she.

---

* *thrill*] i. e., hurl,—an unusual sense of the word; so
Heywood;
   " I'd *thrill* my javelin at the Grecian moysture,
   And spare the Trojan blood."
                   Iron Age, Part First, 1632, Sig. F.
" All which their javelins *thrill* against thy brest."
                   Id., Sig H.

These rude hands ripp'd her, and her innocent
   blood
Flow'd above my elbows.
  Min. Kill'd her willingly?
  Virginius. Willingly, with advice, premedita-
   tion,
And settled purpose; and see, still I wear
Her crimson colours, and these wither'd arms
Are dy'd in her heart-blood.
  Min. Most wretched villain!
  Virginius. But how I lov'd her life! Lend me
   amongst you
One speaking organ to discourse her death:
It is too harsh an imposition
To lay upon a father.—O my Virginia!
  Min. How agrees this? Love her, and murder
   her?
  Virginius. Yes: give me but a little leave to
   drain
A few red tears, for soldiers should weep blood,
And I'll agree them well. Attend me all.
Alas, might I have kept her chaste and free,
This life, so oft gag'd * for ingrateful Rome,
Lay in her bosom: but when I saw her pull'd
By Appius' Lictors to be claim'd a slave,
And dragg'd unto a public sessions-house,
Divorc'd from her fore-spousals with Icilius,
A noble youth, and made a bondwoman,
Enforc'd by violence from her father's arms
To be a prostitute and paramour
To the rude twinings of a lecherous judge;
Then, then, O loving soldiers, (I'll not deny it,
For 'twas mine honour, my paternal pity,
And the sole act for which I love my life,)
Then lustful Appius, he that sways the land,
Slew poor Virginia by this father's hand.
  First Sold. O villain Appius!
  Sec. Sold. O noble Virginius!
  Virginius. To you I appeal; you are my sen-
   tencers:
Did Appius right, or poor Virginius wrong?
Sentence my fact with a free general tongue.
  First Sold. Appius is the parricide.
  Sec. Sold. Virginius guiltless of his daughter's
   death.
  Min. If this be true, Virginius (as the moan
Of all the Roman fry that follows you
Confirms at large), this cause is to be pitied,
And should not die revengeless.
  Virginius. Noble Minutius,
Thou hast a daughter, thou hast a wife too;
So most of you have, soldiers: why might not this

Have happen'd you? Which of you all, dear
   friends,
But now, even now, may have your wives de-
   flower'd,
Your daughters slav'd, and made a Lictor's prey?
Think them not safe in Rome, for mine liv'd
   there.
  *Roman.** It is a common cause.
  First Sold. Appius shall die for 't.
  Sec. Sold. Let's make Virginius general.
  Omnes. A general!
A general! let's make Virginius general!
  Min. It shall be so.—Virginius, take my charge:
The wrongs are thine, so violent and so weighty,
That none but he that lost so fair a child
Knows how to punish. By the gods of Rome,
Virginius shall succeed my full command.
  Virginius. What's honour unto me,—a weak
   old man,
Weary of life, and covetous of a grave?
I am a dead man, now Virginia lives not.
The self-same hand that dar'd to save from shame
A child, dares in the father act the same.
              [*Offers to kill himself.*
  First Sold. Stay, noble general!
  Min. You much forget revenge, Virginius.
Who, if you die, will take your cause in hand,
And proscribe Appius, should you perish thus?
  Virginius. Thou ought'st, Minutius:—soldiers,
   so ought you.
I'm out of fear: my noble wife's expir'd;
My daughter of bless'd memory, the object
Of Appius' lust, lives 'mongst the Elysian vestals;
My house yields none fit for his Lictors' spoil.
You that have wives lodg'd in yon prison, Rome,
Have lands unrified, houses yet unseiz'd,
Your freeborn daughters yet unstrumpeted,
Prevent these mischiefs yet while you have
   time.
  First Sold. We will by you, our noble general.
  Sec. Sold. He that was destin'd to preserve great
   Rome.
  Virginius. I accept your choice, in hope to guard
   you all
From my inhuman sufferings. Be't my pride
That I have bred a daughter, whose chaste blood
Was spilt for you and for Rome's lasting good.
                [*Exeunt.*

---

* *Roman*] i. e., the officer who was to succeed Virginius
in his command (see p. 174). Occasionally our old dramatists neglect, awkwardly enough, to give names to
inferior speakers: so in Shakespeare's *Richard the Second*,
act. IV. sc. I. Aumerle is defied to combat by Fitz-
walter, Percy, and *a Lord.*

---

* gag'd] The old copy "*ingag'd.*"

ACT V.

SCENE I.*

Enter OPPIUS, a Senator, and the Advocate.

Opp. Is Appius, then, committed?

Sen. So 'tis rumour'd.

Opp. How will you bear you in this turbulent
state?
You are a member of that wretched faction:
I wonder how you scape imprisonment.

Adv. Let me alone: I have learnt with the wise
    hedgehog,
To stop my cave that way the tempest drives.
Never did bear-whelp, tumbling down a hill,
With more art shrink his head betwixt his
    claws
Than I will work my safety. Appius
Is in the sand already up to the chin;
And shall I hazard landing on that shelf?
He's a wise friend that first befriends himself.

Opp. What is your course of safety?

Adv. Marry, this:
Virginius, with his troops, is entering Rome,
And it is like that in the market-place
My Lord Icilius and himself shall meet:
Now to encounter these, two such great armies,
Where lies my court of guard?

Sen. Why, in your heels:
There are strange dogs uncoupled.

Adv. You are deceiv'd:
I have studied a most eloquent oration,
That shall applaud their fortune, and distaste
The cruelty of Appius.

Sen. Very good, sir:
It seems, then, you will rail upon your lord,
Your late good benefactor?

Adv. By the way, sir.

Sen. Protest Virginia was no bondwoman,
And read her noble pedigree?

Adv. By the way, sir.

Opp. Could you not, by the way too, find occa-
    sion
To beg Lord Appius' lands?

Adv. And by the way
Perchance I will; for I will gull them all
Most palpably.

Opp. Indeed, you have the art
Of flattery.

Adv. Of rhetoric, you would say:
And I'll begin my smooth oration thus:—
" Most learnèd captains,"——

Sen. Fie, fie, that's horrible! most of your
    captains
Are utterly unlearnèd.

Adv. Yet, I assure you,
Most of them know arithmetic so well,
That in a muster, to preserve dead pays,*
They'll make twelve stand for twenty.

Opp. Very good.

Adv. Then I proceed:—
" I do applaud your fortunes, and commend
In this your observation, noble shake-rags:
The helmet shall no more harbour the spider,
But it shall serve to carouse sack and cider."—
The rest within I'll study.   [*Exit.*

Opp. Farewell, Proteus:
And I shall wish thy eloquent bravado
May shield thee from the whip and bastinado.
Now in this furious tempest let us glide,
With folded sails, at pleasure of the tide.
                         [*Exeunt.*

SCENE II.†

*Enter, from one side, ICILIUS, HORATIUS, VALERIUS, NUMI-
TORIUS, with Soldiers; from the other, VIRGINIUS,
MINUTIUS, and others.*

Icil. Stand!

Virginius. Make a stand!

Icil. A parley with Virginius.

Min. We will not trust our general 'twixt the
    armies,
But upon terms of hostage.

Num. Well advis'd:
Nor we our general. Who for the leaguer?‡

Min. Ourself.

Virginius. Who for the city?

Icil. Numitorius.
    [MINUTIUS and NUMITORIUS *meet, embrace, salute
    the generals.*

Num. How is it with your sorrow, noble brother?

Virginius. I am forsaken of the gods, old man.

---

* *dead pays*] I.e., pay continued to soldiers who were
really dead, which officers of Webster's days scrupled not
sometimes to take for themselves.
† *Scene II.*] The same. The Forum.
‡ *leaguer*] i. e. camp.

* *Scene I.*] Rome. A street.

Num. Preach not that wretched doctrine to
    yourself;
It will beget despair.

  Virginius. What do you call
A burning fever? is not that a devil?
It shakes me like an earthquake. Wilt a, wilt a
Give me some wine?

  Num. O, it is hurtful for you.

  Virginius. Why so are all things that the
    appetite
Of man doth covet in his perfect'st health :
Whatever art or nature have invented
To make the boundless wish of man contented,
Are all his poison.—Give me the wine there!
    when?*
Do you grudge me a poor cup of drink? Say, say.
Now, by the gods, I'll leave enough behind me
To pay my debts; and for the rest, no matter
Who scrambles for 't.

  Num. Here, my noble brother.
Alas, your hand shakes : I will guide it to you.

  Virginius. 'Tis true, it trembles.—Welcome,
    thou just palsy !
'Twere pity this should do me longer service,
Now it hath slain my daughter.—So, I thank you.
Now I have lost all comforts in the world,
It seems I must a little longer live,
Be 't but to serve my belly.

  Min. O my lord,
This violent fever took him late last night:
Since when, the cruelty of the disease
Hath drawn him into sundry passions,
Beyond his wonted temper.

  Icil. 'Tis the gods
Have pour'd their justice on him.

  Virginius. You are sadly met, my lord.

  Icil. Would we had met
In a cold grave together two months since!
I should not then have curs'd you.

  Virginius. Ha ! what's that?

  Icil. Old man, thou hast show'd thyself a noble
    Roman,
But an unnatural father: thou hast turn d
My bridal to a funeral. What devil
Did arm thy fury with the lion's paw,
The dragon's tail, with the bull's double horn
The cormorant's beak, the cockatrice's eyes,
The scorpion's teeth,—and all these by a father
To be employ'd upon his innocent child !

  Virginius. Young man, I love thy true descrip-
    tion :
I am happy now that one beside myself

Doth tax* me for this act. Yet, were I pleas'd,
I could approve the deed most just and noble;
And, sure, posterity, which truly renders
To each man his desert, shall praise me for 't.

  Icil. Come, 'twas unnatural and damnable.

  Virginius. You need not interrupt me : here's
    a fury
Will do it for you. You are a Roman knight :
What was your oath when you receiv'd your
    knighthood?
A parcel of it is, as I remember,
" Rather to die with honour than to live
In servitude." Had my poor girl been ravish'd,
In her dishonour and in my sad grief
Your love and pity quickly had ta'en end :
Great men's misfortunes thus have ever stood,—
They touch none nearly, but their nearest blood.
What do you mean to do? It seems, my lord,
Now you have caught the sword within your hand,
Like a madman you will draw it to offend
Those that best love you ; and perhaps the counsel
Of some loose unthrifts and vile malcontents
Hearten you to it : go to; take your course.
My faction shall not give the least advantage
To murderers, to banquerouts,† or thieves,
To fleece the commonwealth.

  Icil. Do you term us so?
Shall I reprove your rage, or is 't your malice?
He that would tame a lion doth not use
The goad or wirèd whip, but a sweet voice,
A fearful stroking, and with food in hand
Must ply his wanton hunger.

  Virginius. Want of sleep
Will do it better than all these, my lord.
I would not have you wake for others' ruin,
Lest you turn mad with watching.

  Icil. O you gods !
You are now a general: learn to know your place,
And use your noble calling modestly.
Better had Appius been an upright judge
And yet an evil man, than honest man
And yet a dissolute judge ; for all disgrace
Lights less upon the person than the place.
You are i'the city now, where if you raise
But the least uproar, even your father's house
Shall not be free from ransack. Piteous fires,
That chance in towers of stone, are not so fear'd
As those that light in flax-shops; for there's food
For eminent ruin.

  Min. O my noble lord,
Let not your passion bring a fatal end

---

* *tax*] The old copy "teach."
† *banquerouts*] Here for the sake of the metre I have
let the old spelling stand.

To such a good beginning. All the world
Shall honour that deed * in him, which first
Grew to a reconcilement.
　Icil. Come, my lord,
I love your friendship; yes, in sooth, I do;
But will not seal it with that bloody hand.
Join we our armies. No fantastic copy
Or borrow'd precedent will I assume
In my revenge. There's hope yet you may live
To outwear this sorrow.
　Virginius. O, impossible !
A minute's joy to me would quite cross nature ;
As those that long have dwelt in noisome rooms
Swoon presently, if they but scent perfumes.
　Icil. To the senate ! Come, no more of this
　　sad tale ;
For such a tell-tale may we term our grief,
And doth, as 'twere, so listen to her own words,
Envious of others' sleep, because she wakes.
I ever would converse with a griev'd person
In a long journey to beguile the day,
Or winter-evening to pass time away.
March on, and let proud Appius in our view,
Like a tree rotted, fall that way he grow.
　　　　　　　　　　　　　　　　　　[Exeunt.

SCENE III.

APPIUS CLAUDIUS *and* MARCUS CLAUDIUS *discovered in
prison, fettered and gyved.*
　App. Claud. The world is chang'd now. All
　　damnations
Seize on the hydra-headed multitude,
That only gape for innovation !
O, who would trust a people?
　Mar. Claud. Nay, who would not,
Rather than one rear'd on a popular suffrage,
Whose station's built on aves and applause !
There's no firm structure on these airy bases :
O, fie upon such greatness !
　App. Claud. The same hands
That yesterday, to hear me conscionate
And oratorize, rung shrill plaudits forth
In sign of grace, now in contempt and scorn
Hurry me to this place of darkness.
　Mar. Claud. Could not their poisons rather
　　spend themselves
On the judge fully,† but must it needs stretch
To me his servant, and sweep me along?
Curse on the inconstant rabble !
　App. Claud. Grieves it thee
To impart ‡ my sad disaster !

　Mar. Claud. Marry, doth it.
　App. Claud. Thou shared'st a fortune with me
　　in my greatness ;
I hal'd thee after when I clomb * my state ;
And shrink'st thou at my ruin?
　Mar. Claud. I lov'd your greatness,
And would have trac'd you in the golden path
Of sweet promotion : but this your decline
Sours all these hop'd sweets.
　App. Claud. 'Tis the world right :
Such gratitude a great man still shall have
That trusts unto a temporizing slave.
　Mar. Claud. Slave! good. Which of us two
In our dejection is basest? I am most sure
Your loathsome dungeon is as dark as mine ;
Your conscience, for a thousand sentences
Wrongly denounc'd, much more oppress'd than
　　mine :
Then which is the most slave?
　App. Claud. O double baseness,
To hear a drudge thus with his lord compare !
Great men disgrac'd slaves to their servants are.

Enter VIRGINIUS, ICILIUS, MINUTIUS, NUMITORIUS, HORA-
TIUS, VALERIUS, OPPIUS, *with* Soldiers.

　Virginius. Soldiers, keep a strong guard whilst
　　we survey
Our sentenc'd prisoners : and from this deep
　　dungeon
Keep off that great concourse, whose violent hands
Would ruin this stone-building, and drag hence
This impious judge, piecemeal to tear his limbs
Before the law convince † him.
　Icil. See, these monsters,
Whose fronts the fair Virginia's innocent blood
Hath visarded with such black ugliness,
That they are loathsome to all good men's souls !—
Speak, damnèd judge ! how canst thou purge
　　thyself
From lust and blood ?
　App. Claud. I do confess myself
Guilty of both : yet hear me, noble Romans.
Virginius, thou dost but supply my place,
I thine : fortune hath lift thee to my chair,
And thrown me headlong to thy pleading bar.
If in mine eminence I was stern to thee,
Shunning my rigour, likewise shuu my fall ;
And, being mild where I show'd cruelty,
Establish still thy greatness. Make some use
Of this my bondage. With indifference
Survey me, and compare my yesterday

------

* *that deed*] Qy. "that *good* deed"?
† *judge fully*] The old copy "judge's folly."
‡ *impart*] i. e. share

* *clomb*] The old copy "*climb.*"
† *convince*] i. e. convict.

With this sad hour, my height with my decline,
And give them equal balance.

   Virginius. Uncertain fate! but yesterday his
breath
Aw'd Rome, and his least torvèd* frown was
death:
I cannot choose but pity and lament,
So high a rise should have such low descent.

   Icil. He 's ready to forget his injury:
O too relenting age!—Thinks not Virginius,
If he should pardon Appius this black deed,
And set him once more in the ivory chair,
He would be wary to avoid the like,
Become a new man, a more upright judge,
And deserve better of the commonweal?

   Virginius. 'Tis like he would.

   Icil. Nay, if you thus begin,
I'll fetch that shall anatomize his sin.   [*Exit.*

   Num. Virginius, you are too remiss to punish
Deeds of this nature: you must fashion now
Your actions to your place, not to your passion:
Severity to such acts is as necessary
As pity to the tears of innocence.

   Min. He speaks but law and justice.
Make good the streets with your best men-at-arms.
               [*A shout within.*
Valerius and Horatius, know the reason
Of this loud uproar and confusèd noise.
            [*Exeunt* VAL. *and* HOR.
Although my heart be melting at the fall
Of men in place and office, we'll be just
To punish murderous acts, and censure lust.

     Re-enter VALERIUS *and* HORATIUS.

   Val. Icilius, worthy lord, bears through the
street
The body of Virginia towards this prison;
Which, when it was discover'd to the people,
Mov'd such a mournful clamour, that their cries
Pierc'd heaven, and forc'd tears from their sorrow-
ing eyes.

   Hor. Here comes Icilius.

     Re-enter ICILIUS *with the body of* VIRGINIA.

   Icil. Where was thy pity, when thou slew'st this
maid,
Thou wouldst extend to Appius? Pity! See
Her wounds still bleeding at the horrid presence
Of yon stern murderer,† till she find revenge!
Nor will these drops stanch, or these springs be
dry,

---

* *torvèd*] i. e. stern.
† *Her wounds still bleeding at the horrid presence
Of yon stern murderer*] According to the belief of the
time when this play was written.

Till theirs be set a-bleeding. Shall her soul,
(Whose essence some suppose lives in the blood,)
Still labour without rest? Will old Virginius
Murder her once again in this delay?

   Virginius. Pause there, Icilius.
This sight hath stiffen'd all my operant powers,*
Ic'd all my blood, benumb'd my motion quite.
I'll pour my soul into my daughter's belly,
And with a soldier's tears embalm her wounds.—
My only dear Virginia!

   App. Claud. Leave this passion;
Proceed to your just sentence.

   Virginius. We will.—Give me two swords.—
   Appius, grasp this;
You Claudius, that: you shall be your own hang-
men;†
Do justice on yourselves. You made Virginius
Sluice his own blood, lodg'd in his daughter's
breast;
Which your own hands shall act upon yourselves.
If you be Romans, and retain their spirits,
Redeem a base life with a noble death,
And through your lust-burnt veins confine‡ your
breath.

   App. Claud. Virginius is a noble justicer:
Had I my crookèd paths levell'd by thine,
I had not sway'd the balance. Think not, lords,
But he that had the spirit to oppose the gods,
Dares likewise suffer what their powers inflict.
I have not dreaded famine, fire, nor strage,§
Their common vengeance; poison in my cup,
Nor dagger in my bosom,—the revenge
Of private men for private injuries;

---

* *my operant powers*] So in Shakespeare's *Hamlet,* act
iii. sc. 2,—
   " *My operant powers* their functions leave to do," &c.
  † *hangmen*] i. e. executioners.
  ‡ *confine*] i. e. drive out, banish. I subjoin several
passages where the word is used in the same sense: it is
somewhat remarkable that they are all from Heywood:
   " Lycaon's once more fled, we by the helps
   Of these his people have *confined* him hence."
              The Golden Age, 1611, Sig. D.
   " Thy sensuall eyes are fixt upon that wall
   Thou nere shall enter, Rome *confines* you all."
            The Rape of Lucrece, ed. 1630, Sig. I 2
  " *King.* Accept what we most precious hold, thy Life.
  Marshall. Which as your gift I'le keepe, till Heaven
   'and Nature
Confine it hence."
     The Royall King, and the Loyall Subject, 1637, Sig. K 2.
   "Instead of *confin'd,* had his doome beene to have been
coffin'd, there had beene some comfort, he might have
still kept his country, but in plaine Portuguise and
Spanish both, banish."
        A Challenge for Beautie, 1636, Sig. B 2.
   "All that's good and honest I *confine.*"
         The Brazen Age, 1613, Sig. E 2.
  § *strage*] i. e. slaughter.

                        N 2

Nay, more than these, not fear'd to commit evil;—
And shall I tremble at the punishment?
Now, with as much resolvèd constancy
As I offended, will I pay the mulct,
And this black stain laid on my family
(Than which a nobler hath not place in Rome)
Wash with my blood away.—Learn of me,
    Claudius;
I'll teach thee what thou never studied'st yet,
That's bravely how to die.—Judges are term'd
The gods on earth: and such as are corrupt
Read me in this my ruin; those that succeed me
That so offend, thus punish. This the sum of all,—
Appius that sinn'd by Appius' hand shall fall.
                              [*Kills himself.*

Virginius. He died as boldly as he basely err'd;
And so should every true-bred Roman do:
And he whose life was odious, thus expiring,
In his death forceth pity.—Claudius, thou
Wast follower of his fortunes in his being;
Therefore in his not being imitate
His fair example.

Mar. Claud. Death is terrible
Unto a conscience that's oppress'd with guilt.
They say there is Elysium and hell;
The first I have forfeited, the latter fear:
My skin is not sword-proof.

Icil. Why dost thou pause?

Mar. Claud. For mercy; mercy I entreat you
    all.
Is't not sufficient for Virginia slain
That Appius suffer'd? one of noble blood
And eminence in place for a plebeian?
Besides, he was my lord, and might command me:
If I did aught, 'twas by compulsion, lords;
And therefore I crave mercy.

Icil. Shall I doom him?

Virginius. Do, good Icilius.

Icil. Then I sentence thus.
Thou hadst a mercy, most unmeriting slave,
Of which thy base birth was not capable;
Which we take off by taking thence thy sword.
And note the difference 'twixt a noble strain
And one bred from the rabble: both alike
Dar'd to transgress, but, see, their odds in death:
Appius died like a Roman gentleman,
And a man both ways knowing; but this slave
Is only sensible of vicious living,
Not apprehensive of a noble death:
Therefore as a base malefactor we
And timorous slave give him, as he deserves,
Unto the common hangman.

Mar. Claud. What, no mercy?

Icil. Stop's mouth:
Away with him!   [MAR. CLAUD. *is removed.*
                The life of the Decemviri
Expires in them. Rome, thou at length art free,
Restor'd unto thine ancient liberty!

Min. Of consuls; which bold Junius Brutus
    first
Begun in Tarquin's fall.—Virginius, you
And young Icilius shall his place succeed;
So by the people's suffrage 'tis decreed.

Virginius. We marshal, then, our soldiers in
    that name
Of consuls, honour'd with these golden bays.
Two fair, but ladies most infortunate,
Have in their ruins rais'd declining Rome,
Lucretia and Virginia, both renown'd
For chastity.—Soldiers and noble Romans,
To grace her death, whose life hath freed great
    Rome,
March with her corse to her sad funeral tomb.
                              [*Flourish. Exeunt.*

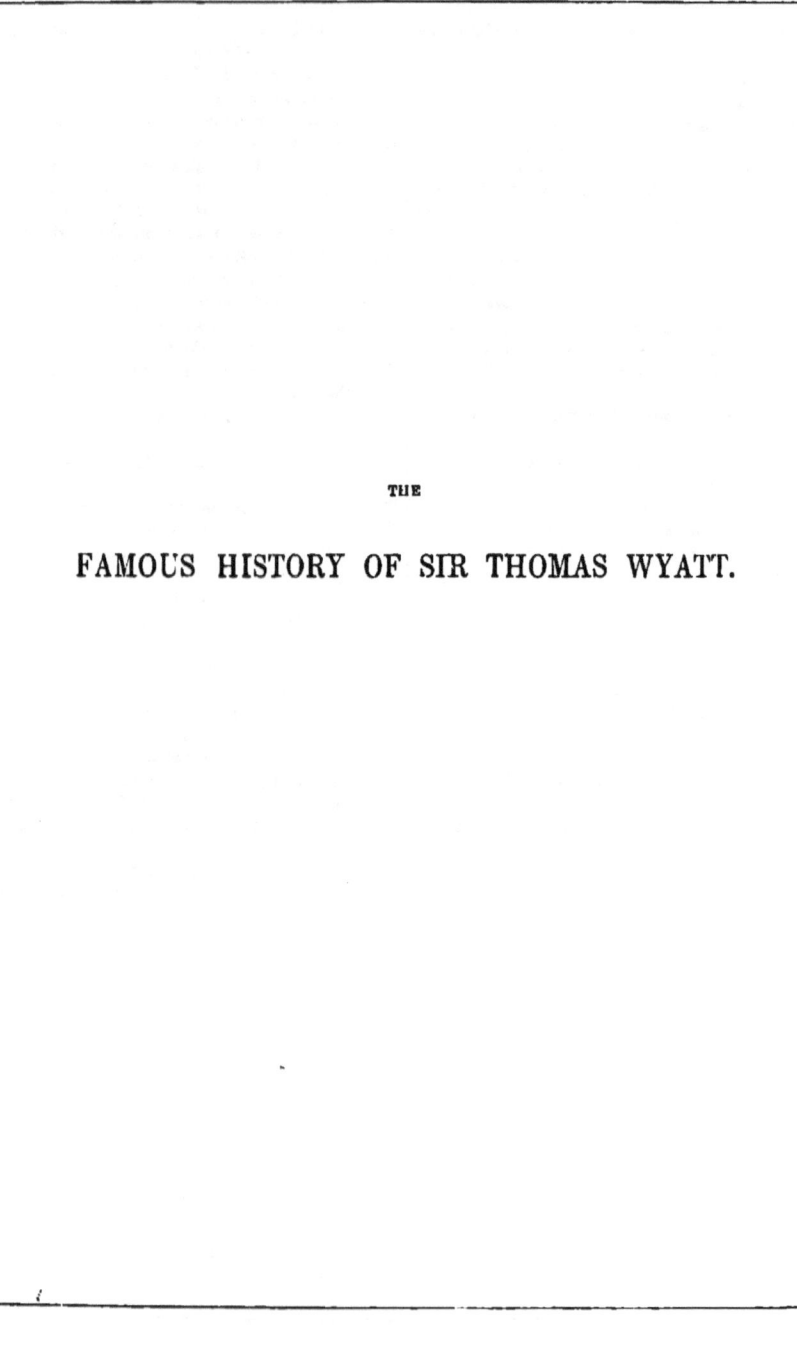

THE

FAMOUS HISTORY OF SIR THOMAS WYATT.

The Famous History of Sir Thomas Wyat. With the Coronation of Queen Mary, and the coming in of King Philip. As it was plaied by the Queens Maiesties Seruants. Written by Thomas Dickers and John Webster. London. Printed by E. A. for Thomas Archer, and are to be solde at his shop in the Pope's-head Pallace: nere the Royall Exchange. 1607. 4to.

The Famous History of Sir Thomas Wyat. With the Coronation of Queen Mary and the comming in of King Philip. As it was plaied by the Queens Maiesties Seruants. Written by Thomas Deckers, and John Webster. London Printed for Thomas Archer, and are to be solde at his shop in the Popes head Pallace, neere the Royall Exchange. 1612. 4to.

When I formerly edited the works of Webster, I was not aware that there existed more than one edition of this play: since that time, a copy of the second quarto has come into my possession (from the sale of Mr. Heber's books).

There can be no doubt that *The Famous History of Sir Thomas Wyatt* consists merely of fragments of two plays, —or rather, a play in Two Parts,—called *Lady June,* concerning which we find the following entries in *The Diary of Henslowe:*

"Lent unto John Thare, the 15 of octobr 1602, to geve unto harey chettell, Thomas Deckers, Thomas Hewode, and Mr. Smyth, and *Mr. Webster,* in earneste of a playe called Ladey Jane, the some of . . . . l[s]

"Lent unto Thomas Hewode, the 21 of octobr 1602, to paye unto Mr. Dickers, chettell, Smythe, *Webster* and Hewode, in fulle payment of ther playe of ladye Jane, the some of . v[ll] x[s]

"Lent unto John Ducke, the 27 of octobr 1602, to geve unto Thomas Deckers, in earneste of the 2 pt of Ladye Jane, the some of . . . . v[s]"

Pp. 242-3, ed. *Shakespeare Soc.*

Whether the present abridgment of *Lady Jane* was made by Dekker and Webster (see its title-page), or by some other play-wright, cannot be determined: that it has suffered cruelly from the hands of the transcriber or printer, is certain.

DRAMATIS PERSONÆ.

Duke of Northumberland.
Guildford Dudley, } his sons.
Ambrose Dudley,
Duke of Suffolk.
Duke of Norfolk.
Earl of Arundel.
Earl of Pembroke.
Earl of Huntingdon.
Bishop of Winchester.
Lord Treasurer.
Sir Thomas Wyatt.
Sir Henry Bedingfield.
Sir George Harper.
Sir Henry Isely.
Sir Robert Rodston.
Captain Brett.
Norroy.
Preacher.
Doctor.
Count Egmont.
Roose.
Homes.
Porter.
Clown.
Headsman, Sheriff, Heralds, Officers, &c.

Queen Mary.
Lady Jane Dudley.
Country Maid.
Ladies.

FAMOUS HISTORY OF SIR THOMAS WYATT.

Enter NORTHUMBERLAND *and* SUFFOLK.*

Suff. How fares the king, my lord? speaks he
cheerly?

North. Even as a dying man, whose life's † like to
Quick lightning,
Which is no sooner seen but is extinct.

Suff. Is the king's will confirm'd?

North. Ay, that's the point that we level at:
But, O, the confirmation of that will,
'Tis all, 'tis all!

Suff. That will confirm my daughter queen.

North. Right; and my son is married to your
daughter.
My lord, in an even plain way I will
Derive the crown unto your daughter's head.
What though the king hath left behind
Two sisters, lawful and immediate heirs,
To succeed him in his throne?
Lies it not in our powers to contradict it?
Have we not the king and council's hands unto it?
Tut, we stand high
In man's opinion and the world's broad eye.

Suff. Here comes Sir Thomas Wyatt.

Enter WYATT.

North. Sir Thomas,
Booted and spurr'd! whither away so fast?

Wyatt. It boots me not to stay,
When in this land rebellion bears such sway.
God's will, a court! 'tis chang'd
Since noble Henry's days. You have set your
hands
Unto a will; a will you well may call it:
So wills Northumberland, so wills great Suffolk,
Against God's will, to wrong those princely
maids.

North. Will you not subscribe
Your hand with other of the lords? Not with me,
That in my hands surprise * the sovereignty?

Wyatt. I'll damn † my soul for no man, no, for
no man.
Who at doomsday must answer for my sin?
Not you, nor you, my lords.
Who nam'd Queen Jane in noble Henry's days?
Which of you all durst once displace his issue?
My lords, my lords, you whet your knives so sharp
To carve your meat, that they will cut your
fingers:
The strength is weakness that you build upon.
The king is sick,—God mend him, ay, God mend
him!—
But were his soul from his pale body free,
Adieu, my lords, the court no court for me.

North. Farewell; I fear thee not.—
[*Exit* WYATT.
The fly is angry, but he wants a sting,
Of ‡ all the council, only this perverse
And peevish lord hath denied his hand
To the investing of your princely daughter.
He's idle, and wants power:
Our ocean shall these petty brooks devour.—
Here comes his highness' doctor.

Enter Doctor.

Suff. How fares his highness?

Doct. His body is past help:

---

* *surprise*] May be right; but qy.?
† *damn*] The old copies "damb'd."
‡ *Of all the council, only this perverse*
And peevish lord hath denied his hand]
The old copies have,
  "*And all the Counsell: onely this peruerse*
  And peuish Lord, hath onely deny'd his haud."
The Rev. J. Mitford (*Gent. Mag.* for June 1833, p. 491)
would read the second line thus,
  "And peevish lord *denied hath* his hand."

---

* *Enter Northumberland, &c.*] Scena. `A room in the
palace at Greenwich.
† *life's*] The old copies "life."

We have left our practice to the divines,
That they may cure his soul.

  Suff. * Past physic's help! why, then, past
    hope of life.—
Here comes his highness' preacher.

Enter Preacher.

Life, reverent man ? †
  Preach. Life, life, though death his body do
    dissever;
Our king lives with the King of Heaven for ever.
  North. Dead !—Send for heralds, call me pur-
    suivants;
Where's the King-at-arms ?
In every market-town proclaim Queen Jane.
  Suff. Best to take the opinion of the council.
  North. You are too timorous; we in ourselves
Are power sufficient : the king being dead,
This hand shall place the crown on Queen Jane's
  head.
Trumpets and drums, with your notes resound
Her royal name, that must in state be crown'd !
                       [Exeunt.

Enter GUILDFORD *and* JANE.‡

  Guild. Our cousin king is dead.
  Jane. Alas, how small an urn contains a king !
He, that rul'd all even with his princely breath,
Is forc'd to stoop now to the stroke of death.
Heard you not the proclamation ?
  Guild. I hear of it, and I give credit to it :
What great men fear to be, their fears make §
  greater.
Our fathers grow ambitious,
And would force us sail in mighty tempests,
And are not lords of what they do possess.
Are not thy thoughts as great ?
  Jane. I have no thoughts so rank, so grown to
As are our fathers' pride.   [head,
Troth, I do enjoy a kingdom, having thee;
And so my pain be prosperous in that,
What care I though a sheep-cote be my palace
Or fairest roof of honour ?
  Guild. See, how thy blood
Keeps course with mine ! Thou must be a queen;
ay me,
A queen ! The flattering bells, that shrilly sound
At the king's funeral, with hollow hearts
Will cowardly call thee sovereign; for, indeed,
Thou wouldst prove but an usurper.

---

* *Suff.*] The old copies "*Aru.*"
† *Life, reverent man ?*] Here the old copies have no
interrogation :—something seems wanting.
‡ *Enter Guildford and Jane*] Scene. A room in Sion
House.
§ *make*] The old copies "grow" (an error occasioned by
that word in the next line).

  Jane. Who would wear fetters,
Though they were all of gold, or to be sick,
Though his faint brows for a wearing nightcap
Wore a crown ? Thou must assume a title
That goes on many feet; but 'tis an office
Wherein the hearts of scholars and of soldiers
Will depend upon thy hearse. Were this rightly
  scann'd,
We scarce should find a king in any land.

Enter ARUNDEL.

  Arun. Honour and happy reign
Attend the new majesty of England !
  Jane. To whom, my lord, bends this your ave ?
  Arun. To your grace, dread sovereign;
You are, by the king's will and the consent
Of all the lords, chosen for our queen.
  Jane. O God ! methinks you sing my death in
  parts
Of music's loudness : 'tis not my turn to rise.

Enter NORTHUMBERLAND, SUFFOLK *with the purse and the
mace, and others.*

  North. The voice of the whole land speaks in
  my tongue :
It is concluded your majesty must ride
From hence unto the Tower, there to stay
Until your coronation.
  Jane. O God !
  Suff. Why sighs your majesty ?
  Jane. My lord and father,
I pray, tell me,—was your father's father
E'er a king ?
  Suff. Never, an it like your grace.
  Jane. Would I might still continue of his line,
Not travel in the clouds ! It is often seen,
The heated blood, that covets to be royal,
Leaves off ere it be noble.—
My learnèd, careful king, what, must we go ?
  Guild. We must.
  Jane. Then it must be so.
  North. Set forward, then.
      [A dead march, and pass round the stage, and
        GUILDFORD *speaks.* *
  Guild. The Tower will be a place of ample state :
Some lodgings in it will, like dead men's sculls,
Remember us of frailty.
  Jane.† We are led
With pomp to prison. O prophetic soul !
Lo, we ascend into our chairs of state,
Like several ‡ coffins, in some funeral pomp.

---

* They are now *supposed* to have reached the Tower.
(The historic fact is, that Jane was conveyed from Sion
House to the Tower *by water.*)
† *Jane*] The old copies "*Gui.*"
‡ *several*] The old copies "*funerall.*" The reading,

Descending to their graves! But we must on.
How can we fare well to keep our court
Where prisoners keep their cave?
　　　　　　　　　　　　　　[A flourish. Exeunt.

Enter QUEEN MARY,* *with a prayer-book in her hand,*
like a nun.

Mary. Thus like a nun, not like a princess born,
Descended from the royal Henry's loins,
Live I environ'd in a house of stone.
My brother Edward lives in pomp and state;
I in a mansion here all ruinate.
Their rich attire, delicious banquetting,
Their several pleasures, all their pride and honour,
I have forsaken for a rich prayer-book.
The golden mines of wealthy India
Are all as dross compar'd to thy sweetness:
Thou art the joy and comfort of the poor;
The everlasting bliss in thee we find.
This little volume, enclos'd in this hand,
Is richer than the empire of this land.

Enter SIR HENRY BEDINOFIELD.

Beding. Pardon me, madam, that so boldly I
　press
Into your chamber: I salute your highness
With the high style of queen.
Mary. Queen! may it be?
Or jest you at my lowering misery?
Beding. Your brother king is dead,
And you the Catholic queen must now succeed.
Mary. I see my God at length hath heard my
　prayer.
You, Sir Harry, for your glad tidings,
Shall be held in honour and due regard.

Enter WYATT.

Wyatt. Health to the Lady Mary!
Mary. And why not queen, Sir Thomas?
Wyatt. Ask that of Suffolk['s] duke, and great
　Northumberland,
Who in your stead have crown'd another.
Mary. Another queen, Sir Thomas, we alive,
The true immediate heiress of our dread father!
Wyatt. Nothing more true than that,
Nothing more true than you are the true heir.
Come, leave this cloister, and be seen abroad:
Your very sight will stir the people's hearts,
And make them cheerly for Queen Mary cry.
One comfort I can tell you: the tenants

Of the Dukes Northumberland and Suffolk
Denied their aid in these unlawful arms;
To all the council I denied my hand,
And for King Henry's issue still will stand.
Mary. Your counsel, good Sir Thomas, is so
　pithy,
That I am won to like it.
Wyatt. Come, let us straight
From hence, from Framlingham. Cheer your
　spirits.
I'll to the dukes at Cambridge, and discharge
Them all.—Prosper me, God, in these affairs!
I lov'd the father well, I lov'd the son,
And for the daughter I through death will run.
　　　　　　　　　　　　　　　　[Exeunt.

Enter NORTHUMBERLAND, SUFFOLK, ARUNDEL, BRETT,
*and Soldiers.**

North. Where's Captain Brett?
Brett. Here, my lord.
Suff. Are all our numbers full?
Brett. They are, my lord.
Suff. See them arraign'd :† I will set forward
　straight.
North. Honourable friends, and native peers,
That have chosen me to be the leader
Of these martial troops, to march against
The sister of our late dead sovereign;
Bear witness of my much unwillingness
In furthering these attempts. I rather joy
To think upon our ancient victories
Against the French and Spaniard, whose high pride
We levell'd with the waves of British shore,
Dying the haven of Britain‡ with guilty blood,
Till all the harbour seem'd a sanguine pool.
Or we desire these arms were now to war
'Gainst the perfidious northern enemy,
Who, trembling at our first shock, voice, and sight,
Like cowards turn'd their backs with shameful
　flight.
But those rich spoils are past: we are now to go,
Being native friends, against a native foe.
In your hands we leave the queen elected:
She hath seizure of the Tower. If you
Be confident, as you have sworn yourselves,
True liegemen to her highness, she no doubt
With royal favour will remunerate
The least of your deserts.

" *several* " (and it is at least a probable emendation) was
proposed by Mr. Collier (*Preface to Coleridge's Seven
Lectures*, &c., p. cv.).

* *Enter Queen Mary,* &c.] Scene. An apartment in the
Castle of Framlingham.

* *Enter Northumberland,* &c.] Scene. London, or in its
neighbourhood?

† *arraign'd*] i. e. arranged: Shakespeare, Spenser, and
other old writers, have *darraign*, in the same sense.

‡ *Britain*] The old copies " Brit;".—The Rev. J. Mitford
(*Gent. Mag.* for June 1833, p. 491) would read " Brute,"—
which helps the metre somewhat, but does not improve
the sense.

Farewell; my tears into your bosoms fall;
With one embrace I do include you all.

Arun. My lord most lov'd, with what a mourning
heart
I take your farewell, let the after-signs
Of my employment witness.   I protest,
Did not the sacred person of my queen,
Whose weal I tender as my soul's chief bliss,
Urge my abode, I would not think it shame
To trail a pike where you were general.
But wishes are in vain; I am bound to stay,
And urgent business calls your grace away:
See, on my knees I humbly take my leave,
And steep my words with tears.

North. Kind Arundel,
I bind thee to my love: once more, farewell.

Arun. Heavens give your grace success!
Commend us to the queen and to your son:
Within one week I hope war will be done. [*Exit.*

Brett. Come, my lords, shall us march?

North. Ay, ay, for God's sake, on:
'Tis more than time, my friends, that we were
gone. [*Exeunt.*

Enter Treasurer and Porter.

Treas. What, ho, porter! open the gate.

Porter. I beseech your honour to pardon me;
The council hath given strict command not
any
Shall pass this way.

Treas. Why, you idle fellow,
Am I not sent upon the queen's affairs,
Commanded by the lords? and know you not
That I am treasurer?   Come, open the gate:
You do you know not what.

Porter. Well, my lord, I do adventure, on your
word,
The dukes' displeasure; all the council-board
Besides may be my heavy enemies;
But go, o' God's name!   I the worst will prove,
And if I die, I die for him I love.

Treas. I thank thee, and will warrant thee from
death.
Is my horse ready?

Porter. It is, my lord.

Treas. Then will I fly this fearful council-board.
[*Exit.*

Porter. My heart misgives me, I have done
amiss;
Yet being a councillor, one of the number,
Nothing can prove amiss.   Now shall I know
The worst; here comes my Lord of Arundel.

Enter ARUNDEL.

Arun. Porter, did the lord treasurer pass this
way?

Porter. But now, my gracious lord.

Arun. Ungracious villain, follow, bring him
back again;
If not by fair means, bring him back by force.
And hear you, sirrah, as you go, will* the lord
mayor,
And some aldermen of his brethren,
And some especial citizens of note,
To attend our further pleasures presently.
The treasurer fled; the duke is but newly arrested;
Some purpose, on my life, to cross their plots:
We'll set strong watches, see gates and walls well
mann'd.
'Tis ten to one but princely innocence
Is these strange turmoils' wisest violence.
[*Exeunt.*

† WINCHESTER, ARUNDEL, *and other Lords, discovered; the
Lord Treasurer kneeling at the council-table.*

Arun. Though your attempt, lord treasurer, be
such
That hath no colour in these troublous times
But an apparent purpose of revolt
From the deceas'd king's will and our decree,
Yet, for you are a councillor of note,
One of our number, and of high degree,
Before we any way presume to judge,
We give you leave to speak in your behalf.

Treas. My lord, the business of these troublous
times,
Binding us all still to respect the good
Of commonweal, yet doth it not debar
Private regard of us and of our own.
The general weal is treasur'd in your breast,
And all my ablest powers have been employ'd
To stir them there; yet have I borne a part,
Laying the commons' troubles next my heart.
My oversight in parting without leave
Was no contempt, but only for an hour,
To order home-affairs, that none of mine
In these nice times should unto faction climb.

Arun. Nay, my good lord, be plain with us, I
pray;
Are you not griev'd that we have given consent
To Lady Jane's election?

Treas. My lords, I am not.

Arun. Speak like a gentleman; upon your word,
Are you not discontent?

Treas. Troth, to be plain,
I am not pleas'd that two such princely maids,

---

* *Enter Treasurer and Porter*] Scene. Court of the
Tower.

* *will*] i. e. desire.
† *Winchester*, &c.] Scene. A room in the Tower.

Lineally descended from our royal king,
And by his testimony confirm'd heir[s],
If that their brother dying issueless,*
And one that never dream'd it, never desir'd
The rule of sovereignty,
But with virgin's tears hath oft bewail'd her
   misery,
Should politicly by us be nam'd a queen.
   Arun. You have said nobly : sit and take your
   place.

       Enter Porter.

Porter. My lords, Sir Thomas Wyatt craves
   access
Unto your honours.
   Arun. Let him come near.
   Porter. Room for Sir Thomas Wyatt !

       Enter WYATT.

Wyatt. A divine spirit teach your honours truth,
Open your eyes of judgment to behold
The true legitimate Mary, your undoubted
   sovereign !
   Arun. Arise, Sir Thomas; sit and take your
   place.——
Now to our former business :
The obligation wherein we all stood bound
To the deceas'd late king's will and our decree,
His cousin Jane and the two absent dukes,
Cannot be conceal'd without great reproach
To us and to our issue. We have sworn,
In presence of the sacred host of heaven,
Unto our late young lord, to both the dukes,
That no impeachment should divert our hearts
From the election of the Lady Jane.†
To this end we have seiz'd her in the Tower,
By public proclamation made her queen ;
To this end we have arm'd the duke[s] with power,

Given them commission under our own hands
To pass against the lady, yea, perform *
In hostile manner ; and no doubt the spleen
Of the undaunted spirit of Northumber's earl
Will not be call'd with writings of repeal.
Advice in this I hold it better far,
To keep the course we run, than, seeking change,
Hazard our lives, our heirs, and the realm.†
   Wyatt. In actions roving from the bent of truth
We have no precedent thus to persist
But the bare name of worldly policy.
If others have ground from justice and the law,
As well divine as politic agreeing,
They are for no cause to be disinherited.
If you not seven years since to that effect
Swore to the father to maintain his seed,
What dispensation hath acquitted you
From your first sacred vows? You'll say, the will
Extorted from a child. O, let mine eyes,
In naming that sweet youth, observe their part,
Pouring down tears, sent from my swelling heart
God's mother, I turn ‡ child ! but I'll go on.
Say that the will were his, forc'd by no trick,
But for religion's love his simple act,
Yet note how much you err. You were sworn
   before
To a man's will, and not a will alone,
But strengthen'd by an act of parliament.
Besides this sacred proof, the princely maids,
Had they no will nor act to prove their right,—
Have birthrights no privilege, being a plea so strong
As cannot be refell'd but by plain wrong?
Now were you touch'd. The lady in [the] Tower,
Alas, she's innocent of any § claim :
Trust me, she'd think it a most happy life,
To leave a queen's and keep a lady's name.
And for the dukes, your warrants sent them forth;
Let the same warrants call them back again :
If they refuse to come, the realm, not they,
Must be regarded. Be strong and bold.
We are the people's factors. Save our sons
From killing one another ; be afraid
To tempt both heaven and earth. So, I have said.
   Arun. Why, then, give order that she shall be
   queen.
Send for the mayor. Her errors we'll forget,
Hoping she will forgive.

---

* There is manifestly a line or lines wanting here.
† *That no impeachment should divert our hearts*
  From the election of the Lady Jane] The old copies
have,—
    " From the *impeachment* of the Lady Jane,"—
the word " *impeachment* " having been repeated from the
preceding line by a mistake of the transcriber or printer.
That the first " *impeachment*,"—i.e. hindrance, let, im-
pediment,—is right, there can be no doubt; and that
in the second line " *election* " is the author's word, seems
equally certain ; compare what Arundel has said a little
before,—
    " Are you not griev'd that we have given consent
      To *Lady Jane's election ?* "
(The reading of this passage proposed by the Rev. J.
Mitford (*Gent. Mag.* for June 1833, p. 492),—
    " That no *impediment* should divert our hearts
      From the *impeachment* of the Lady Jane,"—
alters the right word in the first line, and leaves the
wrong one in the second.)

* *the lady, yea, perform*] The old copies "*the Lady*. You
performe."—As the passage now stands, "*the lady*"
means Mary. But qy. ? "*To pass against the* lady's foes
perforce," &c.,—"the lady's," meaning *the* Lady Jane's?
† *the realm*] The old copies "*the realmes*" (which, though
sense, is at variance with "*the realm*" in the next speech)
‡ *turn*] The old copies "*tearms.*"
§ *any*] The old copies " *my.*"

Wyatt. Never make doubt:
Setting her ceremonious order by,
She is pure within, and mildly chaste without.

Arun. Give order to keep fast the Lady Jane.
Dissolve the council. Let us leave the Tower,
And in the city hold our audience.

Wyatt. You have advis'd well, honourable
    lords:
So will the citizens be wholly ours;
And if the dukes be cross, we'll cross their powers.
                         [*Exeunt.*

Enter BRETT, *Clown, and Soldiers.**

Brett. Lancepersado,† quarter, quarter.

Clown. What shall we quarter, captain?

Brett. Why, the soldiers.

Clown. Why, they are not hanged nor drawn
yet.

Brett. Sir, I mean quarter them, that the offended multitude may pass in safety.

Clown. May we not take tolls of the pies and
the apple-women?

Brett. Not in any sort; the duke's pleasure will
pass free.‡

Clown. The commons shall be used with all
common courtesy, that go in rank like beans,
and cheesecakes on their heads instead of caps.

Brett. Sirrah, this is a famous university,
And those scholars; those lofty buildings and
    goodly houses
Founded by noble patrons. But, no more:
Set a strong watch; that be your chiefest care.

---

* *Enter Brett, &c.*] Scene. A street in Cambridge.

† *Lancepersado*] Written also *lanceprisado, lancepesado,
lancepesada,* or *lancepesata;* (Ital. *lancia spezzata,*) the
lowest officer of foot, one who is under the corporal.
"He is a gentleman of no ancient standing in the
militia, for he draws his pedigree from the time of the
wars between Francis I. and his son, Henry II., kings of
France, on the one part; and the Emperor Charles V.,
and his brother-in-law, the Duke of Savoy, on the other
part. In those wars, when a gentleman of a troop of
horse, in any skirmish, battle, or rencounter, had broke
his lance on the enemy, and lost his horse in the scuffle,
he was entertained (under the name of a broken lance)
by a captain of a foot company as his comrade, till he
was again mounted. But as all good orders fall soon
from their primitive institution, so in a short time our
Monsieur Lancepesata (for so he was called) was forced to
descend from being the captain's comrade, and become
the caporal's companion, and assisted him in the exercise of his charge, and therefore was sometimes called by
the French, *aide caporal.* But when the caporal grew
weary of the comradeship of his lancepesata, he made
him officiate under him, and for that had some allowance
of pay more than the common souldier."—Turner's *Pallas
Armata,* p. 219—(as quoted by Gross, *Mil. Ant.,* v. i.,
p. 262.)

‡ *will pass free*] Qy. "*will have them pass free*"?

Enter a Countryman and a Maid.

Count. What's here? soldiers!

Brett. Fear not good speech. These rude arms
    I bear
Are not to fright sweet gentle peace away,*
But to succour your lives. Pass peaceably away.

Clown. Cry "God save the queen," as you go, and
God send you a good market!

Count. God save the queen! what queen? there
    lies the sense:
When we have none, it can be no offence.

Clown. What carry you there in your basket?

Maid. Eggs, forsooth.

Clown. Well, cry "God save Queen Jane," as you
go, and God send you a good market!

Maid. Is the right queen call'd Jane? alack for
    woe,
[That] at the first she was not christen'd so!
          [*Exeunt Countryman and Maid.*

Brett. Thus old and young still descant on her
    name,
Nor lend no ear when we her style proclaim.
I fear, I fear,—Fear, Brett! what shouldst thou
    fear?
Thou hast a breast compos'd of adamant.
Fall what ill betide,
My anchor is cast, and I in harbour ride.
                [*Exeunt.*

Enter NORTHUMBERLAND, HUNTINGDON, WYATT, *and*
    Soldiers.†

Wyatt. My lord, 'tis true, you sent unto the
    council
For fresh supplies: what succour, what supplies?
Happy is he can draw his neck out of the collar,
And make his peace with Mary.

North. How stands the treasurer addicted to
    us?

Wyatt. I had forgot: when we were at council,
He stole away, and went home to his house,
And by much entreaty was won to return:
In brief, they all incline to Queen Mary.
My lord, farewell:
Each hasty hour will colder tidings tell. [*Exit.*

North. Come they in thunder, we will meet with
    them:
In the loudest language that their ordnance speaks,
Ours shall answer theirs.—Call me a herald,

---

* *Are not to fright sweet gentle peace away*] In the old
copies thus :—
    "*Ist not to fight? Sweet, gentle Peace away.*"
The "*away*" at the end of the next line is very questionable: qy. "along"?

† *Enter Northumberland, &c.*] Scene. Another part of
the same town.

And in the market-place proclaim Queen Jane.
                    [*A Herald called in.*
The streets are full, the town is populous,
The people gape for novelty.—Trumpets, speak
    to them,
That they may answer with an echoing cry,
" God save Queen Jane, God save her majesty ! "
        [*A trumpet sounds, and no answer. The Herald
        sounds a parley, and none answers.*
Ha ! a bare report of trumpets !
Are the slaves hoarse, or want they art to
    speak?
O me ! This town consists on famous colleges,
Such as know both how, and what, and when to
    speak.
Well, yet we will proceed,
And smother what close envy hath decreed.

        Enter AMBROSE DUDLEY.

Ambrose, my son, what news ?
Amb. O my thrice-honour'd father !
North. Boy, speak the worst:
That which sounds deadliest, let me hear that first.
Amb. The lords have all revolted from your fac-
    tion.
North. We in ourselves are strong.
Amb. In Baynard's Castle was a council held,
Whither the mayor and sheriffs did resort,
And 'twas concluded to proclaim Queen Mary. ·
North. Then they revolt the allegiance from my
    daughter,
And give it to another?
Amb. True, my thrice-honour'd father :
Besides, my brother Guildford and his wife,
Where she was proclaim'd queen, are now close
    prisoners,
Namely in the Tower.
North. God take them to his mercy ! they had
    need
Of grace and patience, for they both must bleed.
Poor innocent souls, they both from guilt are free !
Amb. O my thrice-honour'd father, might I ad-
    vise you,
Fly to your manor, there study for your safety.
North. Boy, thou say'st well :
And since the lords have all revolted from me,
Myself will now revolt against myself.
Call me a herald to fill their empty ears :—
Assist me, son :—my good Lord Huntingdon,
Even in this market-town proclaim Queen Mary.

    A trumpet sounds a parley, the Herald proclaims.
Her. Mary, by the grace of God, Queen of Eng-
land, France, and Ireland, defendress of the faith,
Amen !   [*Within, a shout and a flourish.*

North. Amen ! I bear a part ;
Ay, with my tongue,—I do not with my heart.
Now they can cry, now they can bawl and yell :
Base-minded slaves, sink may your souls to hell !

        Enter ROOSE *with letters.*

Roose. My honour'd lord, the council greets you
    with
These letters.
North. Stay, Master Roose ; ere you depart,
    receive
An answer and reward.   [*He readeth the letter.*
" *In the sovereign name of Mary our queen, you
shall, upon the sight hereof, surcease your arms,
discharge your soldiers, and presently repair unto
the court, or else to be held as an arch-traitor.*"
'Tis short and sharp.——
Master Roose, we do obey your warrant:
But, I pray, tell me, how do all our friends at
    court?
Is there not a great mortality amongst them?
Is there not a number of them dead of late,
Since I came thence ?
Roose. My gracious lord, not any.
North. O Master Roose, it cannot be : I will
    assure you,
At my departure thence I left living there at least
Five hundred friends, and now I have not one,
Simply, not one : friends ! ha, ha, ha ! Commission,
Thou must be my friend,
And stand betwixt me and the stroke of death ;
Were thy date out, my life's date were but short :
They are cold friends that kill their friends in
    sport.
Amb. Here comes your honour'd friend, the Earl
    of Arundel.

        Enter ARUNDEL.

North. My honour'd friend,——
Arun. I am no friend to traitors :
In my most high and princely sovereign's name,
I do arrest your honour of high treason.
North. A traitor, Arundel !
Have I not your hand in my commission ?
Let me peruse it : as I take 't, 'tis here ;
And by your warrant have [I] so strict proceeded :
Are the limits of my warrant broke? answer me.
Arun. It may be that it hath pleas'd her
    majesty
To pardon us, and for to punish you ;
I know no other reason : this I must ;
I am commanded, and the act is just.
North. And I obey you. When we parted last,
My lord of Arundel, our farewell was

Better than our greeting now: then you cried,
  "God speed";
Now you come on me, ere you say, "Take heed";
Then you did owe me your best bloods, nay, griev'd
You could not spend them in my service; O, then
It was a double death to stay behind!
But I am overtook, and you are kind,
I am, beshrew you else: but I submit;
My crime is great, and I must answer it.

Arun. You must, with your three sons, be
  guarded safe
Unto the Tower; with you those lords and
  knights
That in this faction did associate you:
For so I am enjoin'd.
Then peaceably let us conduct you thither.

North. O my children, my soul weeps endless
  tears for you!
O, at the general sessions, when all souls
Stand at the bar of justice, and hold up
Their now-immortaliz'd hands, O, then
Let the remembrance of their tragic ends
Be raz'd out of the bead-roll of my sins!
Whene'er the black book of my crime's unclasp'd,
Let not these scarlet letters be found there;
Of all the rest only that page be clear!
But come, to my arraignment, then to death.
The queen and you have long aim'd at this head:
If to my children she sweet grace extend,
My soul hath peace, and I embrace my end.
                         [*Exeunt.*

        Enter SUFFOLK.*

Suff. Three days are past, Monday, Tuesday, and
  Wednesday too,
Yet my protesting servant is not come:
Himself conducted me to this hard lodging,
A simple cabin for so great a prince;
And then he swore, but oaths you see are vain,
That he would hourly come and visit me.
I, that was wont to surfeit in estate,
Am now through hunger almost desolate.

   Enter HOMES, *sweating, with bottle and bag.*

Homes. My lord,—
Suff. Ned Homes, speak, hast thou brought me
  meat?
Homes. With much ado, my lord, meat, bread,
  and wine:
While you refresh yourself, I will record
The cause of my long stay.

Suff. I prithee, do:
Need bids me eat, need bids me hear thee too.
Homes. The night I left you in the hollow tree,
My house was search'd.
Suff. Go on, go on.
Homes. And I no sooner enter'd but attach'd;
Threaten'd the rack, an if I did not yield
Your gracious self into their graceless hands.
Suff. And thou hast done 't, thou hast betray'd
  me!
Homes. Done it! O, betray you! O, no!
First would I see my lovèd wife and children
Murder'd and toss'd on spears, before I would
Deliver your grace unto their hands; for they
Intend your death,—
Suff. Go on, go on.
Homes. And offer'd
A thousand crowns to him that can bring news
Of your abode: 'twas offer'd in my hands,
Which I beseech may stop my vital breath,
When I am fee'd with gold to work your death.

      Enter Sheriff *and* Officers.

Sher. See, yonder sits the duke.
Suff. I kiss thee in requital of this love.
Homes. And, in requital of so great a grace,
I kiss your hand that deign'st * to kiss my face.
Sher. So Judas kiss'd his master.—Seize the
  duke.
Suff. Ah me! Ned Homes, we are undone; both
  thou
And I betray'd!
Sher. My lord, late Duke of Suffolk, in her
  highness'
Name, I do arrest you of high treason.
Suff. I do obey, and only crave this kindness,
You would be good unto my servant Homes,
Who † in relieving me hath but perform'd
The duty of a servant to his lord.
Sher. You are deceiv'd, sir, in your servant
  much;
He is the man that did betray you.—
Here, Master Homes, towards your thousand
  pounds,
Here is a hundred marks;
Come to the Exchequer, you shall have the rest.
Suff. Hast thou betray'd me? yet with such a
  tongue,
So smoothly oil'd, slight off my danger's fear?
O, break, my heart! this grief's too great to bear.

---

* *Enter Suffolk*] If the author intended here to follow
history, the scene is now the Duke's manor of Astley, a
few miles from Coventry; for he was apprehended in
Astley park: see Holinshed's *Chron.* vol. iv. 14, ed. 1808.

* *your hand that deign'st,* &c.] i. e. the hand of thee
that deign'st, &c.—The old copies have "your hand that
dares," &c.,—"*dares*" being evidently a misprint for
"*daines,*"—*daines* (*deignest*).

† *Who*] The old copies "*Where.*"

Homes. Pardon me, my lord.

Suff. God pardon thee,
And lay not to thy soul this grievous sin!
Farewell; and when thou spend'st this ill-got gold,
Remember how thy master's life was sold:
Thy lord that gave thee lordships, made thee great,
Yet thou betray'd'st him as he sat at meat.—
On to my grave! 'tis time that I were dead,
When he that held my heart betrays my head.

[*Exeunt* SUFFOLK, *Sheriff, and Officers.*

Homes. O God, O God, that ever I was born!
This deed hath made me slave to abject scorn.

[*Exit.*

Enter the Clown.

Clown. O poor shrimp, how art thou fallen away
for want of mouching! O, colon* cries out most
tyrannically! the little gut hath no mercy.—
What's here? victuals! O rare, O good!
Feed chops, drink throat; good victuals make
good blood.

Re-enter HOMES, *with a halter about his neck.*

But stay, who's here? more sheriffs, more search-
ers? O, no, this is Homes, that betrayed his
honest master: how, with a halter about his neck!
I hope he doth not mean to hang himself. I'll
step aside.

Homes. This is the place where I betray'd my
lord;
This is the place where oft I have reliev'd,
And villain I betray'd him to the jaws of death.
But here before I further will proceed,
Here will I bury this enticing gold:
Lie there, damn'd fiend, never serve human† more!

Clown. This is rare: now in this mood if he
would hang himself, 'twere excellent.

Homes. Shall I ask mercy? no, it is too late;
Heaven will not hear, and I am desperate.

[*Strangles himself.*

Clown. So, so, a very good ending: would all
false servants might drink of the same sauce!
Gold, you are first mine: you must help [me] to shift
myself into some counterfeit suit of apparel, and
then to London. If my old master be hanged,
why, so: if not, why, rustic and lustic. Yet, before
I go, I do not care if I throw this dog in a ditch.
—Come away, dissembler.—This cannot choose
but be a hundred pound, it weighs so heavy.

[*Exit with the body of* HOMES.

Enter QUEEN MARY,* WINCHESTER, NORFOLK, PEMBROKE,
WYATT, ARUNDEL, *and Attendants.*

Q. Mary. By God's assistance and the power of
heaven,
After our troubles, we are safely set
In our inheritance: for which we do subscribe
The praise and benefit to God; next, thanks
To you, my lords. Now shall the sanctuary,
And the house of the Most High, be newly built;
The ancient honours due unto the church,
Buried within the ruin'd† monasteries,
Shall lift their stately heads and rise again,
To astonish the destroyers' wondering eyes.
Zeal shall be deck'd in gold: religion,
Not like a virgin robb'd of all her pomp,
But bravely‡ shining in her gems of state,
Like a fair bride be offer'd to the Lord.
To build§ large houses, pull no churches down,
Rather enrich the temple with our crown:
Better a poor queen than the subjects poor.

Win. May it please your grace to give release
unto
Such ancient bishops that have lost their honours
In the church-affairs.

Q. Mary. We have given order
To the Duke of Norfolk to release them.

Arun. Your sacred highness will no doubt be
mindful
Of the late oath you took at Framlingham.

Q. Mary. O, my lord of Arundel, we remember
that:
But shall a subject force his prince to swear
Contrary to her conscience and the law?
We here release unto our faithful people
One entire subsidy, due unto the crown
In our dead brother's days. The commonalty
Shall not be overburden'd in our reign:
Let them be liberal in religion,
And we will spare their treasure to themselves.
Better a poor prince than the nation poor:
The subjects' treasure is the sovereign's store.

Arun. What is your highness' pleasure about
the rebels?

Q. Mary. The queen-like rebel,‖ mean you not,
Queen Jane?

Arun. Guildford, and Jane, with great Northumberland,
And haughty Suffolk's duke.

---

* *colon*] A word frequently in the mouth of hungry
personages in our old dramas: it is the largest of the
human intestines, not "the *little* gut," as the Clown here
calls it.

† *human*] Our dictionaries, I believe, do not acknowledge this word as a substantive: but Chapman uses it
frequently as such.

* *Enter Queen Mary*] Scene. London. A room in the
palace.

† *ruin'd*] The old copies "*Ruine.*"

‡ *bravely*] The old copies "*briefly.*"

§ *To build, &c.*] Something that preceded this has
dropt out.

‖ *rebel*] The old copies "*Rebels.*"

o

Q. Mary. The Duke of Suffolk
Is not yet apprehended: therefore, my lords,
Some of you most dear to us in love
Be careful of that charge: the rest we'll leave
For trial of the other prisoners.

Wyatt. The Lady Jane, most mighty sovereign,
Allied to you in blood,—
For she's the daughter of your father's sister,
Mary the Queen of France, Charles Brandon's wife,
Your niece, your next of blood except your
    sister,—
Deserves some pity; so doth youthful Guildford.

Win. Such pity as the law allows to traitors.

Norf. They were misled by their ambitious
    fathers.

Win. What son to obey his father proves a
    traitor,
Must buy their disobedience with their death.

Wyatt. My lord of Winchester still thirsts for
    blood.

Q. Mary. Wyatt, no more; the law shall be
    their judge:
Mercy to mean offenders we'll extend,
Not unto such that dare usurp our crown.

Arun. Count Egmont, the ambassador from
    Spain,
Attends your highness' answer 'bout* those
    letters
Sent from the emperor in his son's behalf.

Q. Mary. In the behalf of lovely, princely Philip,
Whose person we have shrinèd in our heart,
At the first sight of his delightful picture!
That picture should have power to kindle† love
In royal breasts: the darts of love are words,
Pictures, conceit; he will prevail by any.
Your counsel, lords, about this foreign business.

Arun. I say, an it like your royal majesty,
A royal treaty, and to be confirm'd;
And I allow the match.

Win. Allow it, lords! we have cause to thank
    our God
That such a mighty prince as Philip is,
Son to the emperor, heir to wealthy Spain
And many spacious kingdoms, will vouchsafe——

Wyatt. Vouchsafe, my lord of Winchester!
    pray, what?

Win. To grace our mighty sovereign with his
    honourable title.

Wyatt. To marry with our queen, mean you
    not so?

Win. I do; what then?

Wyatt. O God!
Is she a beggar, a forsaken maid,
That she hath need of grace from foreign princes?
By God's dear mother,—O, God pardon! swear I!—
Methinks she is a fair and lovely prince;
Her only beauty, were she of mean birth,
Able to make the greatest potentate,
Ay, the great emperor of the mighty Cham,
That hath more nations under his command
Than Spanish Philip's like to inherit towns,
To come and lay his sceptre at her feet,
And to entreat her to vouchsafe the grace
To take him and his kingdom to her mercy.

Win. Wyatt, you are too hot.

Wyatt. And you too proud.
Vouchsafe! O, base! I hope she'll not vouchsafe
To take the emperor's son to her dear mercy.

Q. Mary. Proceed, my lord of Winchester, I
    pray.

Win. Then still I say we have cause to thank
    our God
That such a mighty prince will look so low
As to respect this island and our queen.

Wyatt. Pardon me, madam; he respects* your
    island
More than your person: think of that.

Norf. Wyatt, you wrong the affection of the
    prince;
For he desires no fortresses nor towns,
Nor to bear any office, rule, or state,
Either by person or by substitute,
Nor yet himself to be a councillor
In our affairs.

Wyatt. What need he, noble lords,
To ask the fruit, when he demands the tree?
No castle, fortresses, nor towers of strength!
It boots not, when the chiefest tower of all,
The key that opens unto all the land,
I mean our gracious sovereign, must be his.
But he will bear no office in the land!
And yet will marry with the queen of all
Nor be of council in the realm's affairs!
And yet the queen enclosèd in his arms.
I do not like this strange marriage:
The fox is subtle, and his head once in,
The slender body easily will follow.
I grant he offers you, in name of dower,
The yearly sum of threescore thousand ducats,
Besides the seventeen famous provinces,
And that the heir succeeding from your loins
Shall have the sovereign rule of both the realms:
What, shall this move your highness to the match?

---

*'bout] The old copies "brought."
† kindle] The old copies "tingle."

*respects] One of the old copies "respect."

Spain is too far for England to inherit,
But England near enough for Spain to woo.

*Q. Mary.** Have not the kings of England, good
Sir Thomas,
Espous'd the daughters of our neighbour kings?

Wyatt. I grant, your predecessors oft have sought
Their queen[s] from France, and sometimes too from
Spain;
But never could I hear that England yet
Has been so base to seek a king from either.
'Tis policy, dear queen, no love at all.

Win. 'Tis love, great queen, no policy at all.

Wyatt. Which of you all dares justify this match,
And not be touch'd in conscience with an oath?
Remember, O, remember, I beseech you,
King Henry's last will and his act at court!
I mean that royal act† of parliament
That does prohibit Spaniards from the land,
That will and act to which you all are sworn;
And do not damn your souls with perjury.

Q. Mary. But that we know thee, Wyatt, to be
true
Unto the crown of England and to us,
Thy over-boldness should be paid with death:
But cease, for fear your liberal ‡ tongue offend.—
With one consent, my lords, you like this match?

Omnes, except WYATT. We do, great sovereign.

Q. Mary. Call in Count Egmont, honourable
lords.

Enter EGMONT.

We have determin'd of your embassy,
And thus I plight our love to Philip's heart.
Embark you straight; the wind blows wondrous
fair:
Till he shall land in England I'm all care.

[*Exeunt all except* WYATT.

Wyatt. And ere he land in England, I will offer
My loyal breast for him to tread upon.
O, who so forward, Wyatt, as thyself
To raise this troublesome queen in this her throne?
Philip is a Spaniard, a proud nation,
Whom naturally our countrymen abhor.
Assist me, gracious heavens, and you shall see
What hate I bear unto their slavery!
I'll into Kent, there muster up my friends,
To save this country, and this realm defend.

[*Exit.*

Enter GUILDFORD, JANE, *and* Lieutenant.§

Guild. Good morrow to the partner‖ of my woe.

Jane. Good morrow to my lord, my lovely Dudley:
Why do you look so sad, my dearest lord?

Guild. Nay, why doth Jane thus with a heavy eye,
And a defected look, salute the day?
Sorrow doth ill become thy silver brow:
Sad grief lies dead, so long as thou liv'st fair;
In my Jane's joy I do not care for care.

Jane. My looks, my love, are sorted with my
heart:
The sun himself doth scantly show his face.
Out of this firm grate you may perceive
The Tower-hill throng'd with store of people,
As if they gap'd for some strange novelty.

Guild. Though sleep do seldom dwell in men
of care,
Yet I did this night sleep, and this night dream'd
My princely father, great Northumberland,
Was married to a stately bride;
And then methought, just on his bridal day,
A poison'd draught did take his life away.

Jane. Let not fond * visions so appal my love;
For dreams do oftentimes contrary prove.

Guild. The nights are tedious, and the days
are sad:
And see you how the people stand in heaps,
Each man sad-looking on his oppos'd object,
As if a general passion possess'd them?
Their eyes do seem as dropping as the moon,
As if prepared for a tragedy;
For never swarms of people there do tread,
But to rob life and to enrich the dead,
And show they wept.†

Lieut. My lord, they did so, for I was there.

Guild. I pray, resolve us, good Master Lieutenant,
Who was it yonder that tender'd up his life
To nature's death?

Lieut. Pardon me, my lord;
'Tis felony to acquaint you with [the] death
Of any prisoner; yet, to resolve your grace,
It was your father, great Northumberland,
That this day lost his head.

Guild. Peace rest his soul!
His sins be buried in his grave,
And not remember'd in his epitaph!‡—
But who comes here?

---

* *Q. Mary.*] The old copies "Win."

† *act*] The old copies "*Court*" (an error occasioned by
"*court*" in the preceding line).

‡ *liberal*] i. e. licentiously free.

§ *Enter Guildford, &c.*] A room in the Tower.

‖ *partner*] The old copies "*Patron.*" (Compare Shake-

speare's *First Part of Henry VI.*, act iii. sc. 2, "And will
be *partner of your* weal or woe.")

* *fond*] i. e. foolish, vain.

† *And show they wept*] Either something which preceded
these words has dropt out, or else they are corrupted.

‡ *His sins be buried in his grave,
And not remember'd in his epitaph*] From Shakespeare;

"Thy ignomy sleep with thee in the grave,
But not remember'd in thy epitaph."
          First Part of Henry IV., act v. sc. iv.

o 2

Jane. My father prisoner !

Enter SUFFOLK, *guarded forth.*

Suff. O Jane, now naught but fear ! thy title and
Thy state thou now must leave for a small grave.
Had I been contented to ha' been great, I had
    stood ;
But now my rising is pull'd down with blood.
Farewell !—Point me my house of prayers.

Jane. Is grief
So short ? 'Twas wont to be full of words, 'tis
    true ;
But now death's lesson bids a cold adieu.
Farewell ! Thus friends on desperate journeys
    part ;
Breaking off words with tears, that swell the
    heart.   [*Exit* SUFFOLK *guarded.*

Lieut. 'Tis the pleasure of the queen that you
    part lodgings
Till your arraignment, which must be to-morrow.

Jane. Good Master Lieutenant, let us pray to-
    gether.

Lieut. Pardon me, madam, I may not ; they
that owe you, sway me.

Guild. Entreat not, Jane : though she our
    bodies part,
Our souls shall meet : farewell, my love !

Jane. My Dudley, my own heart !   [*Exeunt.*

Enter WYATT, HARPER, ISLEY, RODSTON, *and* Soldiers.[*]

Wyatt. Hold, drum ! Stand, gentlemen ! Give
    the word along !

Soldiers. Stand, stand !

Wyatt. Masters, friends, soldiers, and therefore
    gentlemen,
I know
Some of you wear warm purses lin'd with gold :
To them I speak not ; but to such lean knaves
That cannot put up crosses[†] thus I say,—
Fight valiantly, and, by the Mary God,
You that have all your life-time silver lack'd,
Shall now get crowns,—marry, they must be
    crack'd.

First Sold. No matter ; we'll change them for
white money.

Wyatt. But it must needs be so, dear country-
    men ;
For soldiers are the masters of war's mint ;
Blows are the stamps they set upon with bullets,
And broken pates are when the brains lie spilt,
These light crowns that with blood are double-gilt.

<hr>

[*] *Enter* Wyatt, &c.] Scene. A field near Rochester.
[†] *put up crosses*] A quibble : one meaning of *crosses* was
"pieces of money" (many pieces having a cross on one
side).

But that's not all that your stout hearts shall earn :
Stick to this glorious quarrel, and your names
Shall stand in chronicles, rank'd even with kings.
You free your country from base Spanish thrall,
From ignominious slavery : who can
Digest[*] a Spaniard that's a true Englishman ?

First Sold. Would he might choke that digests
him !

Wyatt. He that loves freedom and his country
    cry
" A Wyatt !" he that will not, with my heart,
Let him stand forth, shake hands, and we'll
    depart.[†]

Soldiers. A Wyatt, a Wyatt, a Wyatt !

Enter NORROY, *sounding a trumpet.*

Harp. Forbear, or with the breath thy trumpet
    spends
This shall let forth thy soul.

Norroy. I am a herald,
And challenge safety by the law of arms.

Harp. So shalt thou when thou art lawfully
    employ'd.

Wyatt. What loud knave's that ?

Norroy. No knave, Sir Thomas ; I am a true
    man
To my queen, to whom thou art a traitor.

Soldiers. Knock him down.

Wyatt. Knock him down ! fie, no ;
We'll handle him, he shall sound before he go.

Harp. He comes from Norfolk and those
    fawning lords,
In Mary's name, weighing out life to them
That will with baseness buy[‡] it : seize on him
As a pernicious enemy.

Wyatt. Sir George,
Be rul'd ; since we profess the art of war,
Let's not be hiss'd at for our ignorance :
He shall pass and repass, juggle the best he can.—
Lead him into the city.—Norroy, set forth,
Set forth thy brazen throat, and call all Rochester
About thee ; do thy office ;
Fill their light heads with proclamations, do,
Catch fools with lime-twigs dipt with pardons.—
But, Sir George, and good Sir Harry Isley,
If this gallant open his mouth too wide,
Powder the varlet, pistol him, fire the roof
That's o'er his mouth.
He craves the law of arms, and he shall ha't :
Teach him our law, to cut's throat if he prate.—
If louder reach thy proclamation,
The Lord have mercy upon thee !

<hr>

[*] *Digest*] The old copies " *Digest.*" See note[*], p. 122.
[†] *depart*] i. e. part.   [‡] *buy*] The quarto of 1607 " *burie.*"

Norroy. Sir Thomas, I must do my office.

Harp. Come, we'll do ours too.

Wyatt. Ay, ay, do, blow thyself hence.

[*Exeunt* HARPER, ISLEY, *and* NORROY.

Whorson, proud herald, because he can give arms,

He thinks to cut us off by the elbows.—

Masters, and fellow soldiers, say will you leave

Old Tom Wyatt ?

Omnes. No, no, no.

Wyatt. A march ! 'tis Norfolk's drum, upon my

life.

I pray, see what drum it is.

[*A cry within,* "Arm."

Rod. The word is given ; "arm, arm" flies through

the camp,

As loud, though not so full of dread, as thunder :

For no man's cheeks look pale, but every face

Is lifted up above his foreman's head,

And every soldier does on tiptoe stand,

Shaking a drawn sword in his threatening hand.

Wyatt. At whom, at whose drum ?

Rod. At Norfolk, Norfolk's drum.

With him comes Arundel. You may behold

The silken faces of their ensigns show

Nothing but wrinkles straggling in the wind :

Norfolk rides foremostly, his crest well known ;

Proud as if all our heads were now his own.

Wyatt. Soft ! he shall pay more for them.

Sir Robert Rodston, bring our musketeers

To flank our pikes ; let all our archery fall off

In wings of shot a-both sides of the van,

To gall the first horse of the enemy

That shall come fiercely on our cannoneers :

Bid them to charge :—charge, my hearts !

Omnes. Charge, charge !

Wyatt. Saint George for England ! Wyatt for

poor Kent !

Blood lost in country's quarrel is nobly spent.

Re-enter ISLEY.

Isley. Base slave, hard-hearted fugitive,

He that you sent with Norroy, false Sir George,

Is fled to Norfolk.

Rod. Sir George Harper fled !

Wyatt. I ne'er thought better of a counterfeit :

His name was Harper, was it not ? let him go :

Henceforth all harpers*, for his sake, shall stand

---

* *Henceforth all harpers, for his sake, shall stand
But for plain ninepence*] "The harp first appeared
upon the Irish money in his [Henry the Eighth's] reign."
—Ruding's *Coinage,* vol. ii. p. 443, ed. 1819. By a proclamation, set forth in 1606, it was declared, "that every of
the said *Harp Shillings* should have and bear the name
and value only of twelve Pence Irish, according to the
old standard of that realm ; being in true value no more
than *nine Pence English.*" *Id.* vol. iii. p. 112.

But for plain ninepence throughout all the land.

They come : no man give ground in these hot

cases ;

Be Englishmen, and beard them to their faces.

[*Exeunt.*

Enter NORFOLK, ARUNDEL, BRETT, Clown, *and* Soldiers.*

Norf. Yonder the traitor marcheth with a

steel-bow

Bent on his sovereign and her† kingdom's peace.

To wave him to us with a flag of truce,

And tender him soft mercy, were to call

Our right in question. Therefore put in act

Your resolute intendments : if rebellion

Be suffer'd to take head, she lives too long ;

Treason doth swarm, therefore give signal to the

fight.

Brett. 'Tis good, 'tis good, my lord.

Norf. Where's Captain Brett ?

Brett. Here, my lord.

Norf. To do honour

To you, and those five hundred Londoners

That march after your colours, you shall charge

The traitor in the vanguard, whilst myself,

With noble Arundel and stout Jerningham,

Second you in the main.

God and Saint George this day fight on our side,

While thus we tame a desperate rebel's pride !

[*Exeunt all except* BRETT, Clown, *and some* Soldiers.

Brett. Countrymen and friends, and you the

most valiant sword-and-buckler-men of London,

the Duke of Norfolk in honour has promoted

you to the vanguard ; and why to the vanguard,

but because he knows you to be eager men,

martial men, men of good stomachs, very hot

shots, very actious ‡ for valour, such as scorn to

shrink for a wetting, who will bear off any thing

with head and shoulders ?

Omnes. Well, forwards, good commander, for-

wards !

Brett. I am to lead you ; and whither ? to fight ;

and with whom ? with Wyatt ; and what is Wyatt ?

a most famous and arch-traitor—[*aside*] to nobody,

by this hand, that I know.

Omnes. Nay, speak out, good captain.

Brett. I say again,—Is worthy Norfolk gone ?

Omnes. Ay, ay, gone, gone.

Brett. I say again, that Wyatt for rising thus

in arms, with the Kentish men dangling thus at

---

* *Enter Norfolk,* &c.] Another part of the field.

† *her*] The old copies "his."

‡ *actious*] So Warner ;

"With diuers here not catolog'd, and for a cheefest take

All *actious* Candish, and of these eternall pen-worke

make."

Albion's England, p. 294, ed. 1612.

his tail, is worthy to be hanged—[aside] like a jewel in the kingdom's ear.—Say I well, my lads?

Omnes. Forwards, forwards!

Brett. And whosoever cuts off his head shall have for his labour—

Clown. What shall I have? I'll do't.

Brett. The pox, the plague, and all the diseases the spittle-houses and hospitals can throw upon him.

Clown. I'll not do't, that's flat.

Brett. And wherefore is Wyatt up?

Clown. Because he cannot keep his bed.

Brett. No, Wyatt is up to keep the Spaniards down, to keep King Philip out, whose coming in will give the land such a fillip, 'twill make it reel again.

Clown. 'A would it were come to that, we would; we would leave off fillips and fall to hot-cockles.

Brett. Philip is a Spaniard; and what is a Spaniard?

Clown. A Spaniard is no Englishman, that I know.

Brett. Right, a Spaniard is a Camocho, a Calimanco; nay, which is worse, a Dondego,—and what is a Dondego?

Clown. A Dondego is a kind of Spanish stock-fish or poor-John.

Brett. No, a Dondego is a desperate Viliago, a very Castilian; God bless us. There came but one Dondego* into England, and he made all Paul's stink again: what shall a whole army of Dondegoes do, my sweet countrymen?

Clown. Marry, they will make us all smell abominably: he comes not here, that's flat.

Brett. A Spaniard is called so because he's a Span-yard, his yard is but a span.

Clown. That's the reason our Englishwomen love them not.

Brett. Right, for he carries not the Englishman's yard about him. If you deal with him, look for hard measure: if you give an inch, he'll take an ell; if you† give an ell, he'll take an inch: therefore, my fine, spruce, dapper, finical fellows, if you are now, as you have always been counted, politic Londoners to fly to the stronger side, leave Arundel, leave Norfolk, and love Brett.

Clown. We'll fling our flat-caps at them.

---

* *Dondego*, &c.] i. e. Don Diego.—So Heywood;
   "But for these Spaniards, now *you Don Diegoes,*
   You that made Paules to stinke."
      Fair Maid of the West, 1631, Part 1st, p. 51.
Various other writers allude to the nasty feat of this Don Diego in St. Paul's Cathedral; and it is very plainly told in a letter among the Cottonian MSS. (*Jul. C.* iii.), which must have been written about the beginning of 1597.

† *you*] the old copies "he."

Brett. Wear your own neat's-leather shoes; scorn Spanish leather; cry, "A fig for the Spaniard!" Said I well, bullies?

Omnes. Ay, ay, ay.

Brett. Why, then, fiat, fiat!
And every man die at his foot that cries not "A Wyatt, a Wyatt!"

Omnes. A Wyatt, a Wyatt, a Wyatt!

Enter WYATT.

Wyatt. Sweet music, gallant fellow-Londoners!

Clown. I 'faith, we are the madcaps, we are the lickpennies.

Wyatt. You shall be all Lord Mayors at least.
  [*Exeunt* WYATT, BRETT, Clown, *and* Soldiers.

Alarum sounds, and enter WYATT, BRETT, RODSTON, ISLEY, Clown, *and* Soldiers, *again.**

Wyatt. Those eight brass pieces shall do service now
Against their masters, Norfolk and Arundel:
They may thank their heels·
More than their hands for saving of their lives.
When soldiers turn surveyors, and measure lands,
God help poor farmers. Soldiers and friends, let us all
Play nimble blood-hounds and hunt them step by step.
We hear
The lawyers plead in armour 'stead of gowns;
If they fall out about the case they jar,
Then they may cuff each other from the bar.—
Soft! this is Ludgate: stand aloof; I'll knock.

He knocks; enter PEMBROKE *upon the walls.*

Pem. Who knocks?

Wyatt. A Wyatt, a true friend.
Open your gates, you lowering citizens;
I bring you freedom from a foreign prince:
The queen has heard your suit, and 'tis her pleasure
The city-gates stand open to receive us.

Pem. Avaunt, thou traitor! think'st thou by forgery
To enter London with rebellious arms?
Know that these gates are barr'd against thy entrance;
And it shall cost the lives
Of twenty thousand true subjects to the queen
Before a traitor enters.

Omnes. Shoot him through.

Wyatt. Stay, let's know him first.

Clown. Kill him; then let's know him afterwards.

---

* *and enter . . . . again*] Scene. London,—Ludgate.

Pem. Look on my face, and blushing see with shame

Thy treasons character'd.

Brett. 'Tis the Lord Pembroke.

Wyatt. What have we to do with the Lord Pembroke?
Where's the queen's lieutenant?

Pem. I am lieutenant of the city now.

Wyatt. Are you Lord Mayor?

Pem. The greatest lord that breathes enters not here
Without express command from my dear queen.

Wyatt. She commands by us.

Pem. I do command thee, in her highness' name,
To leave the city-gates, or, by my honour,
A piece of ordnance shall be straight discharg'd
To be thy death's-man and shoot thee to thy grave.

Wyatt. Then here's no entrance?

Pem. No, none. [*Exit.*

Brett. What should we do following Wyatt any longer?

Wyatt. O London, London, thou perfidious town!
Why hast thou broke thy promise to thy friend,
That for thy sake, and for the * general sake,
Hath thrust myself into the mouth of danger?—
March back to Fleet-street.—If that Wyatt die,
London, unjustly, buy† thy treachery!

Brett. Would I could steal away from Wyatt!
it should be the first thing that I would do.
[*Here they all steal away from* WYATT, *and leave him alone.*

Wyatt. Where's all my soldiers? what, all gone,
And left my drum and colours without guard!
O infelicity of careful men!
Yet will I sell my honour'd blood as dear
As e'er did faithful subject to his prince. [*Exit.*

Enter NORFOLK *and* ISLEY.‡

Isley. Pembroke revolts and flies to Wyatt's side.

Norf. He's damn'd in hell that speaks it.

Enter HARPER.§

Harper.§ O my good lord, 'tis spread
That Pembroke and Count Arundel both are fled!

Enter PEMBROKE *and* ARUNDEL.

Pem. 'Sfoot, who said so? what devil dares stir my patience?

---

* *the*] The old copies "*thy*."
† *buy*] i.e. pay dearly for. (Qy. "'by," i.e. abv?)
‡ *Enter Norfolk and Isley*] Scene. A street in London.
§ *Harper*] The old copies "*Isl.*"

Zounds, I was talking with a crew of vagabonds
That lagg'd at Wyatt's tail; and am I thus
Paid for my pains?

Norf. And there being miss'd,
Some villain, finding you out of sight, hath rais'd
This slander on you : but, come, my lord.

Pem. I'll not fight.

Norf. Nay, sweet earl,—

Pem. Zounds, fight, and hear my name dishonour'd!

Arun. Wyatt is march'd down Fleet-street: after him!

Pem. Why do not you, and you, pursue him?

Norf. If I strike one blow, may my hand fall off!

Pem. And if I do, by this ——

Norf. Come, leave your swearing: did not country's care
Urge me to this quarrel, for my part,
I would not strike a blow.

Pem. No more would I :
I'll eat no wrongs : let's all die, and I'll die.

Enter Messenger.

Mess. Stand on your guard,
For this way Wyatt is pursu'd amain.

A great noise within. Enter WYATT, *with his sword drawn, being wounded.*

[*Within.*] Follow, follow!

Norf. Stand, traitor, stand, or thou shalt ne'er stand more.

Wyatt. Lords, I yield :
An easy conquest 'tis to win the field
After all's lost. I am wounded : let me have
A surgeon, that I may go sound unto my grave.
'Tis not the name of traitor
'Pals me, nor plucks my weapon from my hand :
Use me how you can,
Though you say traitor, I am a gentleman.
Your dreadful shaking me, which I defy,
Is a poor loss of life; I wish to die :
Death frights my spirit no more than can my bed,
Nor will I change one hair, losing this head.

Pem. Come, guard him, guard him.

Wyatt. No matter where :
I hope for nothing, therefore nothing fear.
[*Exeunt.*

Enter WINCHESTER, NORFOLK, ARUNDEL, PEMBROKE, *with other lords.**

Win. My Lord of Norfolk, will it please you sit?
By you, the noble Lord of Arundel.
Since it hath pleas'd her sacred majesty.

---

* *Enter Winchester, &c.*] Scene. A room in the Tower.

To nominate us here commissioners,
Let us, without all partiality,
Be open-ear'd to what they can allege.—
Where's the Lieutenant of the Tower?

Enter Lieutenant.

Lieut. Here, my good lord.

Win. Fetch forth the prisoners.   [*Exit* Lieut.

Enter GUILDFORD *and* JANE, *with* Lieutenant.

Place them severally in chairs of state.—
Clerk of the crown, proceed as law requires.

Clerk. Guildford Dudley, hold up thy hand at
the bar.

Guild. Here at the bar of death I hold it up;
And would to God, this hand, heav'd to the law,
Might have advanc'd itself in better place,
For England's good and for my sovereign's weal!

Clerk. Jane Gray, Lady Jane Gray, hold up
thy hand at the bar.

Jane. A hand as pure from treasonous offence*
As the white livery
Worn by the angels in their Maker's sight!

Clerk. You are here indicted by the names of
Guildford Dudley, Lord Dudley, Jane Gray, Lady
Jane Gray, of capital and high treason against our
most sovereign lady the queen's majesty. That
is to say, that you, Guildford Dudley, and Lady
Jane Gray, have, by all possible means, sought
to procure unto yourselves the royalty of the
crown of England, to the disinheriting of our now
sovereign lady the queen's majesty, the true and
lawful issue to that famous king Henry the
Eighth ; and have manifestly adorned yourselves with the state's garland imperial, and have
granted warrants, commissions, and such-like,
for levying of men and soldiers to be sent against
the said majesty : what answer you to this
indictment,—guilty, or not guilty?

Guild. Our answer shall be several like our-
selves :
Yet, noble earl, we confess the indictment.
May we not make some apology unto the court?

Norf. It is against the order of the law ;
Therefore directly plead unto the indictment,
And then you shall be heard.

Guild. Against the law!
Words utter'd, then, as good unspoken were ;
For, whatsoe'er you say, you know your form,
And you will follow it unto our deaths.

Norf. Speak, are you guilty of these crimes or
no?

Jane. I'll answer first ;—I am, and I am not ;
But should we stand unto the last unguilty,

You have large-conscience jurors to besmear
The fairest brow with style of treachery.

Norf. The barons of the land shall be your
jury.

Jane. An honourable and worthy trial ;
And God forbid so many noblemen
Should be made guilty of our timeless deaths !

Arun. You'll answer to the indictment, will
you not?

Guild. My lord, I will : I am——

Norf. What? are you guilty or no?

Guild. I say unguilty still ; yet I am guilty.

Jane. Slander not thyself :
If there be any guilty, it was I ;
I was proclaim'd queen, I the crown should wear.

Guild. Because I was thy husband, I stand here.

Jane. Our loves we sought ourselves, but not
our pride ;
And shall our fathers' faults our lives divide?*

Guild. It was my father that made thee distrest.

Jane. O, but for mine, my Guildford had been
blest.

Guild. My Jane had been as fortunate as fair,

Jane. My Guildford free from this soul-grieving
care.

Guild. If we be guilty, 'tis no fault of ours ;
And shall we die for what's not in our powers?
We sought no kingdom, we desir'd no crown :
It was impos'd upon us by constraint,
Like golden fruit hung on a barren tree ;
And will you count such forcement treachery?
Then make the silver Thames as black as Styx,
Because it was constrain'd to bear the barks†
Whose battering ordnance should have been em-
ploy'd
Against the hinderers of our royalty.

Win. You talk of senseless things.

Guild. Do trees want sense,
That by the power of music have been drawn
To dance a pleasing measure?
We'll come, then, nearer unto living things :
Say we usurp'd the English royalty,
Was't not by your consents?
I tell you, lords, I have your hands to show,
Subscrib'd to the commission of my father,
By which you did authorize him to wage arms.
If they were rebellious against your sovereign,
Who cried so loud as you, "God save Queen
Jane"?
And come you now your sovereign to arraign?
Come down, come down here, at a prisoner's bar :

---

* *treasonous offence*] The old copies "Treasons Innocence."

† *barks*] The old copies "bankes."

* *divide*] The quarto of 1612 "deride."

Better do so than judge yourselves amiss;
For look, what sentence on our heads you lay,
Upon your own may light another day.

Win. The queen hath pardon'd them.

Guild. And we must die
For a less fault,—O partiality!

Jane. Patience, my Guildford; it was ever known,
They that sinn'd least, the punishment have borne.

Guild. True, my fair queen: oft sorrow truly speaks.*
Great men, like great flies,† through law's cob-
webs break,
But the thinn'st frame the prison of the weak.

Norf. Now trust me, Arundel, it doth grieve me much
To sit in judgment of these harmless [souls].

Arun. I help'd to attach the father; but the son—
O, through my blood I feel compassion run!
My lords, we'll be humble suitors to the queen
To save these innocent creatures from their deaths.

Norf. Let's break up court: if Norfolk long should stay,
In tears and passion I should melt away.

Win. Sit still:
What, will you take compassion upon such?
They are heretics.

Jane. We are Christians: leave our conscience to ourselves;
We stand not here about religious causes,
But are accus'd of capital treason.

Win. Then you confess the indictment?

Guild. Even what you will:
Yet save my Jane, although my blood you spill.

Jane. If I must die, save princely Guildford's life.

Norf. Who is not mov'd to see this loving strife?

Arun. Pray, pardon me: do what you will to-
day,

And I'll approve it, though it be my death.

Win. Then hear the speedy sentence of your deaths:
You shall be carried to the place from whence you came,
From thence unto the place of execution,
Through London to be drawn on hurdles,
Where thou, Jane Gray, shalt suffer death by fire,
Thou, Guildford Dudley, hang'd and quarter'd:
So, Lord have mercy upon you!

Guild. Why, this is well,
Since we must die, that we must die together.

Win. Stay, and hear the mercy of the queen:
Because you are of noble parentage,
Although the crime of your offence be great,
She is only pleas'd that you shall——

Both. Will she pardon us?

Win. Only, I say, that you shall lose your heads
Upon the Tower-hill.—So, convey them hence:
Lieutenant, strictly look unto your charge.

Guild. Our dooms are known, our lives have play'd their part.—
Farewell, my Jane!

Jane. My Dudley, mine own heart!

Guild. Fain would I take a ceremonious leave;
But that's to die a hundred thousand deaths.

Jane. I cannot speak, for tears.

Lieut. My lord, come.

Guild. Least griefs speak louder, when the great are dumb.*   [*Exeunt.*

Enter WYATT, *in the Tower.*

Wyatt. The sad aspect this prison doth afford
Jumps† with the measure that my heart doth keep;
And this enclosure here, of naught but stone,
Yields far more comfort than the stony hearts
Of them that wrong'd their country and their friend:
Here are no perjur'd councillors ‡ to swear
A sacred oath, and then forswear the same;
No innovators here do harbour keep:
A stedfast silence doth possess the place:
In this the Tower is noble, being base.

Enter NORFOLK, WINCHESTER, ARUNDEL, *and Officers, to* WYATT.

Norf. Sir Thomas Wyatt,—

Wyatt. That's my name, indeed.

---

* *oft sorrow truly speaks*] The old copies "*of sorrowe truely speakr.*"

† *Great men, like great flies, &c.*] It may be urged that Dekkor wrote this, as the following passage occurs in one of his plays:—
  "*Jovinelli.* You must hang up the lawes.
  Octavio. Like cob-webbe in owle roomes, through
    which great flies
  Breake through, the lesse being caught b'lth wing
    there dies."
If this be not a good play the devil is in it, 1612, Sig. D 3. But the simile is derived from ancient wisdom:—"One of the Seven was wont to say, that lawes were like cob-webs; where the small flies were caught, and the great brake through." Bacon's *Apophthegms*, No. 284.
  See, too, what Delio says in *The Duchess of Malfi*;
    "Then the law to him," &c.   p. 61.

* *Least griefs speak louder, when the great are dumb*] The old copies have,
      "*Great griefes speake louder*
        When the least are dumb'd."
But compare *The White Devil*, p. 15, and note *.

† *Jumps*] i. e. agrees.

‡ *councillors*] i. e. members of the council.

Win. You should say traitor.

Wyatt. Traitor, and Wyatt's name,
Differ as far as Winchester and honour.

Win. I am a pillar of the mother church.

Wyatt. And what am I?

Win. One that subverts the state.

Wyatt. Insult not too much o'er th' unfortunate;
I have no bishop's rochet to declare
My innocency. This is my cross,
That causeless I must suffer my head's loss:
When that hour comes wherein my blood is spilt,
My cross will look as bright as yours twice-gilt.

Norf. Here's for that purpose.

Wyatt. Is your grace so short?
Belike you come to make my death a sport.

Win. We come to bring you to your execution;
You must be hang'd and quarter'd instantly:
At the Park-corner is a gallows set;
Whither make haste to tender nature's debt.

Wyatt. Then here's the end of Wyatt's rising
up: *
I to keep Spaniards from the land was sworn:
Right willingly I yield myself to death;
But sorry such should have my place of birth.
Had London kept his word, Wyatt had stood;
But now King Philip enters through my blood.
                    [*Exeunt* Officers *with* WYATT.

Win. Where's the Lieutenant of the Tower?

Enter Lieutenant.

Lieut. Here, my lord.

Win. Fetch forth your other prisoners.

Lieut. My lord, I will;
Here lies young Guildford, here the Lady Jane.

Norf. Conduct them forth.   [*Exit* Lieut.

Enter GUILDFORD *and* JANE, *with* Lieutenant.

Guild. Good morrow once more to my lovely
Jane.

Jane. The last good-morrow, my sweet love, to
thee.

Guild. What were you reading?

Jane. On a prayer-book.

Guild. Trust me, so was I: we had need to pray,
For, see, the ministers of death draw near.

Jane. To a prepared mind death is a pleasure:
I long in soul till I have spent my breath.

Guild. My lord high chancellor, you are welcome
hither:
What, come you to behold our execution?—
And, my Lord Arundel, thrice welcome: you
help'd

To attach our father; come you now to see
The black conclusion of our tragedy?

Win. We come to do our office.

Guild. So do we;
Our office is to die, yours to look on:
We are beholding unto such beholders.
The time was, lords, when you did flock amain
To see her crown'd; but now to kill my Jane.
The world like to a sickle bends itself:
Men run their course of lives as in a maze:
Our office is to die, yours but to gaze.

Jane. Patience, my Guildford.

Guild. Patience, my lovely Jane!
Patience has blanch'd thy soul as white as snow;
But who shall answer for thy death? This
know,
An innocent to die, what is it less
But to add angels to heaven's happiness?
The guilty dying do applaud the law;
But when the innocent creature stoops his neck
To an unjust doom, upon the judge they check.
Lives are, like souls, requir'd of their neglectors;
Then ours of you that should be our protectors.

Win. Rail not against the law.

Guild. No, God forbid!
My Lord of Winchester is * made of law,
And should I rail against it, 'twere 'gainst you.
If I forget not, you rejoic'd to see
The fall of Cromwell: joy you now at me?
Oft dying men are fill'd with prophecies;
But I'll not be a prophet of your ill.—
Yet know, my lords, they that behold us now
May to the axe of justice one day bow,
And in that plot of ground, where we must die,
Sprinkle their bloods, though I know no cause
why.

Norf. Speak you to me, Lord Guildford?

Guild. Norfolk, no:
I speak to——

Norf. To whom?

Guild. Alas, I do not know.——
Which of us two dies first?

Win. The better part.

Guild. O, rather kill the worst!

Jane. 'Tis I, sweet love, that first must kiss the
block.

Guild. I am a man; men better brook the
shock
Of threatening death: your sex are ever weak;
The thoughts of death a woman's heart will break.

Jane. But I am arm'd to die.

Guild. Likelier to live;

---

* *Wyatt's rising up*] The quarto of 1612 " *Wyats up.*"

* *is*] The old copies "*It's.*"

Death to the unwilling doth his presence give:
He dares not look the bold man in the face,
But on the fearful lays his killing mace.

Win. It is the pleasure of the queen
That the Lady Jane must first suffer death.

Jane. I thank her highness,
That I shall first depart this hapless world,
And not survive to see my dear love dead.

Guild. She dying first, I three times lose my
head.

Enter the Headsman and Ladies.

Heads. Forgive me, lady, I pray, your death.

Guild. Ha! hast thou the heart to kill a face
so fair?

Win. It is her headsman.

Guild. And demands a pardon
Only of her for taking off her head?

Jane. Ay, gentle Guildford, and I pardon him.

Guild. But I'll not pardon him: thou art my
wife,
And he shall ask me pardon for thy life.

Heads. Pardon me, my lord.

Guild. Rise, do not kneel;
Though thou submitt'st, thou hast a lowering steel,
Whose fatal declination brings our death:
Good man of earth, make haste to make us earth.

Heads. Pleaseth the Lady Jane, I'll help her off
With her night-gown.

Jane. Thanks, gentle friend; but I
Have other waiting-women to attend me.—
Good Mistress Ellen,[*] lend me a helping hand
To strip me of these[†] worldly ornaments:
Off with these robes, O, tear them from my side!
Such silken covers are the gilt of pride.
Instead of gowns, my coverture be earth,
My worldly death a new celestial birth![‡]—
What, is it off?

First Lady. Madam, almost.

Jane. Not yet? O God,
How hardly can we shake off this world's pomp,
That cleaves unto us like our body's skin!
Yet thus, O God, shake off thy servant's sin!

First Lady. Here is a scarf to blind your eyes.

Jane. From all the world but from my Guildford's sight:
Before I fasten this beneath my brow,

Let me behold him with a constant look.

Guild. O, do not kill me with that piteous eye!

Jane. 'Tis my last farewell, take it patiently:
My dearest Guildford, let us kiss and part.—
Now blind mine eyes never to see the sky:
Blindfold thus lead me to the block to die.
                    [*Exit with Headsman and Ladies.*

Guild. O!   [*Falls in a trance.*

Norf. How fares my lord?

Arun. He's fall'n into a trance.

Norf. Wake him not until he wake himself.—
O happy Guildford, if thou die in this,
Thy soul will be the first in heavenly bliss!

Win. Here comes the headsman with the head
of Jane.

Re-enter Headsman, with JANE's head.

Guild. Who spake of Jane? who nam'd my
lovely Jane?

Win. Behold her head.

Guild. O, I shall faint again!
Yet let me bear this sight unto my grave,
My sweet Jane's head:—
Look, Norfolk, Arundel, Winchester,
Do malefactors look thus when they die,—
A ruddy lip, a clear reflecting eye,
Cheeks purer than the maiden orient pearl,
That sprinkle[*] bashfulness through the clouds!
Her innocence has given her this look:
The like for me to show so well, being dead,
How willingly would Guildford lose his head!

Win. My lord, the time runs on.

Guild. So does our death:
Here's one has run so fast, she's out of breath.
But the time goes on, and my fair Jane's white
soul;
Will be in heaven before me, if I do stay.
Stay, gentle wife, thy Guildford follows thee:
Though on the earth we part by adverse fate,
Our souls shall knock together at heaven's gate.
The sky is calm, our deaths have a fair day,
And we shall pass the smoother on our way.
My lords, farewell, ay, once farewell to all:
The fathers' pride has caus'd the children's fall.
                    [*Exit GUILDFORD to death.†*

---

[*] *Good Mistress Ellen, &c.*] "Then kneeling downe, she
said the psalme of Miserere mei Deus, in English, and
then stood vp and gaue hir maid (*called mistresse Ellin*)
her gloues and handkercher," &c. Holinshed's *Chron.*
vol. iv. 22, ed. 1808.

[†] *these*] The old copies "*this.*"

[‡] *a new celestial birth*] The old copies "*or new Celestiall
breath.*"

[*] *That sprinkle, &c.*] Corrupted, of course. (The old
copies have "*That* sprinckles," &c.)

[†] Dudley, as every reader of history knows, was put to
death before his wife.
Warner, in describing the end of this unhappy pair,
adheres more closely to fact:—

"Come was the day, the tragicke day, wherein they both
    should die;
When either, passing to their end, ech other did espie,
Shee in her lodging waiting death, prepared her that
    day,
And he in being lead thereto, her lodging in his way."

Norf. Thus have we seen her highness' will
    perform'd :
And now their heads and bodies shall be join'd
And buried in one grave, as fits their loves.

Asending and dissending signes then fly and fall
    apace,
And each bemones the other more than mindes their
    private case.
Their eies, that looked loue ere while, now looke their
    last adew,
And staine their faces, faultles are this dismall enter-
    vew ;
Their eares, earst listning ioies, are deafe, vnlesse to
    sighes profound ;
Their tongs, earst talking ioies, those looks and sighes
    did now confound :
What part soere of them had felt or tasted ioyes ere
    this,
Woare senceles now of any ioy, saue hope of heauenly
    blis.

Thus much I'll say in their behalfs now dead,
Their fathers' pride their lives hath severèd.

                   [*Exeunt.*

Whilst either thus for earthly pompe no longer time
    did looke,
He passeth to the fatall blocke, she praying on her
    booke :
Whence (hauing made a godly end) he was return'd,
    whilst shee
Prepard for like, aud of her lord the senceles tronke
    did see ;
A sight more deathful than her death that should
    coöort him straite,
And for the which her fearcles eies did euery moment
    waite.
She vnalashed, mounting now the skaffold, theare
    attends
The fatall stroke, and vnto God her better parts com-
    monds,
And as she liu'd a vertuous life, so vertuously she euds "
           Albion's England, p. 196, ed. 1612.

WESTWARD HO.

.

West-ward Hoe. As it hath beene diuers times Acted by the Children of Paules. Written by The : Decker, and John Webster. Printed at London, and to be sold by John Hodgets dwelling in Paules Churchyard. 1607. 4to.

I have met with one copy of this comedy, which differs slightly in some passages from the copy I possess. See the prefatory matter to *The White Devil*, p. 2.

The title of *Westward Ho*, that of the play which comes next in the present collection, *Northward Ho*, as well as that of the comedy by Chapman, Jonson, and Marston, *Eastward Ho*, appear to have been derived from the exclamations of the watermen who plied on the Thames:

"[*Make a noise, Westward Ho!*

Queen Elinor. Woman, what noise is this I hear?
Potter's Wife. An like your grace, *it is the watermen that call for passengers to go westward now.*"

Peele's *Edward 1st.—Works*, vol. i. p. 182. sec. ed.

Compare ;

"There lies your way, due west.
. . . Then *westward, ho !*"

Shakespeare's *Twelfth-Night*, act iii. sc. i.

"A stranger? the better welcome: comes hee *Inutward, Westward, or Northward hoe ?*"

Day's *Isle of Gulls*, 1606, Sig. A 2.

" Yea? and will you to the southward y faith? will you to the confines of Italy, my gallants? Take heed how yee goe Northwards ; 'tis a dangerous coast, jest not with 't in winter ; therefore goe Southwards, my gallants, *Southwards hoe !*"

Sharpham's *Fleire*, 1615, Sig. D 4·

Eastward Ho was printed in 1605: the Prologue to it shows that *Westward Ho* was then on the stage;

"Not out of envy, for ther's no effect
Where there's no cause, nor out of imitation,
For we haue euermore been imitated ;
Nor out of our contention to doe better
Then that which is opposde to ours in title ;
For that was good, and better cannot be :
And for the title, if it seeme affected,
We might as well have calde it, *God you good even ;*
Only that eastward, westwards still exceedes,
Honour the sunnes faire rising, not his setting," &c.

DRAMATIS PERSONÆ.

———♦———

EARL.
JUSTINIANO.
HONEYSUCKLE.
TENTERHOOK.
WAFER.
MONOPOLY.
SIR GOSLING GLOWWORM.
LINSTOCK.
WHIRLPOOL.
AMBUSH.
CLUTCH.
Scrivener.
Cashier.
Tailor.
BONIFACE.
Prentice.
Chamberlain.
Boy, Servants, Fiddlers.

MISTRESS JUSTINIANO.
MISTRESS HONEYSUCKLE.*
MISTRESS TENTERHOOK.*
MISTRESS WAFER.*
MISTRESS BIRDLIME.
LUCY.
CHRISTIAN.

---

* *Mistress Honeysuckle.* ⎫ In the old copy (which has no list of dramatis personæ) the Christian names of these
Mistress Tenterhook. ⎬ ladies are generally prefixed to their respective speeches,—*Judith* to Mistress Honey-
Mistress Wafer.   ⎭ suckle's; *Moll,* or *Clare,* to Mistress Tenterhook's; and *Mabel* to Mistress Wafer's.
When our poets make Mistress Tenterhook be addressed "sweet *Clare,*" in the latter part of the play, they must
have forgotten that she had been termed "little *Moll*" in an earlier scene. The name of Mistress Justiniano is
Moll.

WESTWARD HO.

ACT I.

SCENE I.*

Enter MISTRESS BIRDLIME *and* Tailor.

Bird. Stay, tailor, this is the house: pray thee, look the gown be not ruffled; as for the jewels and precious stones, I know where to find them ready presently. She that must wear this gown, if she will receive it, is Master Justiniano's wife, the Italian merchant: my good old lord and master, that hath been a tilter this twenty year, hath sent it. Mum, tailor; you are a kind of bawd. Tailor, if this gentlewoman's husband should chance to be in the way now, you shall tell him that I keep a hot-house † in Gunpowder-alley, near Crutched-Friars, and that I have brought home his wife's foul linen; and, to colour my knavery the better, I have here three or four kinds of complexion, which I will make show of to sell unto her: the young gentlewoman hath a good city wit, I can tell you; she hath read in *The Italian Courtier* ‡ that it is a special ornament to gentlewomen to have skill in painting.

Tailor. Is my lord acquainted with her?

Bird. O, ay.

Tailor. Faith, Mistress Birdlime, I do not commend my lord's choice so well: now, methinks he were better to set up a dairy, and to keep

half a score of lusty, wholesome, honest, country wenches.

Bird. Honest country wenches! in what hundred shall a man find two of that simple virtue?

Tailor. Or to love some lady; there were equality and coherence.

Bird. Tailor, you talk like an ass: I tell thee there is equality enough between a lady and a city dame, if their hair be but of a colour. Name you any one thing that your citizen's wife comes short of to your lady: they have as pure linen, as choice painting, love green-geese in spring, mallard and teal in the fall, and woodcock in winter. Your citizen's wife learns nothing but fopperies of your lady; but your lady or justice-o'-peace madam carries high wit from the city,—namely, to receive all and pay all, to awe their husbands, to check their husbands, to control their husbands; nay, they have the trick on't to be sick for a new gown, or a carcanet,* or a diamond, or so; and I wis† this is better wit than to learn how to wear a Scotch farthingale; nay, more,—Here comes one of the servants: you remember, tailor, that I am deaf; observe that.

Tailor. Ay, thou art in that like one of our young gulls, that will not understand any wrong is done him, because he dares not answer it.

Enter Prentice.

Bird. By your leave, bachelor; is the gentle-woman, your mistress, stirring?

Prent. Yes, she is moving.

Bird. What says he?

Tailor. She is up.

---

* *Scene I.*] London. A street: before the house of Justiniano.

† *I keep a hot-house, &c.*] A *hot-house* meant properly a bagnio; but it also meant a brothel; for brothels were often kept under the pretence of their being *hot-houses*. —"He, sir! a tapster, sir; parcel-bawd; one that serves a bad woman; whose house, sir, was, as they say, plucked down in the suburbs; and now she professes a *hot-house*, which, I think, is a very ill house too." Shakespeare's *Measure for Measure*, act ii. sc. 1.

‡ *The Italian Courtier*] Thomas Hoby's translation of Castiglione's famous *Courtier* appeared in 4to. in 1561.

---

* *carcanet*, i.e., *necklace*.

† *wis*] Some copies of the old ed. "*wist*."

P

Bird. Where's the gentleman, your master, pray you?

Pren. Where many women desire to have their husbands,—abroad.

Bird. I am very thick of hearing.

Pren. Why, abroad:—[*aside*] you smell of the bawd.

Bird. I pray you, tell her here's an old gentlewoman would speak with her.

Pren. So.   [*Exit.*

Tailor. What, will you be deaf to the gentlewoman when she comes too?

Bird. O, no; she's acquainted well enough with my knavery.—She comes.

Enter MISTRESS JUSTINIANO.

How do you, sweet lady?

Mist. Just. Lady!

Bird. By God's me, I hope to call you lady ere you die. What, mistress, do you sleep well on nights?

Mist. Just. Sleep! ay, as quietly as a client having great business with lawyers.

Bird. Come, I am come to you about the old suit: my good lord and master hath sent you a velvet gown here: do you like the colour? three-pile, a pretty fantastical trimming! I would God you would say it, by my troth. I dreamed last night you looked so prettily, so sweetly, methought so like the wisest lady of them all, in a velvet gown.

Mist. Just. What's the forepart?

Bird. A very pretty stuff: I know not the name of your forepart, but 'tis of a hair-colour.

Mist. Just. That it was my hard fortune, being so well brought up, having so great a portion to my marriage, to match so unluckily! Why, my husband and his whole credit is not worth my apparel: well, I shall undergo a strange report in leaving my husband.

Bird. Tush, if you respect your credit, never think of that; for beauty covets rich apparel, choice diet, excellent physic. No German clock,* nor mathematical engine whatsoever, requires so much reparation as a woman's face; and what means hath your husband to allow sweet Doctor Glisterpipe his pension? I have heard that you have threescore smocks that cost three pounds a smock: will these smocks ever hold out with

your husband? no, your linen and your apparel must turn over a new leaf, I can tell you.

Tailor. [*aside*] O admirable bawd! O excellent Birdlime!

Bird. I have heard he loved you, before you were married, entirely: what of that? I have ever found it most true in mine own experience, that they which are most violent dotards before their marriage are most voluntary cuckolds after. Many are honest, either because they have not wit,* or because they have not opportunity, to be dishonest; and this Italian, your husband's countryman, holds it impossible any of their ladies should be excellent witty, and not make the uttermost use of their beauty: will you be a fool, then?

Mist. Just. Thou dost persuade me to ill very well.

Bird. You are nice and peevish:† how long will you hold out, think you? not so long as Ostend.‡

Enter JUSTINIANO.

Passion of me, your husband! Remember that I am deaf, and that I come to sell you complexion:—truly, mistress, I will deal very reasonably with you.

Just. What are you, say ye?

Bird. Ay, forsooth.

Just. What, my most happy wife!

Mist. Just. Why, your jealousy.

Just. Jealousy! in faith, I do not fear to lose That I have lost already.—What are you?

Bird. Please your good worship, I am a poor gentlewoman that cast away myself upon an unthrifty captain that lives now in Ireland: I am fain to pick out a poor living with selling complexion, to keep the frailty, as they say, honest.

Just. What's he?§—Complexion too! you are a bawd.

Bird. I thank your good worship for it.

Just. Do not I know these tricks? That which thou mak'st a colour for thy sin Hath been thy first undoing,—painting, painting.

Bird. I have of all sorts, forsooth: here is the

---

* *No German clock, &c.*] Some copies of the old ed. "*Nor.*"—See the notes of the commentators on—
    "A woman, that is like a German clock,
    Still a-repairing."
Shakespeare's *Love's Labour's Lost*, act iii. sc. 1.

* *wit*] Some copies of the old ed. "*wist*," other copies "*means.*" (Compare what follows.)

† *nice and peevish*] i.e. scrupulous and foolish.

‡ *not so long as Ostend*] After a siege of three years and ten weeks, this place surrendered to the Marquis of Spinola, on the twelfth of September, 1604. In the same year appeared at London *A True Historie of the Memorable Siege of Ostend, and what passed on either side from the beginning of the Siege unto the yeelding up of the Towne, &c. Translated out of French into English. By Edward Grimeston.*

§ *he*] If right, means the Tailor: but qy. "here"?

burned powder of a hog's jaw-bone, to be laid with the oil of white poppy, an excellent fucus to kill morphew, weed out freckles, and a most excellent groundwork for painting; here is ginimony likewise burned and pulverized, to be mingled with the juice of lemons, sublimate mercury, and two spoonfuls of the flowers of brimstone, a most excellent receipt to cure the flushing in the face.

Just. Do you hear, if you have any business to despatch with that deaf goodness there, pray you, take leave—opportunity, that which most of you long for.(though you never be with child), opportunity: I'll find some idle business in the mean time; I will, I will, in truth; you shall not need fear me: or you may speak French; most of your kinds can understand French. God b'wi'you !—

Being certain thou art false, sleep, sleep, my brain;

For doubt was only that which fed my pain.
                                    [*Exit.*

Mist. Just. You see what a hell I live in: I am resolved to leave him.

Bird. O the most fortunate gentlewoman, that will be so wise, and so, so provident ! the caroche shall come.

Mist. Just. At what hour ?

Bird. Just when women and vintners are a-conjuring, at midnight. O the entertainment my lord will make you,—sweet wines, lusty diet, perfumed linen, soft beds! O most fortunate gentlewoman!
                        [*Exeunt* BIRDLIME *and* Tailor.

Re-enter JUSTINIANO.

Just. Have you done? have you despatched? 'tis well: and, in troth, what was the motion ?

Mist. Just. Motion ! what motion ?

Just. Motion ! why, like the motion in law that stays for a day of hearing, yours for a night of hearing. Come, let's not have April in your eyes, I pray you: it shows a wanton month follows your weeping. Love a woman for her tears ! Let a man love oysters for their water: for women, though they should weep liquor enough to serve a dyer or a brewer, yet they may be as stale as wenches that travel every second tide between Gravesend and Billingsgate.

Mist. Just. This madness shows very well.

Just. Why, look you, I am wondrous merry: can any man discern by my face that I am a cuckold? I have known many suspected for men of this misfortune, when they have walked

thorough the streets, wear their hats o'er their eyebrows, like politic penthouses,* which commonly make the shop of a mercer or a linen-draper as dark as a room in Bedlam; his cloak shrouding his face, as if he were a Neopolitan that had lost his beard in April; and if he walk through the street, or any other narrow road (as 'tis rare to meet a cuckold), he ducks at the penthouses, like an ancient† that dares not flourish at the oath-taking of the pretor ‡ for fear of the sign-posts. Wife, wife, do I any of these? Come, what news from his lordship? has not his lordship's virtue once gone against the hair, and coveted corners ?

Mist. Just. Sir, by my soul, I will be plain with you.

Just. Except the forehead, dear wife, except the forehead.

Mist. Just. The gentleman you spake of hath often solicited my love, and hath received from me most chaste denials.

Just. Ay, ay, provoking resistance: 'tis as if you come to buy wares in the city, bid money for't; your mercer or goldsmith says, "Truly, I cannot take it," lets his customer pass his stall, next, nay, perhaps two or three; but if he find he is not prone to return of himself, he calls him back, and back, and takes his money: so you, my dear wife,—O the policy of women and tradesmen ! they'll bite at any thing.

Mist. Just. What would you have me do? all your plate, and most part of your jewels, are at pawn; besides, I hear you have made over all your estate to men in the town here. What would you have me do ? would you have me turn common sinner, or sell my apparel to my waist-coat, and become a laundress ?

Just. No laundress, dear wife, though your credit would go far with gentlemen for taking up of linen; no laundress.

Mist. Just. Come, come, I will speak as my

---

* *like politic penthouses, &c.*] Our old writers have frequent allusions to the roguery of tradesmen in darkening their shops, that customers might be unable to detect the badness of their goods. So Brome; "What should the city do with honesty? . . . Why are your wares gummed, *your shops dark*," &c. *The City Wit,* act i. sc. 1. And Middleton;

"though your shop-wares you vent
With your deceiving lights," &c.

Any thing for a quiet life, act ii. sc. 2,—*Works,* iv. 442, ed. Dyce.

† *ancient*] i.e. flag, standard. (So afterwards, act ii. sc. 1, "I'm as limber as an *ancient that has flourished* in the rain," &c.)

‡ *the pretor*] i.e. the Lord Mayor.

misfortune prompts me. Jealousy hath undone many a citizen; it hath undone you and me. You married me from the service of an honourable lady, and you knew what matches I mought have had. What would you have me to do? I would I had never seen your eyes, your eyes.

Just. Very good, very good.

Mist. Just. Your prodigality, your dicing, your riding abroad, your consorting yourself with noblemen, your building a summer-house, hath undone us, hath undone us. What would you have me do?

Just. Any thing. I have sold my house and the wares in't; I am going for Stode * next tide: what will you do now, wife?

Mist. Just. Have you indeed?

Just. Ay, by this light, all's one: I have done as some citizens at thirty, and most heirs at three-and-twenty, made all away. Why do you not ask me now what you shall do?

Mist. Just. I have no counsel in your voyage, neither shall you have any in mine.

Just. To his lordship,—will you not, wife?

Mist. Just. Even whither my misfortune leads me.

Just. Go; no longer will I make my care thy prison.

Mist. Just. O my fate! Well, sir, you shall answer for this sin which you force me to. Fare you well: let not the world condemn me, if I seek for mine own maintenance.

Just. So, so.

Mist. Just. Do not send me any letters; do not seek any reconcilement; by this light, I'll receive none: if you will send me my apparel, so; if not, choose. I hope we shall ne'er meet more.
                                        [*Exit.*

Just. So, farewell the acquaintance of all the mad devils that haunt jealousy! Why should a man be such an ass to play the antic for his wife's appetite? Imagine that I, or any other great man, have on a velvet night-cap, and put case that this night-cap be too little for my ears or forehead, can any man tell me where my night-cap wrings me, except I be such an ass to proclaim it? Well, I do play the fool with my misfortune very handsomely. I am glad that I am certain of my wife's dishonesty; for a secret strumpet is like mines prepared to ruin goodly buildings. Farewell my care! I have told my wife I am

going for Stode: that's not my course; for I resolve to take some shape upon me, and to live disguised here in the city. They say, for one cuckold to know that his friend is in the like head-ache, and to give him counsel, is as if there were two partners, the one to be arrested, the other to bail him. My estate is made over to my friends, that do verily believe I mean to leave England. Have amongst you, city dames! you that are indeed the fittest and most proper persons for a comedy: nor let the world lay any imputation upon my disguise; for court, city, and country, are merely as masks one to the other, envied of some, laughed at of others: and so, to my comical business.   [*Exit.*

SCENE II.*

Enter TENTERHOOK, MISTRESS TENTERHOOK, MONOPOLY, *a Scrivener, and a Cashier.*

Ten. Moll,—

Mist. Ten. What would, heart?

Ten. Where's my cashier? are the sums right? are the bonds sealed?

Cash. Yea, sir.

Ten. Will you have the bags sealed?

Mon. O, no, sir, I must disburse instantly; we that be courtiers have more places to send money to than the devil hath to send his spirits. There's a great deal of light gold.

Ten. O, sir, 'twill away in play: an you will stay till to-morrow, you shall have it all in new sovereigns.

Mon. No, in troth, 'tis no matter, 'twill away in play. Let me see the bond, when this money is to be paid [*looks at the bond*]: the tenth of August, the first day that I must tender this money, is the first of dog-days.

Scriv. I fear 'twill be hot staying for you in London then.

Ten. Scrivener, take home the bond with you.
                                    [*Exit Scrivener.*
Will you stay to dinner, sir?—Have you any partridge, Moll?

Mist. Ten. No, in troth, heart; but an excellent pickled goose, a new service.—Pray you, stay.

Mon. Sooth, I cannot.—By this light, I am so infinitely, so unboundably beholding to you!

Ten. Well, signior, I'll leave you.—My cloak, there!

Mist. Ten. When will you come home, heart?

---

* *I am going for Stode next tide*] By *Stode*, I suppose, we are to understand *Stade*.—Here the spelling of the old ed. is "Stoad"; but in act iii. sc. 3, it has "*Stode*."

* *Scene II.*] The same. A room in the house of Tenterhook.

Ten. In troth, self, I know not; a friend of yours and mine hath broke.

Mist. Ten. Who, sir?

Ten. Master Justiniano, the Italian.

Mist. Ten. Broke, sir?

Ten. Yea, sooth: I was offered forty yesterday upon the Exchange, to assure a hundred.

Mist. Ten. By my troth, I am sorry.

Ten. And his wife is gone to the party.

Mist. Ten. Gone to the party! O wicked creature!

Ten. Farewell, good Master Monopoly: I prithee, visit me often.   [*Exit.*

Mon. Little Moll, send away the fellow.

Mist. Ten. Philip, Philip,—

Cash. Here, forsooth.

Mist. Ten. Go into Bucklersbury,* and fetch me two ounces of preserved melons: look there be no tobacco taken in the shop when he weighs it.

Cash. Ay, forsooth.   [*Exit.*

Mon. What do you eat preserved melons for, Moll?

Mist. Ten. In troth, for the shaking of the heart: I have here sometime such a shaking, and downwards such a kind of earthquake, as it were.

Mon. Do you hear, let your man carry home my money to the ordinary, and lay it in my chamber: but let him not tell my host that it is money: I owe him but forty pound, and the rogue is hasty; he will follow me when he thinks I have money, and pry into me as crows perch upon carrion, and when he hath found it out, prey upon me as heralds do upon funerals.

Mist. Ten. Come, come, you owe much money in town: when you have forfeited your bond, I shall ne'er see you more.

Mon. You are a monkey: I'll pay him fore's day: I'll see you to-morrow too.

Mist. Ten. By my troth, I love you very honestly; you were never the gentleman offered any uncivility to me, which is strange, methinks, in one that comes from beyond seas: would I had given a thousand pound, I could not love thee so!

Mon. Do you hear, you shall feign some scurvy disease or other, and go to the Bath next spring: I'll meet you there.

Enter MISTRESS HONEYSUCKLE *and* MISTRESS WAFER.

Mist. Honey. By your leave, sweet Mistress Tenterhook.

* *Bucklersbury*] In our author's time, was chiefly occupied by druggists.

Mist. Ten. O, how dost, partner?

Mon. Gentlewomen, I stayed for a most happy wind, and now the breath from your sweet, sweet lips should set me going. Good Mistress Honeysuckle, good Mistress Wafer, good Mistress Tenterhook, I will pray for you, that neither rivalship in loves, pureness of painting, or riding out of town, nor acquainting each other with it, be a cause your sweet beauties do fall out, and rail one upon another.

Mist. Wafer. Rail, sir! we do not use to rail.

Mon. Why, mistress, railing is your mother tongue, as well as lying.

Mist. Honey. But do you think we can fall out?

Mon. In troth, beauties, as one spake seriously that there was no inheritance in the amity of princes, so think I of women; too often interviews amongst women, as amongst princes, breed envy oft to other's fortune: there is only in the amity of women an estate for will; and every puny knows that is no certain inheritance.

Mist. Wafer. You are merry, sir.

Mon. So may I leave you, most fortunate gentlewoman!   [*Exit.*

Mist. Ten. [*aside*] Love shoots here.

Mist. Wafer. Tenterhook, what gentleman is that gone out? is he a man?

Mist. Honey. O God, and an excellent trumpeter. He came lately from the university, and loves city dames only for their victuals. He hath an excellent trick to keep lobsters and crabs sweet in summer, and calls it a device to prolong the days of shell-fish; for which I do suspect he hath been clerk to some nobleman's kitchen. I have heard he never loves any wench till she be as stale as Frenchmen eat their wild-fowl.—[*Aside*] I shall anger her.

Mist. Ten. How stale, good Mistress Nimblewit?

Mist. Honey. Why, as stale as a country hostess, an Exchange sempster, or a court laundress.

Mist. Ten. He is your cousin: how your tongue runs!

Mist. Honey. Talk and make a noise, no matter to what purpose; I have learned that with going to puritan lectures. I was yesterday at a banquet: will you discharge my ruffs of some wafers?— And how doth thy husband, Wafer?

Mist. Wafer. Faith, very well.

Mist. Honey. He is just like a torchbearer to maskers; he wears good clothes, and is ranked in good company, but he doth nothing: thou art fain to take all and pay all.

Mist. Ten. The more happy she: would I could

make such an ass of my husband too!—I hear
say he breeds thy child in his teeth, every
year.

Mist. Wafer. In faith, he doth.

Mist. Honey. By my troth, 'tis pity but the fool
should have the other two pains incident to the
head.

Mist. Wafer. What are they?

Mist. Honey. Why, the head-ache and horn-
ache. I heard say that he would have had thee
nursed thy child thyself too.

Mist. Wafer. That he would, truly.

Mist. Honey. Why, there's the policy of husbands to keep their wives in. I do assure you, if
a woman of any markable face in the world give
her child suck, look, how many wrinkles be in
the nipple of her breast, so many will be in her
forehead by that time twelvemonth. But, sirrah,[*]
we are come to acquaint thee with an excellent
secret; we two learn to write.

Mist. Ten. To write!

Mist. Honey. Yes, believe it, and we have the
finest schoolmaster, a kind of precisian, and yet
an honest knave too. By my troth, if thou beest
a good wench, let him teach thee: thou mayst
send him of any errand, and trust him with any
secret; nay, to see how demurely he will bear
himself before our husbands, and how jocund
when their backs are turned!

Mist. Ten. For God's love, let me see him.

Mist. Wafer. To-morrow we'll send him to
thee: till then, sweet Tenterhook, we leave thee,
wishing thou mayst have the fortune to change
thy name often.

Mist. Ten. How! change my name!

Mist. Wafer. Ay; for thieves and widows love
to shift many names, and make sweet use of it
too. -

Mist. Ten. O, you are a wag, indeed. Good
Wafer, remember my schoolmaster.—Farewell,
good Honeysuckle.

Mist. Honey. Farewell, Tenterhook. [*Exeunt.*

ACT II.

SCENE I.†

Enter BONIFACE, *an apprentice, brushing his master's cloak
and cap, and singing; enter* HONEYSUCKLE *in his
night-cap, trussing himself‡.*

Honey. Boniface, make an end of my cloak and
cap.

Bon. I have despatched 'em, sir; both of them
lie flat at your mercy.

Honey. 'Fore God, methinks my joints are
nimbler every morning since I came over than
they were before. In France, when I rise,§ I
was so stiff and so stark, I would ha' sworn my

legs had been wooden pegs; a constable new-
chosen kept not such a peripatetical gait: but
now I'm as limber as an ancient[*] that has
flourished in the rain, and as active as a Norfolk
tumbler.

Bon. You may see what change of pasture is
able to do.

Honey. It makes fat calves in Romney-Marsh,
and lean knaves in London: therefore, Boniface,
keep your ground. God's my pity, my forehead
has more crumples than the back part of a
counsellor's gown, when another rides upon his
neck at the bar. Boniface, take my helmet: give
your mistress my night-cap. Are my antlers swoln
so big, that my biggen pinches my brows? So,
request her to make my head-piece a little wider.

Bon. How much wider, sir?

Honey. I can allow her almost an inch: go, tell
her so, very near an inch.

Bon. [*aside*] If she be a right citizen's wife, now
her husband has given her an inch, she'll take an
ell, or a yard at least. [*Exit.*

Enter JUSTINIANO *like a writing mechanical pedant.*

Honey. Master Parenthesis! *salve, salve, domine.*

---

* *sirrah*] "*Sirrah* Iras, go."

    Shakespeare's *Antony and Cleopatra*, act. v. sc. 2.

    "*Julia.* Why, Ile tell thee, *sirrah.*

    Dorigene. No, *sirrah*, you shannot tell me."

       The Two Merry Milke-Maids, 1620, sig. B 4.

And in *The Wit of a Woman*, 1604, Erinta says to
Gianetta, "But harke, *sirra*, tell me one thing, if it fall
out," &c. sig. B.

A female was sometimes addressed "*sirrah*," long after
our author's days: in Etherege's *Man of Mode, or Sir
Fopling Flutter,* 1676, old Bellair says to Harriet, "Adod,
sirrah, I like thy wit well." Act ii. sc. 1.

In the north of Scotland I have frequently heard
persons in the lower ranks of life use the word "*Sirs*,"
when speaking to two or three women.

† *Scene I.*] London. A room in the house of Honeysuckle.

‡ *trussing himself*] i.e. tying the tagged laces which
fastened the breeches to the doublet.

§ *rise*] Or *ris*, was formerly often used for *rose.*

* *ancient*] See note †, p. 211.

Just. Salve tu quoque; jubeo te salvere plurimum.

Honey. No more *plurimums*, if you love me: Latin whole-meats are now minced, and served in for English gallimawfries; let us, therefore, cut out our uplandish neats' tongues, and talk like regenerate Britons.

Just. Your worship is welcome to England: I poured out orisons for your arrival.

Honey. Thanks, good Master Parenthesis: and *que nouvelles?* what news flutters abroad? do jackdaws dung the top of Paul's steeple still?

Just. The more is the pity, if any daws do come into the temple, as I fear they do.

Honey. They say Charing-cross is fallen down since I went to Rochelle: but that's no such wonder; 'twas old, and stood awry, as most part of the world can tell: and though it lack under-propping, yet, like great fellows at a wrestling, when their heels are once flying up, no man will save 'em; down they fall, and there let them lie, though they were bigger than the guard: Charing-cross was old, and old things must shrink, as well as new northern cloth.

Just. Your worship is in the right way, verily; they must so: but a number of better things between Westminster-bridge and Temple-bar, both of a worshipful and honourable erection, are fallen to decay, and have suffered putre-faction, since Charing fell, that were not of half so long standing as the poor wry-necked monument.

Honey. Who's within there? One of you call up your mistress: tell her here's her writing schoolmaster.—I had not thought, Master Paren-thesis, you had been such an early stirrer.

Just. Sir, your vulgar and fourpenny penmen, that, like your London sempsters, keep open shop and sell learning by retail, may keep their beds and lie at their pleasure; but we, that edify in private and traffic by wholesale, must be up with the lark, because, like country attorneys, we are to shuffle up many matters in a forenoon. Certes, Master Honeysuckle, I would sing *Laus Deo,* so I may but please all those that come under my fingers; for it is my duty and function, perdy, to be fervent in my vocation.

Honey. Your hand: I am glad our city has so good, so necessary, and so laborious a member in it; we lack painful and expert penmen amongst us. Master Parenthesis, you teach many of our merchants, sir, do you not?

Just. Both wives, maids, and daughters; and I thank God the very worst of them lie by very good men's sides: I pick out a poor living amongst 'em, and I am thankful for it.

Honey. Trust me, I am not sorry: how long have you exercised this quality?

Just. Come Michael-tide next, this thirteen year.

Honey. And how does my wife profit under you, sir? hope you to do any good upon her?

Just. Master Honeysuckle, I am in great hope she shall fructify: I will do my best, for my part; I can do no more than another man can.

Honey. Pray, sir, ply her, for she is capable of any thing.

Just. So far as my poor talent can stretch, it shall not be hidden from her.

Honey. Does she hold her pen well yet?

Just. She leans somewhat too hard upon her pen yet, sir, but practice and animadversion will break her from that.

Honey. Then she grubs her pen?

Just. It's but my pains to mend the neb again.

Honey. And whereabouts is she now, Master Parenthesis? She was talking of you this morning, and commending you in her bed, and told me she was past her letters.

Just. Truly, sir, she took her letters very suddenly, and is now in her minims.

Honey. I would she were in her crotchets too, Master Parenthesis: ha, ha! I must talk merrily, sir.

Just. Sir, so long as your mirth be void of all squirrility,* 'tis not unfit for your calling. I trust, ere few days be at an end, to have her fall to her joining, for she has her letters *ad unguem;* her A, her great B, and her great C, very right; D and E delicate; her double F of a good length, but that it straddles a little too wide; at the G very cunning.

Honey. Her H is full, like mine; a goodly big H.

Just. But her double L is well; her O of a rea-sonable size; at her P and Q, neither merchant's daughter, alderman's wife, young country gentle-woman, nor courtier's mistress, can match her.

Honey. And how her U?

Just. U, sir! she fetches up U best of all; her single U she can fashion two or three ways, but her double U is as I would wish it.

Honey. And, faith, who takes it faster,—my wife or Mistress Tenterhook?

Just. O, your wife, by odds; she'll take more in one hour than I can fasten either upon Mistress Tenterhook, or Mistress Wafer, or Mistress Flap-dragon the brewer's wife, in three.

---

* *squirrility*] A corrupt form of *scurrility,* sometimes found in old writers.

Enter MISTRESS HONEYSUCKLE.

Honey. Do not thy cheeks burn, sweet chuckaby, for we are talking of thee?

Mist. Honey. No, goodness, I warrant: you have few citizens speak well of their wives behind their backs; but to their faces they'll cog worse and be more suppliant than clients that sue in *forma paper.**—How does my master? troth, I am a very truant: have you your ruler about you, master? for, look you, I go clean awry.

[*Shows copy-book.*

Just. A small fault; most of my scholars do so.—Look you, sir, do not you think your wife will mend? mark her dashes, and her strokes, and her breakings, and her bendings.

Honey. She knows what I have promised her, if she do mend.—Nay, by my fay, Jude, this is well, if you would not fly out thus, but keep your line.

Mist. Honey. I shall in time, when my hand is in.—Have you a new pen for me, master? for, by my truly, my old one is stark naught, and will cast no ink.—Whither are you going, lamb?

Honey. To the Custom-house, to the 'Change, to my warehouse, to divers places.

Mist. Honey. Good Cole, tarry not past eleven, for you turn my stomach then from my dinner.

Honey. I will make more haste home than a stipendiary Switzer does after he's paid.—Fare you well, Master Parenthesis.

Mist. Honey. I am so troubled with the rheum too! Mouse, what's good for't?

Honey. How often have I told you you must get a patch!† I must hence. [*Exit.*

Mist. Honey. I think, when all's ‡ done, I must follow his counsel, and take a patch; I['d] have had one long ere this, but for disfiguring my face: yet I had noted that a mastic patch upon some women's temples hath been the very rheum § of beauty.

---

* *forma paper*] Our early dramatists have a pleasure in making their characters miscall terms of law: *so* Rowley; "I, by my troth, he is now but a Knight under *Forma Papris.*" *When you see mee you know mee*, 1632. Sig. O 3.

† *you must get a patch*] "Even as blacke patches are worne, some for pride, *some to stay the Rheume*, and some to hide the scab," &c. *Jacke Drums Entertainment*, 1616, Sig. I 2.

   "For when they did but happen for to see
     Those that with Rhume a little troubled be
     Weare on their faces a round mastick patch,
   Their fondness I perceiv'd sometime to catch
   That for a Fashion."

     Wither's *Abuses Stript and Whipt*, B. ii. Sat. I, p. 171, ed. 1615.

‡ *all's*] Some copies of the old ed. "*all.*"

§ *rheum*]. A misprint, I believe: but qy. for what?

Just. Is he departed? is old Nestor marched into Troy?

Mist. Honey. Yes, you mad Greek; the gentleman's gone.

Just. Why, then, clap up copy-books, down with pens, hang up ink-horns: and now, my sweet Honeysuckle, see what golden-winged bee from Hybla flies humming with *crura thymo plena,** which he will empty in the hive of your bosom.

[*Giving letter.*

Mist. Honey. From whom?

Just. At the skirt of that sheet, in black work, is wrought his name: break not up the wild-fowl† till anon, and then feed upon him all night for their money, and walk to your gardens with young men i'the daytime for your pleasure. O you delicate damnations! you do but as I would do: were I the properest, sweetest, plumpest, cherry-checked, coral-lipped woman in a kingdom, I would not dance after one man's pipe.

Mist. Honey. And why?

Just. Especially after an old man's.

Mist. Honey. And why, pray?

Just. Especially after an old citizen's.

Mist. Honey. Still, and why?

Just. Marry, because the suburbs, and those without the bars, have more privilege than they within the freedom. What need one woman dote upon one man? or one man be mad, like Orlando, for one woman?

Mist. Honey. Troth, 'tis true, considering how much flesh is in every shambles.

Just. Why should I long to eat of baker's bread only, when there's so much sifting, and bolting, and grinding in every corner of the city? Men and women are born, and come running into the world faster than coaches do into Cheapside upon Simon and Jude's day; and are eaten up by death faster than mutton and porridge in a term-time. Who would pin their hearts to any sleeve? This world is like a mint: we are no sooner cast into

---

* *crura thymo plena*]

   "At fessam multa referunt se nocte minores,
     Crura thymo plenæ." Virgil. Georg. iv. 181.

† *break not up the wildfowl*] To *break up* was an old term for carving. (So in Shakespeare's *Love's Labour's Lost*, act iv. sc. 1, "*Break up* this capon," i. e. Open this letter.)

the fire, taken out again, hammered, stamped, and made current, but presently we are changed: the new money, like a new drab, is catched at by Dutch, Spanish, Welsh, French, Scotch, and English; but the old cracked King-Harry groats are shovelled up, feel bruising and battering, clipping and melting,—they smoke for't.

Mist. Honey. The world's an arrant naughty pack I see, and is a very scurvy world.

Just. Scurvy! worse than the conscience of a broom-man, that carries out new ware and brings home old shoes. A naughty pack! why, there's no minute, no thought of time passes, but some villany or other is a-brewing. Why, even now-now, at holding up of this finger, and before the turning down of this, some are murdering, some lying with their maids, some picking of pockets, some cutting purses, some cheating, some weighing out bribes; in this city some wives are cuckolding some husbands; in yonder village some farmers are now-now grinding the jawbones of the poor. Therefore, sweet scholar, sugared Mistress Honeysuckle, take summer before you, and lay hold of it: why, even now must you and I hatch an egg of iniquity.

Mist. Honey. Troth, master, I think thou wilt prove a very knave.

Just. It's the fault of many that fight under this band.

Mist. Honey. I shall love a puritan's face the worse, whilst I live, for that copy of thy countenance.

Just. We are all weathercocks, and must follow the wind of the present, from the bias.

Mist. Honey. Change a bowl, then.*

Just. I will so; and now for a good cast: there's the knight, Sir Goeling Glowworm.

Mist. Honey. He's a knight made out of wax.†

Just. He took up silks upon his bond, I confess; nay, more, he's a knight in print: but let his knighthood be of what stamp it will, from him come I, to entreat you, and Mistress Wafer, and Mistress Tenterhook, being both my scholars, and your honest pew-fellows, to meet him this afternoon at the Rhenish wine-house i'the Stilliard.‡ Captain Whirlpool will be there;

young Linstock, the alderman's son and heir, there too. Will you steal forth, and taste of a Dutch bun and a keg of sturgeon?

Mist. Honey. What excuse shall I coin now?

Just. Phew! excuses! You must to the Pawn to buy lawn; * to Saint Martin's for lace; to the garden; to the glass-house; to your gossip's; to the poulter's:† else take out an old ruff, and go to your sempster's. Excuses! why, they are more ripe than medlars at Christmas.

Mist. Honey. I'll come. The hour!

Just. Two: the way through Paul's; every wench take a pillar, there clap on your masks: your men will be behind you; and, before your prayers be half done, be before you, and man you out at several doors. You'll be there?

Mist. Honey. If I breathe.

Just. Farewell. [*Exit* MIST. HONEY.
So: now must I go set the t'other wenches the self-same copy: a rare schoolmaster for all kind

Marchantes of Almaine," &c. Stow's *Survey of London*, 1598, p. 184.

"Stilliard is a place in London, where the fraternitie of the Easterling Merchants, otherwise the Merchants of the Haunse and Almaine, are wont to have their abode. It is so called Stilliard, of a broad place or court wherein steele was much sould, q. *Steelyard*, upon which that house is now founded." Minshew's *Guide into Tongues*, 1617.

"They [The Hans Town Merchants] were permitted to sell Rhenish wine by retail." Malcolm's *London*, vol. i. p. 48.

Compare with the passage in the text;

"Men when they are idle, and know not what to do, saith one, Let us go *to the stillyard and drinke Rhenish wine*, &c." Nash's *Pierce Pennilesse*, Sig. E 2, ed. 1595.

"Who would let a Cit (whose teeth are rotten out with sweet meates his mother brings him from goshippings) breathe upon her vernish for the promise of a dry neat's tongue and *a pottle of Rhenish at the stillyard*, when she may command a blade to toss and tumble her?" Nabbes's *Bride*, 1640, Sig. E.

To this note I now (1857) add, on the authority of Mr. P. Cunningham's *Handbook of London*—that the Steel-yard, Stelyard, or Stilliard (in Upper Thames Street, in the ward of Dowgate) appears to have been so called from its being the place where the King's steelyard, or beam, was erected for weighing the tonnage of goods imported into London.—In the present passage the old ed. has "Stillyard," but twice afterwards it has "*Stilliard*."

* *to the Pawn to buy lawn*] So in the curious poetical dialogue '*Tis merry when gossips meet*, 1609, the Wife says:

"In truth (kind cousse) my comming's from the *Pawn*,
But I protest I lost my labour there:
A Gentleman promist to give me *lawne*,
And did not meet me, which he well shall heare."
Stanza 2nd.

The *Pawn* (*Bahn*, Germ., a path or walk; *Baan*, Dutch, a pathway) was a corridor, which formed a kind of Bazaar, in the Royal Exchange (Gresham's). See Cunningham's *Handbook of London*.

† *poulter's*] i. e. poulterer's.

---

* *from the bias.*

MIST. HONEY. *Change a bowl, then*] Here the metaphor is, of course, from the game of bowls.

† *He's a knight made out of wax*] So in Shakespeare's *Romeo and Juliet*, act i. sc. 3, the Nurse says of Paris, "Why, he's a man of wax."

‡ *the Rhenish wine-house i'the Stilliard*] "Next to this lane on the East [Cosin Lane, Dowgate Ward] is the Stele house, or *Stele yards* (as they terme it), a place for

of hands I. O, what strange curses are poured
down with one blessing!
Do all tread on the heel? Have all the art
To hoodwink wise men thus? and, like those
builders
Of Babel's tower, to speak unknown tongues,
Of all, save by their husbands, understood?
Well, if, as ivy 'bout the elm does twine,
All wives love clipping,* there's no fault in
mine.
But if the world lay speechless, even the dead
Would rise, and thus cry out from yawning graves,
Women make men or fools, or beasts, or slaves.

[*Exit.*

SCENE II.*

Enter EARL *and* MISTRESS BIRDLIME.

Earl. Her answer! talk in music; will she
come?

Bird. O, my sides ache in my loins, in my
bones: I ha' more need of a posset of sack, and
lie in my bed and sweat, than to talk in music.
No honest woman would run hurrying up and
down thus, and undo herself for a man of honour,
without reason. I am so lame, every foot that I
set to the ground went to my heart; I thought I
had been at mum-chance,† my bones rattled so
with jaunting: had it not been for a friend in a
corner [*Takes aqua-vitæ*], I had kicked up my
heels.

Earl. Minister comfort to me,—will she come?

Bird. All the castles of comfort that I can
put you into is this, that the jealous wittol her
husband came, like a mad ox, bellowing in whilst
I was there. O, I ha' lost my sweet breath with
trotting.

Earl. Death to my heart! her husband! What
saith he?

Bird. The frize-jerkin rascal out with his purse,
and called me plain bawd to my face.

Earl. Affliction to me! then thou spak'st not
to her?

Bird. I spake to her, as clients do to lawyers
without money, to no purpose; but I'll speak
with him, and hamper him too, if ever he fall
into my clutches: I'll make the yellow-hammer
her husband know (for all he's an Italian) that
there's a difference between a cogging bawd and
an honest motherly gentlewoman. Now, what

cold whetstones lie over your stomacher? will
you have some of my *aqua?* Why, my lord!

Earl. Thou hast kill'd me with thy words.

Bird. I see bashful lovers and young bullocks
are knocked down at a blow. Come, come, drink
this draught of cinnamon-water, and pluck up
your spirits; up with 'em, up with 'em. Do you
hear? the whiting-mop* has nibbled.

Earl. Ha!

Bird. O, I thought I should fetch you: you
can "ha" at that; I'll make you hem anon. As
I'm a sinner, I think you'll find the sweetest,
sweetest bedfellow of her. O, she looks so
sugaredly, so simperingly, so gingerly, so amorously, so amiably! Such a red lip, such a white
forehead, such a black eye, such a full cheek, and
such a goodly little nose, now she's in that
French gown, Scotch falls, Scotch bum, and
Italian head-tire you sent her, and is such an
enticing she-witch, carrying the charms of your
jewels about her! O!

Earl. Did she receive them? speak,—here's
golden keys   [*Giving money.*
To unlock thy lips,—did she vouchsafe to take
them?

Bird. Did she vouchsafe to take them? there's
a question! you shall find she did vouchsafe.
The troth is, my lord, I got her to my house,
there she put off her own clothes, my lord, and
put on your's, my lord; provided her a coach;
searched the middle aisle in Paul's,† and with
three Elizabeth twelve-pences pressed three
knaves, my lord; hired three liveries in Long-
lane,‡ to man her: for all which, so God mend
me, I'm to pay this night before sun-set.

Earl. This shower shall fill them all: rain in
their laps
What golden drops thou wilt.

Bird. Alas, my lord, I do but receive it with

---

* *clipping*] i. e. embracing.
† *Scene II.*] The same. A room in the house of the Earl.
‡ *mum-chance*] A game played either with dice or
cards: Mistress Birdlime alludes to the former method.

---

* *whiting-mop*] i. e. young whiting,—a cant term for a
nice young woman, a tender creature.
† *searched the middle aisle in Paul's, and with three
Elizabeth twelve-pences pressed three knaves*] Persons of
every description, with a strange want of reverence for
the sanctity of the spot, used daily to frequent the body
of old St. Paul's. There the young gallant gratified his
vanity by strutting about in the most fashionable attire;
there the politician discussed the latest news; there he
who could not afford to dine loitered during the dinner-
hour; *there the servant out of place came to be engaged*;
there the pickpocket found the best opportunities for
the exercise of his talents, &c.
‡ *hired three liveries in Long-lane*] "The lane, truelie
called Long," (Stow's *Survey*, p. 311, ed. 1598,) running
out of Aldersgate-street, and falling into West Smith-
field, abounded in shops where second-hand apparel
might be procured.

one hand, to pay it away with another: I'm but your baily.

Earl. Where is she?

Bird. In the green-velvet chamber: the poor sinful creature pants like a pigeon under the hands of a hawk; therefore use her like a woman, my lord; use her honestly, my lord, for, alas, she's but a novice and a very green thing.

Earl. Farewell: I'll in unto her.

Bird. Fie upon't, that were not for your honour; you know gentlewomen use to come to lords' chambers, and not lords to the gentle-women's: I'd not have her think you are such a rank rider. Walk you here: I'll beckon; you shall see I'll fetch her with a wet finger.

Earl. Do so.

Bird. Hist! why, sweetheart, Mistress Justiniano! why, pretty soul, tread softly, and come into this room: here be rushes;* you need not fear the creaking of your cork shoes.

Enter MISTRESS JUSTINIANO.

So, well said!†—There's his honour.—I have business, my lord: very now the marks are set up, I'll get me twelve score off, and give aim.‡
              [*Exit.*

Earl. You're welcome, sweet, you're welcome.
   Bless my hand
With the soft touch of yours. Can you be cruel
To one so prostrate to you? even my heart,
My happiness, and state lie at your feet.
My hopes me flatter'd that the field was won,
That you had yielded (though you conquer me),
And that all marble scales, that barr'd your eyes
From throwing light on mine, were quite ta'en off
By the cunning woman's hand that works for me:
Why, therefore, do you wound me now with frowns?
Why do you fly me? Do not exercise
The art of woman on me; I'm already
Your captive, sweet. Are those your hate or fears?

Mist. Just. I wonder lust can hang at such white hairs.

Earl. You give my love ill names, it is not lust;
Lawless desires well temper'd may seem just.
A thousand mornings with the early sun,
Mine eyes have 'fore § your windows watch'd to steal
Brightness from those: as oft upon the days
That consecrated to devotion are,
Within the holy temple have I stood

---

* *rushes*] See note †, p. 21.
† *well said!*] In our early writers is often equivalent to *Well done!*   ‡ *give aim*] See note *, p. 20.
§ *'fore*] The old ed. "from."

Disguis'd, waiting your presence; and when your hands
Went up towards heaven to draw some blessing down,
Mine, as if all my nerves by yours did move,
Begg'd in dumb signs some pity for my love:
And thus being feasted only with your sight,
I went more pleas'd than sick men with fresh health,
Rich men with honour, beggars do with wealth.

Mist. Just. Part now so pleas'd; for now you more enjoy me.

Earl. O, you do wish me physic to destroy me!

Mist. Just. I have already leap'd beyond the bounds
Of modesty, in piecing out my wings
With borrow'd feathers: but you sent a sorceress
So perfect in her trade, that did so lively
Breathe forth your passionate accents, and could draw
A lover languishing so piercingly,
That her charms wrought upon me, and, in pity
Of your sick heart, which she did counterfeit
(O, she's a subtle beldam!), see, I cloth'd
My limbs, thus player-like, in rich attires
Not fitting mine estate; and am come forth,—
But why I know not.

Earl. Will you love me?

Mist. Just. Yes;
If you can clear me of a debt that's due
But to one man, I'll pay my heart to thee.

Earl. Who's that?

Mist. Just. My husband.

Earl. Um.

Mist. Just. The sum's so great,
I know a kingdom cannot answer it;
And therefore I beseech you, good my lord,
To take this gilding off, which is your own,
And henceforth cease to throw out golden hooks
To choke mine honour: though my husband's poor,
I'll rather beg for him than be your whore.

Earl. 'Gainst beauty you plot treason, if you suffer
Tears to do violence to so fair a cheek.
That face was ne'er made to look pale with want:
Dwell here, and be the sovereign of my fortunes:
Thus shall you go attir'd.

Mist. Just. Till lust be tir'd.
I must take leave, my lord.

Earl. Sweet creature, stay.
My coffers shall be yours, my servants yours,
Myself will be your servant; and I swear
By that which I hold dear in you, your beauty

(And which I'll not profane), you shall live here
As free from base wrong as you are from blackness,
So you will deign but let me enjoy your sight.
Answer me, will you?

Mist. Just. I will think upon't.

Earl. Unless you shall perceive that all my
    thoughts
And all my actions be to you devoted,
And that I very justly earn your love,
Let me not taste it.

Mist. Just. I will think upon it.

Earl. But when you find my merits of full
    weight,
Will you accept their worth?

Mist. Just. I'll think upon't.
I'd speak with the old woman.

Earl. She shall come.—
Joys, that are born unlook'd for, are born dumb.
                        [*Exit.*

Mist. Just. Poverty, thou bane of chastity,
Poison of beauty, broker of maidenheads!
I see when force nor wit can scale the hold,
Wealth must; she'll ne'er be won that defies gold:
But lives there such a creature? O, 'tis rare
To find a woman chaste that's poor and fair.

Re-enter BIRDLIME.

Bird. Now, lamb, has not his honour dealt
like an honest nobleman with you? I can tell
you, you shall not find him a Templar, nor one of
these cogging Catherine-pear-coloured* beards,
that by their good wills would have no pretty
woman scape them.

Mist. Just. Thou art a very bawd, thou art a
devil
Cast in a reverend shape: thou stale damnation,†
Why hast thou me entic'd from mine own
    paradise,
To steal fruit in a barren wilderness?

Bird. Bawd, and devil, and stale damnation!
Will women's tongues, like bakers' legs, never go
straight?

Mist. Just. Had thy Circæan magic me trans-
    form'd
Into that sensual shape for which thou conjur'st,
And I were turn'd common venturer,
I could not love this old man.

Bird. This old man, um! this old man! do
his hoary hairs stick in your stomach? yet,

methinks, his silver hairs should move you: they
may serve to make you bodkins. Does his age
grieve you? Fool! is not old wine wholesomest,
old pippins toothsomest, old wood burn brightest,
old linen wash whitest? Old soldiers, sweetheart,
are surest, and old lovers are soundest: I ha'
tried both.

Mist. Just. So will not I.

Bird. You'd have some young perfumed
beardless gallant* board you, that spits all his
brains out at's tongue's end, would you not?

Mist. Just. No, none at all; not any.

Bird. None at all! what do you make there,
then? why are you a burden to the world's
conscience, and an eye-sore to well-given men?
I dare pawn my gown, and all the beds in my
house, and all the gettings in Michaelmas-term
next, to a tavern-token,† that thou shalt never be
an innocent.

Mist. Just. Who are so?

Bird. Fools: why, then, are you so precise?
Your husband's down the wind; and will you,
like a haggler's arrow, be down the weather?
Strike whilst the iron is hot. A woman, when
there be roses in her cheeks, cherries on her lips,
civet in her breath, ivory in her teeth, lilies in
her hand, and liquorice in her heart, why, she's
like a play; if new, very good company, very
good company; but if stale, like old Jeronimo,
go by, go by:‡ therefore, as I said before, strike.
Besides, you must think that the commodity of
beauty was not made to lie dead upon any young
woman's hands: if your husband have given up
his cloak, let another take measure of you in his
jerkin; for as the cobbler in the night-time
walks with his lantern, the merchant and the

---

* *gallant*] The old ed. "*Gallants.*"

† *a tavern-token*] There being a scarcity of small change,
tradesmen were allowed to coin *tokens*—promissory pieces
of brass or copper, of the value of a farthing. Reed
(note on the First Part of *The Honest Whore*, act i. sc. 4,)
thinks they were called *tavern-tokens*, because they were
"probably at first coined chiefly by tavern keepers;"
but Gifford (note on Ben Jonson's *Works*, vol. i. p. 29,)
observes, "that most of them would travel to the tavern
may be easily supposed, and hence, perhaps, the name."

‡ *like old Jeronimo, go by, go by*] An allusion to a pas-
sage in Kyd's *Spanish Tragedy*, which has been ridiculed
by a host of poets;
"*Hieronimo.* Justice, O, justice to Hieronimo!
Lorenzo. Back! see'st thou not the king is busie?
Hieronimo. O, is he so?
King. Who is he that interrupts our business?
Hieronimo. Not I.—Hieronimo, beware; *got by, goe by.*"
                  Sig. G 4. Allde's ed. n. d.
It may be just necessary to add, that the *Spanish
Tragedy* is a continuation of *The First Part of Jeronimo*,
which was most probably also the work of Kyd.

---

* *Catherine-pear-coloured*] i. e. red.

† *stale damnation*] So Juliet, in Shakespeare's *Romeo
and Juliet*, act iii. sc. 5; and Malevole, in *The Malcontent*,
act v. sc. 2 (see the present edition); use "ancient damnation" as a term of reproach.

lawyer with his link, and the courtier with his torch, so every lip has his lettuce to himself; the lob has his lass, the collier his dowdy, the western-man his pug, the serving-man his punk, the student his nun in White-friars, the puritan his sister, and the lord his lady ; which worshipful vocation may fall upon you, if you'll but strike whilst the iron is hot.

Mist. Just. Witch, thus I break thy spells: were I kept brave *
On a king's cost, I am but a king's slave. [*Exit.*

Bird. I see, that, as Frenchmen love to be bold, Flemings to be drunk, Welshmen to be called Britons, and Irishmen to be costermongers, so cockneys, especially she cockneys, love not aqua-vitæ when 'tis good for them.

Enter MONOPOLY.†

Mon. Saw you my uncle?

Bird. I saw him even now going the way of all flesh, that's to say, towards the kitchen. Here's a letter to your worship from the party.
[*Giving letter.*

Mon. What party?

Bird. The Tenterhook, your wanton.

Mon. From her! phew! pray thee, stretch me no more upon your Tenterhook : pox on her! are there no pothecaries i' the town to send her physic bills to, but me? She's not troubled with the green-sickness still, is she?

Bird. The yellow jaundice, as the doctor tells me. Troth, she's as good a peat! she is fallen away so, that she's nothing but bare skin and bone ; for the turtle so mourns for you!

Mon. In black?

Bird. In black! you shall find both black and blue, if you look under her eyes.

Mon. Well, sing over her ditty when I'm in tune.

Bird. Nay, but will you send her a box of mithridatum and dragon-water,—I mean some restorative words? Good Master Monopoly, you know how welcome you're to the city; and will you, Master Monopoly, keep out of the city? I know you cannot : would you saw how the poor gentlewoman lies!

Mon. Why, how lies she?

Bird. Troth, as the way lies over Gads-hill, very dangerous : you would pity a woman's case,

---

* *brave*] i. e. finely dressed.
† *Enter* MONOPOLY.·
Mon. Saw you my uncle?] Qy. is the Earl the uncle of Monopoly? and the latter, in consequence of that relationship, now under the Earl's roof? Or were the audience to *suppose*, after Mrs. Justiniano's *exit*, a change of place?

---

if you saw her. Write to her some treatise of pacification.

Mon. I'll write to her to-morrow.

Bird. To-morrow! she'll not sleep, then, but tumble ; an if she might have it to-night, it would better please her.

Mon. Perhaps I'll do't to-night: farewell.

Bird. If you do't to-night, it would better please her than to-morrow.

Mon. God's so, dost hear! I'm to sup this night at the Lion in Shoreditch with certain gallants : canst thou not draw forth some delicate face that I ha' not seen, and bring it thither? wut thou?

Bird. All the painters in London shall not fit for colour as I can : but we shall have some swaggering?

Mon. All as civil, by this light, as lawyers.

Bird. But, I tell you, she's not so common as lawyers, that I mean to betray to your table; for, as I'm a sinner, she's a knight's cousin,—a Yorkshire gentlewoman, and only speaks a little broad, but of very good carriage.

Mon. Nay, that's no matter ; we can speak as broad as she : but wut bring her?

Bird. You shall call her cousin, do you see? two men shall wait upon her, and I'll come in by chance : but shall not the party be there?

Mon. Which party?

Bird. The writer of that simple hand.

Mon. Not for as many angels as there be letters in her paper: speak not of me to her, nor our meeting, if you love me. Wut come?

Bird. Mum, I'll come.

Mon. Farewell.

Bird. Good Master Monopoly, I hope to see you one day a man of great credit.

Mon. If I be, I'll build chimneys with tobacco, but I'll smoke some : and be sure, Birdlime, I'll stick wool upon thy back.

Bird. Thanks, sir, I know you will; for all the kindred of the Monopolies are held to be great fleecers.   [*Exeunt.*

SCENE III.*

Enter SIR GOSLING GLOWWORM, LINSTOCK, WHIRLPOOL; *and the three* Citizens' Wives, *masked, viz.,* MISTRESS HONEYSUCKLE, MISTRESS WAFER, *and* MISTRESS TENTERHOOK.

Sir Gos. So, draw those curtains, and let's see the pictures under 'em.   [*The ladies unmask.*]

Lin. Welcome to the Stilliard, fair ladies.

---

* *Scene III.*] The same. A room in the Rhenish wine-house in the Stilliard. See note ‡, p. 217.

Mist. Honey., Mist. Wafer., Mist. Ten. Thanks, good Master Linstock.

Whirl. Hans, some wine, Hans!

Enter HANS *with cloth and buns.*

Hans. Yaw, yaw, you sall hebben it, mester: old vine or new vine?

Sir Gos. Speak, women.

Mist. Honey. New wine, good Sir Gosling:—wine in the must, good Dutchman, for must is best for us women.

Hans. New vine,—voll; two pots of new vine!
                              [*Exit.*

Mist. Honey. An honest butterbox; for if it be old, there's none of it comes into my belly.

Mist. Wafer. Why, Tenterhook, pray thee, let's dance friskin, and be merry.

Lin. Thou art so troubled with Monopolies; they so hang at thy heart-strings.

Mist. Ten. Pox o' my heart, then.

Re-enter HANS *with wine.*

Mist. Honey. Ay, and mine too: if any courtier of them all set up his gallows there, wench, use him as thou dost thy pantables,* scorn to let him kiss thy heel, for he feeds thee with nothing but court-holy-bread,† good words, and cares not for thee.—Sir Gosling, will you taste a Dutch what's you call 'em?

Mist. Wafer. Here, Master Linstock, half mine is yours: bun, bun, bun, bun.

Just. [*within*] Which room? where are they?—Wo-ho, ho, ho, so-ho, boys!

Sir Gos. 'Sfoot, who's that? lock our room.

Just. [*within*] Not till I am in; and then lock out the devil, though he come in the shape of a puritan.

Enter JUSTINIANO *disguised as before.*

Mist. Honey., Mist. Wafer., Mist. Ten. Schoolmaster, welcome; welcome, in troth.

Just. Who would not be scratched with the briers and brambles to have such burs sticking on his breeches?—Save you, gentlemen!—O noble knight!

Sir Gos. More wine, Hans!

Just. Am not I, gentlemen, a ferret of the right hair, that can make three conies bolt at a clap into your purse-nets?‡ Ha, little do their three husbands dream what copies I am setting their wives now: were't not a rare jest, if they should come sneaking upon us, like a horrible noise of fiddlers?§

---

* *pantables*] i.e. slippers.

† *court-holy-bread*] Or, as we more usually find it, *court-holy-water*,—i. e. flattery, insincere compliments.

‡ *purse-nets*] See note *, p. 150.

§ *noise of fiddlers*] i. e. company of fiddlers.

Mist. Honey. 'Troth, I'd not care; let 'em come; I'd tell 'em we'd ha' none of their dull music.

Mist. Wafer. [*drinking*] Here, Mistress Tenterhook.

Mist. Ten. Thanks, good Mistress Wafer.

Just. Who's there? peepers, intelligencers, eavesdroppers?

Omnes. Uds foot, throw a pot at's head!

Just. O Lord! O gentlemen, knight, ladies that may be, citizens' wives that are, shift for yourselves, for a pair of your husbands' heads are knocking together with Hans his, and inquiring for you.

Omnes. Keep the door locked.

Mist. Honey. O, ay, do, do; and let Sir Gosling (because he has been in the Low Countries) swear *Gots Sacrament,* and drive 'em away with broken Dutch.

Just. Here's a wench has simple sparks in her: she's my pupil, gallants.—[*Aside*] Good God! I see a man is not sure that his wife is in the chamber, though his own fingers hung on the padlock: trap-doors, false drabs, and spring-locks, may cozen a covey of constables. How the silly husbands might here ha' been gulled with Flemish money!—Come, drink up Rhine, Thames, and Meander dry; there's nobody.

Mist. Honey. Ah, thou ungodly master!

Just. I did but make a false fire, to try your valour, because you cried "Let'em come." By this glass of woman's wine, I would not ha' seen their spirits walk here, to be dubbed deputy of a ward, I: they would ha' chronicled me for a fox in a lamb's skin. But, come; is this merry midsummer-night agreed upon? when shall it be? where shall it be?

Lin. Why, faith, to-morrow at night.

Whirl. We'll take a coach and ride to Ham or so.

Mist. Ten. O, fie upon't, a coach! I cannot abide to be jolted.

Mist. Wafer. Yet most of your citizens' wives love jolting.

Sir Gos. What say you to Blackwall or Limehouse?

Mist. Honey. Every room there smells too much of tar.

Lin. Let's to mine host Dogbolt's at Brainford,* then: there you are out of eyes, out of ears; private rooms, sweet linen, winking attendance, and what cheer you will.

Omnes. Content, to Brainford.

---

* *Brainford*] i. e. Brentford. (I retain the old spelling on account of the pun in p. 243.)

Mist. Wafer. Ay, ay, let's go by water; for, Sir Gosling, I have heard you say you love to go by water.

Mist. Honey. But, wenches, with what pulleys shall we slide, with some cleanly excuse, out of our husbands' suspicion, being gone westward for smelts * all night?

Just. That's the block now we all stumble at: wind up that string well, and all the consort's† in tune.

Mist. Honey. Why, then, goodman scraper, 'tis wound up, I have it.—Sirrah Wafer, thy child's at nurse :—if you that are the men could provide some wise ass that could keep his countenance,—

Just. Nay, if he be an ass, he will keep his countenance.

Mist. Honey. Ay, but I mean, one that could set out his tale with audacity, and say that the child were sick, and ne'er stagger at it; that last should serve all our feet.

Whirl. But where will that wise ass be found now?

Just. I see I'm born still to draw dun out o'the mire‡ for you; that wise beast will I be. I'll be that ass that shall groan under the burden of that abominable lie: heaven pardon me, and pray God the infant be not punished for't! Let me see : I 'll break out in some filthy shape like a thrasher, or a thatcher, or a sowgelder, or something : and speak dreamingly, and swear how the child pukes, and eats nothing (as perhaps it does not), and lies at the mercy of God (as all children and old folks do); and then, scholar Wafer, play you your part.

Mist. Wafer. Fear not me for a veney§ or two.

Just. Where will you meet i'the morning?

Sir Gos. At some tavern near the water-side, that's private.

Just. The Greyhound, the Greyhound in Blackfriars, an excellent rendezvous.

Lin. Content, the Greyhound by eight.

Just. And then you may whip forth, two first, and two next, on a sudden, and take boat at Bridewell-dock most privately.

Omnes. Be't so : a good place.

Just. I'll go make ready my rustical properties.* Let me see :—scholar, hie you home, for your child shall be sick within this half hour.　　[*Exit.*

Enter BIRDLIME.

Mist. Honey. 'Tis the uprightest-dealing man!— God's my pity, who's yonder?

Bird. I'm bold to press myself under the colours of your company, hearing that gentlewoman was in the room.—[*To Mist. Ten.*] A word, mistress.

Mist. Ten. How now! what says he?

Sir Gos. Zounds, what's she? a bawd, by the Lord, is't not?

Mist. Wafer. No, indeed, Sir Gosling; she's a very honest woman and a midwife.

Mist. Ten. At the Lion in Shoreditch? and would he not read it? nor write to me? I'll poison his supper.

Bird. But no words that I bewrayed him.

Mist. Ten. Gentlemen, I must be gone; I cannot stay, in faith: pardon me; I'll meet to-morrow :—come, nurse :—cannot tarry, by this element.

Sir Gos. Mother, you, grannam, drink ere you go.

Bird. I am going to a woman's labour; indeed, sir, cannot stay.

[*Exeunt* MISTRESS TENTERHOOK *and* BIRDLIME.

Mist. Wafer. I hold my life,† the black-bird her husband whistles for her.

---

* *westward for smelts*] A proverbial expression. In 1603 appeared a story-book (which suggested to Shakespeare some of the circumstances in *Cymbeline*) entitled *Westward for Smelts, or the Waterman's Fare of Mad Merry Western Wenches,* &c.

† *consort's*] See note on *Northward Ho,* act ii. sc. i., p. 260.

‡ *to draw dun out o' the mire*] Gifford thus satisfactorily describes a game, the allusion to which in *Romeo and Juliet,* act i. sc iv., had completely puzzled all Shakespeare's commentators. "*Dun is in the mire* is a Christmas gambol, at which I have often played. A log of wood is brought into the midst of the room : this is *Dun,* (the cart-horse,) and a cry is raised, that he is *stuck in the mire.* Two of the company advance, either with or without ropes, to draw him out. After repeated attempts, they find themselves unable to do it, and call for more assistance. The game continues till all the company take part in it, when Dun is extricated of course ; and the merriment arises from the awkward and affected efforts of the rustics to lift the log, and from sundry arch contrivances to let the ends of it fall on one another's toes." Note on Ben Jonson's *Works,* vol. vii. p. 283.

§ *veney*] Or *venue,* a technical term for a *hit* or *thrust* in playing with different weapons, was a subject of dispute

between Messrs. Steevens and Malone : Douce has made himself their umpire in his *Illustrations of Shakespeare,* vol. i. p. 233, to which I refer the reader. In fencing, *venue,* the French term, answered to the Italian *stoccata :* see Gifford's note on Ben Jonson, vol. i. p. 39. I wonder that Malone, in his contest with Steevens, failed to quote the following passage of a play which he must surely have read :—

"1 *Law.* Women, look to't, the fencer gives you a *veney.*
2 *Law.* Believe it, he *hits* home."
　　　　　Swetnam, the Woman-hater, 1620, Sig. F 2.

* *properties*] Used here in a theatrical sense—articles necessary for the scene.

† *Mist. Wafer. I hold my life,* &c.] The old ed. prefixes to this speech "*Amb.*," which in early plays often stands for "*Both*": but here it would seem to be a mistake for "*Mab*"; see note on the *Dramatis Personæ* of this play.

Mist. Honey. A reckoning! Break one, break all.

Sir Gos. Here, Hans!—Draw not; I'll draw for all, as I'm true knight.

Mist. Honey. Let him: 'mongst women this does stand for law,
The worthiest man, though he be fool, must draw.
                                        [*Exeunt.*

ACT III.

SCENE I.*

Enter TENTERHOOK *and* MISTRESS TENTERHOOK.

Ten. What book is that, sweetheart?

Mist. Ten. Why, the book of bonds that are due to you.

Ten. Come, what do you with it? why do you trouble yourself to take care about my business?

Mist. Ten. Why, sir, doth not that which concerns you concern me? You told me Monopoly had discharged his bond; I find by the book of accounts here that it is not cancelled. Ere I would suffer such a cheating companion to laugh at me, I'd see him hanged, I. Good sweetheart, as ever you loved me, as ever my bed was pleasing to you, arrest the knave: we were never beholding to him for a pin, but for eating up our victuals: good mouse, enter an action against him.

Ten. In troth, love, I may do the gentleman much discredit; and besides, it may be other actions may fall very heavy upon him.

Mist. Ten. Hang him! to see the dishonesty of the knave!

Ten. O wife, good words: a courtier, a gentleman.

Mist. Ten. Why may not a gentleman be a knave? that were strange, in faith: but, as I was a-saying, to see the dishonesty of him that would never come, since he received the money, to visit us! You know, Master Tenterhook, he hath hung long upon you: Master Tenterhook, as I am virtuous, you shall arrest him.

Ten. Why, I know not when he will come to town.

Mist. Ten. He's in town; this night he sups at the Lion in Shoreditch: good husband, enter your action, and make haste to the Lion presently. There's an honest fellow, Sergeant Ambush, will do it in a trice; he never salutes a man in courtesy, but he catches him as if he would arrest him: good heart, let Sergeant Ambush lie in wait for him.

Ten. Well, at thy entreaty I will do it.—[*To*

Servant *within.*] Give me my cloak, there! Buy a link, and meet me at the Counter in Wood-street. —Buss me, Moll.

Mist. Ten. Why, now you love me: I'll go to bed, sweetheart.

Ten. Do not sleep till I come, Moll.

Mist. Ten. No, lamb.   [*Exit* TENTERHOOK.
Baa, sheep! If a woman will be free in this intricate labyrinth of a husband, let her marry a man of a melancholy complexion; she shall not be much troubled with him. By my sooth, my husband hath a hand as dry as his brains, and a breath as strong as six common gardens. Well, my husband is gone to arrest Monopoly: I have dealt with a sergeant privately, to entreat him, pretending that he is my aunt's son: by this means shall I see my young gallant that in this has played his part. When they owe money in the city once, they deal with their lawyers by attorney, follow the court, though the court do them not the grace to allow them their diet. O, the wit of a woman when she is put to the pinch!   [*Exit.*

SCENE II.*

Enter TENTERHOOK, SERGEANT AMBUSH, *and* YEOMAN CLUTCH.

Ten. Come, Sergeant Ambush,—come, Yeoman Clutch: yon's the tavern; the gentleman will come out presently. Thou art resolute?

Amb. Who, I? I carry fire and sword that fight for me, here and here. I know most of the knaves about London, and most of the thieves too, I thank God and good intelligence.

Ten. I wonder thou dost not turn broker, then.

Amb. Phew! I have been a broker already; for I was first a puritan, then a bankrupt, then a broker, then a fencer, and then sergeant: were not these trades would make a man honest?— Peace! the door opes: wheel about, Yeoman Clutch.

---

* *Scene I.*] London. A room in the house of Tenterhook.

* *Scene II.*] The same. Before the Lion in Shoreditch.

Enter WHIRLPOOL, LINSTOCK, *and* MONOPOLY, *unbraced.*

Mon. An e'er I come to sup in this tavern again! there's no more attendance than in a gaol: an there had been a punk or two in the company, then we should not have been rid of the drawers. Now were I in an excellent humour to go to a vaulting-house: I would break down all their glass windows, hew in pieces all their joint-stools, tear [their] silk petticoats, ruffle their periwigs, and spoil their painting,—O the gods, what I could do! I could undergo fifteen bawds, by this darkness; or if I could meet one of these varlets that wear Pannier-alley on their backs, sergeants, I would make them scud so fast from me, that they should think it a shorter way between this and Ludgate, than a condemned cutpurse thinks it between Newgate and Tyburn.

Lin. You are for no action to-night?

Whirl. No, I'll to bed.

Mon. Am not I drunk now? *Implentur veteris Bacchi pinguisque tobacco.**

Whirl. Faith, we are all heated.

Mon. Captain Whirlpool, when wilt come to court and dine with me?

Whirl. One of these days, Frank; but I'll get me two gauntlets for fear I lose my fingers in the dishes: there be excellent shavers, I hear, in the most of your under-offices. I protest I have often come thither, sat down, drawn my knife, and, ere I could say grace, all the meat hath been gone: I have risen and departed thence as hungry as ever came country attorney from Westminster. Good night, honest Frank: do not swagger with the watch, Frank.

[*Exeunt* WHIRLPOOL *and* LINSTOCK.

Ten. So, now they are gone, you may take him.

Amb. Sir, I arrest you.

Mon. Arrest me! at whose suit, you varlets?

Clutch. At Master Tenterhook's.

Mon. Why, you varlets, dare you arrest one of the court?

Amb. Come, will you be quiet, sir?

Mon. Pray thee, good yeoman, call the gentle-men back again. There's a gentleman hath carried a hundred pound of mine, home with him to his lodging, because I dare not carry it over the fields: I'll discharge it presently.

Amb. That's a trick, sir; you would procure a rescue.

Mon. Catchpoll, do you see? I will have the hair of your head and beard shaved off for this, an e'er I catch you at Gray's Inn, by this light, la.

---

* *Implentur, &c.*] "Implentur veteris Bacchi pinguis-que *ferinæ*." Virgil, *Æneid*, l. 215.

Amb. Come, will you march?

Mon. Are you sergeants Christians? Sirrah, thou lookest like a good pitiful rascal, and thou art a tall man too it seems; thou hast backed many a man in thy time, I warrant.

Amb. I have had many a man by the back, sir.

Mon. Well said! in troth, I love your quality: 'las, 'tis needful every man should come by his own. But, as God mend me, gentlemen, I have not one cross* about me, only you two. Might not you let a gentleman pass out of your hands, and say you saw him not? is there not such a kind of mercy in you now and then, my masters? As I live, if you come to my lodging to-morrow morning, I'll give you five brace of angels. Good yeoman, persuade your graduate here: I know some of you to be honest faithful drunkards: respect a poor gentleman in my case.

Ten. Come, it will not serve your turn.—Officers, look to him upon your peril.

Mon. Do you hear, sir? you see I am in the hands of a couple of ravens here: as you are a gentleman, lend me forty shillings: let me not live, if I do not pay you the forfeiture of the whole bond, and never plead conscience.

Ten. Not a penny, not a penny: good night, sir.

[*Exit.*

Mon. Well, a man ought not to swear by any thing, in the hands of sergeants, but by silver; and because my pocket is no lawful justice to minister any such oath unto me, I will patiently encounter the Counter. Which is the dearest ward in prison, sergeant? the Knight's ward?†

Amb. No, sir, the Master's side.†

Mon. Well the knight is above the master, though his table be worse furnished: I'll go thither.

Amb. Come, sir, I must use you kindly: the gentleman's wife that hath arrested you——

Mon. Ay, what of her!

Amb. She says you are her aunt's son.

Mon. I am?

Amb. She takes on so pitifully for your arrest-ing: 'twas much against her will, good gentle-woman, that this affliction lighted upon you.

Mon. She hath reason, if she respect her poor kindred.

Amb. You shall not go to prison.

Mon. Honest sergeant, conscionable officer, did

---

* *I have not one cross about me, only you two*] This quibbling on the word *cross* has occurred before: see note †, p. 196.

† *the Knight's ward?*
AMB. *No, sir, the Master's side*] See note ‡, p. 168.

Q

I forget myself even now, a vice that sticks to me always when I am drunk, to abuse my best friends? Where didst buy this buff? Let me not live, but I'll give thee a good suit of durance.* Wilt thou take my bond, sergeant? Where's a scrivener, a scrivener, good yooman? you shall have my sword and hangers † to pay him.

Amb. Not so, sir; but you shall be prisoner in my house: I do not think but that your cousin will visit you there i'the morning, and take order for you.

Mon. Well said! Was't not a most treacherous part to arrest a man in the night, and when he is almost drunk? when he hath not his wits about him, to remember which of his friends is in the subsidy? Come, did I abuse you, I recant: you are as necessary in a city as tumblers in Norfolk, sumners in Lancashire, or rake-hells in an army.

[Exeunt.

SCENE III.‡

Enter JUSTINIANO *like a collier, and a* Boy.

Just. Buy any small coal, buy any small coal?§

Boy. Collier, collier!

Just. What sayest, boy?

Boy. 'Ware the pillory!

Just. O, boy, the pillory assures many a man that he is no cuckold; for how impossible were

---

it a man should thrust his head through so small a loop-hole, if his forehead were branched, boy!

Boy. Collier, how came the goose to be put upon you, ha?

Just. I'll tell thee. The term lying at Winchester, in Henry the Third's days, and many Frenchwomen coming out of the Isle of Wight thither, (as it hath always been seen, though the Isle of Wight could not of long time neither endure foxes nor lawyers, yet it could brook the more dreadful cockatrice,*) there were many punks in the town, as you know our term is their term. Your farmer, that would spend but threepence on his ordinary, would lavish half-a-crown on his lechory; and many men, calves as they were, would ride in a farmer's foul boots before breakfast: the commonest sinner had more fluttering about her than a fresh punk hath when she comes to a town of garrison or to a university. Captains, scholars, servingmen, jurors, clerks, townsmen, and the black guard,† used all to one ordinary, and most of them were called to a pitiful reckoning; for, before two returns of Michaelmas, surgeons were full of business; the care of most, secrecy, grew as common as lice in Ireland, or as scabs in France. One of my tribe, a collier, carried in his cart forty maimed soldiers to Salisbury, looking as pitifully as Dutchmen first made drunk, then carried to beheading: every one that met him cried "'Ware the goose,‡ collier!" and from that day to this there's a record to be seen at Croydon, how that pitiful waftage, which indeed was virtue in the collier, that all that time would carry no coals, laid this imputation on all the posterity.

Boy. You are full of tricks, collier.

Just. Boy, where dwells Master Wafer?

Boy. Why, here: what wouldst? I am one of his juvenals.

Just. Hath he not a child at nurse at Moreclacke?§

Boy. Yes: dost thou dwell there?

Just. That I do: the child is wondrous sick; I was willed‖ to acquaint thy master and mistress with it.

Boy. I'll up and tell them presently. *[Exit.*

Just. So, if all should fail me, I could turn collier. O the villany of this age! how full of secrecy and silence (contrary to the opinion of the world) have I ever found most women! I

---

* Where didst buy this buff? Let me not live, but I'll give thee a good suit of durance] So, in Shakespeare's *First Part of Henry IV.*, act i. sc. 2, the Prince says to Falstaff with a pun, "And is not a *buff* jerkin a most sweet robe of *durance?*"—*Durance* was a strong and lasting kind of stuff: Mr. Halliwell (*Shakespeare Society Papers*, vol. iii. 35) cites from *The Book of Rates*, ed. 1675, p. 35,—

		£	s.	d.
"Durance, or }	with thred, the yard	..	00	06 08
Duretty. }	with silk, the yard	..	00	10 00."

† *hangers]* i. e. fringed and ornamented loops, attached to the girdle, in which the small sword or dagger was suspended:—

"Mens swords in *hangers* hang, fast by their side."

Taylor the water poet's *Vertue of a Jayle and necessitie of Hanging, Works*, 1630, p. 133.

‡ *Scene III.]* The same. A street: before the house of Wafer.

§ *Buy any small coal, buy any small coal?]* This was the common cry of colliers: so in one of the rarest of plays, *A Knacke to know an honest man*, 1596;

"*Enter* LELIO, *like a colliar.*

Le. Will you buy any coles, fine small coles?" Sig. G.

Let me here make a remark on a note of Gifford. "With our ancestors," says he, "*colliers,* I know not for what reason, lay, like Mrs. Quickly, *under an ill name.*" *Ben Jonson's Works*, vol. ii. p. 169. I believe they were in bad repute because they used to cheat most grossly the purchasers of coals by giving false measure: R. Greene, in his *Pleasant Discovery of the Coosnage of Colliers*, appended to his *Notable Discovery of Coosnage*, 1591, lays open all their knavery.

* cockatrice] A cant name for a prostitute.

† *the black guard]* See note **, p. 8.

‡ *the goose]* See note on *A Cure for a Cuckold*, act iv. sc. 1.

§ *More-clacke]* A common corruption of *Mortlake.*

‖ *willed]* i. e. desired.

have sat a whole afternoon many times by my wife, and looked upon her eyes, and felt if her pulses have beat, when I have named a suspected love; yet all this while have not drawn from her the least scruple of confession. I have lain awake a thousand nights, thinking she would have revealed somewhat in her dreams, and when she has begun to speak any thing in her sleep, I have jogged her, and cried, "Ay, sweet-heart, but when will your love come?" or "What did he say to thee over the stall?" or "What did he do to thee in the garden-chamber?" or "When will he send to thee any letters?" or "When wilt thou send to him any money?" What an idle coxcomb jealousy will make a man! Well, this is my comfort, that here comes a creature of the same head-piece.

Enter WAFER *and* MISTRESS WAFER, *with* Boy.

Mist. Wafer. O my sweet child!—Where's the collier?

Just. Here, forsooth.

Mist. Wafer [*to* Boy]. Run into Bucklersbury* for two ounces of dragon-water, some spermaceti, and treacle.—What is it sick of, collier? a burning fever?

Just. Faith, mistress, I do not know the infirmity of it.—Will you buy any small coal, say you?

Wafer. Prithee, go in and empty them.—Come, be not so impatient.

Mist. Wafer. Ay, ay, ay, if you had groaned for't as I have done, you would have been more natural. —[*To* Servant *within*] Take my riding-hat and my kirtle, there!—I'll away presently.

Wafer. You will not go to-night, I am sure.

Mist. Wafer. As I live, but I will.

Wafer. Faith, sweetheart, I have great business to-night: stay till to-morrow, and I'll go with you.

Mist. Wafer. No, sir, I will not hinder your business. I see how little you respect the fruits of your own body. I shall find somebody to bear me company.

Wafer. Well, I will defer my business for once, and go with thee.

Mist. Wafer. By this light, but you shall not; you shall not hit me i'the teeth that I was your hindrance.—Will you to Bucklersbury, sir?
          [*Exit* Boy.

Wafer. Come, you are a fool; leave your weeping.

Mist. Wafer. You shall not go with me, as I live.   [*Exit* WAFER.

Just. Pupil!

Mist. Wafer. Excellent master!

Just. Admirable mistress! How happy be our Englishwomen that are not troubled with jealous husbands! Why, your Italians, in general, are so sun-burnt with these dog-days, that your great lady there thinks her husband loves her not, if he be not jealous: what confirms the liberty of our women more in England than the Italian proverb which says,—If there were a bridge over the narrow seas, all the women in Italy would show their husbands a million of light pair of heels, and fly over into England!

Mist. Wafer. The time of our meeting? come.

Just. Seven.

Mist. Wafer. The place?

Just. In Blackfriars: there take water, keep aloof from the shore, on with your masks, up with your sails, and, Westward ho!

Mist. Wafer. So.   [*Exit.*

Just. O the quick apprehension of women! they'll grope out a man's meaning presently. Well, it rests now that I discover myself in my true shape to these gentlewomen's husbands; for though I have played the fool a little, to beguile the memory of mine own misfortune, I would not play the knave, though I be taken for a bankrupt: but, indeed, as in other things, so in that, the world is much deceived in me; for I have yet three thousand pounds in the hands of a sufficient friend, and all my debts discharged. I have received here a letter from my wife, directed to Stode,* wherein she most repentently entreateth my return, with protestation to give me assured trial of her honesty: I cannot tell what to think of it, but I will put it to the test. There is a great strife between beauty and chastity; and that which pleaseth many is never free from temptation. As for jealousy, it makes many cuckolds, many fools, and many bankrupts; it may have abused me, and not my wife's honesty: I'll try it:—but first to my secure and doting companion[s]. [*Exit.*

SCENE IV.†

Enter MONOPOLY *and* MISTRESS TENTERHOOK.

Mon. I beseech you, Mistress Tenterhook,— before God, I'll be sick, if you will not be merry.

Mist. Ten. You are a sweet beagle.

Mon. Come, because I kept from town a little,

---

* *Bucklersbury*] See note *, p. 213.

* *Stode*] See note *, p. 212.
† *Scene IV.*] The same. A room in the house of Ambush.

q 2

—let me not live, if I did not hear the sickness was in town very hot. In troth, thy hair is of an excellent colour since I saw it; O those bright tresses, like to threads of gold! *

Mist. Ten. Lie and ashes suffer much in the city for that comparison.

Mon. Here's an honest gentleman will be here by and by was born at Fulham; his name is Gosling Glowworm.

Mist. Ten. I know him [not]: what is he?

Mon. He is a knight. What ailed your husband to be so hasty to arrest me?

Mist. Ten. Shall I speak truly? shall I speak not like a woman?

Mon. Why not like a woman?

Mist. Ten. Because women's tongues are like to clocks; if they go too fast, they never go true: 'twas I that got my husband to arrest thee, I have.

Mon. I am beholding to you.

Mist. Ten. Forsooth, I could not come to the speech of you: I think you may be spoken withal now.

Mon. I thank you: I hope you'll bail me, cousin?

Mist. Ten. And yet why should I speak with you? I protest I love my husband.

Mon. Tush, let not any young woman love a man in years too well.

Mist. Ten. Why?

Mon. Because he'll die before he can requite it.

Mist. Ten. I have acquainted Wafer and Honeysuckle with it, and they allow† my wit for 't extremely.

Enter AMBUSH.

O honest sergeant!

Amb. Welcome, good Mistress Tenterhook.

Mist. Ten. Sergeant, I must needs have my cousin go a little way out of town with me, and to secure thee, here are two diamonds; they are worth two hundred pound; keep them till I return him.

Amb. Well, 'tis good security.

Mist. Ten. Do not come in my husband's sight in the mean time.

Enter WHIRLPOOL, SIR GOSLING GLOWWORM, LINSTOCK, MISTRESS HONEYSUCKLE, *and* MISTRESS WAFER.

Amb. Welcome, gallants.

Whirl. How now! Monopoly arrested!

---

* *O those bright tresses, like to threads of gold!*] Reads very like a quotation; but I have searched several poems and plays for it in vain.

† *allow*] i. e. approve, praise.

Mon. O my little Honeysuckle, art come to visit a prisoner?

Mist. Honey. Yes, faith, as gentlemen visit merchants, to fare well, or as poets young quaint revellers, to laugh at them.—Sirrah,* if I were some foolish justice, if I would not beg thy wit, never trust me.

Mist. Ten. Why, I pray you?

Mist. Honey. Because it hath been concealed all this while. But, come, shall we to boat? we are furnished for attendants as ladies are; we have our fools and our ushers.

Sir Gos. I thank you, madam; I shall meet your wit in the close one day.

Mist. Wafer. Sirrah, thou knowest my husband keeps a kennel of hounds?

Mist. Honey. Yes.

Whirl. Doth thy husband love venery?

Mist. Wafer. Venery!

Whirl. Ay, hunting and venery are words of one signification.

Mist. Wafer. Your two husbands† and he have made a match to go find a hare about Busty Causy.‡

Mist. Ten. They'll keep an excellent house till we come home again.

Mist. Honey. O, excellent! a Spanish dinner,— a pilcher, and a Dutch supper,—butter and onions.

Lin. O, thou art a mad wench!

Mist. Ten. Sergeant, carry this ell of cambric to Mistress Birdlime: tell her, but that it is a rough tide and that she fears the water, she should have gone with us.

Sir Gos. O, thou hast an excellent wit!

Whirl. To boat, boy!

Mist. Honey. Sir Gosling, I do take it your legs are married.

Sir Gos. Why, mistress?

Mist. Honey. They look so thin upon it.

Sir Gos. Ever since I measured with your husband, I have shrunk in the calf.

Mist. Honey. And yet you have a sweet tooth in your head.

Sir Gos. O, well dealt for the calf's head! You may talk what you will of legs, and rising in the small, and swelling beneath the garter; but 'tis certain, when lank thighs brought long stockings out of fashion, the courtier's leg and his slender tilting-staff grew both of a bigness.—Come, for Brainford! [*Exeunt.*

---

* *Sirrah*] See note *. p. 214.

† *husbands*] The old ed. "*husband.*"

‡ *Busty Causy*] Qy. "*Bushy Causy*"?

ACT IV.

SCENE I.*

Enter Mistress Birdlime *and* Luce.

Bird. Good morrow, Mistress Luce: how did you take your rest to-night? how doth your good worship like your lodging? what will you have to breakfast?

Luce. A pox of the knight that was here last night! he promised to have sent me some wild-fowl: he was drunk, I'll be stewed else.

Bird. Why, do not you think he will send them?

Luce. Hang them, 'tis no more in fashion for them to keep their promises, than 'tis for men to pay their debts: he will lie faster than a dog trots. What a filthy knocking was at door last night! some puny Inn-o'-court-men, I'll hold my contribution.

Bird. Yes, in troth, were they, civil gentlemen without beards; but to say the truth, I did take exceptions at their knocking, took them aside, and said to them, "Gentlemen, this is not well, that you should come in this habit, cloaks and rapiers, boots and spurs: I protest to you, those that be your ancients in the house would have come to my house in their caps and gowns, civilly and modestly. I promise you, they might have been taken for citizens, but that they talk more liker fools." [*Knocking within.*]—Who knocks there?—Up into your chamber.

[*Exit* Luce.

Enter Honeysuckle.

Who are you? some man of credit, that you come in muffled thus?

Honey. Who's above?

Bird. Let me see your face first. O, Master Honeysuckle! Why, the old party, the old party.

Honey. Phew, I will not go up to her. Nobody else?

Bird. As I live. Will you give me some sack? —Where's Opportunity?

Enter Christian.

Honey. What dost call her?

Bird. Her name is Christian; but Mistress Luce cannot abide that name, and so she calls her Opportunity.

Honey. Very good, good.   [*Gives money.*]

Bird. Is't a shilling? bring the rest in aqua-vitæ.   [*Exit* Christian.

Come, shall's go to noddy?*

Honey. Ay, an thou wilt, for half-an-hour.

Bird. Here are the cards: deal. [*They play.*] God send me deuces and aces with a court-card, and I shall get by it.

Honey. That can make thee nothing.

Bird. Yes, if I have a coat-card turn up.

Honey. I show four games.

Bird. By my troth, I must show all and little enough too, six games: play your single game, I shall double with you anon. Pray you, lend me some silver to count my games.

Re-enter Christian *with sack.*

How now, is it good sack?

Chris. There's a gentleman at door would speak with you.

Honey. God's so, I will not be seen by any means.

Bird. Into that closet, then.

[*Exit* Honeysuckle.

What, another muffler?

Enter Tenterhook.

Ten. How dost thou, Mistress Birdlime?

Bird. Master Tenterhook! The party is above in the dining-chamber.

Ten. Above!

Bird. All alone.   [*Exit* Tenterhook.

Re-enter Honeysuckle.

Honey. Is he gone up? who was't, I pray thee!

Bird. By this sack, I will not tell you: say that you were a country gentleman, or a citizen that hath a young wife, or an Inn-of-Chancery-man, should I tell you? pardon me. This sack tastes of horse-flesh:† I warrant you the leg of a dead horse hangs in the butt of sack to keep it quick.

---

* *Scene I.*] London. A room in the house of Mistress Birdlime.

* *noddy*] A game on the cards, which appears, from passages in our old writers, to have been played in more ways than one.

† *This sack tastes of horse-flesh, &c.*] So Glapthorne; "This coller spoyles my drinking, or else *this sack has horse-flesh* in't, it rides upon my stomacko."
     The Hollander, 1640, Sig. II 2.
The statute 12 Car. ii. c. 25, sect. 11, which forbids the adulteration of wines, mentions, among other ingredients used for that purpose, "nor any sort of *flesh* whatsoever."

Honey. I beseech thee, good Mistress Birdlime, tell me who it was.

Bird. O God, sir, we are sworn to secrecy as well as surgeons. Come, drink to me, and let's to our game.

Enter TENTERHOOK *and* LUCE, *above*.

Ten. Who am I?

Luce. You?—pray you, unblind me:—Captain Whirlpool? no; Master Linstock?—pray, unblind me:—you are not Sir Gosling Glowworm, for he wears no rings of his fingers:—Master Freeze-leather?—O, you are George the drawer at the Mitre:—pray you, unblind me:—Captain Puck-foist?—Master Counterpane the lawyer?—What the devil mean you? beshrew your heart, you have a very dry hand:—are you not mine host Dog-bolt of Brainford?—Mistress Birdlime?—Master Honeysuckle?—Master Wafer?

Ten. What, the last of all your clients!

Luce. O, how dost thou, good cousin?

Ten. Ay, you have many cousins.

Luce. Faith, I can name many that I do not know: and suppose I did know them, what then? I will suffer one to keep me in diet, another in apparel, another in physic, another to pay my house-rent. I am just of the nature of alchemy; I will suffer every plodding fool to spend money upon me; marry, none but some worthy friend to enjoy my more retired and useful faithfulness.

Ten. Your love, your love.

Luce. O, ay, 'tis the curse that is laid upon our quality; what we glean from others we lavish upon some trothless well-faced younger brother, that loves us only for maintenance.

Ten. Hast a good term, Luce?

Luce. A pox on the term! and now I think on 't, says a gentleman last night, let the pox be in the town seven year, Westminster never breeds cobwebs, and yet 'tis as catching as the plague, though not all so general. There be a thousand bragging Jacks in London, that will protest they can wrest comfort from me, when, I swear, not one of them know whether my palm be moist or not. In troth, I love thee: you promised me seven ells of cambric. [*Knocking within.*] Who's that knocks?

Honey. What, more sacks to the mill! I 'll to my old retirement. [*Exit.*

Enter WAFER.

Bird. How doth your good worship?—[*Aside*]

Passion of my heart, what shift shall I make?—How hath your good worship done a long time?

Wafer. Very well, Godamercy.

Bird. Your good worship, I think, be riding out of town.

Wafer. Yes, believe me, I love to be once a week a-horseback, for methinks nothing sets a man out better than a horse.

Bird. 'Tis certain nothing sets a woman out better than a man.

Wafer. What, is Mistress Luce above?

Bird. Yes, truly.

Wafer. Not any company with her?

Bird. Company! shall I say to your good worship and not lie, she hath had no company,—let me see how long it was since your worship was here; you went to a butcher's feast at Cuckold's-haven* the next day after Saint Luke's day,—not this fortnight, in good truth.

Wafer. Alas, good soul!

Bird. And why was it? go to, go to, I think you know better than I. The wench asketh every day, when will Master Wafer be here? and if knights ask for her, she cries out at stair-head, "As you love my life, let 'em not come up: I 'll do myself violence, if they enter." Have not you promised her somewhat?

Wafer. Faith, I think she loves me.

Bird. Loves! well, would you know what I know! then you would say somewhat. In good faith, she's very poor: all her gowns are at pawn; she owes me five pound for her diet, besides forty shillings I lent her to redeem two half silk kirtles from the broker's: and do you think she needed be in debt thus, if she thought not of somebody?

Wafer. Good, honest wench.

Bird. Nay, in troth, she's now entering into bond for five pounds* more; the scrivener is but new gone up to take her bond.

Wafer. Come, let her not enter into bond; I 'll lend her five pound; I 'll pay the rest of her debts: call down the scrivener.

Bird. I pray you, when he comes down, stand muffled, and I'll tell him you are her brother.

Wafer. If a man have a good honest wench that lives wholly to his use, let him not see her want.

[*Exit* MISTRESS BIRDLIME, *and then enter above.*

Bird. O Mistress Luce, Mistress Luce, you are the most unfortunate gentlewoman that ever breathed! Your young wild brother came newly out of the country: he calls me bawd, swears I keep a bawdy-house, says his sister is turned

---

* *above*] See note *, p. 100

* *Cuckhold's-haven.*) See note on *Northward Ho,* act iii. sc. ii, p. 266.

whore, and that he will kill and slay any man
that he finds in her company.

Ten. What conveyance will you make with me,
Mistress Birdlime?

Luce. O God, let him not come up! 'tis the
swaggeringest wild-oats.

Bird. I have pacified him somewhat, for I
told him that you were a scrivener come to take
a band * of her: now, as you go forth, say, "she
might have had so much money if she had
pleased," and say, "she is an honest gentlewoman,"
and all will be well.

Ten. Enough.—Farewell, good Luce.

Bird. Come, change your voice, and muffle you.
　　　[*Exeunt, above,* BIRDLIME *and* TENTERHOOK.

Luce. What trick should this be? I have never
a brother. I'll hold my life, some franker customer is come, that she slides him off so
smoothly.

　　Re-enter, below, TENTERHOOK *and* BIRDLIME.

Ten. The gentlewoman is an honest gentlewoman as any is in London, and should have had
thrice as much money upon her single bond, for
the good report I hear of her.

Wafer. No, sir, her friends can furnish her
with money.

Ten. By this light, I should know that voice.
Wafer! Od's-foot, are you the gentlewoman's
brother?

Wafer. Are you turned a scrivener, Tenterhook?

Bird. [*aside*] I am spoiled.

Wafer. Tricks of Mistress Birdlime, by this
light.

　　　　Re-enter HONEYSUCKLE.

Honey. Hoick, covert! hoick, covert! why, gentlemen, is this your hunting?

Ten. A consort! What make you here, Honeysuckle?

Honey. Nay, what make you two here?—O
excellent Mistress Birdlime! thou hast more
tricks in thee than a punk hath uncles, cousins,
brothers, sons, or fathers,—an infinite company.

Bird. If I did it not to make your good wor-
ships merry, never believe me. I will drink to
your worship[s] a glass of sack.

　　　　Enter JUSTINIANO.

Just. God save you!

Honey., Wafer. Master Justiniano! welcome
from Stode!†

Just. Why, gentlemen, I never came there.

Ten. Never there! where have you been,
then?

Just. Marry, your daily guest, I thank you.

Ten., Honey., Wafer. Ours!

Just. Ay, yours. I was the pedant that learned
your wives to write; I was the collier that
brought you news your child was sick: but the
truth is, for aught I know, the child is in health,
and your wives are gone to make merry at
Brainford.

Wafer. By my troth, good wenches, they little
dream where we are now.

Just. You little dream what gallants are with
them.

Ten. Gallants with them! I'd laugh at that.

Just. Four gallants, by this light; Master
Monopoly is one of them.

Ten. Monopoly! I'd laugh at that, in faith.

Just. Would you laugh at that? why, do ye
laugh at it, then. They are there by this time.
I cannot stay to give you more particular intelligence: I have received a letter from my wife
here. If you will call me at Putney, I'll bear
you company.

Ten. Od's-foot, what a rogue is Sergeant Ambush! I'll undo him, by this light.

Just. I met Sergeant Ambush, and willed* him
come to this house to you presently. So, gentlemen, I leave you.—Bawd, I have nothing to
say to you now.—Do not think too much in so
dangerous a matter; for in women's matters 'tis
more dangerous to stand long deliberating than
before a battle.　　　　　　　　[*Exit.*

Wafer. This fellow's poverty hath made him
an arrant knave.

Bird. Will your worship drink any aqua-vitæ?

Ten. A pox on your aqua-vitæ!—Monopoly,
that my wife urged me to arrest, gone to
Brainford!—Here comes the varlet.

　　　　Enter AMBUSH.

Amb. I am come, sir, to know your pleasure.

Ten. What, hath Monopoly paid the money
yet?

Amb. No, sir, but he sent for money.

Ten. You have not carried him to the Counter?
he is at your house still?

Amb. O Lord, ay, sir, as melancholic, &c.†

---

* *band*] i. e. bond.
† *Stode*] See note *, p. 212.

* *willed*] i. e. desired.
† *as melancholic, &c.*] Was the performer to conclude
this speech with any simile that he thought proper?
Our old dramatists sometimes trusted to the player's
powers of extemporizing: so Greene;
　" Faire Polyxena, the pride of Ilion,

Ten. You lie like an arrant varlet. By this caudle, I laugh at the jest:

Bird. [*aside*] And yet he's ready to cry.

Ten. He's gone with my wife to Bruinford: an there be any law in England, I'll tickle ye for this.

Amb. Do your worst, for I have good security, and I care not; besides, it was his cousin your wife's pleasure that he should go along with her.

Ten. Hoy-day, her cousin! Well, sir, your security?

Amb. Why, sir, two diamonds here.

Ten. [*aside*] O my heart! my wife's two diamonds!—Well, you'll go along and justify this?

Amb. That I will, sir.

Enter LUCE, *below.*

Luce. Who am I?

Ten. What the murrain care I who you are? hold off your fingers, or I'll cut them with these diamond[s].

Luce. I'll see 'em, i'faith. So, I'll keep these diamonds till I have my silk gown and six ells of cambric.

Ten. By this light, you shall not.

Luce. No? what, do you think you have fops in hand? sue me for them.

Wafer, Honey. As you respect your credit, let's go.

Ten. Good Luce, as you love me, let me have them; it stands upon my credit: thou shalt have any thing; take my purse.

Luce. I will not be crossed in my humour, sir.

Ten. You are a damned filthy punk.—What an unfortunate rogue was I, that ever I came into this house!

Bird. Do not spurn any body in my house, you were best.

Ten. Well, well.

[*Exeunt* TENTERHOOK, WAFER, HONEYSUCKLE, *and* AMBUSH.

Bird. Excellent Luce! the getting of these two diamonds may chance to save the gentle-women's credit. Thou heardest all?

Luce. O, ay, and, by my troth, pity them: what a filthy knave was that betrayed them!

Fear not Achilles' over-madding boy;
Pyrrhus shall not, &c.

Souns, Orgalio, why sufferest thou this old trot to come so nigh me?"
Orlando Furioso, Dram. Works, i. 43, ed. Dyce.
And Heywood;
"Jockie is led to whipping over the stage, *speaking some words, but of no importance.*"
Edward the Fourth, Part Sec., ed. 1619, sig. Y.

Bird. One that put me into pitiful fear: Master Justiniano here hath layed lurking, like a sheep-biter, and, in my knowledge, hath drawn these gentlewomen to this misfortune. But I'll down to Queenhive;* and the watermen, which were wont to carry you to Lambeth-Marsh,† shall carry me thither. It may be I may come before them. I think I shall pray more, what for fear of the water, and for my good success, than I did this twelvemonth. [*Exeunt.*

SCENE II.‡

Enter the EARL *and three* Servingmen.

Earl. Have you perfum'd this chamber?

Omnes. Yes, my lord.

Earl. The banquet?

Omnes. It stands ready.

Earl. Go, let music
Charm with her excellent voice an awful silence
Through all this building, that her sphery soul
May, on the wings of air, in thousand forms
Invisibly fly, yet be enjoy'd. Away!

First Serv. Does my lord mean to conjure, that he draws these strange characters?

Sec. Serv. He does; but we shall see neither the spirit that rises, nor the circle it rises in.

Third Serv. 'Twould make our hair stand up an end, if we should. Come, fools, come; meddle not with his matters: lords may do any thing. [*Exeunt* Servingmen.

Earl. This night shall my desires be amply crown'd,
And all those powers that taste of man in us
Shall now aspire that point of happiness,
Beyond which sensual eyes ne'er look,—sweet pleasure,
Delicious pleasure, earth's supremest good,
The spring of blood, though it dry up our blood.
Rob me of that,—though to be drunk with pleasure,
As rank excess even in best things is bad,
Turns man into a beast,—yet that being gone,
A horse, and this, the goodliest shape, all one.
We feed, wear rich attires, and strive to cleave
The stars with marble towers, fight battles, spend
Our blood to buy us names, and, in iron hold,

* *Queenhive*] i. e. Queenhithe.
† *Lambeth-Marsh*] A noted haunt of prostitutes and sharpers.
‡ *Scene II.*] The same. A room in the house of the Earl.

Will we eat roots, to imprison fugitive gold :
But to do thus, what spell can us excite ?
This, the strong magic of our appetite ;
To feast which richly, life itself undoes.
Who'd not die thus ? to see, and then to choose.
Why, even those that starve in voluntary wants,
And, to advance the mind, keep the flesh poor,
The world enjoying them, they not the world,
Would they do this, but that they are proud to
　　　　suck
A sweetness from such sourness ? Let 'em so :
The torrent of my appetite shall flow
With happier stream.　A woman !　O, the spirit
And extract of creation !　This, this night,
The sun shall envy.　What cold checks our
　　　　blood ?
Her body is the chariot of my soul,
Her eyes my body's light, which if I want,
Life wants, or if possess, I undo her,
Turn her into a devil, whom I adore,
By scorching her with the hot steam of lust.
'Tis but a minute's pleasure, and the sin
Scarce acted is reported : shun it, than :*
O, he that can abstain is more than man !
Tush !　Resolv'st thou to do ill, be not precise :
Who write of virtue best, are slaves to vice.
　　　　　　　　　　　　　　　　[Music.
The music sounds alarum to my blood :
What's bad I follow, yet I see what's good.†

　　[*Whilst the song is heard, the* EARL *draws a curtain,
　　and sets forth a banquet.　He then exit, and re-
　　enters presently with* JUSTINIANO. *attired like his
　　wife, masked ; leads him to the table, places him
　　in a chair, and in dumb signs courts him till the
　　song be done.*

Fair, be not doubly mask'd with that and
　　night :
Beauty, like gold, being us'd becomes more bright.

　Just. [*taking off his mask*].　Will it please your
lordship to sit ?　I shall receive small pleasure,
if I see your lordship stand.

　Earl. Witch ! hag ! what art thou ; proud damnation ?

　Just. A merchant's wife.

　Earl. Fury, who rais'd thee up ? what com'st
thou for ?

　Just. For a banquet.

　Earl. I am abus'd, deluded.—Speak, what art
thou ?
Ud's death, speak, or I'll kill thee.　In that habit
I look'd to find an angel, but thy face
Shows thou'rt a devil.

　Just. My face is as God made it, my lord : I
am no devil, unless women be devils ; but men
find 'em not so, for they daily hunt for them.

　Earl. What art thou that dost cozen me thus ?

　Just. A merchant's wife, I say, Justiniano's
wife ; she whom that long birding-piece of yours,
I mean that wicked Mother Birdlime, caught for
your honour.　Why, my lord, has your lordship
forgot how ye courted me last morning ?

　Earl. The devil, I did !

　Just. Kissed me last morning.

　Earl. Succubus, not thee.

　Just. Gave me this jewel last morning.

　Earl. Not to thee, harpy.

　Just. To me, upon mine honesty ; swore you
would build me a lodging by the Thames side
with a water-gate to it, or else take me a lodging
in Cole-harbour.*

　Earl. I swore so ?

　Just. Or keep me in a labyrinth, as Harry kept
Rosamond, where the Minotaur, my husband,
should not enter.

　Earl. I swore so, but, gipsey, not to thee.

　Just. To me, upon my honour : hard was the
siege which you laid to the crystal walls of my
chastity, but I held out you know ; but because
I cannot be too stony-hearted, I yielded, my
lord, by this token, my lord, (which token lies at
my heart like lead,) but by this token, my lord,
that this night you should commit that sin which
we all know with me.

　Earl. Thee !

　Just. Do I look ugly, that you put "thee" upon
me ? did I give you my hand to horn my head,
that's to say my husband, and is it come to
"thee" ? is my face a filthier face, now it is yours,
than when it was his ? or have I two faces under
one hood ?　I confess I have laid mine eyes in
brine, and that may change the copy : but, my
lord, I know what I am.

　Earl. A sorceress : thou shalt witch mine ears
　　no more ;
If thou canst pray, do't quickly, for thou diest.

　Just. I can pray, but I will not die,—thou liest.
My lord, there drops your lady ; and now know,

---

　* *than*] A form of *then*, common in old poets.
　† *What's bad*, &c.] "video meliora proboque, deteriora
sequor."　Ovid, *Met.* vii. 20.

　* *Cole-harbour*] Or *Coal-harbour*—a corruption of Cold-
harbour, or Coldharborough, was an old building in
Dowgate Ward.　Stow (*Survey*, p. 188, ed. 1598,) tells
us, "The last deceased Earle [of Shrewsbury] tooke it
down, and in place thereof builded a great number of
small tenements, now letten out for great rents to
people of all sorts."—Debtors and persons not of the
most respectable character used to take refuge there.
Middleton calls it "the devil's sanctuary."　*A Trick to
catch the old one*,—*Works*, ii. 55, ed. Dyce.

Thou unseasonable lecher, I am her husband,
Whom thou wouldst make whore. Read; she
  speaks there thus:
  [Mistress Justiniano is discovered, lying as if dead*.
Unless I came to her, her hand should free
Her chastity from blemish: proud I was
Of her brave mind; I came, and seeing what
  slavery,
Poverty, and the frailty of her sex,
Had, and was like to make her subject to,
I begg'd that she would die; my suit was granted;
I poison'd her; thy lust there strikes her dead:
Horns fear'd plague worse than sticking on the
  head.
  Earl. O God, thou hast undone thyself and me!
None live to match this piece: thou art too
  bloody:
Yet for her sake, whom I'll embalm with tears,
This act with her I bury; and to quit
Thy loss of such a jewel, thou shalt share
My living with me: come, embrace.
  Just. My lord!
  Earl. Villain, damn'd merciless slave, I'll
  torture thee
To every inch of flesh.—What, ho! help! who's
  there?
Come hither! here's a murderer, bind him!—
  How now!
What noise is this?

          Re-enter the Servingmen.

  First Serv. My lord, there are three citizens
face me down that here's one Master Parenthesis,
a schoolmaster, with your lordship, and desire he
may be forthcoming to 'em.
  Just. That borrow'd name is mine.—[*Calling to
  those within*] Shift for yourselves;
Away, shift for yourselves; fly; I am taken!
  Earl. Why should they fly, thou screech-owl?
  Just. I will tell thee:
Those three are partners with me in the murder;
We four commix'd the poison.—[*Calling to those
  within*] Shift for yourselves!
  Earl. Stop's mouth, and drag him back: en-
  treat'em enter.   [*Exit* First Serv.
O, what a conflict feel I in my blood!
I would I were less great to be more good.

Enter Tenterhook, Wafer, *and* Honeysuckle, *with*
            First Servingman.

Ye're welcome: wherefore came you?—Guard
  the doors.—

  ———————————
  * *Mistress Justiniano is discovered, lying as if dead*]
  This stage-direction is not in the old ed.—Here probably
  Justiniano drew back a curtain.

When I behold that object, all my senses
Revolt from reason.—He that offers flight
Drops down a corse.
  Ten., Wafer, Honey. A corse!
  First Serv. Ay, a corse: do you scorn to be
worms' meat more than she?
  Just. See, gentlemen, the Italian that does
  scorn,
Beneath the moon, no baseness like the horn,
Has pour'd through all the veins of yon chaste
  bosom
Strong poison to preserve it from that plague.
This fleshly lord, be doted on my wife;
He would have wrought on her and play'd on me:
But to pare off these brims, I cut off her,
And gull'd him with this lie, that you had hands
Dipt in her blood with mine; but this I did,
That his stain'd age and name might not be hid.
My act, though vile, the world shall crown as just;
I shall die clear, when he lives soil'd with lust.—
But, come, rise, Moll; awake, sweet Moll; thou'st
  play'd
The woman rarely, counterfeited well.
            [Mistress Justiniano *rises*.
  First Serv. Sure, sh'as nine lives.
  Just. See, Lucrece is not slain:
Her eyes, which lust call'd suns, have their first
  beams,
And all those frightments are but idle dreams:
Yet, afore Jove, she had her knife prepar'd
To let her * blood forth ere it should run black.
Do not these open cuts now cool your back?
Methinks they should: when vice sees with
  broad eyes
Her ugly form, she does herself despise.
  Earl. Mirror of dames, I look upon thee now,
As men long blind having recover'd sight,
Amaz'd, scarce able are to endure the light.
Mine own shame strikes me dumb: henceforth
  the book
I'll read shall be thy mind, and not thy look.
  Honey. I would either we were at Brainford to
see our wives, or our wives here to see this pa-
geant.
  Ten. So would I; I stand upon thorns.
  Earl. The jewels which I gave you, wear; your
  fortunes
I'll raise on golden pillars: fare you well.
Lust in old age, like burnt straw, does even choke
The kindlers, and consumes in stinking smoke.
                              [*Exit.*
  Just. You may follow your lord by the smoke,
badgers.

  ———————————
  * *her*] The old ed., "*his*."

First Serv. If fortune had favoured him, we might have followed you by the horns.

Just. Fortune favours fools; your lord's a wise lord. [*Exeunt* Servingmen.] So.—How now! ha! This is that makes me fat now: is't not ratsbane to you, gentlemen, as pap was to Nestor? but I know the invisible sins of your wives hang at your eye-lids, and that makes you so heavy-headed.

Ten. If I do take 'em napping, I know what I'll do.

Honey. I'll nap some of them.

Ten. That villain Monopoly, and that Sir Gosling, treads 'em all.

Wafer. Would I might come to that treading!

Just. Ha, ha, so would I.—Come, Moll: the book of the siege of Ostend,* writ by one that dropped in the action, will never sell so well as a report of the siege between this grave, this wicked elder and thyself; an impression of you two would away in a May morning. Was it ever heard that such tirings were brought away from a lord by any wench but thee, Moll, without paying, unless the wench conycatched him? Go thy ways: if all the great Turk's concubines were but like thee, the ten-penny infidel† should

never need keep so many geldings to neigh over 'em.—Come, shall this western voyage hold, my hearts?

Ten., Wafer, Honey. Yes, yes.

Just. Yes, yes! s'foot, you speak as if you had no hearts, and look as if you were going westward indeed.* To see how plain-dealing women can pull down men!—Moll, you'll help us to catch smelts† too?

Mist. Just. If you be pleased.

Just. Never better since I wore a smock.

Honey. I fear our oars have given us the bag.‡

Wafer. Good, I'd laugh at that. ·

Just. If they have, would theirs § might give them the bottle! Come, march whilst the women double their files. Married men, see, there's comfort; the moon's up: 'fore Don Phœbus, I doubt we shall have a frost this night, her horns are so sharp: do you not feel it bite?

Ten. I do, I'm sure.

Just. But we'll sit upon one another's skirts i' the boat, and lie close in straw, like the hoary courtier. Set on

To Brainford now, where if you meet frail wives,
Ne'er swear 'gainst horns in vain Dame Nature
    strives. [*Exeunt.*

ACT V.

SCENE I.‡

Enter MONOPOLY, WHIRLPOOL, LINSTOCK ; MISTRESS HONEY-SUCKLE, MISTRESS WAFER, *and* MISTRESS TENTERHOOK, *their hats off.*

Mon. Why, chamberlain!—Will not these fiddlers be drawn forth? are they not in tune yet? or are the rogues afraid o' the statute,§ and dare not travel so far without a passport?

Whirl. What, chamberlain!

Lin. Where's mine host?—What, chamberlain!

Enter CHAMBERLAIN.

Cham. Anon, sir; here, sir; at hand, sir.

Mon. Where's this noise?|| What a lousy town's this! Has Brainford no music in't?

Cham. They are but rosining, sir, and they'll scrape themselves into your company presently.

Mon. Plague o' their cat's-guts and their scraping! Dost not see women here, and can we, thinkest thou, be without a noise, then?

Cham. The troth is, sir, one of the poor instruments caught a sore mischance last night: his most base bridge fell down; and belike they are making a gathering for the reparations of that.

Whirl. When they come, let's have 'em, with a pox.

Cham. Well, sir, you shall, sir.

Mon. Stay, chamberlain; where's our knight, Sir Gosling? where's Sir Gosling?

Cham. Troth, sir, my master and Sir Gosling are guzzling; they are dabbling together fathom-

---

* *the siege of Ostend*] See note ‡, p. 210.
† *the ten-penny infidel*] So Dekker ;
    "Wilt fight, *Turke-a-tenpence!*"
        Satiromastix, 1602, sig. H 2.
‡ *Scene I.*] Brentford. A room in an inn.
§ *the statute*] "Statute against vagabonds." MS. note
by Malone.
   || *noise*] See note §, p. 222.

* *westward indeed*] i. e. to Tyburn.
† *to catch smelts*] See note *, p. 223.
‡ *I fear our oars have given us the bag*] *To give the bag*
means *to cheat*.
§ *theirs*] Old ed., "*wheres*."

deep: the knight hath drunk so much health to
the gentlemen yonder, on his knees,* that he
has almost lost the use of his legs.

Mist. Honey. O, for love, let none of 'em enter
our room, fie !

Mist. Wafer. I would not have 'em cast up
their accounts here, for more than they mean to
be drunk this twelvemonth.

Mist. Ten. Good chamberlain, keep them and
their healths out of our company.

Cham. I warrant you, their healths shall not
hurt you.　　　　　　　　　　　　[*Exit.*

Mon. Ay, well said ! they're none of our
giving : let 'em keep their own quarter.　Nay, I
told you the men would soak him, if he were
ten knights ; if he were a knight of gold, they'd
fetch him over.

Mist. Ten. Out upon him !

Whirl. There's a lieutenant and a captain
amongst 'em too.

Mon. Nay, then, look to have somebody lie on
the earth for't : it's ordinary for your lieutenant
to be drunk with your captain, and your captain
to cast with your knight.

Mist. Ten. Did you never hear how Sir Fabian
Scarecrow (even such another) took me up one
night before my husband, being in wine ?

Mist. Wafer. No, indeed : how was it ?

Mist. Ten. But I think I took him down with
a witness.

Mist. Honey. How, good Tenterhook ?

Mist. Ten. Nay, I'll have all your ears take
part of it.

Omnes. Come, on then.

Mist. Ten. He used to frequent me and my
husband divers times ; and at last comes he out
one morning to my husband, and says, " Master
Tenterhook," says he, " I must trouble you to
lend me two hundred pound about a commodity
which I am to deal in :" and what was that commodity but his knighthood ?

Omnes. So.

Mist. Ten. " Why, you shall, Master Scarecrow,"
says my good man : so within a little while after,
Master Fabian was created knight.

Mon. Created a knight ! that's no good heraldry ; you must say dubbed.

Mist. Ten. And why not created, pray ?

Omnes, except Mon. Ay, well done ! put him
down at's own weapon.

Mist. Ten. Not created ! why, all things have
their being by creation.

Lin. Yes, by my faith, is't.

Mist. Ten. But to return to my tale,—

Whirl. Ay, marry ; mark now.

Mist. Ten. When he had climbed up this costly
ladder of preferment, he disburses the money
back again very honourably ; comes home, and
was by my husband invited to supper.　There
supped with us, besides, another gentleman
incident to the court, one that had bespoke me
of my husband to help me into the banquetting-
house and see the revelling, a young gentlewoman,* and that was our schoolmaster, Master
Parenthesis, for I remember he said grace,—
methinks I see him yet, how he turned up the
white o' the eye, when he came to the last gasp,
and that he was almost past grace !—

Mist. Wafer. Nay, he can do't.

Mist. Ten. All supper-time my new-minted
knight made wine the waggon to his meat, for it
ran down his throat so fast, that, before my
chamber-maid had taken half up, he was not
scarce able to stand.

Mon. A general fault at citizens' tables.

Mist. Ten. And I, thinking to play upon him,
asked him, " Sir Fabian Scarecrow," quoth I,
" what pretty gentlewoman will you raise up now
to stall her your lady ?" But he, like a foul-
mouthed man, swore, " Zounds, I'll stall never a
punk in England a lady ; there's too many
already." " O, fie, Sir Fabian," quoth I, " will
you call her that shall be your wife such an
odious name ?" And then he sets out a throat,
and swore again, like a stinking-breathed knight
as he was, that women were like horses.

Mist. Honey., Mist. Wafer. O filthy knave !

Mist. Ten. They'd break over any hedge to
change their pasture, though it were worse.
" Fie, man, fie," says the gentlewoman,—

Mon. Very good.

Mist. Ten. And he, bristling up his beard to
rail at her too, I cut him over the thumbs thus ;
" Why, Sir Fabian Scarecrow, did I incense my
husband to lend you so much money upon your
bare word, and do you backbite my friends and
me to our faces ? I thought you had had more
perseverance : if you bore a knightly and a de-
generous mind, you would scorn it : you had
wont to be more deformable amongst women :
fie, that you'll be so humoursome ! here was
nobody so egregious towards you, Sir Fabian ;"

---

* *the knight hath drunk so much health to the gentleman
yonder on his knees.*] This was a foolish custom of the day,
at which the Puritans expressed the highest indignation.

* *gentlewoman*] The old copy " Gentleman "; but see
what presently follows.

and thus, in good sadness, I gave him the best words I could pick out, to make him ashamed of his doings.

Whirl. And how took he this correction?

Mist. Ten. Very heavily, for he slept presently upon't; and in the morning was the sorriest knight, and, I warrant, is so to this day, that lives by bread in England.

Mon. To see what wine and women can do! the one makes a man not to have a word to throw at a dog, the other makes a man to eat his own words, though they were never so filthy.

Whirl. I see these fiddlers cannot build up their bridge, that some music may come over us.

Lin. No, faith, they are drunk too: what shall's do therefore?

Mon. Sit up at cards all night.

Mist. Wafer. That's serving-man's fashion.

Whirl. Drink burnt wine and eggs, then.

Mist. Honey. That's an exercise for your suburb wenches.

Mist. Ten. No, no, let's set upon our posset, and so march to bed; for I begin to wax light with having my natural sleep pulled out o' mine eyes.

Omnes. Agreed, be't so; the sack-posset and to bed.

Mon. What, chamberlain!—I must take a pipe of tobacco.

Mist. Honey., Mist. Wafer, Mist. Ten. Not here, not here, not here.

Mist. Wafer. I'll rather love a man that takes a purse than him that takes tobacco.

Mist. Ten. By my little finger, I'll break all your pipes, and burn the case and the box too, an you draw out your stinking smoke afore me.

Mon. Prithee, good Mistress Tenterhook,—I'll ha' done in a trice.

Mist. Ten. Do you long to have me swoon?

Mon. I'll use but half a pipe, in troth.

Mist. Ten. Do you long to see me lie at your feet?

Mon. Smell to't; 'tis perfumed.

Mist. Ten. O God, O God, you anger me; you stir my blood; you move me; you make me spoil a good face with frowning at you. This was ever your fashion, so to smoke my husband when you come home, that I could not abide him in mine eye; he was a mote in it, methought, a month after. Pray, spawl in another room: fie, fie, fie!

Mon. Well, well: come, we'll for once feed her humour.

Mist. Honey. Get two rooms off at least, if you love us.

Mist. Wafer. Three, three, Master Linstock, three.

Lin. 'Sfoot, we'll dance to Norwich,* and take it there, if you'll stay till we return again. Here's a stir! You'll ill abide a fiery face, that cannot endure a smoky nose.

Mon. Come, let's satisfy our appetite.

Whirl. And that will be hard for us; but we'll do our best.

[*Exeunt* MONOPOLY, WHIRLPOOL, *and* LINSTOCK.

Mist. Ten. So; are they departed? What string may we three think that these three gallants harp upon, by bringing us to this sinful town of Brainford, ha?

Mist. Honey. I know what string they would harp upon, if they could put us into the right tune.

Mist. Wafer. I know what one of 'em buzzed in mine ear, till, like a thief in a candle, he made mine ears burn; but I swore to say nothing.

Mist. Ten. I know as verily they hope, and brag one to another, that this night they'll row westward in our husbands' wherries as we hope to be rowed to London to-morrow morning in a pair of oars. But, wenches, let's be wise, and make rooks of them that, I warrant, are now setting purse-nets† to conycatch us.

Mist. Honey., Mist. Wafer. Content.

Mist. Ten. They shall know that citizens' wives have wit enough to outstrip twenty such gulls: though we are merry, let's not be mad; be as wanton as now-married wives, as fantastic and light-headed to the eye as feather-makers, but as pure about the heart as if we dwelt amongst 'em in Blackfriars.‡

Mist. Wafer. We'll eat and drink with 'em.

Mist. Ten. O, yes; eat with 'em as hungerly as soldiers; drink as if we were froes;§ talk as freely as jesters: but do as little as misers, who, like dry nurses, have great breasts, but give no milk. It were better we should laugh at their popinjays than live in fear of their prating

---

* *dance to Norwich*] An allusion to a feat of Kempe, the actor, of which he published an account, called *Kemps Nine Daies Wonder, performed in a daunce from London to Norwich,* 1600, 4to. It has been reprinted by the Camden Society from the unique copy in the Bodleian Library.

† *purse-nets*] See note *, p. 130.

‡ *as fantastic and light-headed to the eye as feather-makers, but as pure about the heart as if we dwelt amongst 'em in Blackfriars*] Blackfriars was famed for the residence of Puritans, some of whom, most inconsistently with their religious opinions, followed the trade of feather-making.

§ *froes*] i. e. frows.

tongues. Though we lie all night out of the city, they shall not find country wenches of us; but since we ha' brought 'em thus far into a fool's paradise, leave 'em in't: the jest shall be a stock to maintain us and our pewfellows in laughing at christenings, cryings-out, and upsittings this twelve-month. How say you, wenches? have I set the saddle on the right horse?

Mist. Wafer, Mist. Honey. O, 'twill be excellent!

Mist. Wafer. But how shall we shift 'em off?

Mist. Ten. Not as ill debtors do their creditors, with good words; but as lawyers do their clients when they're overthrown, by some new knavish trick: and thus it shall be; one of us must dissemble to be suddenly very sick.

Mist. Honey. I'll be she.

Mist. Ten. Nay, though we can all dissemble well, yet I'll be she; for men are so jealous, or rather envious of one another's happiness, especially in these out-of-town gossipings, that he who shall miss his hen, if he be a right cock indeed, will watch the other from treading.

Mist. Wafer. That's certain; I know that by myself.

Mist. Ten. And, like Æsop's dog, unless himself might eat hay, will lie in the manger and starve, but he'll hinder the horse from eating any: besides, it will be as good as a Welsh hook for you to keep out the other at the staves-end; for you may boldly stand upon this point, that unless every man's heels may be tript up, you scorn to play at football.

Mist. Honey. That's certain :—peace! I hear them spitting after their tobacco.

Mist. Ten. A chair, a chair! one of you keep as great a coil and calling as if* you ran for a midwife; th'other hold my head; whilst I cut my lace.

Mist. Wafer. Passion of me! Master Monopoly! Master Linstock! an you be men, help to daw† Mistress Tenterhook! O, quickly, quickly! she's sick and taken with an agony.

Re-enter, as she cries, MONOPOLY, WHIRL-POOL, *and* LINSTOCK.

Mon., Whirl., Lin. Sick! How! how now! what's the matter?

Mon. Sweet Clare, call up thy sp rits.

Mist. Ten. O Master Monopoly, my spirits will not come at my calling! I am terrible and ill. Sure, sure, I'm struck with some wicked planet, for it hit my very heart. O, I feel myself worse and worse!

Mon. Some burnt sack for her, good wenches, or posset-drink. Pox o' this rogue chamberlain! one of you call him. How her pulses beat! a draught of cinnamon-water now for her were better than two tankards out of the Thames.— How now, ha?

Mist. Ten. Ill, ill, ill, ill, ill.

Mon. I'm accursed to spend money in this town of iniquity; there's no good thing ever comes out of it; and it stands upon such musty ground, by reason of the river, that I cannot see how a tender woman can do well in't. 'Sfoot, sick now, cast down, now 'tis come to the push!

Mist. Ten. My mind misgives me that all's not sound at London.

Whirl. Pox on 'em that be not sound! what need that touch you?

Mist. Ten. I fear you'll never carry me thither.

Mon., Whirl., Lin. Pooh, pooh, say not so.

Mist. Ten. Pray, let my clothes be utterly undone, and then lay me in my bed.

Lin. Walk up and down a little.

Mist. Ten. O Master Linstock, 'tis no walking will serve my turn.—Have me to bed, good sweet Mistress Honeysuckle.—I doubt that old hag, Gillian of Brainford,* has bewitched me.

---

* *Gillian of Brainford*] Gillian, Julian, or Joan of Brentford was a reputed witch of some celebrity.

Jyl of breyntfords testament. Newly compiled, n. d. 4to., consisting of eight leaves, is among the rarest of black-letter tracts; it was written by Robert, and printed by William, Copland. In this very low and vulgar production no mention is made of Gillian's being addicted to witchcraft: as the Bodleian copy is now before me, I quote a few lines from it;

    " At Brentford on the west of London
      Nygh to a place yᵗ called is Syon
      There dwelt a widow of a homly sort
      Honest in substaunce and full of sport
      Dally she cowd wᵗ pastim and Jestes
      Among her neyghbours and her gestes
      She kept an Ihe of ryght good lodgyng
      For all estates that thyder was comyng."

The reader who has any curiosity to know what Gillian bequeathed to her friends, may gratify it by turning to Nash's *Summers last will and testament,* 1600, Sig. B. 2.

It appears from Henslowe's *Diary* that she was a character in a play written by Thomas Dowton [or Downton] and Samuel Redly [Rowley?], produced in February, 1598-9, and mentioned there under the title of " *Fryer Fox and gyllen of Branforde.*"

In the 4to. of Shakespeare's *Merry Wives of Windsor,* 1602, when Mistress Page says that Falstaff

    " might put on a gowne and a muffler,
     And so escape,"

Mistress Ford answers,

    " Thats wel remembred, my maids aunt,
     Gillian of Brainford, hath a gowne aboue."

        p. 37, Shakespeare Soc. reprint.

---

* *as if*] The old copy " *and as if.*"
† *daw*] i. e. revive.

Mon. Look to her, good wenches.

Mist. Wafer. Ay, so we will,—[*aside*] and to you too. [*Aside to* MIST. TEN. *and* MIST. HONEY.] This was excellent.

[*Exeunt* MISTRESS TENTERHOOK, MISTRESS HONEY- SUCKLE, *and* MISTRESS WAFER.

Whirl. This is strange.

Lin. Villanous spiteful luck! No matter, th'other two hold bias.

Whirl. Peace! mark how he's nipt: nothing grieves me so much as that poor Pyramus here must have a wall this night between him and his Thisbe.

Mon. No remedy, trusty Troilus: and it grieves me as much that you'll want your false Cressida to-night, for here's no Sir Pandarus to usher you into your chamber.

Lin. I'll summon a parley to one of the wenches, and see how all goes.

Mon. No whispering with the common enemy, by this iron: he sees the devil that sees how all goes amongst the women to-night. Nay, 'sfoot, if I stand piping till you dance, damn me.

Lin. Why, you'll let me call to 'em but at the key-hole?

Mon. Pooh, good Master Linstock, I'll not stand by whilst you give fire at your key-holes. I'll hold no trencher till another feeds; no stirrup till another gets up; be no door-keeper. I ha' not been so often at court, but I know what the backside of the hangings are made of; I'll trust none under a piece of tapestry, namely a coverlet.

Whirl. What will you say if the wenches do this to gull us?

Mon. No matter, I'll not be doubly gulled, by them and by you: go, will you take the lease of the next chamber, and do as I do?

Whirl., Lin. And what's that?

Mon. Any villany in your company, but nothing out on't. Will you sit up, or lie by't?

Whirl. Nay, lie, sure; for lying is most in fashion.

Mon. Troth, then, I'll have you before me.

Whirl., Lin. It shall be yours.

Mon. Yours, i' faith: I'll play Janus with two faces, and look asquint both ways for one night.

Lin. Well, sir, you shall be our door-keeper.

Mon. Since we must swim, let's leap into one flood:

We'll either be all naught, or else all good.

Exeunt.

SCENE II.*

Enter a Noise of Fiddlers,† following the CHAMBERLAIN.

Cham. Come, come, come, follow me, follow me. I warrant, you ha' lost more by not falling into a sound‡ last night, than ever you got at one job since it pleased to make you a noise: I can tell you, gold is no money with 'em. Follow me, and fum as you go: you shall put something into their ears, whilst I provide to put something into their bellies. Follow close, and fum.

[*Exeunt.*

SCENE III.§

Enter SIR GOSLING GLOWWORM *and* MISTRESS BIRDLIME *pulled along by him.*

Sir Gos. What kin art thou to Long Meg of Westminster?‖ thou'rt like her.

Bird. Somewhat alike, sir, at a blush; nothing akin, sir, saving in height of mind, and that she was a goodly woman.

Sir Gos. Mary Ambree,¶ do not you know me? had not I a sight of this sweet phisnomy at Rhenish wine-house, ha? last day, i'the Stilliard, ha?** Whither art bound, galleyfoist?†† whither art bound? whence comest thou, female yeoman-o'-the-guard?

Bird. From London, sir.

Sir Gos. Dost come to keep the door, Ascapart?‡‡

Bird. My reparations hither is to speak with the gentlewomen here that drunk with your worship at the Dutch house of meeting.

Sir Gos. Drunk with me! you lie, not drunk with me: but, faith, what wouldst with the

---

* *Scene II.*] The same. A lobby in the same.

† *a Noise of Fiddlers*] See note §, p. 222.

‡ *sound*] I need hardly observe that the Chamberlain is quibbling here,—*sound* being the usual form of *swoon* when this play was written.

§ *Scene III.*] The same. A room in the same.

‖ *Long Meg of Westminster*] An Amazon often alluded to by our old writers. She was the heroine of a play, named after her, and first acted in 1594, as we learn from Henslowe's *Diary.* She also figured in a ballad entered on the Stationers' books in that year. In 1635 appeared a tract entitled *The Life of Long Meg of Westminster*, containing the mad merry prankes she played in her lifetime, &c.

¶ *Mary Ambree*] Was as famous as the lady last mentioned. *The valorous acts performed at Gaunt by the brave bonnie lass Mary Ambree, who in revenge of her lovers death did play her part most gallantly*, may be found in Percy's *Reliques*, vol. ii. p. 240, ed. 1812.

** *the Rhenish wine-house . . . i'the Stilliard*] See note ‡, p. 217.

†† *galleyfoist*] A large barge with oars. When our old writers talk of "*the* galleyfoist," they mean the Lord Mayor of London's barge. The word is formed of *galley*, and *foist*, a light vessel,—Fr. *fuste*.

‡‡ *Ascapart*] A renowned giant, whom Sir Bevis of Southampton conquered.

womon? they are a-bed. Art not a midwife? ono of 'om told me thou wert a nightwoman.

[*Music within: the* Fiddlers.

Bird. I ha' brought some women a-bed in my time, sir.

Sir Gos. Ay, and some young men too, hast not, Pandora?—How now! where's this noise?

Bird. I'll commit your worship—

Sir Gos. To the stocks? art a justice? shalt not commit me.

Enter Fiddlers.

Dance first, faith.—Why, scrapers, appear under the wenches' comical window,* by the Lord! U'ds daggers, cannot sin be set ashore once in a reign upon your country quarters, but it must have fiddling? what set of villains are you, you perpetual ragamuffins?

First Fid. The town-consort,† sir.

Sir Gos. Consort, with a pox! cannot the shaking of the sheets ‡ be danced without your town-piping? nay, then, let all hell roar.

First Fid. I beseech you, sir, put up yours, and we'll put up ours.

Sir Gos. Play, you lousy Hungarians:§ see, look the Maypole is set up, we'll dance about it. —Keep this circle, maquerelle.||

Bird. I am no mackerel, and I'll keep no circles.

Sir Gos. Play, life of Pharaoh, play: the bawd shall teach me a Scotch jig.

Bird. Bawd! I defy thee and thy jigs, whatsoever thou art: were I in place where, I'd make thee prove thy words.

Sir Gos. I would prove 'em, Mother Best-betrust: why, do not I know you, grannam? and that sugar-loaf? ¶ ha! do I not, Megæra?

Bird. I am none of your Megs: do not nickname me so; I will not be nicked.

---

* *Why, scrapers, appear under the wenches' comical window*] If this be right, I cannot explain it: if it be wrong, I cannot set it right. (In the first ed. of the present work I quoted *"the comical wenches' window"?*)

† *consort*] See note on *Northward Ho*, act ii. sc. i., p. 260.

‡ *the shaking of the sheets*] The name of an old dance, often mentioned with a double entendre by our early dramatists.

§ *Hungarians*] A cant term, alluding either to the Hungarians who once overran a considerable part of Europe, or to the condition of the persons addressed,— *hungry fellows.* See notes of Shakespeare's commentators on *The Merry Wives of Windsor*, act i. sc. iii.

|| *maquerelle*] i. e. bawd, panderess. Brathwait has;
   "Yet, howsoere this *Maquerella* trade,
   She's tane in court and city for a maid."
         The Honest Ghost, 1658, p. 19.
And the old panderess in *The Malcontent* (which forms a ortion of this collection) is named *Maquerelle.*

¶ *sugar-loaf*] i. e. high-crowned hat.

Sir Gos. You will not, you will not! how many of my name, of the Glowworms, have paid for your furred gowns, thou woman's broker?

Bird. No, sir, I scorn to be beholding to any glowworm that lives upon earth for my fur: I can keep myself warm without glowworms.

Sir Gos. Canst sing, woodpecker? come, sing, and wake 'em.

Bird. Would you should well know it, I am no singing woman.

Sir Gos. Howl, then: 'sfoot, sing or howl, or I'll break your ostrich egg-shell there.

Bird. My egg hurts not you: what do you mean, to flourish so?

Sir Gos. Sing, Madge, Madge; sing, owlet.

Bird. How can I sing with such a sour face? I am haunted with a cough and cannot sing.

Sir Gos. One of your instruments, mountebanks.—Come, here, clutch, clutch.

Bird. Alas, sir, I'm an old woman, and know not how to clutch an instrument.

Sir Gos. Look, mark: to and fro, as I rub it; make a noise; it's no matter; any hunt's-up* to waken vice.

Bird. I shall never rub it in tune.

Sir Gos. Will you scrape?

Bird. So you will let me go in to the parties, I will saw and make a noise.

Sir Gos. Do, then: sha't in to the parties, and part 'em; sha't, my lean lena.

Bird. If I must needs play the fool in my old days, let me have the biggest instrument, because I can hold that best: I shall cough like a broken-winded horse, if I gape once to sing once.

Sir Gos. No matter; cough out thy lungs.

Bird. No, sir, though I'm old and worm-eaten, I'm not so rotten.   [*Coughs.*

A Song.†

Will your worship be rid of me now?

Sir Gos. Fain, as rich men's heirs would be of their gouty dads. That's the hot-house where your parties are sweating: amble; go, tell the he parties I have sent 'em a mast to their ship.

Bird. Yes, forsooth, I'll do your errand. [*Exit.*

Sir Gos. Half musty still, by thundering Jove! With what wedge of villany might I cleave out an hour or two?—Fiddlers, come, strike up; march before me: the chamberlain shall put a crown for you into his bill of items. You shall sing bawdy songs under every window i'the

---

* *hunt's-up*] Means properly a tune played to rouse sportsmen in the morning.

† *A Song*] See note †, p. 45.

town: up will the clowns start, down come the wenches; we'll set the men a-fighting, the women a-scolding, the dogs a-barking; you shall go on fiddling, and I follow dancing Lantæra: curry your instruments, play, and away.

[*Exeunt.*

———◆———

SCENE IV.*

Enter TENTERHOOK, HONEYSUCKLE, WAFER, JUSTINIANO, *and* MISTRESS JUSTINIANO, *with* AMBUSH *and* Chamberlain.

Honey. Sergeant Ambush, as thou'rt an honest fellow, scout in some back-room, till the watchword be given for sallying forth.

Amb. Dun's the mouse.†   [*Exit.*

Ten. A little low woman, sayest thou, in a velvet cap, and one of 'em in a beaver?—Brother Honeysuckle, and brother Wafer, hark, they are they.

Wafer. But art sure their husbands are a-bed with 'em?

Cham. I think so, sir; I know not: I left 'em together in one room; and what division fell amongst 'em the fates can discover, not I.

Ten. Leave us, good chamberlain; we are some of their friends; leave us, good chamberlain; be merry a little; leave us, honest chamberlain.

[*Exit Chamberlain.*

We are abused, we are bought and sold in Brainford-market: never did the sickness of one belied nurse-child stick so cold to the hearts of three fathers; never were three innocent citizens so horribly, so abominably wrung under the withers.

Honey., Wafer. What shall we do? how shall we help ourselves?

Honey. How shall we pull this thorn out of our foot, before it rankle?

Ten. Yes, yes, yes, well enough: one of us stay here to watch, do you see? to watch; have an eye, have an ear. I, and my brother Wafer, and Master Justiniano, will set the town in an insurrection, bring hither the constable and his bill-men, break open upon 'em, take 'em in their wickedness, and put 'em to their purgation.

Honey., Wafer. Agreed.

Just. Ha, ha, purgation!

Ten. We'll have 'em before some country justice of coram (for we scorn to be bound to the peace); and this justice shall draw his sword in our defence: if we find 'em to be malefactors, we'll tickle 'em.

Honey. Agreed: do not say, but do't, come.

Just. Are you mad? do you know what you do? whither will you run?

Ten., Honey., Wafer. To set the town in an uproar.

Just. An uproar! will you make the townsmen think that Londoners never come hither but upon Saint Thomas's night? Say you should rattle up the constable, thrash all the country together, hedge in the house with flails, pike-staves, and pitch-forks, take your wives napping, these western smelts nibbling, and that, like so many Vulcans, every smith should discover his Venus dancing with Mars in a net,—would this plaster cure the headache?

Ten. Ay, it would.

*Honey., Wafer.** Nay, it should.

Just. Nego, nego; no, no, it shall be proved unto you, your heads would ache worse: when women are proclaimed to be light, they strive to be more light; for who dare disprove a proclamation?

Ten. Ay, but when light wives make heavy husbands, let these husbands play mad Hamlet,† and cry "Revenge!" Come, and we'll do so.

Mist. Just. Pray, stay, be not so heady, at my entreaty.

Just. My wife entreats you, and I entreat you, to have mercy on yourselves, though you have none over the women. I'll tell you a tale. This last Christmas, a citizen and his wife, as it might be one of you, were invited to the revels one night at one of the Inns-o'-court. The husband, having business, trusts his wife thither to take up a room for him before: she did so; but before she went, doubts arising what blocks her husband would stumble at to hinder his entrance, it was consulted upon by what token, by what trick, by what banner or brooch, he should be known to be he when he rapped at the gate.

Ten., Honey., Wafer. Very good.

Just. The crowd, he was told, would be greater, their clamours greater, and able to drown the throats of a shoal of fishwives: he himself, therefore, devises an excellent watchword, and the sign at which he would hang out himself should be a horn; he would wind his horn, and that should give 'em warning that he was come.

---

* *Scene IV.*] The same. An outer-room in the same.
† *Dun's the mouse*] See the notes of the commentators on
   "Tut, dun's the mouse, the constable's own word."
        Shakespeare's *Romeo and Juliet*, act i. sc.

* HONEY., WAFER] The old ed. "*All 3.*"
† *play mad Hamlet, and cry "Revenge!*"] One of the numerous passages in contemporary writers which attest the popularity of Shakespeare's *Hamlet.*

Ten., Honey., Wafer. So.

Just. The torchmen and whifflers* had an item
to receive him: he comes, rings out his horn with
an alarum, enters with a shout; all the house
rises, thinking some sow-gelder pressed in;† his
wife blushed, the company jested; the simple
man, like a beggar going to the stocks, laughed,
as not being sensible of his own disgrace: and
hereupon the punies set down this decree, that
no man shall hereafter come to laugh at their
revels, if his wife be entered before him, unless
he carry his horn about him.

Wafer. I'll not trouble them.

Just. So, if you trumpet abroad and preach at
the market-cross your wives' shame, 'tis your own
shame.

Ten., Honey., Wafer. What shall we do, then ?

Just. Take my counsel, I'll ask no fee for't:
bar out host, banish mine hostess, beat away the
chamberlain, let the ostlers walk, enter you the
chambers peaceably, lock the doors gingerly, look
upon your wives woefully, but upon the evil-
doers most wickedly.

Ten. What shall we reap by this ?

Just. An excellent harvest, this : you shall hear
the poor mouse-trapped guilty gentlemen call for
mercy ; your wives you shall see kneeling at your
feet, and weeping, and wringing, and blushing,
and cursing Brainford, and crying Pardonnez moi,
pardonnez moi, pardonnez moi ! whilst you have
the choice to stand either as judges to condemn
'em, beadles to torment 'em, or confessors to
absolve 'em. And what a glory will it be for
you three, to kiss your wives like forgetful husbands, to exhort and forgive the young men like
pitiful fathers ; then to call for oars, then to cry
"Hey for London !" then to make a supper,

then to drown all in sack and sugar, then to go
to bed, and then to rise and open shop, where
you may ask any man what he lacks, with your
cap off, and none shall perceive whether the
brims wring you.

Ten. We'll raise no towns.

Honey. No, no; let's knock first.

Wafer. Ay, that's best : I'll summon a parley.
                                          [Knocks.

Mist. Ten. [within] Who's there? have you
stock-fish in hand, that you beat so hard? who
are you ?

Ten. That's my wife : let Justiniano speak, for
all they know our tongues.

Mist. Ten. [within] What a murrain ail these
colts, to keep such a kicking?—Monopoly ?

Just. Yes.

Mist. Ten. [within] Is Master Linstock up too,
and the captain ?

Just. Both are in the field : will you open your
door ?

Mist. Ten. [within] O, you are proper gamesters,
to bring false dice with you from London to
cheat yourselves ! Is't possible that three shallow
women should gull three such gallants ?

Ten. What means this ?

Mist. Ten. [within]. Have we defied you upon
the walls all night, to open our gates to you i' the
morning ? Our honest husbands, they (silly men)
lie praying in their beds now, that the water
under us may not be rough, the tilt that covers
us may not be rent, and the straw about our feet
may keep our pretty legs warm. I warrant they
walk upon Queenhive, as Leander did for Hero,
to watch for our landing : and should we wrong
such kind hearts? would we might ever be
troubled with the toothache, then !

Ten. This thing that makes fools of us thus, is
my wife.   [Knocks.

Mist. Wafer. [within] Ay, ay, knock your
bellies' full : we hug one another a-bed, and lie
laughing till we tickle again, to remember how
we sent you a bat-fowling.

Wafer. An almond, parrot :* that's my Mab's
voice ; I know by the sound.

---

* whifflers] "The term is, undoubtedly, borrowed from
whiffle, another name for a fife or small flute ; for
whifflers were originally those who preceded armies or
processions, as fifers or pipers. . . . In process of
time, the term whiffler, which had always been used in
the sense of a fifer, came to signify any person who went
before in a procession. Minsheu, in his Dictionary, 1617,
describes him to be a club or staff-bearer. Sometimes
the whifflers carried white staves," &c.—Douce's Illustrations of Shakespeare, vol. i. p. 507.

† thinking some sow-gelder pressed in]
  "Have ye any work for the sow-gelder, ho ?
  My horn goes to high, to low, to high, to low !"
    Song by Higgen, disguised as a sow-gelder, in
    Fletcher's Beggars' Bush, act iii. sc. i.
"And so much credit now attends it [i. e. the horn] daily,
That euery common crier, petie baily,
Swine-heards, and braue sow-gelders, in a pride
Doe beare a horne low dangling by their side."
  Breton's Cornu-copiæ, Pasquils Night-cap, &c., p. 108,
  ed. 1612.

* An almond, parrot !] A sort of proverbial expression :
  "An almon now for Parrot, dilycatly drest."
    Skelton's Speke, Parrot,—Works, ii. 4. ed. Dyce.
  "An Almonde for Parret, a Rope for Parrat."
  Houghton's Englishmen for my money, 1616, Sig. G 3.
  "Here's an almond for parrot."
  Dekker and Middleton's Honest Whore (Part First),—
    Middleton's Works, iii. 112, ed. Dyce.
  An Almond for a Parrat, n. d., attributed to Nash, is a
  memorable production ; and one of the poems of the

Just. 'Sfoot, you ha' spoiled half already, and you'll spoil all, if you darn not up your moutha. Villany! nothing but villany! I'm afraid they have smelt your breaths at the key-hole, and now they set you to catch flounders, whilst in the meantime the concupiscentious malefactors make 'em ready, and take London napping.

Ten., Honey., Wafer. I'll not be gulled so.

Ten. Show yourselves to be men, and break open doors.

Just. Break open doors, and show yourselves to be beasts! If you break open doors, your wives may lay flat burglary to your charge.

Honey. Lay a pudding! burglary!

Just. Will you, then, turn Corydons* because you are among clowns? Shall it be said you have no brains, being in Brainford?

Ten., Honey., Wafer. Master Parenthesis, we will enter and set upon 'em.

Just. Well, do so; but enter not so that all the country may cry shame of your doings: knock 'em down, burst open Erebus, and bring an old house over your heads, if you do.

Wafer. No matter, we'll bear it off with head and shoulders. [*Knocks.*

Mist. Wafer. [*within*] You cannot enter, indeed, la.—[*Looks out*] God's my pittikin, our three husbands summon a parley: let that long old woman either creep under the bed, or else stand upright behind the painted cloth. [*Disappears.*

Wafer. Do you hear, you Mabel?

Mist. Wafer. [*looking out*] Let's never hide our heads now, for we are discovered.

Honey. But all this while my Honeysuckle appears not.

Just. Why, then, two of them have pitched their tents there, and yours lies in ambuscado with your enemy there.

Honey. Stand upon your guard there, whilst I batter here. [*Knocks.*

Mon. [*within*] Who's there?

Just. Hold, I'll speak in a small voice, like one of the women.—Here's a friend: are you up? rise, rise; stir, stir.

Mon. [*within*] Ud's foot, what weasel are you? are you going to catch quails, that you bring your pipes with you? I'll see what troubled ghost it is that cannot sleep. [*Looks out.*

Ten. O, Master Monopoly, God save you!

Mon. Amen; for the last time I saw you, the devil was at mine elbow in buff. What! three merry men, and three merry men, and three merry men* be we too.

Hon. How does my wife, Master Monopoly?

Mon. Who? my overthwart† neighbour?— passing well:—this is kindly done: Sir Gosling is not far from you; we'll join our armies presently; here be rare fields to walk in.— Captain, rise; Captain Linstock, bestir your stumps, for the Philistines are upon us.
[*Disappears.*

Ten. This Monopoly is an arrant knave, a cogging knave, for all he's a courtier: if Monopoly be suffered to ride up and down with other men's wives, he'll undo both city and country.

Enter MISTRESS TENTERHOOK, MISTRESS HONEYSUCKLE, *and* MISTRESS WAFER.

Just. Moll, mask thyself; they shall not know thee.

Mist. Ten.,
Mist. Honey., } How now, sweethearts! what
Mist. Wafer. make you here?

Wafer. Not that which you make here.

Ten. Marry, you make bulls of your husbands.

Mist. Ten. Buzzards, do we not? out, you yellow infirmities! do all flowers show in your eyes like columbines?

Wafer. Wife, what says the collier? is not thy soul blacker than his coals? how does the child? how does my flesh and blood, wife?

Mist. Wafer. Your flesh and blood is very well recovered now, mouse.

Wafer. I know 'tis: the collier has a sackful of news to empty.

Ten. Clare, where be your two rings with diamonds?

Mist. Ten. At hand, sir, here, with a wet finger.

Ten. I dreamed you had lost 'em.—[*Aside*] What a profane varlet is this shoulder-clapper, to lie thus upon my wife and her rings!

Enter MONOPOLY, WHIRLPOOL, *and* LINSTOCK.

Mon.,
Whirl., } Save you, gentlemen!
Lin.

---

indefatigable Wither is called *Amygdala Britannica, Almonds for Parrets,* 1647.

* *Corydons*] "The name of this unfortunate shepherd of Virgil [Corydon] seems to have suggested to our old writers a certain mixture of rusticity and folly."

Gifford's Note on Ben Jonson's *Works,* vol. i. p. 40.

* *three merry men, and three merry men, &c.*] A fragment of an old song. See my edition of Peele's *Works,* vol. i. p. 208, sec. ed.; and the notes of the commentators on Shakespeare's *Twelfth Night,* act ii. sc. 3.

† *overthwart*] Generally used for cross, contradictious —but here it seems merely to mean opposite, as in *The Merry Devil of Edmonton,* 1626: "Body of Saint George, this is mine *overthwart neighbour* hath done this." Sig. F 2.

Ten.,
Honey., } And you, and our wives from you !
Wafer.

Mon. Your wives have saved themselves, for one.

Ten. Master Monopoly, though I meet you in High Germany, I hope you can understand broken English; have you discharged your debt ?

Mon. Yes, sir, with a double charge; your harpy, that set his ten commandments upon my back, had two diamonds to save him harmless.

Ten. Of you, sir ?

Mon. Me, sir: do you think there be no diamond courtiers ?

Ten. Sergeant Ambush, issue forth !

Re-enter AMBUSH.

Monopoly, I'll cut off your convoy.—Master Sergeant Ambush, I charge you, as you hope to receive comfort from the smell of mace, speak not like a sergeant, but deal honestly: of whom had you the diamonds ?.

Amb. Of your wife, sir, if I'm an honest man.

Mist. Ten. Of me, you pewter-buttoned rascal !

Mon. Sirrah, you that live by nothing but the carrion of Poultry,—

Mist. Ten. Schoolmaster, hark hither.

Mon. Where are my gems and precious stones, that were my bail ?

Amb. Forthcoming, sir, though your money is not; your creditor has 'em.

Just. Excellent ! peace !—Why, Master Tenterhook, if the diamonds be of the reported value, I'll pay your money, receive 'em, keep 'em till Master Monopoly be fatter i' the purse;—for, Master Monopoly, I know you will not be long empty, Master Monopoly.

Mist. Ten. Let him have 'em, good Tenterhook: where are they ?

Ten. At home; I locked 'em up.

Enter MISTRESS BIRDLIME.

Bird. No, indeed, forsooth, I locked 'em up, and those are they your wife has, and those are they your husband, like a bad liver as he is, would have given to a niece of mine, that lies in my house to take physic, to have committed fleshly treason with her.

Ten. I at your house ! you old ——

Bird. You, perdy; and that honest bachelor: never call me old for the matter.

Mist. Honey. Motherly woman, he's my husband, and no bachelor's buttons are at his doublet.

Bird. 'Las, I speak innocently: and that lean

gentleman set in his staff there. But, as I'm a sinner, both I and the young woman had an eye to the main chance; and though they brought more about 'em than Captain Ca'ndish's voyage * came to, they should not, nor could not, unless I had been a naughty woman, have entered the straits.

Mist. Ten.,
Mist. Honey., } Have we smelt you out, foxes ?
Mist. Wafer.

Mist. Ten. Do you come after us with hue and cry, when you are the thieves yourselves ?

Mist. Honey. Murder, I see, cannot be hid: but if this old sibyl of yours speak oracles, for my part, I'll be like an almanac that threatens nothing but foul weather.

Ten. That bawd has been damned five hundred times; and is her word to be taken ?

Just. To be damned once is enough for any one of her coat.

Bird. Why, sir, what is my coat, that you sit thus upon my skirts ?

Just. Thy coat is an ancient coat; one of the seven deadly sins put thy coat first to making: but do you hear ? you mother of iniquity ! you that can lose and find your ears when you list ! go, sail with the rest of your bawdy traffickers to the place of sixpenny sinfulness, the suburbs.

Bird. I scorn the sinfulness of any suburbs in Christendom: 'tis well known I have up-risers and down-liers within the city, night by night, like a profane fellow as thou art.

Just. Right, I know thou hast.—I'll tell you, gentlefolks; there's more resort to this fortune-teller, than of forlorn wives married to old husbands, and of green-sickness wenches that can get no husbands, to the house of a wise woman: she has tricks to keep a vaulting-house under the law's nose.

Bird. Thou dost the law's nose wrong, to belie me so.

---

* *Captain Ca'ndish's voyage*] The name of Thomas Cavendish (—who, sailing from Plymouth in 1586, with three insignificant vessels, plundered the coast of New Spain and Peru, captured, off California, a Spanish admiral of seven hundred tons, and having circumnavigated the globe, returned to England with a very large fortune, in 1588—) is frequently abbreviated by our old writers: so Brome;

"Ca'ndish and Hawkins, Furbisher, all our voyagers,
    Went short of Mandevile."
                    The Antipodes, 1640, Sig. C 3.
This contraction is scarce yet out of use;
" When Chatsworth tastes no Ca'ndish bounties,
    Let fame forget this costly countess."
            Epitaph by Horace Walpole, in his *Letters to Montagu*, p. 207.

Just. For either a cunning woman has a chamber in her house, or a physician, or a picture-maker, or an attorney, because all these are good cloaks for the rain. And then, if the female party that's cliented above-stairs be young, she's a squire's daughter of low degree, that lies there for physic, or comes up to be placed with a countess; if of middle age, she's a widow, and has suits at the term or so.

Mist. Honey. O, fie upon her! burn the witch out of our company.

Mist. Ten. Let's hem her out of Brainford, if she get not the faster to London.

Mist. Wafer. O, no, for God's sake! rather hem her out of London, and let her keep in Brainford still.

Bird. No, you cannot hem me out of London. —Had I known this, your rings should ha' been poxed ere I would ha' touched 'em. I will take a pair of oars and leave you. [*Exit.*

Just. Let that ruin of intemperance be raked up in dust and ashes. And now tell me, if you had raised the town, had not the tiles tumbled upon your heads! for you see your wives are chaste, these gentlemen civil; all is but a merriment, all but a May-game: she has her diamonds, you shall have your money; the child is recovered, the false collier discovered; they came to Brainford to be merry; you were caught in Bird-lime: and therefore set the hare's-head against the goose-giblets,* put all instruments in tune, and every husband play music upon the lips of his wife, whilst I begin first.

Ten.,
Honey, } Come, wenches; be't so.
Wafer.

---

* *set the hare's-head against the goose-giblets*] A pro-verbial expression, signifying to balance things, to set one against another: compare Field's *Amends for Ladies*, Sig. B 3, ed. 1639; and Middleton's *A Trick to catch the old one.—Works*, ii. 73, ed. Dyce. Sometimes it occurs with a slight variation: " set the Hare *Pye* against the Goose gibleta." Rowley's *Match at Midnight*, 1633, Sig. I 2. " Ide set mine olde debts against my new driblets, and the hare's *foot* against the goose giblets." Dekker's *Shoemakers Holiday*, 1600, Sig. C.

Mist. Ten. Mistress Justiniano, is't you were ashamed all this while of showing your face?— Is she your wife, schoolmaster?

Just. Look you, your schoolmaster has been in France, and lost his hair;* no more Parenthesis now, but Justiniano: I will now play the merchant with you. Look not strange at her, nor at me: the story of us both shall be as good as an old wife's tale, to cut off our way to London.

Enter Chamberlain.

How now!

Cham. Alas, sir, the knight yonder, Sir Gosling, has almost his throat cut by poulterers and towns-men and rascals; and all the noise that went with him, poor fellows, have their fiddle-cases pulled over their ears.

Omnes. Is Sir Gosling hurt?

Cham. Not much hurt, sir[s]; but he bleeds like a pig, for his crown's cracked.

Mist. Honey. Then has he been twice cut i' the head since we landed, once with a pottle-pot, and now with old iron.

Just. Gentlemen, hasten to his rescue some, whilst others call for oars.

Omnes. Away, then, to London.

Just. Farewell, Brainford.——
Gold that buys health can never be ill spent,
Nor hours laid out in harmless merriment.

SONG.

Oars, oars, oars, oars!
To London, hey! to London, hey!
Hoist up sails, and let's away;
For the safest bay
For us to land is London shores.
Oars, oars, oars, oars!
Quickly shall we get to land,
If you, if you, if you
Lend us but half a hand:
O, lend us half a hand!
 [*Exeunt.*

---

* *Look you, your schoolmaster has been in France, and lost his hair*] Here we must suppose Justiniano to pull off the false hair which assisted his disguise: he alludes to the effects of the venereal, or, as it was called, the French disease.

NORTHWARD HO.

North-ward Hoe. Sundry times Acted by the Children of Paules. By Thomas Decker, and John Webster. Imprinted at London by G. Eld. 1607. 4to.

Concerning the origin of the title of this comedy, see the prefatory remarks to the proceding play.

DRAMATIS PERSONÆ.

———◆———

Mayberry.
Bellamont.
Philip.
Greenshield.
Featherstone.
Leverpool.
Chartley.
Hornet.
Hans Van Belch.
Allum.
Captain Jenkins.
Leapfrog.
Squirrel.
Chamberlain.
Prentice.
Tailor.
Fullmoon.
Musician, Sergeants, Keepers, Fiddlers, Tapsters, Servants.

Mistress Mayberry
Kate.
Doll.
Bawd.
Hostess.
Maids.

NORTHWARD HO.

ACT I.

SCENE I.*

Enter GREENSHIELD *and* FEATHERSTONE, *booted.*

Feath. Art sure old Mayberry inns here to-night?

Green. 'Tis certain: the honest knave chamberlain, that hath been my informer, my bawd, ever since I knew Ware, assures me of it; and more, being a Londoner, though altogether unacquainted, I have requested his company at supper.

Feath. Excellent occasion! how we shall carry ourselves in this business is only to be thought upon.

Green. Be that my undertaking: if I do not take a full revenge of his wife's puritanical coyness!

Feath. Suppose it she should be chaste?

Green. O, hang her! this art of seeming honest makes many of our young sons and heirs in the city look so like our prentices.—Chamberlain!

Enter Chamberlain.

Cham. Here, sir.

Green. This honest knave is called Innocence: is't not a good name for a chamberlain? He dwelt at Dunstable not long since, and hath brought me and the two butcher's daughters there to interview twenty times, and not so little, I protest.—How chance you left Dunstable, sirrah?

Cham. Faith, sir, the town drooped ever since the peace in Ireland. Your captains were wont to take their leaves of their London pole-cats (their wenches I mean, sir,) at Dunstable: the next morning, when they had broke their fast together, the wenches brought them to Hockley-i'-the-Hole; and so the one for London, the other

for West-Chester.* Your only road now, sir, is York, York, sir.

Green. True; but yet it comes scant of the prophecy,—Lincoln was, London is, and York shall be.

Cham. Yes, sir, 'tis fulfilled; York shall be, that is, it shall be York still: surely, it was the meaning of the prophet.—Will you have some cray-fish and a spitchcock?

Feath. And a fat trout.

Cham. You shall, sir.—The Londoners you wot of. [*Exit.*

Enter MAYBERRY *and* BELLAMONT.

Green. Most kindly welcome: I beseech you hold our boldness excused, sir.

Bell. Sir, it is the health of travellers to enjoy good company: will you walk?

Feath. Whither travel you, I beseech you?

May. To London, sir: we came from Sturbridge.

Bell. I tell you, gentlemen, I have observed very much with being at Sturbridge;† it hath

---

* *West-Chester*] On their way to Ireland: "My refuge is *Ireland* or Virginia; necessity cries out, and I will presently to *Westchester*." Cook's *Green's Tu Quoque*, Sig. B, ed. 1622. "Hee came into *Ireland*, where at Dubblin hee was strucke lame; but recovering new strength and courage, hee ship'd himselfe for England, landed at *West-Chester*, whence taking poste towards London, hee lodg'd at Hockley in the Hole, in his way," &c. Taylor the water poet's *Praise of cleane Linnen*,—*Works*, 1630, p. 170. It may perhaps be necessary to add, that the ancient city of Chester is called *West Chester*, from its relative situation, to distinguish it from several other towns which bear the name of Chester with some addition.

† *I have observed very much with being at Sturbridge*] Sturbridge fair, from which our two travellers are just come, is mentioned by old Skelton;

"And *syllogisari* was drowned at *Sturbridge fayre*."

Speke, Parrot,—Works, ii. 9, ed. Dyce. And it was resorted to both for business and pleasure

---

* *Scene I.*] Ware. A room in an inn.

afforded me mirth beyond the length of five Latin comedies. Here should you meet a Norfolk yeoman full-butt, with his head able to overturn you, and his pretty wife, that followed him, ready to excuse the ignorant hardness of her husband's forehead; in the goose-market number of freshmen, stuck here and there with a graduate, like cloves with great heads in a gammon of bacon; here two gentlemen making a marriage between their heirs over a woolpack; there a minister's wife that could speak false Latin very lispingly; here two in one corner of a shop, Londoners, selling their wares, and other gentlemen courting their wives; where they take up petti-coats, you should find scholars and town's-men's wives crowding together, while their husbands were in another market busy amongst the oxen;—'twas like a camp, for in other countries so many punks do not follow an army: I could make an excellent description of it in a comedy.—But whither are you travelling, gentlemen?

Feath. Faith, sir, we purposed a dangerous voyage; but upon better consideration we altered our course.

May. May we without offence partake the ground of it?

Green. 'Tis altogether trivial, in sooth; but, to pass away the time till supper, I'll deliver it to you, with protestation before hand, I seek not to publish every gentlewoman's dishonour, only by the passage of my discourse to have you censure * the state of our quarrel.

Bell. Forth, sir.

Green. Frequenting the company of many mer-chants' wives in the city, my heart by chance leaped into mine eye to affect the fairest, but withal the falsest, creature that ever affection stooped to.

May. Of what rank was she, I beseech you?

Feath. Upon your promise of secrecy?

Bell. You shall close it up like treasure of

your own, and yourself shall keep the key of it.*

Green. She was, and by report still is, wife to a most grave and well-reputed citizen.

May. And entertained your love?

Green. As meadows do April. The violence, as it seemed, of her affection—but, alas, it proved her dissembling—would, at my coming and de-parting, bedew her eyes with love-drops: O, she could† the art of woman most feelingly!

Bell. Most feelingly!

May. I should not have liked that feelingly, had she been my wife.—Give us some sack, here! —and, in faith,—we are all friends, and in private, —what was her husband's name?—I'll give you a carouse by and by.

Green. O, you shall pardon me his name: it seems you are a citizen; it would be discourse enough for you upon the Exchange this fortnight, should I tell his name.

Bell. Your modesty in this wife's commenda-tion!—On, sir.

Green. In the passage of our loves, amongst other favours of greater value, she bestowed upon me this ring, which, she protested, was her hus-band's gift.

May. The posy, the posy?—[*Aside*] O my heart! that ring?—Good, in faith.

Green. Not many nights coming to her, and being familiar with her,——

May. Kissing, and so forth?

Green. Ay, sir.

May. And talking to her feelingly?

Green. Pox on't, I lay with her.

May. Good, in faith; you are of a good com-plexion.

Green. Lying with her, as I say, and rising somewhat early from her in the morning, I lost this ring in her bed.

May. [*aside*] In my wife's bed!

Feath. How do you, sir?

May. Nothing.—Let's have a fire, chamberlain! —I think my boots have taken water, I have such a shuddering.—I' the bed, you say?

Green. Right, sir, in Mistress Mayberry's sheets.

May. Was her name Mayberry?

Green. Beshrew my tongue for blabbing! I presume upon your secrecy.

---

long after the present play was produced. Ned Ward wrote a piece full of low humour, called *A Step to Stir-Bitch Fair;* see the second vol. of his works, p. 248, ed. 1706. The reader who is desirous of authentic informa-tion on such matters will find a long and curious account of Sturbridge fair in Defoe's *Tour through Britain,* vol. i. p. 83, sqq., ed. 1742: "It is not only," says he, "the greatest in the whole nation, but I think in Europe; nor is the Fair at Leipsick in Saxony, the Mart at Frankfort on the Main, or the Fairs at Nurem-berg or Augsburg, reputed any way comparable to this at Sturbridge."

* *censure*] i. e. judge of, give an opinion on.

* *and yourself shall keep the key of it*] From Shake-speare;

"'Tis in my memory lock'd,
And you yourself shall keep the key of it."
Hamlet, act i. sc. 3.

† *could*] i. e. knew, understood.

May. O God, sir! but where did you find your losing?

Green. Where I found her falseness,—with this gentleman, who, by his own confession, partaking the like enjoyment, found this ring the same morning on her pillow, and shamed not in my sight to wear it.

May. What, did she talk feelingly to him too? I warrant, her husband was forth o' town all this while; and he, poor man, travelled with hard eggs in's pocket, to save the charge of a bait, whilst she was at home with her plovers, turkey, chickens. Do you know that Mayberry?

Feath. No more than by name.

May. He's a wondrous honest man.—Let's be merry.—Will not your mistress—gentlemen, you are tenants in common, I take it?—

Feath., }
Green. } Yes.

May. Will not your mistress make much of her husband when he comes home, as if no such legerdemain had been acted?

Green. Yes, she hath reason for't: for in some countries, where men and women have good travelling stomachs, they begin with porridge; then they fall to capon or so forth; but if capon come short of filling their bellies, to their porridge again, 'tis their only course: so for our women in England.

May. This, with taking of long journeys, kindred that comes in o'er the hatch, and sailing to Westminster, makes a number of cuckolds.

Bell. Fie, what an idle quarrel is this! Was this her ring?

Green. Her ring, sir.

May. A pretty idle toy: would you would take money for't!

Feath., }
Green. } Money, sir!

May. The more I look on't, the more I like it.

Bell. Troth, 'tis of no great value; and considering the loss and finding of this ring made breach into your friendship, gentlemen, with this trifle purchase his love: I can tell you he keeps a good table.

Green. What, my mistress' gift!

Feath. Faith, you are a merry old gentleman; I'll give you my part in't.

Green. Troth, and mine, with your promise to conceal it from her husband.

May. Doth he know of it yet?

Green. No, sir.

May. He shall never, then, I protest: look you, this ring doth fit me passing well.

Feath. I am glad we have fitted you.

May. This walking is wholesome: I was a-cold even now; now I sweat for't.

Feath. Shall's walk into the garden, Luke?— Gentlemen, we'll down and hasten supper.

May. Look you, we must be better acquainted, that's all.

Green. Most willingly.—[*Aside to* FEATH.] Excellent! he's heat to the proof: let's withdraw, and give him leave to rave a little.

    [*Exeunt* GREENSHIELD *and* FEATHERSTONE.

May. Chamberlain, give us a clean towel!

Re-enter Chamberlain *with towel.*

Bell. How now, man!

May. I am foolish old Mayberry, and yet I can be wise Mayberry too: I'll to London presently.— Be gone, sir.   [*Exit* Chamberlain.

Bell. How, how!

May. Nay, nay, God's precious, you do mistake me, Master Bellamont: I am not distempered; for to know a man's wife is a whore, is to be resolved of it; and to be resolved of it, is to make no question of it; and when a case is out of question,—what was I saying?

Bell. Why, look you, what a distraction are you fallen into!

May. If a man be divorced, do you see, divorced *forma juris,* whether may he have an action or no 'gainst those that make horns at him?

Bell. O madness! that the frailty of a woman should make a wise man thus idle! Yet, I protest, to my understanding, this report seems as far from truth as you from patience.

May. Then am I a fool; yet I can be wise, an I list, too: what says my wedding-ring?

Bell. Indeed, that breeds some suspicion: for the rest, most gross and open; for two men both to love your wife, both to enjoy her bed, and to meet you as if by miracle, and, not knowing you, upon no occasion in the world, to thrust upon you a discourse of a quarrel, with circumstance so dishonest, that not any gentleman but of the country blushing would have published, ay, and to name you. Do you know them?

May. Faith, now I remember, I have seen them walk muffled by my shop.

Bell. Like enough: pray God they do not borrow money of us 'twixt Ware and London! Come, strive to blow over those clouds.

May. Not a cloud; you shall have clean moonshine. They have good smooth looks, the fellows.

Bell. As jet: they will take up, I warrant you, where they may be trusted. Will you be merry?

May. Wondrous merry :—let's have some sack to drown this cuckold; down with him!—wondrous merry. One word and no more; I am but a foolish tradesman, and yet I'll be a wise tradesman. [*Exeunt.*

SCENE II.*

Enter DOLL, *led between* LEVERPOOL *and* CHARTLEY; *after them,* PHILIP *arrested, and Sergeants.*

Philip. Arrest me ! at whose suit?—Tom Chartley, Dick Leverpool, stay; I'm arrested.

Chart., Lever., Doll. Arrested !

First Serg. Gentlemen, break not the head of the peace: it's to no purpose, for he's in the law's clutches; you see he's fanged.

Doll. Ud's life, do you stand with your naked weapons in your hand, and do nothing with 'em? Put one of 'em into my fingers, I'll tickle the pimple-nosed varlets.

Phil. Hold, Doll.—Thrust not a weapon upon a mad woman.—Officers, step back into the tavern: you might ha' ta'en me i' the street, and not i' the tavern-entry, you cannibals.

Sec. Serg. We did it for your credit, sir.

Chart. How much is the debt?—Drawer, some wine !

Enter Drawer with wine.

First Serg. Fourscore pound.—Can you send for bail, sir ? or what will you do? we cannot stay.

Doll. You cannot, you pasty-footed rascals! you will stay one day in hell.

Phil. Fourscore pounds draws deep.—Farewell, Doll.—Come, sergeants, I'll step to mine uncle not far off, hereby in Pudding-lane, and he shall bail me:—if not, Chartley, you shall find me playing at span-counter†: —and so, farewell: send me some tobacco.

First Serg. Have an eye to his hands.

Sec. Serg. Have an eye to his legs.

[*Exeunt* PHILIP *and Sergeants.*

Doll. I'm as melancholy now !

Chart. Villanous, spiteful luck! I'll hold my life, some of these saucy drawers betrayed him.

Draw. We, sir ! no, by gad, sir, we scorn to have a Judas in our company.

Lever. No, no; he was dogged in : this is the end of all dicing.

Doll. This is the end of all whores, to fall into the hands of knaves.—Drawer, tie my shoe, prithee; the new knot, as thou seest this— Philip is a good honest gentleman : I love him because he'll spend; but when I saw him on his father's hobby, and a brace of punks following him in a coach, I told him he would run out.— Hast done, boy ?

Draw. Yes, forsooth : by my troth, you have a dainty leg.

Doll. How now, goodman rogue !

Draw. Nay, sweet Mistress Doll.

Doll. Doll ! you reprobate ! out, you bawd for seven years by the custom of the city !

Draw. Good Mistress Dorothy, the pox take me, if I touched your leg but to a good intent.

Doll. Prate you?—The rotten-toothed rascal will for sixpence fetch any whore to his master's customers :—and is every one that swims in a taffeta gown lettuce for your lips? Ud's life, this is rare, that gentlewomen and drawers must suck at one spiggot. Do you laugh, you unseasonable puckfist?* do you grin?

Chart. Away, drawer !—Hold, prithee, good rogue ; hold, my sweet Doll : a pox o' this swaggering ! [*Exit Drawer.*

Doll. Pox o' your guts, your kidneys! mew, hang ye, rook !—I'm as melancholy now as Fleet-street in a long vacation.

Lever. Melancholy ! come, we'll ha' some mulled sack.

Doll. When begins the term ?

Chart. Why, hast any suits to be tried at Westminster?

Doll. My suits, you base ruffian, have been tried at Westminster already. So soon as ever the term begins, I'll change my lodging; it stands out o' the way : I'll lie about Charing-cross, for if there be any stirrings, there we shall have 'em ; or if some Dutchman would come from the States—O, these Flemings pay soundly for what they take.

Lever. If thou't have a lodging westward, Doll, I'll fit thee.

Doll. At Tyburn, will you not? a lodging of your providing ! to be called a lieutenant's or a captain's wench ! O, I scorn to be one of your Low-country commodities, I ! Is this body made to be maintained with provant and dead pay?†

---

* *Scene II.*] London. An outer-room in a tavern.

† *span-counter*] A pun is intended here: *span-counter* being a common game among boys, *counter*, the prison, to which, if he could procure no bail, Philip was to be consigned.

* *puckfist*] This word, used often by our old writers in the sense of an empty, insignificant fellow, meant originally a sort of fungus : "all the sallets are turn'd to Jewes-cars, mushrooms, and *Puckfists.*" Heywood and Bromo's *Lancashire Witches,* 1634, Sig. F 4.

† *provant and dead pay*] "Provant" is—provender, military allowance : for "dead pay," see note *, p. 176.

no; the mercer must be paid, and satin gowns must be ta'en up.

Chart. And gallon pots must be tumbled down.

Doll. Stay; I have had a plot a-breeding in my brains—Are all the quest-houses broken up?*

Lever. Yes, long since: what then?

Doll. What then! marry, then is the wind come about, and so † those poor wenches, that before Christmas fled westward with bag and baggage, come now sailing alongst the lee shore with a northerly wind; and we that had warrants to lie without the liberties come now dropping into the freedom by owl-light sneakingly.

Chart. But, Doll, what's the plot thou speakest of?

Doll. Marry, this. Gentlemen, and tobacco-stinkers, and such-like, are still buzzing where sweet-meats are, like flies; but they make any flesh stink that they blow upon: I will leave those fellows, therefore, in the hands of their laundresses. Silver is the king's stamp, man God's stamp, and a woman is man's stamp; we are not current till we pass from one man to another.

Lever., }
Chart. } Very good.

Doll. I will, therefore, take a fair house in the city; no matter though it be a tavern that has blown up his master; it shall be in trade still, for I know divers taverns i' the town that have but a wall between them and a hot-house.‡ It shall then be given out that I'm a gentlewoman of such a birth, such a wealth, have had such a breeding, and so forth, and of such a carriage,

and such qualities, and so forth : to set it off the better, old Jack Hornet shall take upon him to be my father.

Lever. Excellent! with a chain about his neck, and so forth.

Doll. For that Saint Martin's and we will talk.* I know we shall have gudgeons bite presently; if they do, boys, you shall live like knights fellows : as occasion serves, you shall wear liveries and wait; but when gulls are my windfalls, you shall be gentlemen and keep them company. Seek out Jack Hornet incontinently.

Lever. We will.—Come, Chartley.—We'll play our parts, I warrant.

Doll. Do so.
The world's a stage, from which strange shapes we borrow;
To-day we are honest, and rank knaves tomorrow.   [*Exeunt.*

<hr/>

SCENE III.†

Enter MAYBERRY, BELLAMONT, *and a* Prentice.

May. Where is your mistress, villain? when went she abroad?

Pren. Abroad, sir! why, as soon as she was up, sir.

May. Up, sir, down, sir! so, sir.—Master Bellamont, I will tell you a strange secret in nature; this boy is my wife's bawd.

Bell. O, fie, sir, fie! the boy, he does not look like a bawd; he has no double chin.‡

Pren. No, sir; nor my breath does not stink, I smell not of garlic or aqua-vitæ: I use not to be drunk with sack and sugar; I swear not, "God damn me, if I know where the party is," when 'tis a lie and I do know: I was never carted, but in harvest; never whipt, but at school; never had the grincomes;§ never sold one maidenhead ten several times, first to an

---

* *Are all the quest-houses broken up?*] About Christmas, I believe, the aldermen and citizens of each ward in the city, used to hold a quest to inquire concerning misdemeanours and annoyances, brothels, &c. *Quest-houses* were the houses where the quest was held, and which were usually the chief watchhouses. Doll, in her next speech, alludes to the shifts made by the ladies when driven out of the city, and their private return when they no longer feared the quest.

From a passage in one of Middleton's plays it appears that gaming was sometimes carried on there : "Such a day I lost fifty pound in hugger-mugger at dice, at the *quest-house.*" *Any thing for a quiet life.—Works,* iv. 425, ed. Dyce.

Quest-houses generally adjoined churches. "But you may say, it is like a farthing candle in a great church : I answer, that light will not enlighten the by-chapels of the church, nor *the quest-house,* nor the belfry; neither doth the light move the church, though it enlightens it." *Philosophical Letters* by the Duchess of Newcastle, 1664, p. 139.

† *so*] The old ed. "*for.*"

‡ *a hot-house*] See note †, p. 209.

* *with a chain about his neck* . . . *For that Saint Martin's and we will talk*] So Brathwait:

"By this bee travells *to Saint Martins lane,*
And to the shops he goes *to buy a chaine.*"
The Honest Ghost, &c., 1658, p. 167.

† *Scene III.*] The same. A room in the house of Mayberry.

‡ *double chin*] The characteristic of a bawd, according to many of our old dramatists:

"The bawds will be so fat with what they earn,
Their chins will hang like udders, by Easter-eve."
Middleton's *Chaste Maid in Cheapside,—Works,*
iv. 32, ed. Dyce.

§ *grincomes*] Or *crincomes,* a cant term for the venereal disease: "Grinkcomes," says Taylor, the water poet, "is an Utopian word, which is in English a P. at Paris." *Works,* 1630, p. 111.

Englishman, then to a Welshman, then to a Dutchman, then to a pocky Frenchman : I hope, sir, I am no bawd, then.

May. Thou art a baboon, and holdest me with tricks, whilst my wife grafts, grafts. Away, trudge, run, search her out by land and by water.

Pren. Well, sir, the land I'll ferret, and, after that, I'll search her by water, for it may be she's gone to Brainford.

May. Inquire at one of mine aunts.[*]

Bell. One of your aunts ! are you mad ?

May. Yes, as many of the twelve companies are,—troubled, troubled.   [*Exit* Prentice.

Bell. I'll chide you ; go to, I'll chide you soundly.

May. O Master Bellamont !

Bell. O Master Mayberry ! before your servant to dance a Lancashire hornpipe ! it shows worse to me than dancing does to a deaf man that sees not the fiddles : 'sfoot, you talk like a player.

May. If a player talk like a madman, or a fool, or an ass, and knows not what he talks, then I'm one. You are a poet, Master Bellamont ; I will bestow a piece of plate upon you to bring my wife upon the stage : would not her humour please gentlemen ?

Bell. I think it would. Yours would make gentlemen as fat as fools : I would give two pieces of plate to have you stand by me when I were to write a jealous man's part. Jealous men are either knaves or coxcombs ; be you neither : you wear yellow hose without cause.

May. Without cause, when my mare bears double ! without cause !

Bell. And without wit.

May. When two virginal-jacks[†] skip up, as the key of my instrument goes down !—

Bell. They are two wicked elders.

May. When my wife's ring does smoke for't !

Bell. Your wife's ring may deceive you.

May. O Master Bellamont ! had it not been my wife had made me a cuckold, it should never have grieved me.

Bell. You wrong her, upon my soul.

May. No, she wrongs me upon her body.

Enter a Servingman.

Bell. Now, blue-bottle ?[*] what flutter you for, sea-pie ?

Serv. Not to catch fish, sir : my young master, your son, Master Philip, is taken prisoner.

Bell. By the Dunkirks ?[†]

Serv. Worse ; by catchpolls[‡] he's encountered.

Bell. Shall I never see that prodigal come home ?

Serv. Yes, sir, if you'll fetch him out, you may kill a calf for him.

Bell. For how much lies he ?

Serv. The debt is four-score pound : marry, he charged me to tell you it was four-score and ten, so that he lies only for the odd ten pound.

Bell. His child's part[§] shall now be paid : this money shall be his last, and this vexation the last of mine.—If you had such a son, Master Mayberry !

May. To such a wife ; 'twere an excellent couple.

Bell. [*giving money to* Serv.] Release him, and release me of much sorrow : I will buy a son no more : go, redeem him.   [*Exit* Servingman.

Re-enter Prentice *with* MISTRESS MAYBERRY.

Pren. Here's the party, sir.

May. Hence, and lock fast the doors : now is my prize.

Pren. [*aside*] If she beat you not at your own weapon, would her buckler were cleft in two pieces !   [*Exit.*

Bell. I will not have you handle her too roughly.

May. No, I will, like a justice of peace, grow to the point.—Are not you a whore ? never start ; thou art a cloth-worker, and hast turned me—

Mist. May. How, sir ! into what, sir, have I turn'd you ?

May. Into a civil suit, into a sober beast, a land-rat, a cuckold : thou art a common bed-fellow ; art not, art not ?

---

[*] *aunts*] Few readers of old plays require to be told that *aunt* was a cant name for a bawd or prostitute.

[†] *virginal-jacks*] A virginal was a kind of spinnet : "In a *virginal*," says Bacon, "as soon as ever the *jack* falleth, and toucheth the string, the sound ceaseth." And Brathwait ;

     " For, like to *jacks* mov'd in a *virginal*,
     I thought ones rising was anothers fall."
               Honest Ghost, 1658, p. 128.

[*] *blue-bottle*] Blue was the colour usually worn by servants of the time.

[†] *Dunkirks*] i. e. privateers of Dunkirk.

[‡] *by catchpolls he's encountered*] So Sir John Harington ;
     " Till at the last two *catch-poles him encounter.*"
                 Epigram 99, Book II.

[§] *His child's part*] Compare Heywood ;
     "But putst them [moneys] to increase, where in short time
     They grow a *child's part*, or a daughter's portion."
          The Fair Maid of the Exchange, 1637, Sig. D 3.
And *The Famous Historye of Thomas Stukely*, 1605 ;
     "Not so sick, sir, but I hope to have a *child's part* by your last will and testament." Sig C 3.

Mist. May. Sir, this language
To me is strange; I understand it not.

May. O, you study the French now.

Mist. May. Good sir, lend me patience.

May. I made a sallad of that herb :* dost see
these flesh-hooks? I could tear out those false
eyes, those cat's eyes, that can see in the night ;
punk, I could.

Bell. Hear her answer for herself.

· *Mist. May.* Good Master Bellamont,
Let him not do me violence.—Dear sir,
Should any but yourself shoot out those names,
I would put off all female modesty,
To be reveng'd on him.

May. Know'st thou this ring?
There has been old running at the ring† since I
went.

Mist. May. Yes, sir, this ring is mine : he was
a villain
That stole it from my hand ; he was a villain
That put it into yours.

May. They were no villains
When they stood stoutly for me, took your part,
And, 'stead of colours, fought under my sheets.

Mist. May. I know not what you mean.

May. They lay with thee :
I mean plain dealing.

Mist. May. With me ! if ever I had thought
unclean,
In detestation of your nuptial pillow,
Let sulphur drop from heaven, and nail my body
Dead to this earth ! That slave, that damnèd Fury,
Whose whips are in your tongue to torture me,
Casting an eye unlawful on my cheek,
Haunted your threshold daily, and threw forth
All tempting baits which lust and credulous
youth
Apply to our frail sex : but those being weak,
The second siege he laid was in sweet words.

May. And then the breach was made.

Bell. Nay, nay, hear all.

Mist. May. At last he takes me sitting at your
door,
Seizes my palm, and, by the charm of oaths
Back to restore it straight, he won my hand
To crown his finger with that hoop of gold.
I did demand it ; but he, mad with rage
And with desires unbridled, fled, and vow'd
That ring should me undo : and now belike

His spells have wrought on you. But I beseech
you
To dare him to my face, and in mean time
Deny me bed-room, drive me from your board,
Disgrace me in the habit of your slave,
Lodge me in some discomfortable vault,
Where neither sun nor moon may touch my
sight,
Till of this slander I my soul acquite.

Bell. Guiltless, upon my soul !

May. Troth, so think I.
I now draw in your bow, as I before
Suppos'd they drew in mine : my stream of
jealousy
Ebbs back again, and I, that like a horse
Ran blind-fold in a mill, all in one circle,
Yet thought I had gone fore-right, now spy my
error.—
Villains, you have abus'd me, and I vow
Sharp vengeance on your heads !—Drive in your
tears :
I take your word you're honest ; which good
men,
Very good men, will scarce do to their wives.
I will bring home these serpents, and allow them
The heat of mine own bosom : wife, I charge you, ·
Set out your haviours towards them in such
colours
As if you had been their whore ; I'll have it so.
I'll candy o'er my words, and sleek my brow,
Entreat 'em that they would not point at me,
Nor mock my horns : with this arm I'll embrace
'em,
And with this——go to !

Mist. May. O, we shall have murder !
You kill my heart.

May. No, I will shed no blood ;
But I will be reveng'd ; they that do wrong
Teach others way to right. I'll fetch my blow
Fair and afar off, and, as fencers use,
Though at the foot I strike, the head I'll bruise.

Bell. I'll join with you : let's walk.—O, here's
my son.

Enter PHILIP *with* Servingman.

Welcome ashore, sir : from whence come you,
pray?

Phil. From the house of prayer and fasting,
the Counter.

Bell. Art not thou ashamed to be seen come
out of a prison?

Phil. No, God's my judge ; but I was ashamed
to go into prison.

Bell. I am told, sir, that you spend your credit and your coin upon a light woman.

---

* *a sallad of that herb*] *Patience* was the name of an
herb : "you may recover it with a sallet of parsly and
the heurbe patience." *A pleasant commodie called Looks
about you*, 1600, Sig. C 3.

† *running at the ring*] See note *, p. 60.

Phil. I ha' seen light gold, sir, pass away amongst mercers.

Bell. And that you have laid thirty or forty pounds upon her back in taffeta gowns and silk petticoats.

Phil. None but tailors will say so : I ne'er laid any thing upon her back. I confess I took up a petticoat and a raised fore-part for her ; but who has to do with that ?

May. Marry, that has every body, Master Philip.

Bell. Leave her company, or leave me ; for she's a woman of an ill name.

Phil. Her name is Dorothy, sir ; I hope that's no ill name.

Bell. What is she ? what wilt thou do with her ?

*May.** 'Sblood, sir, what does he with her !

Bell. Dost mean to marry her ? of what birth is she ? what are her comings in ? what does she live upon ?

Phil. Rents, sir, rents,† she lives upon her rents ; and I can have her.

Bell. You can ?

Phil. Nay, father, if destiny dog me, I must have her. You have often told me the nine Muses are all women, and you deal with them : may not I the better be allowed one than you so many ? Look you, sir, the northern man loves white-meats, the southern man sallads, the Essex man a calf, the Kentish man a wag-tail, the Lancashire man an egg-pie, the Welshman leeks and cheese, and your Londoners raw mutton ; so, father, God b'wi'you, I was born in London.

Bell. Stay, look you, sir : as he that lives upon sallads without mutton feeds like an ox (for he eats grass, you know), yet rises as hungry as an ass ; and as he that makes a dinner of leeks will have lean cheeks : so thou, foolish Londoner, if nothing but raw mutton can diet thee, look to live* like a fool and a slave, and to die like a beggar and a knave.—Come, Master Mayberry.—Farewell, boy.

Phil. Farewell, Father Snot.†—Sir[s], if I have her, I'll spend more in mustard and vinegar in a year than both you in beef.

Bell.,
May. } More saucy knave thou.　　　[*Exeunt.*

ACT II.

SCENE I.‡

Enter HORNET, DOLL, LEVERPOOL *and* CHARTLEY *like Servingmen.*

Hor. Am I like a fiddler's base-viol, new set up, in a good case, boys ? is't neat, is it terse ? am I handsome, ha ?

Omnes. Admirable, excellent !

Doll. An under-sheriff cannot cover a knave more cunningly.

Lever. 'Sfoot, if he should come before a church-warden, he would make him pew-fellow with a lord's steward at least.

Hor. If I had but a staff in my hand, fools would think I were one of Simon and Jude's gentlemen-ushers, and that my apparel were hired. They say three tailors go to the making up of a man ; but I'm sure I had four tailors and a half went to the making of me thus : this suit, though it ha' been canvassed well, yet 'tis no lawsuit, for 'twas despatched sooner than a posset on a wedding-night.

Doll. Why, I tell thee, Jack Hornet, if the devil and all the brokers in Long-lane had rifled their wardrobe, they would ha' been damned before they had fitted thee thus.

Hor. Punk, I shall be a simple father for you. How does my chain show, now I walk ?

Doll. If thou wert hung in chains, thou couldst not show better.

Chart. But how sit our blue coats on our backs ?

---

* MAY] The old ed. "*Phil.*"

† *Rents, sir, rents,* &c.] The reader who is curious in parallel passages may turn to Middleton's *Blurt, Master Constable.*—*Works,* i. 268, ed. Dyce.

‡ *Scene I.*] London. A room in Doll's house. (A tavern,—the Shipwreck Tavern,—it would seem : she has previously said, p. 253, "I will, therefore, take a fair house in the city ; no matter though it be a *tavern* that has blown up his master," &c. ; and compare her words at the close of the present scene ; "So will we four be drunk i' *the Shipwreck Tavern.*"

* *look to live*] Qy. was a couplet intended here ?

† *Farewell, Father Snot*] This elegant valediction (after which, in the old copy, is a short break) was, perhaps, a parody on, or a quotation from, some song : in *The Wit of a Woman,* 1604, I find,

"My bush and my pot
　Cares not a groate
For such a lob-coats,
　Farewell, Sinior snot."—Sig. G 3.

Doll. As they do upon bankrupt retainers' backs at Saint George's feast in London; but at Westminster it makes 'em scorn the badge of their occupation; there the bragging velure-cushioned* hobby-horses prance up and down as if some o' the tilters had ridden 'em.

Hor. Nay, 'afoot, if they be bankrupts, 'tis like some have ridden 'em; and thereupon the citizen's proverb rises, when he says, he trusts to a broken staff.

Doll. Hornet, now you play my father, take heed you be not out of your part, and shame your adopted daughter.

Hor. I will look gravely, Doll,—do you see, boys?—like the foreman of a jury; and speak wisely, like a Latin schoolmaster; and be surly and dogged and proud, like the keeper of a prison.

Lever. You must lie horribly when you talk of your lands.

Hor. No shopkeeper shall outlie me, nay, no fencer. When I hem, boys, you shall duck; when I cough and spit gobbets, Doll,——

Doll. The pox shall be in your lungs, Hornet.

Hor. No, Doll; these with their high shoes shall tread me out.

Doll. All the lessons that I ha' pricked out for 'em is, when the weathercock of my body turns towards them, to stand bare.

Hor. And not to be saucy as servingmen are.

Chart. Come, come, we are no such creatures as you take us for.

Doll. If we have but good draughts in my poterboat, fresh salmon, you sweet villains, shall be no meat with us.

Hor. 'Sfoot, nothing moves my choler but that my chain is copper; but 'tis no matter, better men than old Jack Hornet have rode up Holborn with as bad a thing about their necks as this : your right whiffler*, indeed, hangs himself in Saint Martin's,† and not in Cheapside.

Doll. Peace ! somebody rings.—Run both, whilst he has the rope in's hand : if it be a prize, hale him ; if a man o' war, blow him up, or hang him out at the main-yard's end.

            [*Exeunt* LEVERPOOL *and* CHARTLEY.

Hor. But what ghosts—hold up, my fine girl —what ghosts haunt thy house ?

Doll. O, why, divers. I have a clothier's factor or two, a grocer that would fain pepper me, a Welsh captain that lays hard siege, a Dutch merchant that would spend all that he's able to make i'the Low-Countries but to take measure of my Holland sheets when I lie in 'em —I hear trampling; 'tis my Flemish boy.

Re-enter LEVERPOOL *and* CHARTLEY, *with* HANS VAN BELCH.

Hans. Dar is vor you, and vor you,—een, twen, drie, vier, and vive skilling : drinks skellum upsie freese, nempt dats u drinck gelt.

Lever. Till our crowns crack again, Master Hans Van Belch.

Hans. How is't met you, how is't, vro ! vrolick ?

Doll. Ick vare well, God danke you : nay, I'm an apt scholar, and can take.

Hans. Dat is good, dat is good. Ick can neet stay long, for Ick heb en skip come now upon de vater. O mine schonen vro, we sall dance lanteera teera, and sing Ick brincks to you, Mynheer Van.—Wat man is dat, vro ?

Hor. Nay, pray, sir, on.

Hans. Wat bonds foot is dat, Dorothy ?

Doll. 'Tis my father.

Hans. Got's sacrament, your vader ! why seyghen you niet so to me !—Mine heart, 'tis mine all great desire to call you mine vader ta, for Ick love dis schonen vro your dochterkin.

Hor. Sir, you are welcome in the way of honesty.

Hans. Ick bedanck you : Ick heb so ghe founden vader.

---

* *velure-canioned*] *Velure* is velvet.

"Cannions, of breeches. G. canóns : on les appele ainsi pource qu'ils sont aucunement semblables aux canóns d'artillerie,—because they are like cannons of artillery, or cans or pots."—Minsheu's *Guide into the tongues,* p. 61, ed. 1617.

Strutt explains *canions* to be "ornamental tubes or tags at the ends of the ribbands and laces, which were attached to the extremities of the breeches."—*Dress and Habits, &c.,* vol. ii. p. 263.

Cannon-hose, decorated at the knees with a quantity of ribbons, were fashionable in the time of Charles the Second.

In a MS. copy of a comedy called *The Humourous Lovers,* by the Duke of Newcastle, among the Harleian MSS., 7367, the following song (not given in the printed copy of the play, 1677,) occurs at the beginning of the 4th act ;

     " I conjure thee, I conjure thee,
       By the Ribands in thy Hatt,
       By thy pritty lac'd Cravat,
       By the Ribands round thy Bum,
       Which is brac'd much like a Drum,
       By thy dangling Pantaloons,
       And thy ruffling Port *Cannons,*
       By thy freezeld Perriwige,
       Which does make thee look so bigg,
       By thy Sword of Silver guilt,
       And the Riband at thy Hilt,—
       Apeare, apear."

---

       * *whiffler*] See note *, p. 242.
       † *Saint Martin's*] See note *, p. 253.

Hor. What's your name, I pray?

Hans. Mun nom biu Hans Van Belch.

Hor. Hans Van Belch!

Hans. Yau, yau, 'tis so, 'tis so; de dronken man is altcet remenber me.

Hor. Do you play the merchant, son Belch?

Hans. Yau, vader. Ick heb de skip swim now upon de vater: if you endouty, go up in de little skip dat go so, and be pulled up to Wapping. Ick sall bear you on my back, and hang you about min neck into min groet skip.

Hor. He says, Doll, he would have thee to Wapping, and hang thee.

Doll. No, father, I understand him.—But, Master Hans, I would not be seen hanging about any man's neck, to be counted his jowel, for any gold.

Hor. Is your father living, Master Hans?

Hans. Yau, yau, min vader heb schonen husen in Ausburgh; groet mynheer is mine vader's broder: mine vader heb land, and bin full of fee, dat is, beasts, cattle.

Chart. He's lousy, belike.

Hans. Min vader bin de grotest fooker in all Ausburgh.

Doll. The greatest what?

Lever. Fooker, he says.

Doll. Out upon him!

Hans. Yau, yau, fooker is en groet mynheer, he's en elderman vane city. Got's sacrament, wat is de clock? Ick met stay.

Hor. [*aside to Doll*] Call his watch before you, if you can.   [*A watch.**]

Doll. Here's a pretty thing: do these wheels spin up the hours? what's o'clock?

Hans. Acht; yau, 'tis acht.

Doll. We can hear neither clock nor jack going; we dwell in such a place, that I fear I shall never find the way to church, because the bells hang so far: such a watch as this would make me go down with the lamb and be up with the lark.

Hans. Seghen you so? dor it to.

Doll. O, fie, I do but jest; for, in truth, I could never abide a watch.

Hans. Got's sacrament, Ick niet heb it any more.

   [*Bell rings: exeunt* LEVERPOOL *and* CHARTLEY.

Doll. Another peal! Good father, launch out this Hollander.

Hor. Come, Master Belch, I will bring you to

the water-side, perhaps to Wapping, and there I'll leave you.

Hans. Ick bedanck you, vader.

   [*Exeunt* HANS VAN BELCH *and* HORNET.

Doll. They say whores and bawds go by clocks; but what a Manasses is this to buy twelve hours so dearly, and then be begged out of 'em so easily! He'll be out at heels shortly sure, for he's out about the clocks already. O foolish young man, how dost thou spend thy time!

     Re-enter LEVERPOOL.

Lever. Your grocer.

Doll. Nay, 'sfoot, then I'll change my tune.

    Enter ALLUM *with* CHARTLEY.

I may curse* such leaden-heeled rascals!—Out of my sight!—A knife, a knife, I say!—O Master Allum, if you love a woman, draw out your knife, and undo me, undo me!

All. Sweet Mistress Dorothy, what should you do with a knife? it's ill meddling with edge-tools.—What's the matter, masters? Knife! God bless us!

Lever. [*aside*] 'Sfoot, what tricks at noddy† are these?

Doll. O, I shall burst, if I cut not my lace, I'm so vexed! My father he's rid to court one way‡ about a matter of a thousand pound weight: and one of his men, like a rogue as he is, is rid another way for rents; I looked to have had him up yesterday, and up to-day, and yet he shows not his head; sure, he's run away, or robbed and run thorough. And here was a scrivener but even now, to put my father in mind of a bond that will be forfeit this night, if the money be not paid, Master Allum. Such cross fortune!

All. How much is the bond?

Chart. [*aside*] O rare little villain!

Doll. My father could take up, upon the bareness of his word, five hundred pound, and five too,—

All. What is the debt?

Doll. But he scorns to be—and I scorn to be—

All. Prithee, sweet Mistress Dorothy, vex not. How much is it?

Doll. Alas, Master Allum, 'tis but poor fifty pound!

All. If that be all, you shall upon your word take up so much with me: another time I'll run as far in your books.

Doll. Sir, I know not how to repay this kind-ness; but when my father—

---

* *curse*] The old ed. "cause."

† *tricks at noddy*] Leverpool plays on the double meaning of the word *noddy*, which signifies both a game at cards (see note *, p. 239,) and a fool.

‡ *way*] The old ed. "was."

---

* *A watch*] So the old ed. We are left to guess how Doll contrives to make Hans produce his watch.

All. Tush, tush, 'tis not worth the talking: just fifty pound! when is it to be paid?

Doll. Between one and two.

Lever. [*aside*] That's we three.

All. Let one of your men go along, and I'll send your fifty pound.

Doll. You so bind me, sir!—[*To* LEVERPOOL] Go, sirrah.—Master Allum, I ha' some quinces brought from our house i'the country to preserve: when shall we have any good sugar come over? The wars in Barbary make sugar at such an excessive rate! you pay sweetly now, I warrant, sir, do you not?

All. You shall have a whole chest of sugar, if you please.

Doll. Nay, by my faith, four or five loaves will be enough, and I'll pay you at my first child, Master Allum.

All. Content, i'faith: your man shall bring all under one. I'll borrow a kiss of you at parting.

Enter CAPTAIN JENKINS.

Doll. You shall, sir; I borrow more of you. [*Exeunt* ALLUM *and* LEVERPOOL.

Chart. Save you, captain.

Doll. Welcome, good Captain Jenkins.

Capt. Jen. What, is he a barber-surgeon that dressed your lips so?

Doll. A barber! he's my tailor: I bid him measure how high he would make the standing-collar of my new taffeta gown before, and he, as tailors will be saucy and lickerish, laid me o'er the lips.

Capt. Jen. Ud's blood, I'll lay him 'cross upon his coxcomb next day.

Doll. You know 'tis not for a gentlewoman to stand with a knave for a small matter, and so I would not strive with him, only to be rid of him.

Capt. Jen. If I take Master Prick-louse ramping so high again, by this iron, which is none o' God's angel,* I'll make him know how to kiss your blind cheeks sooner. Mistress Dorothy Hornet, I would not have you be a hornet to lick at cowshards, but to sting such shreds of rascality: will you sing "A tailor shall have me, my joy"?

Doll. Captain, I'll be led by you in any thing. A tailor, foh!

Capt. Jen. Of what stature or size have you a stomach to have your husband now?

Doll. Of the meanest stature, captain; not a size longer than yourself nor shorter.

Capt. Jen. By God, 'tis well said; all your best captain in the Low-Countries are as taller as I: but why of my pitch, Mistress Doll?

Doll. Because your smallest arrows fly farthest. Ah, you little hard-favoured villain, but sweet villain, I love thee because thou't draw o' my side: hang the rogue that will not fight for a woman!

Capt. Jen. Ud's blood, and hang him for urse than a rogue that will slash and cut for an oman, if she be a whore.

Doll. Prithee, good Captain Jenkins, teach me to speak some Welsh: methinks a Welshman's tongue is the neatest tongue—

Capt. Jen. As any tongue in the urld, unless Cra ma crees, that's urse.

Doll. How do you say, "I love you with all my heart"?

Capt. Jen. Mi cara whee en hellon.*

Doll. Mi cara whee en hell-hound.

Capt. Jen. Hell-hound! *O mon dieu!—Mi cara whee en hellon.*

Doll. O, *Mi cara whee en hellon.*

Capt. Jen. O, an you went to writing-school twenty-score year in Wales, by Sesu, you cannot have better utterance for Welsh.

Doll. "Come tit me, come tat me, come throw a kiss at me"—how is that?

Capt. Jen. By gad, I kanow not what your tit-mes and tat-mes are, but *mee uatha*: 'sblood, I know what kisses be as well as I know a Welsh hook. If you will go down with Shropshire carriers, you shall have Welsh enough in your pellies forty weeks.

Doll. Say, captain, that I should follow your colours into your country, how should I fare there?

Capt. Jen. Fare! by Sesu, O, there is the most abominable seer,† and wider silver pots to drink in, and softer peds to lie upon and do our necessary pusiness, and fairer houses, and parks, and holes for conies, and more money, besides toasted scese and butter-milk in North Wales, diggon, besides harps, and Welsh frize, and goats, and cow-heels, and metheglin: ouh, it may be set in the kernicles. Will you march thither?

---

* *which is none o' God's angel*] Compare Dekker; "I markt, by this candle, *which is none of God's Angels.*" *Satiromastix*, 1602, Sig. C.

* Qy. *Mi gara chwi yn nghalon?*

† *abominable seer*] The captain does not use *abominable* in a bad sense, quite the reverse: so in Field's *A Woman is a Weathercock*, 1612;

"*Abraham.* Does she so love me say you?

Pendant. Yes, yes, out of all question the whore does love you *abhominable.*" Sig. F. 4.

Is it necessary to add that by "*seer*" he means *cheer*, and, a little after, by "*kernicles*" *chronicles?*

s 2

Doll. Not with your Shropshire carriers, captain.

Capt. Jen. Will you go with Captain Jenkin, and see his cousin Madoc ap-an-Jenkin there? and I'll run headlongs by and by, and batter away money for a new coach to jolt you in,

Doll. Bestow your coach upon me, and two young white mares, and you shall see how I'll ride.

Capt. Jen. Will you? by all the leeks that are worn on Saint Davy's day, I will buy not only a coach with four wheels, but also a white mare and a stone-horse too, because they shall traw you very lustily, as if the devil were in their arses.

As he is going, enter PHILIP.

How now! more tailors?

Phil. How, sir! tailors!

Doll. O good captain, 'tis my cousin.

Capt. Jen. Is he?—I will cousin you then, sir, too one day.

Phil. I hope, sir, then to cozen you too.

Capt. Jen. By gad, I hobe so.— Farewell, Sidanen.*   [*Exit.*

Re-enter LEVERPOOL *at another door.*

Lever. Here's both money and sugar.

Doll. O sweet villain! set it up.

[*Exit* LEVERPOOL, *and re-enter presently.*

Phil. 'Sfoot, what tame swaggerer was this I met, Doll?

Doll. A captain, a captain. But hast scaped the Dunkirks, honest Philip? Philip-rials are not more welcome: did thy father pay the shot?

Phil. He paid that shot, and then shot pistolets into my pockets; hark, wench;—

Chink, chink,

Makes the punk wanton and the bawd to wink.

[*Capers.*

Chart. O rare music!

Lever. Heavenly consort, better than old Moon's!†

Phil. But why, why, Doll, go these two like bendles in blue, ha?

Doll. There's a moral in that.—Flay off your skins, you precious canuibals.—O, that the Welsh captain were here again, and a drum with him! I could march now, ran, tan, tan, tara, ran, tan, tan.—Sirrah Philip, has thy father any plate in's house?

Phil. Enough to set up a goldsmith's shop.

Doll. Canst not borrow some of it? We shall have guests to-morrow or next day, and I would serve the hungry ragamuffins in plate, though 'twere none of mine own.

Phil. I shall hardly borrow it of him; but I could get one of mine aunts to beat the bush for me, and she might get the bird.

Doll. Why, prithee, let me be one of thine aunts,* and do it for me, then: as I'm virtuous and a gentlewoman, I'll restore.

Phil. Say no more; 'tis done.

Doll. What manner of man is thy father? 'sfoot, I'd fain see the witty monkey, because thou sayest he's a poet. I'll tell thee what I'll do. Leverpool or Chartley shall, like my gentleman-usher, go to him, and say such a lady sends for him about a sonnet or an epitaph for her child that died at nurse, or for some device about a mask or so: if he comes, you shall stand in a corner, and see in what state I'll bear myself. He does not know me nor my lodging?

Phil. No, no.

Doll. Is't a match, sirs? shall's be merry with him and his Muse?

Phil., Lever., Chart. Agreed; any scaffold to execute knavery upon.

Doll. I'll send, then, my vaunt-courier presently: in the mean time march after the captain, scoundrels.—Come, hold me up; Look, how Sabrina sunk i'the river Severn, So will we four be drunk i'the Shipwreck Tavern.

[*Exeunt.*

SCENE II.†

Enter BELLAMONT, MAYBERRY, *and* MISTRESS MAYBERRY.

May. Come, wife, our two gallants will be here presently: I have promised them the best of entertainment, with protestation never to reveal

---

* *Sidanen*] The old copy "*Sidanien*."—"Sidanen, s. f. dim. (sidan) that is silken, or made of silk. It is the name of an old tune; *also an epithet for a fine woman; and has been applied particularly to Queen Elizabeth.*" Owen's *Dictionary of the Welsh Language.*

In reference to the latter part of the preceding quotation from Owen, I have to observe, that there was licensed to Richard Jones, the 13th of August, 1579, *A Ballad of Brittishe Sidanen, applied by a courtier to the praise of the Queue,* which is printed (from a MS.) in the *British Bibliographer,* vol. i. p. 338, and entitled *A Dittie to the tune of Welshe Sydänen, made to the Queenes maj.' Eliz. by Lodov. Lloyd.*

† *Heavenly consort, better than old Moon's*] "Sirrah wag, this rogue was son and heire to Antony Nowe-Now, and *Blind Moone:* and hee must needs be a scurvy musitian that hath *two fidlers* to his fathers." Wilkins's *Miseries of Inforst Marriage,* Sig. A. 2, 1607.

Anthony Now-Now figures in Chettle's *Kind-Harts Dream,* 1592.

When the present play was written, and long after, a set of musicians playing or singing together was called a *consort;* the term concert is comparatively modern.

* *aunts*] See note *, p. 254.

† *Scene II.*] The same. A room in the house of Mayberry.

to thee their slander. I will have thee bear
thyself as if thou madest a feast upon Simon
and Jude's day to country gentlewomen that
came to see the pageant: bid them extremely
welcome, though thou wish their throats cut; 'tis
in fashion.

Mist. May. O God! I shall never endure them.

Bell. Endure them! you are a fool. Make it
your case, as it may be many women's of the
freedom, that you had a friend in private whom
your husband should lay to his bosom, and he in
requital should lay his wife to his bosom; what
treads of the toe, salutations by winks, discourse
by bitings of the lip, amorous glances, sweet
stolen kisses, when your husband's back's turned,
would pass between them! Bear yourself to
Greenshield as if you did love him for affecting
you so entirely, not taking any notice of his
journey: they'll put more tricks upon you.—
You told me, Greenshield means to bring his
sister to your house, to have her board here.

May. Right. She's some cracked demi-culverin
that hath miscarried in service: no matter though
it be some charge to me for a time, I care not.

Mist. May. Lord, was there ever such a husband!

May. Why, wouldst thou have me suffer their
tongues to run at large in ordinaries and cockpits!
Though the knaves do lie, I tell you, Master Bellamont, lies that come from stern looks and satin
outsides, and gilt rapiers also, will be put up and
go for current.

Bell. Right, sir; 'tis a small spark gives fire to
a beautiful woman's discredit.

May. I will therefore use them like informing
knaves in this kind; make up their mouths with
silver, and after be revenged upon them. I was
in doubt I should have grown fat of late: au it
were not for law-suits and fear of our wives, we
rich men should grow out of all compass.—They
come.

Enter GREENSHIELD *and* FEATHERSTONE.

My worthy friends, welcome: look, my wife's
colour rises already.

Green. You have not made her acquainted with
the discovery?

May. O, by no means. Ye see, gentlemen, the
affection of an old man: I would fain make all
whole again.—Wife, give entertainment to our
new acquaintance: your lips, wife; any woman
may lend her lips without her husband's privity;
'tis allowable.

Mist. May. You are very welcome. I think it

be near dinner-time, gentlemen: I'll will * the
maid to cover, and return presently.   [*Exit.*

Bell. [aside to May.] God's precious, why doth
she leave them?

May. [aside to Bell.] O, I know her stomach: she is
but retired into another chamber, to ease her heart
with crying a little. It hath ever been her humour:
she hath done it five or six times in a day, when
courtiers have been here, if any thing hath been
out of order, and yet, every return, laughed and
been as merry!—And how is it, gentlemen? you
are well acquainted with this room, are you not?

Green. I had a delicate banquet once on that
table.

May. In good time: but you are better acquainted with my bed-chamber.

Bell. Were the cloth-of gold cushions set forth
at your entertainment?

Feath. Yes, sir.

May. And the cloth-of-tissue vallance?

Feath. They are very rich ones.

May. [aside] God refuse me, they are lying
rascals! I have no such furniture.

Green. I protest it was the strangest, and yet
withal the happiest fortune, that we should meet
you two at Ware, that ever redeemed such dis-
solute† actions. I would not wrong you again for
a million of Londons.

May. No? Do you want any money? or if you
be in debt (I am a hundred pound i'the subsidy),
command me.

Feath. Alas, good gentleman! Did you ever
read of the like patience in any of your ancient
Romans?

Bell. You see what a sweet face in a velvet cap
can do: your citizen's wives are like partridges,
the hens are better than the cocks.

Feath. I believe it, in troth: sir, you did observe
how the gentlewoman could not contain herself
when she saw us enter?

Bell. Right.

Feath. For thus much I must speak in allowance
of her modesty; when I had her most private, she
would blush extremely.

Bell. Ay, I warrant you, and ask you if you
would have such a great sin lie upon your conscience as to lie with another man's wife?

Feath. In troth, she would.

Bell. And tell you there were maids enough in
London, if a man were so viciously given, whose
portions would help them to husbands, though
gentlemen gave the first onset?

---

* *will*].i. e. desire. † *dissolute*] The old ed. "desolate."

Feath. You are a merry old gentleman, in faith, sir: much like to this was her language.

Bell. And yet clip * you with as voluntary a bosom as if she had fallen in love with you at some Inns-o'-court revels, and invited you by letter to her lodging?

Feath. Your knowledge, sir, is perfect without any information.

May. I'll go see what my wife is doing, gentlemen: when my wife enters, show her this ring, and 'twill quit all suspicion.   [*Exit.*

Feath. [*aside to Green.*] Dost hear, Luke Greenshield? will thy wife be here presently?

Green.† [*aside to Feath.*] I left my boy to wait upon her. By this light, I think God provides; for if this citizen had not, out of his overplus of kindness, proffered her her diet and lodging under the name of my sister, I could not have told what shift to have made, for the greatest part of my money is revolted: we'll make more use of him. The whoreson rich innkeeper of Doncaster, her father, showed himself a rank ostler, to send her up at this time o' year, and by the carrier too; 'twas but a jade's trick of him.

Feath. [*aside to Green.*] But have you instructed her to call you brother?

Green. [*aside to Feath.*] Yes; and she'll do it. I left her at Bosoms Inn:‡ she'll be here presently.

Re-enter MAYBERRY.

May. Master Greenshield, your sister is come; my wife is entertaining her: by the mass, I have been upon her lips already.

Re-enter MISTRESS MAYBERRY *with* KATE.

Lady, you are welcome.—Look you, Master Greenshield, because your sister is newly come out of the fresh air, and that to be pent up in a narrow lodging here i'the city may offend her health, she shall lodge at a garden-house of mine in Moorfields; where if it please you and my worthy friend here to bear her company, your several lodgings and joint commons, to the poor ability of a citizen, shall be provided.

Feath. O God, sir!

May. Nay, no compliment; your loves command it. Shall's to dinner, gentlemen?—Come, Master Bellamont.—I'll be the gentleman-usher to this fair lady.*

          [*Exeunt* MAYBERRY *and* BELLAMONT.

Green. Here is your ring, mistress: a thousand times, ——† and would have willingly lost my best of maintenance, that I might have found you half so tractable.

Mist. May. Sir, I am still myself. I know not by what means you have grown upon my husband: he is much deceived in you, I take it. Will you go in to dinner?—[*Aside*] O God, that I might have my will of him! an it were not for my husband, I'd scratch out his eyes presently.

          [*Exeunt* GREENSHIELD *and* MISTRESS MAYBERRY.

Feath. Welcome to London, bonny Mistress Kate: thy husband little dreams of the familiarity that hath passed between thee and I, Kate.

Kate. No matter, if he did. He ran away from me, like a base slave as he was, out of Yorkshire, and pretended he would go the Island voyage:‡ since I ne'er heard of him till within this fortnight. Can the world condemn me for entertaining a friend, that am used so like an infidel?

Feath. I think not: but if your husband knew of this, he'd be divorced.

Kate. He were an ass, then. No: wise men should deal by their wives as the sale of ordnance passeth in England: if it break the first discharge, the workman is at the loss of it; if the second, the merchant and the workman jointly; if the third, the merchant: so in our case, if a woman prove false the first year, turn her upon her father's neck; if the second, turn her home to her father, but allow her a portion; but if she hold pure metal two year and fly to several pieces in the third, repair the ruins of her honesty at your charges: for the best piece of ordnance may be cracked in the casting; and for women to have cracks and flaws, alas, they are born to them. Now, I have held out four year.—Doth my husband do any things about London? doth he swagger?

Feath. O, as tame as a fray in Fleet-street, when there are nobody to part them.

---

* *clip*] i. e. embrace.

† *Green.*] The old ed. "*May.*"

‡ *Bosoms Inn*] "Antiquities in this Lane [St. Lawrence Lane] I find none other than that, among many fair Houses, there is one large Inne for receit of Travellers, called *Blossoms Inne*, but corruptly *Bosoms Inne*, and hath to sign S. Laurence the Deacon, in a border of Blossoms or Flowers." Stow's *Survey of London*, &c. B. iii. p. 40, ed. 1720.

---

* *I'll be the gentleman-usher to this fair lady*] In the first edition of this work I transferred these words to Greenshield,—wrongly, I now believe.

† ——] This break is found in the old ed., occasioned by some defect in the MS.

‡ *the Island Voyage*] Undertaken against Hispaniola, in 1585: the fleet, commanded by Sir Francis Drake, consisted of twenty-one ships, carrying above two thousand volunteers: they took possession of St. Domingo.

Kate. I ever thought so. We have notable valiant fellows about Doncaster; they'll give the lie and the stab both in an instant.

Feath. You like such kind of manhood best, Kate.

Kate. Yes, in troth; for I think any woman that loves her friend had rather have him stand by it than lie by it. But, I pray thee, tell me why must I be quartered at this citizen's garden-house, say you?

Feath. The discourse of that will set thy blood on fire to be revenged on thy husband's forehead-piece.

Re-enter MISTRESS MAYBERRY *and* BELLAMONT.

Mist. May. Will you go in to dinner, sir?

Kate. Will you lead the way, forsooth?

Mist. May. No, sweet, forsooth, we'll follow you. [*Exeunt* KATE *and* FEATHERSTONE.] O Master Bellamont, as ever you took pity upon the simplicity of a poor abused gentlewoman, will you tell me one thing?

Bell. Any thing, sweet Mistress Mayberry.

Mist. May. Ay, but will you do it faithfully?

Bell. As I respect your acquaintance, I shall do it.

Mist. May. Tell me, then, I beseech you, do not you think this minx is some naughty pack whom my husband hath fallen in love with, and means to keep under my nose at his garden-house?*

Bell. No, upon my life, is she not.

Mist. May. O, I cannot believe it. I know by her eyes she is not honest. Why should my husband proffer them such kindness that have abused him and me so intolerable? and will not suffer me to speak—there's the hell on't—not suffer me to speak?

Bell. Fie, fie! he doth that like a usurer that will use a man with all kindness, that he may be careless of paying his money upon his day, and afterwards take the extremity of the forfeiture. Your jealousy is idle: say this were true; it lies in the bosom of a sweet wife to draw her husband from any loose imperfection, from wenching, from jealousy, from covetousness, from crabbedness (which is the old man's common disease), by her politic yielding. She may do it from crabbedness; for example, I have known as tough blades as any are in England broke upon a feather-bed. Come to dinner.

Mist. May. I'll be ruled by you, sir, for you are very like mine uncle.

Bell. Suspicion works more mischief, grows more strong,
To sever chaste beds, than apparent wrong.†
[*Exeunt.*

ACT III.

SCENE I.*

Enter DOLL, CHARTLEY, LEVERPOOL, *and* PHILIP.

Phil. Come, my little punk, with thy two compositors to this unlawful painting-house, thy pounders:† my old poetical dad will be here presently. Take up thy state in this chair, and bear thyself as if thou wert talking to thy pothecary after the receipt of a purgation: look scurvily upon him; sometimes be merry, and stand upon thy pantofles,‡ like a new-elected scavenger.

Doll. And by and by melancholic, like a tilter that hath broke his staves foul before his mistress.

Phil. Right, for he takes thee to be a woman of a great count. [*Knocking within.*] Hark! upon my life, he's come.   [*Hides himself.*

Doll. See who knocks. [*Exit* LEVERPOOL.] Thou shalt see me make a fool of a poet, that hath made five hundred fools.

Re-enter LEVERPOOL.

Lever. Please your new ladyship, he's come.

Doll. Is he? I should for the more state let him walk some two hours in an outer-room: if I did owe him money, 'twere not much out of fashion. But come, enter him:—stay; when we are in private conference, send in my tailor.

Enter BELLAMONT, *brought in by* LEVERPOOL.

Lever. Look you, my lady's asleep: she'll wake presently.

---

* *Scene I.*] London. A room in Doll's house (see note ‖, p. 256).

† *thy pounders: my old poetical dad, &c.*] The old ed. has "*thy pounders a my old poeticall dad,*" &c. I am doubtful about the right reading.

‡ *pantofles*] i. e. slippers.

* *at his garden-house*] Garden-houses were used for such purposes : so in the opening of Barry's *Ram-Alley*, 1611 ;

"what makes he heere,
In the skirts of Holborne, so neere the field,
And at a garden-house? a has some punke,
Upon my life."

† *wrong*] The old ed. "*wrongs.*"

Bell. I come not to teach a starling, sir ; God b' wi' you !

Lever. Nay, in truth, sir, if my lady should but dream you had been here,——

Doll. Who's that keeps such a prating ?

Lever. 'Tis I, madam.

Doll. I'll have you preferred to be a crier ; you have an excellent throat for't.—Pox o' the poet, is he not come yet ?

Lever. He's here, madam.

Doll. Cry you mercy : I ha' cursed my monkey for shrewd turns a hundred times, and yet I love it never the worse, I protest.

Bell. 'Tis not in fashion, dear lady, to call the breaking out of a gentlewoman's lips scabs, but the heat of the liver.

Doll. So, sir :—if you have a sweet breath, and do not smell of sweaty linen, you may draw nearer, nearer.

Bell. I am no friend to garlic, madam.

Doll. You write the sweeter verse a great deal, sir. I have heard much good of your wit, master poet ; you do many devices for citizen's wives : I care not greatly, because I have a city-laundress already, if I get a city-poet too : I have such a device for you, and this it is——

Enter Tailor.

O, welcome, tailor.—Do but wait till I despatch my tailor, and I'll discover my device to you.

Bell. I'll take my leave of your ladyship.

Doll. No, I pray thee, stay : I must have you sweat for my device, master poet.

Phil. [*aside*] He sweats already, believe it.

Doll. A cup of wine, there !—What fashion will make a woman have the best body, tailor ?

Tailor. A short Dutch waist with a round Catherine-wheel farthingale ; a close sleeve with a cartoose * collar and a piccadel.†

Doll. And what meat will make a woman have a fine wit, master poet ?

Bell. Fowl, madam, is the most light, delicate, and witty feeding.

Doll. Fowl, sayest thou ? I know them that feed of it every meal, and yet are as arrant fools as any are in a kingdom, of my credit.—Hast thou done, tailor ? [*Exit* Tailor.] Now to discover my device, sir : I'll drink to you, sir.

Phil. [*aside*] God's precious, we ne'er thought

of her device before ; pray God it be any thing tolerable.

Doll. I'll have you make twelve posies for a dozen of cheese-trenchers.*

Phil. [*aside*] O horrible !

Bell. In Welsh, madam ?

Doll. Why in Welsh, sir ?

Bell. Because you will have them served in with your cheese, lady.

Doll. I will bestow them, indeed, upon a Welsh captain, one that loves cheese better than venison ; for if you should but get three or four Cheshire cheeses, and set them a-running down Highgate-hill, he would make more haste after them than after the best kennel of hounds in England. What think you of my device ?

Bell. 'Fore God, a very strange device and a cunning one.

Phil. [*aside*] Now he begins to eye the goblet.

Bell. You should be akin to the Bellamounts ; you give the same arms, madam.

Doll. Faith, I paid sweetly for the cup, as it may be you and some other gentlemen have done for their arms.

Bell. Ha ! the same weight, the same fashion ! I had three nest of them † given me by a nobleman at the christening of my son Philip.

Phil. [*Discovering himself*] Your son is come to full age, sir, and hath ta'en possession of the gift of his godfather.

Bell. Ha ! thou wilt not kill me ?

Phil. No, sir, I'll kill no poet, lest his ghost write satires against me.

---

* *twelve posies for a dozen of cheese-trenchers*] Cheese-trenchers, at the time this play was written, used frequently to have posies inscribed on them. In Dekker and Middleton's *Honest Whore, Part First*, George quotes six lines, "as one of our *cheese-trenchers* says very learnedly." Middleton's *Works*, iii. 98, ed. Dyce. Compare too Middleton's *No Wit, no Help, like a Woman's ;*

"*L. Gold.* Twelve trenchers, upon every one a month ! January, February, March, April—

Pep. Ay, and their posies under 'em.

L. Gold. Pray, what says May ? she's the spring lady.

Pep. [*reads*]
      Now gallant May, in her array,
      Doth make the field pleasant and gay," &c.
                              Id. v. 40.

† *three nest of them*] So in the opening of Marston's *Dutch Courtezan*, 1605 ; "cogging Cocledemoy is runne away with a neast of goblets ;" and so in Armin's *Two Maides of Moreclacke*, 1609 ;

"Place your plate, and pile your vitriall boales
      Nest upon nest." Sig. II 2,

Mr. Crossley, of Manchester, observes to me that the term *nest of goblets* is still made use of in the West Riding of Yorkshire ; a near relative of his possesses one of these *nests*,—a large goblet containing many smaller ones of gradually diminishing sizes, which fit into each other and fill it up.

---

* *cartoose*] Qy. "*cartouch*"?

† *piccadel*] Is described as an upright collar with stiffened plaits : here it seems to mean a sort of edging to the collar.

Bell. What's she? a good commonwealth's woman, she was born—

Phil. For her country, and has borne her country.

Bell. Heart of virtue, what make I here?

Phil. This was the party you railed on. I keep no worse company than yourself, father. You were wont to say, venery is like usury, that it may be allowed though it be not lawful.

Bell. Wherefore come I hither?

Doll. To make a device for cheese-trenchers.

Phil. I'll tell you why I sent for you; for nothing but to show you that your gravity may be drawn in; white hairs may fall into the company of drabs, as well as red-beards into the society of knaves. Would not this woman deceive a whole camp i'the Low-Countries, and make one commander believe she only kept her cabin for him, and yet quarter twenty more in't?

Doll. Prithee, poet, what dost thou think of me?

Bell. I think thou art a most admirable, brave, beautiful whore.

Doll. Nay, sir, I was told you would rail: but what do you think of my device, sir? nay, but you are not to depart yet, master poet: wut sup with me? I'll cashier all my young barnacles, and we'll talk over a piece of mutton and a partridge wisely.

Bell. Sup with thee, that art a common undertaker! thou that dost promise nothing but watchet eyes, bombast * calves, and false periwigs!

Doll. Prithee, comb thy beard with a comb of black lead; it may be I shall affect thee.

Bell. O thy unlucky star! I must take my leave of your worship; I cannot fit your device at this instant. I must desire to borrow a nest of goblets of you [*Taking them*].—O villany! I would some honest butcher would beg all the queans and knaves i'the city, and carry them into some other country: they'd sell better than beeves and calves. What a virtuous city would this be, then! marry, I think there would be a few people left in't. Ud's foot, gulled with cheese-trenchers, and yoked in entertainment with a tailor! good, good. [*Exit.*

Phil. How dost, Doll?

Doll. Scurvy, very scurvy.

Lever. Whore shall's sup, wench?

Doll. I'll sup in my bed. Get you home to your lodging, and come when I send for you. O filthy rogue that I am!

Phil. How, how, Mistress Dorothy?

Doll. Saint Antony's fire light in your Spanish slops! ud's life, I'll make you know a difference between my mirth and melancholy, you panderly rogue.

Omnes. We observe your ladyship.

Phil. The punk's in her humour, pax*.

Doll. I'll humour you, an you pox me.

[*Exeunt* CHARTLEY, LEVERPOOL, *and* PHILIP.

Ud's life, have I lien with a Spaniard of late, that I have learnt to mingle such water with my Malaga? O, there's some scurvy thing or other breeding! How many several loves of players, of vaulters, of lieutenants, have I entertained, besides a runner o' the ropes, and now to let blood when the sign is at the heart! Should I send him a letter with some jewel in't, he would requite it as lawyers do, that return a woodcock-pie to their clients, when they send them a bason and a ewer.† I will instantly go and make myself drunk till I have lost my memory. Love‡ a scoffing poet! [*Exit.*

SCENE II.§

Enter LEAPFROG *and* SQUIRREL.

Leap. Now, Squirrel, wilt thou make us acquainted with the jest thou promised to tell us of?

Squir. I will discover it, not as a Derbyshire woman discovers her great teeth, in laughter, but softly, as a gentleman courts a wench behind an arras; and this it is. Young Greenshield, thy master,|| with Greenshield's sister, lie in my master's garden-house here in Moorfields.

Leap. Right: what of this?

---

* *pax*] For *pox;* it was perhaps an affected mode of pronouncing the word. So Heywood and Brome in *The late Lancashire Witches*, 1634, "Pax, I think not on't,"—Sig. E 3; Brome in the *Joviall Crew*, 1652, "Pax o' your fine thing,"—Sig. L; and Middleton, in *Your Five Gallants,* "Pax on't, we spoil ourselves for want of these things at university,"—*Works,* ii. 235, ed. Dyce.

† *Should I send him a letter,* &c. . . . . *a bason and a ewer*] I once imagined that "*a woodcock-pie*" meant here *long bills;* but I now think it is a mere derision, as woodcocks were reckoned foolish birds: when this play was written, *basons* and *ewers* of silver used frequently to be given as presents; "One of Lord Timon's men? a gift, I warrant. Why, this hits right; I dreamt of a *silver bason and ewer* to-night." Shakespeare's *Timon of Athens,* act iii. sc. 1.

‡ *Love*] The old ed. "*liue.*"

§ *Scene II.*] The lobby in Mayberry's garden-house, Moorfields.

|| *thy master*] i. e. Featherstone.

* *bombast*] i. e. *bombasted,*—stuffed.

Squir. Marry, sir, if the gentlewoman be not his wife, he commits incest, for I'm sure he lies with her every night.

Leap. All this I know; but to the rest.

Squir. I will tell thee the most politic trick of a woman that e'er made a man's face look withered and pale, like the tree in Cuckold's-haven * in a great snow; and this it is. My mistress makes her husband believe that she walks in her sleep o' nights ; and to confirm this belief in him, sundry times she hath risen out of her bed, unlocked all the doors, gone from chamber to chamber, opened her chests, toused among her linen, and when he hath waked and missed her,

* *the tree in Cuckold's-haven*] As perhaps this work may be read by some who are unacquainted with the neighbourhood of London, and have never sailed down the Thames to eat white-bait at Greenwich, it may be necessary to inform them that a little below Rotherhithe is a spot, close on the river, called Cuckold's Point, which is distinguished by a tall pole with a pair of horns on the top. Tradition says that near this place there lived, in the reign of King John, a miller who had a handsome wife; that his majesty had an intrigue with the fair dame, and gave the husband, as a compensation, all the land on that side, which he could see from his house, looking down the Thames,—which land, however, he was to possess only on the condition of walking on that day (the 18th of October) annually to the farthest bounds of his estate with a pair of buck's horns on his head; and that the miller, having cleared his eyesight, saw as far as Charlton, and enjoyed the land on the above-mentioned terms. (In several books which condescend to notice this story we are told that the miller lived at Charlton and saw as far as Cuckold's Point; but the version of it which I have given is what the watermen on the Thames even now repeat.) Horn-fair is still held at Charlton, on the 18th of October, in commemoration of the event.

In *A Discovery by Sea, &c.* by Taylor the water-poet, (*Works*, folio, p. 21, 1630,) are the following lines :—

"And passing further, I at first observ'd
That Cuckold's-Haven was but badly serv'd ;
For there old Time had such confusion wrought,
That of that ancient place remained nought.
No monumentall memorable Horne,
Or Tree, or Post, which hath those trophees borne,
Was left, whereby posterity may know
Where their forefathers crests did grow, or show."

"Why, then, for shame this worthy port maintaine,
Let's have our Tree and Horns set up againe ;
That passengers may shew obedience to it,
In putting off their hats, and homage doe it."

"But holla, Muse, no longer be offended,
'Tis worthily repair'd, and bravely mended.
For which great meritorious worke, my pen
Shall give the glory unto Greenwich men :
It was their onely cost, they were the actors
Without the helpe of other benefactors ;
For which my pen their prayses here adornes,
As they have beautifi'd the Hav'n with Hornes."

The custom here alluded to, of doing homage to the pole-horns, is not yet obsolete among the vulgar.

coming to question why she conjured thus at midnight, he hath found her fast asleep : marry, it was cat's sleep, for you shall hear what prey she watched for.

Leap. Good : forth.

Squir. I overheard her last night talking with thy master, and she promised him that as soon as her husband was asleep, she would walk according to her custom, and come ·to his chamber : marry, she would do it so puritanically, so secretly, I mean, that nobody should hear of it.

Leap. Is't possible ?

Squir. Take but that corner and stand close, and thine eyes shall witness it.

Leap. O intolerable wit ! what hold can any man take of a woman's honesty ?

Squir. Hold ! no more hold than of a bull 'nointed with soap, and baited with a shoal of fiddlers in Staffordshire.—Stand close ; I hear her coming.

Enter KATE.

Kate. What a filthy knave was the shoemaker that made my slippers ! what a creaking they keep ! O Lord, if there be any power that can make a woman's husband sleep soundly at a pinch, as I have often read in foolish poetry that there is, now, now, an it be thy will, let him dream some fine dream or other, that he's made a knight or a nobleman or somewhat, whilst I go and take but two kisses, but two kisses, from sweet Featherstone !   [*Exit.*

Squir. 'Sfoot, he may well dream he's made a knight, for I'll be hanged if she do not dub him.

Enter GREENSHIELD.

Green. Was there ever any walking spirit like to my wife ? what reason should there be in nature for this ? I will question some physician. Nor here neither ! Ud's life, I would laugh if she were in Master Featherstone's chamber : she would fright him.—Master Featherstone, Master Featherstone !

Feath. [*within*] Ha ! how now ! who calls ?

Green. Did you leave your door open last night ?

Feath. [*within*] I know not ; I think my boy did.

Green. God's light, she's there, then.—Will you know the jest ? my wife hath her old tricks. I'll hold my life, my wife's in your chamber ; rise out of your bed, and see an you can feel her.

Squir. [*aside to Leap.*] He will feel her, I warrant you.

Green. Have you her, sir ?

Feath. [*within*] Not yet, sir :—she's here. ·sir.

Green. So I said even now to myself, before God, la.—Take her up in your arms, and bring her hither softly for fear of waking her.—I never knew the like of this, before God, la.

Enter FEATHERSTONE *with* KATE *in his arms.*

Alas, poor Kate!—Look, before God, she's asleep with her eyes open: pretty little rogue! I'll wake her, and make her ashamed of it.

Feath. O, you'll make her sicker, then.

Green. I warrant you.—Would all women thought no more hurt than thou dost now, sweet villain!—Kate, Kate!

Kate. I longed for the merrythought of a pheasant.

Green. She talks in her sleep.

Kate. And the foul-gutted tripe-wife had got it, and eat half of it; and my colour went and came, and my stomach wambled, till I was ready to swoon; but a midwife perceived it, and marked which way my eyes went, and helped me to it: but, Lord, how I picked it! 'twas the sweetest meat, methought.

Squir. [*aside*] O politic mistress!

Green. Why, Kate, Kate!

Kate. Ha, ha, ha! ay, beshrew your heart—Lord, where am I?

Green. I pray thee, be not frighted.

Kate. O, I am sick, I am sick, I am sick! O, how my flesh trembles! O, some of the angelica-water! I shall have the mother* presently.

Green. Hold down her stomach, good Master Featherstone, while I fetch some.   · [*Exit.*

Feath. Well dissembled, Kate.

Kate. Pish, I am like some of your ladies that can be sick when they have no stomach to lie with their husbands.

Feath. What mischievous fortune is this! We'll have a journey to Ware, Kate, to redeem this misfortune.

Kate. Well, cheaters do not win always: that woman that will entertain a friend must as well provide a closet or backdoor for him as a feather-bed.

Feath. By my troth, I pity thy husband.

Kate. Pity him! no man dares call him cuckold, for he wears satin: pity him! he that will pull down a man's sign and set up horns, there's law for him.

Feath. Be sick again, your husband comes.

Re-enter GREENSHIELD *with a broken shin.*

Green. I have the worst luck; I think I get more bumps and shrewd turns i'the dark—How does she, Master Featherstone?

Feath. Very ill, sir, she's troubled with the mother extremely: I held down her belly even now, and I might feel it rise.

Kate. O, lay me in my bed, I beseech you!

Green. I will find a remedy for this walking, if all the doctors in town can sell it: a thousand pound to a penny she spoil not her face, or break her neck, or catch a cold that she may ne'er claw off again.—How dost, wench?

Kate. A little recovered. Alas, I have so troubled that gentleman!

Feath. None i'the world, Kate: may I do you any farther service?

Kate. An I were where I would be, in your bed,—pray, pardon me, was't you, Master Featherstone?—hem, I should be well then.

Squir. [*aside to Leap.*] Mark how she wrings him by the fingers.

Kate. Good night.—Pray you, give the gentleman thanks for patience.

Green. Good night, sir.

Feath. You have a shrewd blow; you were best have it searched.

Green. A scratch, a scratch.

.   [*Exeunt* GREENSHIELD *and* KATE.

Feath. Let me see, what excuse should I frame, to get this wench forth o'town with me? I'll persuade her husband to take physic, and presently have a letter framed from his father-in-law, to be delivered that morning, for his wife to come and receive some small parcel of money in Enfield-chase, at a keeper's that is her uncle: then, sir, he, not being in case to travel, will entreat me to accompany his wife: we'll lie at Ware all night, and the next morning to London. I'll go strike a tinder, and frame a letter presently.   [*Exit.*

Squir. And I'll take the pains to discover all this to my master, old Mayberry. There hath gone a report a good while my master hath used them kindly, because they have been over familiar with his wife; but I see which way Featherstone looks. Sfoot, there's ne'er a gentleman of them all shall gull a citizen, and think to go scot-free. Though your commons shrink for this, be but secret, and·my master shall entertain thee; make thee, instead of handling false dice, finger nothing but gold and silver, wag: an old servingman turns to a young beggar, whereas a young prentice may turn to an old alderman. Wilt be secret?

Leap. O God, sir, as secret as rushes* in an old lady's chamber.   [*Exeunt.*

---

* *the mother*] i. e. hysterical passion.

* *rushes*] See note †, p. 21.

ACT IV.

SCENE I.*

Enter BELLAMONT, in his nightcap, with leaves in his hand; his Servingman after him, with lights, standish, and paper.

Bell. Sirrah, I'll speak with none.

Serv. Not a player?

Bell. No, though a sharer bawl;
I'll speak with none, although it be the mouth
Of the big company; I'll speak with none: away!
                     [*Exit* Servingman.
Why should not I be an excellent statesman? I
can in the writing of a tragedy make Cæsar speak
better than ever his ambition could; when I
write of Pompey, I have Pompey's soul within
me; and when I personate a worthy poet, I am
then truly myself, a poor unpreferred scholar.

Re-enter Servingman hastily.

Serv. Here's a swaggering fellow, sir, that
speaks not like a man of God's making,† swears
he must speak with you, and will speak with
you.

Bell. Not of God's making! what is he? a
cuckold?

Serv. He's a gentleman, sir, by his clothes.

Bell. Enter him and his clothes [*Exit* Serving-
man]: clothes sometimes are better gentlemen
than their masters.

Enter CAPTAIN JENKINS *with* Servingman.

Is this he?—Seek you me, sir?
                     [*Exit* Servingman.

Capt. Jen. I seek, sir, God pless you, for a
sentleman that talks besides to himself when he's
alone, as if he were in Bedlam; and he's a poet.

Bell. So, sir, it may be you seek me, for I'm
sometimes out o' my wits.

Capt. Jen. You are a poet, sir, are you?

Bell. I'm haunted with a fury, sir.

Capt. Jen. Pray, master poet, shoot off this
little pot-gun, and I will conjure your fury: 'tis
well lay‡ you, sir. My desires are to have some

amiable and amorous sonnet or madrigal composed
by your fury, see you.

Bell. Are you a lover, sir, of the nine Muses?

Capt. Jen. Ow, by gad, out o'cry.*

Bell. You're, then, a scholar, sir?

Capt. Jen. I ha' picked up my cromes in Sesus
College in Oxford, one day a gad while ago.

Bell. You're welcome, you're very welcome.
I'll borrow your judgment: look you, sir, I'm
writing a tragedy, the tragedy of *Young Astyanax.*

Capt. Jen. Styanax' tragedy! is he living, can
you tell? was not Styanax a Monmouth man?

Bell. O, no, sir, you mistake; he was a Trojan,
great Hector's son.

Capt. Jen. Hector was grannam to Cadwallader:
when she was great with child, God udge me,
there was one young Styanax of Monmouthshire
was a madder Greek as any is in all England.

Bell. This was not he, assure ye. Look you,
sir, I will have this tragedy presented in the
French court by French gallants.

Capt. Jen. By God, your Frenchmen will do a
tragedy-enterlude poggy well.

Bell. It shall be, sir, at the marriages of the
Duke of Orleans, and Chatillon the Admiral of
France; the stage —

Capt. Jen. Ud's bluod, does Orleans marry
with the Admiral of France, now?

Bell. O, sir, no, they are two several marriages.
As I was saying, the stage hung all with black
velvet, and, while 'tis acted, myself will stand
behind the Duke of Biron, or some other chief
minion or so, who shall, ay, they shall take some
occasion, about the music of the fourth act, to
step to the French king, and say, *Sire, voila, il
est votre tres humble serviteur, le plus sage et divin
esprit, Monsieur Bellamont,* all in French thus,
pointing at me, or, *Yon is the learned old English
gentleman, Master Bellamont, a very worthy man
to be one of your privy chamber or poet laureat.*

Capt. Jen. But are you sure Duke Pepper-noon
will give you such good urds behind your back
to your face?

---

* *Scene* I.] London. A room in the house of Bellamont.

† *that speaks not like a man of God's making]*
"*Prin.* Doth this man serve God?
  Biron. Why ask you?
  Prin. He speaks not like a man of God's making."
    Shakspeare's *Love's Labour's Lost,* act v. sc. 2.

‡ *lay*] Qy.?

* *out o' cry*] i. e. out of measure. Malone (note on *As
you like it,* act iii. sc. 2) thinks it alludes to the custom of
giving notice by a crier of things to be sold: I rather believe it is derived from the circumstance of a person
being so far distant as to be unable to hear another
person crying after him. *Out of all ho,* and *out of all
whooping,* seem to have the same meaning.

Bell. O, ay, ay, ay, man; he's the only courtier that I know there. But what do you think that I may come to by this?

Capt. Jen. God udge me, all France may hap die in your debt for this.

Bell. I am now writing the description of his death.

Capt. Jen. Did he die in his ped?

Bell. You shall hear. [*Reads.*

" *Suspicion is the minion of great hearts*"——No, I will not begin there. Imagine a great man were to be executed about the seventh hour in a gloomy morning.

Capt. Jen. As it might be Samson or so, or great Golias that was killed by my countryman?

Bell. Right, sir: thus I express it in *Young Astyanax*; [*Reads.*

" *Now the wild people, greedy of their griefs,*

Longing to see that which their thoughts abhorr'd,

Prevented day, and rode on their own roofs,"——

Capt. Jen. Could the little horse that ambled on the top of Paul's* carry all the people? else how could they ride on the roofs?

Bell. O, sir, 'tis a figure in poetry: mark how 'tis followed; [*Reads.*

" *rode on their own roofs,*

Making all neighbouring houses til'd with men."

" Til'd with men,"—is't not good?

Capt. Jen. By Sesu, an it were tiled all with naked imen, 'twere better.

Bell. You shall hear no more; pick your ears, they are foul, sir. What are you, sir, pray?

Capt. Jen. A captain, sir, and a follower of god Mars.

Bell. Mars, Bacchus, and I love Apollo: a captain! then I pardon you, sir; and, captain, what would you press me for?

Capt. Jen. For a witty ditty to a sentleoman that I am fallen in withal, over head and ears in affections and natural desires.

Bell. An acrostic were good upon her name, methinks.

Capt. Jen. Cross sticks! I would not be too cross, master poet; yet, if it be best to bring her name in question, her name is Mistress Dorothy Hornet.

Bell. [*aside*] The very consumption that wastes

my son, and the ay-me that hung lately upon me!—Do you love this Mistress Dorothy?

Capt. Jen. Love her! there is no captain's wife in England can have more love put upon her; and yet, I'm sure, captains' wives have their pellies-full of good men's loves.

Bell. And does she love you? has there passed any great matter between you?

Capt. Jen. As great a matter as a whole coach and a horse and his wife are gone to and fro between us.

Bell. Is she—i'faith, captain, be valiant and tell truth—is she honest?

Capt. Jen. Honest! God udge me, she's as honest as a punk that cannot abide fornication and lechery.

Bell. Look you, captain, I'll show you why I ask: I hope you think my wenching days are past; yet, sir, here's a letter that her father brought me from her, and enforced me to take, this very day.

Capt. Jen. 'Tis for some love-song to send to me, I hold my life.

Re-enter Servingman, *and whispers* BELLAMONT.

Bell. This falls out pat.—My man tells me the party is at my door: shall she come in, captain?

Capt. Jen. O, ay, ay, put her in, I pray now. [*Exit* Servingman.

Bell. The letter says here that she's exceeding sick, and entreats me to visit her. Captain, lie you in ambush behind the hangings, and perhaps you shall hear the piece of a comedy: she comes, she comes, make yourself away.

Capt. Jen. [*aside*] Does the poet play Torkin, and cast my Lucresie's water too in huggermuggers? if he do, Styanax' tragedy was never so horrible bloody-minded as his comedy shall be. *Taw a son,** Captain Jenkins.

[*Hides himself.*

Enter DOLL.

Doll. Now, master poet, I sent for you.

Bell. And I came once at your ladyship's call.

Doll. My ladyship and your lordship lie both in one manor. You have conjured up a sweet spirit in me, have you not, rhymer?

Bell. Why, Medea, what spirit? Would I were a young man for thy sake!†

Doll. So would I, for then thou couldst do me no hurt; now thou dost.

---

* *the little horse that ambled on the top of Paul's*] Banks's famous horse, called Morocco (with which learned animal the commentators on our old poets have made their readers so familiar), is said, among other feats, to have mounted to the top of St. Paul's church. (See note *, p. 17.)

* *Taw a son*] i. e. hold your tongue.

† *Would I were a young man for thy sake!*] So Shallow in Shakespeare's *Merry Wives of Windsor*, act i. sc. 1; "Would I were young for your sake, Mistress Anne!"

Bell. If I were a younker, it would be no immodesty in me to be seen in thy company; but to have snow in the lap of June, vile, vile! Yet, come; garlic has a white head and a green stalk; * then why should not I? Let's be merry: what says the devil to all the world? for I'm sure thou art carnally possessed with him.

Doll. Thou hast a filthy foot, a very filthy carrier's foot.

Bell. A filthy shoe, but a fine foot: I stand not upon my foot, I.

Capt. Jen. [aside] What stands he upon, then, with a pox, God bless us?

Doll. A leg and a calf! I have had better of a butcher forty times for carrying a body,—not worth begging by a barber-surgeon.

Bell. Very good; you draw me and quarter me: fates keep me from hanging!

Doll. And which most turns up a woman's stomach, thou art an old hoary man; thou hast gone over the bridge of many years, and now art ready to drop into a grave : what do I see, then, in that withered face of thine?

---

* *garlic has a white head and a green stalk*] So in *The Honest Lawyer*, 1616; "I'm like a leeke, though I have a gray head, I have a greene," &c. Sig. G 2. And so in various old plays and poems, Chaucer's *Reve's Prologue*, &c. This piece of wit may be traced to Boccaccio; "E quagli che contro alla mia età parlando vanno, mostra mal che conoscano che, *perche il porro abbia il capo bianco, che la coda sia verde.*" *Decamerone,*—Introduction to *Giornata quarta.*

Having quoted *The Honest Lawyer*, I cannot refrain from pointing out the resemblance between a passage in it, and one in *The Widow*, a joint production of Jonson, Fletcher, and Middleton ;

"*Gripe.* The stone, the stone, I am pittifully grip'd with the stone. . . . .
Valentine. Sir, the disease is somewhat dangerous.

I must awhile withdraw to study, sir.
Now am I puzzled : bloud, what medicine
Should I devise to do't? It must be violent.
Give him some aqua-fortis ; that would speed him.
Let's see. Me thinks, a little gun-powder
Should have some strange relation to this fit.
I have seen gun-powder oft drive out stones
From forts and castle-walls," &c.
            The Honest Lawyer. Written by S. S. 1616, Sig. F 2.

"*Occulto.* I warrant you: your name's spread, sir, for an emperick.
There's an old mason troubled with the stone
Has sent to you this morning for your counsell ;
He would have ease fain. . . . . . .
Latrocinio. Le' me see, ile send him a whole musket-charge of gunpowder.
Occulto. Gun-powder ! what sir, to break the stone?
Latrocinio. I, by my faith, sir :
It is the likeliest thing I know to do't.
I'm sure it breaks stone-walls and castles down :
I see no reason but't should break the stone."
    The Widow (first printed in 1652), act iv. sc. 2, p. 42.

Bell. Wrinkles, gravity.

Doll. Wretchedness, grief : old fellow, thou hast bewitched me ; I can neither eat for thee, nor sleep for thee, nor lie quietly in my bed for thee.

Capt. Jen. [aside] Ud's blood, I did never see a white flea before. I will cling you.

Doll. I was born, sure, in the dog-days, I'm so unlucky : I, in whom neither a flaxen hair, yellow beard, French doublet, nor Spanish hose, youth nor personage, rich face nor money, could ever breed a true love to any, ever to any man, am now besotted, dote, am mad, for the carcass of a man ; and, as if I wore a bawd, no ring pleases me but a Death's head.*

Capt. Jen. [aside] Sesu, are men so arsy-varsy?

Bell. Mad for me ! why, if the worm of lust were wriggling within me as it does in others, do't think I'd crawl upon thee? would I low after thee, that art a common calf-bearer?

Doll. I confess it.

Capt. Jen. [aside] Do you? are you a town-cow, and confess you bear calves?

Doll. I confess I have been an inn for any guest.

Capt. Jen. [aside] A poga o' your stable-room ! is your inn a bawdy-house, now?

Doll. I confess, (for I ha' been taught to hide nothing from my surgeon, and thou art he,) I confess that old stinking surgeon like thyself, whom I call father, that Hornet, never sweat for me ; I'm none of his making.

Capt. Jen. [aside] You lie; he makes you a punk,—Hornet minor.

Doll. He's but a cheater, and I the false die he plays withal. I pour all my poison out before thee, because hereafter I will be clean. Shun me not, loathe me not, mock me not. Plagues confound thee ! I hate thee to the pit of hell ;

---

* *as if I wore a bawd, no ring pleases me but a Death's head*] The bawds of those days, probably from an affectation of piety, used to wear rings with Death's heads on them, as several passages from old writers might be adduced to show. But the wearing of such rings was not confined to those motherly gentlewomen : " the olde Countesse spying on the finger of Seignior Cosimo a *Ring with a Death's head ingraven,* circled with this Posie, Gressus ad vitam, demaunded whether hee adornde the Signet for profit or pleasure : Seignior Cosimo speaking in truth as his conscience wild him, told her, that it was a favour which a Gentlewoman had bestowed upon him, and that onely hee wore it for her sake." Greene's *Farewell to Follie,* Sig. B 2, ed. 1617.—Underwood the player bequeathed "to his daughter Elizabeth two seal-rings of gold, *one with a death's-head.*" See his will in Malone's *Hist. Acc. of the English Stage,* p. 215, ed. Boswell.

yet if thou goest thither, I'll follow thee: run,
ay,* do what thou canst, I'll run and ride over
the world after thee.

Capt. Jen. [*aside*] Cockatrice !—[*Comes out*]
You, Mistress Salamanders, that fear no burning,
let my mare and my mare's horse, and my coach,
come running home again; and run to an hospital
and your surgeons, and to knaves and panders,
and to the tivel and his tame too.

Doll. Fiend, art thou raised to torment me?

Bell. She loves you, captain, honestly.

Capt. Jen. I'll have any man, oman, or cild, by
his ears, that says a common drab can love a
sentleman honestly.—I will sell my coach for a
cart to have you to punk's hall, Pridewell.—I
sarge you in Apollo's name, whom you belong to,
see her forthcoming, till I come and tiggle her
by and by.—'Sblood, I was never cozened with a
more rascal piece of mutton, since I came out
o'the Lawer-Countries.   [*Exit.*

Bell. My doors are open for thee: be gone,
woman.

Doll. This goat's-pizzle of thine—

Bell. Away ! I love no such implements in my
house.

Doll. Dost not? am I but an implement? By
all the maidenheads that are lost in London in a
year (and that's a great oath), for this trick other
manner of women than myself shall come to this
house only to laugh at thee; and if thou wouldst
labour thy heart out, thou shalt not do withal.†
                                                [*Exit.*

Bell. Is this my poetical fury?

Re-enter Servingman.

How now, sir !

Serv. Master Mayberry and his wife, sir, i'the
next room.

Bell. What are they doing, sir?

Serv. Nothing, sir, that I see; but only would
speak with you.

Bell. Enter 'em. [*Exit* Servingman.] This
house will be too hot for me: if this wench cast
me into these sweats, I must shift myself for
pure necessity. Haunted with sprites in my old
days !

Enter MAYBERRY *booted, and* MISTRESS MAYBERRY.

May. A comedy ! a Canterbury tale smells not

half so sweet as the comedy I have for thee, old
poet: thou shalt write upon't, poet.

Bell. Nay, I will write upon't, if't be a comedy,
for I have been at a most villanous female tragedy:
come, the plot, the plot.

May. Let your man give you the boots presently : the plot lies in Ware, my white * poet.—
Wife, thou and I this night will have mad sport
in Ware ; mark me well, wife, in Ware.

Mist. May. At your pleasure, sir.

May. Nay, it shall be at your pleasure, wife.—
Look you, sir, look you : Featherstone's boy, like
an honest crack-halter, laid open all to one of my
prentices ; for boys, you know, like women, love
to be doing.

Bell. Very good : to the plot.

May. Featherstone, like a crafty mutton-
monger, persuades Greenshield to be run through
the body.

Bell. Strange ! through the body?

May. Ay, man, to take physic : he does so, he's
put to his purgation. Then, sir, what does me
Featherstone but counterfeits a letter from an
inn-keeper of Doncaster, to fetch Greenshield
(who is needy, you know) to a keeper's lodge in
Enfield-chase, a certain uncle, where Greenshield
should receive money due to him in behalf of his
wife?

Bell. His wife ! is Greenshield married? I have
heard him swear he was a bachelor.

Mist. May. So have I, a hundred times.

May. The knave has more wives than the
Turk ; he has a wife almost in every shire in
England : this parcel-gentlewoman is that inn-
keeper's daughter of Doncaster.

Bell. Hath she the entertainment of her forefathers? will she keep all comers company?

May. She helps to pass away stale capons, sour
wine, and musty provender. But to the purpose:
this train was laid by the baggage herself, and
Featherstone, who it seems makes her husband a
unicorn; and to give fire to't, Greenshield, like an
arrant wittol, entreats his friend to ride before
his wife and fetch the money, because, taking
bitter pills, he should prove but a loose fellow if
he went, and so durst not go.

---

* *ay*] The old ed. "*ayde.*"
† *thou shalt not do withal*] i.e. thou shalt not be able to
help it. "It is my infirmity, and I cannot *doe withall,*
to die for't." Chapman's *May-Day*, 1611, Sig. A 4.
"Beare witnes, my masters, if hee dye of a surfet, I cannot *doe withall,* it is his owne seeking, not mine." Nash's
Have with you to Saffron-walden, Sig. G 4, ed. 1596.

* *white*] Was employed formerly as an epithet to
express fondness : "*white* boy," "*white* son," and "*white*
girl," occur frequently in our old writers. I do not remember to have found it in any author after the time of
poor mad Lee, who uses it in a strange passage of the
Dedication of his *Rival Queens* to the Earl of Mulgrave.
(Though Mayberry a little after calls Bellamont "my
little hoary poet," we are not to conclude that "*white*"
in the present instance means *hoary*.)

Bell. And so the poor stag is to be hunted in Enfield-chase.

May. No, sir; master poet, there you miss the plot. Featherstone and my Lady Greenshield are rid to batter away their light commodities in Ware; Enfield-chase is too cold for 'em.

Bell. In Ware!

May. In dirty Ware.—I forget myself.—Wife, on with your riding-suit, and cry "Northward ho!" as the boy at Paul's says:* let my prentice get up before thee, and man thee to Ware: lodge in the inn I told thee: spur, cut, and away!

Mist. May. Well, sir.   [*Exit.*

Bell. Stay, stay; what's the bottom of this riddle? why send you her away?

May. For a thing, my little hoary poet. Look thee, I smelt out my noble stinker Greenshield in his chamber, and as though my heart-strings had been cracked, I wept and sighed, and thumped and thumped, and raved and randed and railed, and told him how my wife was now grown as common as bribery,† and that she had hired her tailor to ride with her to Ware, to meet a gentleman of the court.

Bell. Good; and how took he this drench down?

May. Like eggs and muscadine, at a gulp. He cries out presently, "Did not I tell you, old man, that she'd win any ‡ game when she came to bearing?" § He rails upon her, wills me to take her in the act, to put her to her white sheet, to be divorced, and, for all his guts are not fully scoured by his pothecary, he's pulling on his boots, and will ride along with us. Let's muster as many as we can.

Bell. It will be excellent sport to see him and his own wife meet in Ware, will't not? Ay, ay, we'll have a whole regiment of horse with us.

May. I stand upon thorns ‖

Till I shake him by the horns.—

---

* *cry "Northward ho!" as the boy at Paul's says*] I presume Paul's Wharf is meant: "Paul's Wharf, or St. Benets Paul's Wharf, a noted Stairs for Watermen."
Stow's *Survey of London,* &c. B. iii. p. 229, ed. 1720.
                    "*and I'll*
Take water at Paul's wharf, and overtake you."
Middleton's *Chaste Maid in Cheapside,*—Works, iv. 76, ed. Dyce.

† *bribery*] The old ed. "baibery" (which, supposing it to mean "finery fit to please a babe," cannot be right).

‡ *any*] The old ed. "my."

§ *bearing*] Was a term at the games of Irish and backgammon.
"O, the trial is *when she comes to bearing.*"
Middleton and Dekker's *Roaring Girl,*—Middleton's *Works,* ii. 520, ed. Dyce.
"*Bear as fast as you can* . . . *when you come to bearing,* have a care," &c. The *Compleat Gamester,* pp. 155-6, ed. 1674.   ‖ *I stand,* &c.] Qy. Is this a quotation?

Come, boots, boy! we must gallop all the way; for the sin, you know, is done with turning up the white of an eye: will you join your forces?

Bell. Like a Hollander against a Dunkirk.*

May. March, then.—This curse is on all lechers thrown,
They give horns, and at last horns are their own.
                    [*Exeunt.*

SCENE II.†

Enter CAPTAIN JENKINS *and* ALLUM.

Capt. Jen. Set the best of your little diminutive legs before, and ride post, I pray.

Allum. Is it possible that Mistress Doll should be so bad?

Capt. Jen. Possible! 'sblood, 'tis more easy for an oman to be naught than for a soldier to beg; and that's horrible easy, you know.

Allum. Ay, but to cony-catch us all so grossly!

Capt. Jen. Your Norfolk tumblers are but zanies to cony-catching punks.

Allum. She gelded my purse of fifty pounds in ready money.

Capt. Jen. I will geld all the horses in five hundred shires but I will ride over her and her cheaters and her Hornets. She made a stark ass of my conch-horse: and there is a putter-box whom she spread thick upon her white bread, and eat him up; I think she has sent the poor fellow to Gelder-land: but I will marse pravely in and out, and pack again, upon all the Low-Countries in Christendom, as Holland and Zealand and Netherland, and Cleveland too; and I will be drunk and cast‡ with Master Hans Van Belch but I will smell him out.

Allum. Do so, and we'll draw all our arrows of revenge up to the head but we'll hit her for her villany.

Capt. Jen. I will traw as petter and as urse weapons as arrows up to the head, lug you; it shall be warranta to give her the whip-doodle.

Allum. But now she knows she's discovered, she'll take her bells § and fly out of our reach.

Capt. Jen. Fly with her pells! ounds, I know a parish that sal tag down all the pells and sell 'em to Captain Jenkins, to do him good; and if pell[s] will fly, we'll fly too, unless the pell-ropes hang us. Will you amble up and down to Master Justice by my side, to have this rascal Hornet in

---

* *a Dunkirk*] See note †, p. 254.
† *Scene II.*] The same.   A street.
‡ *cast*] i. e. vomit.
§ *take her bells,* &c.] i. e. like a falcon.

corum, and so to make her hold her whore's
peace?

Allum. I'll amble or trot with you, captain.
You told me she threatened her champions
should cut for her: if so, we may have the peace
of her.

Capt. Jen. O *mon dieu! Duw gwyn!** Follow
your leader. Jenkins shall cut and slice as worse
as they: come, I scorn to have any peace of her
or of any *oman,†* but open wars. [*Exeunt.*

SCENE III.‡

Enter BELLAMONT, MAYBERRY, GREENSHIELD, PHILIP,
LEVERPOOL, *and* CHARTLEY, *all booted.*

Bell. What, will these young gentlemen too
help us to catch this fresh salmon, ha? Philip,
are they thy friends?

Phil. Yes, sir.

Bell. We are beholding to you, gentlemen, that
you'll fill our consort: I ha'§ seen your faces
methinks before, and I cannot inform myself
where.

Lever.,
Charl., } May be so, sir.

Bell. Shall's to horse? here's a tickler: || heigh,
to horse!

May. Come, switch and spurs! let's mount
our chevals: merry, quoth a.'

Bell. Gentlemen, shall I shoot a fool's bolt out
among you all, because we'll be sure to be merry?

Omnes. What is't?

Bell. For mirth on the highway will make us
rid ground¶ faster than if thieves were at our
tails. What say ye to this? let's all practise
jests one against another, and he that has the
best jest thrown upon him, and is most galled,
between our riding forth and coming in, shall
bear the charge of the whole journey. .

Omnes. Content, i'faith.

Bell. We shall fit one o'you with a coxcomb at
Ware, I believe.

May. Peace!

Green. Is't a bargain?

Omnes. And hands clapt upon it.

Bell. Stay, yonder's the Dolphin without
Bishopsgate, where our horses are at rack and
manger, and we are going past it. Come, cross
over:—and what place is this?

May. Bedlam, is't not?

Bell. Where the madmen are: I never was
amongst them: as you love me, gentlemen, let's
see what Greeks are within.

Green. We shall stay too long.

Bell. Not a whit: Ware will stay for our
coming, I warrant you. Come, a spurt and
away! let's be mad once in our days. This is
the door. [*Knocks.*

Enter FULLMOON.

May. Save you, sir! may we see some o' your
mad folks? do you keep 'em?

Full. Yes.

Bell. Pray, bestow your name, sir, upon us.

Full. My name is Fullmoon.

Bell. You well deserve this office, good Master
Fullmoon: and what madcaps have you in your
house?

Full. Divers.

Enter a Musician.*

May. God's so, see, see! what's he walks
yonder? is he mad?

Full. That's a musician: yes, he's besides
himself.

Bell. A musician! how fell he mad, for God's
sake?

Full. For love of an Italian dwarf.

Bell. Has he been in Italy, then?

Full. Yes, and speaks, they say, all manner of
languages.

Enter a Bawd.

Omnes. God's so, look, look! what's she?

Bell. The dancing bear, a pretty well-favoured
little woman.

Full. They say, but I know not, that she was
a bawd, and was frighted out of her wits by fire.

Bell. May we talk with 'em, Master Fullmoon?

Full. Yes, as you will. I must look about, for
I have unruly tenants. [*Exit.*

Bell. What have you in this paper, honest
friend?

Green. Is this he has all manner of languages,
yet speaks none?

Bawd. How do you, Sir Andrew? will you
send for some aqua-vitæ for me? I have had no
drink never since the last great rain that fell.

---

* *Duw gwyn*] i. e. white God: the old copy "*u dgnin.*"
† *oman*] The old ed. "*onam.*"
‡ *Scene III*] Near Bedlam; to which they presently
"cross over."
§ *ha'*] The old ed. "*ha.*"
|| *a tickler*] He means his switch.
¶ *rid ground*] i. e. get over ground: the expression is
now, I believe, obsolete; and I was rather surprised to
find it used so recently as in a letter from Richardson,
the novelist, to Lady Bradshaigh; "a regular even
pace, stealing away ground, rather than seeming to *rid
it.*" *Correspondence,* vol. iv. 291.

* *Musician*] The old ed., by a misprint, "*Phisition.*"

T

Bell. No? that's a lie.

Bawd. Nay, by gad, then, you lie, for all you're Sir Andrew. I was a dapper rogue in Portingal voyage,* not an inch broad at the heel, and yet thus high: I scorned, I can tell you, to be drunk with rain-water then, sir, in those golden and silver days; I had sweet bits then, Sir Andrew. How do you, good brother Timothy?

Bell. You have been in much trouble since that voyage?

Bawd. Never in Bridewell, I protest, as I'm a virgin, for I could never abide that Bridewell, I protest. I was once sick, and I took my water in a basket, and carried it to a doctor's.

Philip. In a basket!

Bawd. Yes, sir: you arrant fool, there was a urinal in it.

Philip. I cry you mercy.

Bawd. The doctor told me I was with child. How many lords, knights, gentlemen, citizens, and others, promised me to be godfathers to that child! 'twas not God's will: the prentices made a riot upon my glass windows, the Shrove-Tuesday following,† and I miscarried.

Omnes. O, do not weep!

Bawd. I ha' cause to weep: I trust gentlewomen their diet sometimes a fortnight; lend gentlemen holland shirts, and they sweat 'em out at tennis; and no restitution, and no restitution. But I'll take a new order: I will have but six stewed prunes‡ in a dish, and some of Mother Wall's cakes;§ for my best customers are tailors.

Omnes. Tailors! ha, ha!

Bawd. Ay, tailors: give me your London prentice; your country gentlemen are grown too politic.

Bell. But what say you to such young gentlemen as these are?

Bawd. Foh! they, as soon as they come to their lands, get up to London, and, like squibs that run upon lines,* they keep a spitting of fire and cracking till they ha' spent all; and when my squib is out, what says his punk? foh, he stinks!
[*Sings.*

Methought, this other night I saw a pretty sight,
  Which pleased me much,—
A comely country maid, not squeamish nor afraid
  To let gentlemen touch:
I sold her maidenhead once, and I sold her maidenhead twice,
  And I sold it last to an alderman of York;
And then I had sold it thrice.

Mus.† You sing scurvily.

Bawd. Marry, muff,‡ sing thou better, for I'll go sleep my old sleeps. [*Exit.*

Bell. What are you a-doing, my friend?

Mus. Pricking, pricking.

Bell. What do you mean by pricking?

Mus. A gentleman-like quality.

Bell. This fellow is somewhat prouder and sullener than the other.

May. O, so be most of your musicians.

Mus. Are my teeth rotten?

Omnes. No, sir.

Mus. Then I am no comfit-maker nor vintner: I do not get wenches in my drink.—Are you a musician?

Bell. Yes.

Mus. We'll be sworn brothers, then, look you, sweet rogue.

Green. God's so, now I think upon't, a jest is crept into my head: steal away, if you love me.

---

* *Portingal voyage*] The *Portugal voyage* was the expedition in 1589, consisting of one hundred and eighty vessels, and twenty-one thousand men, commanded by Sir Francis Drake and Sir John Norris: it is generally said to have been undertaken for the purpose of seating Antonio on the throne of Portugal; but the brave volunteers who composed it were most probably excited to the enterprise by the wish of revenging themselves on Spain, and by the hopes of gain and glory.

† *the prentices made a riot upon my glass windows, the Shrove-Tuesday following*] Shrove-Tuesday was a holiday for apprentices, during which they used to be exceedingly riotous, and to attempt to demolish houses of bad fame:

  "It was the day of all dayes in the yeare,
    That unto Bacchus hath his dedication,
  When mad-braynd prentises, that no men feare,
    O'rethrow the dens of bawdie recreation."
          Pasquils Palinodia, 1634, Sig. D.

‡ *stewed prunes*] A favourite dainty in brothels, as the commentators on Shakespeare have abundantly shown.

§ *Mother Wall's cakes*] I learn where this dame resided from the following passage of Haughton's *English-men for my money*, 1616; "I have the scent of London-stone as full in my nose, as Abchurch-lane of *Mother Walles pasties*." Sig. G.

* *like squibs that run upon lines, &c.*] So Marston, in his *Parasitaster, or the Fawne,* 1606;
"*Page.* There be squibs, sir, which squibs running upon lines, like some of our gawdie gallants, sir, keepe a smother, sir, with flishing and flashing, and in the end, sir, they doe, sir—
Nymphadoro. What, sir?
Page. Stink, sir." Sig. B.
In *A Rich Cabinet, with Variety of Inventions, &c.,* 1651, by J. White, are instructions "How to make your fireworks to run upon a line backward and forward." Sig. I 2.

† *Musician*] Before the Bawd's song in the old ed. is a stage-direction, "*Enter the Musition;*" but it does not appear that he had quitted the scene.

‡ *Marry, muff*] A not uncommon expression in our old writers (equivalent, I believe, to—Stuff, nonsense). So Middleton; "Wearied, sir! *marry, muff!*" *Blurt, Master Constable,—Works,* i. 258, ed. Dyce.

[*Exeunt* GREENSHIELD, MAYBERRY, PHILIP, LEVERPOOL, and CHARTLEY. *Musician sings.**]

Mus. Was ever any merchant's band set better? I set it. Walk, I'm a-cold: this white satin is too thin unless it be cut, for then the sun enters. Can you speak Italian too? *sapete Italiano?*

Bell. Un poco.

Mus. 'Sblood, if it be in you, I'll poke it out of you: *un poco!* Come, march: lie here with me but till the fall of the leaf, and if you have but *poco Italiano* in you, I'll fill you full of more *poco*: march.

Bell. Come on. [*Exeunt.*

Re-enter GREENSHIELD, MAYBERRY, PHILIP, LEVERPOOL, CHARTLEY, and FULLMOON.

Green. Good Master Mayberry, Philip, if you be kind gentlemen, uphold the jest: your whole voyage is paid for.

May. Follow it, then.

Full. The old gentleman, say you? why, he talked even now as well in his wits as I do myself, and looked as wisely.

Green. No matter how he talks, but his pericranion's perished.

Full. Where is he, pray?

Philip. Marry, with the musician, and is madder by this time.

Chart. He's an excellent musician himself, you must note that.

May. And having met one fit for his own tooth, you see he skips from us.

Green. The troth is, Master Fullmoon, divers trains have been laid to bring him hither without gaping of people, and never any took effect till now.

Full. How fell he mad?

Green. For a woman. Look you, sir; here's a crown, to provide his supper. He's a gentleman of a very good house: you shall be paid well if you convert him. To-morrow morning bedding and a gown shall be sent in, and wood and coal.

Full. Nay, sir, he must ha' no fire.

Green. No? why, look what straw you buy for him shall return you a whole harvest.

Omnes. Let his straw be fresh and sweet, we beseech you, sir.

Green. Get a couple of your sturdiest fellows, and bind him, I pray, whilst we slip out of his sight.

Full. I'll hamper him, I warrant, gentlemen. [*Exit.*

Omnes. Excellent!

May. But how will my noble poet take it at my hands, to betray him thus?

Omnes. Foh, 'tis but a jest. He comes.

Re-enter the Musician *and* BELLAMONT.

Bell. Perdonate mi, si io dimando del vostro nome.—O, whither shrunk you? I have had such a mad dialogue here.

Omnes. We ha' been with the other mad folks.

May. And what says he and his prick-song?

Bell. We were up to the ears in Italian, i'faith.

Omnes. In Italian! O good Master Bellamont, let's hear him.

Re-enter FULLMOON *with two* Keepers: *they lay hold on* BELLAMONT, *while* MAYBERRY, GREENSHIELD, PHILIP, LEVERPOOL *and* CHARTLEY *steal away.*

Bell. How now! 'sdeath, what do you mean? are you mad?

Full. Away, sirrah!—Bind him; hold fast.—You want a wench, sirrah, do you?

Bell. What wench? will you take mine arms from me, being no heralds? let go, you dogs.

Full. Bind him.—Be quiet: come, come; dogs! fie, and a gentleman!

Bell. Master Mayberry, Philip, Master Mayberry, ud's foot!

Full. I'll bring you a wench: are you mad for a wench?

Bell. I hold my life, my comrades have put this fool's-cap upon thy head, to gull thee*: I smell it now: why, do you hear, Fullmoon? let me loose, for I'm not mad; I'm not mad, by Jesu.

Full. Ask the gentlemen that.

Bell. By the Lord, I'm as well in my wits as any man i'the house, and this is a trick put upon thee by these gallants in pure knavery.

Full. I'll try that; answer me to this question:—loose his arms a little:—look you, sir; three geese nine pence, every goose three pence, what's that a goose, roundly, roundly, one with another?

Bell. 'Sfoot, do you bring your geese for me to cut up? [*Strikes him soundly, and kicks him.*

Re-enter MAYBERRY, GREENSHIELD, PHILIP, LEVERPOOL, and CHARTLEY.

Omnes. Hold, hold!—Bind him, Master Fullmoon.

Full. Bind him you: he has paid me all; I'll have none of his bonds, not I, unless I could recover them better.

Green. Have I given it you, master poet? did the lime-bush take?

May. It was his warrant sent thee to Bedlam,

---

* *Musician sings*] See note †, p. 46.

* *thee*] Old ed. "me." (compare Bellamont's next speech.)

T 2

old Jack Bellamont: and, Master Full-i'-the-moon, our warrant discharges him.—Poet, we'll all ride upon thee to Ware, and back again, I fear, to thy cost.

Bell. If you do, I must bear you.—Thank you, Master Greenshield; I will not die in your debt. —Farewell, you mad rascals.—To horse, come.— 'Tis well done, 'twas well done. You may laugh, you shall laugh, gentlemen. If the gudgeon had been swallowed by one of you, it had been vile;

but, by gad, 'tis nothing, for your best poets, indeed, are mad for the most part.—Farewell, goodman Fullmoon.

Full. Pray, gentlemen, if you come by, call in.
[*Exit.*

Bell. Yes, yes, when they are mad.—Horse yourselves now, if you be men.

May. He gallop must that after women rides: Get our wives out of town, they take long strides.
[*Exunt.*

ACT V.

SCENE I.*

Enter MAYBERRY *and* DELLAMONT.

May. But why have you brought us to the wrong inn, and withal possessed Greenshield that my wife is not in town? when my project was, that I would have brought him up into the chamber where young Featherstone and his wife lay, and so all his artillery should have recoiled into his own bosom.

Bell. O, it will fall out far better: you shall see my revenge will have a more neat and unexpected conveyance. He hath been all up and down the town to inquire for a Londoner's wife: none such is to be found, for I have mewed your wife up already. Marry, he hears of a Yorkshire gentlewoman at next inn, and that's all the commodity Ware affords at this instant. Now, sir, he very politicly imagines that your wife is rode to Puckeridge, five mile further; for, saith he, in such a town, where hosts will be familiar, and tapsters saucy, and chamberlains worse than thieves' intelligencers, they'll never put foot out of stirrup; either at Puckeridge or Wade's-Mill, saith he, you shall find them; and because our horses are weary, he's gone to take up post-horse. My counsel is only this,—when he comes in, feign yourself very melancholy, swear you will ride no further; and this is your part of the comedy: the sequel of the jest shall come like money borrowed of a courtier, and paid within the day, a thing strange and unexpected.

May. Enough, I ha't.

Bell. He comes.

Enter GREENSHIELD.

Green. Come, gallants, the post-horse are ready; 'tis but a quarter of an hour's riding; we'll ferret them and firk them, in faith.

Bell. Are they grown politic? when do you see honesty covet corners, or a gentleman that's no thief lie in the inn of a carrier?

May. Nothing hath undone my wife but too much riding.

Bell. She was a pretty piece of a poet indeed, and in her discourse would, as many of your goldsmiths' wives do, draw her simile from precious stones so wittily, as "redder than your ruby," "harder than your diamond," and so from stone to stone in less time than a man can draw on a strait boot, as if she had been an excellent lapidary.

Green. Come, will you to horse, sir?

May. No, let her go to the devil, an she will: I'll not stir a foot further.

Green. God's precious, is't come to this?— Persuade him, as you are a gentleman: there will be ballads made of him, and the burden thereof will be,—

" *If you* * *had rode out five mile forward,*
He had found the fatal house of Brainford northward;
O hone, hone, hone, O nonero!"

Bell. You are merry, sir.

Green. Like your citizen, I never think of my debts when I am a-horseback.

Bell. You imagine you are riding from your creditors.

Green. Good, in faith.—Will you to horse?

May. I'll ride no further.   [*Exit.*

Green. Then I'll discharge the postmaster.— Was't not a pretty wit of mine, master poet, to have had him rode into Puckeridge with a horn before him? ha, was't not?

Bell. Good sooth, excellent: I was dull in

---

* *Scene* I.] Ware. A room in an inn.

* *If you had,* &c.] Qy. " *If* he *had,*" &c.? or else in the next line "You *had found,*" &c? Compare what Kate sings in p. 279.

apprehending it. But, come, since we must stay, we'll be merry.—Chamberlain, call in the music, bid the tapsters and maids come up and dance !—What ! we'll make a night of it.

Enter CHAMBERLAIN, Fiddlers, Tapsters, *and* Maids.

Hark you, masters, I have an excellent jest to make old Mayberry merry : 'sfoot, we'll have him merry.

Green. Let's make him drunk, then : a simple catching wit ! !

Bell. Go thy ways : I know a nobleman would take such a delight in thee.

Green. Why, so he would in his fool.

Bell. Before God, but he would make a difference ; he would keep you in satin. But as I was a-saying, we'll have him merry. His wife is gone to Puckeridge : 'tis a wench makes him melancholy, 'tis a wench must make him merry : we must help him to a wench. When your citizen comes into his inn, dropping-wet and cold,* either the hostess or one of her maids warms his bed, pulls on his night-cap, cuts his corns, puts out the candle, bids him command aught, if he want aught; and so after, master citizen† sleeps as quietly as if he lay in his own Low-Country of Holland, his own linen, I mean, sir. We must have a wench for him.

Green. But where's this wench to be found ? here are all the moveable petticoats of the house.

Bell. At the next inn there lodged to-night——

Green. God's precious, a Yorkshire gentlewoman. I ha't, I'll angle for her presently : we'll have him merry.

Bell. Procure some chamberlain to pander for you.

Green. No, I'll be pander myself, because we'll be merry.

Bell. Will you, will you ?

Green. But how ! be a pander ! as I am a gentleman, that were horrible. I'll thrust myself into the outside of a falconer in town here; and now I think on't, there are a company of country players, that are come to town here, shall furnish me with hair and beard. If I do not bring her !—We'll be wondrous merry.

Bell. About it : look you, sir, though she bear her far aloof, and her body out of distance, so her mind be coming, 'tis no matter.

Green. Get old Mayberry merry. That any man should take to heart thus the downfal

---

* *dropping-wet and cold*] The old ed. "wet and cold dropping."

† *citizen*] The old ed. "*cittiner.*"

---

of a woman ! I think when he comes home, poor snail, he'll not dare to peep forth of doors lest his horns usher him.   [*Exit.*

Bell. Go thy ways. There be more in England wear large ears and horns than stags and asses. Excellent ! he rides post with a halter about his neck.

Re-enter MAYBERRY.

May. How now ! will't take ?

Bell. Beyond expectation : I have persuaded him the only way to make you merry is to help you to a wench, and the fool is gone to pander his own wife hither.

May. Why, he'll know her.

Bell. She hath been masked ever since she came into the inn for fear of discovery.

May. Then she'll know him.

Bell. For that his own unfortunate wit helped my lazy invention, for he hath disguised himself like a falconer in town here, hoping in that procuring shape to do more good upon her than in the outside of a gentleman.

May. Young Featherstone will know him.

Bell. He's gone into the town, and will not return this half hour.

May. Excellent, if she would come.

Bell. Nay, upon my life, she'll come. When she enters, remember some of your young blood, talk as some of your gallant commoners will, dice, and drink freely; do not call for sack, lest it betray the coldness of your manhood; but fetch a caper now and then, to make the gold chink in your pockets,—ay, so.

May. Ha, old poet, let's once stand to it for the credit of Milk-street ! Is my wife acquainted with this ?

Bell. She's perfect, and will come out upon her cue, I warrant you.

May. Good wenches, in faith.—Fill's some more sack here.

Bell. God's precious, do not call for sack by any means.

May. Why, then, give us a whole lordship for life in Rhenish, with the reversion in sugar.

Bell. Excellent !

May. It were not amiss, if we were dancing.

Bell. Out upon't ! I shall never do it.

Re-enter GREENSHIELD *disguised, with* KATE *masked.*

Green. Out of mine nostrils, tapster ! thou smellest, like Guildhall two days after Simon and Jude, of drink most horribly.—Off with thy mask; sweet sinner of the north : these masks are foils to good faces, and to bad ones they are like new satin outsides to lousy linings.

Kate. O, by no means, sir. Your merchant will not open a whole piece to his best customer: he that buys a woman must take her as she falls. I'll unmask my hand; here's the sample.

Green. Go to, then, old poet. I have ta'en her up already as a pinnace bound for the straits: she knows her burden yonder.

Bell. Lady, you are welcome. Yon is the old gentleman; and observe him, he's not one of your fat city chuffs, whose great belly argues that the felicity of his life consists in capon, sack, and sincere honesty; but a lean, spare, bountiful gallant, one that hath an old wife and a young performance; whose reward is not the rate of a captain newly come out of the Low-Countries, or a Yorkshire attorney in good contentious practice, some angel,—no, the proportion of your wealthy citizen to his wench is her chamber, her diet, her physic, her apparel, her painting, her monkey, her pander, her every thing. You'll say, your young gentleman is your only service, that lies before you like a calf's head, with his brains some half yard from him; but, I assure you, they must not only have variety of foolery, but also of wenches: whereas your conscionable greybeard of Farringdon-within will keep himself to the ruins of one cast waiting-woman an age, and perhaps, when he's past all other good works, to wipe out false weights and twenty i' the hundred, marry her.

Green. O, well bowled, Tom !* we have precedents for't.

Kate. But I have a husband, sir.

Bell. You have ? If the knave thy husband be rich, make him poor, that he may borrow money of this merchant, and be laid up in the Counter or Ludgate: so it shall be conscience in you [r] old gentleman, when he hath seized all thy goods, to take thee home † and maintain thee.

Green. O, well bowled, Tom !* we have precedents for't.

Kate. Well, if you be not a nobleman, you are some great valiant gentleman by your breath ‡ and the fashion of your beard, and do but thus to make the citizen merry, because you owe him some money.

Bell. O, you are a wag.

May. You are very welcome.

Green. He is ta'en ; excellent, excellent ! there's one will make him merry. Is it any imputation to help one's friend to a wench ?

Bell. No more than at my lord's entreaty to help my lady to a pretty waiting woman. If he had given you a gelding, or the reversion of some monopoly, or a new suit of satin, to have done this, happily* your satin would have smelt of the pander : but what's done freely, comes, like a present to an old lady, without any reward ; and what is done without any reward, comes, like wounds to a soldier, very honourably notwithstanding.

May. This is my breeding, gentlewoman : and whither travel you ?

Kate. To London, sir, as the old tale goes, to seek my fortune.

May. Shall I be your fortune, lady ?

Kate. O, pardon me, sir; I'll have some young landed heir to be my fortune, for they favour she-fools more than citizens.

May. Are you married ?

Kate. Yes, but my husband is in garrison i' the Low-Countries, is his colonel's bawd, and his captain's jester : he sent me word over that he will thrive, for though his apparel lie i' the Lombard, he keeps his conscience i' the muster-book.

May. He may do his country good service, lady.

Kate. Ay, as many of your captains do, that fight, as the geese saved the Capitol, only with prattling. Well, well, if I were in some nobleman's hands now, may be he would not take a thousand pounds for me.

May. No ?

Kate. No, sir; and yet may be at year's end would give me a brace of hundred pounds to marry me to his baily or the solicitor of his law-suits.—Who's this, I beseech you ?

Enter Mistress Mayberry, *her hair loose, with the Hostess.*

Host. I pray you, forsooth, be patient.

Bell. Passion of my heart, Mistress Mayberry ! [*Exeunt* Chamberlain, Fiddlers, Tapsters, *and* Maids.

Green. [*aside*] Now will she put some notable trick upon her cuckoldly husband.

May. Why, how now, wife ! what means this, ha ?

Mist. May. Well, I am very well. O my unfortunate parents, would you had buried me quick, when you linked me to this misery !

May. O wife, be patient ! I have more cause to rail, wife.

---

* *Tom*] After this word, the old ed. has "( )"
† *thee home*] The old ed. "the home."
‡ *breath*] The old ed. "bearth."

* *happily*] i. e. haply.

Mist. May. You have! prove it, prove it. Where's the courtier you should have ta'en in my bosom? I'll spit my gall in's face that can tax me of any dishonour. Have I lost the pleasure of mine eyes, the sweets of my youth, the wishes of my blood, and the portion of my friends, to be thus dishonoured, to be reputed vile in London, whilst my husband prepares common diseases for me at Ware? O God, O God!

Bell. [*aside*] Prettily well dissembled.

Host. As I am true hostess, you are to blame, sir.—What are you, mistress *? I'll know what you are afore you depart, mistress. Dost thou leave thy chamber in an honest inn, to come and inveigle my customers?—An you had sent for me up, and kissed me, and used me like an hostess, 'twould never have grieved me; but to do it to a stranger!

Kate. I'll leave you, sir.

May. Stay.—[*To Mist. May.*] Why, how now, sweet gentlewoman! cannot I come forth to breathe myself, but I must be haunted?—[*Aside to her*] Rail upon old Bellamont, that he may discover them.—You remember Featherstone, Greenshield?

Mist. May. I remember them! Ay, they are two as cogging, dishonourable, damned, forsworn, beggarly gentlemen as are in all London; and there's a reverend old gentleman, too, your pander, in my conscience.

Bell. Lady, I will not, as the old gods were wont, swear by the infernal Styx; but by all the mingled wine in the cellar beneath, and the smoke of tobacco that hath fumed over the vessels, I did not procure your husband this banqueting-dish of sucket. Look you, behold the parenthesis.

[*Pulls off* GREENSHIELD'S *false hair and beard.*]

Host. Nay, I'll see your face too.

[*Pulls off* KATE'S *mask.*]

Kate. My dear unkind husband, I protest to thee I have played this knavish part only to be witty.

Green. That I might be presently turned into a matter more solid than horn,—into marble!

Bell. Your husband, gentlewoman! why, he never was a soldier.

Kate. Ay, but a lady got him pricked for a captain: I warrant you, he will answer to the name of captain, though he be none; like a lady that will not think scorn to answer to the name of her first husband, though he were a soap-boiler.

Green. Haug off, thou devil, away!

Kate [*sings*].

" *No, no : you fled me t'other day;*
When I was with child you ran away,
But since I have caught you now"—

Green. A pox of your wit and your singing!

Bell. Nay, look you, sir, she must sing, because we'll be merry:

" *What though* * *you rode not five mile forward,*
You have found that fatal house at Brainford northward,
O hone, hono, nanero!"

Green. God refuse me,† gentlemen, you may laugh and be merry; but I am a cuckold, and I think you knew of it.—Who lay i'the segs with you to-night, wild-duck?

Kate. Nobody with me, as I shall be saved; but Master Featherstone came to meet me as far as Royston.

Green. Featherstone!

May. See, the hawk, that first stooped my pheasant, is killed by the spaniel that first sprang all of our side, wife.

Bell. 'Twas a pretty wit of you, sir, to have had him rode into Puckeridge with a horn before him; ha, was't not?

Green. Good.

Bell. Or, where a citizen keeps his house, you know, 'tis not as a gentleman keeps his chamber, for debt, but, as you said even now very wisely, lest his horns should usher him.

Green. Very good.—Featherstone!—he comes.

Enter FEATHERSTONE.

Feath. Luke Greenshield, Master Mayberry, old poet, Moll, and Kate, most happily encountered: ud's life, how came you hither? By my life, the man looks pale.

Green. You are a villain, and I'll make't good upon you: I am no servingman to feed upon your reversion.

Feath. Go to the ordinary, then.

Bell. This is his ordinary, sir; and in this she is like a London ordinary,—her best getting comes by the box.

Green. You are a damned villain.

Feath. O, by no means.

Green. No? Ud's life, I'll go instantly take a purse, be apprehended, and hanged for't; better than be a cuckold.

Feath. Best first make your confession, sirrah.

---

* *mistress*] Here, and in the next line, the old ed. "maisters."

* *What though, &c.*] See p. 276.
† *God refuse me*] See note §, p. 7.

Green. 'Tis this; thou hast not used me like a gentleman.

Feath. A gentleman! thou a gentleman! thou art a tailor.

Bell. 'Ware peaching!

Feath. No, sirrah, if you will confess aught, tell how thou hast wronged that virtuous gentlewoman: how thou layest at her two year together, to make her dishonest; how thou wouldst send me thither with letters; how duly thou wouldst watch the citizens'-wives' vacation, which is twice a-day, namely the Exchange-time, twelve at noon, and six at night; and where she refused thy importunity and vowed to tell her husband, thou wouldst fall down upon thy knees, and entreat her for the love of heaven, if not to ease thy violent affection, at least to conceal it,—to which her pity and simple virtue consented; how thou tookest her wedding-ring from her; met those two gentlemen at Ware; feigned a quarrel; and the rest is apparent. This only remains,—what wrong the poor gentlewoman hath since received by our intolerable lie, I am most heartily sorry for, and to thy bosom will maintain all I have said to be honest.

May. Victory, wife! thou art quit by proclamation.

Bell. Sir, you are an honest man: I have known an arrant thief for peaching made an officer: give me your hand, sir.

Kate. O filthy, abominable husband, did you all this!

May. Certainly he is no captain; he blushes.

Mist. May. Speak, sir, did you ever know me answer your wishes?

Green. You are honest; very virtuously honest.

Mist. May. I will, then, no longer be a loose woman: I have at my husband's pleasure ta'en upon me this habit of jealousy. I'm sorry for you: virtue glories not in the spoil, but in the victory.

Bell. How say you by that good[l]y sentence? Look you, sir, you gallants visit citizens' houses, as the Spaniard first sailed to the Indies: you pretend buying of wares or selling of lands; but the end proves 'tis nothing but for discovery and conquest of their wives for better maintenance. Why, look you, was he aware of those broken patience * when you met him at Ware and possessed him of the downfall of his wife? You are a cuckold; you have pandered your own wife to this gentleman; better men have done it, honest

Tom; * we have precedents for't. Hie you to London. What is more catholic i'the city than for husbands daily for to forgive the nightly sins of their bedfellows? If you like not that course, but do † intend to be rid of her, rifle her at a tavern,‡ where you may swallow down some fifty wiseacres, sons and heirs to old tenements and common gardens, like so many raw yolks with muscadine to bedward.

Kate. O filthy knave, dost compare a woman of my carriage to a horse?

Bell. And no disparagement; for a woman to have a high forehead, a quick ear, a full eye, a wide nostril, a sleek skin, a straight back, a round hip, and so forth, is most comely.

Kate. But is a great belly comely in a horse, sir?

Bell. No, lady.

Kate. And what think you of it in a woman, I pray you?

Bell. Certainly I am put down at my own weapon: I therefore recant the rifling. No, there is a new trade come up for cast gentlewomen, of periwig-making: let your wife set up i'the Strand; and yet I doubt whether she may or no, for they say the women have got it to be a corporation. If you can, you may make good use of it, for you shall have as good a coming-in by hair (though it be but a falling commodity), and by other foolish tiring, as any between Saint Clement's and Charing.

Feath. Now you have run yourself out of breath, hear me. I protest the gentlewoman is honest; and since I have wronged her reputation in meeting her thus privately, I'll maintain her. —Wilt thou hang at my purse, Kate, like a pair of Barbary buttons,§ to open when 'tis full, and close when 'tis empty?

Kate. I'll be divorced, by this Christian element: and because thou thinkest thou art a

---

* *patience*] Qy. "*patients*?" but the whole passage is otherwise corrupted.

* *Tom*] See note *, p. 278.

† *but do intend*] The old ed. "*but to intend.*"

‡ *rifle her at a tavern*] Our old writers used *rifle* in the sense of *raffle:* so Chapman,—"Why, then, thus it shal be, weele strike up a drumme, set up a tent, call people together, put crownes a peece, let's *rifle* for her." *The Blinde begger of Alexandria*, 1598, Sig. B 3. And Minsheu, in his *Guide into the tongues*, ed. 1617, explains *rifling* to be "a kinde of game, where he that in casting doth throw most on the dice, takes up all that is laid down." Dr. Nott therefore is quite wrong, when in a note on his reprint of Dekker's *Gull's Horn-book*, p. 165, he says that "any *rifling*" means "any *cheating* or *plundering*."

§ *Barbary buttons*] Moorish buttons, I believe, of gold or silver filigree-work.

cuckold, lest I should make thee an infidel in causing thee to believe an untruth, I'll make thee a cuckold.

Bell. Excellent wench!

Feath. Come, let's go, sweet; the nag I ride upon bears double : we'll to London.

May. Do not bite your thumbs, sir.

Kate. Bite his thumb!   [*Sings.*

> " *I'll make him do a thing worse than this :*
> *Come love me whereas I lay.*"

Feath. What, Kate?

Kate [*sings*].

> " *He shall father a child is none of his,*
> *O, the clean contrary way.*"

Feath. O lusty Kate!

       [*Exeunt* FEATHERSTONE *and* KATE.

May. Methought he said even now you were a tailor.

Green. You shall hear more of that hereafter : I'll make Ware and him stink ere he goes : if I be a tailor, the rogue's naked weapon shall not fright me; I'll beat him and my wife both out o'the town with a tailor's yard.   [*Exit.*

May. O valiant Sir Tristram!—Room there!

Enter PHILIP, LEVERPOOL, *and* CHARTLEY.

Phil. News, father, most strange news out of the Low-Countries : your good lady and mistress, that set you to work upon a dozen of cheese-trenchers, is now lighted at the next inn, and the old venerable gentlewoman's * father with her.

Bell. Let the gates of our inn be locked up closer than a nobleman's gates at dinner-time.

Omnes. Why, sir, why?

Bell. If she enter here, the house will be infected : the plague is not half so dangerous as a she-hornet.—Philip, this is your shuffling o'the cards, to turn up her for the bottom card at Ware.

Philip. No, as I'm virtuous, sir : ask the two gentlemen.

Lever. No, in troth, sir. She told us, that, inquiring at London for you or your son, your man chalked out her way to Ware.

Bell. I would Ware might choke 'em both.—Master Mayberry, my horse and I will take our leaves of you : I'll to Bedlam again rather than stay her.

May. Shall a woman make thee fly thy country? Stay, stand to her, though she were greater than Pope Joan. What are thy brains conjuring for, my poetical bay-leaf-eater?

Bell. For a sprite o'the buttery, that shall make us all drink with mirth, if I can raise it. Stay, the chicken is not fully hatched.—Wit,* I beseech thee! so, come!—Will you be secret, gentlemen, and assisting?

Omnes. With brown bills, if you think good.

Bell. What will you say if by some trick we put this little hornet into Featherstone's bosom, and marry 'em together?

Omnes. Fuh! 'tis impossible.

Bell. Most possible. I'll to my trencher-woman; let me alone for dealing with her: Featherstone, gentlemen, shall be your patient.

Omnes. How, how?

Bell. Thus. I will close with this country pedler, Mistress Dorothy, that travels up and down to exchange pins for conyskins, very lovingly; she shall eat of nothing but sweatmeats in my company, good words; whose taste when she likes, as I know she will, then will I play upon her with this artillery,—that a very proper man and a great heir, naming Featherstone, spied her from a window, when she lighted at her inn, is extremely fallen in love with her, vows to make her his wife, if it stand to her good liking, even in Ware; but being, as most of your young gentlemen are, somewhat bashful, and ashamed to venture upon a woman,——

May. City and suburbs can justify it : so, sir.

Bell. He sends me, being an old friend, to undermine for him. I'll so whet the wench's stomach, and make her so hungry, that she shall have an appetite to him, fear it not. Greenshield shall have a hand in it too; and, to be revenged of his partner, will, I know, strike with any weapon.

Lever. But is Featherstone of any means? else you undo him and her.

May. He has land between Fulham and London : he would have made it over to me.—To your charge, poet : give you the assault upon her; and send but Featherstone to me, I'll hang him by the gills.

Bell. He's not yet horsed, sure.—Philip, go thy ways, give fire to him, and send him hither with a powder presently.

Phil. He's blown up already.   [*Exit.*

Bell. Gentlemen, you'll stick to the device, and look to your plot?

Omnes. Most poetically : away to your quarter.

Bell. I march : I will cast my rider, gallants. I hope you see who shall pay for our voyage.

       [*Exit.*

---

* *gentlewoman's*] The old ed. "*Gentlemans.*"

* *Wit*] The old ed. "hit."

May. That must be that comes here.

Re-enter PHILIP *and* FEATHERSTONE.

Master Featherstone, O Master Featherstone, you may now make your fortunes weigh ten stone of feathers more than ever they did! leap but into the saddle now that stands empty for you, you are made for ever.

Lever. [*aside*] An ass, I'll be sworn.

Feather. How, for God's sake, how!

May. I would you had what I could wish you. I love you, and because you shall be sure to know where my love dwells, look you, sir, it hangs out at this sign: you shall pray for Ware, when Ware is dead and rotten. Look you, sir, there is as pretty a little pinnace struck sail hereby, and come in lately: she's my kinswoman, my father's youngest sister, a ward; her portion three thousand; her hopes, if her grannam die without issue, better.

Feath. Very good, sir.

May. Her guardian goes about to marry her to a stone-cutter; and rather than she'll be subject to such a fellow, she'll die a martyr: will you have all out? she's run away, is here at an inn i'the town. What parts soever you have played with me, I see good parts in you; and if you now will catch Time's hair that's put into your hand, you shall clap her up presently.

Feath. Is she young, and a pretty wench?

Lever. Few citizens' wives are like her.

Phil. Young! why, I warrant sixteen hath scarce gone over her.

Feath. 'Sfoot, where is she? If I like her personage as well as I like that which you say belongs to her personage, I'll stand thrumming of caps no longer, but board your pinnace whilst 'tis hot.

May. Away, then, with these gentlemen, with a French gallop, and to her! Philip here shall run for a priest, and despatch you.

Feath. Will you, gallants, go along? We may be married in a chamber for fear of hue and cry after her, and some of the company shall keep the door.

May. Assure your soul she will be followed: away, therefore. [*Exeunt* FEATHERSTONE, PHILIP, LEVERPOOL, *and* CHARTLEY.] He's in the Curtian gulf,* and swallowed, horse and man. He will have somebody keep the door for him! she'll look to that. I am younger than I was two nights ago for this physic.—How now!

Enter CAPTAIN JENKINS, ALLUM, HANS VAN BELCH, *and others, booted.*

Capt. Jen. God pless you! is there not an arrant scurvy trab in your company, that is a sentlewoman born, sir, and can tawg Welsh, and Dutch, and any tongue in your head?

May. How so? Drabs in my company! do I look like a drab-driver?

Capt. Jen. The trab will drive you, if she put you before her, into a pench-hole.*

Allum. Is not a gentleman here, one Master Bellamont, sir, of your company?

May. Yes, yes: come you from London? he'll be here presently.

Capt. Jen. Will he? tawson, this oman hunts at his tail, like your little goats in Wales follow their mother. We have warrants here from master austice of this shire, to show no pity nor mercy to her: her name is Doll.

May. Why, sir, what has she committed? I think such a creature is i'the town.

Capt. Jen. What has she committed! ounds, she has committed more than manslaughters, for she has committed herself, God pless us, to everlasting prison. Lug you, sir, she is a punk: she shifts her lovers (as captains and Welsh gentlemen and such) as she does her trenchers; when she has well fed upon't, and that there is left nothing but pare bones, she calls for a clean one, and scrapes away the first.

Re-enter BELLAMONT *with* HORNET, DOLL *between them;* FEATHERSTONE, GREENSHIELD, KATE, PHILIP, LEVERPOOL, *and* CHARTLEY.

May. God's so, Master Featherstone, what will you do? here's three come from London to fetch away the gentlewoman with a warrant.

Feather. All the warrants in Europe shall not fetch her now: she's mine sure enough.—What have you to say to her? she's my wife.

Capt. Jen. Ow! 'sblood, do you come so far to fish, and catch frogs? your wife is a tilt-boat; any man or oman may go in her for money: she's a cony-catcher.—Where is my moveable goods called a coach, and my two wild peasts? pogs on you, would they had trawn you to the gallows!

Allum. I must borrow fifty pound of you, mistress bride.

Hans. Yaw, vro, and you make me de gheck, de groet fool: you heb mine gelt too; war is it?

---

* *He's in the Curtian gulf*] Every schoolboy knows the story of M. Curtius.

* *pench-hole*] He means *bench-hole*. So in Shakespeare's *Antony and Cleopatra*, act iv. sc. 7; "We'll beat 'em into *bench-holes*"; where Malone observes that *bench-hole* means "the hole in a bench *ad levandum alvum*."

Doll. Out, you base scums! come you to disgrace me in my wedding-shoes?

Feath. Is this your three-thousand-pound ward? ye told me, sir, she was your kinswoman.

May. Right, one of mine aunts.*

Bell. Who pays for the northern voyage now, lads?

Green. Why do you not ride before my wife to London now? The woodcock's i'the springe.

Kate. O, forgive me, dear husband! I will never love a man that is worse than hanged, as he is.

May. Now a man may have a course in your park?

Feath. He may, sir.

Doll. Never, I protest: I will be as true to thee as Ware and Wade's-Mill are one to another.

Feath. Well, it's but my fate. Gentlemen, this is my opinion, it's better to shoot in a bow that has been shot in before, and will never start, than to draw a fair new one, that for every arrow will be warping.—Come, wench, we are joined, and all the dogs in France shall not part us.—I have some lands; those I'll turn into money, to pay you, and you, and any.—I'll pay all that I can for thee, for I'm sure thou hast paid me.

Omnes. God give you joy!

May. Come, let's be merry.—[*To Greenshield.*] Lie you with your own wife, to be sure she shall not walk in her sleep.—A noise of musicians,* chamberlain!—

This night let's banquet freely: come. we'll dare Our wives to combat i'the great bed in Ware.

[*Exeunt.*

---

* *aunts*] See note *, p. 254.

* *A noise of musicians*] See note §, p. 222.

A CURE FOR A CUCKOLD.

A Cure for a Cuckold. A pleasant Comedy, As it hath been several times Acted with great Applause. Written by John Webster and William Rowley. Placere Cupio. London, Printed by Tho. Johnson, and are to be sold by Francis Kirkman, at his Shop at the Sign of John Fletchers Head, over against the Angel-Inne, on the Back-side of St. Clements, without Temple-Bar. 1661. 4to.

We have no other authority than that of Kirkman for attributing this play to Webster and Rowley : I believe, however, that it is rightly assigned. A great portion of it, which the authors meant for blank verse, Kirkman has printed as prose : in some passages the integrity of the text is very questionable.

William Rowley, Webster's coadjutor in this drama, flourished in the reign of James the First. Meres mentions among the best writers of comedy, "Maister Rowley, once a rare Scholler of learned Pembrooke Hall in Cambridge," (*Palladis Tamia, Wits Treasury, Being the Second Part of Wits Commonwealth*, 1598, fol. 283,): but he doubtless alludes to another dramatist of the same name, *Samuel* Rowley. It appears that William was an actor, as well as an author, and he is said to have been more excellent in comedy than in tragedy. "There was one Will. Rowley was Head of the Princes Company of Comedians in 1613 to 1616. See the Office Books of the Ld. Stanhope, Treasurer of the Chamber in those years, in Dr. Rich. Rawlinson's Possession." MS. note by Oldys on Langbaine's *Acc. of Eng. Dram. Poets*, in the Brit. Museum. "William Rowley, the author-actor, was married to Isabel Tooley at Cripplegate Church, in 1637."—Collier's *Memoirs of the Principal Actors in the Plays of Shakespeare*, p. 233.

Of his plays there remain four of which he was the sole author,—(the best of them, *A new Wonder, a Woman never vext*, was revived with alterations at Covent-Garden Theatre, in 1824,)—and twelve which he composed in conjunction with other writers, Day, Wilkins, Middleton, Fletcher, Massinger, Ford, Heywood, Dekker, and Webster. His name is associated with Shakespeare's on the title-page of *The Birth of Merlin*; but certainly the bard of Avon at least had no hand in that wretched drama.

THE STATIONER TO THE JUDICIOUS READER.

GENTLEMEN,

It was not long since I was only a bookreader, and not a bookseller, which quality (my former employment somewhat failing, and I being unwilling to be idle,) I have now lately taken on me. It hath been my fancy and delight, e'er since I knew any thing, to converse with books; and the pleasure I have taken in those of this nature, viz. plays, hath been so extraordinary, that it hath been much to my cost; for I have been, as we term it, a gatherer of plays for some years, and I am confident I have more of several sorts than any man in England, bookseller or other: I can at any time show seven hundred in number, which is within a small matter all that were ever printed. Many of these I have several times over, and intend, as I sell, to purchase more; all, or any of which, I shall be ready either to sell or lend to you upon reasonable considerations.

In order to the encreasing of my store, I have now this term printed and published three, viz. this called *A Cure for a Cuckold*, and another called *The Thracian Wonder*, and the third called *Gammer Gurton's Needle*. Two of these three were never printed; the third, viz., *Gammer Gurton's Needle*, hath been formerly printed, but it is almost an hundred years since. As for this play, I need not speak any thing in its commendation; the authors' names, Webster and Rowley, are (to knowing men) sufficient to declare its worth: several persons remember the acting of it, and say that it then pleased generally well; and let me tell you, in my judgment it is an excellent old play. The expedient of curing a cuckold, after the manner set down in this play, hath been tried to my knowledge, and therefore I may say *probatum est*. I should, I doubt, be too tedious, or else I would say somewhat in defence of this, and in commendation of plays in general; but I question not but you have read what abler pens than mine have writ in their vindication. Gentlemen, I hope you will so encourage me in my beginnings, that I may be induced to proceed to do you service, and that I may frequently have occasion, in this nature, to subscribe myself

Your servant,

FRANCIS KIRKMAN.

DRAMATIS PERSONÆ.

WOODROFF, a justice of the peace, father to Annabel.
FRANCKFORD, a merchant, brother-in-law to Woodroff.
LESSINGHAM, a gentleman, in love with Clare.
BONVILE, a gentleman, the bridegroom and husband to Annabel.
RAYMOND,
EUSTACE,
LIONEL,   } gallants invited to the wedding.
GROVER,
ROCHFIELD, a young gentleman and a thief.*
COMPASS, a seaman,
PETTIFOG,
DODGE,   } two attorneys.
A Counsellor.
Two Clients.
Two Boys.
A Sailor.

LUCE, wife to Franckford, and sister to Woodroff.
ANNABEL, the bride and wife to Bonvile.
CLARE, Lessingham's mistress.
URSE, wife to Compass.
Nurse.
A Waitingwoman.

---

* a young gentleman and a thief] I must observe, that it is Kirkman who so characterises Rochfield. I give the Dram. Per. from the old ed.

A CURE FOR A CUCKOLD.

ACT I.

SCENE I.*

Enter LESSINGHAM *and* CLARE.

Less. This is a place of feasting and of joy,
And, as in triumphs and ovations, here
Nothing save state and pleasure.

Clare. 'Tis confess'd.

Less. A day of mirth and solemn jubilee,——

Clare. For such as can be merry.

Less. A happy nuptial,
Since a like pair of fortunes suitable,
Equality in birth, parity in years,
And in affection no way different,
Are this day sweetly coupled.

Clare. 'Tis a marriage.

Less. True, lady, and a noble precedent
Methinks for us to follow.   Why should these
Outstrip us in our loves, that have not yet
Outgone us in our time?   If we thus lose
Our best and not-to-be recover'd hours
Unprofitably spent, we shall be held
Mere truants in love's school.

Clare. That's a study
In which I never shall ambition have.
To become graduate.

Less. Lady, you are sad:
This jovial meeting puts me in a spirit
To be made such.   We two are guests invited,
And meet by purpose, not by accident:
Where's, then, a place more opportunely fit,
In which we may solicit our own loves,
Than before this example?

Clare. In a word,
I purpose not to marry.

Less. By your favour;
For as I ever to this present hour
Have studied your observance, so from henceforth

* *Scene I.*] The garden belonging to Woodroft's house.

I now will study plainness:—I have lov'd you
Beyond myself, mis-spended for your sake
Many a fair hour which might have been employ'd
To pleasure or to profit; have neglected
Duty to them from whom my being came,
My parents, but my hopeful studies most:
I have stol'n time from all my choice delights
And robb'd myself, thinking to enrich you:
Matches I have had offer'd, some have told me
As fair, as rich,—I never thought 'em so:
And lost all these in hope to find out you.
Resolve me, then, for Christian charity;
Think you an answer of that frozen nature
Is a sufficient satisfaction for
So many more than needful services?

Clare. I have said, sir.

Less. Whence might this distaste arise?
Be at least so kind to perfect me in that.
Is it of some dislike lately conceiv'd
Of this my person, which perhaps may grow
From calumny and scandal? if not that,
Some late-received melancholy in you?
If neither, your perverse and peevish will,—
To which I most imply it?

Clare. Be it what it can or may be, thus it is;
And with this answer pray rest satisfied.
In all these travels, windings, and indents,
Paths, and by-paths, which many have sought out,
There's but one only road, and that alone,
To my fruition: which whoso finds out,
'Tis like he may enjoy me; but that failing,
I ever am mine own.

Less. O, name it, sweet!
I am already in a labyrinth,
Until you guide me out.

Clare. I'll to my chamber.
May you be pleas'd unto your mis-spent time

U

To add but some few minutes, by my maid
You shall hear further from me.
    Less. I'll attend you.   [*Exit* CLARE.
What more can I desire than be resolv'd
Of such a long suspense? Here's now the period
Of much expectation.

    Enter RAYMOND, EUSTACE, LIONEL, *and* GROVER.

    Ray. What, you alone retir'd to privacy
Of such a goodly confluence, all prepar'd
To grace the present nuptials!
    Less. I have heard some say,
Men are ne'er less alone than when alone,
Such power hath meditation.
    Eust. O these choice beauties
That are this day assembled! but of all
Fair Mistress Clare, the bride excepted still,
She bears away the prize.
    Lion. And worthily;
For, setting off her present melancholy,
She is without taxation.*
    Grov. I conceive
The cause of her so sudden discontent.
    Ray. 'Tis far out of my way.
    Grov. I'll speak it, then.
In all estates, professions, or degrees,
In arts or sciences, there is a kind
Of emulation; likewise so in this.
There's a maid this day married, a choice beauty:
Now, Mistress Clare, a virgin of like age
And fortunes correspondent, apprehending
Time lost in her that's in another gain'd,
May upon this—for who knows women's
    thoughts?—
Grow into this deep sadness.
    Ray. Like enough.
    Less. You are pleasant, gentlemen, or else
    perhaps,
Though I know many have pursu'd her love——
    Grov. And you amongst the rest, with pardon,
    sir;
Yet she might cast some more peculiar eye
On some that not respects her.
    Less. That's my fear,
Which you now make your sport.

    Enter Waitingwoman.

    Wait. A letter, sir.
    Less. From whom?
    Wait. My mistress.   [*Gives letter.*
    Less. [*aside*] She has kept her promise;
And I will read it, though I in the same
Know my own death included.

    * *without taxation*] i. e. irreproachable.

    Wait. Fare you well, sir.   [*Exit.*
    Less. [*reads*] " *Prove all thy friends, find out the
    best and nearest ;*
Kill for my sake that friend that loves thee dearest."
Her servant, nay, her hand and character,
All meeting in my ruin!—Read again.
" *Prove all thy friends, find out the best and
    nearest ;*
Kill for my sake that friend that loves thee dearest."
And what might that one be? 'tis a strange
    difficulty,
And it will ask much counsel.   [*Exit.*
    Ray. Lessingham
Hath left us on the sudden.
    Eust. Sure, the occasion
Was of that letter sent him.
    Lion. It may be
It was some challenge.
    Grov. Challenge! never dream it :
Are such things sent by women?
    Ray. 'Twere an heresy
To conceive but such a thought.
    Lion. Tush, all the difference
Begot this day must be at night decided
Betwixt the bride and bridegroom.—Here both
come.

    Enter WOODROFF, ANNABEL, BONVILE, FRANCKFORD,
    LUCE, *and* Nurse.

    Wood. What did you call the gentleman we met
But now in some distraction?
    Bon. Lessingham
A most approv'd and noble friend of mine,
And one of our prime guests.
    Wood. He seem'd to me
Somewhat in mind distemper'd. What concern
Those private humours our so public mirth,
In such a time of revels? Mistress Clare,
I miss her too: why, gallants, have you suffer'd
    her
Thus to be lost amongst you?
    Anna. Dinner done,
Unknown to any, she retir'd herself.
    Wood. Sick of the maid perhaps, because she
    sees
You, mistress bride, her school and playfellow,
So suddenly turn'd wife.
    Franck. 'Twas shrewdly guess'd.
    Wood. Go find her out.—Fie, gentlemen, within
The music plays unto the silent walls,
And no man there to grace it: when I was young,
At such a meeting I have so bestirr'd me
Till I have made the pale green-sickness girls
Blush like the ruby, and drop pearls apace

Down from their ivory foreheads; in those days
I have cut capers thus high. Nay, in, gentlemen,
And single out the ladies.

Ray. Well advis'd.—

Nay, mistress bride, you shall along with us,
For without you all's nothing.

Anna. Willingly,
With master bridegroom's leave.

Bon. O my best joy,
This day I am your servant.

Wood. True, this day;
She his, her whole life after,—so it should be;
Only this day a groom to do her service,
For which, the full remainder of his age,
He may write master. I have done it yet,
And so, I hope, still shall do.—Sister Luce,
May I presume my brother Franckford can
Say as much and truly?

Luce. Sir, he may;
I freely give him leave.

Wood. Observe that, brother;
She freely gives you leave: but who gives leave,
The master or the servant?

Franck. You are pleasant,
And it becomes you well, but this day most,
That having but one daughter, have bestow'd her
To your great hope and comfort.

Wood. I have one:
Would you could say so, sister! but your
    barrenness
Hath given your husband freedom, if he please,
To seek his pastime elsewhere.

Luce. Well, well, brother,
Though you may taunt me, that have never yet
Been bless'd with issue, spare my husband, pray,
For he may have a by-blow or an heir
That you never heard of.

Franck. O, fie, wife! make not
My fault too public.

Luce. Yet himself keep within compass.

Franck. If you love me, sweet,——

Luce. Nay, I have done.

Wood. But if
He have not, wench, I would he had the hurt
I wish you both. Prithee, thine ear a little.

Nurse. [*to* FRANCKFORD] Your boy grows up,
    and 'tis a chopping lad,
A man even in the cradle.

Franck. Softly, nurse.

Nurse. One of the forward'st infants! how it
    will crow,
And chirrup like a sparrow! I fear shortly
It will breed teeth: you must provide him
    therefore

A coral with a whistle and a chain.

Franck. He shall have any-thing.

Nurse. He's now quite out of blankets.

Franck. There's a piece; [*Gives money.*
Provide him what he wants: only, good nurse,
Prithee, at this time be silent.

Nurse. A charm to bind
Any nurse's tongue that's living.

Wood. Come, we are miss'd
Among the younger fry: gravity ofttimes
Becomes the sports of youth, especially
At such solemnities; and it were sin
Not in our age to show what we have bin.
        [*Exeunt.*

SCENE II.*

Enter LESSINGHAM, *sad, with a letter in his hand.*

Less. Amicitiâ nihil dedit Natura majus nec
    rarius:
So saith my author.† If, then, powerful Nature,
In all her bounties shower'd upon mankind,
Found none more rare and precious than this one
We call Friendship, O, to what a monster
Would this trans-shape me,—to be made that he
To violate such goodness! To kill any,
Had been a sad injunction; but a friend!
Nay, of all friends the most approv'd! a task
Hell, till this day, could never parallel.
And yet this woman has a power of me
Beyond all virtue,—virtue! almost grace.
What might her hidden purpose be in this,
Unless she apprehend some fantasy,
That no such thing has being, and as kindred,
And claims to crowns, are worn out of the world,
So the name friend? 't may be 'twas her conceit.
I have tried those that have profess'd much
For coin, nay, sometimes, slighter courtesies,
Yet found 'em cold enough: so, perhaps, she;
Which makes her thus opinion'd. If in the
    former,
And therefore better days, 'twas held so rare,
Who knows but in these last and worser times
It may be now with Justice banish'd th' earth?
I'm full of thoughts, and this my troubled breast
Distemper'd with a thousand fantasies.
Something I must resolve. I'll first make proof
If such a thing there be; which having found,
'Twixt love and friendship 'twill be a brave fight,
To prove in man which claims the greatest right.

---

* *Scene II.*] A room in the same house.
† *So saith my author*] A passage somewhat resembling
this occurs in Cicero.

U 2

Enter RAYMOND, EUSTACE, LIONEL, *and* GROVER.

Ray. What, Master Lessingham!
You that were wont to be compos'd of mirth,
All spirit and fire, alacrity itself,
Like the lustre of a late-bright-shining sun,
Now wrapt in clouds and darkness!
　Lion. Prithee, be merry;
Thy dulness sads the half part of the house,
And deads that spirit which thou wast wont to
　　quicken,
And, half-spent, to give life to.
　Less. Gentlemen,
Such as have cause for sport, I shall wish ever
To make of it the present benefit,
While it exists; content is still short-breath'd :
When it was mine, I did so; if now yours,
I pray make your best use on't.
　Lion. Riddles and paradoxes:
Come, come, some crotchet's come into thy pate,
And I will know the cause on't.
　Grov. So will I,
Or, I protest, ne'er leave thee.
　Less. 'Tis a business*
Proper to myself, one that concerns
No second person.
　Grov. How's that! not a friend?
　Less. Why, is there any such?
　Grov. Do you question that? what do you take
me for?
　Eust. Ay, sir, or me? 'Tis many months ago
Since we betwixt us interchang'd that name,
And, of my part, ne'er broken.
　Lion. Troth, nor mine.
　Ray. If you make question of a friend, I pray
Number not me the last in your account,
That would be crown'd in your opinion first.
　Less. You all speak nobly; but amongst you all
Can such a one be found?
　Ray. Not one amongst us
But would be proud to wear the character
Of noble friendship : in the name of which,
And of all us here present, I entreat,
Expose to us the grief that troubles you.
　Less. I shall, and briefly. If ever gentleman
Sunk beneath scandal, or his reputation,
Never to be recover'd, suffer'd, and
For want of one whom I may call a friend,
Then mine is now in danger.
　Ray. I'll redeem 't,
Though with my life's dear hazard.
　Eust. I pray, sir,
Be to us open-breasted.

---

* *'Tis a business, &c.*] The old ed. gives this speech to
Eustace.

　Less. Then 'tis thus.
There is to be perform'd a monomachy,
Combat, or duel,—time, place, and weapon,
Agreed betwixt us. Had it touch'd myself
And myself only, I had then been happy;
But I by composition am engag'd
To bring with me my second, and he too,
Not as the law of combat is, to stand
Aloof and see fair play, bring off his friend,
But to engage his person : both must fight,
And either of them dangerous.
　Eust. Of all things
I do not like this fighting.
　Less. Now, gentlemen,
Of this so great a courtesy I am
At this instant merely * destitute.
　Ray. The time?
　Less. By eight o'clock to-morrow.
　Ray. How unhappily
Things may fall out! I am just at that hour,
Upon some late-conceivèd discontents,
To atone† me to my father; otherwise
Of all the rest you had commanded me
Your second and your servant.
　Lion. Pray, the place?
　Less. Calais-sands.‡
　Lion. It once was fatal to a friend of mine
And a near kinsman; for which I vow'd then,
And deeply too, never to see that ground:
But if it had been elsewhere, one of them
Had before nine§ been worms'-meat.
　Grov. What's the weapon?
　Less. Single-sword.
　Grov. Of all that you could name,
A thing I never practis'd : had it been
Rapier, or that and poniard, where men use
Rather sleight than force, I had been then your
　　man.
Being young, I strain'd the sinews of my arm;
Since then to me 'twas never serviceable.
　Eust. In troth, sir, had it been a money-matter,
I could have stood your friend ; but as for fighting,
I was ever out at that.
　Less. Well, farewell, gentlemen.
　　[*Exeunt* RAYMOND, EUSTACE, LIONEL, *and* GROVER.
But where's the friend in all this? Tush, she's
　　wise,

---

* *merely*] i. e. utterly.
† *atone*] i. e. reconcile.
‡ *Calais-sands*] As duelling was punishable by the
English law, it was customary for gallants, who had
affairs of honour to settle, to betake themselves to Calais-
sands.
§ *nine*] The old ed. "*mine.*"

And knows there's no such thing beneath the
    moon :
I now applaud her judgment.

Enter BONVILE.

Bon. Why, how now, friend I This discontent,
    which now
Is so unseason'd, makes me question what
I ne'er durst doubt before, your love to me :
Doth it proceed from envy of my bliss,
Which this day crowns me with? or have you
    been
A secret rival in my happiness,
And grieve to see me owner of those joys
Which you could wish your own?

Less. Banish such thoughts,
Or you shall wrong the truest faithful friendship
Man e'er could boast of. O, mine honour, sir !
'Tis that which makes me wear this brow of
    sorrow :
Were that free from the power of calumny,—
But pardon me, that being now a-dying,
Which is so near to man, if part we cannot
With pleasant looks.

Bon. Do but speak the burden,
And I protest to take it off from you,
And lay it on myself.

Less. 'Twere a request,
Impudence without blushing could not ask,
It bears with it such injury.

Bon. Yet must I know't.

Less. Receive it, then :—but I entreat you, sir,
Not to imagine that I apprehend
A thought to further my intent for you ;
From you 'tis least suspected :—'twas my fortune
To entertain a quarrel with a gentleman,
The field betwixt us challeng'd, place an I time,
And these to be perform'd not without seconds :
I have relied on many seeming friends,
But cannot bless my memory with one
Dares venture in my quarrel.

Bon. Is this all?

Less. It is enough to make all temperature
Convert to fury. Sir, my reputation,
The life and soul of honour, is at stake,
In danger to be lost ; the word of coward
Still printed in the name of Lessingham.

Bon. Not while there is a Bonvile. May I live
    poor,
And die despis'd, not having one sad friend
To wait upon my hearse, if I survive
The ruin of that honour! Sir, the time?

Less. Above all spare me [that], for that once
    known,

You'll cancel this your promise, and unsay
Your friendly proffer ; neither can I blame you :
Had you confirm'd it with a thousand oaths,
The heavens would look with mercy, not with
    justice,
On your offence, should you infringe 'em all.
Soon after sun-rise, upon Calais-sands,
To-morrow we should meet : now to defer
Time one half-hour. I should but forfeit all.
But, sir, of all men living, this, alas,
Concerns you least ; for shall I be the man
To rob you of this night's felicity,
And make your bride a widow, her soft bed
No witness of those joys this night expects?

Bon. I still prefer my friend before my pleasure,
Which is not lost for ever, but adjourn'd
For more mature employment.

Less. Will you go, then?

Bon. I am resolv'd I will.

Less. And instantly?

Bon. With all the speed celerity can make.

Less. You do not weigh those inconveniences
This action meets with : your departure hence
Will breed a strange distraction in your friends,
Distrust of love in your fair virtuous bride,
Whose eyes perhaps may never more be bless'd
With your dear sight, since you may meet a grave,
And that not 'mongst your noble ancestors,
But amongst strangers, almost enemies.

Bon. This were enough to shake a weak resolve ;
It moves not me. Take horse as secretly
As you well may : my groom shall make mine ready
With all speed possible, unknown to any.

Less. But, sir, the bride.

Enter ANNABEL.

Anna. Did you not see the key that's to unlock
My carcanet * and bracelets? now, in troth,
I am afraid 'tis lost.

Bon. No, sweet, I ha't ;
I found it lie at random in your chamber,
And knowing you would miss it, laid it by :
'Tis safe, I warrant you.

Anna. Then my fear's past :
But till you give it back, my neck and arms
Are still your prisoners.

Bon. But you shall find
They have a gentle gaoler.

Anna. So I hope.
Within you're much inquir'd of.

Bon. Sweet, I follow. [*Exit* ANNABEL.] Dover

Less. Yes, that's the place.

---

* carcanet] i. e. necklace.

Ron. If you be there before me, hire a bark :
I shall not fail to meet you.   [*Exit.*
    Less. Was ever known
A man so miserably bless'd as I ?
I have no sooner found the greatest good
Man in this pilgrimage of life can meet,

But I must make the womb where 'twas con-
    ceiv'd
The tomb to bury it, and the first hour it lives
The last it must breathe. Yet there is a fate
That sways and governs above woman's hate.
                                                [*Exit.*

ACT II.

SCENE I.*

Enter ROCHFIELD.

Roch. A younger brother ! 'tis a poor calling ;
Though not unlawful, very hard to live on :
The elder fool inherits all the lands,
And we that follow, legacies of wit,
And get 'em when we can too. Why should law,
If we be lawful and legitimate,
Leave us without an equal divident ?
Or why compels it not our fathers else
To cease from getting, when they want to give ?
No, sure, our mothers will ne'er agree to that ;
They love to groan, although the gallows echo
And groan together for us : from the first
We travel forth, t'other's our journey's end.
I must forward. To beg is out of my way,
And borrowing is out of date. The old road,
The old high-way, 't must be, and I am in't :
The place will serve for a young beginner,
For this is the first day I set ope shop.
Success, then, sweet Laverna ! I have heard
That thieves adore thee for a deity :
I would not purchase by thee but to eat ;
And 'tis too churlish to deny me meat.—
Soft ! here may be a booty.

Enter ANNABEL *and a Servant.*

    Anna. Hors'd, says't thou ?
    Serv. Yes, mistress, with Lessingham.
    Anna. Alack, I know not what to doubt or fear !
I know not well whether't be well or ill ;
But, sure, it is no custom for the groom
To leave his bride upon the nuptial day.
I am so young and ignorant a scholar—
Yes, and it proves so ; I talk away perhaps
That might be yet recover'd. Prithee, run :
The fore-path may advantage thee to meet 'em,
Or the ferry, which is not two miles before,
May trouble 'em until thou com'st in ken ;
And if thou dost, prithee, enforce thy voice

To overtake thine eyes, cry out, and crave
For me but one word 'fore his departure ;
I will not stay him, say, beyond his pleasure,
Nor rudely ask the cause, if he be willing
To keep it from me. Charge him by all the love—
But I stay thee too long : run, run.
    Serv. If I had wings, I would spread 'em now,*
        mistress.   [*Exit.*
    Anna. I'll make the best speed after that I can ;
Yet I 'm not well acquainted with the path :
My fears, I fear me, will misguide me too. [*Exit.*
    Roch. There's good movables,
I perceive, whate'er the ready coin be :
Whoever owns her, she's mine now ; the next
        ground
Has a most pregnant hollow for the purpose.
                                                [*Exit.*

SCENE II.†

Enter Servant, *who runs over, and exit : then enter* ANNABEL ;
        after her, ROCHFIELD.

    Anna. I'm at a doubt already where I am.
    Roch. I'll help you, mistress : well overtaken.
    Anna. Defend me, goodness !—What are you ?
    Roch. A man.
    Anna. An honest man, I hope.
    Roch. In some degrees hot, not altogether cold,
So far as rank poison, yet dangerous,
As I may be dress'd : I am an honest thief.
    Anna. Honest and thief hold small affinity ;
I never heard they were akin before :
Pray heaven I find it now !
    Roch. I tell you my name.
    Anna. Then, honest thief, since you have taught
        me so,
For I'll inquire no other, use me honestly.
    Roch. Thus, then, I'll use you. First, then,‡
        to prove me honest,

---

* *I would spread 'em now*] Qy. "*I now would spread 'em*"?
† *Scene II.*] Another part of the same.
‡ *then*] Repeated, it would seem, by mistake.

I will not violate your chastity
(That's no part yet of my profession),
Be you wife or virgin.

Anna. I am both, sir.

Roch. This, then, it seems should be your
    wedding-day,
And these the hours of interim to keep you
In that double state : come, then, I'll be brief,
For I'll not hinder your desirèd hymen.
You have about you some superfluous toys,
Which my lank hungry pockets would contain *
With much more profit and more privacy ;
You have an idle chain which keeps your neck
A prisoner ; a manacle, I take it,
About your wrist too. If these prove emblems
Of the combinèd hemp to halter mine,
The Fates take their pleasure ! these are set
    down
To be your ransom, and there the thief is prov'd.

Anna. I will confess both, and the last forget.
You shall be only honest in this deed:
Pray you, take it ; I entreat you to it,
And then you steal 'em not.

Roch. You may deliver 'em.

Anna. Indeed, I cannot. If you observe, sir,
They are both lock'd about me, and the key
I have not : happily † you are furnish'd
With some instrument that may unloose 'em.

Roch. No, in troth, lady ; I am but a freshman ;
I never read further than this book you see,
And this very day is my beginning too :
These picking-laws I am to study yet.

Anna. O, do not show me that, sir, 'tis too
    frightful !
Good, hurt me not, for I do yield 'em freely :
Use but your hands ; perhaps their strength will
    serve
To tear 'em from me without much detriment :
Somewhat I will endure.

Roch. Well, sweet lady,
You're the best patient for a young physician,
That I think e'er was practis'd on. I'll use you
As gently as I can, as I'm an honest thief.
No ! will't not do ? Do I hurt you, lady ?

Anna. Not much, sir.

Roch. I'd be loth at all. I cannot do't.

Anna. Nay, then, you shall not, sir. You a thief,
    [*She draws his sword.*
And guard yourself no better ? no further read ?
Yet out in your own book ! a bad clerk, are you
    not !

Roch. Ay, by Saint Nicholas :*—lady, sweet
    lady,—

Anna. Sir, I have now a masculine vigour,
And will redeem myself with purchase † too.
What money have you ?

Roch. Not a cross,‡ by this foolish hand of
    mine.

Anna. No money ? 'twere pity, then, to take
    this from thee ;
I know thou'lt use me ne'er the worse for this ;
Take it again, I know not how to use it :
A frown had taken't from me, which thou hadst
    not.
And now hear and believe me,—on my knees
I make the protestation ; forbear
To take what violence and danger must
Dissolve, if I forgo 'em now. I do assure
You would not strike my head off for my chain,
Nor my hand for this : how to deliver 'em
Otherwise, I know not. Accompany
Me back unto my house, 'tis not far off :
By all the vows which this day I have tied
Unto my wedded husband, the honour
Yet equal with my cradle-purity,
(If you will tax me,) to the hopèd joys,
The blessings of the bed, posterity,
Or what aught else by woman may be pledg'd,
I will deliver you in ready coin
The full and dear'st esteem § of what you crave.

Roch. Ha ! ready money is the prize I look for :
It walks without suspicion any where,
When chains and jewels may be stay'd and call'd
Before the constable : but——

Anna. But ! can you doubt ?
You saw I gave you my advantage up :
Did you e'er think a woman to be true ?

Roch. Thought's free ; I have heard of some
    few, lady,
Very few indeed.

Anna. Will you add one more to your belief ?

Roch. They were fewer than the articles of my
    belief ;
Therefore I have room for you, and will believe
    you.

Stay ; you'll ransom your jewels with ready coin ;
So may you do, and then discover me.

Anna. Shall I reiterate the vows I made
To this injunction, or new ones coin ?

Roch. Neither ; I'll trust you : if you do destroy

---

* *contain*] The old ed. "contrive."
† *happily*] i. e. haply.

* *a bad clerk, are you not ? Ay, by Saint Nicholas*] A cant
name for thieves was *St. Nicholas' clerks.*
† *purchase*] i. e. booty.
‡ *a cross*] See note †, p. 196.
§ *esteem*] i. e. value.

A thief that never yet did robbery,
Then farewell I, and mercy fall upon me!
I know one once fifteen years courtier old,
And he was buried ere he took a bribe:
It may be my case in the worser way.
Come, you know your path back.

Anna. Yes, I shall guide you.

Roch. Your arm: I'll lead with greater dread
than will;
Nor do you fear, though in thief's handling still.
[*Exeunt.*

SCENE III.*

Enter Two Boys, *one with a Child in his arms.*

First Boy. I say 'twas fair play.

Sec. Boy. To snatch up stakes! I say you should
not say so, if the child were out of mine arms.

First Boy. Ay, then thou'dst lay about like a
man: but the child will not be out of thine arms
this five years; and then thou hast a prenticeship
to serve to a boy afterwards.

Sec. Boy. So, sir: you know you have the
advantage of me.

First Boy. I'm sure you have the odds of me;
you are two to one.—But, soft, Jack! who comes
here! if a point will make us friends, we'll not
fall out.

Sec. Boy. O, the pity! 'tis gaffer Compass:
they said he was dead three years ago.

First Boy. Did not he dance the hobby-horse
in Hackney-morris once?

Sec. Boy. Yes, yes, at Green-goose fair; as honest
and as poor a man.

Enter COMPASS.

Comp. Blackwall, sweet Blackwall, do I see thy
white cheeks again? I have brought some brine
from sea for thee; tears that might be tied in a
true-love knot, for they're fresh salt indeed. O
beautiful Blackwall! If Urse, my wife, be living
to this day, though she die to-morrow, sweet Fates!

Sec. Boy. Alas, let's put him out of his dumps,
for pity sake.—Welcome home, gaffer Compass.

First Boy. Welcome home, gaffer.

Comp. My pretty youths, I thank you.— Honest
Jack, what a little man art thou grown since I
saw thee! Thou hast got a child since, methinks.

Sec. Boy. I am fain to keep it, you see, whosoever got it, gaffer· it may be another man's case
as well as mine.

* *Scene III.*] Blackwall.

Comp. Sayest true, Jack: and whose pretty
knave is it?

Sec. Boy. One that I mean to make a younger
brother, if he live to't, gaffer. But I can tell you
news: you have a brave boy of your own wife's;
O, 'tis a shot to this pig!

Comp. Have I, Jack? I'll owe thee a dozen of
points* for this news.

Sec. Boy. O, 'tis a chopping boy! it cannot
choose, you know, gaffer, it was so long a-breeding.

Comp. How long, Jack?

Sec. Boy. You know 'tis four year ago since you
went to sea, and your child is but a quarter old
yet.

Comp. What plaguy boys are bred now-a-days!

First Boy. Pray, gaffer, how long may a child
be breeding before 'tis born?

Comp. That is as things are and prove, child;
the soil has a great hand in't too, the horizon,
and the clime: these things you'll understand
when you go to sea. In some parts of London
hard by you shall have a bride married to-day,
and brought to bed within a month after, sometimes within three weeks, a fortnight.

First Boy. O horrible!

Comp. True, as I tell you, lads. In another
place you shall have a couple of drones, do what
they can, shift lodgings, beds, bedfellows, yet not
a child in ten years.

Sec. Boy. O pitiful!

Comp. Now it varies again by that time you
come at Wapping, Ratcliff, Limehouse, and here
with us at Blackwall; our children come uncertainly, as the wind serves. Sometimes here
we are supposed to be away three or four year
together: 'tis nothing so; we are at home and
gone again, when nobody knows on't. If you'll
believe me, I have been at Surat, as this day; I
have taken the long-boat, (a fair gale with me,)
been here a-bed with my wife by twelve o'clock
at night, up and gone again i'the morning, and
no man the wiser, if you'll believe me.

Sec. Boy. Yes, yes, gaffer, I have thought so
many times,—that you or somebody else have been
at home: I lie at next wall, and I have heard a
noise in your chamber all night long.

Comp. Right: why, that was I; yet thou never
sawest me.

Sec. Boy. No, indeed, gaffer.

Comp. No, I warrant thee; I was a thousand
leagues off ere thou wert up. But, Jack, I have

* *points*] i.e. the tagged laces which fastened the
breeches to the doublet.

been loth to ask all this while, for discomforting myself, how does my wife? is she living?

Sec. Boy. O, never better, gaffer, never so lusty: and truly she wears better clothes than she was wont in your days, especially on holidays,—fair gowns, brave petticoats, and fine smocks, they say that have seen 'em; and some of the neighbours report that they were taken up at London.

Comp. Like enough: they must be paid for, Jack.

Sec. Boy. And good reason, gaffer.

Comp. Well, Jack, thou shalt have the honour on't: go tell my wife the joyful tidings of my return.

Sec. Boy. That I will, for she heard you were dead long ago. [*Exit.*

First Boy. Nay, sir, I'll be as forward as you, by your leave. [*Exit.*

Comp. Well, wife, if I be one of the livery, I thank thee. The horners are a great company; there may be an alderman amongst us one day: 'tis but changing our copy, and then we are no more to be called by our old brother-hood.

Enter URSE.

Urse. O my sweet Compass, art thou come again?

Comp. O Urse, give me leave to shed! the fountains * of love will have their course: though I cannot sing at first sight, yet I can cry before I see. I am new come into the world, and children cry before they laugh a fair while.

Urse. And so thou art, sweet Compass, new-born indeed,

For rumour laid thee out for dead long since.
I never thought to see this face again:
I heard thou wert div'd to the bottom of the sea,
And taken up a lodging in the sands,
Never to come to Blackwall again.

Comp. I was going, indeed, wife; but I turned back: I heard an ill report of my neighbours,—sharks and sword-fishes, and the like, whose companies I did not like. Come kiss my tears, now, sweet Urse: sorrow begins to ebb.

Urse. A thousand times welcome home, sweet Compass!

Comp. An ocean of thanks; and that will hold 'em. And, Urse, how goes all at home? or cannot all go yet? lank still? will't never be full sea at our wharf?

Urse. Alas, husband!

Comp. A lass or a lad, wench? I should be glad of both: I did look for a pair of Compasses before this day.

Urse. And you from home?

Comp. I from home! why, though I be from home, and other of our neighbours from home, it is not fit all should be from home; so the town might be left desolate, and our neighbours of Bow might come further from the Itacus,* and inhabit here.

Urse. I'm glad you're merry, sweet husband.

Comp. Merry! nay, I'll be merrier yet: why should I be sorry? I hope my boy's well, is he not? I looked for another by this time.

Urse. What boy, husband?

Comp. What boy! why, the boy I got when I came home in the cock-boat one night about a year ago: you have not forgotten't, I hope. I think I left behind for a boy, and a boy I must be answered: I'm sure I was not drunk; it could be no girl.

Urse. Nay, then, I do perceive my fault is known:

Dear man, your pardon!

Comp. Pardon! why, thou hast not made away my boy, hast thou? I'll hang thee, if there were ne'er a whore in London more, if thou hast hurt but his little toe.

Urse. Your long absence, with rumour of your death,—

After long battery I was surpris'd.

Comp. Surprised! I cannot blame thee: Blackwall, if it were double black-walled, can't hold out always, no more than Limehouse, or Shadwell, or the strongest suburbs about London; and when it comes to that, woe be to the city too!

Urse. Pursu'd by gifts and promises, I yielded ·
Consider, husband, I am a woman,
Neither the first nor last of such offenders.
'Tis true I have a child.

Comp. Ha' you? and what shall I have, then, I pray? Will not you labour for me, as I shall do for you? Because I was out o' the way when 'twas gotten, shall I lose my share? There's better law amongst the players yet; for a fellow shall have his share, though he do not play that day. If you look for any part of my four years' wages, I will have half the boy.

Urse. If you can forgive me, I shall be joy'd at it.

Comp. Forgive thee! for what? for doing me a pleasure? And what is he that would seem to father my child?

---

* *fountains*] The old ed. "fountain."

* *Itacus*] Seems to be a misprint.

Urse. A man, sir, whom in better courtesies
We have been beholding to, the merchant
Master Franckford.

Comp. I'll acknowledge no other courtesies:
for this I am beholding to him, and I would
requite it, if his wife were young enough. Though
he be one of our merchants at sea, he shall give
me leave to be owner at home. And where's my
boy? shall I see him?

Urse. He's nurs'd at Bednal-Green:* 'tis now
too late;
To-morrow I'll bring you to it, if you please.

Comp. I would thou couldst bring me another
by to-morrow. Come, we'll eat, and to bed; and
if a fair gale come, we'll hoist sheets, and set
forwards.
Let fainting fools lie sick upon their scorns;
I'll teach a cuckold how to hide his horns.

[*Exeunt.*

SCENE IV.†

Enter WOODROFF, FRANCKFORD, RAYMOND, EUSTACE,
GROVER, LIONEL, CLARE, *and* LUCE.

Wood. This wants a precedent, that a bride-
groom
Should so discreet and decently observe
His forms, postures, all customary rites
Belonging to the table, and then hide himself
From his expected wages in the bed.

Franck. Let this be forgotten too, that it
remain‡ not
A first example.

Ray. Keep it amongst us,
Lest it beget too much unfruitful sorrow.
Most likely 'tis, that love to Lessingham
Hath fastened on him, we all denied.

Eust. 'Tis more certain than likely: I know
'tis so.

Grov. Conceal, then: the event may be well
enough.

Wood. The bride, my daughter, she is hidden
too;
This last hour she hath not been seen with us.

Ray. Perhaps they are together.

Eust. And then we make too strict an inqui-
sition:
Under correction of fair modesty,
Should they be stol'n away to bed together,
What would you say to that?

Wood. I would say, speed 'em well;
And if no worse news comes, I'll never weep
for't.

Enter NURSE.

How now! hast thou any tidings?

Nurse. Yes, forsooth, I have tidings.

Wood. Of any one that's lost?

Nurse. Of one that's found again, forsooth.

Wood. O, he was lost, it seems, then.

Franck. This tidings comes to me, I guess, sir.

Nurse. Yes, truly, does it, sir.

Ray. Ay, have old lads work for young nurses?

Eust. Yes, when they groan towards their second infancy.

Clare. [*aside*] I fear myself most guilty for the
absence
Of the bridegroom. What our wills will do
With over-rash and headlong peevishness
To bring our calm discretions to repentance!
Lessingham's mistaken, quite out o' the way
Of my purpose too.

Franck. Return'd!

Nurse. And all discover'd.

Franck. A fool rid him further off! Let him not
Come near the child.

Nurse. Nor see't, if it be your charge.

Franck. It is, and strictly.

Nurse. To-morrow morning, as I hear, he pur-
poseth
To come to Bednal-Green, his wife with him.

Franck. He shall be met there: yet if he fore-
stall
My coming, keep the child safe.

Nurse. If he be
The earlier up, he shall arrive at the proverb.*

[*Exit.*

Wood. So, so;
There's some good luck yet, the bride's in sight
again.

Enter ANNABEL *and* ROCHFIELD.

Anna. Father, and gentlemen all, beseech you
Entreat this gentleman with all courtesy:
He is a loving kinsman of my Bonvile's,
That kindly came to gratulate our wedding;
But as the day falls out, you see alone
I personate both groom and bride; only
Your help to make this welcome better.

Wood. Most dearly.

---

* *Bednal-Green*] i. e. Bethnal-Green.
† *Scene IV.*] A room in the house of Woodroff.
‡ *remain*] The old ed. "remains."

* *the proverb*] "Early up and never the nearer." .
Ray's *Proverbs*, p. 101, ed. 1768.
"You say true, Master Subtle; I have beene *early up*,
but, as God helps me, I was *never the neere.*"
Field's *Amends for Ladies*, sig. F 3, ed. 1639.

Ray. To all, assure you, sir.

Wood. But where's the bridegroom, girl?
We are all at a nonplus, here, at a stand,
Quite out; the music ceas'd, and dancing sur-
    bated,*
Not a light heel amongst us; my cousin Clare too
As cloudy here as on a washing-day.

Clare. It is because you will not dance with me;
I should then shake it off.

Anna. 'Tis I have cause
To be the sad one now, if any be:
But I have question'd with my meditations,
And they have render'd well and comfortably
To the worst fear I found.   Suppose this day
He had long since appointed to his foe
To meet, and fetch a reputation from him,
Which is the dearest jewel unto man:
Say he do fight, I know his goodness such,
That all those powers that love it are his guard,
And ill cannot betide him.

Wood. Prithee, peace;
Thou'lt make us all cowards to hear a woman
Instruct so valiantly.—Come, the music!
I'll dance myself rather than thus put down:
What! I am rife † a little yet.

Anna. Only this gentleman
Pray you be free in welcome to: I tell you
I was in a fear when first I saw him.

Roch. [*aside*] Ha! she'll tell.

Anna. I had quite lost my way in
My first amazement; but he so fairly came
To my recovery, in his kind conduct
Gave me such loving comforts to my fears;
'Twas he instructed me in what I spake,
And many better than I have told you yet;
You shall hear more anon.

Roch. [*aside*] So, she will out with't.

Anna. I must, I see, supply both places still.—
Come, when I have seen you back to your pleasure,
I will return to you, sir: we must discourse
More of my Bonvile yet.

Omnes. A noble bride, faith.

Clare. You have your wishes, and you may be
    merry:
Mine have over-gone me.
                    [*Exeunt all except* ROCHFIELD.

Roch. It is the trembling trade to be a thief!
H'ad need have all the world bound to the peace,
Besides the bushes and the vanes of houses:
Every thing that moves, he goes in fear of 's life on;
A fur-gown'd cat, an meet her in the night,

She stares with a constable's eye upon him,
And every dog a watchman; a black cow,
And a calf with a white face after her,
Shows like a surly justice and his clerk;
And if the baby go but to the bag,
'Tis ink and paper for a mittimus.
Sure, I shall never thrive on't; and it may be
I shall need take no care,—I may be now
At my journey's end, or but the goal's distance,
And so to the t'other place.   I trust a woman
With a secret worth a hanging; is that well?
I could find in my heart to run away yet:
And that were base too, to run from a woman:
I can lay claim to nothing but her vows,
And they shall strengthen me.

              Re-enter ANNABEL.

Anna. See, sir, my promise:
[*Giving money*] There's twenty pieces, the full
              value, I vow,
Of what they cost.

Roch. Lady, do not trap me
Like a sumpter-horse, and then spur-gall me
Till I break my wind.   If the constable
Be at the door, let his fair staff appear:
Perhaps I may corrupt him with this gold.

Anna. Nay, then, if you mistrust me,—Father,
              gentlemen,
Master Raymond, Eustace!

Re-enter WOODROFF, FRANCKFORD, RAYMOND, EUSTACE,
    GROVER, LIONEL, CLARE, *and* LUCE, *with a* Sailor.

Wood. How now! what's the matter, girl?

Anna. For shame, will you bid your kinsman
              welcome?
No one but I will lay a hand on him:
Leave him alone, and all a-revelling!

Wood. O, is that it?—Welcome, welcome
              heartily!—
I thought the bridegroom had been return'd.—But
I have news, Annabel; this fellow brought it.—
Welcome, sir! why, you tremble methinks, sir.

Anna. Some agony of anger 'tis, believe it,
His entertainment is so cold and feeble.

Ray. Pray, be cheer'd, sir.

Roch. I'm wondrous well, sir; 'twas the gentle-
              man's mistake.

Wood. 'Twas my hand shook belike, then; you
              must pardon
Age, I was stiffer once.   But as I was saying,
I should by promise see the sea to-morrow
('Tis meant for physic) as low as Lee or Margate:*

---

* *the dancing surbated*] Equivalent to—the dancers fa-
tigued.   To *surbate* is to batter or weary with treading.
† *rife*] Seems to be used here in the sense of—active.

* *Margate*] Here, and in Act III. sc. 3, the old ed. has
"Margets"; but in Act V. sc. 1, it has "Margot."

I have a vessel riding forth, gentlemen,
'Tis call'd the God-speed too,
Though I say't, a brave one, well and richly
    fraughted;
And I can tell you she carries a letter of mart
In her mouth too, and twenty roaring boys
On both sides on her, starboard and larboard.
What say you now, to make you all adventurers?
You shall have fair dealing, that I'll promise you.
  Ray. A very good motion, sir: I begin;
[*Giving money*] There's my ten pieces.
  Eust. [*Giving money*] I second 'em with these.
  Grov. [*Giving money*] My ten in the third place.
  Roch. [*Giving money*] And, sir, if you refuse not
  a proffer'd love,
Take my ten pieces with you too.
  Wood. Yours above all the rest, sir.
  Anna. Then make 'em above, venture ten more.
  Roch. Alas, lady, 'tis a younger brother's
    portion,
And all in one bottom!
  Anna. At my encouragement, sir:
Your credit, if you want, sir, shall not sit down
Under that sum return'd.

  Roch. With all my heart, lady.—[*Giving money*]
    There, sir.—
[*Aside*] So, she has fish'd for her gold back, and
    caught it;
I am no thief now.
  Wood. I shall make here a pretty assurance.
  Roch. Sir, I shall have a suit to you.
  Wood. You are likely to obtain it, then, sir.
  Roch. That I may keep you company to sea,
And attend you back: I am a little travell'd.
  Wood. And heartily thank you too, sir.
  Anna. Why, that's well said.—
Pray you be merry: though your kinsman be ab-
    sent,
I am here, the worst part of him; yet that shall
    serve
To give you welcome: to-morrow may show you
What this night will not; and be full assur'd,
Unless your twenty pieces be ill-lent,
Nothing shall give you cause of discontent.
[*Giving money*] There's ten more, sir.
  Roch. [*aside*] Why should I fear? Foutre on't!
I will be merry now, spite of the hangman.
                          [*Exeunt.*

ACT III.

SCENE I.*

Enter LEASINGHAM *and* BONVILE.

  Bon. We are first i'the field: I think your enemy
Is stay'd at Dover or some other port,
We hear not of his landing.
  Less. I am confident
He is come over.
  Bon. You look, methinks, fresh-colour'd.
  Less. Like a red morning, friend, that still fore-
    tells
A stormy day to follow: but, methinks,
Now I observe your face, that you look pale;
There's death in't already.
  Bon. I could chide your error.
Do you take me for a coward? A coward
Is not his own friend, much less can he be
Another man's. Know, sir, I am come hither
To instruct you, by my generous example,
To kill your enemy, whose name as yet
I never question'd.
  Less. Nor dare I name him yet
For disheartening you.

  Bon. I do begin to doubt
The goodness of your quarrel.
  Less. Now you have't;
For I protest that I must fight with one
From whom, in the whole course of our ac-
    quaintance,
I never did receive the least injury.
  Bon. It may be the forgetful * wine begot
Some sudden blow, and thereupon this† challenge.
Howe'er you are engag'd; and, for my part,
I will not take your course, my unlucky friend,
To say your conscience grows pale and heartless,
Maintaining a bad cause. Fight as lawyers plead,
Who gain the best of reputation
When they can fetch a bad cause smoothly off:
You are in, and must through.
  Less. O my friend,
The noblest ever man had! When my fate
Threw me upon this business, I made trial

---

* *forgetful*] So Milton:
           "If the sleepy drench -
  Of that *forgetful* lake benumb not still," &c.
                    Par. Lost, ii. 73.
† *this*] The old ed. "'tis."

Of divers had profess'd to me much love,
And found their friendship, like the effects that
　　kept
Our company together, wine and riot:
Giddy and sinking I had found 'em oft,
Brave seconds at pluralities of healths;
But when it came to the proof, my gentlemen
Appear'd to me as promising and failing
As cozening lotteries. But then I found
This jewel worth a thousand counterfeits:
I did but name my engagement, and you flew
Unto my succour with that cheerfulness
As a great general hastes to a battle,
When that the chief of the adverse part
Is a man glorious and * of ample fame;
You left your bridal bed to find your death-bed;
And herein you most nobly express'd
That the affection 'tween two loyal friends
Is far beyond the love of man to woman,
And is more near allied to eternity.
What better friend's part could be show'd i'the
　　world!
It transcends all: my father gave me life,
But you stand by my honour when 'tis falling,
And nobly underprop† it with your sword.
But now you have done me all this service,
How, how, shall I requite this? how return
My grateful recompense for all this love?
For it am I come hither with full purpose
To kill you.
　　Bon. Ha!
　　Less. Yes, I have no opposite i'the world but
Yourself: [*Giving letter*] there, read the warrant
　　for your death.
　　Bon. 'Tis a woman's hand.
　　Less. And 'tis a bad hand too:
The most of 'em speak fair, write foul, mean worse.
　　Bon. Kill me! Away, you jest.
　　Less. Such jest as your sharp-witted gallants use
To utter, and lose their friends. Read there how I
Am fetter'd in a woman's proud command:
I do love madly, and must do madly.
Deadliest hellebore or vomit of a toad
Is qualified poison to the malice of a woman.
　　Bon. And kill that friend? strange!
　　Less. You may see, sir,
Although the tenure by which land was held
In villanage be quite extinct in England,
Yet you have women there at this day living
Make a number of slaves.
　　Bon. And kill that friend!
She mocks you, upon my life, she does equivocate:

Her meaning is, you cherish in your breast
Either self-love, or pride, as your best friend,
And she wishes you'd kill that.
　　Less. Sure, her command
Is more bloody; for she loathes me, and has put,
As she imagines, this impossible task,
For ever to be quit and free from me:
But such is the violence of my affection,
That I must undergo it. Draw your sword,
And guard yourself: though I fight in fury,
I shall kill you in cold blood, for I protest
'Tis done in heart-sorrow.
　　Bon. I'll not fight with you,
For I have much advantage: the truth is,
I wear a privy coat.
　　Less. Prithee, put it off, then,
If thou* beest manly.
　　Bon. The defence I mean is the justice of my
　　cause;
That would guard me, and fly to thy destruction.
What confidence thou wear'st in a bad cause!
I am likely to kill thee, if I fight;
And then you fail to effect your mistress' bidding,
Or to enjoy the fruit of 't. I have ever
Wishèd thy happiness, and vow I now
So much affect it, in compassion
Of my friend's sorrow: make thy way to it.†
　　Less. That were a cruel murder.
　　Bon. Believe't, 'tis ne'er intended otherwise,
When 'tis a woman's bidding.
　　Less. O the necessity of my fate!
　　Bon. You shed tears.
　　Less. And yet must on in my cruel purpose:
A judge, methinks, looks loveliest when he weeps
Pronouncing of death's sentence. How I stagger
In my resolve! Guard thee, for I came hither
To do and not to suffer. Wilt not yet
Be persuaded to defend thee? turn the point,
Advance it from the ground above thy head,
And let it underprop thee otherwise
In a bold resistance.
　　Bon. Stay. Thy injunction was
Thou shouldst kill thy friend.
　　Less. It was.
　　Bon. Observe me.
He wrongs me most ought to offend me least,
And they that study man say of a friend,
There's nothing in the world that's harder found,
Nor sooner lost. Thou cam'st to kill thy friend,
And thou mayst brag thou hast done't; for here
　　for ever

---

* *and*] The old ed. "but."
† *underprop*] The old ed. "*under-prop*."

* *thou*] The old ed. "then."
† *make thy way to it*] Something seems to have dropt
out here.

All friendship dies between us, and my heart,
For bringing forth any effects of love,
Shall be as barren to thee as this sand
We tread on, cruel and inconstant as
The sea that beats upon this beach. We now
Are severèd : thus hast thou slain thy friend,
And satisfied what the witch, thy mistress, bade
 thee.
Go, and report that thou hast slain thy friend.

 Less. I am serv'd right.

 Bon. And now that I do cease to be thy friend,
I will fight with thee as thine enemy :
I came not over idly to do nothing.

 Less. O friend !

 Bon. Friend !
The naming of that word shall be the quarrel.
What do I know but that thou lov'st my wife,
And feign'dst this plot to divide me from her bed,
And that this letter here is counterfeit ?
Will you advance, sir ?

 Less. Not a blow :
'Twould appear ill in either of us to fight,
In you unmanly ; for believe it, sir,
You have disarm'd me already, done away
All power of resistance in me. It would show
Beastly to do wrong to the dead : to me you say
You are dead for ever, lost on Calais-sands
By the cruelty of a woman. Yet remember
You had a noble friend, whose love to you
Shall continue after death. Shall I go over
In the same bark with you ?

 Bon. Not for yon town
Of Calais : you know 'tis dangerous living
At sea with a dead body.

 Less. O, you mock me.
May you enjoy all your noble wishes !

 Bon. And may you find a better friend than I,
And better keep him !   [*Exeunt.*

SCENE II.*

Enter Nurse, Compass, *and* Urse.

 Nurse. Indeed, you must pardon me, goodman
Compass ; I have no authority to deliver, no, not
to let you see the child : to tell you true, I have
command unto the contrary.

 Comp. Command ! from whom ?

 Nurse. By the father of it.

 Comp. The father ! who am I ?

 Nurse. Not the father, sure : the civil law has
found it otherwise.

 Comp. The civil law ! why, then, the uncivil law
shall make it mine again. I'll be as dreadful as a
Shrove-Tuesday* to thee : I will tear thy cottage,
but I will see my child.

 Nurse. Speak but half so much again, I'll call
the constable, and lay burglary to thy charge.

 Urse. My good husband, be patient.—And, prithee, nurse, let him see the child.

 Nurse. Indeed, I dare not.
The father first deliver'd me the child :
He pays me well and weekly for my pains,
And to his use I keep it.

 Comp. Why, thou white bastard-breeder, is not
this the mother ?

 Nurse. Yes, I grant you that.

 Comp. Dost thou ? and I grant it too : and is not
the child mine own, then, by the wife's copyhold ?

 Nurse. The law must try that.

 Comp. Law ! dost think I'll be but a father-in-
law ? All the law betwixt Blackwall and Tuthill-
street (and there's a pretty deal) shall not keep
it from me, mine own flesh and blood : who does
use to get my children but myself ?

 Nurse. Nay, you must look to that : I ne'er
knew you get any.

 Comp. Never ? Put on a clean smock and try
me, if thou darest ; three to one I get a bastard on
thee to-morrow morning between one and three.

 Nurse. I'll see thee hanged first.

 Comp. So thou shalt too.

Enter Franckford *and* Luce.

 Nurse. O, here's the father : now, pray, talk
with him.

 Franck. Good morrow, neighbour : morrow to
you both.

 Comp. Both ! Morrow to you and your wife
too.

 Franck. I would speak calmly with you.

 Comp. I know what belongs to a calm and a
storm too. A cold word with you : you have tied
your mare in my ground.

 Franck. No, 'twas my nag.

 Comp. I will cut off your nag's tail, and make
his rump make hair-buttons, if e'er I take him
there again.

 Franck. Well, sir : but to the main.

 Comp. Mane ! yes, and I'll clip his mane too,
and crop his ears too, do you mark ? and backgall
him, and spurgall him, do you note ? and slit his
nose, do you smell me now, sir ? unbreech his
barrel, and discharge his bullets ; I'll gird him
till he stinks : you smell me now I'm sure.

Franck. You are too rough, neighbour. To
maintain——

Comp. Maintain! you shall not maintain no
child of mine: my wife does not bestow her
labour to that purpose.

Franck. You are too speedy. I will not maintain——

Comp. No, marry, shall you not.

Franck. The deed to be lawful:
I have repented it, and to the law
Given satisfaction; my purse has paid for't.

Comp. Your purse! 'twas my wife's purse: you
brought in the coin indeed, but it was found base
and counterfeit.

Franck. I would treat colder with you, if you
be pleased.

Comp. Pleased! yes, I am pleased well enough:
serve me so still. I am going again to sea one of
these days: you know where I dwell. Yet you'll
but lose your labour: get as many children as
you can, you shall keep none of them.

Franck. You are mad.

Comp. If I be born-mad, what's that to you?

Franck. I leave off milder phrase, and then tell
you plain, you are a——

Comp. A what? what am I?

Franck. A coxcomb.

Comp. A coxcomb! I knew 'twould begin with
a C.

Franck. The child is mine, I am the father
of it:
As it is past the deed, 'tis past the shame;
I do acknowledge and will enjoy it.

Comp. Yes, when you can get it again. Is it
not my wife's labour? I'm sure she's the mother:
you may be as far off the father as I am, for my
wife's acquainted with more whoremasters besides
yourself, and crafty merchants too.

Urse. No, indeed, husband; to make my offence
Both least and most, I knew no other man:
He's the begetter, but the child is mine;
I bred and bore it, and I will not lose it.

Luce. The child's my husband's, dame, and he
must have it.
I do allow my sufferance to the deed,
In lieu I never yet was fruitful to him,
And in my barrenness excuse my wrong.

Comp. Let him dung his own ground better at
home, then: if he plant his radish-roots in my
garden, I'll eat 'em with bread and salt, though I
get no mutton to 'em. What though your husband lent my wife your distaff, shall not the yarn
be mine? I'll have the head; let him carry the
spindle home again.

Franck. Forbear more words, then; let the law
try it.—
Meantime, nurse, keep the child; and to keep it
better,
Here take more pay beforehand; there's money
for thee.

Comp. There's money for me too: keep it for
me, nurse. Give him both thy dugs at once:
I pay for thy right dug.

Nurse. I have two hands you see: gentlemen,
this does but show how the law will hamper you:
even thus you must be used.

Franck. The law shall show which is the
worthier gender:
A schoolboy can do't.

Comp. I'll whip that schoolboy that declines
the child from my wife and her heirs: do not I
know my wife's case, the genitive case, and that's
hujus, as great a case as can be?

Franck. Well, fare you well: we shall meet in
another place.—
Come, Luce. [*Exeunt* FRANCKFORD *and* LUCE.

Comp. Meet her in the same place again, if you
dare, and do your worst. Must we go to law for
our children now-a-days? No marvel if the
lawyers grow rich: but ere the law shall have a
limb, a leg, a joint, a nail,
I will spend more than a whole child in getting:
Some win by play, and others by by-betting.
[*Exeunt.*

————◆————

SCENE III.*

Enter RAYMOND, EUSTACE, LIONEL, GROVER, ANNABEL,
and CLARE.

Lion. Whence was that letter sent?

Anna. From Dover, sir.

Lion. And does that satisfy you what was the
cause
Of his going over?

Anna. It does: yet had he
Only sent this, it had been sufficient.

Ray. Why, what's that?

Anna. His will, wherein
He has estated me in all his land.

Eust. He's gone to fight.

Lion. Lessingham's second, certain.

Anna. And I am lost, lost in't for ever.

Clare. [*aside*] O fool Lessingham,
Thou hast mistook my injunction utterly,
Utterly mistook it! and I am mad, stark mad
With my own thoughts, not knowing what event

* *Scene III.*] The garden belonging to Woodroff's house.

Their going-o'er will come to. 'Tis too late
Now for my tongue to cry my heart mercy.
Would I could be senseless till I hear
Of their return! I fear me both are lost.

Ray. Who should it be Lessingham's gone to
　　fight with?

Eust. Faith, I cannot possibly conjecture.

Anna. Miserable creature! a maid, a wife,
And widow in the compass of two days!

Ray. Are you sad too?

Clare. I am not very well, sir.

Ray. I must put life in you.

Clare. Let me go, sir.

Ray. I do love you in spite of your heart.

Clare. Believe it,
There was never a fitter time to express it,
For my heart has a great deal of spite in't.

Ray. I will discourse to you fine fancies.

Clare. Fine fooleries, will you not?

Ray. By this hand, I love you and will court you.

Clare. Fie!
You can command your tongue, and I my ears
To hear you no further.

Ray. [*aside*] On my reputation,
She's off o' the hinges strangely.

Enter WOODROFF, ROCHFIELD, *and a* Sailor

Wood. Daughter, good news.

Anna. What, is my husband heard of?

Wood. That's not the business: but you have
　　here a cousin
You may be mainly proud of; and I am sorry
'Tis by your husband's kindred, not your own,
That we might boast to have so brave a man
In our alliance.

Anna. What, so soon return'd?
You have made but a short voyage: howsoever
You are to me most welcome.

Roch. Lady, thanks:
'Tis you have made me your own creature;
Of all my being, fortunes, and poor fame,
(If I have purchas'd any, and of which
I no way boast,) next the high providence,
You have been the sole creatress.

Anna. O dear cousin,
You are grateful above merit.—What occasion
Drew you so soon from sea?

Wood. Such an occasion,
As I may bless heaven for, you thank their bounty,
And all of us be joyful.

Anna. Tell us how.

Wood. Nay, daughter, the discourse will best
　　appear
In his relation: where he fails, I'll help.

Roch. Not to molest your patience with recital
Of every vain and needless circumstance,
'Twas briefly thus. Scarce having reach'd to
　　Margate,*
Bound on our voyage, suddenly in view
Appear'd to us three Spanish men-of-war.
These, having spied the English cross advance,
Salute us with a piece to have us strike:
Ours, better spirited, and no way daunted
At their unequal odds, though but one bottom,
Return'd 'em fire for fire. The fight begins,
And dreadful on the sudden: still they proffer'd
To board us, still we bravely beat 'em off.

Wood. But, daughter, mark the event.

Roch. Sea-room we got: our ship being swift
　　of sail,
It help'd us much. Yet two unfortunate shot,
One struck the captain's head off, and the other,
With an unlucky splinter, laid the master
Dead on the hatches: all our spirits then fail'd us.

Wood. Not all: you shall hear further, daughter.

Roch. For none was left to manage: nothing now
Was talk'd of but to yield up ship and goods,
And mediate for our peace.

Wood. Nay, coz, proceed.

Roch. Excuse me, I entreat you, for what's more
Hath already pass'd my memory.

Wood. But mine it never can.—Then he stood
　　up,
And with his oratory made us again
To recollect our spirits, so late dejected.

Roch. Pray, sir,—

Wood. I'll speak 't out.—By unite consent
Then the command was his, and 'twas his place
Now to bestir him. Down he went below,
And put the linstocks in the gunners' hands;
They ply their ordnance bravely: then again
Up to the decks; courage is there renew'd,
Fear now not found amongst us. Within less
Than four hours' fight two of their ships were
　　sunk,
Both founder'd, and soon swallow'd. Not long
　　after,
The third† begins to wallow, lies on the lee
To stop her leaks: then boldly we come on,
Boarded, and took her, and she's now our prize.

Sailor. Of this we were eye-witness.

Wood. And many more brave boys of us
　　besides,
Myself for one. Never was, gentlemen,
A sea-fight better manag'd.

Roch. Thanks to heaven

---

* *Margate*] The old ed. "Margets." See note *, p. 299.
† *third*] The old ed. "three."

We have sav'd our own, damag'd the enemy,
And to our nation's glory we bring home
Honour and profit.
 Wood. In which, cousin Rochfield,
You, as a venturer, have a double share,
Besides the name of captain, and in that
A second benefit; but, most of all,
Way to more great employment.
 Roch. [*to* ANNABEL.] Thus your bounty
Hath been to me a blessing.

 Ray. Sir, we are all
Indebted to your valour: this beginning
May make us of small venturers to become
Hereafter wealthy merchants.
 Wood. Daughter, and gentlemen,
This is the man was born to make us all.
Come, enter, enter: we will in and feast:
He's in the bridegroom's absence my chief guest.
                                   [*Exeunt.*

ACT IV.

SCENE I.*

Enter COMPASS, URSE, LIONEL, PETTIFOG *the Attorney,*
and First Boy.

 Comp. Three Tuns do you call this tavern?
It has a good neighbour of Guildhall, Master
Pettifog.—Show a room, boy.
 First Boy. Welcome, gentlemen.
 Comp. What, art thou here, Hodge?
 First Boy. I am glad you are in health, sir.
 Comp. This was the honest crack-rope first gave
me tidings of my wife's fruitfulness.—Art bound
prentice?
 First Boy. Yes, sir.
 Comp. Mayst thou long jumble bastard† most
artificially, to the profit of thy master and plea-
sure of thy mistress!
 First Boy. What wine drink ye, gentlemen?
 Lion. What wine relishes your palate, good
Master Pettifog?
 Pett. Nay, ask the woman.
 Comp. Elegant‡ for her: I know her diet.
 Pett. Believe me, I con her thank for't §: I am
of her side.

 Comp. Marry, and reason, sir: we have enter-
tained you for our attorney.
 First Boy. A cup of neat Allegant?
 Comp. Yes, but do not make it speak Welsh,
boy.
 First Boy. How mean you?
 Comp. Put no metheglin in't, ye rogue.
 First Boy. Not a drop, as I am true Briton. [*Exit.*
           [*They sit down :* PETTIFOG *pulls out papers.*

Enter, to another table, FRANCKFORD, EUSTACE, LUCE,
MASTER DODGE *a lawyer, and a Drawer.*

 Franck. Show a private room, drawer.
 Drawer. Welcome, gentlemen.*
 Eust. As far as you can from noise, boy.
 Drawer. Further this way, then, sir; for in the
next room there are three or four fishwives
taking up a brabbling business.
 Franck. Let's not sit near them by any means.
 Dodge. Fill canary, sirrah.
         [*Drawer fills their glasses, and then exit.*
 Franck. And what do you think of my cause,
Master Dodge?
 Dodge. O, we shall carry it most indubitably.
You have money to go through with the business,
and ne'er fear it but we'll trounce 'em: you are
the true father.
 Luce. The mother will confess as much.
 Dodge. Yes, mistress, we have taken her
affidavit—Look you, sir, here's the answer to
his declaration.

---

* *Scene I.*] The Three Tuns Tavern. (But the audience
was not to suppose that the present party were within
the house, till the Boy had said "Welcome, gentlemen.")
 † *bastard*] The commentators on Shakespeare's First
Part of *Henry IVth.*, act ii. sc. 4, quote various passages
from old writers where *bastard* is mentioned.
 "That it was a sweetish wine, there can be no doubt;
and that it came from some of the countries which
border the Mediterranean, appears equally certain. . . .
There were two sorts, white and brown."—Henderson's
Hist. of Wines, p. 290-1.
 ‡ *Elegant*] A quibble is intended here: *Allegant* or
Alligant (for our old poets write it both ways) is wine of
Alicant; or perhaps the following lines may illustrate
Compass's meaning;
 "In dreadful darknesse *Alligant* lies drown'd,
   Which marryed men invoke for procreation."
               Pasquil's Palinodia, 1634, Sig. C 3.
 § *I con her thank for't*] Annotators and dictionary-

makers have given various examples from Elizabethan
writers of the use of the expression "to con thanks,"
which answers to the French *sçavoir gré*,—"con" signifying *know :* it occurs in our old ballads ;
 "Therefore I *cun the* more thanks,
   Thou arte come at thy day."
           A Lytell geste of Robyn Hode.
         (Ritson's *Robin Hood*, vol. i. p. 4 &.)
 * *Drawer. Welcome gentlemen*] See first note in this page.
                                                    x

Franck. You may think strange, sir, that I am
 at charge
To call a charge upon me; but 'tis truth
I made a purchase lately, and in that
I did estate the child, 'bout which I'm su'd,
Joint-purchaser in all the land I bought.
Now that's one reason that I should have care,
Besides the tie of blood, to keep the child
Under my wing, and see it carefully
Instructed in those fair abilities
May make it worthy hereafter to be mine,
And enjoy the land I have provided for't.
 Luce. Right: and I counsell'd you to make
  that purchase;
And therefore I'll not have the child brought up
By such a coxcomb as now sues for him.
He'd bring him up only to be a swabber:
He was born a merchant and a gentleman,
And he shall live and die so.

Dodge. Worthy mistress, I drink to you: you
are a good woman, and but few of so noble a
patience.

Re-enter First Boy.

First Boy. Score a quart of Allegant to the
Woodcock.

Enter Second Boy, *like a musician.*

Sec. Boy. Will you have any music, gentlemen?
Comp. Music amongst lawyers! here's nothing
but discord.—What, Ralph?*—Here's another of
my young cuckoos I heard last April, before I
heard the nightingale.†—No music, good Ralph:
here, boy; your father was a tailor, and methinks
by your leering eye you should take after him:
a good boy; make a leg handsomely; scrape
yourself out of our company. [*Exit* Second Boy.]
And what do you think of my suit, sir?

Pett. Why, look you, sir: the defendant was
arrested first by *Latitat* in an action of trespass.
Comp. And a lawyer told me it should have
been an action of the case :—should it not, wife?

---

* *Ralph*] In act ii. sc. 3, one of these boys is *Jack*, the
other not being named :—but here Compass calls one of
them *Ralph*, and at the commencement of this scene
addresses the other as *Hodge*.
† *Here's another of my young cuckoos I heard last April,
before I heard the nightingale*] He who happened to hear
the cuckoo sing before the nightingale was supposed not
to prosper in his love-affairs:
 "Thy liquid notes that close the eye of day,
 First heard before the shallow cuckoo's bill,
 Portend success in love: O, if Jove's will
 Have link'd that amorous power to thy soft lay,
 Now timely sing, ere the rude bird of hate
 Foretell my hopeless doom in some grove nigh."
  Milton's *Sonnet to the Nightingale.*

Urse. I have no skill in law, sir: but you heard
a lawyer say so.

Pett. Ay; but your action of the case is in
that point too ticklish.

Comp. But what do you think? shall I overthrow my adversary?

Pett. Sans question. The child is none of
yours: what of that? I marry a widow is
possessed of a ward: shall not I have the
tuition of that ward? Now, sir, you lie at a
stronger ward; for *partus sequitur ventrem*, says
the civil law; and if you were within compass of
the four seas, as the common law goes, the child
shall be yours certain.

Comp. There's some comfort in that yet. O,
your attorneys in Guildhall have a fine time on't!

Lion. You are in effect both judge and jury
yourselves.

Comp. And how you will laugh at your clients,
when you sit in a tavern, and call them coxcombs,
and whip up a cause, as a barber trims his
customers on a Christmas-eve, a snip, a wipe, and
away!

Pett. That's ordinary, sir: you shall have the
like at a *nisi prius.*

Enter First Client.

O, you are welcome, sir.
First Client. Sir, you'll be mindful of my suit?
Pett. As I am religious. I'll drink to you.
First Client. I thank you.—By your favour,
mistress.—I have much business, and cannot
stay; but there's money for a quart of wine.
Comp. By no means.
First Client. I have said, sir. [*Exit.*
Pett. He's my client, sir, and he must pay.
This is my tribute: custom is not more truly
paid in the Sound of Denmark.

Enter Second Client.

Sec. Client. Good sir, be careful of my business.
Pett. Your declaration's drawn, sir. I'll drink
to you.
Sec. Client. I cannot drink this morning; but
there's money for a pottle of wine.
Pett. O good sir!
Sec. Client. I have done, sir.—Morrow, gentle-
men. [*Exit.*
Comp. We shall drink good cheap, Master
Pettifog.
Pett. An we sat here long, you'd say so. I
have sat here in this tavern but one half-hour,
drunk but three pints of wine, and what with
the offering of my clients in that short time, I

have got nine shillings clear, and paid all the reckoning.

Lion. Almost a counsellor's fee.

Pett. And a great one, as the world goes in Guildhall; for now our young clerks share with 'em, to help 'em to clients.

Comp. I don't think but that the cucking-stool is an enemy to a number of brabbles that would else be determined by law.

Pett. 'Tis so, indeed, sir. My client that came in now sues his neighbour for kicking his dog, and using the defamatory speeches, "Come out, cuckold's cur!"

Lion. And what shall you recover upon this speech?

Pett. In Guildhall,* I assure you: the other that came in was an informer, a precious knave.

Comp. Will not the ballad of Flood,† that was pressed, make them leave their knavery?

Pett. I'll tell you how he was served: this informer comes into Turnbull-street to a victualling-house,‡ and there falls in league with a wench,—

Comp. A tweak or bronstrops: I learned that name in a play.§

Pett. Had, belike, some private dealings with her, and there got a goose. ||

Comp. I would he had got two: I cannot away with ¶ an informer.

Pett. Now, sir, this fellow, in revenge of this,

---

* *In Guildhall*] Something seems wanting here.

† *the ballad of Flood*] This ballad, I believe, has not come down to us, nor do I remember to have seen any other allusion to it. Several gentlemen very conversant with ballad literature had never heard of it till I mentioned it to them; and the Rev. J. Lodge most obligingly sought for it in the Pepysian Collection, at Cambridge, without success.

‡ *into Turnbull-street to a victualling-house*] Turnbull-street (more properly called *Turnmill*-street) was a noted haunt of harlots, between Clerkenwell-Green and Cowcross: brothels were often kept under pretence of their being victualling-houses or taverns.

§ *A tweak, or bronstrops: I learned that name in a play*] *Tweak* and *bronstrops* were cant terms for a prostitute, employed by the Roarers of the time, as we learn from several passages of Middleton and Rowley's *Fair Quarrel*, the play to which, in all probability, our text alludes: but in the following passage of that curious drama a distinction is made between the signification of the two words, *tweak* being used for harlot, and *bronstrops* for bawd; "Now for thee, little fucus, mayst thou first serve out thy time as a *tweak*, and then become a *bronstrops*, as she is!"—Middleton's *Works*, iii. 531, ed. Dyce. The first ed. of the *Fair Quarrel*, 1617, does not contain the passage just quoted.

|| *a goose*] i.e. a Winchester goose (—see Pettifog's next speech—) which means a venereal swelling: the public stews were under the control of the Bishop of Winchester.

¶ *away with*] i.e. endure.

---

informs against the bawd that kept the house that she used cans in her house: but the cunning jade comes me into the court, and there deposes that she gave him true Winchester measure.

Comp. Marry, I thank her with all my heart for't.

Re-enter Drawer.

Drawer. Here's a gentleman, one Justice Woodroff, inquires for Master Franckford.

Franck. O, my brother, and the other compromiser, come to take up the business.

Enter Counsellor and WOODROFF.

Wood. We have conferr'd and labour'd for your peace,
Unless your stubbornness prohibit it;
And be assur'd, as we can determine it,
The law will end, for we have sought the cases.

Comp. If the child fall to my share, I am content to end upon any conditions: the law shall run on head-long else.

Franck. Your purse must run by like a footman, then.

Comp. My purse shall run open-mouthed at thee.

Coun. My friend, be calm: you shall hear the reasons.
I have stood up for you, pleaded your cause,
But am overthrown; yet no further yielded
Than your own pleasure: you may go on in law,
If you refuse our censure.*

Comp. I will yield to nothing but my child.

Coun. 'Tis, then, as vain in us to seek your peace:
Yet take the reasons with you. This gentleman
First speaks, a justice, to me; and observe it,
A child that's base and illegitimate born,
The father found, who (if the need require it)
Secures the charge and damage of the parish
But the father? who charg'd with education
But the father? then, by clear consequence,
He ought, for what he pays for, to enjoy.
Come to the strength of reason, upon which
The law is grounded: the earth brings forth,
This ground or that, her crop of wheat or rye:
Whether shall the seedsman enjoy the sheaf,
Or leave it to the earth that brought it forth?
The summer tree brings forth her natural fruit,
Spreads her large arms: who but the lord of it
Shall pluck [the] apples, or command the lops?
Or shall they sink into the root again?
'Tis still most clear upon the father's part.

Comp. All this law I deny, and will be mine own lawyer. Is not the earth our mother? and

---

* *censure*] i.e. judgment, opinion.

x 2

shall not the earth have all her children again? I
would see that law durst keep any of us back;
she'll have lawyers and all first, though they be
none of her best children: my wife is the mother:
and so much for the civil law. Now I come
again; and you're gone at the common law.
Suppose this is my ground: I keep a sow upon it,
as it might be my wife; you keep a boar, as it
might be my adversary here; your boar comes
foaming into my ground, jumbles with my sow,
and wallows in her mire; my sow cries "Weke,"
as if she had pigs in her belly:—who shall keep
these pigs? he the boar, or she the sow?

Wood. Past other alteration, I am chang'd;
The law is on the mother's part.

Coun. For me, I am strong in your opinion.
I never knew my judgment err so far;
I was confirm'd upon the other part,
And now am flat against it.

Wood. Sir, you must yield;
Believe it, there's no law can relieve you.

Franck. I found it in myself.—Well, sir,
The child's your wife's, I'll strive no further in it;
And being so near unto agreement,
Let us go quite through to't: forgive my fault,
And I forgive my charges, nor will I
Take back the inheritance I made unto it.

Comp. Nay, there you shall find me kind too:
I have a pottle of claret and a capon to supper
for you; but no more mutton for you, not a bit.

Ray. Yes, a shoulder, and we'll be there too;
or a leg opened with venison-sauce.

Comp. No legs opened, by your leave, nor no
such sauce.

Wood. Well, brother and neighbour, I am glad
you are friends.

Omnes. All, all joy at it.

[*Exeunt* WOODROFF, FRANCKFORD, LUCE, *and Lawyers.*

Comp. Urse, come kiss, Urse; all friends.

Ray.* Stay, sir, one thing I would advise you;
'tis counsel worth a fee, though I be no lawyer;
'tis physic indeed, and cures cuckoldry, to keep
that spiteful brand out of your forehead, that
it shall not dare to meet or look out at any
window to you; 'tis better than an onion to a
green wound i' the left hand made by fire, it takes
out scar and all.

Comp. This were a rare receipt; I'll content
you for your skill.

Ray. Make here a flat divorce between yourselves,
Be you no husband, nor let her be no wife:

Within two hours you may salute again,
Woo, and wed a-fresh; and then the cuckold's
blotted.
This medicine is approv'd?

Comp. Excellent; and I thank you.—Urse, I
renounce thee, and I renounce myself from thee;
thou art a widow, Urse. I will go hang myself
two hours, and so long thou shalt drown thyself:
then will we meet again in the pease-field by
Bishop's-Hall,* and, as the swads and the cods
shall instruct us, we'll talk of a new matter.

Urse. I will be ruled: fare you well, sir.

Comp. Farewell, widow; remember time and
place: change your clothes too, do ye hear,
widow? [*Exit* URSE.] Sir, I am beholding to
your good counsel.

Ray. But you'll not follow your own so far, I
hope; you said you'd hang yourself.

Comp. No, I have devised a better way; I will
go drink myself dead for an hour: then when I
awake again, I am a fresh new man, and so I go
a-wooing.

Ray. That's handsome, and I'll lend thee a
dagger.

Comp. For the long weapon let me alone, then.
[*Exeunt.*

SCENE II.†

Enter LESSINGHAM *and* CLARE.

Clare. O sir, are you return'd? I do expect
To hear strange news now.

Less. I have none to tell you;
I am only to relate I have done ill
At a woman's bidding; that's, I hope, no news.
Yet wherefore do I call that ill, begets
My absolute happiness? You now are mine,
I must enjoy you solely.

Clare. By what warrant?

Less. By your own condition. I have been at
Calais,
Perform'd your will, drawn my revengeful sword,
And slain my nearest and best friend i' the world
I had for your sake.

Clare. Slain your friend for my sake?

Less. A most sad truth.

Clare. And your best friend?

Less. My chiefest.

Clare. Then of all men you are most miserable:

* *the pease-field by Bishop's-Hall*] "Bishop's-Hall, about
a quarter of a mile to the east of Bethnal-Green, (lately
taken down,) is said to have been the palace of Bishop
Bonner. Hence *Bonner's Fields* adjoining."—Cunningham's *Handbook of London*, sub "Bethnal-Green."

† *Scene II.*] A room in Woodroff's house.

Nor have you aught further'd your suit in this,
Though I enjoin'd you to't; for I had thought
That I had been the best esteeméd friend
You had i'the world.

Less. Ye did not wish, I hope,
That I should have murder'd you?

Clare. You shall perceive more
Of that hereafter: but I pray, sir, tell me,—
For I do freeze with expectation of it,
It chills my heart with horror till I know
What friend's blood you have sacrific'd to your
　　fury
And to my fatal sport,—this bloody riddle;
Who is it you have slain?

Less. Bonvile, the bridegroom.

Clare. Say? O, you have struck him dead
　　thorough my heart!
In being true to me you have prov'd in this
The falsest traitor. O, I am lost for ever!
Yet, wherefore am I lost? rather recover'd
From a deadly witchcraft; and upon his grave
I will not gather rue but violets
To bless my wedding-strowings. Good sir, tell me
Are you certain he is dead?

Less. Never, never
To be recover'd.

Clare. Why, now, sir, I do love you
With an entire heart. I could dance methinks:
Never did wine or music stir in woman
A sweeter touch of mirth. I will marry you,
Instantly marry you.

Less. [*aside.*] This woman has strange changes.
　　—You are ta'en
Strangely with his death.

Clare. I'll give the reason
I have to be thus ecstasied with joy:
Know, sir, that you have slain my dearest friend
And fatalest enemy.

Less. Most strange!

Clare. 'Tis true:
You have ta'en a mass of lead from off my heart
For ever would have sunk it in despair.
When you beheld me yesterday, I stood
As if a merchant walking on the downs
Should see some goodly vessel of his own
Sunk 'fore his face i'the harbour; and my heart
Retain'd no more heat than a man that toils
And vainly labours to put out the flames
That burn his house to the bottom. I will tell
　　you
A strange concealment, sir, and till this minute
Never reveal'd, and I will tell it now
Smiling, and not blushing. I did love that Bon-
　　vile,

Not as I ought, but as a woman might,—
That's beyond reason: I did dote upon him,
Though he ne'er knew oft; and beholding him
Before my face wedded unto another,
And all my interest in him forfeited,
I fell into despair; and at that instant
You urging your suit to me, and I thinking
That I had been your only friend i'the world,
I heartily did wish you would have kill'd
That friend yourself, to have ended all my sorrow,
And had prepar'd it, that unwittingly
You should have done't by poison.

Less. Strange amazement!

Clare. The effects of a strange love.

Less. 'Tis a dream, sure.

Clare. No, 'tis real, sir, believe it.

Less. Would it were not!

Clare. What, sir! you have done bravely: 'tis
　　your mistress
That tells you you have done so.

Less. But my conscience
Is of counsel 'gainst you, and pleads otherwise.
Virtue in her past actions glories still,
But vice throws loathéd looks on former ill.
But did you love this Bonvile?

Clare. Strangely, sir;
Almost to a degree of madness.

Less. [*aside.*] Trust a woman!
Never, henceforward: I will rather trust
The winds which Lapland witches sell to men.
All that they have is feign'd, their teeth, their
　　hair,
Their blushes, nay, their conscience too is feign'd:
Let 'em paint, load themselves with cloth of
　　tissue,
They cannot yet hide woman; that will appear
And disgrace all. The necessity of my fate!
Certain this woman has bewitch'd me here,
For I cannot choose but love her. O, how fatal
This might have prov'd! I would it had for me!
It would not grieve me though my sword had
　　split
His heart in sunder; I had then destroy'd
One that may prove my rival. O, but then
What had my horror been, my guilt of conscience!
I know some do ill at women's bidding
I' the dog-days, and repent all the winter after:
No, I account it treble happiness
That Bonvile lives; but 'tis my chiefest glory
That our friendship is divided.

Clare. Noble friend,
Why do you talk to yourself?

Less. Should you do so,
You'd talk to an ill woman. Fare you well,

For ever fare you well.—[*Aside*] I will do
    somewhat
To make as fatal breach and difference
In Bonvile's love as mine: I am fix'd in't:
My melancholy and the devil shall fashion 't.
  Clare. You will not leave me thus?
  Less. Leave you for ever:
And may my friend's blood, whom you lov'd so
    dearly,
For ever lie imposthum'd in your breast,
And i' the end choke you! Woman's cruelty
This black and fatal thread hath ever spun;
It must undo, or else it is undone.   [*Exit.*
  Clare. I am every way lost, and no means to
    raise me
But bless'd repentance. What two unvalu'd
    jewels
Am I at once depriv'd of! Now I suffer
Deservedly. There's no prosperity settled:
Fortune plays ever with our good or ill,
Like cross and pile,* and turns up which she will.

           Enter BONVILE.

  Bon. Friend!
  Clare. O, you are the welcom'st under heaven!
Lessingham did but fright me: yet I fear
That you are hurt to danger.
  Bon. Not a scratch.
  Clare. Indeed, you look exceeding well, me-
    thinks.
  Bon. I have been sea-sick lately, and we count
That excellent physic. How does my Annabel?
  Clare. As well, sir, as the fear of such a loss
As your esteem'd self will suffer her.
  Bon. Have you seen Lessingham since he re-
    turn'd?
  Clare. He departed hence but now, and left
    with me
A report had almost kill'd me.
  Bon. What was that?
  Clare. That he had kill'd you.
  Bon. So he has.
  Clare. You mock me.
  Bon. He has kill'd me for a friend, for ever
    silenc'd
All amity between us. You may now
Go and embrace him, for he has fulfill'd
The purpose of that letter.   [*Gives letter.*
  Clare. O, I know't.

---

* *cross and pile*] The same as *Head or tail*, is a game
still practised by the vulgar, who play it by tossing up a
halfpenny. Our Edward the Second was partial to it.
There can be no doubt it is derived from the Ostrachinda
of the Grecian boys. See Strutt's *Sports and Pastimes of
the People of England*, p. 296, ed. 1810.

And had you known this, which I meant to have
    sent you   [*She gives him another.*
An hour 'fore you were married to your wife,
The riddle had been constru'd.
  Bon. Strange! this expresses
That you did love me.
  Clare. With a violent affection.
  Bon. Violent, indeed; for it seems it was your
    purpose
To have ended it in violence on your friend:
The unfortunate Lessingham unwittingly
Should have been the executioner.
  Clare. 'Tis true.
  Bon. And do you love me still?
  Clare. I may easily
Confess it, since my extremity is such
That I must needs speak or die.
  Bon. And you would enjoy me,
Though I am married?
  Clare. No, indeed, not I, sir:
You are to sleep with a sweet bed-fellow
Would knit the brow at that.
  Bon. Come, come, a woman's telling truth
Makes amends for her playing false: you would
    enjoy me?
  Clare. If you were a bachelor or widower,
Afore all the great ones living.
  Bon. But 'tis impossible
To give you present satisfaction; for
My wife is young and healthful, and I like
The summer and the harvest of our love,
Which yet I have not tasted of, so well
That, an you'll credit me, for me her days
Shall ne'er be shorten'd. Let your reason, there-
    fore,
Turn you another way, and call to mind,
With best observance, the accomplish'd graces
Of that brave gentleman whom late you sent
To his destruction; a man so every way
Deserving, no one action of his
In all his life-time e'er degraded him
From the honour he was born to. Think how
    observant
He'll prove to you in nobler request than so
Obey'd you in a bad one; and remember
That afore you engag'd him to an act
Of horror, to the killing of his friend,
He bore his steerage true in every part,
Led by the compass of a noble heart.
  Clare. Why do you praise him thus? You said
    but now
He was utterly lost to you; now't appears
You are friends, else you'd not deliver of him
Such a worthy commendation.

Bon. You mistake,
Utterly mistake that I am friends with him
In speaking this good of him.   To what purpose
Do I praise him ? only to this fatal end,
That you might fall in love and league with him :
And what worse office can I do i' the world
Unto my enemy than to endeavour
By all means possible to marry him
Unto a whore ? and there, I think, she stands.

Clare. Is whore a name to be belov'd ? if not,
What reason have I ever to love that man
Puts it upon me falsely ? You have wrought
A strange alteration in me : were I a man,
I would drive you with my sword into the field,
And there put my wrong to silence.   Go, you're
    not worthy
To be a woman's friend in the least part
That concerns honourable reputation ;
For you are a liar.

Bon. I will love you now
With a noble observance, if you will continue
This hate unto me : gather all those graces,
From whence you have fall'n, yonder, where you
    have left 'em
In Lessingham, he that must be your husband ;
And though henceforth I cease to be his friend,
I will appear his noblest enemy,
And work reconcilement 'tween you.

Clare. No, you shall not ;
You shall not marry him to a strumpet : for that
    word
I shall ever hate you.

Bon. And for that one deed
I shall ever love you.   Come, convert your
    thoughts
To him that best deserves 'em, Lessingham.
It is most certain you have done him wrong ;
But your repentance and compassion now
May make amends : disperse this melancholy,
And on that turn of Fortune's wheel depend,
When all calamities will mend or end.   [*Exeunt.*

SCENE III.[*]

Enter COMPASS, RAYMOND, EUSTACE, LIONEL, *and* GROVER.

Comp. Gentlemen, as you have been witness to
our divorce, you shall now be evidence to our
next meeting, which I look for every minute, if
you please, gentlemen.

Ray. We came for the same purpose, man.

Comp. I do think you'll see me come off with

---

as smooth a forehead, make my wife as honest a
woman once more as a man sometimes would
desire, I mean of her rank, and a teeming woman
as she has been.   Nay, surely I do think to make
the child as lawful a child too as a couple of un-
married people can beget, and let it be begotten
when the father is beyond sea, as this was : do
but note.

Eust. 'Tis that we wait for.

Comp. You have waited the good hour : see,
she comes.   A little room, I beseech you, silence
and observation.

Ray. All your own, sir.

Enter URSE.

Comp. Good morrow, fair maid.

Urse. Mistaken in both, sir, neither fair nor maid.

Comp. No ? a married woman ?

Urse. That's it I was, sir ; a poor widow now.

Comp. A widow !   Nay, then I must make a
little bold with you : 'tis akin to mine own case ;
I am a wifeless husband too.   How long have
you been a widow, pray ? nay, do not weep.

Urse. I cannot choose, to think the loss I had.

Comp. He was an honest man to thee it seems.

Urse. Honest, quoth 'a, O !

Comp. By my feck, and those are great losses.
An honest man is not to be found in every hole
nor every street : if I took a whole parish in
sometimes,
I might say true,
For stinking mackarel may be cried for new.

Ray. Somewhat sententious.

Eust. O, silence was an article enjoin'd.

Comp. And how long is it since you lost your
honest husband ?

Urse. O, the memory is too fresh, and your
sight makes my sorrow double.

Comp. My sight ! why, was he like me ?

Urse. Your left hand to your right is not more
like.

Comp. Nay, then I cannot blame thee to weep :
an honest man, I warrant him, and thou hadst a
great loss of him.   Such a proportion, so limbed,
so coloured, so fed !

Ray. Yes, faith, and so taught too.

Eust. Nay, will you break the law !

Urse. Twins were never liker.

Comp. Well, I love him the better, whatsoever
is become of him.   And how many children did
he leave thee at his departure ?

Urse. Only one, sir.

Comp. A boy or a girl ?

Urse. A boy, sir.

Comp. Just mine own case still : my wife, rest her soul ! left me a boy too. A chopping boy, I warrant ?

Urse. Yes, if you call 'em so.

Comp. Ay, mine is a chopping boy : I mean to make either a cook or a butcher of him, for those are your chopping boys. And what profession was your husband of ?

Urse. He went to sea, sir, and there got his living.

Comp. Mine own faculty too. And you can like a man of that profession well ?

Urse. For his sweet sake whom I so dearly lov'd,

More dearly lost, I must think well of it.

Comp. Must you ? I do think, then, thou must venture to sea once again, if thou'lt be ruled by me.

Urse. O, sir, but there's one thing more burdensome

To us than most of others' wives, which moves me

A little to distaste it : long time we endure

The absence of our husbands, sometimes many years ;

And then if any slip in woman be,—

As long vacations may make lawyers hungry,

And tradesmen cheaper pennyworths afford,

Than otherwise they would, for ready coin,—

Scandals fly out, and we poor souls [are] branded

With wanton living and incontinency ;

When, alas ! consider, can we do withal ? *

Comp. They are fools, and not sailors, that do not consider that : I'm sure your husband was not of that mind, if he were like me.

Urse. No, indeed, he would bear kind and honestly.

Comp. He was the wiser. Alack, your land and fresh-water men never understand what wonders are done at sea: yet they may observe ashore that a hen, having tasted the cock, kill him, and she shall lay eggs afterwards.

Urse. That's very true, indeed.

Comp. And so may women, why not ? may not a man get two or three children at once ? one must be born before another, you know.

Urse. Even this discretion my sweet husband had :

You more and more resemble him.

Comp. Then, if they knew what things are done at sea, where the winds themselves do copulate and bring forth issue, as thus :—in the old world there

were but four in all, as nor', east, sou', and west : these dwelt far from one another, yet by meeting they have engendered nor'-east, sou'-east, sou'-west, nor'-west,—then they were eight ; of them were begotten nor'-nor'-east, nor'-nor'-west, sou'-sou'-east, sou'-sou'-west, and those two sou's were sou'-east' and sou'-west' daughters ; and indeed, there is a family now of thirty-two of 'em, that they have filled every corner of the world : and yet for all this, you see these bawdy bellows-menders, when they come ashore, will be offering to take up women's coats in the street.

Urse. Still my husband's discretion.

Comp. So I say, if your landmen did understand that we send winds from sea, to do our commendations to our wives, they would not blame you as they do.

Urse. We cannot help it.

Comp. But you shall help it. Can you love me, widow ?

Urse. If I durst confess what I do think, sir, I know what I would say.

Comp. Durst confess ! Why, whom do you fear ? here's none but honest gentlemen, my friends : let them hear, and never blush for't.

Urse. I shall be thought too weak, to yield at first.

Ray. Tush, that's niceness : come, we heard all the rest :

The first true stroke of love sinks the deepest ; If you love him, say so.

Comp. I have a boy of mine own ; I tell you that aforehand : you shall not need to fear me that way.

Urse. Then I do love him.

Comp. So, here will be man and wife to-morrow, then : what though we meet strangers, we may love one another ne'er the worse for that.—Gentlemen, I invite you all to my wedding.

Omnes. We'll all attend it.

Comp. Did not I tell you I would fetch it off fair ? Let any man lay a cuckold to my charge, if he dares, now.

Ray. 'Tis slander, whoever does it.

Comp. Nay, it will come to petty-lassery * at least, and without compass of the general pardon too, or I'll bring him to a foul sheet, if he has ne'er a clean one : or let me hear him that will say I am not father to the child I begot.

Eust. None will adventure any of those.

---

* *do withal*] See note †, p. 271.

* *petty-lassery*] So in *The Fleire* by Sharpham ; "you cannot be hanged for't, 'tis but *pettilassery* at most." Sig D 3. ed. 1615.

Comp. Or that my wife that shall be is not as honest a woman as some other men's wives are.

Ray. No question of that.

Comp. How fine and sleek my brows are now !

Eust. Ay, when you are married they'll come to themselves again.

Comp. You may call me bridegroom, if you please, now, for the guests are bidden.

Omnes. Good master bridegroom !

Comp. Come, widow, then : ere the next ebb and tide,

If I be bridegroom, thou shalt be the bride.

             [*Exeunt.*

ACT V.

SCENE I.*

Enter ROCHFIELD *and* ANNABEL.

Roch. Believe me, I was never more ambitious,
Or covetous, if I may call it so ;
Of any fortune greater than this one,
But to behold his face.

Anna. And now's the time ;
For from a much-fear'd danger, as I heard,
He's late come over.

Roch. And not seen you yet !
'Tis some unkindness.

Anna. You may think it so ;
But for my part, sir, I account it none.
What know I but some business of import
And weighty consequence, more near to him
Than any formal compliment to me,
May for a time detain him ? I presume
No jealousy can be aspers'd on him
For which he cannot well apology.

Roch. You are a creature every way complete,
As good a wife as woman ; for whose sake,
As I in duty am endear'd to you,
So shall I owe him service.

Enter LESSINGHAM.

Less. [*aside*] The ways to love and crowns lie
both through blood,
For in 'em both all lets must be remov'd
It could be styl'd no true ambition else.
I am grown big with project :—project, said I ?
Rather with sudden mischief ; which, without
A speedy birth, fills me with painful throes,
And I am now in labour.—Thanks, occasion,
That giv'st me a fit ground to work upon !
It should be Rochfield, once since our departure
It seems engrafted in this family :
Indeed, the house's minion, since, from the lord
To the lowest groom, all with unite consent
Speak him so largely ; nor, as it appears

By this their private conference, is he grown
Least in the bride's opinion,—a foundation
On which I will erect a brave revenge.

Anna. Sir, what kind offices lie in your way
To do for him, I shall be thankful for,
And reckon them mine own.

Roch. In acknowledgement,
I kiss your hand : so, with a gratitude
Never to be forgot, I take my leave.

Anna. I mine of you, with hourly expectation
Of a long-look'd-for husband.

Roch. May it thrive
According to your wishes !   [*Exit* ANNABEL.

Less. [*aside*] Now's my turn.—
Without offence, sir, may I beg your name ?

Roch. 'Tis that I never yet denied to any,
Nor will to you that seem a gentleman ;
'Tis Rochfield.

Less. Rochfield ! You are, then, the man
Whose nobleness, virtue, valour, and good parts
Have voic'd you loud : Dover, and Sandwich,
Margate,
And all the coast is full of you :
But more, as an eye-witness of all these,
And with most truth, the master of this house
Hath given them large expressions.

Roch. Therein his love
Exceeded much my merit.

Less. That's your modesty.
Now I, as one that goodness love in all men,
And honouring that which is but found in few,
Desire to know you better.

Roch. Pray, your name ?

Less. Lessingham.

Roch. A friend to Master Bonvile ?

Less. In the number
Of those which he esteems most dear to him
He reckons me not last.

Roch. So I have heard.

Less. Sir, you have cause to bless the lucky
planet

---

        * *Scene I.*] A hall in Woodroff's house.

Beneath which you were born; 'twas a bright star
And then shin'd clear upon you: for as you
Are every way well-parted, so I hold you
In all designs mark'd to be fortunate.

Roch. Pray, do not stretch your love to flattery;
'T may call it, then, in question: grow, I pray you,
To some particulars.

Less. I have observ'd
But late your parting with the virgin bride,
And therein some affection.

Roch. How!

Less. With pardon, —
In this I still applaud your happiness,
And praise the blessèd influence of your stars:
For how can it be possible that she,
Unkindly left upon the bridal day,*
And disappointed of those nuptial sweets
That night expected, but should take the occasion
So fairly offer'd I may, and stand excus'd,
As well in detestation of a scorn
Scarce in a husband heard of, as selecting
A gentleman in all things so complete
To do her those neglected offices
Her youth and beauty justly challengeth?

Roch. [*aside*] Some plot to wrong the bride; and
I now
Will marry craft with cunning: if he'll bite,
I'll give him line to play on.—Were't your case,
You being young as I am, would you intermit
So fair and sweet occasion?
Yet,† misconceive me not, I do entreat you,
To think I can be of that easy wit
Or of that malice to defame a lady,
Were she so kind as to expose herself;
Nor is she such a creature.

Less. [*aside*] On this foundation
I can build higher still.—Sir, I believe't.
I hear you two call cousins: comes your kindred
By the Woodroffs or the Bonviles?

Roch. From neither; 'tis a word of courtesy
Late interchang'd betwixt us; otherwise
We are foreign as two strangers.

Less. [*aside*] Better still.

Roch. I would not have you grow too inward‡
with me
Upon so small a knowledge: yet to satisfy you,
And in some kind too to delight myself,
Those bracelets and the carcanet § she wears
She gave me once.

---

* *bridal day*] The old ed. "Bride-day."
† *Yet, &c.*] The old ed. gives the last five lines of this
speech to Leessingham.
‡ *inward*] i. e. intimate.
§ *carcanet*] i.e. necklace.

Less. They were the first and special tokens
pass'd
Betwixt her and her husband.

Roch. 'Tis confess'd;
What I have said, I have said. Sir, you have power
Perhaps to wrong me or to injure her:
This you may do; but, as you are a gentleman,
I hope you will do neither.

Less. Trust upon't.   [*Exit* ROCHFIELD.
If I drown, I will sink some along with me;
For of all miseries I hold that chief,
Wretched to be when none coparts our grief.
Here's another anvil to work on: I must now
Make this my master-piece, for your old foxes
Are seldom ta'en in springes.

Enter WOODROFF.

Wood. What, my friend!
You are happily return'd; and yet I want
Somewhat to make it perfect. Where's your friend,
My son-in-law?

Less. O sir!

Wood. I pray, sir, resolve me;
For I do suffer strangely till I know
If he be in safety.

Less. Fare you well: 'tis not fit
I should relate his danger.

Wood. I must know't.
I have a quarrel to you already
For enticing my son-in-law to go over:
Tell me quickly, or I shall make it greater.

Less. Then truth is, he is dangerously wounded.

Wood. But he's not dead, I hope.

Less. No, sir, not dead:
Yet, sure, your daughter may take liberty
To choose another.

Wood. Why, that gives him dead.

Less. Upon my life, sir, no: your son's in health,
As well as I am.

Wood. Strange! you deliver riddles.

Less. I told you he was wounded, and 'tis true;
He is wounded in his reputation.
I told you likewise, which I am loth to repeat,
That your fair daughter might take liberty
To embrace another: that's the consequence
That makes my best friend wounded in his fame.
This is all I can deliver.

Wood. I must have more of't;
For I do sweat already, and I'll sweat more:
'Tis good, they say, to cure aches; and o'the
sudden
I am sore from head to foot. Let me taste the worst.

Less. Know, sir, if ever there were truth in
falsehood,

Then 'tis most true your daughter plays most
    false
With Bonvile, and hath chose for her favourite
The man that now pass'd by me, Rochfield.
    Wood. Say?
I would thou hadst spoke this on Calais-sands,
And I within my sword and poniard's length
Of that false throat of thine ! I pray, sir, tell me
Of what kin or alliance do you take me
To the gentlewoman you late mention'd?
    Less. You are her father.
    Wood. Why, then, of all men living, do you
    address
This report to me, that ought of all men breathing
To have been the last o'the roll, except the
    husband,
That should have heard of 't?
    Less. For her honour, sir, and yours;
That your good counsel may reclaim her.
    Wood. I thank you.
    Less. She has departed,* sir, upon my know-
    ledge,
With jewels and with bracelets, the first pledges
And confirmation of the unhappy contract
Between herself and husband.
    Wood. To whom?
    Less. To Rochfield.
    Wood. Be not abus'd: but now,
Even now, I saw her wear 'em.
    Less. Very likely:
'Tis fit, hearing her husband is return'd,
That he† should re-deliver 'em.
    Wood. But pray, sir, tell me,
How is it likely she could part with 'em,
When they are lock'd about her neck and wrists,
And the key with her husband?
    Less. O, sir, that's but practice:*
She has got a trick to use another key
Besides her husband's.
    Wood. Sirrah, you do lie;
And were I to pay down a hundred pounds
For every lie given, as men pay twelve-pence,
And worthily, for swearing, I would give thee
The lie, nay, though it were in the court of honour,
So oft, till of the thousands I am worth
I had not left a hundred. For is't likely
So brave a gentleman as Rochfield is,
That did so much at sea to save my life,
Should now on land shorten my wretched days
In ruining my daughter? A rank lie!
Have you spread this to any but myself?

    Less. I am no intelligencer.
    Wood. Why, then, 'tis yet a secret:
And that it may rest so, draw ! I'll take order
You shall prate of it no further.
    Less. O, my sword
Is enchanted, sir, and will not out o'the scabbard.
I will leave you, sir: yet say not I give ground,
For 'tis your own you stand on.

    Enter BONVILE *and* CLARE.

[*Aside.*] Clare here with Bonvile! excellent! on
    this
I have more to work: this goes to Annabel,
And it may increase the whirlwind.   [*Exit.*
    Bon. How now, sir!
Come, I know this choler bred in you
For the voyage which I took at his entreaty:
But I must reconcile you.
    Wood. On my credit,
There's no such matter. I will tell you, sir,
And I will tell it in laughter, the cause of it
Is so poor, so ridiculous, so impossible
To be believ'd: ha, ha! he came even now
And told me that one Rochfield, now a guest
(And most worthy, sir, to be so) in my house,
Is grown exceedingly familiar with
My daughter.
    Bon. Ha!
    Wood. Your wife; and that he has had favours
    from her.
    Bon. Favours!
    Wood. Love-tokens I did call 'em in my youth;
Lures to which gallants spread their wings, and
    stoop
In ladies' bosoms. Nay, he was so false
To truth and all good manners, that those jewels
You lock'd about her neck, he did protest
She had given to Rochfield. Ha! methinks o'the
    sudden
You do change colour. Sir, I would not have you
Believe this in least part: my daughter's honest,
And my guess* is a noble fellow; and for this

---

    * *departed*] i. e. parted.
    † *he*] The old ed. "*she.*"
    ‡ *practice*] i. e. artifice.

    * *guess*] A corruption of *guest*, not unfrequently used
by old writers:
    "Sir, my maisters *gesse* be none of my copesmates."
    A pleasant Commodie called Looke about you. 1600, Sig. F 3.
       "It greatly at my stomacke stickes
      That all this day we had no *guesse,*
      And have of meate so many a messe."
        The Downfall of Robert, Earl of Huntingdon.
          (by Chettle), 1601, Sig. H 4.
    "*Guesse* will come in, 'tis almost supper-time."
    Yarington's *Two Lamentable Tragedies*, 1601, Sig. B 3.
      "The nuptials being done,
    To which the king came willingly a *guest,*
    Each one repair'd unto their business."
        Chalkhill's *Thealma and Clearchus,* 1683, p. 28.

Slander deliver'd me by Lessingham,
I would have cut his throat.

Bon. As I your daughter's,
If I find not the jewels 'bout her.

Clare. Are you return'd
With the Italian plague upon you, jealousy?

Wood. Suppose that Lessingham should love
    my daughter,
And thereupon fashion your going over,
As now your jealousy, the stronger way
So to divide you, there were a fine crotchet!
Do you stagger still? If you continue thus,
I vow you are not worth a welcome home
Neither from her nor me.—See, here she comes.

Re-enter ROCHFIELD *and* ANNABEL.

Clare. I have brought you home a jewel.

Anna. Wear it yourself;
For these I wear are fetters, not favours.

Clare. I look'd for better welcome.

Roch. Noble sir,
I must woo your better knowledge.

Bon. O dear sir,
My wife will bespeak it for you.

Roch. Ha, your wife!

Wood. Bear with him, sir, he's strangely off
    o'the hinges.

Bon. [*aside*] The jewels are i'the right place:
but the jewel
Of her heart sticks yonder.—You are angry with
    me
For my going over.

Anna. Happily more angry for your coming
    over.

Bon. I sent you my will from Dover.

Anna. Yes, sir.

Bon. Fetch it.

Anna. I shall, sir, but leave your self-will with
    you.   [*Exit.*

Wood. This is fine; the woman will be mad
    too.

Bon. Sir, I would speak with you.

Roch. And I with you of all men living.

Bon. I must have satisfaction from you.

Roch. Sir, it grows upon the time of payment.

Wood. What's that, what's that? I'll have no
    whispering.

Re-enter ANNABEL *with the will.*

Anna. Look you, there's the patent
Of your deadly affection to me.

Bon. 'Tis welcome.
When I gave myself for dead, I then made over

My land unto you: now I find your love
Dead to me, I will alter't.

Anna. Use your pleasure.
A man may make a garment for the moon,
Rather than fit your constancy.

Wood. How's this?
Alter your will!

Bon. 'Tis in mine own disposing:
Certainly I will alter't.

Wood. Will you so, my friend?
Why, then, I will alter mine too.
I had estated thee, thou peevish fellow,
In forty thousand pounds after my death:
I can find another executor.

Bon. Pray, sir, do.
Mine I'll alter without question.

Wood. Dost hear me?
An if I change not mine within this two hours,
May my executors cozen all my kindred
To whom I bequeath legacies!

Bon. I am for a lawyer, sir.

Wood. And I will be with one as soon as
    thyself,
Though thou rid'st post to the devil. [*Exit* BON.

Roch. Stay, let me follow and cool him.

Wood. O, by no means:
You'll put a quarrel upon him for the wrong
H' as done my daughter.

Roch. No, believe it, sir;
He's my wish'd friend.

Wood. O, come, I know the way of't;
Carry it like a French quarrel, privately whisper,
Appoint to meet, and cut each other's throats
With cringes and embraces. I protest
I will not suffer you exchange a word
Without I overhear't.

Roch. Use your pleasure.
        [*Exeunt* WOODROFF *and* ROCHFIELD.

Clare. You are like to make fine work now.

Anna. Nay, you are like
To make a finer business of't.

Clare. Come, come,
I must solder you together.

Anna. You! why, I heard
A bird sing lately, you are the only cause
Works the division.

Clare. Who, as thou ever lov'dst me?
For I long, though I am a maid, for't.

Anna. Lessingham.

Clare. Why, then, I do protest myself first
    cause
Of the wrong which he has put upon you both;
Which, please you to walk in, I shall make good
In a short relation. Come, I'll be the clew

To lead you forth this labyrinth, this toil
Of a suppos'd and causeless jealousy.
Cankers touch choicest fruit with their infection,
And fevers seize those of the best complexion.
                                        [*Exeunt.*

SCENE II.*

Enter WOODROFF *and* ROCHFIELD.

Wood. Sir, have I not said I love you? if I have,
You may believe 't before an oracle,
For there's no trick in 't, but the honest sense.
    Roch. Believe it! that I do, sir.
    Wood. Your love must, then,
Be as plain with mine, that they may suit together.
I say you must not fight with my son Bonvile.
    Roch. Not fight with him, sir?
    Wood. No, not fight with him, sir.
I grant you may be wrong'd, and I dare swear
So is my child; but he is the husband, you know,
The woman's lord, and must not always be told
Of his faults neither: I say you must not fight.
    Roch. I'll swear it, if you please, sir.
    Wood. And forswear, I know 't,
Ere you lay ope the secrets of your valour:
It is enough for me I saw you whisper,
And I know what belongs to 't.
    Roch. To no such end, assure you.
    Wood. I say you cannot fight with him,
If you be my friend, for I must use you:
Yonder's my foe, and you must be my second.

Enter LESSINGHAM.

Prepare thee, slanderer, and get another
Better than thyself too; for here's my second,
One that will fetch him up, and firk him too :—
Get your tools: I know the way to Calais-sands,
If that be your fence-school:—he'll show you
            tricks, faith;
He'll let blood your calumny: your best guard
Will come to a *peccavi*, I believe.
    Less. Sir, if that be your quarrel,
He's a party in it, and must maintain
The side with me: from him I collected
All those circumstances concern your daughter,
His own tongue's confession.
    Wood. Who! from him?
He will belie to do thee a pleasure, then,
If he speak any ill upon himself:
I know he ne'er could do an injury.
    Roch. So please you, I'll relate it, sir.

Enter BONVILE, ANNABEL, *and* CLARE.

Wood. Before her husband, then,—and here
            he is,
In friendly posture with my daughter too :
I like that well.—Son bridegroom and lady bride,
If you will hear a man defame himself,
For so he must if he say any ill,
Then listen.
    Bon. Sir, I have heard this story,
And meet with your opinion in his goodness:
The repetition will be needless.
    Roch. Your father has not, sir: I will be brief
In the delivery.
    Wood. Do, do, then : I long to hear it.
    Roch. The first acquaintance I had with your
            daughter
Was on the wedding-eve.
    Wood. So; 'tis not ended yet, methinks.
    Roch. I would have robb'd her.
    Wood. Ah, thief!
    Roch. That chain and bracelet which she wears
            upon her,
She ransom'd with the full esteem in gold,
Which was with you my venture.
    Wood. Ah, thief again!
    Roch. For any attempt against her honour, I vow
I had no thought on.
    Wood. An honest thief, faith, yet.
    Roch. Which she as nobly recompens'd, brought
            me home,
And in her own discretion thought it meet
For cover of my shame, to call me cousin.
    Wood. Call a thief cousin! why, and so she might,
For the gold she gave thee she stole from her
            husband;
'Twas all his now: yet 'twas a good girl too.
    Roch. The rest you know, sir.
    Wood. Which was worth all the rest,—
Thy valour, lad; but I'll have that in print,
Because I can no better utter it.
    Roch. Thus jade* unto my wants,
And spurr'd by my necessities, I was going,
But by that lady's counsel I was stay'd
(For that discourse was our familiarity):
And this you may take for my recantation;
I am no more a thief.
    Wood. A blessing on thy heart!
And this was the first time, I warrant thee, too.
    Roch. Your charitable censure is not wrong'd
            in that.
    Wood. No; I knew 't could be but the first
            time at most :

---

* *Scene II.*] Before Woodroff's house.

* *jade*] i. e. jaded.

But for thee, brave valour, I have in store
That thou shalt need to be a thief no more.
                  [*Soft music within.*

Ha! what's this music?

  Bon. It chimes an Io pæan to your wedding, sir,
If this be your bride.

  Less. Can you forgive me? some wild distractions
Had overturn'd my own condition,
And spilt the goodness you once knew in me:
But I have carefully recover'd it,
And overthrown the fury on 't.

  Clare. It was my cause
That you were so possess'd; and all these troubles
Have from my peevish will original:
I do repent, though you forgive me not.

  Less. You have no need for your repentance, then,
Which is due to it: all's now as at first
It was wish'd to be.

  Wood. Why, that's well said of all sides.
But, soft! this music has some other meaning:
Another wedding towards!

Enter COMPASS, RAYMOND, EUSTACE, LIONEL, GROVER, URSE *between* FRANCKFORD *and another,* LUCE, Nurse, *and* Child.

Good speed, good speed!

  Comp. We thank you, sir.

  Wood. Stay, stay; our neighbour Compass, is it not?

  Comp. That was, and may be again to-morrow; this day Master Bridegroom.

  Wood. O, give you joy! But, sir, if I be not mistaken, you were married before now: how long is't since your wife died?

  Comp. Ever since yesterday, sir.

  Wood. Why, she's scarce buried yet, then.

  Comp. No, indeed: I mean to dig her grave soon: I had no leisure yet.

  Wood. And was not your fair bride married before?

  Urse. Yes, indeed, sir.

  Wood. And how long since · your husband departed?

  Urse. Just when my husband's wife died.

  Wood. Bless us, Hymen!
Are not these both the same parties?

  Bon. Most certain, sir.

  Wood. What marriage call you this?

  Comp. This is called "Shedding of horns," sir.

  Wood. How!

  Less. Like enough; but they may grow again next year.

  Wood. This is a new trick.

  Comp. Yes, sir, because we did not like the old trick.

  Wood. Brother, you are a helper in this design too?

  Franck. The father to give the bride, sir.

  Comp. And I am his son, sir, and all the sons he has; and this is his grandchild, and my elder brother: you'll think this strange now.

  Wood. Then it seems he begat this before you.

  Comp. Before me! not so, sir; I was far enough off when 'twas done: yet let me see him dares say, this is not my child and this my father.

  Bon. You cannot see him here, I think, sir.

  Wood. Twice married! can it hold?

  Comp. Hold! it should hold the better, a wise man would think, when 'tis tied of two knots.

  Wood. Methinks it should rather unloose the first,
And between 'em both make up one negative.

  Eust. No, sir; for though it hold on the contrary,
Yet two affirmatives make no negative.

  Wood. Cry you mercy, sir.

  Comp. Make what you will, this little negative was my wife's laying, and I affirm it to be mine own.

  Wood. This proves the marriage before substantial,
Having this issue.

  Comp. 'Tis mended now, sir: for, being double-married, I may now have two children at a birth, if I can get 'em. D' ye think I'll be five years about one as I was before?

  Eust. The like has been done for the loss of the wedding-ring,
And to settle a new peace before disjointed.

  Lion. But this, indeed, sir, was especially done,
To avoid the word of scandal, that foul word
Which the fatal monologist cannot alter.

  Wood. Cuckoo.

  Comp. What's that? the nightingale?

  Wood. A night-bird;
Much good may do you, sir!*

---

* *Much good may do you, sir!*] In the first edition of the present collection, I printed "Much good may [it] do you, sir!" But, according to our old phraseology, the "it" was frequently omitted in expressions of this kind. Let me observe that in several places of the present scene (as in some earlier passages of the play) it is difficult to determine whether the author wrote prose or a very loose sort of blank-verse (which perhaps through the carelessness of the transcriber has become still more akin to prose).

Comp. I'll thank you when I'm at supper.—
Come, father, child, and bride: and for your
part, father,
Whatsoever he, or he, or t'other says,
You shall be as welcome as in my t'other wife's
    days.
    Franck. I thank you, sir.
    Wood. Nay, take us with you,* gentlemen:

   * *take us with you*] i. e. understand us.

One wedding we have yet to solemnize;
The first is still imperfect, such troubles
Have drown'd our music; but now, I hope, all's
    friends:
Get you to bed, and there the wedding ends.
    Comp. And so, good night. My bride and I'll
    to bed:
He that has horns, thus let him learn to shed.

              [*Exeunt.*

THE MALCONTENT.

The Malcontent. By John Marston. 1604. Printed at London by V. S., for William Aspley, and are to be solde at his shop in Paules Church-yard.

The Malcontent. Augmented by Marston. With the Additions played by the Kings Maiesties servants. Written by Ihon Webster. 1604. At London Printed by V. S. for William Aspley, and are to be sold at his shop in Paules Church-yard.

Both Marston and Webster, it appears from the last title-page, made additions to this play. It is impossible to distinguish the portions which the latter contributed; but he is generally supposed to have written the Induction. What is not found in the first 4to, I have marked by inverted commas: other variations of the two editions, I have given in the notes.

I have had occasion several times in the course of this work to observe, that different copies of the *same editions* of old plays often present various readings: such is the case with the copies of the second 4to of the *Malcontent;* my copy does not altogether agree with that in the Garrick Collection.

The Malcontent has been reprinted in the different editions of Dodsley's *Old Plays,* and in the *Ancient British Drama;* and more recently in Mr. Halliwell's edition of Marston's *Works.*

The hero of this play, Malevole, was performed by Burbadge: see the Induction ; see also *A Funeral Elegy on the death of the famous actor, Richard Burbadge,* printed in Mr. Collier's *Memoirs of the Principal Actors in the plays of Shakespeare,* p. 52, ed. Shakes. Soc.

BENIAMINO* JONSONIO,
POETÆ
ELEGANTISSIMO,
GRAVISSIMO,
AMICO
SVO, CANDIDO ET CORDATO,
IOHANNES MARSTON,
MVSARVM ALVMNVS,
ASPERAM HANC SUAM THALIAM
D. D.

TO THE READER.

I AM an ill orator ; and, in truth, use to indite more honestly than eloquently, for it is my custom to speak as I think, and write as I speak.

In plainness, therefore, understand, that in some things I have willingly erred, as in supposing a Duke of Genoa, and in taking names different from that city's families : for which some may wittily accuse me ; but my defence shall be as honest as many reproofs unto me have been most malicious. Since, I heartily protest, it was my care to write so far from reasonable offence, that even strangers, in whose state I laid my scene, should not from thence draw any disgrace to any, dead or living. Yet, in despite of my endeavours, I understand some have been most unadvisedly over-cunning in misinterpreting me, and with subtlety as deep as hell have maliciously spread ill rumours, which springing from themselves, might to themselves have heavily returned. Surely I desire to satisfy every firm spirit, who, in all his actions, proposeth to himself no more ends than God and virtue do, whose intentions are always simple : to such I protest that, with my free understanding, I have not glanced at disgrace of any, but of those whose unquiet studies labour innovation, contempt of holy policy, reverend, comely superiority, and established unity : for the rest of my supposed tartness, I fear not but unto every worthy mind it will be approved so general and honest as may modestly pass with the freedom of a satire. I would fain leave the paper ; only one thing afflicts me, to think that scenes, invented merely to be spoken, should be enforcively published to be read, and that the least hurt I can receive is to do myself the wrong. But, since others otherwise would do me more, the least inconvenience is to be accepted. I have myself, therefore, set forth this comedy ; but so, that my enforced absence must much rely upon the printer's discretion : but I shall entreat, slight errors in orthography may be as slightly over-passed, and that the unhandsome shape, which this trifle in reading presents, may be pardoned for the pleasure it once afforded you when it was presented with the soul of lively action.

Sine aliqua dementia nullus Phœbus.†

J. M.

---

* BENIAMINO] The second 4to. "BENIAMINI."
† *Sine aliqua, &c.*] Instead of this, the first 4to has "*Me mea sequentur fata.*"

DRAMATIS PERSONÆ.

GIOVANNI ALTOFRONTO, disguised as MALEVOLE, sometime Duke of Genoa.
PIETRO JACOMO, Duke of Genoa.
MENDOZA, a minion to the Duchess of Pietro Jacomo.
CELSO, a friend to Altofronto.
BILIOSO, an old choleric marshal.
PREPASSO, a gentleman-usher.
FERNEZE, a young courtier, and enamoured on the Duchess.
FERRARDO, a minion to Duke Pietro Jacomo.
EQUATO, } two courtiers.
GUERRINO, }
"PASSARELLO, fool to Bilioso."

AURELIA, Duchess to Duke Pietro Jacomo.
MARIA, Duchess to Duke Altofronto.
EMILIA, } two ladies attending on Aurelia.
BIANCA, }
MAQUERELLE, an old panderess.

"THE INDUCTION

"TO

"THE MALCONTENT, AND THE ADDITIONS ACTED BY THE KING'S "MAJESTY'S ·SERVANTS.

"WRITTEN BY JOHN WEBSTER.

" *Enter* W. SLY*, *a Tire-man following him with a stool.*

" *Tire-man.* Sir, the gentlemon will be angry "if you sit here.

" *Sly.* Why, we may sit upon the stage at the "private house. Thou dost not take me for a "country-gentleman, dost? dost think I fear "hissing? I'll hold my life thou tookest me for "one of the players.

" *Tire-man.* No, sir.

" *Sly.* By God's slid,† if you had, I would have "given you but six-pence‡ for your stool. Let "them that have stale suits sit in the galleries. "Hiss at me! Ho that will be laughed out of a "tavern or an ordinary, shall seldom feed well, or "be drunk in good company.—Where's Harry "Condell, Dick Burbadge, and William Sly? Let "me speak with some of them.

" *Tire-man.* An't please you to go in, sir, you may.

" *Sly.* I tell you, no: I am one that hath seen "this play often, and can give them intelligence "for their action: I have most of the jests here "in my table-book.

" *Enter* SINKLO.§

" *Sinklo.* Save you, coz!

" *Sly.* O, cousin, come, you shall sit between "my legs here.

" *Sinklo.* No, indeed, cousin: the audience "then will take me for a viol-de-gambo, and "think that you play upon me.

" *Sly.* Nay, rather that I work upon you, coz.

" *Sinklo.* We stayed for you at supper last "night at my cousin Honey-moon's, the woollen- "draper. After supper we drew cuts for a score "of apricocks, the longest cut still to draw an "apricock: by this light, 'twas Mistress Frank "Honeymoon's fortune still to have the longest "cut: I did measure for the women.—What be "these, coz?

" *Enter* D. BURBADGE, H. CONDELL, *and* J. LOWIN.*

" *Sly.* The players.—God save you!

" *Burbadge.* You are very welcome.

" *Sly.* I pray you, know this gentleman, my "cousin; 'tis Master Doomsday's son, the usurer.

" *Condell.* I beseech you, sir, be covered.

" *Sly.* No †, in good faith, for mine ease: look "you, my hat's the handle to this fan: God's "so, what a beast was I, I did not leave my "feather at home! Well, but I'll take an order "with you.

[*Puts his feather in his pocket.*

---

* *W. Sly*] See an account of William Sly in Mr. Collier's *Memoirs of the Principal Actors in the plays of Shakespeare,* p. 151.—The reader must observe that here Sly is per-sonating the "cousin" of young "Master Doomsday," who (acted by Sinklo) presently enters.

† *By God's slid*] This petty oath (more usually "'Slid") is, I believe, equivalent to "*By God's lid.*" (Compare several other profane expressions formerly in use,—"*By God's body,*" "*By God's head,*" &c.)

‡ *six-pence for your stool*] "From chap. vi. in Dekker's *Guls Horn-book,* it appears that it was the fashion for the gallants of the time to sit on the stage on stools."—*Reed.*

§ *Sinklo*] A performer of no eminence: see Mr. Collier's

Memoirs of the Principal Actors, &c.—*Introd.,* p. xxvii.— He is noting (as already noticed) young "Master Doomsday."

* *D. Burbadge, H. Condell, and J. Lowin*] For all that can be told concerning Richard Burbadge, Henry Condell, and John Lowin, see Mr. Collier's *Memoirs of the Principal Actors,* &c., pp. 1, 132, 165.

† *No, in good faith, for mine ease*] "A quotation from the part of Osrick in *Hamlet.* Sly might have been the original performer of that character."—*Stevens.*

" *Burbadge.* Why do you conceal your feather,
" sir?

" *Sly.* Why, do you think I'll have jests broken
" upon me in the play, to be laughed at? this
" play hath beaten all your gallants out of the
" feathers: Black-friars hath almost spoiled
" Black-friars for feathers.*

" *Sinklo.* God's so, I thought 'twas for some-
" what our gentlewomen at home counselled me
" to wear my feather to the play: yet I am loth
" to spoil it.

" *Sly.* Why, coz?

" *Sinklo.* Because I got it in the tilt-yard;
" there was a herald broke my pate for taking it
" up: but I have worn it up and down the
" Strand, and met him forty times since, and yet
" he dares not challenge it.

" *Sly.* Do you hear, sir? this play is a bitter
" play.

" *Condell.* Why, sir, 'tis neither satire nor
" moral, but the mean passage of a history: yet
" there are a sort of discontented creatures that
" bear a stingless envy to great ones, and these will
" wrest the doings of any man to their base,
" malicious appliment; but should their inter-
" pretation come to the test, like your marmoset,
" they presently turn their teeth to their tail and
" eat it.

" *Sly.* I will not go so far with you; but I say,
" any man that hath wit may censure,† if he sit
" in the twelve-penny room;‡ and I say again, the
" play is bitter.

" *Burbadge.* Sir, you are like a patron that, pre-
" senting a poor scholar to a benefice, enjoins
" him not to rail against any thing that stands
" within compass of his patron's folly. Why
" should not we enjoy the ancient freedom of
" poesy? Shall we protest to the ladies that
" their painting makes them angels? or to my
" young gallant that his expense in the brothel
" shall gain him reputation? No, sir, such vices
" as stand not accountable to law should be cured
" as men heal tetters, by casting ink upon them.
" Would you be satisfied in any thing else, sir?

" *Sly.* Ay, marry, would I: I would know how
" you came by this play?

---

* *Black-friars hath almost spoiled Black-friars for
feathers*] See note ‡, p. 237.—"The following passage, in
act v. sc. 2, is probably alluded to as having produced
this change. 'For as now-a-days no courtier but has
his mistress, no captain but has his cockatrice, no cuckold but has his horns, and *no fool but has his feather,* &c.'"
—Collier.

† *censure*] i.e. judge.

‡ *room*] i.e. box.

" *Condell.* Faith, sir, the book was lost; and
" because 'twas pity so good a play should be
" lost, we found it, and play it.

" *Sly.* I wonder you would play it, another
" company having interest in it.

" *Condell.* Why not Malevole in folio with us,
" as Jeronimo in decimo-sexto with them? They
" taught us a name for our play; we call it *One
" for another.**

" *Sly.* What are your additions?

" *Burbadge.* Sooth, not greatly needful; only
" as your salad to your great feast, to entertain a
" little more time, and to abridge the not-received
" custom of music in our theatre. I must leave
" you, sir. [*Exit.*

" *Sinklo.* Doth he play the Malcontent?

" *Condell.* Yes, sir.

" *Sinklo.* I durst lay four of mine ears the play
" is not so well acted as it hath been.

" *Condell.* O, no, sir, nothing *ad Parmenonis
" suem.* †

---

* *One for another*] " From this preliminary portion of
the play we learn that it had, in the first instance, been
performed by a rival company, under the title of 'The
Malcontent,' but that, with additions, it was that night
to be represented by the King's players, with the new
name of 'One for Another.' Collier's *Memoirs of the
Principal Actors,* &c., p. 26.—"The meaning I conceive
to be this: 'I wonder,' says Sly, 'you play the Malcontent, another company having interest in it.' 'Why
not?' says Condell: 'they took little *Jeronymo* (16°)
from us; why should we not therefore take the Malcontent in large (folio) from them? This is what we call
one for another, an exchange of plays.' Jonson's additions
to *Jeronymo* were done for Henslowe, and Mr. Collier has
shown it likely that *The Malcontent* was written for
Henslowe." P. *Cunningham* (*Notes and Queries,*—Sec.
Ser., vol. i. 71).

† *nothing* ad Parmenonis suem] " ' *Nihil ad Parmenonis
suem*' is a proverb directed against those who, from
prejudice or prepossession, pass a hasty judgment, without having any good grounds on which to found their
decision. Phædrus, without mentioning the name of
Parmeno, has turned the incident which gave rise to the
proverb into a fable; Fab. l. v. f. v.

"The following extract from Plutarch, 'in the very
words of Creech,' would have suited the annotator's
purpose somewhat better than the fabricated quotation
from Terence [which Steevens gave in a note on the present
passage]. 'For upon what other account should men be
moved to admire *Parmeno's sow* so much as to pass it
into a proverb? Yet 'tis reported, that Parmeno being
very famous for imitating the grunting of a pig, some
endeavoured to rival and outdo him. And when the
hearers, being prejudiced, cried out, 'Very well, indeed,
but *nothing comparable to Parmeno's sow,*' one took a pig
under his arm, and came upon the stage; and when,
tho' they heard the very pig, they still continued, '*This
is nothing comparable to Parmeno's sow,*' he threw his pig
amongst them, to shew that they judged according to
opinion and not truth.' Plutarch, *Sympos.* lib. v. prob. i."
L.S. in *The Shakespeare Society's Papers,* vol. iii. 85.

" *Lowin.* Have you lost your ears, sir, that you
" are so prodigal of laying them?

" *Sinklo.* Why did you ask that, friend?

" *Lowin.* Marry, sir, because I have heard of a
" fellow would offer to lay a hundred-pound
" wager that was not worth five baubees: and in
" this kind you might venture four of your
" elbows; yet God defend* your coat should have
" so many!

" *Sinklo.* Nay, truly, I am no great censurer;
" and yet I might have been one of the college of
" critics once. My cousin here hath an excellent
" memory indeed, sir.

" *Sly.* Who, I? I'll tell you a strange thing of
" myself; and I can tell you, for one that never
" studied the art of memory, 'tis very strange
" too.

" *Condell.* What's that, sir?

" *Sly.* Why, I'll lay a hundred pound, I'll walk
" but once down by the Goldsmiths' Row in
" Cheap, take notice of the signs, and tell you
" them with a breath instantly.

" *Lowin.* 'Tis very strange.

" *Sly.* They begin as the world did, with Adam
" and Eve. There's in all just five and fifty.† I
" do use to meditate much when I come to plays
" too. What do you think might come into a
" man's head now, seeing all this company?

" *Condell.* I know not, sir.

" *Sly.* I have an excellent thought. If some
" fifty of the Grecians that were crammed in the
" horse'-belly had eaten garlic, do you not think
" the Trojans might have smelt out their knavery?

" *Condell.* Very likely.

" *Sly.* By God, I would they‡ had, for I love
" Hector horribly.

" *Sinklo.* O, but, coz, coz!

" ' Great Alexander,' when he came to the tomb
" of Achilles,

" 'Spake with a big loud voice, O thou thrice-
" blessèd and happy!'

" *Sly.* Alexander was an ass to speak so well of
" a filthy cullion.†

" *Lowin.* Good sir, will you leave the stage?
" I'll help you to a private room.‡

" *Sly.* Come, coz, let's take some tobacco.—
" Have you never a prologue?

" *Lowin.* Not any, sir.

" *Sly.* Let me see, I will make one extempore.

[*Come to them, and fencing of a congey with arms
and legs, be round with them.§*]

" Gentlemen,|| I could wish for the women's
" sakes you had all soft cushions; and, gentle-
" women, I could wish that for the men's sakes
" you had all more easy standings.

" What would they wish more but the play
" now? and that they shall have instantly.

[*Exeunt.*"

---

* *Great Alexander,* &c.] "His afternoones theame," (says Gabriel Harvey, writing to Spenser,) "was borrowed out of him, whom one in your coate, they say, is as much beholding unto, as any planet or starre in heaven is unto the sunne; and is quoted, as yourself best remember, in the Glose of your October:

Giunto Alessandro a la famosa tomba
Del fero Achille, sospirando disse,
O fortunato, che si chiara tromba
Trovasti! [Petrarch, *Son.* cliii.]

Within an houre or thereaboutes, he brought me these foure lustie hexameters; altered since not past in a worde or two:

Noble Alexander, when he came to the tombe of Achilles,
Sighing spake with a bigge voyce,—O thrice blessed Achilles, [found,
That such a trump, so great, so loude, so glorious hast
As the renowned and surprizing archpoet Homer!"

Three Proper, and wittie, familiar Letters: lately passed betweene two Universitie men: touching the Earthquake in Aprill last, and our English reformed Versifying. 4to. 1580, p. 39. The "foure lustie hexameters" just quoted were by John Harvey, Gabriel's brother. Long before the present play was written, Peele had ridiculed on the stage Gabriel's own hexameters: see *The Old Wiues Tale,* in Peele's *Works,* vol. i. p. 238, sec. ed. 1829.

† *cullion*] i.e. scoundrel.

‡ *room*] i.e. box.

§ *Come to them,* &c.] I have made this a stage-direction, at the suggestion of Mr. Collier: it is printed in the old copy as a portion of the text.

|| *Gentlemen,* &c.] "This seems intended as a burlesque on the Epilogue to *As you like it.*"—*Reed.*

---

* *defend*] i.e. forbid.

† *There's in all just five and fifty*] "This is a pleasant exaggeration on the part of Sly. There were in all, as Stow tells us, 'ten fair dwelling-houses and fourteen shops.' See 'Goldsmiths' Row' in *Handbook of London,* ed. 1850." *P. Cunningham* (*Notes and Queries,*—Sec. Ser., vol. i, 71).

‡ *they.*] The old ed. "*he.*"

THE MALCONTENT.*

ACT I.

SCENE I.†

The vilest out-of-tune music being heard, enter BILIOSO *and* PREPASSO.

Bil. Why, how now! are ye mad, or drunk, or both, or what?

Pre. Are ye building Babylon there?

Bil. Here's a noise in court! you think you are in a tavern, do you not?

Pre. You think you are in a brothel-house, do you not?—This room is ill-scented.

Enter One with a perfume.

So, perfume, perfume; some upon me, I pray thee.—The duke is upon instant entrance: so, make place there!

Enter PIETRO, FERRARDO, EQUATO; CELSO *and* GUERRINO *before.*

Pietro. Where breathes that music?

Bil. The discord rather than the music is heard from the malcontent Malevole's chamber.

Fer. [*calling*] Malevole!

Mal. [*above, out of his chamber*] Yaugh, god-a-man, what dost thou there? Duke's Ganymede, Juno's jealous of thy long stockings: shadow of a woman, what wouldst, weasel? thou lamb o' court, what dost thou bleat for? ah, you smooth-chinned catamite!

Pietro. Come down, thou rugged ‡ cur, and snarl here; I give thy dogged sullenness free liberty: trot about and bespurtle whom thou pleasest.

Mal. I'll come among you, you goatish-blooded toderers,* as gum into taffata, to fret, to fret: I'll fall like a sponge into water, to suck up, to suck up. [*Howls again†.*] I'll go to church,‡ and come to you. [*Exit above.*

Pietro. This Malevole is one of the most prodigious affections that ever conversed with nature: a man, or rather a monster; more discontent than Lucifer when he was thrust out of the presence. His appetite is unsatiable as the grave; as far from any content as from heaven: his highest delight is to procure others vexation, and therein he thinks he truly serves heaven; for 'tis his position, whosoever in this earth can be contented is a slave and damned; therefore does he afflict all in that to which they are most affected. The elements struggle within him; his own soul is at variance "within herself"; his speech is halter-worthy at all hours. I like him, faith: he gives good intelligence to my spirit, makes me understand those weaknesses which others' flattery palliates.—Hark! they sing. [*A song.§* See, he comes. Now shall you hear the extremity of a malcontent: he is as free as air; he blows over every man.

Enter MALEVOLE *below.*

And, sir, whence come you now?

Mal. From the public place of much dissimulation, "the church."

---

* *toderers*] "I suppose this is a word coined from *tod*, a certain weight of sheep's wool. He seems willing to intimate that the duke, &c. are *mutton-mongers*. The meaning of *laced mutton* is well known."—*Steevens.*

† *Howls again*] The old eds. have "Howle *againe*," and as a portion of the dialogue; but the words are evidently a stage-direction. Just before Malevole has exclaimed, "Yaugh, god-a-man," &c.,—which is a sort of *howling*.

‡ *go to church*] The first 4to. "*pray:*" but compare what Malevole says when he enters below.

§ *A song*] See note †, p. 45.

---

* *The Malcontent.*] Opposite these words, on the margin of both 4tos, is "*Vexat censura columbas.*" [Juvenal, *Sat.* ii. 63.]

† *Scene I.*] A room in the palace, with a gallery, it would seem. Prepasso says, "This *room* is ill-scented;" and, presently after, Malevole appears "*above*," i.e. on what was called *the upper stage.*

‡ *rugged.*] The second 4to. "*ragged.*"

Pietro. What didst there?

Mal. Talk with a usurer; take up at interest.

Pietro. I wonder what religion thou art "of"?

Mal. Of a soldier's religion.

Pietro. And what dost thou think makes most infidels now?

Mal. Sects, sects. I have seen seeming piety change her robe so oft, that sure none but some arch-devil can shape her a new* petticoat.

Pietro. O, a religious policy.

Mal. But, damnation on a politic religion! "I am weary: would I were one of the duke's hounds now!"

Pietro. But what's the common news abroad, Malevole? thou doggest rumour still.

Mal. Common news! why, common words are, God save ye, Fare ye well; common actions, flattery and cozenage; common things, women and cuckolds.—And how does my little Ferrard? Ah, ye lecherous animal!—my little ferret, he goes sucking up and down the palace into every hen's nest, like a weasel:—and to what dost thou addict thy time to now more than to those antique painted drabs that are still affected of young courtiers,—flattery, pride, and venery?

Fer. I study languages. Who dost think to be the best linguist of our age?

Mal. Phew! the devil: let him possess thee; he'll teach thee to speak all languages most readily and strangely; and great reason, marry, he's travelled greatly i' the world, and is every where.

Fer. Save i' the court.

Mal. Ay, save i' the court.— [*To Bilioso*] And how does my old muckhill, overspread with fresh snow! thou half a man, half a goat, all a beast! how does thy young wife, old huddle?

Bil. Out, you improvident rascal!

Mal. Do, kick, thou hugely-horned old duke's ox, good Master Make-pleas.

Pietro. How dost thou live now-a-days, Malevole?

Mal. Why, like the knight Sir Patrick Penlolians,† with killing o' spiders for my lady's monkey.

Pietro. How dost spend the night? I hear thou never sleepest.

Mal. O, no; but dream the most fantastical! O heaven! O fubbery, fubbery!

Pietro. Dream! what dreamest?

Mal. Why, methinks I see that signior pawn his foot-cloth,‡ that metreza her plate: this

madam takes physic, that t'other monsieur may minister to her: here is a pander jewelled; there "is" a fellow in shift of satin this day, that could not shift a shirt t'other night: here a Paris supports that Helen; there's a Lady Guinever bears up that Sir Lancelot: dreams, dreams, visions, fantasies, chimeras, imaginations, tricks, conceits!—[*To Prepasso*] Sir Tristram Trimtram, come aloft, Jack-an-apes,* with a whim-wham: here's a knight of the land of Catito shall play at trap with any page in Europe; do the sword-dance with any morris-dancer in Christendom; ride at the ring,† till the fin of his eyes look as blue as the welkin;‡ and run the wildgoose-chase even with Pompey the Huge.§

Pietro. You run!

Mal. To the devil.—Now, signior Guerrino, that thou from a most pitied prisoner shouldst grow a most loathed flatterer!—Alas, poor Celso, thy star's oppressed: thou art an honest lord: 'tis pity.

Equato. Is't pity?

Mal. Ay, marry is't, philosophical Equato; and 'tis pity that thou, being so excellent a scholar by art, shouldst be so ridiculous a fool by nature.—I have a thing to tell you, duke: bid 'em avaunt, bid 'em avaunt.

Pietro. Leave us, leave us.

[*Exeunt all except* Pietro *and* Malevole

Now, sir, what is't?

Mal. Duke, thou art a becco,‖ a cornuto.

Pietro. How!

Mal. Thou art a cuckold.

Pietro. Speak, unshale¶ him quick.

Mal. With most tumbler-like nimbleness.

Pietro. Who? by whom? I burst with desire.

Mal. Mendoza is the man makes thee a horned beast; duke, 'tis Mendoza cornutes thee.

Pietro. What conformance? relate; short, short.

Mal. As a lawyer's beard.

There is an old crone in the court, her name is Maquerelle,

She is my mistress, sooth to say, and she doth ever tell me.

---

* *new*] Omitted in the second 4to.
† *Penlohans*] The second 4to. "Peulolians."
‡ *foot cloth*] See note *, p. 7.

* *come aloft, Jack-an-apes, &c.*] The exclamation of an ape-ward to his ape.
† *ride at the ring*] See note *, p. 60.
‡ *till the fin of his eyes look as blue as the welkin*] See note ‡, p. 67.
§ *Pompey the Huge*] So in Shakespeare's *Love's Labour's Lost*, act v., sc. 2.; "Greater than Great, great, great, great Pompey! *Pompey the Huge!*"
‖ *becco*] "i.e. cuckold, Ital."—*Steevens.*
¶ *unshale*] A form of *unshell.*

Blirt, a rhyme, blirt, a rhyme ! Maquerelle is a
cunning bawd; I am an honest villain; thy wife
is a close drab; and thou art a notorious cuckold.
Farewell, duke.

Pietro. Stay, stay.

Mal. Dull, dull duke, can lazy patience make
lame revenge ? O God, for a woman to make a
man that which God never created, never made !

Pietro. What did God never make ?

Mal. A cuckold : to be made a thing that's
hoodwinked with kindness, whilst every rascal
fillips his brows; to have a coxcomb with egregious horns pinned to a lord's back, every page
sporting himself with delightful laughter, whilst
he must be the last must know it: pistols and
poniards ! pistols and poniards !

Pietro. Death and damnation !

Mal. Lightning and thunder !

Pietro. Vengeance and torture !

Mal. Catso ! *

Pietro. O, revenge !

" *Mal.* Nay, to select among ten thousand fairs
" A lady far inferior to the most,
" In fair proportion both of limb and soul ;
" To take her from austerer check of parents,
" To make her his by most devoutful rites,
" Make her commandress of a better essence
" Than is the gorgeous world, even of a man ;
" To hug her with as rais'd an appetite
" As usurers do their delv'd-up treasury
" (Thinking none tells it but his private self) ;
" To meet her spirit in a nimble kiss,
" Distilling panting ardour to her heart ;
" True to her sheets, nay, diets strong his blood,
" To give her height of hymeneal sweets,——

" *Pietro.* O God !

" *Mal.* Whilst she lisps, and gives him some
" court-*quelquechose,*
" Made only to provoke, not satiate :
" And yet even then the thaw of her delight
" Flows from lewd heat of apprehension,
" Only from strange imagination's rankness,
" That forms the adulterer's presence in her soul,
" And makes her think she clips† the foul knave's
" loins.

" *Pietro.* Affliction to my blood's root !

" *Mal.* Nay, think, but think what may proceed
" of this ;
" Adultery is often the mother of incest.

" *Pietro.* Incest !

---

*   *Catso*] An Italian exclamation (of obscene meaning)
still in use.
    † *clips*] i.e. embraces.

" *Mal.* Yes, incest: mark :—Mendoza of his wife
" begets perchance a daughter : Mendoza dies;
" his son marries this daughter: say you ? nay,
" 'tis frequent, not only probable, but no question
" often acted, whilst ignorance, fearless ignorance,
" clasps his own seed.

" *Pietro.* Hideous imagination !

" *Mal.* Adultery ? why, next to the sin of simony,
" 'tis the most horrid transgression under the
" cope of salvation.

" *Pietro.* Next to simony !

" *Mal.* Ay, next to simony, in which our men
" in next age shall not sin.

" *Pietro.* Not sin ! why ?

" *Mal.* Because (thanks to some church-men)
" our age will leave them nothing to sin with.
" But adultery, O dulness! should show * exem-
" plary punishment, that intemperate bloods may
" freeze but to think it." I would damn him
and all his generation : my own hands should do
it; ha, I would not trust heaven with my vengeance :—any thing.

Pietro. Any thing, any thing, Malevole : thou
shalt see instantly what temper my spirit holds.
Farewell; remember I forget thee not; farewell.

[*Exit* PIETRO.

" *Mal.* Farewell.

" Lean thoughtfulness, a sallow meditation,
" Suck thy veins dry, distemperance rob thy
" sleep !
" The heart's disquiet is revenge most deep :
" He that gets blood, the life of flesh but spills,
" But he that breaks heart's peace, the dear soul
" kills.
" Well, this disguise doth yet afford me that
" Which kings do seldom hear, or great men
" use,—
" Free speech : and though my state's usurp'd,
" Yet this affected strain gives me a tongue
" As fetterless as is an emperor's.
" I may speak foolishly, ay, knavishly,
" Always carelessly, yet no one thinks it fashion
" To poise my breath ; for he that laughs and
" strikes
" Is lightly felt, or seldom struck again.
" Duke, I'll torment thee now; my just revenge
" From thee than crown a richer gem shall part :
" Beneath God, naught's so dear as a calm heart."

Re-enter CELSO.

Celso. My honour'd lord,—

Mal. Peace, speak low, peace ! O Celso, constant lord,

---

*   *should show*] The old ed. "*shue should.*"

(Thou to whose faith I only rest discover'd,
Thou, one of full ten millions of men,
That lovest virtue only for itself;
Thou in whose hands old Ops may put her soul,)
Behold for-ever-banish'd Altofront,
This Genoa's last year's duke. O truly noble!
I wanted those old instruments of state,
Dissemblance and suspect: I could not time it,
         Celso;
My throne stood like a point midst * of a circle,
To all of equal nearness; bore with none;
Rein'd all alike; so slept in fearless virtue,
Suspectless, too suspectless; till the crowd,
(Still liquorous of untried novelties,)
Impatient with soverer government,
Made strong with Florence, banish'd Altofront.

   Celso. Strong with Florence! ay, thence your
         mischief rose;
For when the daughter of the Florentine
Was match'd once with this Pietro, now duke,
No stratagem of state untried was left,
Till you of all——

   Mal. Of all was quite bereft:
Alas, Maria too close prison'd,
My true-faith'd duchess, i'the citadel!

   Celso. I'll still adhere: let's mutiny and die.

   Mal. O, "no," climb not a falling tower, Celso;
'Tis well held desperation, no zeal,
Hopeless to strive with fate: peace; temporize.
Hope, hope, that ne'er forsakes † the wretched'st
         man,
Yet bids me live, and lurk in this disguise.
What, play I well the free-breath'd discontent?
Why, man, we are all philosophical monarchs
Or natural fools. Celso, the court's a-fire;
The duchess' sheets will smoke for't ere 't be long:
Impure Mendoza, that sharp-nos'd lord, that made
The curs'd match link'd Genoa with Florence,
Now broad-horns the duke, which he now knows.
Discord to malcontents is very manna:
When the ranks are burst, then scuffle, Altofront.

   Celso. Ay, but durst——

   Mal. 'Tis gone; 'tis swallow'd like a mineral:
Some way 'twill work; pheut, I'll not shrink:
He's resolute who can no lower sink.

   "Biliosо *re-entering,* Malevole *shifteth his speech.*
" O the father of May-poles! did you never see a
" fellow whose strength consisted in his breath, re-
" spect in his office, religion in ‡ his lord, and love
" in himself? why, then, behold.

---

* *midst*] The second 4to "*in* middest."
† *forsakes*] The old eds. "forsak'st," and in the next
line "bidst."
‡ *in*] The old ed. "*on.*"

   " *Bil.* Signior,—

   " *Mal.* My right worshipful lord, your court
" night-cap makes you have a passing high fore-
" head.

   " *Bil.* I can tell you strange news, but I am sure
" you know them already: the duke speaks much
" good of you.

   " *Mal.* Go to, then: and shall you and I now
" enter into a strict friendship?

   " *Bil.* Second one another?

   " *Mal.* Yes.

   " *Bil.* Do one another good offices?

   " *Mal.* Just: what though I called thee old ox,
" egregious wittol, broken-bellied coward, rotten
" mummy? yet, since I am in favour——

   " *Bil.* Words of course, terms of disport. His
" grace presents you by me a chain, as his grateful
" remembrance for—I am ignorant for what;
" marry, ye may impart: yet howsoever—come—
" dear friend; dost know my son?

   " *Mal.* Your son?

   " *Bil.* He shall eat wood-cocks, dance jigs, make
" possets, and play at shuttle-cock with any young
" lord about the court: he has as sweet a lady
" too; dost know her little bitch?

   " *Mal.* 'Tis a dog, man.

   " *Bil.* Believe me, a she-bitch: O, 'tis a good
" creature! thou shalt be her servant. I'll make
" thee acquainted with my young wife too: what!
" I keep her not at court for nothing. 'Tis grown
" to supper-time; come to my table: that, any
" thing I have, stands open to thee.

   " *Mal.* [*aside to* Celso] How smooth to him
" that is in state of grace,
" How servile is the rugged'st courtier's face!
" What profit, nay, what nature would keep down,
" Are heav'd to them are minions to a crown.
" Envious ambition never sates his thirst,
" Till sucking all, he swells and swells, and burst.*

   " *Bil.* I shall now leave you with my always-best
" wishes; only let's hold betwixt us a firm corre-
" spondence, a mutual-friendly-reciprocal kind of
" steady-unanimous-heartily-leagued——

   " *Mal.* Did your signiorship ne'er see a pigeon-
" house that was smooth, round, and white with-
" out, and full of holes and stink within? ha' ye
" not, old courtier?

   " *Bil.* O, yes, 'tis the form, the fashion of them
" all.

   " *Mal.* Adieu, my true court-friend; farewell,
" my dear Castilio. †   [*Exit* Bilioso.

---

* *burst*] The old ed. "*burstes.*"
† *Castilio*] An allusion to Baldassar Castiglione: see
note ‡, p. 209.

Celso. Yonder's Mendoza.

Mal. True, the privy-key. [*Descries* MENDOZA.

Celso. I take my leave, sweet lord.

Mal. 'Tis fit; away!   [*Exit* CELSO.

Enter MENDOZA *with three or four Suitors.*

Men. Leave your suits with me; I can and will: attend my secretary; leave me.   [*Exeunt* Suitors.

Mal. Mendoza, hark ye, hark ye. You are a treacherous villain: God b' wi' ye!

Men. Out, you base-born rascal!

Mal. We are all the sons of heaven, though a tripe-wife were our mother: ah, you whoreson, hot-reined he-marmoset! Ægisthus! didst ever hear of one Ægisthus?

Men. Gisthus?

Mal. Ay, Ægisthus: he was a filthy incontinent flesh-monger, such a one as thou art.

Men. Out, grumbling rogue!

Mal. Orestes, beware Orestes!

Men. Out, beggar!

Mal. I once shall rise.

Men. Thou rise!

Mal. Ay, at the resurrection.
No vulgar seed but once may rise and shall;
No king so huge but 'fore he die may fall. [*Exit.*

Men. Now, good Elysium! what a ´delicious heaven is it for a man to be in a prince's favour! O sweet God! O pleasure! O fortune! O all thou best of life! what should I think, what say, what do to be a favourite, a minion? to have a general timorous respect observe a man, a stateful silence in his presence, solitariness in his absence, a confused hum and busy murmur of obsequious suitors training him; the cloth held up, and way proclaimed before him; petitionary vassals licking the pavement with their slavish knees, whilst some odd palace-lampreels that engender with snakes, and are full of eyes on both sides, with a kind of insinuated * humbleness, .fix all their delights † upon his brow. O blessed state! what a ravishing prospect doth the Olympus of favour yield! Death, I cornute the duke! Sweet women! most sweet ladies! nay, angels! by heaven, he is more accursed than a devil that hates you, or is hated by you; and happier than a god that loves you, or is beloved by you: you preservers of mankind, life-blood of society, who would live, nay, who can live without you? O paradise! how majestical is your austerer presence! how imperiously chaste is your more modest face! but, O, how full of ravishing

* *insinuated*] The first 4to. "*insinuating.*"
† *delights*] The first 4to. "*lights.*"

attraction is your pretty, petulant, languishing, lasciviously-composed countenance! these amorous smiles, those soul-warming sparkling glances, ardent as those flames that singed the world by heedless Phaeton! in body how delicate,* in soul how witty, in discourse how pregnant, in life how wary, in favours how judicious, in day how sociable, and in night how ——
O pleasure unutterable! indeed, it is most certain, one man cannot deserve only to enjoy a beauteous woman: but a duchess! in despite of Phœbus, I'll write a sonnet instantly in praise of her.

Exit.

————

SCENE II.†

Enter FERNEZE *ushering* AURELIA, EMILIA *and* MAQUERELLE *bearing up her train,* BIANCA *attending: then exeunt* EMILIA *and* BIANCA.

Aurel. And is't possible! Mendoza slight me! possible?

Fer. Possible!
What can be strange in him that's drunk with favour,‡
Grows insolent with grace?—Speak, Maquerelle, speak.

Maq. To speak feelingly, more, more richly in solid sense than worthless words, give me those jewels of your ears to receive my enforced duty. As for my part, 'tis well known I can put up § any thing [FERNEZE *privately feeds* MAQUERELLE'S *hands with jewels during this speech*]; can bear patiently with any man: but when I heard he wronged your precious sweetness, I was enforced to take deep offence. 'Tis most certain he loves Emilia with high appetite: and, as she told me (as you know we women impart our secrets one to another), when she repulsed his suit, in that he was possessed with your endeared grace, Mendoza most ingratefully renounced all faith to you.

Fer. Nay, called you—Speak, Maquerelle, speak.

Maq. By heaven, witch, dried biscuit; and contested blushlessly he loved you but for a spurt or so.

* *in body how delicate,* &c.] The author had here an eye to the well-known passage of Shakespeare;—"What a piece of work is man! How noble in reason! how infinite in faculties! in form, and moving, how express and admirable! in action, how like an angel! in apprehension, how like a god! the beauty of the world! the paragon of animals!" *Hamlet,* act ii. sc. 2.
† *Scene II.*] Another room in the same.
‡ *with favour*] Omitted in the copy of the second 4to. in the Garrick Collection.
§ *up*] Not in the second 4to.

Fer. For maintenance.

Maq. Advancement and regard.

Aurel. O villain! O impudent Meudoza!

Maq. Nay, he is the rustiest-jawed,* the foulest-mouthed knave in railing against our sex: he will rail against† women—

Aurel. How! how!

Maq. I am ashamed to speak't, I.

Aurel. I love to hate him : speak.

Maq. Why, when Emilia scorned his base unsteadiness, the black-throated rascal scolded, and said—

Aurel. What?

Maq. Troth, 'tis too shameless.

Aurel. What said he?

Maq. Why, that, at four, women were fools; at fourteen, drabs; at forty, bawds; at fourscore, witches; and [at] a hundred, cats.

Aurel. O unlimitable impudency!

Fer. But as for poor Ferneze's fixèd heart,
Was never shadeless meadow drier parch'd
Under the scorching heat of heaven's dog,
Than is my heart with your enforcing eyes.

Maq. A hot simile.

Fer. Your smiles have been my heaven, your frowns my hell:
O, pity, then! grace should with beauty dwell.

Maq. Reasonable perfect, by'r lady.

Aurel. I will love thee, be it but in despite
Of that Mendoza :—witch!—Ferneze,—witch!—
Ferneze, thou art the duchess' favourite:
Be faithful, private: but 'tis dangerous.

Fer. His love is lifeless that for love fears breath :
The worst that's due to sin, O, would 'twere death!

Aurel. Enjoy my favour. I will be sick instantly and take physic: therefore in depth of night visit—

Maq. Visit her chamber, but conditionally you shall not offend her bed : by this diamond!

Fer. By this diamond. [*Giving diamond to* MAQ.

Maq. Nor tarry longer than you please : by this ruby!

Fer. By this ruby.   [*Giving ruby to* MAQ.

Maq. And that the door shall not creak.

Fer. And that the door shall not creak.

Mac. Nay, but swear.'

Fer. By this purse.   [*Giving purse to* MAQ.

Maq. Go to, I'll keep your oaths for you: remember, visit.

---

* *rustiest-jawed*] The second 4to. "rustiest *jawle;*" a misprint which is followed in modern editions of this play.

† *against*] The first 4to "*agen.*"

Aurel. Dried biscuit!—Look where the base wretch comes.

Enter MENDOZA, *reading a sonnet.*

Men. "*Beauty's life, heaven's model, love's queen,*"—

Maq. That's his Emilia.

Men. "*Nature's triumph, best on* earth,*"—

Maq. Meaning Emilia.

Men. "*Thou only wonder that the world hath seen,*"—

Maq. That's Emilia.

Aurel. Must I, then, hear her praised?—Mendoza!

Men. Madam, your excellency is graciously encountered : I have been writing passionate flashes in honour of—   [*Exit* FERNEZE.

Aurel. Out, villain, villain!
O judgment, where have been my eyes? what
Bewitch'd election made me dote on thee?
What sorcery made me love thee! But, be gone;
Bury thy head. O, that I could do more
Than loathe thee! hence, worst of ill!
No reason ask, our reason is our will.†
                    [*Exit with* MAQUERELLE.

Men. Women! nay, Furies; nay, worse; for they torment only the bad, but women good and bad. Damnation of mankind! Breath, hast thou praised them for this? and is't you, Ferneze, are wriggled into smock-grace? sit sure. O, that I could rail against these monsters in nature, models of hell, curse of the earth, women! that dare attempt any thing, and what they attempt they care not how they accomplish; without all premeditation or prevention; rash in asking, desperate in working, impatient in suffering, extreme in desiring, slaves unto appetite, mistresses in dissembling, only constant in unconstancy,‡ only perfect in counterfeiting: their

---

* *on*] The first 4to "*of.*"

† *No reason, &c.*] The first 4to;
      "No reason *else*, my reason is *my* will."

‡ *only constant in unconstancy*] Compare a striking passage in *The Fair Maide of Bristow*, 1605;
"A harlot's love is like a chimney-smoke,
    Quivering in the aire betweene two blasts of winde,
    Borne heere and there by either of the same,
    And properly to none of both inclind :
    Hate and despaire is painted in their eies,
    Deceit and treason in their bosome lies:
    Their promises are made of brittle glasse,
    Ground like a phillip to the finest dust ;
    Their thoughts like streaming rivers swiftly passe ;
    Their words are oyle, and yet they geather rust :
    True are they never found but in untruth,
    Constant in nought but in unconstancie,
    Devouring cankars of mans liberty." Sig E 3.
(The play just quoted was no doubt written several

words are feigned, their eyes forged, their sighs*
dissembled, their looks counterfeit, their hair
false, their given hopes deceitful, their very
breath artificial: their blood is their only god;
bad clothes, and old age, are only the devils they
tremble at. That I could rail now!

Enter PIETRO, his sword drawn.

Pietro. A mischief fill thy throat, thou foul-
jaw'd slave!
Say thy prayers.

Men. I ha' forgot 'em.

Pietro. Thou shalt die.

Men. So shalt thou. I am heart-mad.

Pietro. I am horn-mad.

Men. Extreme mad.

Pietro. Monstrously mad.

Men. Why?

Pietro. Why! thou, thou hast dishonoured my
bed.

Men. I! Come, come, sit;† here's my bare
heart to thee,
As steady as is the centre to this‡ glorious world:
And yet, hark, thou art a cornuto,—but by me?

Pietro. Yes, slave, by thee.

Men. Do not, do not with tart and spleenful
breath
Lose him can lose thee. I offend my duke!
Bear record, O ye dumb and raw-air'd nights,
How vigilant my sleepless eyes have been
To watch the traitor! record, thou spirit of truth,
With what debasement I ha' thrown myself
To under-offices, only to learn
The truth, the party, time, the means, the place,
By whom, and when, and where thou wert
disgrac'd!
And am I paid with slave? hath my intrusion
To places private and prohibited,
Only to observe the closer passages,
Heaven knows with vows of revelation,
Made me suspected, made me deem'd a villain?
What rogue hath wrong'd us?

Pietro. Mendoza, I may err.

Men. Err! 'tis too mild a name: but err and err,
Run giddy with suspect, 'fore through me thou
know
That which most creatures, save thyself, do know:

years before it was given to the press.) So also in a volume
of poems by Philip Jenkins, entitled *Amorea*, 1660:
    "What, *only constant in unconstancie?*
      And true alone to mutability?" p. 52.
  * *sighs*] Both 4tos. "*sights*"; and, indeed, so the word
was sometimes written.
  † *sit*] Qy. "sir"?
  ‡ *the centre to this*] The first 4to. "*this* center to this;"
the second 4to. "*this* centre to *the.*"

Nay, since my service hath so loath'd reject,
'Fore I'll reveal, shalt find them clipt* together.

Pietro. Mendoza, thou knowest I am a most
plain-breasted man.

Men. The fitter to make a cornuto:† would
your brows were most plain too!

Pietro. Tell me: indeed, I heard thee rail—

Men. At women, true: why, what cold phlegm
could choose,
Knowing a lord so honest, virtuous,
So boundless loving, bounteous, fair-shap'd, sweet,
To be contemn'd, abus'd, defam'd, made cuckold?
Heart! I hate all women for't: sweet sheets, wax
lights, antic bed-posts, cambric smocks, villanous
curtains, arras pictures, oiled hinges, and all the‡
tongue-tied lascivious witnesses of great creatures'
wantonness,—what salvation can you expect?

Pietro. Wilt thou tell me?

Men. Why, you may find it yourself; observe,
observe.

Pietro. I ha' not the patience: wilt thou deserve me, § tell, give it.

Men. Take't: why, Ferneze is the man, Ferneze: I'll prove't; this night you shall take him
in your sheets: will't serve?

Pietro. It will; my bosom's in some peace: till
night—

Men. What?

Pietro. Farewell.

Men. God! how weak a lord are you!
Why, do you think there is no more but so?

Pietro. Why!

Men. Nay, then, will I presume to counsel you:
It should be thus. You with some guard upon
the sudden
Break into the princess' chamber: I stay behind,
Without the door, through which he needs must
pass:
Ferneze flies; let him: to me he comes; he's kill'd
By me, observe, by me: you follow: I rail,
And seem to save the body. Duchess comes,
On whom (respecting her advancèd birth,
And your fair nature), I know, nay, I do know,
No violence must be us'd; she comes: I storm,
I praise, excuse Ferneze, and still maintain
The duchess' honour: she for this loves me.
I honour you; shall know her soul, you mine:
Then naught shall she contrive in vengeance
(As women are most thoughtful in revenge)
Of her Ferneze, but you shall sooner know't

  * *clipt*] i.e. joined in embraces.
  † *cornuto*] The second 4to. "*cuckolde.*"
  ‡ *the*] The first 4to. "*yee.*"
  § *deserve me*] i.e. deserve of me.

Than she can think't. Thus shall his death come
      sure,
Your duchess brain-caught: so your life secure.

Pietro. It is too well: my bosom and my heart,
When nothing helps, cut off the rotten part.
                                              [*Exit.*

Men. Who cannot feign friendship can ne'er
produce the effects of hatred. Honest fool duke!
subtle lascivious duchess! silly novice Ferneze!
I do laugh at ye. My brain is in labour till it
produce mischief, and I feel sudden throes, proofs
sensible, the issue is at hand.
As bears shape young, so I'll form my device,
Which grown proves horrid: vengeance makes
      men wise.   [*Exit.*

"SCENE III.*

"Enter MALEVOLE *and* PASSARELLO.

"Mal. Fool, most happily encountered: canst
"sing, fool?

"Pass. Yes, I can sing, fool, if you'll bear the
"burden; and I can play upon instruments,
"scurvily, as gentlemen do. O, that I had been
"gelded! I should then have been a fat fool for
"a chamber, a squeaking fool for a tavern, and a
"private fool for all the ladies.

"Mal. You are in good case since you came to
"court, fool: what, guarded, guarded!†

"Pass. Yes, faith, even as footmen and bawds
"wear velvet, not for an ornament of honour,
"but for a badge of drudgery; for, now the duke
"is discontented, I am fain to fool him asleep
"every night.

"Mal. What are his griefs?

"Pass. He hath sore eyes.

"Mal. I never observed so much.

"Pass. Horrible sore eyes; and so hath every
"cuckold, for the roots of the horns spring in the
"eyeballs, and that's the reason the horn of a
"cuckold is as tender as his eye, or as that
"growing in the woman's forehead twelve years
"since,‡ that could not endure to be touched.
"The duke hangs down his head like a columbine.

---

* *Scene III.*] Another room in the same.

† *guarded*] Adorned with facings, trimmings.

‡ *as that growing in the woman's forehead twelve years
since*] The woman with the horn in her forehead was
probably Margaret Griffith, wife of David Owen, of Llan
Gaduain, in Montgomery. A portrait of her is in
existence, prefixed to a scarce pamphlet, entitled,
"*A miraculous and monstrous, but yet most true and
certayne Discourse of a Woman, now to be seen in London,*

"Mal. Passarello, why do great men beg
"fools?*

"Pass. As the Welshman stole rushes, when
"there was nothing else to filch; only to keep
"begging in fashion.

"Mal. Pooh, thou givest no good reason; thou
"speakest like a fool.

"Pass. Faith, I utter small fragments, as your
"knight courts your city widow with jingling of
"his gilt spurs, advancing his bush-coloured
"beard,† and taking tobacco: this is all the
"mirror of their knightly compliments.‡ Nay, I
"shall talk when my tongue is a-going once; 'tis
"like a citizen on horse-back, evermore in a false
"gallop.

"Mal. And how doth Macquerelle fare now-a-
"days?·

"Pass. Faith, I was wont to salute her as our
"English women are at their first landing in
"Flushing;§ I would call her whore: but now
"that antiquity leaves her as an old piece of
"plastic|| to work by, I only ask her how her
"rotten teeth fare every morning, and so leave
"her. She was the first that ever invented
"perfumed smocks for the gentlewomen, and
"woollen shoes, for fear of creaking, for the visitant.
"She were an excellent lady, but that her face
"peeleth like Muscovy glass.¶

---

*of the age of threescore yeares or thereabouts, in the midst of
whose forehead there groweth out a crooked Horne of four
ynches long. Imprinted at London, by Thomas Orwin, and
are to be sold by Edward White, dwelling at the little north
dore of Paules Church, at the signe of the Gun, 1588."*
O. *Gilchrist.*

If she is the person alluded to, this additional scene
must have been composed about 1600.

* *beg fools*] i.e. apply to become their guardians, and
to enjoy the profits of their lands; which, under the
writ, in the old common law, *de idiota inquirendo,* might
be granted by the king to any subject.

† *with jingling of his gilt spurs, advancing his bush-
coloured beard*] The gallants of the time considered it high
fashion to wear spurs which jingled as they walked.—I
here follow the text of my own copy of the second 4to.:
the copy in the Garrick Collection (*the same edition*) has
"*with something of his guilt: some aduancing his high-
colored beard.*"

‡ *compliments*] i.e. accomplishments.

§ *as our English women are at their first landing in
Flushing*] "At this time *Flushing* was in the hands of
the English as part of the security for money advanced
by Queen Elizabeth to the Dutch. The governor and
garrison were all Englishmen."—*Reed.*

|| *an old piece of plastic*] "i.e. an ancient model made of
wax or clay, by which an artist might work."—*Steevens.*

¶ *Muscovy glass*] i.e. talc. Here Reed cites the following passages:
"In the province of Corelia, and about the river
"Dwyna towards the North-sea, there groweth a soft
"rocke which they call Slude. This they cut into
"pieces, and so tear it into thin *flakes, which naturally it*

" *Mal.* And how doth thy old lord, that hath
"wit enough to be a flatterer, and conscience
"enough to be a knave?

" *Pass.* O, excellent: he keeps beside me fifteen
"jesters, to instruct him in the art of fooling,
"and utters their jests in private to the duke
"and duchess: he'll lie like to your Switzer
"or lawyer; he'll be of any side for most
"money.

" *Mal.* I am in haste, be brief.

" *Pass.* As your fiddler when he is paid.—He'll
"thrive, I warrant you, while your young courtier
"stands like Good-Friday in Lent; men long to
"see it, because more fatting days come after it;

"else he's the leanest and pitifullest actor in the
"whole pageant. Adieu, Malevole.

" *Mal.* [*aside*] O world most vile, when thy
"loose vanities,
"Taught by this fool, do make the fool seem
"wise !

" *Pass.* You'll know me again, Malevole.

" *Mal.* O, ay, by that velvet.

" *Pass.* Ay, as a pettifogger by his buckram
"bag. I am as common in the court as an
"hostess's lips in the country; knights, and
"clowns, and knaves, and all share me: the
"court cannot possibly be without me. Adieu,
"Malevole."   [*Exeunt.*

ACT II.

SCENE I.[*]

Enter MENDOZA *with a sconce,[†] to observe* FERNEZE'S *entrance, who, whilst the act is playing, enters unbraced,*
Two Pages before him with lights; is met by MAQUE-
RELLE *and conveyed in; the Pages are[‡] sent away.*

Men. He's caught, the woodcock's head is i'the
    noose.
Now treads Ferneze in dangerous path of lust,
Swearing his sense is merely[§] deified :
The fool grasps clouds, and shall beget Centaurs :
And now, in strength of panting faint delight,
The goat bids heaven envy him. Good goose,
I can afford thee nothing

But the poor comfort of calamity, pity.
Lust's like the plummets hanging on clock-lines,
Will ne'er ha' done till all is quite undone ;
Such is the course salt sallow lust doth run ;
Which thou shalt try. I'll be reveng'd. Duke,
    thy suspect ;
Duchess, thy disgrace ; Ferneze, thy rivalship ;
Shall have swift vengeance. Nothing so holy,
No band of nature so strong,
No law of friendship so sacred,
But I'll profane, burst, violate, 'fore I'll
Endure disgrace, contempt, and poverty.
Shall I, whose very hum struck all heads bare,
Whose face made silence, creaking of whose shoe
Forc'd the most private passages fly ope,
Scrape like a servile dog at some latch'd door?
Learn now to make a leg, and cry "Beseech ye,
Pray ye, is such a lord within?" be aw'd
At some odd usher's scoff'd formality?
First sear my brains ! *Unde cadis, non quo,*
    refert ;[*]
My heart cries, "Perish all !" How ! how ! what
    fate
Can once avoid revenge, that's desperate?
I'll to the duke: if all should ope—if I tush,
Fortune still dotes on those who cannot blush.
    [*Exit.*

" *is apt for,* and so use it for glasse lanthorns and such
"like. It giveth both inwards and outwards a clearer
"light then glasse, and for this respect is better than
"either glasse or horne; for that it neither breaketh like
"glasse, nor yet will burne like the lanthorne."
    Giles Fletcher's *Russe Commonwealth*, 1591, p. 10.
"They have no English glass : of slices of a rocke,
    Hight *Sluda*, they their windowes make, that English
    glass doth mocke.
They cut it very thinne, and sew it with a thred
In pretie order, like to panes, to serve their present
    needs :
No other glasse, good faith, doth give a better light,
And sure the rocke is nothing rich, the cost is very
    slight."
    Turbervile's *Letter to Spenser*, *Hackluyt*, 1589, p. 410.
  * *Scene I.*] Ante-chamber to the apartments of the
Duchess in the palace.
  † *sconce*] i.e. lantern.
  ‡ *the payes are*] The first 4to. "the *Dutches* pages."
  § *merely*] i.e. absolutely.

  * *Unde cadis, non quo, refert*]
               "Magis unde cadas,
  Quam quo, refert." Seneca,—*Thyest.* 925.

SCENE II.*

Enter MALEVOLE *at one door;* BIANCA, EMILIA, *and* MAQUERELLE *at the other door.*

Mal. Bless ye, cast o' ladies!†—Ha, dipsas!‡ how dost thou, old coal?

Maq. Old coal!

Mal. Ay, old coal: methinks thou liest like a brand under these§ billots of green wood. He that will inflame a young wench's heart, let him lay close to her an old coal that hath first been fired, a panderess, my half-burnt lint, who though thou canst not flame thyself, yet art able to set a thousand virgins' tapers afire.—And how does‖ Jauivere thy husband, my little periwinkle? is he troubled with the cough o' the lungs still? does he hawk o'nights still? he will not bite.

Bian. No, by my troth, I took him with his mouth empty of old teeth.

Mal. And he took thee with thy belly full of young bones: marry, he took his maim by the stroke of his enemy.

Bian. And I mine by the stroke of my friend.

Mal. The close stock!¶ O mortal wench! Lady, ha' ye now no restoratives for your decayed Jasons?** look ye, crab's guts baked, distilled ox-pith, the pulverized hairs of a lion's upper-lip, jelly of cock-sparrows, he-monkey's marrow, or powder of fox-stones?—And whither are all†† you ambling now?

Bian. Why,* to bed, to bed.

Mal. Do your husbands lie with ye?

Bian. That were country fashion, i'faith.

Mal. Ha' ye no foregoers about you? come, whither in good deed, la, now?

Maq.† In good indeed, la, now, to eat the most miraculously, admirably, astonishable composed posset with three curds, without any drink. Will ye help me with a he-fox?—Here's the duke.

"*Mal.* Fried frogs are very good, and French-"like too." '[*Exeunt* Ladies.

Enter PIETRO, CELSO, EQUATO, BILIOSO, FERRARDO, *and* MENDOZA.

Pietro. The night grows deep and foul: what hour is't?

Celso. Upon the stroke of twelve.

Mal. Save ye, duke!

Pietro. From thee: be gone, I do not love thee; let me see thee no more; we are displeased.

Mal. Why, God b'wi' thee!‡ Heaven hear my curse,—may thy wife and thee live long together!

Pietro. Be gone, sirrah!

Mal. When Arthur first in court began,§—Agamemnon—Menelaus—was ever any duke a cornuto?

Pietro. Be gone, hence!

Mal. What religion wilt thou be of next?

Men. Out with him!

Mal. With most servile patience.—Time will come

When wonder of thy error will strike dumb Thy bezzled‖ sense.—

The slave's in favour: ay, marry, shall he rise:¶ Good God! how subtle hell doth flatter vice! Mounts** him aloft, and makes him seem to fly, As fowl the tortoise mock'd, who to the sky The ambitious shell-fish rais'd! the end of all Is only, that from height he might dead fall.

"*Bil.* Why, when?†† out, ye rogue! be gone, "ye rascal!

"*Mal.* I shall now leave ye with all my best "*Bil.* Out, ye cur! ["wishes.

---

* *Scene II.*] A room in the same.

† *cast o' ladies*] i.e. brace, couple of ladies. (Dodsley, whom all the editors have followed here, printed "*chaste* ladies" !). The expression is drawn from falconry:
"A *cast of faulcons* (in their pride
At passage scouring) fowle espide
Securely feeding from the spring:
At one both ayme with nimble wing.
They first mount up above mans sight,
Flying for life this emulous flight
In equall compasse, and maintaine
Their pitch without a lazie plaine.
Then stooping freely (lightning-like)
They (counter) dead each other strike.
The fowle escapes, and with her wings
Their funerall dirge, this lesson, sings,—
Who aims at glory not aright
Meetes death, but glorie takes her flight."
Scott's *Certaine Pieces of this Age Parabolis'd*, p. 89, printed with his *Philomythie*, 1616.

‡ *dipsas*] A kind of serpent; those whom it bit were said to die tormented with thirst; hence Lucan, "*torrida dipsas.*"

§ *these*] Not in the second 4to.

‖ *does*] The second 4to. "*dooth.*"

¶ *stock*] i.e. stoccata. See note §, p. 223.

** *Jasons*] The first 4to. "*Jason.*"

†† *all*] Not in the second 4to.

---

* *Why*] Not in the second 4to.

† *Maq.*] The second 4to. gives this speech to Bianca.

‡ *b'wi' thee*] The second 4to. "*be with thee.*"

§ *When Arthur, &c.*] "This entire ballad (which Falstaff likewise begins to sing in the Second Part of *King Henry IV.*) is published in the first volume of Dr. Percy's *Reliques of Ancient English Poetry.*"—Reed.

‖ *bezzled*] i.e. besotted: to *bezzle* is to drink hard.

¶ *The slave's in favour: ay, marry, shall he rise*] The true reading here is uncertain. The 4tos. have "*slaues* I *fauour, I marry shall he rise,*" &c. Dodsley gave "Slaves to favour, marry, shall *arise*," &c.

** *Mounts*] The first 4to. "*mount.*"

†† *when*] See note *, p. 68.

"*Mal.* Only let's hold together a firm corre-
"*Bil.* Out!   ["spondence.
"*Mal.* A mutual*-friendly-reciprocal-perpetual
"kind of steady-unanimous-heartily-leagued—
"*Bil.* Hence, ye gross-jawed, peasantly—out, go!
"*Mal.* Adieu, pigeon-house; thou burr, that
"only stickest to nappy fortunes. The serpigo,
"the strangury, an eternal uneffectual priapism
"seize thee!
"*Bil.* Out, rogue!
"*Mal.* Mayst thou be a notorious wittolly
"pander to thine own wife, and yet get no office,
"but live to be the utmost misery of mankind, a
"beggarly cuckold!"   [*Exit.*
Pietro. It shall be so.
Men. It must be so, for where great states
     revenge,
'Tis requisite the parties with piety   \
And soft respect ever be closely dogg'd.†
Lay one into his breast shall sleep with him,
Feed in the same dish, run in self-faction,
Who may discover‡ any shape of danger;
For once disgrac'd, displayèd§ in offence,
It makes man blushless, and man is (all confess)
More prone to vengeance than to gratefulness.
Favours are writ in dust; but stripes we feel
Depravèd nature stamps in lasting steel.
Pietro. You shall be leagu'd with the duchess.
Equato. The plot is very good.
Pietro.‖ You shall both kill, and seem the corse
Fer. A most fine brain-trick.   [to *savu.*
Celso. [*aside*] Of a most cunning knave.
Pietro. My lords, the heavy action we intend
Is death and shame, two of the ugliest shapes
That can confound a soul; think, think of it:
I strike, but yet, like him that 'gainst stone walls
Directs, his shafts rebound in his own face;
My lady's shame is mine, O God, 'tis mine!
Therefore I do conjure all secrecy:
Let it¶ be as very little as may be,
Pray ye, as may be.

Make frightless entrance, salute her with soft eyes,
Stain naught with blood; only Ferneze dies,
But not before her brows. O gentlemen,
God knows I love her! Nothing else, but this:—
I am not well: if grief, that sucks veins dry,
Rivels the skin, casts ashes in men's faces,
Be-dulls the eye, unstrengthens all the blood,
Chance to remove me to another world,
As sure I once must die, let him succeed:
I have no child; all that my youth begot
Hath been your loves, which shall inherit me:
Which as it ever shall, I do conjure it,
Mendoza may succeed: he's nobly* born;
With me of much desert.
Celso. [*aside*] Much!†
Pietro. Your silence answers, "Ay:"
I thank you. Come on now. O, that I might die
Before her shame's display'd! would I were
     forc'd
To burn my father's tomb, unheal‡ his bones,
And dash them in the dirt, rather than this!
This both the living and the dead offends:
Sharp surgery where naught but death amends.
     [*Exeunt.*

SCENE II.§

Enter MAQUERELLE, EMILIA, *and* BIANCA, *with a posset.*

Maq. Even here it is, three curds in three
     regions individually distinct,
Most methodically‖ according to art compos'd,
     without any drink.
Bian. Without any drink!
Maq. Upon my honour. Will ye sit and eat?
Emil. Good the composure: the receipt, how
     is't?
Maq. 'Tis a pretty pearl; by this pearl, (how
does't with me!) thus it is. Seven and thirty
yolks of Barbary hens' eggs; eighteen spoonfuls
and a half of the juice of cock-sparrow bones;
one ounce, three drams, four scruples, and one
quarter of the syrup of Ethiopian dates;
sweetened with three quarters of a pound of
pure candied Indian eringoes; strewed over with

---

* *A mutual, &c.*] Billoso's words in p. 332.
† *'Tis requisite the parties with piety
   And soft respect ever be closely dogg'd*] The 4tos. have;
" *Tis requisite, the parts* [sec. 4to. "*partes*"] *with piety
   And soft* [sec. 4to. "*loft*"] *respect forbeares, be closely
   dogd,*" &c.
It seems impossible to ascertain what the author really
wrote. Mr. W. N. Lettsom proposes;
   " *Men.*   It must be so, for where
   Great states revenge, 'tis requisite the parties
   With *spy of close suspect* be closely dogg'd," &c.
‡ *discover*] The first 4to. "*disseuer.*"
§ *displayèd*] The first 4to. "*discoured.*"
‖ *Pietro*] The 4tos. "*Mend.*"
¶ *it*] i.e. the shame.

* *nobly*] The second 4to. "*noble.*"
† *Much!*] A contemptuous and ironical exclamation,
frequently used by our old dramatists, and expressing
denial. ("*Much of that,*"=Little or none of it.)
‡ *unheal*] i.e. uncover. To *heal* in Sussex signifies to
cover."—*Steevens.*—The first 4to. "*unhill.*"
§ *Scene III.*] Antechamber to the apartments of the
duchess in the same.
‖ *methodically*] The second 4to. "*methodicall.*"

the powder of pearl of America, amber of Cataia, and lamb-stones of Muscovia.

Bian. Trust me, the ingredients are very cordial, and, no question, good, and most powerful in restauration.*

Maq. I know not what you mean by restauration; but this it doth,—it purifieth the blood, smootheth the skin, enliveneth the eye, strengtheneth the veins, mundifieth the teeth, comforteth the stomach, fortifieth the back, and quickeneth the wit; that's all.

Emil. By my troth, I have eaten but two spoonfuls, and methinks I could discourse most swiftly and wittily already.

Maq. Have you the art to seem honest?

Bian. Ay, thank advice and practice.

Maq. Why, then, eat me o' this posset, quicken your blood, and preserve your beauty. Do you know Doctor Plaster-face? by this curd, he is the most exquisite in forging of veins, sprightening of eyes, dying of hair, sleeking of skins, blushing of cheeks, surphling † of breasts, blanching and bleaching of teeth, that ever made an old lady gracious by torch-light; by this curd, la.

Bian. Well,‡ we are resolved, what God has given us we'll cherish.

Maq. Cherish any thing saving your husband; keep him not too high, lest he leap the pale: but, for your beauty, let it be your saint; bequeath two hours to it every morning in your closet. I ha' been young, and yet, in my conscience, I am not above five-and-twenty: but, believe me, preserve and use your beauty; for youth and beauty once gone, we are like bee-hives without honey, out-o'-fashion apparel that no man will wear: therefore use me your beauty.

Emil. Ay, but men say—

Maq. Men say! let men say what they will! life o' woman! they are ignorant of our § wants. The more in years, the more in perfection they grow; if they lose youth and beauty, they gain wisdom and discretion: but when our beauty fades, good-night with us. There cannot be an uglier thing to see than an old woman : from

which, O pruning, pinching, and painting, deliver all sweet beauties !   [*Music within.*

Bian. Hark ! music !

Maq. Peace, 'tis i' the duchess' bed-chamber. Good rest, most prosperously-graced ladies.

Emil. Good night, sentinel.

Bian. Night, dear Maquerelle.

Maq. May my posset's operation send you my wit and honesty; and me, your youth and beauty: the pleasingest rest !
        [*Exeunt, at one door,* Bianca *and* Emilia ; *at another,* Maquerelle.

A Song* within.

Whilst the song is singing, enter Mendoza *with his sword drawn, standing ready to murder* Ferneze *as he flies from the duchess' chamber.—Tumult within.*

[*Within.*] Strike, strike !

[*Aur. within.*] Save my Ferneze ! O, save my Ferneze !

[*Within.*] Follow, pursue !

[*Aur. within.*] O, save Ferneze !

Enter Ferneze *in his shirt, and is received upon* Mendoza's *sword.*

Men. Pierce, pierce !—Thou shallow fool, drop there !   [*Thrusts his rapier in* Ferneze.
He that attempts a princess' lawless love
Must have broad hands, close heart, with Argus' eyes,
And back of Hercules, or else he dies.

Enter Aurelia, Pietro, Ferrardo, Bilioso, Celso, *and* Equato.

All. Follow, follow !

Men. Stand off, forbear, ye most uncivil lords !

Pietro. Strike !

Men. Do not; tempt not a man resolv'd :
            [Mendoza *bestrides the wounded body of* Ferneze, *and seems to save him.*
Would you, inhuman murderers, more than death ?

Aur. O poor Ferneze !

Men. Alas, now all defence too late !

Aur. He's dead.

Pietro. I am sorry for our shame.—Go to your bed :
Weep not too much, but leave some tears to shed
When I am dead.

Aur. What, weep for thee ! my soul no tears shall find.

Pietro. Alas, alas, that women's souls are blind !

Men. Betray such beauty !

---

* *restauration*] The first 4to. "operation."

† *surphling of breasts*] i.e. beautifying breasts by cosmetics. "To *surphule* or *surfel* the cheeks," says Gifford, "is to wash them with mercurial or sulphur water," &c. Note on Ford's *Works,* i. 405.—All the editors of this play read "*soupling of breasts*" !

‡ *Well*] The second 4to. "*We.*"

§ *our*] The second 4to. "*your.*"

* *A Song*] See note †, p. 45.

Murder such youth! contemn civility!
He loves him not that rails not at him.

Pietro. Thou canst not move us: we have
blood enough.—
An please you, lady, we have quite forgot
All your defects: if not, why, then—

Aur. Not.

Pietro. Not: the best of rest; good-night.

[*Exeunt* PIETRO, FERRARDO, BILIOSO, CELSO,
and EQUATO.

Aur. Despite go with thee!

Men. Madam, you ha' done me foul disgrace;
you have wronged him much loves you too much:
go to; your soul knows you have.

Aur. I think I have.

Men. Do you but think so?

Aur. Nay, sure, I have : my eyes have witnessed
thy love : thou hast stood too firm for me.

Men. Why, tell me, fair-cheeked lady, who
even in tears art powerfully beauteous, what un-
advised passion struck ye into such a violent heat
against me? Speak, what mischief wronged us?
what devil injured us? speak.

Aur. The thing ne'er worthy of the name of
man, Ferneze;
Ferneze swore thou lov'[d]st Emilia;
Which to advance, with most reproachful breath
Thou both didst blemish and denounce my love.

Men. Ignoble villain! did I for this bestride
Thy wounded limbs? for this rank opposite
Even to my sovereign?* for this, O God, for this,
Sunk all my hopes, and with my hopes my life?
Ripp'd bare my throat unto the hangman's axe?—
Thou most dishonour'd trunk!—Emilia!
By life, I know her not—Emilia!—
Did you believe him?

Aur. Pardon me, I did.

Men. Did you? and thereupon you graced him?

Aur. I did.

Men. Took him to favour, nay, even clasp'd
with him?

Aur. Alas, I did!

Men. This night?

Aur. This night.

Men. And in your lustful twines the duke
took you?

Aur. A most sad truth.

Men. O God, O God! how we dull honest
souls,
Heavy-brain'd men, are swallow'd in the bogs
Of a deceitful ground! whilst nimble bloods,

Light-jointed spirits speed,* cut good men's
throats,
And scape. Alas, I am too honest for this age,
Too full of phlegm and heavy steadiness;
Stood still whilst this slave cast a noose about
me;
Nay, then to stand in honour of him and her,
Who had even slic'd my heart!

Aur. Come, I did err,
And am most sorry I did err.

Men. Why, we are both but dead : the duke
hates us;
And those whom princes do once groundly hate,
Let them provide to die, as sure as fate.
Prevention is the heart of policy.

Aur. Shall we murder him?

Men. Instantly?

Aur. Instantly; before he casts a plot,
Or further blaze my honour's much-known blot,
Let's murder him.

Men. I would do much for you : will yo marry
me?

Aur. I'll make thee duke. We are of Medicis;
Florence our friend; in court my faction †
Not meanly strengthful; the duke then dead;
We well prepar'd for change; the multitude
Irresolutely reeling; we in force;
Our party seconded; the kingdom maz'd;
No doubt of ‡ swift success all shall be grac'd.

Men. You do confirm me; we are resolute:
To-morrow look for change; rest confident.
'Tis now about the immodest waist of night:
The mother of moist dew with pallid light
Spreads gloomy shades about the numbed earth.
Sleep, sleep, whilst we contrive our mischief's
birth.
This man I'll get inhum'd. Farewell: to bed;
Ay, kiss thy § pillow, dream the duke is dead.
So, so, good night.   [*Exit* AURELIA.
          How fortune dotes on impudence! ||
I am in private the adopted son
Of yon good prince :
I must be duke; why, if I must, I must.
Most silly lord, name me! O heaven! I see
God made honest fools to maintain crafty knaves.

* *speed*] The first 4to. "pent," the second "spent."—
The reading in the text is Dodsley's,—and a doubtful one.
† *in court my faction, &c.*] "I would recommend the
following regulation, &c., of this speech :
—————— 'in court my faction
Not meanly strengthen'd (the duke then *being dead*)
We're well prepar'd for change.'"—*Steevens.*
‡ *of*] i.e. *with.*
§ *thy*] The second 4to. "the."
|| *How fortune dotes on impudence!*] So at p. 337;
"Fortune still dotes on those who cannot blush."

*   *for this rank opposite*
Even to my sovereign?] Not in the second 4to.

The duchess is wholly mine too; must kill her
    husband
To quit her shame; much! * then marry her: ay.
O, I grow proud in prosperous treachery!
As wrestlers clip,† so I'll embrace you all,
Not to support, but to procure your fall.

Enter MALEVOLE.

Mal. God arrest thee!

Men. At whose suit?

Mal. At the devil's. Ah, you treacherous
damnable monster, how dost? how dost, thou
treacherous rogue? Ah, ye rascal! I am banished
the court, sirrah.

Men. Prithee, let's be acquainted; I do love
thee, faith.

Mal. At your service, by the Lord, la: shall's
go to supper? Let's be once drunk together, and
so unite a most virtuously-strengthened friendship: shall's, Huguenot? shall's?

Men. Wilt fall upon my chamber to-morrow
morn?

Mal. As a raven to a dunghill. They say
there's one dead here; pricked for the pride of
the flesh.

Men. Ferneze: there he is; prithee, bury him.

Mal. O, most willingly: I mean to turn pure
Rochelle churchman,‡ I.

Men. Thou churchman! why, why?

Mal. Because I'll live lazily, rail upon authority,
deny kings' supremacy in things indifferent, and
be a pope in mine own parish.

Men. Wherefore dost thou think churches were
made?

Mal. To scour plough-shares: I ha' § seen oxen
plough up altars; *et nunc seges ubi Sion fuit.*‖

---

* *much!*] See note †, p. 339.
† *clip*] i. e. embrace.
‡ *Rochelle churchman*] "*Rochelle* was at this time held by
the Huguenots or Protestants, with the privilege of professing their religion unmolested. It was besieged, in
1573, by the duke of Anjou without success; but fell
into the hands of its enemies in 1629, after a long,
obstinate, and brave defence."—*Reed.*
§ *ha'*] The second 4to. "*have.*"
‖ *et nunc seges ubi Sion fuit*] "Jam seges est ubi Troja
fuit." *Ovid.—Her. Epist.* i. 53.

Men. Strange!

Mal. Nay, monstrous! I ha' seen a sumptuous
steeple turned to a stinking privy; more beastly,
the sacredest place made a dogs' kennel; nay, most
inhuman, the stoned coffins of long-dead Christians burst up, and made hogs' troughs: *hic finis
Priami.** Shall I ha' some sack and cheese at
thy chamber? Good night, good mischievous
incarnate devil; good night, Mendoza; ah, ye
inhuman villain, good night! night, rub.

Men. Good night: to-morrow morn?

Mal. Ay, I will come, friendly damnation, I will
come. [*Exit* MENDOZA.] I do descry cross-points;
honesty and courtship straddle as far asunder as
a true Frenchman's legs.

Fer. O!

Mal. Proclamations! more proclamations!

Fer. O! a surgeon!

Mal. Hark! lust cries for a surgeon. What
news from Limbo? how does† the grand cuckold,
Lucifer?

Fer. O, help, help! conceal and save me.

[FERNEZE *stirs, and* MALEVOLE *helps him up.*

Mal. Thy shame more than thy wounds do
    grieve me far:
Thy wounds but leave upon thy flesh some scar;
But fame ne'er heals, still rankles worse and worse;
Such is of uncontrollèd lust the curse.
Think what it is in lawless sheets to lie;
But, O Ferneze, what in lust to die!
Then thou that shame respect'st, O, fly converse
With women's eyes and lisping wantonness!
Stick candles 'gainst a virgin wall's white back,
If they not burn, yet at the least they'll black.
Come, I'll convey thee to a private port,
Where thou shalt live (O happy man!) from court.
The beauty of the day begins to rise,
From whose bright form night's heavy shadow flies.
Now gin close plots to work; the scene grows full,
And craves his eyes who hath a solid skull.

[*Exit, conveying* FERNEZE *away.*

---

* *hic finis Priami*] "Hæc finis Priami fatorum." *Virgil,
—Æn.* ii. 554.
† *does*] The second 4to. "*dooth.*"

ACT III.

SCENE I.*

Enter PIETRO, MENDOZA, EQUATO, *and* BILIOSO.

Pietro. 'Tis grown to youth of day : how shall
we waste this light ?
My heart's more heavy than a tyrant's crown.
Shall we go hunt ? Prepare for field.
                  [*Exit* EQUATO.

Men. Would ye could be merry !
Pietro. Would God I could ! Mendoza, bid 'em
haste.   [*Exit* MENDOZA.
I would fain shift place ; O vain relief !
Sad souls may well change place, but not change
grief :
As deer, being struck, fly thorough many soils,†
Yet still the shaft sticks fast, so——
  Bil. A good old simile, my honest lord.
  Pietro. I am not much unlike to some sick man
That long desired hurtful drink ; at last
Swills in and drinks his last, ending at once
Both life and thirst. O, would I ne'er had known
My own dishonour ! Good God, that men should
desire
To search out that, which, being found, kills all
Their joy of life ! to taste the tree of knowledge,
And then be driven from out paradise !—
Canst give me some comfort ?
  Bil. My lord, I have some books which have
been dedicated to my honour, and I ne'er read 'em,
and yet they had very fine names, *Physic for
Fortune*,‡ *Lozenges of sanctified sincerity ;*§ very
pretty works of curates, scriveners, and school-
masters. Marry, I remember one Seneca, Lucius
Annæus Seneca——
  Pietro. Out upon him ! he writ of temperance
and fortitude, yet lived like a voluptuous epicure,
and died like an effeminate coward.—Haste thee
to Florence :
Here, take our letters ; see 'em seal'd : away !
Report in private to the honour'd duke
His daughter's forc'd disgrace ; tell him at length
We know too much : due compliments* advance :
There's nought that's safe and sweet but igno-
rance.   [*Exit.*

" *Enter* BIANCA.

  " *Bil.* Madam, I am going ambassador for
" Florence ; 'twill be great charges to me.
  " *Bian.* No matter, my lord, you have the lease
" of two manors come out next Christmas ; you
" may lay your tenants on the greater rack for it :
" and when you come home again, I'll teach you
" how you shall get two hundred pounds a-year
" by your teeth.
  " *Bil.* How, madam ?
  " *Bian.* Cut off so much from house-keeping :
" that which is saved by the teeth, you know, is
" got by the teeth.
  " *Bil.* 'Fore God, and so I may ; I am in won-
" drous credit, lady.
  " *Bian.* See the use of flattery : I did ever
" counsel you to flatter greatness, and you have
" profited well : any man that will do so shall be
" sure to be like your Scotch barnacle,† now a
" block, instantly a worm, and presently a great
" goose : this it is to rot and putrify in the bosom
" of greatness.
  " *Bil.* Thou art ever my politician. O, how
" happy is that old lord that hath a politician to
" his young lady ! I'll have fifty gentlemen shall
" attend upon me : marry, the most of them
" shall be farmers' sons, because they shall bear
" their own charges ; and they shall go apparelled
" thus,—in sea-water-green suits, ash-colour cloaks,
" watchet‡ stockings, and popinjay-green feathers :
" will not the colours do excellent ?

---

* *Scene I.*] A room in the palace.
† *soils*] i.e., I believe, streams. At least, *to take soil* was
a common hunting-term, meaning *to take refuge in the
water.* So Petowe in his *Second Part of Hero and Leander*,
1598 :

   "The chased deare hath *soils* to coole his heate," &c.
See Appendix iii. to Marlowe's *Works*, iii. 344, ed. Dyce.
  ‡ *Physic for Fortune*] "In 1579 was published a book,
entitled *Physic against Fortune, as well prosperous as
adverse, contained in two Books. Written in Latin by Francis
Petrarch, a most famous poet and oratour, and now first
Englished by Thomas Twyne.* 4to. B. L."—*Reed.*
  § *Lozenges of sanctified sincerity*] "I have not met with
this book, but from the ridicule thrown out in *The Wits*,
I believe some one with a similar title had before
appeared."—*Reed.*
  The passage of Davenant's *Wits*, 1636, alluded to by
Reed, is the following :

   " 'A pill to purge phlebotomy,'—'A balsamum
    For the spiritual back,'—'*A lozenge against lust.*"
                       Act ii. sc. 1.

* *compliments*] The first 4to. "*complaints.*"
† *Scotch barnacle,* &c.] See, concerning this fiction, the
notes of the commentators on the *Tempest*, act iv. sc. last.
Malone's *Shakespeare*, by Boswell, vol. xv., pp. 155-6.
  ‡ *watchet*] i.e. pale blue.

" *Bian.* Out upon't! they'll look like citizens
" riding to their friends at Whitsuntide ; their
" apparel just so many several parishes.

" *Bil.* I'll have it so ; and Passarello, my fool,
" shall go along with me ; marry, he shall be in
" velvet.

" *Bian.* A fool in velvet!

" *Bil.* Ay, 'tis common for your fool to wear
" satin ; I'll have mine in velvet.

" *Bian.* What will you wear, then, my lord ?

" *Bil.* Velvet too ; marry, it shall be em-
" broidered, because I'll differ from the fool
" somewhat. I am horribly troubled with the
" gout : nothing grieves me, but that my doctor
" hath forbidden me wine, and you know your
" ambassador must drink. Didst thou ask thy
" doctor what was good for the gout ?

" *Bian.* Yes ; he said, ease, wine, and women,
" were good for it.

" *Bil.* Nay, thou hast such a wit ! What was
" good to cure it, said he ?

" *Bian.* Why, the rack. All your empirics
" could never do the like cure upon the gout the
" rack did in England, or your Scotch boot.*
" The French harlequin † will instruct you.

" *Bil.* Surely, I do wonder how thou, having
" for the most part of thy life-time been a country
" body, shouldst have so good a wit.

" *Bian.* Who, I ? why, I have been a courtier
" thrice two months.

" *Bil.* So have I this twenty year, and yet
" there was a gentleman-usher called me coxcomb
" t'other day, and to my face too : was't not a
" back-biting rascal ? I would I were better tra-
" velled, that I might have been better acquainted
" with the fashions of several countrymen : but
" my secretary, I think, he hath sufficiently in-
" structed me.

" *Bian.* How, my lord ?

" *Bil.* 'Marry, my good lord,' quoth he, 'your
" lordship shall ever find amongst a hundred
" Frenchmen forty hot-shots ; amongst a hundred
" Spaniards, three-score braggarts ; amongst a
" hundred Dutchmen, four-score drunkards ;
" amongst a hundred Englishmen, four-score and
" ten madmen ; and amongst an hundred Welsh-
" men'——

" *Bian.* What, my lord ?

" *Bil.* 'Four-score and nineteen gentlemen.'

" *Bian.* But since you go about a sad embassy,
" I would have you go in black, my lord.

" *Bil.* Why, dost think I cannot mourn, unless
" I wear my hat in cipres,* like an alderman's
" heir ? that's vile, very old, in faith.

" *Bian.* I'll learn of you shortly : O, we should
" have a fine gallant of you, should not I instruct
" you ! How will you bear yourself when you
" come into the Duke of Florence' court ?

" *Bil.* Proud enough, and 'twill do well enough :
" as I walk up and down the chamber, I'll spit
" frowns about me, have a strong perfume in my
" jerkin, let my beard grow to make me look
" terrible, salute no man beneath the fourth
" button ; and 'twill do excellent.

" *Bian.* But there is a very beautiful lady
" there ; how will you entertain her ?

" *Bil.* I'll tell you that, when the lady hath
" entertained me : but to satisfy thee, here comes
" the fool.

" *Enter* PASSARELLO.

" Fool, thou shalt stand for the fair lady.

" *Pass.* Your fool will stand for your lady
" most willingly and most uprightly.

" *Bil.* I'll salute her in Latin.

" *Pass.* O, your fool can understand no Latin.

" *Bil.* Ay, but your lady can.

" *Pass.* Why, then, if your lady take down
" your fool, your fool will stand no longer for
" your lady.

" *Bil.* A pestilent fool ! 'fore God, I think the
" world be turned upside down too.

" *Pass.* O, no, sir ; for then your lady and all
" the ladies in the palace should go with their
" heels upward, and that were a strange sight,
" you know.

" *Bil.* There be many will repine at my prefer-
" ment.

" *Pass.* O, ay, like the envy of an elder sister,
" that hath her younger made a lady before her.

" *Bil.* The duke is wondrous discontented.

" *Pass.* Ay, and more melancholic than a
" usurer having all his money out at the death of
" a prince.

" *Bil.* Didst thou see Madam Floria to-day ?

" *Pass.* Yes, I found her repairing her face to-
" day ; the red upon the white showed as if her

---

* *Scotch boot*] The very powerful description of the
infliction of torture by this instrument, given in the
universally-read *Tales of my Landlord*, renders any account
of it unnecessary here.

† *harlequin*] The old ed. "*herlakene.*"

---

* *my hat in cipres*] Cipres (written, also, *cypress*, and
cyprus) was a fine kind of gauze, nearly the same as
crape :

   "*Gorg. Goddess of Cyprus*—
Bub. Stay, I do not like that word *cyprus*, for she'll
think I mean to make hatbands of her."
              Shirley's *Love-Tricks.*—*Works*, i. 42.

"cheeks should have been served in for two
"dishes of barberries in stewed broth, and the
"flesh to them a woodcock.

" *Bil.* A bitter fool!*—Come, madam, this
"night thou shalt enjoy me freely, and to-morrow
"for Florence.

" *Pass.* What a natural fool is he that would
"be a pair of boddice to a woman's petticoat, to
"be trussed and pointed to them! Well, I'll
"dog my lord; and the word is proper: for when
"I fawn upon him, he feeds me; when I snap
"him by the fingers, he spits in my mouth. If a
"dog's death were not strangling, I had rather be
"one than a serving-man; for the corruption of
"coin is either the generation of a usurer or a
"lousy beggar. [*Exeunt* BLANCA *and* PASSARELLO."

Enter MALEVOLE *in some frize gown, whilst* BILIOSO *reads
his patent.*

Mal. I cannot sleep; my eyes' ill-neighbouring
    lids
Will hold no fellowship. O thou pale sober
    night,
Thou that in sluggish fumes all sense dost steep;
Thou that giv'st all the world full leave to play,
Unbend'st the feebled veins of sweaty labour!
The galley-slave, that all the toilsome day
Tugs at his oar against the stubborn wave,
Straining his rugged veins, snores fast;
The stooping scythe-man, that doth barb† the
    field,
Thou mak'st wink sure: in night all creatures
    sleep;
Only the malcontent, that 'gainst his fate
Repines and quarrels,—alas, he's goodman tell-
    clock!
His sallow jaw-bones sink with wasting moan;
Whilst others' beds are down, his pillow's stone.

Bil. Malevole!

Mal. Elder of Israel, thou honest defect of
wicked nature and obstinate ignorance, when did
thy wife let thee lie with her?

Bil. I am going ambassador to Florence.

Mal. Ambassador! Now, for thy country's
honour, prithee, do not put up mutton and
porridge i' thy cloak-bag. Thy young lady
wife goes to Florence with thee too, does she
not?

Bil. No, I leave her at the palace.

Mal. At the palace! Now, discretion shield,
man; for God's love, let's ha' no more cuckolds!
Hymen begins to put off his saffron robe: keep

thy wife i'the state of grace. Heart o' truth, I
would sooner leave my lady singled in a bordello
than in the Genoa palace:
Sin there appearing in her sluttish shape,
Would soon grow loathsome, even to blushes'
    sense;
Surfeit would choke* intemperate appetite,
Make the soul scent the rotten breath of lust.
When in an Italian lascivious palace,
A lady guardian-less, .
Left to the push of all allurement,
The strongest incitements to immodesty,
To have her bound, incens'd with wanton sweets,
Her veins fill'd high with heating delicates,
Soft rest, sweet music, amorous masquerers,
Lascivious banquets, sin itself gilt-o'er,
Strong fantasy tricking up strange delights,
Presenting it dress'd pleasingly to sense,
Sense leading it unto the soul, confirm'd
With potent example, impudent custom,
Entic'd by that great bawd, opportunity;†
Thus being prepar'd, clap to her easy ear
Youth in good clothes, well-shap'd, rich,
Fair-spoken, promising, noble, ardent, blood-full,
Witty, flattering,—Ulysses absent,
O Ithaca, can‡ chastest Penelope hold out?

Bil. Mass, I'll think on't. Farewell.

Mal. Farewell. Take thy wife with thee.
Farewell.   [*Exit* BILIOSO.
To Florence; um! it may prove good, it may;
And we may once unmask our brows.

Enter CELSO.

Celso. My honour'd lord,—

Mal. Celso, peace! how is't? speak low: pale
    fears
Suspect that hedges, walls, and trees, have ears:
Speak, how runs all? .

Celso. I'faith, my lord, that beast with many
    heads,
The staggering multitude, recoils apace:
Though thorough great men's envy, most men's
    malice,
Their much-intemperate heat hath banish'd you,
Yet now they find§ envy and malice ne'er
Produce faint reformation.

---

* *fool*] The old ed. "*fowl.*"
† *barb*] "i.e. mow."—*Steevens.*

* *choke*] The old eds. "*cloake*" and "*cloke.*"
† *Entic'd by that great bawd, opportunity*] So in Shakespeare's *Lucrece:*
    "O Opportunity, thy guilt is great!
    Thou foul abettor! thou notorious bawd!"
‡ *O Ithaca, can*] The second 4to. "*O Ithacan.*"
§ *find*] The first 4to. "*faind.*"

The duke, the too soft duke, lies as a block,
For which two tugging factions seem to saw;
But still the iron through the ribs they draw.

Mal. I tell thee, Celso, I have over found
Thy breast most far from shifting cowardice
And fearful baseness: therefore I'll tell thee,
   Celso,
I find the wind begins to come about;
I'll shift my suit of fortune.
I know the Florentine, whose only force,
By marrying his proud daughter to this prince,
Both banish'd me, and made this weak lord duke,
Will now forsake them all; be sure he will:
I'll lie in ambush for conveniency,
Upon their severance to confirm myself.

Celso. Is Ferneze interr'd?

Mal. Of that at leisure: he lives.

Celso. But how stands Mendoza? how is't with
him?

Mal. Faith, like a pair of snuffers, snibs filth
in other men, and retains it in himself.*

Celso. He does fly from public notice, methinks,
as a hare does from hounds; the feet whereon
he flies betray him.

Mal. I can track him, Celso.
O, my disguise fools him most powerfully!
For that I seem a desperate malcontent,
He fain would clasp with me: he 's the true slave
That will put on the most affected grace
For some vile second cause.

Celso. He's here.

Mal. Give place.   [*Exit* Celso.

Enter Mendoza.

Illo, ho, ho, ho! art there, old truepenny?†
Where hast thou spent thyself this morning?
I see flattery in thine eyes, and damnation in thy
soul. Ha, ye‡ huge rascal!

Men. Thou art very merry.

Mal. As a scholar *futuens gratis.* How does §
the devil go with thee now?

Men. Malevole, thou art an arrant knave.

Mal. Who, I? I have been a sergeant, man.

Men. Thou art very poor.

Mal. As Job, an alchymist, or a poet.

Men. The duke hates thee.

Mal. As Irishmen do bum-cracks.

Men. Thou hast lost his amity.

Mal. As pleasing as maids lose their virginity.

Men. Would thou wert of a lusty spirit! would
thou wert noble!

Mal. Why, sure my blood gives me I am noble,
sure I am of noble kind; for I find myself possessed with all their qualities;—love dogs, dice,
and drabs, scorn wit in stuff-clothes; have bent
my shoemaker, knocked my semstress, cuckold *
my pothecary, and undone my tailor. Noble!
why not? since the stoic said, *Neminem servum
non ex regibus, neminem regem non ex servis esse
oriundum;* † only busy Fortune touses, and the
provident Chances‡ blend them together. I'll
give you a simile: did you e'er see a well with
two buckets, whilst one comes up full to be
emptied, another goes down empty to be filled?
such is the state of all humanity. Why, look
you, I may be the son of some duke; for, believe
me, intemperate lascivious bastardy makes
nobility doubtful: I have a lusty daring heart,
Mendoza.

Men. Let's grasp; I do like thee infinitely: wilt
enact one thing for me?

Mal. Shall I get by it? [Men. *gives him his
purse.*] Command me; I am thy slave, beyond
death and hell.

Men. Murder the duke.

Mal. My heart's wish, my soul's desire, my
fantasy's dream, my blood's longing, the only
height of my hopes! How, O God, how! O,
how my united spirits throng together, to §
strengthen my resolve!

Men. The duke is now a-hunting.

Mal. Excellent, admirable, as the devil would
have it! Lend me, lend me, rapier, pistol, cross-
bow: so, so, I'll do it.

Men. Then we agree.

Mal. As Lent and fish-mongers. Come, a-cap-
a-pe, how? inform.

Men. Know that this weak-brain'd duke, who
   only stands
On Florence' stilts, hath out of witless zeal
Made me his heir, and secretly confirm'd
The wreath to me after his life's full point.

Mal. Upon what merit?

Men. Merit! by heaven, I horn him:

---

* *Himself*] The second 4to. "itself."
† *Illo, ho, ho, ho! art there, old truepenny?*]
   "*Hor.* [*within*] Illo, ho, ho, my lord!
   Ham. Hillo, ho, ho, boy! come, bird, come.
   .   .   .   .
   .   .   .   .   art thou there, truepenny?"
                  Shakespeare's *Hamlet*, act. i. sc. 5.
‡ *ye*] The second 4to. "thou."
§ *does*] The second 4to. "dooth."

* *cuckold*] i.e. cuckolded.
† *Neminem, &c.*] "Plato ait: Neminem regem non ex
servis esse oriundum, neminem non servum ex regibus."
                                      Seneca,—*Epist.* xliv.
‡ *Chances*] i.e. Fates.
§ *to*] Both 4tos. "so."

Only Ferneze's death gave me state's life.
Tut, we are politic, he must not live now.

Mal. No reason, marry: but how must he die now?

Men. My utmost project is to murder the duke, that I might have his state, because he makes me his heir; to banish the duchess, that I might be rid of a cunning Lacedæmonian, because I know Florence will forsake her; and then to marry Maria, the banished Duke Alto-front's wife, that her friends might strengthen me and my faction: this is all, la.

Mal. Do you love Maria?

Men. Faith, no great affection, but as wise men do love great women, to ennoble their blood and augment their revenue. To accomplish this now, thus now. The duke is in the forest next the sea: single him, kill him, hurl him i' the main, and proclaim thou sawest wolves eat him.

Mal. Um! not so good. Methinks when he is slain,
To get some hypocrite, some dangerous wretch
That's muffled o'er * with feignèd holiness,
To swear he heard the duke on some steep cliff
Lament his wife's dishonour, and, in an agony
Of his heart's torture, hurl'd his groaning sides
Into the swollen sea,—this circumstance
Well made sounds probable: and hereupon
The duchess——

Men. May well be banish'd:
O unpeerable invention! rare!
Thou god of policy! it honeys me.

Mal. Then fear not for the wife of Altofront;
I'll close to her.

Men. Thou shalt, thou shalt. Our excellency is pleas'd:
Why wert not thou an emperor? when we
Are duke, I'll make thee some great man, sure.

Mal. Nay,
Make me some rich knave, and I'll make myself
Some great man.

Men. In thee be all my spirit:
Retain ten souls, unite thy virtual powers:
Resolve; ha, remember greatness! heart, farewell:
The fate of all my hopes in thee doth dwell.
                                        [*Exit.*

Re-enter CELSO.

Mal. Celso, didst hear?—O heaven, didst hear
Such devilish mischief? suffer'st thou the world
Carouse damnation even with greedy swallow,
And still dost wink, still does thy vengeance slumber?
If now thy brows are clear, when will they thunder?   [*Exeunt.*

* *o'er*] The 4tos. "*or.*"

SCENE II.*

Enter PIETRO, FERRARDO, PREPASSO, *and* Three Pages.

Fer. The dogs are at a fault.
                        [*Cornets like horns within.*

Pietro. Would God nothing but the dogs were at it! Let the deer pursue safety,† the dogs follow the game, and do you follow the dogs: as for me, 'tis unfit one beast should hunt another; I ha' one chaseth me: an't ‡ please you, I would be rid of ye a little.

Fer. Would your grief would, as soon as we, leave you to quietness!§

Pietro. I thank you.
                [*Exeunt* FERRARDO *and* PREPASSO.
Boy, what dost thou dream of now?

First Page. Of a dry summer, my lord; for here's a hot world towards: but, my lord, I had a strange dream last night.

Pietro. What strange dream?

First Page. Why, methought I pleased you with singing, and then I dreamt you gave me that short sword.

Pietro. Prettily begged: hold thee, I'll prove thy dream true; take't.   [*Giving sword.*

First Page. My duty: but still I dreamt on, my lord; and methought, an't shall please your excellency, you would needs out of your royal bounty give me that jewel in your hat.

Pietro. O, thou didst but dream, boy; do not believe it: dreams prove not always true; they may hold in a short sword, but not in a jewel. But now, sir, you dreamt you had pleased me with singing; make that true, as I ha' made the other.

First Page. Faith, my lord, I did but dream, and dreams, you say, prove not always true; they may hold in a good sword, but not in a good song: the truth is, I ha' lost my voice.

Pietro. Lost thy voice! how?

First Page. With dreaming, faith: but here's a couple of sirenical rascals shall enchant ye: what shall they sing, my good lord?

Pietro. Sing of the nature of women; and then the song shall be surely full of variety, old crotchets, and most sweet closes: it shall be humorous, grave, fantastic, amorous, melancholy, sprightly, one in all, and all in one.

First Page. All in one!

Pietro. By'r lady, too many. Sing: my speech grows culpable of unthrifty idleness: sing.

* *Scene II.*] A forest near the sea.
† *safety*] The 4tos. "*safely.*"
‡ *an't*] The first 4to. "*and*" (and so afterwards).
§ *as soon as we, leave you to quietness*] The second 4to. "*as soone leave you as we to quietnesse.*"

Ah, so, so, sing.

Song * *by* Second *and* Third Pages.

I am heavy : walk off; I shall talk in my sleep :
walk off.   [*Exeunt* Pages.

Enter MALEVOLE, *with cross-bow and pistol.*

Mal. Brief, brief : who? the duke! good heaven, that fools

Should stumble upon greatness!—Do not sleep,
duke;

Give ye good-morrow : I must† be brief, duke;
I am foe'd to murder thee : start not : Mendoza,
Mendoza hir'd me; here's his gold, his pistol,
Cross-bow, and ‡ sword : 'tis all as firm as earth.
O fool, fool, chokèd with the common maze
Of easy idiots, credulity !

Make him thine heir! what, thy sworn murderer!

Pietro. O, can it be?

Mal. Can!

Pietro. Discover'd he not Ferneze?

Mal. Yes, but why? but why? for love to thee?
Much, much !§ to be reveng'd upon his rival,
Who had thrust his jaws awry;
Who being slain, suppos'd by thine own hands,

Defended by his sword, made thee most loathsome,
Him most gracious with thy loose princess :
Thou, closely yielding egress and regress to her,
Madest him heir; whose hot unquiet lust
Straight tous'd thy sheets, and now would seize
thy state.

Politician! wise man! death! to be
Led to the stake like a bull by the horns;
To make even kindness cut a gentle throat !
Life, why art thou numb'd? thou foggy dulness,
speak :
Lives not more faith in a home-thrusting tongue
Than in these fencing tip-tap courtiers?

Enter CELSO, *with a hermit's gown and beard.*

Pietro.* Lord Malevole, if this be true——

Mal. If I come, shade thee with this disguise.
If! thou shalt handle it; he shall thank thee for
killing thyself. Come, follow my directions, and
thou shalt see strange sleights.

Pietro. World, whither wilt thou?

Mal. Why, to the devil. Come, the morn grows
late :

A steady quickness is the soul of state. [*Exeunt.*

ACT IV.

SCENE I.‖

Enter MAQUERELLE.

Maq. [*knocking at the ladies' door.*] Medam,¶ medam, are you stirring, medam? if you be stirring,
medam,—if I thought I should disturb ye—

Enter Page.

Page. My lady is up, forsooth.

Maq. A pretty boy, faith : how old art thou?

Page. I think fourteen.

Maq. Nay, an ye be in the teens—are ye a

gentleman born? do you know me? my name is
Medam Maquerelle; I lie in the old Cunny-court.

Page.† See, here the ladies.

Enter BIANCA *and* EMILIA.

Bian. A fair day to ye, Maquerelle.

Emil. Is the duchess up yet, sentinel?

Maq. O ladies, the most abominable mischance!
O dear ladies, the most piteous disaster! Ferneze
was taken last night in the duchess' chamber :
alas, the duke catched him and killed him!

Bian. Was he found in bed?

Maq. O, no; but the villanous certainty is, the
door was not bolted, the tongue-tied hatch held
his peace : so the naked troth is, he was found
in his shirt, whilst I, like an arrant beast, lay in
the outward chamber, heard nothing; and yet
they came by me in the dark, and yet I felt them
not, like a senseless creature as I was. O beauties,
look to your busk-points ; ‡ if not chastely, yet

---

* *Song*] See note †, p. 45.

† *I must*] The first 4to. "*must*"; the second 4to. "*you
must.*"

‡ *and*] Not in the first 4to.

§ *Much, much?*] See note †, p. 330.

‖ *Scene I.* . . . . . *knocking at the ladies'. door*]
It is not easy to determine in what particular part of the
Genoan Palace the present scene passes ; nor do I believe
that the author himself could have cleared up the difficulty. By "*the ladies'* door" we are certainly to understand the door of the chamber of Bianca and Emilia :
but presently the Duchess Aurelia says to Celso on his
entering, "We are not pleased with your intrusion upon
our private retirement."

¶ *Medam*] I allow this spelling to remain, as, I suppose,
it is meant to mark the affected pronunciation of the
speaker.

* *Pietro*] Both 4tos. "Cel."

† *Page*] Not in the old eds.

‡ *busk-points*] i.e. the tagged laces which fastened the
busk of the stays.

charily: be sure the door be bolted.—Is your lord gone to Florence?

Bian. Yes, Maquerelle.

Maq. I hope you'll find the discretion to purchase a fresh gown 'fore his return.—Now, by my troth, beauties, I would ha' ye once wise: he loves ye; pish! he is witty; bubble! fair-proportioned; mew! nobly born; wind! Let this be still your fixed position: esteem me every man according to his good gifts, and so ye shall ever remain most dear, and most worthy to be, most dear ladies.

Emil. Is the duke returned from hunting yet?

Maq. They say not yet.

Bian. 'Tis now in midst of day.

Emil. How bears the duchess with this blemish now?

Maq. Faith, boldly; strongly defies defame, as one that has a duke to her father. And there's a note to you: be sure of a stout friend in a corner, that may always awe your husband. Mark the haviour of the duchess now: she dares defame; cries, "Duke, do what thou canst, I'll quit mine honour:" nay, as one confirmed in her own virtue against ten thousand mouths that mutter her disgrace, she's presently for dances.

Bian. For dances!

Maq. Most true.

Emil. Most strange.

Enter FERRARDO.

See, here's my servant young Ferrardo: how many servants thinkest thou I have, Maquerelle?

Maq. The more, the merrier: 'twas well said, use your servants as you do your smocks; have many, use one, and change often; for that's most sweet and courtlike.

Fer. Save ye, fair ladies! Is the duke return'd?

Bian. Sweet sir, no voice of him as yet in court.

Fer. 'Tis very strange.

Bian. And how like you my servant, Maquerelle?

Maq. I think he could hardly draw Ulysses' bow; but, by my fidelity, were his nose narrower, his eyes broader, his hands thinner, his lips thicker, his legs bigger, his feet lesser, his hair blacker, and his teeth whiter, he were a tolerable sweet youth, i'faith. An he will come to my chamber, I will read him the fortune of his board. [*Cornets sound within.*

Fer. Not yet returned! I fear—but the duchess approacheth.

Enter MENDOZA *supporting* AURELIA, *and* GUERRINO: *the ladies that are on the stage rise:* FERRARDO *ushers in* AURELIA, *and then takes a lady to tread a measure.**

Aur. We will dance:—music!—we will dance.

Guer. Les quanto,† lady, *Pensez bien, Passa regis*, or *Bianca's brawl?*

Aur. We have forgot the brawl.‡

Fer. So soon? 'tis wonder.

Guer. Why, 'tis but two singles on the left, two on the right, three doubles § forward, a traverse of six round: do this twice, three singles side, galliard-trick of twenty, coranto-pace; a figure of eight, three singles broken down, come up, meet, two doubles, fall back, and then honour.

Aur. O Dædalus, thy maze! I have quite forgot it.

Maq. Trust me, so have I, saving the falling-back, and then honour.

Aur. Music, music!

Enter PREPASSO.

Prep. Who saw the duke? the duke?

Aur. Music!

Enter EQUATO.

Equato. The duke? is the duke returned?

Aur. Music!

Enter CELSO.

Celso. The duke is either quite invisible, or else is not.

Aur. We are not pleased with your intrusion upon our private retirement; we are not pleased: you have forgot yourselves.

Enter a Page.

Celso. Boy, thy master? where's the duke?

Page. Alas, I left him burying the earth with his spread joyless limbs: he told me he was

---

* *tread a measure*] A *measure* was a slow and solemn dance. It was not thought indecorous in the most grave and dignified personages to *tread a measure*.

† *Les quanto*] Qy. "*Los guantes?*" Mr. Collier (*Shakespeare Soc. Papers*, i. 28), quotes, from Rawlinson's MS. No. 108, Bodl. Lib., a list of dances, among which is "Quarto dispayne"; while Mr. Halliwell (*Dict. of Arch. and Prov. Words*) gives, from the same MS., "Quantodispaine."—In Munday's *Banquet of Daintie Conceits*, 1588, is:

"A Dyttie expressing a familiar controversie between Wit and Will: wherein Wit mildlie rebuketh the follies of Will, and sheweth him (as in a glasse) the fall of wilfull heads.

"This Dittie may be sung after the note of a courtlie daunce, called *Les Guanto*."

‡ *the brawl*] Reed has a long unnecessary note here: the figure of this dance is no where so minutely described as in Guerrino's next speech.

§ *doubles*] The first 4to. "*double.*"

heavy, would sleep; bade* me walk off, for that
the strength of fantasy oft made him talk †in his
dreams. I straight obeyed, nor never‡ saw him
since: but wheresoe'er he is, he's sad.

Aur. Music, sound high, as is our heart! sound
high!

Enter MALEVOLE, *and* PIETRO *disguised like an Hermit.*

Mal. The duke,—peace!—the duke is dead.

Aur. Music!

Mal. Is't music?

Men. Give proof.

Fer. How?

Celso. Where?

Prep. When?

Mal. Rest in peace, as the duke does; quietly
sit: for my own part, I behold him but dead;
that's all: marry, here's one can give you a more
particular account of him.

Men. Speak, holy father, nor let any brow
Within this presence fright thee from the truth:
Speak confidently and freely.

Aur. We attend.

Pietro. Now had the mounting sun's all-
ripening wings
Swept the cold sweat of night from earth's dank
breast,
When I, whom men call Hermit of the Rock,
Forsook my cell, and clamber'd up a cliff,
Against whose base the heady Neptune dash'd
His high-curl'd brows; there 'twas I eas'd my
limbs:
When, lo! my entrails melted with the moan
Some one, who far 'bove me was climb'd, did
make—
I shall offend.

Men. Not.

Aur. On.

Pietro. Methinks I hear him yet:—'O female
faith!
Go sow the ingrateful sand, and love a woman:
And do I live to be the scoff of men?
To be the§ wittol-cuckold, even to hug
My poison? Thou knowest, O truth!
Sooner hard steel will melt with southern wind,
A seaman's whistle calm the ocean,
A town on fire be extinct with tears,
Than women, vow'd to blushless impudence,

With sweet behaviour and soft minioning*
Will turn from that where appetite is fix'd.
O powerful blood! how thou dost slave their
soul!
I wash'd an Ethiop, who, for recompense,
Sullied my name: and must I, then, be forc'd
To walk, to live thus black? must! must! fie!
He that can bear with must, he cannot die.'
With that, he sigh'd so† passionately deep,
That the dull air even groan'd: at last he cries,
'Sink shame in seas, sink deep enough!' so dies;
For then I view'd his body fall, and souse ‡
Into the foamy main. O, then I saw,
That which methinks I see, it was the duke;
Whom straight the nicer-stomach'd sea belch'd up:
But then——

Mal. Then came I in; but, 'las, all was too
late!
For even straight he sunk.

Pietro. Such was the duke's sad fate.

Celso. A better fortune to our Duke Mendoza!

Omnes. Mendoza!   [*Cornets flourish.*

Men. A guard, a guard!

Enter a Guard.

       We, full of hearty tears
For our good father's loss,
(For so we well may call him
Who did beseech your loves for our succession,)
Cannot so lightly over-jump his death
As leave his woes revengeless.—Woman of shame,
       [*To* AURELIA.
We banish thee for ever to the place
From whence this good man comes; nor permit,

---

* *minioning*] "i.e. being treated as a *minion* or darling."
—*Steevens.* In the last edition of Dodsley's *Old Plays,*
the note by Gilchrist on this word, and the quotation
from Burton, are altogether "from the purpose."

† *so*] The second 4to. "*too.*"

‡ *souse*] From the occurrence of the word, I take the
opportunity of noticing that the late excellent editor of
Ben Jonson has, I think, unfortunately adopted it, in the
following passage of *The Devil is an ass:*
       "Madam, this young Wittipol
Would have debauch'd my wife, and made me cuckold
Thorough a casement; he did fly her home
To mine own window; but, I think, I *sous'd* him,
And ravish'd her away out of his *pounces.*"
"All the copies of the folio which I have examined,"
says Mr. Gifford, "read *sou't*, of which I can make
nothing but *sought* or *sous'd;* and I prefer the latter.
Whalley reads *fought;* but he evidently had not consulted
the old copy."—Gifford's *Ben Jonson,* vol. v. p. 126.
Sou't is nothing more than a variety in the spelling of
shu'd: to *shu* is to scare away a bird. See Cotgrave in v.
"*chou,*" Tim Bobbin's *Lancashire Dialect,* and Jamieson's
Scottish Dictionary in v. "*shu.*"
That such is the meaning of the word in *Ben Jonson* is
plain from the rest of the passage where it occurs, "*fly
her home,*" and "*out of his pounces.*"

---

* *bade*] The second 4to. "*bid.*"
† *talk*] The first 4to. "*talking.*"
‡ *nor never*] The second 4to. "*nor euer*": but the
double negative was formerly very common.
§ *the*] The first 4to. "*their.*"

On death, unto thy * body any ornament;
But, base as was thy life, depart away.

Aur. Ungrateful!

Men. Away!

Aur. Villain, hear me!

Men. Be gone!

[PREPASSO and GUERRINO *lead away* AURELIA *guarded.*

My lords,
Address to public council; 'tis most fit:
The train of fortune is borne up by wit.
Away! our presence shall be sudden; haste.

[*All depart, except* MENDOZA, MALEVOLE, *and* PIETRO.

Mal. Now, you egregious devil! ha, ye murdering politician! how dost, duke? how dost look now? brave duke, i'faith.

Men. How did you kill him?

Mal. Slatted † his brains out, then soused him in the briny sea.

Men. Brained him, and drowned him too?

Mal. O, 'twas best, sure work; for he that strikes a great man, let him strike home, or else 'ware, he'll prove no man: shoulder not a huge fellow, unless you may be sure to lay him in the kennel.

Men. A most sound brain-pan! I'll make you both emperors.

Mal. Make us Christians, make us Christians.

Men. I'll hoist ye, ye shall mount.

Mal. To the gallows, say ye? come ;‡ *præmium incertum petit certum scelus.*§ How stands the progress?

Men. Here, take my ring unto the citadel;
[*Giving ring.*
Have entrance to Maria, the grave duchess
Of banish'd Altofront. Tell her we love her;
Omit no circumstance to grace our person: do't.

Mal. I'll ‖ make an excellent pander: duke, farewell; 'dieu, adieu, duke.

Men. Take Maquerelle with thee; for 'tis found
None cuts a diamond but a diamond.
[*Exit* MALEVOLE.
Hermit,
Thou art a man for me, my confessor:
O thou selected spirit, born for my good!
Sure thou wouldst make

An excellent elder in a deform'd church.
Come, we must be inward, * thou and I all one.

Pietro. I am glad I was ordained for ye.

Men. Go to, then; thou must know that Malevole is a strange villain; dangerous, very dangerous: you see how broad 'a speaks; a gross-jawed rogue: I would have thee poison him: he's like a corn upon my great toe, I cannot go for him; he must be cored out, he must. Wilt do't, ha?

Pietro. Any thing, any thing.

Men. Heart of my life! thus, then. To the citadel:
Thou shalt consort with this Malevole;
There being at supper, poison him: it shall be laid
Upon Maria, who yields love or dies:
Scud † quick.

Pietro. Like lightning: good deeds crawl, but mischief flies. [*Exit.*

Re-enter MALEVOLE.

Mal. Your devilship's ring has no virtue: the buff-captain, the sallow Westphalian gammon-faced zaza cries, "Stand out;" must have a stiffer warrant, or no pass into the castle of comfort.

Men. Command our sudden letter.—Not enter! sha't: what place is there in Genoa but thou shalt? into my heart, into my very heart: come, let's love; we must love, we two, soul and body.

Mal. How didst like the hermit? a strange hermit, sirrah.

Men. A dangerous fellow, very perilous: He must die.

Mal. Ay, he must die.

Men. Thou'st‡ kill him. We are wise; we must be wise.

Mal. And provident.

Men. Yea, provident: beware an hypocrite; A church-man once corrupted, O, avoid!
A fellow that makes religion his stalking-horse,§
He breeds a plague: thou shalt poison him.

Mal. O, 'tis wondrous necessary: how?

Men. You both go jointly to the citadel;

---

* *inward*] i.e. intimate.

† *Scud, &c.*] The second 4to.;
　"Skud quicke like lightning.
　　Pie. Good deedes crawle, but mischiefe flies."

‡ *Thou's*] A contraction of "*Thou must.*"

§ *stalking-horse*] "*The stalking-horse* was one either real or factitious, by which the fowler anciently sheltered himself from the sight of the game. See Steevens's note on *Much ado about Nothing*, act ii. sc. 3."—*Reed.*

"In the margin at this place [only in the second 4to.], the words "*shoots under his belly*" are inserted; which is merely an explanation of the manner in which a corrupted churchman makes religion his *stalking-horse*, viz. by shooting at his object under its belly."—*Collier.*

---

* *thy*] Both 4tos. "*the.*"

† *Slatted*] "i.e. *dashed.* It is a North-country word. See Ray's *Collection of English words.* p. 54, ed. 1768."—*Reed.*

‡ *come*] The first 4to. "*O d me.*"

§ *præmium incertum, &c.*]:
　　　　"præmium incertum petis,
　　Certum scelus." Seneca,—*Phœn.* 632.

‖ *I'll*] The first 4to. "*Iste.*"

There sup, there poison him : and Maria,
Because she is our opposite, shall bear
The sad suspect ; on which she dies or loves us.
    Mal. I run.   [*Exit.*
    Men. We that are great, our sole self-good still
    moves us.
They shall die both, for their deserts crave more
Than we can recompense : their presence still
Imbraids * our fortunes with beholdingness,†
Which we abhor ; like deed, not doer : then con-
    clude,
They live not to cry out " Ingratitude !"
One stick burns t'other, steel cuts steel alone :
'Tis good trust few ; but, O, 'tis best trust none!
                             [*Exit.*

SCENE II.‡

Enter MALEVOLE *and* PIETRO, *still disguised, at several doors.*

    Mal. How do you ? how dost, duke ?
    Pietro. O, let
The last day fall ! drop, drop on § our curs'd heads !
Let heaven unclasp itself, vomit forth flames !
    Mal. O, do not rave,‖ do not turn player ;
there's more of them than can well live one by
another already. What, art an infidel still ?
    Pietro. I am amaz'd ; ¶ struck in a swoon with
    wonder :
I am commanded to poison thee—
    Mal. I am commanded to poison thee at
supper—
    Pietro. At supper—
    Mal. In the citadel—
    Pietro. In the citadel.
    Mal. Cross capers ! tricks ! truth o' heaven !
he** would discharge us as boys do elder††-guns,
one pellet to strike out another. Of what faith
art now ?
    Pietro. All is damnation ; wickedness extreme :
There is no faith in man.
    Mal. In none but usurers and brokers ; they
deceive no man : men take 'em for blood-suckers,
and so they are. Now, God deliver me from my
friends !

    Pietro. Thy friends !
    Mal. Yes, from my friends ; for from mine
enemies I'll deliver myself. O, cut-throat friendship is the rankest villany ! Mark this Mendoza ;
mark him for a villain : but heaven will send a
plague upon him for a rogue.
    Pietro. O world !
    Mal. World ! 'tis the only region of death, the
greatest shop of the devil ; the cruelest prison of
men, out of the which none pass without paying
their dearest breath for a fee ; there's nothing
perfect in it but extreme, extreme calamity, such
as comes yonder.

Enter AURELIA, *two halberts before and two after, supported by* CELSO *and* FERRARDO ; AURELIA *in base mourning attire.*

    Aur. To banishment ! lead * on to banishment !
    Pietro. Lady, the blessedness of repentance to
you !
    Aur. Why, why, I can desire nothing but
death,
Nor deserve any thing but hell.
If heaven should give sufficiency of grace
To clear my soul, it would make heaven graceless :
My sins would make the stock of mercy poor ;
O, they would tire† heaven's goodness to reclaim
    them !
Judgment is just yet from that vast villain ; ‡
But, sure, he shall not miss sad punishment
'Fore § he shall rule.—On to my cell of shame !
    Pietro. My cell 'tis, lady ; where, instead of
    masks,
Music, tilts, tourneys, and such court-like shows,
The hollow murmur of the checkless winds
Shall groan again ; whilst the unquiet sea
Shakes the whole rock with foamy battery.
There usherless the air comes in and out :
The rheumy vault will force your eyes to weep,
Whilst you behold true desolation :
A rocky barrenness shall pain ‖ your eyes,
Where all at once one reaches where he stands,
With brows the roof, both walls with both his
    hands.
    Aur. It is too good.—Bless'd spirit of my lord,
O, in what orb soe'er thy soul is thron'd,

---

    * *Imbraids*] i.e. upbraids.
    † *beholdingness*] "The state of being beholden."—
Steevens.
    ‡ *Scene II.*] The court of the palace.
    § *on*] The first 4to. "*in.*"
    ‖ *rave*] The second 4to. "*rand.*"
    ¶ *amazed*] The first 4to. "*mazde.*"
    ** *he*] Not in the first 4to.
    †† *elder*] The second 4to. "*elderne.*"

    * *lead*] The old eds. "*led*" and "*ledde.*"
    † *tire*] The first 4to. "*try.*"
    ‡ *Judgment is just yet from that vast villain*] If the text
be right, Aurelia means, "My doom is just, though it be
passed by that villain Mendoza." Dodsley, however,
reads :
        "Judgment is just ; yet *for* that vast villain,
         Be sure he shall not miss," &c.
    § *'Fore*] The first 4to. "*For.*"
    ‖ *pain*] The second 4to. "*pierce.*"

Behold me worthily most miserable!
O, let the anguish of my contrite spirit
Entreat some reconciliation!
If not, O, joy, triumph in my just grief!
Death is the end of woes and tears' relief.

Pietro. Belike your lord not lov'd you, was unkind.

Aur. O heaven!
As the soul loves* the body, so lov'd he:
'Twas death to him to part my presence, heaven
To see me pleas'd.
Yet I, like to a wretch given o'er to hell,
Brake all the sacred rites of marriage,
To clip † a base ungentle faithless villain;
O God! a very pagan reprobate—
What should I say? ungrateful, throws me out,
For whom I lost soul, body, fame, and honour.
But 'tis most fit: why should a better fate
Attend on any who forsake chaste sheets;
Fly the embrace of a devoted heart,
Join'd by a solemn vow 'fore God and man,
To taste the brackish flood ‡ of beastly lust
In an adulterous touch? O ravenous immodesty!
Insatiate impudence of appetite!
Look, here's your end; for mark, what sap in dust,
What good in sin, § even so much love in lust.
Joy to thy ghost, sweet lord! pardon to me!

Celso. 'Tis the duke's pleasure this night you
    rest in court.

Aurelia. Soul, lurk in shades; run, shame, from
    brightsome skies:
In night the blind man misseth not his eyes.

    [*Exit with* CELSO, FERRARDO, *and halberts.*]

Mal. Do not weep, kind cuckold: take comfort,
man; thy betters have been beccos: Agamemnon,
emperor of all the merry Greeks, that tickled all
the true Trojans, was a cornuto; Prince Arthur,
that cut off twelve kings' beards, was a cornuto;
Hercules, whose back bore up heaven, and got
forty wenches with child in one night,—

Pietro. Nay, 'twas fifty.

Mal. Faith, forty's enow, o' conscience,—yet
was a cornuto. Patience; mischief grows proud:
be wise.

Pietro. Thou pinchest too deep; art too keen
upon me.

Mal. Tut, a pitiful surgeon makes a dangerous
sore: I'll tent thee to the ground. Thinkest I'll
sustain myself by flattering thee, because thou art
a prince? I had rather follow a drunkard, and live
by licking up his vomit, than by servile flattery.

Pietro. Yet great men ha' done 't.

Mal. Great slaves fear better than love, born
naturally for a coal-basket;* though the common
usher of princes' presence, Fortune, ha'† blindly
given them better place. I am vowed to be thy
affliction.

Pietro. Prithee, be;
I love much misery, and be thou son to me.

Mal. Because you are an usurping duke.——

    Enter BILIOSO.

Your lordship's well returned from‡ Florence.

Bil. Well returned, I praise my horse.

Mal. What news from the Florentines?

Bil. I will conceal the great duke's pleasure;
only this was his charge: his pleasure is, that his
daughter die; Duke Pietro be banished for banishing his blood's dishonour; and that Duke
Altofront be re-accepted. This is all: but I hear
Duke Pietro is dead.

Mal. Ay, and Mendoza is duke: what will
you do?

Bil. Is Mendoza strongest?

Mal. Yet he is.

Bil. Then yet I'll hold with him.

Mal. But if that Altofront should turn straight
again?

Bil. Why, then, I would turn straight again.
'Tis good run still with him that has most might:
I had rather stand with wrong, than fall with right.

" *Mal.* What religion will you be of now?

" *Bil.* Of the duke's religion, when I know what
" it is.

" *Mal.* O Hercules!

" *Bil.* Hercules! Hercules was the son of Jupiter
" and Alcmena.

" *Mal.* Your lordship is a very wit-all.

" *Bil.* Wittal!

" *Mal.* Ay, all-wit.

" *Bil.* Amphitryo was a cuckold."

Mal. Your lordship sweats; your young lady
will get you a cloth for your old worship's brows.
[*Exit* BILIOSO.] Here's a fellow to be damned:
this is his inviolable maxim,—flatter the greatest
and oppress the least: a whoreson flesh-fly, that
still gnaws upon the lean galled backs.

Pietro. Why dost, then, salute him?

Mal. Faith,§ as bawds go to church, for fashion
sake. Come, be not confounded; thou'rt but

---

* *lores*] Both 4tos. " lou'd."
† *clip*] i. e. embrace.   ‡ *flood*] Both 4tos. " bloud."
§ *What good in sin*, &c.] Both 4tos. " *What sinne in
good*," &c.

* *born naturally for a coal-basket*] In great families the
carriers of coals were the lowest of all drudges; hence,
to carry coals meant to submit to insults.
† *ha'*] The second 4to. " *hath*."
‡ *from*] The first 4to. " *for*."
§ *Faith*] The second 4to. " *Yfaith*."

A A

in danger to lose a dukedom. Think this :—this
earth is the only grave and Golgotha wherein all
things that live must rot; 'tis but the draught
wherein the heavenly bodies discharge their
corruption; the very muck-hill on which the
sublunary orbs cast their excrements : man is the
slime of this dung-pit, and princes are the gov-
ernors of these men; for, for our souls, they are
as free as emperors, all of one piece; there * goes
but a pair of shears betwixt an emperor and the
son of a bag-piper; only the dying, dressing,
pressing, glossing, makes the difference. Now,
what art thou like to lose?
A gaoler's office to keep men in bonds,
Whilst toil and treason all life's good confounds.

　Pietro. I here renounce for ever regency:
O Altofront, I wrong thee to supplant thy right,
To trip thy heels up with a devilish sleight!
For which I now from throne am thrown: world-
　tricks abjure;
For vengeance though't † comes slow, yet it comes
　sure.
O, I am chang'd! for here, 'fore the dread power,
In true contrition, I do dedicate
My breath to solitary holiness,

My lips to prayer, and my breast's care shall be,
Restoring Altofront to regency.
　Mal. Thy vows are heard, and we accept thy
　　faith.　　　　　　　[*Undisguiseth himself.*

Re-enter FERNEZE *and* CELSO.

Banish amazement : come, we four must stand
Full shock of fortune: be not so wonder-stricken.
　Pietro. Doth Ferneze live?
　Fer. For your pardon.
　Pietro. Pardon and love. Give leave to recollect
My thoughts dispers'd in wild astonishment.
My vows stand fix'd in heaven, and from hence
I crave all love and pardon.
　Mal. Who doubts of providence,
That sees this change? a hearty faith to all !
He needs must rise who * can no lower fall :
For still impetuous vicissitude
Tosseth † the world; then let no maze intrude
Upon your spirits : wonder not I rise;
For who can sink that close can temporise?
The time grows ripe for action : I'll detect
My privat'st plot, lest ignorance fear suspect.
Let's close to counsel, leave the rest to fate :
Mature discretion is the life of state.　　[*Exeunt.*

ACT V.

SCENE I.‡

"*Enter* BILIOSO *and* PASSARELLO.

　"*Bil.* Fool, how dost thou like my calf in a
"long stocking?
　"*Pas.* An excellent calf, my lord.
　"*Bil.* This calf hath been a reveller this twenty
"year. When Monsieur Gundi lay here am-
"bassador, I could have carried a lady up and
"down at arm's end in a platter; and I can
"tell you, there were those at that time who, to
"try the strength of a man's back and his arm,
"would be coistered.§ I have measured calves

　"with most of the palace, and they come nothing
"near me : besides, I think there be not many
"armours in the arsenal will fit me, especially for
"the head-piece. I'll tell thee—
　"*Pass.* What, my lord?
　"*Bil.* I can eat stewed broth as it comes
"seething off the fire; or a custard as it comes
"reeking out of the oven; and I think there are
"not many lords can do it. A good pomander,‡
"a little decayed in the scent; but six grains of
"musk, ground with rose-water, and tempered
"with a little civet, shall fetch her again
"presently.
　"*Pass.* O, ay, as a bawd with aqua-vitæ.
　"*Bil.* And, what, dost thou rail upon the
"ladies as thou wert wont?

---

* *there goes but a pair of shears, &c.*] "i.e. they are both
of the same piece. The same expression is in [Shake-
speare's] *Measure for Measure,* act i. sc. 2."—*Reed.*
† *though't*] The first 4to. "*that.*"
‡ *Scene I.*] A room in the palace.
§ *coistered*] "The meaning of this passage is plain
enough without an explanation. The word *coistered* I
have not found in any ancient writer, but it seems to be
derived from the French word *coisser*, incommoder, faire
de la peine; or perhaps *coiter*, presser, exciter. See
Lacombe's *Dictionaire du vieux language Francois,* 1767."
—*Reed.* Nares (in his *Gloss.*) says that *coistered* "seems
to mean coiled up into a small compass."

* *who*] Omitted in the second 4to.
† *Tosseth*] The first 4to. "*Looseth.*"
‡ *pomander*] Perfumed paste, generally rolled into a
ball, but sometimes moulded into other forms: it was
carried in the pocket, or hung about the neck, and was
considered a preservative against infection. A silver case
filled with perfumes was sometimes called a *pomander.*—
Something seems to have dropped out of the text here.

" *Pass.* I were better roast a live cat, and might
"do it with more safety. I am as secret to
"them* as their painting. There's Maquerelle,
"oldest bawd and a perpetual beggar—did you
"never hear of her trick to be known in the city?

" *Bil.* Never.

" *Pass.* Why, she gets all the picture-makers to
"draw her picture; when they have done, she
"most courtly finds fault with them one after
"another, and never fetcheth them: they, in
"revenge of this, execute her in pictures as they
"do in Germany, and hang her in their shops:
"by this means is she better known to the
"stinkards than if she had been five times
"carted.

" *Bil.* 'Fore God, an excellent policy.

" *Pass.* Are there any revels to-night, my lord?

" *Bil.* Yes.

" *Pass.* Good my lord, give me leave to break
"a fellow's pate that hath abused me.

" *Bil.* Whose pate?

" *Pass.* Young Ferrardo, my lord.

" *Bil.* Take heed, he's very valiant; I have
"known him fight eight quarrels in five days,
"believe it.

" *Pass.* O, is he so great a quarreller? why,
"then, he's an arrant coward.

" *Bil.* How prove you that?

" *Pass.* Why, thus. He that quarrels seeks to
"fight; and he that seeks to fight seeks to die;
"and he that seeks to die seeks never to fight
"more; and he that will quarrel, and seeks means
"never to answer a man more, I think he's a
"coward.

" *Bil.* Thou canst prove any thing.

" *Pass.* Any thing but a rich knave; for I can
"flatter no man.

" *Bil.* Well, be not drunk, good fool: I shall
"see you anon in the presence."   [*Exeunt.*

SCENE II.†

Enter, from opposite sides, MALEVOLE *and* MAQUERELLE,
singing.

Mal. The Dutchman for a drunkard,—

Maq. The Dane for golden locks,—

Mal. The Irishman for usquebaugh,—

Maq. The Frenchman for the pox.

Mal. O, thou art a blessed creature! had I a
modest woman to conceal, I would put her to

thy custody; for no reasonable creature would
ever suspect her to be in thy company: ah, thou
art a melodious Maquerelle,—thou picture of a
woman, and substance of a beast!

" *Enter* PASSARELLO *with wine.*

" *Maq.* O fool, will ye be ready anon to go with
"me to the revels? the hall will be so pestered*
"anon.

" *Pass.* Ay, as the country is with attorneys.

" *Mal.* What hast thou there, fool?

" *Pass.* Wine; I have learned to drink since I
"went with my lord ambassador: I'll drink to
"the health of Madam Maquerelle.

" *Mal.* Why, thou wast wont to rail upon her.

" *Pass.* Ay; but since I borrowed money of
"her, I'll drink to her health now; as gentlemen
"visit brokers, or as knights send venison to the
"city, either to take up more money, or to
"procure longer forbearance.

" *Mal.* Give me the bowl. I drink a health to
"Altofront, our deposed duke. [*Drinks.*

" *Pass.* I'll take it [*Drinks*]:—so. Now I'll
"begin a health to Madam Maquerelle. [*Drinks.*

" *Mal.* Pooh! I will not pledge her.

" *Pass.* Why, I pledged your lord.

" *Mal.* I care not.

" *Pass.* Not pledge Madam Maquerelle! why,
"then, will I spew up your lord again with this
"fool's finger.

" *Mal.* Hold; I'll take it. [*Drinks.*

" *Maq.* Now thou hast drunk my health, fool,
"I am friends with thee.

" *Pass.* Art? art?

"When Griffon† saw the reconcilèd quean

"Offering about his neck her arms to cast,

"He threw off sword and heart's malignant
"stream,

"And lovely her below the loins embrac'd.—

"Adieu, Madam Maquerelle."   [*Exit.*

Mal. And how dost thou think o' this transfor-
mation of state now?

Maq. Verily,‡ very well; for we women always
note, the falling of the one is the rising of the
other; some must be fat, some must be lean;
some must be fools, and some must be lords;
some must be knaves, and some must be officers;
some must be beggars, some must be knights;
some must be cuckolds, and some must be

---

* *them*] The old ed. "*thieues.*"—Dodsley substituted
"*ladies.*"

† *Scene II.*] Before the citadel.

* *pestered*] i.e. crowded.

† *When Griffon, &c.*] "*Griffon* is one of the heroes of
Orlando Furioso, from whence one might suspect these
lines to be taken. I do not, however, find them there."—
Reed.

‡ *Verily*] The first 4to. "*Verie.*"

A A 2

citizens. As for example, I have two court-dogs, most * fawning curs, the one called Watch, the other Catch: now I, like Lady Fortune, sometimes love this dog, sometimes raise † that dog; sometimes favour Watch, most commonly fancy Catch. Now, that dog which I favour I feed; and he's so ravenous, that what I give he never chaws it, gulps it down whole, without any relish of what he has, but with a greedy expectation of what he shall have. The other dog now——

Mal. No more dog, sweet Maquerelle, no more dog. And what hope hast thou of the Duchess Maria? will she stoop to the duke's lure? will she come, ‡ thinkest?

Maq. Let me see, where's the sign now? ha' ye e'er a calendar? where's the sign, trow you?

Mal. Sign! why, is there any moment in that?

Maq. O, believe me, a most secret power: look ye, a Chaldean or an Assyrian, I am sure 'twas a most sweet Jew, told me, court any woman in the right sign, you shall not miss. But you must take her in the right vein then; as, when the sign is in Pisces, a fishmonger's wife is very sociable; in Cancer, a precisian's wife is very flexible; in Capricorn, a merchant's wife hardly holds out; in Libra, a lawyer's wife is very tractable, especially if her husband be at the term; only in Scorpio 'tis very dangerous meddling. Has the duke sent any jewel, any rich stones?

Mal. Ay, I think those are the best signs to take a lady in.

Enter Captain.

By your favour, signior, I must discourse with the Lady Maria, Altofront's duchess; I must enter for the duke.

Capt. She here shall give you interview: I received the guardship of this citadel from the good Altofront, and for his use I'll keep't, till I am of no use.

Mal. Wilt thou? O heaven,§ that a Christian should be found in a buff-jerkin! Captain Conscience, I love thee, captain. We attend.

[*Exit* Captain.

And what hope hast thou of this duchess' easiness?

Maq. 'Twill go hard, she was a cold creature

ever; she hated monkeys, fools, jesters, and gentlemen-ushers extremely; she had the vile trick on't, not only to be truly modestly honourable in her own conscience, but she would avoid the least wanton carriage that might incur suspect; as, God bless me, she had almost brought bed-pressing out of fashion; I could scarce get a fine for the lease of a lady's favour once in a fortnight.

Mal. Now, in the name of immodesty, how many maidenheads hast thou brought to the block?

Maq. Let me see: heaven forgive us our misdeeds!—Here's the duchess.

Enter MARIA *with* Captain.

Mal. God bless thee, lady!

Maria. Out of thy company!

Mal. We have brought thee tender of a husband.

Maria. I hope I have one already.

Maq. Nay, by mine honour, madam, as good ha' ne'er a husband as a banished husband; he's in another world now. I'll tell ye, lady, I have heard of a sect that maintained, when the husband was asleep the wife might lawfully entertain another man, for then her husband was as dead; much more when he is banished.

Maria. Unhonest creature!

Maq. Pish, honesty is but an art to seem so: Pray ye, what's honesty, what's constancy, But fables feign'd, odd old fools' chat, devis'd By jealous fools * to wrong our liberty?

Mal. Molly, he that loves thee is a duke, Mendoza; he will maintain thee royally, love thee ardently, defend thee powerfully, marry thee sumptuously, and keep thee, in despite of Rosiclear or Donzel del Phebo.† There's jewels: if thou wilt, so; if not, so.

Maria. Captain, for God's love, ‡ save poor wretchedness
From tyranny of lustful insolence!
Enforce me in the deepest dungeon dwell,
Rather than here; here round about is hell.—
O my dear'st Altofront! where'er thou breathe,
Let my soul sink into the shades beneath,
Before I stain thine honour! 'tis§ thou has 't,
And long as I can die, I will live chaste.

Mal. 'Gainst him that can enforce how vain is strife!

---

* *most*] The second 4to. "*the most.*"
† *raise*] The first 4to. "*rouse.*"
‡ *come*] i.e. yield to his wishes. The second 4to. has, by a misprint, "*cowe,*" in consequence of which Dodsley and the other editors of this play read "*coo!*"
§ *heaven*] The second 4to. "*heauens.*"

* *fools*] Qy. "*souls*"?
† *Rosiclear or Donzel del Phebo*] "See *The Mirror of Knighthood.*"—*Steevens.*
‡ *love*] The second 4to. "*sake.*"
§ *'tis*] The second 4to. "*this.*"

Maria. She that can be enforc'd has ne'er a
    knife:
She that through force her limbs with lust enrolls,
Wants Cleopatra's asps and Portia's coals.
God amend you!   [*Exit with* Captain.

Mal. Now, the fear of the devil for ever go
with thee!—Maquerelle, I tell thee, I have found
an honest woman: faith, I perceive, when all is
done, there is of women, as of all other things,
some good, most bad; some saints, some sinners:
for as now-a-days no courtier but has his mistress,
no captain but has his cockatrice,* no cuckold
but has his horns, and no fool but has his feather;
even so, no woman but has her weakness and
feather too, no sex but has his—I can hunt the
letter no farther.—[*Aside*] O God, how loathsome
this toying is to me! that a duke should be forced
to fool it! well, *stultorum plena sunt omnia :†*
better play the fool lord than be the fool lord.—
Now, where's your sleights, Madam Maquerelle?

Maq. Why, are ye ignorant that 'tis said a
squeamish affected niceness is natural to women,
and that the excuse of their yielding is only,
forsooth, the difficult obtaining? You must put
her to't: women are flax, and will fire in a
moment.

Mal. Why, was [not] the flax put into thy
mouth, and yet thou, thou set fire, thou inflame
her!

Maq. Marry, but I'll tell ye now, you were
too hot.

Mal. The fitter to have inflamed the flax,
woman.

Maq. You were too boisterous, spleeny, for,
indeed——

Mal. Go, go, thou art a weak pandress: now
I see,
Sooner earth's fire heaven itself shall waste,
Than all with heat can melt a mind that's chaste.
Go : thou the duke's lime-twig ! I'll make the duke
turn thee out of thine office: what, not get one
touch of hope, and had her at such advantage !

Maq. Now, o' my conscience, now I think in my
discretion, we did not take her in the right sign;
the blood was not in the true vein, sure.   [*Exit.*

" *Enter* BILIOSO.

" *Bil.* Make way there ! the duke returns from
" the enthronement.—Malevole,—

" *Mal.* Out, rogue !

" *Bil.* Malevole,—

" *Mal.* Hence, ye gross-jawed, peasantly—out,
" go !"

" *Bil.* Nay, sweet Malevole, since my return I
" hear you are become the thing I always prophe-
" sied would be,—an advanced virtue, a worthily-
" employed faithfulness, a man o' grace, dear
" friend. Come; what! *Si quoties peccant*
" *homines†*—if as often as courtiers play the
" knaves, honest men should be angry—why,
" look ye, we must collogue‡ sometimes, forswear
" sometimes.

" *Mal.* Be damned sometimes.

" *Bil.* Right: *nemo omnibus horis sapit;* no
" man can be honest at all hours : necessity often
" depraves virtue.

" *Mal.* I will commend thee to the duke.

" *Bil.* Do : let us be friends, man.

" *Mal.* And knaves, man.

" *Bil.* Right: let us prosper and purchase:§
" our lordships shall live, and our knavery be
" forgotten.

" *Mal.* He that by any ways gets riches, his
" means never shames‖ him.

" *Bil.* True.

" *Mal.* For impudency and faithlessness are the
" main stays to greatness.

" *Bil.* By the Lord, thou art a profound lad.

" *Mal.* By the Lord, thou art a perfect knave :
" out, ye ancient damnation !¶

" *Bil.* Peace, peace ! an thou wilt not be a
" friend to me as I am a knave, be not a knave
" to me as I am thy friend, and disclose me.
" Peace ! cornets !"**

Enter PREPASSO *and* FERRARDO, *two Pages with lights,*
CELSO *and* EQUATO, MENDOZA *in duke's robes, and*
GUERRINO.

Men. On, on ; leave us, leave us.
     [*Exeunt all except* MALEVOLE *and* MENDOZA.
Stay, where is the hermit ?

---

* *cockatrice*] A cant name for a prostitute.
† *stultorum plena,* &c.] Cicero,—*Epist. ad Fam.* ix. 22.

* *Hence,* &c.] A repetition of what Bilioso had said to
Malevole, see p. 339.
† *Si quoties peccant homines*] "Si, quoties homines
peccant," &c. Ovid,—*Trist.* ii. 33.
‡ *collogue*] " In cant language, the word *collogue* means
to *wheedle.*"—Reed. " To collogue, *adulor, adblandior.*"
Coles's *Dict.* It properly means, I believe, to confer,
converse together, for some unlawful or deceitful purpose.
§ *purchase*] i.e. acquire riches. See note †, p. 74.
‖ *means never shames*] Here (as frequently in our old
writers), *means* is the singular.
¶ *ancient damnation*] See note †, p. 220.
** *cornets*] I should have thought that this word belonged to the immediately following stage-direction, had
I not afterwards (p. 359) found,
" ——— So, cornets, cornets !
    Re-enter PREPASSO," &c.

Mal. With Duke Pietro, with Duke Pietro.

Men. Is he dead? is he poisoned?

Mal. Dead, as the duke is.

Men. Good, excellent: he will not blab; secureness lives in secrecy. Come hither, come hither.

Mal. Thou hast a certain strong villanous scent about thee my nature cannot endure.

Men. Scent, man! What returns Maria, what answer to our suit?

Mal. Cold, frosty; she is obstinate.

Men. Then she's but dead; 'tis resolute, she dies: Black deed only through black deed* safely flies.

Mal. Pooh! *per scelera semper sceleribus tutum est iter.*†

Men. What, art a scholar? art a politician? sure, thou art an arrant knave.

Mal. Who, ‡ I? I ha' been twice an under-sheriff, man. "Well, I will go rail upon some "great man, that I may purchase the bastinado, "or else go marry some rich Genoan lady, and "instantly go travel.

"*Men.* Travel, when thou art married?

"*Mal.* Ay, 'tis your young lord's fashion to do "so, though he was so lazy, being a bachelor, "that he would never travel so far as the "university: yet when he married her, tales off, "and, Catso,§ for England!

"*Men.* And why for England?

"*Mal.* Because there is no brothel-houses there.

"*Men.* Nor courtezans?

"*Mal.* Neither; your whore went down with "the stews, and your punk came up with your "puritan."

Men. Canst thou empoison? canst thou empoison?

Mal. Excellently; no Jew, pothecary, or politician better. Look ye, here's a box: whom wouldst thou empoison? here's a box [*Giving it*], which, opened and the fume ta'en‖ up in conduits ¶ thorough which the brain purges

itself, doth instantly for twelve hours' space bind up all show of life in a deep senseless sleep: here's another [*Giving it*], which, being opened under the sleeper's nose, chokes all the pores* of life, kills him suddenly.

Men. I'll try experiments; 'tis good not to be deceived.—So, so; catso!

    [*Seems to poison* MALEVOLE, *who falls.*

Who would fear that may destroy?
    Death hath no teeth nor† tongue;
And he that's great, to him are ‡ slaves,
    Shame, murder, fame, and wrong.—
Celso!

      Enter CELSO.

Celso. My honour'd lord?

Men. The good Malevole, that plain-tongu'd man,
Alas, is dead on sudden, wondrous strangely!
He held in our esteem good place. Celso,
See him buried, see him buried.

Celso. I shall observe ye.

Men. And, Celso, prithee, let it be thy care
    to-night
To have some pretty show, to solemnize
Our high instalment; some music, maskery.
We'll give fair entertain unto Maria,
The duchess to the banish'd Altofront:
Thou shalt conduct her from the citadel
Unto the palace. Think on some maskery.

Celso. Of what shape, sweet lord?

Men. What§ shape! why, any quick-done fiction;
As some brave spirits of the Genoan dukes,
To come out of Elysium, forsooth,
Led in by Mercury, to gratulate
Our happy fortune; some such anything,
Some far-fet trick good for ladies,‖ some stale toy
Or other, no matter, so't be of our devising.
Do thou prepare't; 'tis but for fashion ¶ sake;
Fear not, it shall be grac'd, man, it shall take.

Celso. All service.

Men. All thanks; our hand shall not be close
    to thee: farewell.

[*Aside*] Now is my treachery secure, nor can we
    fall:
Mischief that prospers, men do virtue call.

---

* deed] The first 4to. "*deedes.*"
† per scelera, &c.,] Seneca,—*Agam.* 115.
‡ *Mal. Who, I, &c.*] There is some confusion in the second 4to. at this place; it reads:
"MAL. Who, I? I haue bene twice an vnder sherife, man.

      Enter MALEVOLE *and* MENDOZA.

MEND. Hast bin with Maria?
MAL. As your scriuener to your vsurer I haue delt about taking of this commoditie, but shes could-frosty. well, I will go raile," &c.
Mr. Collier conjectures that perhaps when it was wished to shorten the performance, the scene began here.
§ *Catso*] See note *, p. 331.
‖ ta'en] The second 4to. "*taken.*"
¶ conduits] The second 4to. "*cōmodites.*"

---

* *pores*] The second 4to. "*power.*"
† *nor*] The second 4to. "*or*" (but our early writers often preferred using the former where we should now use the latter).
‡ *are*] The first 4to. "*one.*"
§ *What*] Both 4tos. "*Why.*"
‖ *Some far-fet trick good for ladies*]—far-fet, i.e. far-fetched.—An allusion to the proverb, "*Far-fet is good for ladies.*" So in Jonson's *Cynthia's Revels*, act iv. sc. 1. "Marry, and this may be *good for us ladies;* for it seems *'tis far-fet* by their stay."
¶ *fashion*] The second 4to. "*a fashion.*"

I'll trust no man: he that by tricks gets wreaths
Keeps them with steel; no man securely breathes
Out of's deservèd rank*; the crowd will mutter,
     " fool :"
Who cannot bear with spite, he cannot rule.
The chiefest secret for a man of state
Is, to live senseless of a strengthless hate. [*Exit.*

  Mal. [*starting up*] Death of the damned thief!
I'll make one i'the mask; thou shalt ha' some
brave spirits of the antique dukes.

  Cel. My lord, what strange delusion?

  Mal. Most happy, dear Celso, poisoned with an
empty box: I'll give thee all anon: my lady
comes to court; there is a whirl of fate comes
tumbling on; the castle's captain stands for me,
the people pray for me, and the great leader of
the just stands for me: then courage, Celso;
For no disastrous chance can ever move him
That leaveth nothing but a God above him.
                                        [*Exeunt.*

SCENE III.†

Enter BILIOSO *and* PREPASSO, *two Pages before them;*
     MAQUERELLE, BIANCA, *and* EMILIA.

  Bil. Make room there, room for the ladies!
why, gentlemen, will not ye suffer the ladies to
be entered in the great chamber? why, gallants!
and you, sir, to drop your torch where the
beauties must sit too!

  Pre. And there's a great fellow plays the
knave; why dost not strike him?

  Bil. Let him play the knave, o' God's name;
thinkest thou I have no more wit than to strike
a great fellow?—The music! more lights!
revelling-scaffolds! do you hear? Let there
be oaths enow ready at the door, swear out the
devil himself. Let's leave the ladies, and go see
if the lords be ready for them.
             [*Exeunt* BILIOSO, PREPASSO, *and Pages.*

  Maq. And, by my troth, beauties, why do you
not put you into the fashion? this is a stale cut;
you must come in fashion: look ye, you must be
all felt, felt and feather, a felt upon your bare
hair: ‡ look ye, these tiring things are justly out
of request now: and, do ye hear? you must wear
falling-bands, you must come into the falling
fashion: there is such a deal o' pinning these
ruffs, when the fine clean fall is worth all: and

again, if you should chance to take a nap in the
afternoon, your falling-band requires no poting-
stick* to recover his form: believe me, no fashion
to the falling,† I say.

  Bian. And is not Signior St. Andrew ‡ a gallant
fellow now;

  Maq. By my maidenhead, la, honour and he
agree as well together as a satin suit and woollen
stockings.

  Emilia. But is not Marshal Make-room, my
servant in reversion, a proper gentleman?

  Maq. Yes, in reversion, as he had his office;
as, in truth, he hath all things in reversion: he
has his mistress in reversion, his clothes in
reversion, his wit in reversion; and, indeed, is a
suitor to me for my dog in reversion: but, in
good verity, la, he is as proper a gentleman in
reversion as—and, indeed, as fine a man as may
be, having a red beard and a pair of warpt § legs.

  Bian. But, i'faith, I am most monstrously in
love with Count Quidlibet-in-quodlibet: is he not
a pretty, dapper, unidle‖ gallant?

  Maq. He is even one of the most busy-fingered
lords; he will put the beauties to the squeak
most hideously.

Re-enter BILIOSO.

  Bil. Room! make a lane there! the duke is
entering: stand handsomely for beauty's sake,
take up the ladies there! So, cornets, cornets!

Re-enter PREPASSO, *joins to* BILIOSO; *then enter two Pages
with lights,* FERRARDO, MENDOZA; *at the other door, two
Pages with lights, and the* Captain *leading in* MARIA;
MENDOZA *meets* MARIA, *and closeth with her; the rest fall
back.*

  Men. Madam, with gentle ear receive my suit;
A kingdom's safety should o'er-peise ¶ slight rites;
Marriage is merely nature's policy:
Then, since unless our royal beds be join'd,
Danger and civil tumult frights the state,
Be wise as you are fair, give way to fate.

  Maria. What wouldst thou, thou affliction to
our house?

---

* *poting-stick*] Generally written *poking-stick*,—a piece
of stick, or iron, or bone, with which the plaits of ruffs
were adjusted:
     "A boy arm'd with a *poating-sticke*
     Will dare to challenge Cutting Dicke."
                    Kempe's Nine daies wonder, 1600.
† *falling*] The first 4to. "*falling band.*"
‡ *St. Andrew*] The first 4to. "St. Andrew *Jaques.*"
§ *warpt*] The second 4to. "*wrapt.*"
‖ *unidle*] The first 4to. "*windle.*" As Maquerelle
immediately after terms him "*busy-fingered,*" "*unidle*"
seems the right reading.
¶ *o'er-peise*] i.e. over-weigh.

---

* *Out of's deservèd rank*] The first 4to. "*Out of distuned
rankes*"; the second 4to. "*Out of deserued* ranckes."
† *Scene III.*] The presence-chamber.
‡ *bare hair*] The first 4to. "*head.*"

Thou ever-devil, 'twas thou that banished'st
My truly noble lord !

Men. I !

Maria. Ay, by thy plots, by thy black strata-
gems :
Twelve moons have suffer'd change since I beheld
The loved presence of my dearest lord.
O thou far worse than death ! he parts but soul
From a weak body ; but thou soul from soul
Dissever'st, that which God's own hand did knit ;
Thou scant of honour, full of devilish wit !

Men. We'll check your too-intemperate lavish-
ness :
I can, and will.

Maria. What canst ?

Men. Go to ; in banishment thy husband dies.

Maria. He ever is at home that's ever wise.

Men. You'st* ne'er meet more : reason should
love control.

Maria. Not meet !
She that dear loves, her love's still in her soul.

Men. You are but a woman, lady, you must
yield.

Maria. O, save me, thou innated bashfulness,
Thou only ornament of woman's modesty !

Men. Modesty ! death, I'll torment thee.

Maria. Do, urge all torments, all afflictions try ;
I'll die my lord's as long as I can die.

Men. Thou obstinate, thou shalt die.—Captain,
that lady's life
Is forfeited to justice : we have examin'd her,
And we do find she hath empoisonèd
The reverend hermit ; therefore we command
Severest custody.—Nay, if you'll do's no good,
You'st do's no harm : a tyrant's peace is blood.

Maria. O, thou art merciful ; O gracious devil,
Rather by much let me condemnèd be
For seeming murder than be damn'd for thee !
I'll mourn no more ; come, girt my brows with
flowers :
Revel and dance, soul, now thy wish thou hast ;
Die like a bride, poor heart, thou shalt die chaste.

Enter AURELIA *in mourning habit.*

Life is a frost of cold felicity,†—

Aur. And death the thaw of all our vanity :
Was't not an honest priest that wrote so ?

Men. Who let her in ?

Bil. Forbear !

Pre. Forbear !

Aur. Alas, calamity is every where :
Sad misery, despite your double doors,
Will enter even in court.

Bil. Peace !

Aur. I ha' done.*

Bil. One word,—take heed !

Aur. I ha' done.

Enter MERCURY *with loud music.*

Mer. Cyllenian Mercury, the god of ghosts,
From gloomy shades that spread the lower coasts,
Calls four high-famèd Genoan † dukes to come,
And make this presence their Elysium,
To pass away this high triumphal night
With song and dances, court's more soft delight.

Aur. Are you god of ghosts ? I have a suit
depending in hell betwixt me and my conscience ;
I would fain have thee help me to an advocate.

Bil. Mercury shall be your lawyer, lady.

Aur. Nay, faith, Mercury has too good a face
to be a right lawyer.

Pre. Peace, forbear ! Mercury presents the mask.

*Cornets : the song to the cornets, which playing, the mask
enters ;* MALEVOLE, PIETRO, FERNEZE, *and* CELSO, *in
white robes, with dukes' crowns upon laurel-wreaths,
pistolets and short swords under their robes.*

Men. Celso, Celso, court ‡ Maria for our love.—
Lady, be gracious, yet grace.

Maria. With me, sir ?

[MALEVOLE *takes* MARIA *to dance.*

Mal. Yes, more lovèd than my breath ;
With you I'll dance.

Maria. Why, then, you dance with death.
But, come, sir, I was ne'er more apt for § mirth.
Death gives eternity a glorious breath :
O, to die honour'd, who would fear to die ?

Mal. They die in fear who live in villany.

Men. Yes, believe him, lady, and be rul'd by
him.

Pietro. Madam, with me.

[PIETRO *takes* AURELIA *to dance.*

Aur. Wouldst, then, be miserable ?

Pietro. I need not wish.

Aur. O, yet forbear my hand ! away ! fly ! fly !
O, seek not her that only seeks to die !

Pietro. Poor lovèd soul !

Aur. What, wouldst court misery ?

Pietro. Yes.

Aur. She'll come too soon :—O my griev'd
heart !

---

* *You'st*] A contraction of *you must :* so *thou'st* is put
for *thou must,* p. 351.

† *Life is a frost of cold felicity*] This line is given to
Aurelia in the second 4to.

* *I ha' done, &c.*] The old eds. have,—
"AUR. I ha done ; one word, take heede, I ha done."

† *Genoan*] The first 4to. "*Genoa.*"

‡ *court*] The second 4to. "*count.*"

§ *for*] The second 4to. "*to.*"

Pietro. Lady, ha' done, ha' done :
Come,* let us dance ; be once from sorrow free.

Aur. Art a sad man ?

Pietro. Yes, sweet.

Aur. Then we'll agree.

[*FERNEZE takes* MAQUERELLE, *and* CELSO BIANCA :
*then the cornets sound the measure, one change,
and rest.*

Fer. [*to* BIANCA.] Believe it, lady ; shall I
swear? let me enjoy you in private, and I'll
marry you, by my soul.

Bian. I had rather you would swear by your
body : I think that would prove the more regarded
oath with you.

Fer. I'll swear by them both, to please you.

Bian. O, damn them not both to please me,
for God's sake !

Fer. Faith, sweet creature, let me enjoy you
to-night, and I'll marry you to-morrow fortnight,
by my troth, la.

Maq. On his troth, la ! believe him not ; that
kind of cony-catching is as stale as Sir Oliver
Anchovy's perfumed jerkin : promise of matrimony by a young gallant, to bring a virgin lady
into a fool's paradise ; make her a great woman,
and then cast her off ;—'tis as common and† natural
to a courtier, as jealousy to a citizen, gluttony to a
puritan, wisdom to an alderman, pride to a tailor,
or an empty hand-basket‡ to one of these sixpenny damnations : of his troth, la! believe him
not ; traps to catch pole-cats.

Mal. [*to* MARIA.] Keep your face constant, let
no sudden passion
Speak in your eyes.

Maria. O my Altofront !

Pietro. [*to* AURELIA.] A tyrant's jealousies
Are very nimble : you receive it all?

Aur. My heart, though not my knees, doth
Low as the earth, to thee.   [*humbly fall,*

Mal.§ Peace ! next change ; no words.

Maria. Speech to such, ay, O, what will affords !
[*Cornets sound the measure over again : which
danced, they unmask.*

Men. Malevole !

[*They environ* MENDOZA, *bending their pistols on him.*

Mal. No.

Men. Altofront ! Duke Pietro !‖ Ferneze ! ha !

All. Duke Altofront ! Duke Altofront !

[*Cornets, a flourish.—They seize upon* MENDOZA.

Men. Are we surpris'd ? what strange delusions
mock

Our senses ? do I dream ? or have I dreamt
This two days' space ? where am I ?

Mal. Where an arch-villain is.

Men. O, lend me breath till I am fit to die !*
For peace with heaven, for your own souls' sake,
Vouchsafe me life !

Pietro. Ignoble villain ! whom neither heaven
     nor hell,
Goodness of God or man, could once make good !

Mal. Base, treacherous wretch ! what grace
     canst thou expect,
That hast grown impudent in gracelessness ?

Men. O, life !

Mal. Slave, take thy life.
Wert thou defencèd, th[o]rough blood and wounds,
The sternest horror of a civil fight,
Would I achieve thee ; but prostrate at my feet,
I scorn to hurt thee : 'tis the heart of slaves
That deigns to triumph over peasants' graves ;
For such thou art, since birth doth ne'er enroll
A man 'mong monarchs, but a glorious soul.
" O, I have seen strange accidents of state !
" The flatterer, like the ivy, clip † the oak,
" And waste it to the heart ; lust so confirm'd,
" That the black act of sin itself not sham'd
" To be term'd courtship.
" O, they that are as great as be their sins,
" Let them remember that th' inconstant people
" Love many princes‡ merely for their faces
" And outward shows ; and they do covet more
" To have a sight of these than of their virtues.
" Yet thus much let the great ones still conceive,§
" When they observe not heaven's impos'd condi-
     tions,
" They are no kings,‖ but forfeit their commissions.
     " *Maq.* O good my lord, I have lived in the
" court this twenty year : they that have been old
" courtiers, and come to live in the city, they are
" spited at, and thrust to the walls like apricocks,
" good my lord.
     " *Bil.* My lord, I did know your lordship in
" this disguise ; you heard me ever say, if Altofront
" did return, I would stand for him : besides, 'twas
" your lordship's pleasure to call me wittol and
" cuckold : you must not think, but that I knew
" you, I would have put it up so patiently."

---

* *Come*] The first 4to. "*Come downe.*"
† *and*] Both 4tos. "*as.*"
‡ *hand-basket*] Not in the first 4to.
§ *Mal.*] Both 4tos. "*Pietro.*"
‖ *Pietro*] The first 4to. "*Lorenzo.*"

* *till I am fit to die*] The first 4to. "*to liue* til I am fit
to dy."
† *clip*] i. e. embrace.
‡ *princes*] So my copy of the second 4to. ; that in the
Garrick collection, "*men.*"
§ *conceive*] The old ed. "*conceale.*"
‖ *kings*] So my copy of the second 4to. ; that in the
Garrick collection, "*men.*"

Mal. You o'er-joy'd * spirits, wipe your long-
    wet eyes.   [*To* PIETRO *and* AURELIA.
Hence with this man [*Kicks out* MENDOZA]: an
    eagle takes not flies.
You to your vows [*To* PIETRO *and* AURELIA]: and
    thou unto the suburbs.† [*To* MAQUERELLE.

---

  * o'er-joy'd] The first 4to. "are ioy'd."
  † the suburbs] "Where in most countries the stews are
situated."—*Reed.*

You to my worst friend I would hardly give;
Thou art a perfect old knave [*To* BILIOSO]: all-
    pleas'd live
You two unto my breast [*To* CELSO *and the*
    Captain]: thou to my heart. [*To* MARIA.
" The rest of idle actors idly part : "
And as for me, I here assume my right,
To which I hope all's pleas'd : to all good night.
          [*Cornets, a flourish.*   *Exeunt.*

" AN IMPERFECT ODE, BEING BUT ONE STAFF,

" SPOKEN BY THE PROLOGUE.

" To wrest each hurtless thought to private sense
" Is the foul use of ill-bred impudence :
    " Immodest censure now grows wild,
      " All over-running.
    " Let innocence be ne'er so chaste,
      " Yet at the last
      " She is defil'd
    " With too-nice-brainèd cunning.

    " O you of fairer soul,
      " Control
    " With an Herculean arm
      " This harm ;
" And once teach all old freedom of a pen,
" Which still must write of fools, whiles't writes
    " of men ! "

" EPILOGUS.

" Your modest silence, full of heedy stillness,
" Makes me thus speak : a voluntary illness
" Is merely senseless ; but unwilling error,
" Such as proceeds from too rash youthful fervour,
" May well be call'd a fault, but not a sin :
" Rivers take names from founts where they begin.
    " Then let not too severe an eye peruse
" The slighter brakes of our reformèd Muse,*
" Who could herself herself of faults detect,
" But that she knows 'tis easy to correct,

---

  * The slighter brakes of our reformed Muse] "I suppose
by this expression is meant the uncultivated parts of our
performance ; brakes (i.e. fern) commonly grow in ground
that is never tilled or broken up."—*Steevens.* Here
"brakes" seems to mean—flaws, breaks. See Mr. Halliwell's Dict. of Arch. and Prov. Words, sub "Brake."

" Though some men's labour : troth, to err is fit,
" As long as wisdom's not profess'd, but wit.
" Then till another's happier Muse appears,*
" Till his Thalia feast your learnèd ears,
" To whose desertful lamps pleas'd Fates impart
" Art above nature, judgment above art,
" Receive this piece, which hope nor fear yet
    " daunteth :
" He that knows most knows most how much he
    " wanteth."

---

  * Then till another's happier Muse appears, &c.] An
allusion to Ben Jonson : see Gifford's Memoirs of that
poet, p. lxxii.

MONUMENTS OF HONOUR.

Monuments of Honor. Derived from remarkable antiquity, and celebrated in the Honorable City of London, at the sole munificent charge and expences of the Right Worthy and Worshipfull Fraternity of the Eminent Merchant-Taylors. Directed in their most affectionate loue, at the Confirmation of their Right Worthy Brother John Gore in the High Office of his Maiesties Lieutenant ouer this his Royall Chamber. Expressing in a Magnificent Tryumph, all the Pageants, Chariots of Glory, Temples of Honor, besides a specious and goodly Sea Tryumph, as well particularly to the honor of the City as generally to the glory of this our Kingdome. Inuented and written by John Webster Merchant-Taylor. Non norunt hæc monumenta mori. Printed at London by Nicholas Okes. 1624. 4to.

TO THE

RIGHT WORTHY DESERVER OF THIS SO NOBLE A CEREMONY THIS DAY CONFERRED
UPON HIM, JOHN GORE, LORD MAYOR AND CHANCELLOR OF THE
RENOWNED CITY OF LONDON.

My worthy lord,

These presentments, which were intended principally for your honour, and for illustrating the worth of that worthy corporation whereof you are a member, come now humbly to kiss your lordship's hands, and to present the inventor of them to that service which my ability expressed in this may call me to, under your lordship's favour, to do you * honour, and the city service, in the quality of a scholar; assuring your lordship I shall never either to your ear or table press unmannerly or impertinently. My endeavours this way have received grace and allowance from your worthy brothers that were supervisors of the cost of these Triumphs; and my hope is, that they shall stand no less respected in your eye, nor undervalued in your worthy judgment : which favours done to one born free of your company, and your servant, shall ever be acknowledged by him stands interested

To your lordship in all duty,

JOHN WEBSTER.

---

* *to do you*] The old ed. "*! to you, do you.*"

MONUMENTS OF HONOUR.

I could in this my preface, by as great light of learning as any formerly employed in this service can attain to, deliver to you the original and cause of all Triumphs, their excessive cost in the time of the Romans; I could likewise with so noble amplification make a survey of the worth and glory of the Triumphs of the precedent times in this honourable city of London, that, were my work of a bigger bulk, they should remain to all posterity. But both my pen and ability this way are confined in too narrow a circle; nor have I space enough in this so short a volume to express only with rough lines and a faint shadow, as the painters' phrase is, first, the great care and alacrity of the right worshipful the Master and Wardens, and the rest of the selected and industrious committees, both for the curious and judging election of the subject for the present spectacles, and next that the working or mechanic part of it might be answerable to the invention. Leaving, therefore, these worthy gentlemen to the embraces and thanks of the right honourable and worthy Pretor,* and myself under the shadow of their crest, which is a safe one, for 'tis the Holy Lamb in the Sunbeams, I do present to all modest and indifferent judges these my present endeavours.

I fashioned, for the more amplifying the show upon the water, two eminent spectacles in manner of a Sea-triumph. The first furnished with four persons : in the front Oceanus and Thetis ; behind them, Thamesis and Medway, the two rivers on whom the Lord Mayor extends his power as far as from Staines to Rochester. The other show is of a fair Terrestrial Globe, circled about, in convenient seats, with seven of our most famous navigators; as Sir Francis Drake, Sir John Hawkins, Sir Martin Frobisher, Sir Humphrey Gilbert, Captain Thomas Cavendish, Captain Christopher Carlisle, and Captain John Davis. The conceit of this device to be, that, in regard the two rivers pay due tribute of waters to the seas, Oceanus in grateful recompense returns the memory of these seven worthy captains, who have made England so famous in remotest parts of the world. These two spectacles, at my Lord Mayor's taking water at the Three Cranes, approaching my Lord's barge, after a peal of sea-thunder from the other side the water, these speeches between Oceanus and Thetis follow:

OCEANUS AND THETIS.

Thetis.

What brave sea-music bids us welcome, hark !
Sure, this is Venice, and the day Saint Mark,
In which the Duke and Senates their course hold
To wed our empire with a ring of gold.

Oceanus.

No, Thetis, you're mistaken: we are led
With infinite delight from the land's head
In ken of goodly shipping and yon bridge :
Venice had ne'er the like : survey that ridge
Of stately buildings which the river hem,
And grace the silver stream as the stream them.
That beauteous seat is London, so much fam'd
Where any navigable sea is nam'd ;
And in that bottom eminent merchants plac'd,
As rich and venturous as ever grac'd
Venice or Europe : these two rivers here,
Our followers, may tell you where we are ;
This Thamesis, that Medway, who are sent
To yon* most worthy Pretor, to present
Acknowledgement of duty ne'er shall err
From Staines unto the ancient Rochester.
And now to grace their Triumph, in respect
These pay us tribute, we are pleas'd to select

---

* *Pretor*] i. e. Lord Mayor.

* *yon*] The old ed. "you."

Seven worthy navigators out by name,
Seated beneath this Globe; whose ample fame
In the remotest part o' the earth is found,
And some of them have circled the globe round.
These, you observe, are living in your eye,
And so they ought, for worthy men ne'er die;
Drake, Hawkins, Frobisher, Gilbert, brave knights,
That brought home gold and honour from sea-
   fights,
Ca'ndish, Carlisle, and Davis; and to these
So many worthies I could add at seas
Of this bold nation, it would envy strike
I' the rest o' the world who cannot show the like:
'Tis action values honour, as the flint
Look[s] black and feels like ice, yet from within't
There are struck sparks which to the darkest
   nights
Yield quick and piercing food for several lights.

Thetis.

You have quicken'd well my memory; and now
Of this your grateful Triumph I allow.
Honour looks clear, and spreads her beams at
   large
From the grave Senate seated in that barge.—
Rich lading swell your bottoms! a blest gale
Follow your ventures, that they never fail!
And may you live successively to wear
The joy of this day, each man his whole year!

This show, having tendered this service to my
Lord upon the water, is after to be conveyed
ashore, and in convenient place employed for
adorning the rest of the Triumph. After my
Lord Mayor's landing, and coming past Paul's-
Chain, there first attends for his honour, in Paul's
Church-yard, a beautiful spectacle called the
Temple of Honour; the pillars of which are
bound about with roses and other beautiful
flowers, which shoot up to the adorning of
the King's Majesty's Arms on the top of the
Temple.

In the highest seat a person representing Troynovant or the City, enthroned, in rich habiliments:
beneath her, as admiring her peace and felicity,
sit five eminent cities, as Antwerp, Paris, Rome,
Venice, and Constantinople: under these sit five
famous scholars and poets of this our kingdom,
as Sir Geoffrey Chaucer, the learned Gower, the
excellent John Lydgate, the sharp-witted Sir
Thomas More, and last, as worthy both soldier
and scholar, Sir Philip Sidney,—these being
celebrators of honour, and the preservers both of

the names of men and memories of cities above
to posterity.

I present, riding afore this Temple, Henry de
Royal, the first pilgrim or gatherer of quarterago
for this Company, and John of Yeackaley, King
Edward the Third's pavilion-maker, who pur-
chased our Hall in the sixth year of the aforesaid
king's government. These lived in Edward the
First's time likewise; in the sixth of whose reign
this Company was confirmed a guild or corporation
by the name of Tailors and Linen-armour[er]s,
with power to choose a Master and Wardens at
midsummer. These are decently habited and
hooded according to the ancient manner. My
Lord is here saluted with two speeches; first by
Troynovant in these lines following:

THE SPEECH OF TROYNOVANT.

History, Truth, and Virtue seek by name
To celebrate the Merchant-Tailors' fame.
That Henry de Royal, this we call
Worthy John Yeacksley purchas'd first this Hall:
And thus from low beginnings there oft springs
Societies claim brotherhoods of kings.
I, Troynovant, plac'd eminent in the eye
Of these admire at my felicity,*
Five cities, Antwerp, and the spacious Paris,
Rome, Venice, and the Turk's metropolis:
Beneath these, five learn'd poets, worthy men,
Who do eternize brave acts by their pen,
Chaucer, Gower, Lydgate, More, and for our time
Sir Philip Sidney, glory of our clime:
These beyond death a fame to monarchs give,
And these make cities and societies live.

The next delivered by him represents Sir Philip
Sidney:

To honour by our writings worthy men,
Flows as a duty from a judging pen;
And when we are employ'd in such sweet praise,
Bees swarm and leave their honey on our bays:
Ever more musically verses run
When the loath'd vein of flattery they shun.
Survey, most noble Pretor, what succeeds,
Virtue low-bred aspiring to high deeds.

These passing on, in the next place my Lord
is encountered with the person of Sir John Hawkwood, in complete armour, his plume, and feather
for his horse's chaffron,† of the Company's colours,

---

* *Of these admire at my felicity, &c.*] i. e. of these *which*
admire at my felicity, namely, five cities, &c.

† *chaffron*] i. e. chamfron, a head-piece with a project-
ing spike.—Old ed. "*shafforne.*

whito and watchet.* This worthy knight did most worthy service, in the time of Edward the Third, in France; after, served as general divers princes of Italy; went to the Holy Land; and in his return back died at Florence, and there lies buried with a fair monument over him. This worthy gentleman was free of our Company; and thus I prepare him to give my Lord entertainment:

SIR JOHN HAWKWOOD'S SPEECH.

My birth was mean, yet my deservings grew
To eminence, and in France a high pitch flew:
From a poor common soldier I attain'd
The style of captain, and then knighthood gain'd;
Serv'd the Black Prince in France in all his wars;
Then went i'the Holy Land; thence brought my
And wearied body which no danger fear'd, [scars,
To Florence, where it nobly lies inteer'd :†
There Sir John Hawkwood's memory doth live,
And to the Merchant-Tailors fame doth give.

After him follows a Triumphant Chariot with the Arms of the Merchant-Tailors coloured and gilt in several places of it; and over it there is supported, for a canopy, a rich and very spacious Pavilion coloured crimson, with a Lion Passant: this is drawn with four horses; for porters would have made it move tottering and improperly. In the Chariot I place for the honour of the Company, of which records remain in the Hall, eight famous kings of this land, that have been free of this worshipful Company.

First, the victorious Edward the Third, that first quartered the arms of France with England: next, the munificent Richard the Second, that kept ten thousand daily in his court in checkroll: by him, the grave and discreet Henry the Fourth: in the next chairs, the scourge and terror of France, Henry the Fifth, and by him, his religious though unfortunate son, Henry the Sixth: the two next chairs are supplied with the persons of the amorous and personable Edward the Fourth, for so Philip Commineus and Sir Thomas More describe him; the other with the bad man but the good king, Richard the Third, for so the laws he made in his short government do illustrate him: but lastly in the most eminent part of the Chariot I place the wise and politic Henry the Seventh, holding the charter by which the Company was improved from the title of Linen-armourers into the name of Master and Wardens of Merchant-Tailors of Saint John

Baptist. The chairs of these kings that were of the house of Lancaster are garnished with artificial red roses, the rest with white; but the uniter of the division and houses, Henry the Seventh, both with white and red; from whence his Royal Majesty now reigning took his motto for one piece of his coin, *Henricus rosas, regna Jacobus.*

The speaker in this Pageant is Edward the Third: the last line of his speech is repeated by all the rest in the Chariot:

Edward the Third.

View whence the Merchant-Tailors' honour springs,—
From this most royal conventicle of kings:
Eight that successively wore England's crown,
Held it a special honour and renown,
(The Society was so worthy and so good,)
T'unite themselves into their Brotherhood.
Thus time and industry attain the prize,
As seas from brooks, as brooks from hillocks rise:
Let all good men this sentence oft repeat,—
By unity the smallest things grow great.

The Kings.

By unity the smallest things grow great:

and this repetition was proper, for it is the Company's motto, *Concordiâ parvæ res crescunt.*

After this pageant, rides Queen Anne, wife to Richard the Second, free likewise of this Company: nor let it seem strange; for, besides her, there were two duchesse[s], five countesses, and two baronesses, free of this Society, seventeen princes and dukes, one archbishop, one-and-thirty earls, besides those made with noble Prince Henry, one viscount, twenty-four bishops, sixty-six barons, seven abbots, seven priors or sub-prior[s]; and with Prince Henry, in the year 1607,* the Duke of Lennox, the Earls of Nottingham, Suffolk, Arundel, Oxford, Worcester, Pembroke, Essex, Northampton, Salisbury, Montgomery, the Earl of Perth, Viscount Cranbourne, barons the Lord Eures, Hunsdon, Hayes,† Burleigh, Master Howard, Master Sheffield, Sir John Harington, Sir Thomas Chaloner, besides states‡ of the Low-Countries, and Sir Noel Caroon their lieger§ ambassador.

---

* *watchet*] i. e. pale blue.
† *inteer'd*] So the old ed. for the sake of the rhyme.

* *and with Prince Henry, in the year* 1607, &c.] The King and Prince Henry dined in Merchant-Tailors' Hall, July 16th, 1607; on which occasion the Prince and the noblemen, &c., here mentioned, were made free of the Company. See Nichols's *Progresses of King James*, &c., vol. ii. 140.
† *Eures . . Hayes*, &c.] Properly "*Eure . . Hay.*" &c.
‡ *states*] i. e. persons of high rank.
§ *lieger*] i. e. resident.

And iu regard our Company are styled Brethren of the Fraternity of Saint John Baptist, and that the ancient Knights of Saint John of Jerusalem,—to which now-demolished house in Saint John's Street our Company then using to go to offer, it is recorded Henry the Seventh, then accompanying them, gave our Master the upper-hand,—because these knights, I say, were instituted to secure the way for pilgrims in the desert, I present therefore two of the worthiest Brothers of this Society of Saint John Baptist I can find out in history; the first, Amade le Grand, by whose aid Rhodes was recovered from the Turks, and the Order of Annuntiade or Salutation instituted with that of four letters, FERT, signifying *Fortitudo ejus Rhodum tenuit;* and the other, Monsieur* Jean Valet, who defended Malta from the Turks' invasion, and expelled them from that impregnable key of Christendom; this styled Great Master of Malta, that Governor of Rhodes.

Next I bring our two Sea-triumphs; and after that, the Ship called the Holy Lamb, which brings hanging in her shrouds the Golden Fleece; the conceit of this being, that God is the guide and protector of all prosperous ventures.

To second this, follow the two beasts, the Lion and Camel, proper to the Arms of the Company: on the Camel rides a Turk, such as use to travel with caravans; and on the Lion a Moor or wild Numidian.

The fourth eminent Pageant I call the Monument of Charity and Learning: this fashioned like a beautiful Garden with all kinds of flowers; at the four corners four artificial birdcages with variety of birds in them; this for the beauty of the flowers and melody of the birds to represent a spring in winter. In the midst of the Garden, under an elm-tree, sits the famous and worthy patriot, Sir Thomas White: who had a dream that he should build a college where two bodies of an elm sprang from one root; and being inspired to it by God, first rode to Cambridge to see if he could find any such; failing of it there, went to Oxford, and surveying all the grounds in and near the University, at last in Gloster-Hall-garden he found one that somewhat resembled it; upon which he resolved to endow it with larger revenue and to increase the foundation: having set men at work upon it, and riding one day out at the North-Gate at Oxford, he spied

on his right hand the self-same elm had been figured him in his dream; whereupon he gives o'er his former purpose of so amply enlarging Gloster-Hall (yet not without a large exhibition to it), purchases the ground where the elm stood, and in the same place built the College of Saint John Baptist; and to this day the elm grows in the garden carefully preserved, as being, under God, a motive to their worthy foundation.

This I have heard Fellows of the House, of approved credit and no way superstitiously given, affirm to have been delivered from man to man since the first building of it; and that Sir Thomas White, inviting the Abbot of Osney to dinner in the aforesaid Hall, in the Abbot's presence and the hearing of divers other grave persons, affirmed, by God's inspiration, in the former-recited manner, he built and endowed the College.

This relation is somewhat with the largest; only to give you better light of the figure, the chief person in this is Sir Thomas White, sitting in his eminent habit of Lord Mayor: on the one hand sits Charity with a pelican on her head; on the other, Learning with a book in one hand and a laurel-wreath in the other: behind him is the College of Saint John Baptist in Oxford exactly modelled: two cornets, which for more pleasure answer one and another interchangeably; and round about the Pageant sit twelve of the four-and-twenty Cities (for more would have overburdened it) to which this worthy gentleman hath been a charitable benefactor. When my Lord approaches to the front of this piece, Learning humbles herself to him in these ensuing verses:

THE SPEECH OF LEARNING.

To express what happiness the country yields,
The poets feign'd heaven in th' Elysian fields:
We figure here a Garden fresh and new,
In which the chiefest of our blessings grew.
This worthy patriot here, Sir Thomas White,
Whilst he was living, had a dream one night
He had built a college and given living to't,
Where two elm-bodies sprang up from one root:
And as he dream'd, most certain 'tis he found
The elm near Oxford; and upon that ground
Built Saint John's College. Truth can testify
His merit, whilst his Faith and Charity
Was the true compass, measur'd every part,
And took the latitude of his Christian heart;
Faith kept the centre, Charity walk'd this round
Until a true circumference was found:

---

* *the other, Monsieur*] The old od. *"the other of Moun-sieur."*

And may the impression of this figure strike
Each worthy senator to do the like!

The last I call the Monument of Gratitude,
which thus dilates itself:

Upon an Artificial Rock, set with mother-of-
pearl and such other precious stones as are found
in quarries, are placed four curious Pyramids,
charged with the Prince's Arms, the Three
Feathers; which by day yield a glorious show;
and by night a more goodly, for they have lights
in them, that, at such time as my Lord Mayor
returns from Paul's, shall make certain ovals and
squares resemble precious stones. The Rock
expresses the richness of the kingdom Prince
Henry was born heir to; the Pyramids, which
are monuments for the dead, that he is deceased.*
On the top of this rests half a Celestial Globe;
in the midst of this hangs the Holy Lamb in the
Sunbeams; on either side of these an Angel.
Upon a pedestal of gold stands the figure of
Prince Henry with his coronet, george, and
garter: in his left hand he holds a circlet of
crimson velvet, charged with four Holy Lambs,
such as our Company choose Masters with. In
several cants† beneath sits, first, Magistracy,
tending a Bee-hive; to express his gravity in
youth and forward industry to have proved an
absolute governor: next, Liberality, by her a
Dromedary; showing his speed and alacrity in
gratifying his followers: Navigation with a
Jacob's-staff and Compass; expressing his‡ desire
that his reading that way might in time grow to
the practic and building to that purpose one of
the goodliest ships was ever launched in the
river: in the next, Unanimity with a Chaplet of
Lilies, in her lap a Sheaf of Arrows; showing he
loved nobility and commonalty with an entire
heart: next, Industry on a hill where Ants are
hoarding up corn; expressing his forward inclination to all noble exercise: next, Chastity, by her
a Unicorn; showing it is guide to all other
virtues, and clears the fountain-head from all
poison: Justice, with her properties: then
Obedience, by her an Elephant, the strongest
beast, but most observant to man of any creature:
then Peace sleeping upon a Cannon; alluding to the
eternal peace he now possesses: Fortitude, a Pillar
in one hand, a Serpent wreathed about the other;

to express * his height of mind and the expectation of an undaunted resolution. These twelve
thus seated, I figure Loyalty, as well sworn
servant to this City as to this Company; and
at my Lord Mayor's coming from Paul's and
going down Wood-street, Amado le Grand
delivers this speech unto him:

THE SPEECH OF AMADE LE GRAND.

Of all the Triumphs which your eye has view'd,
This the fair Monument of Gratitude,
This chiefly should your eye and ear employ,
That was of all your Brotherhood the joy;
Worthy Prince Henry, fame's best president,
Call'd to a higher court of parliament
In his full strength of youth and height of blood,
And, which crown'd all, when he was truly good:
On virtue and on worth he still was throwing
Most bounteous showers, where'er he found them
　　growing;
He never did disguise his ways by art,
But suited his intents unto his heart;
And lov'd to do good more for goodness' sake
Than any retribution man could make.
Such was this Prince: such are the noble hearts
Who, when they die, yet die not in all parts,
But from the integrity of a brave mind
Leave a most clear and eminent fame behind:
Thus hath this jewel not quite lost his ray,
Only cas'd-up 'gainst a more glorious day.
And be't remember'd that our Company
Have not forgot him who ought ne'er to die:
Yet wherefore should our sorrow give him dead,
When a new Phœnix † springs up in his stead,
That, as he seconds him in every grace,
May second him in brotherhood and place?

Good rest, my Lord! Integrity, that keeps
The safest watch and breeds the soundest sleeps,
Make the last day of this your holding seat
Joyful as this, or rather, more complete!

I could a more curious and elaborate way have
expressed myself in these my endeavours; but
to have been rather too tedious in my speeches,
or too weighty, might have troubled my noble
Lord and puzzled the understanding of the
common people: suffice it, I hope 'tis well; and
if it please his Lordship and my worthy employ-
ers, I am amply satisfied.

---

* *deceased*] See p. 371.
† *cants*] i. e. niches.
‡ *expressing his*] The old ed. "*expressing that his.*"

* *express*] The old ed. "*expect.*"
† *a new Phœnix*] i. e. Prince Charles.

A MONUMENTAL COLUMN.

A Monvmental Colvmne, Erected to the liuing Memory of the euer-glorious Henry, late Prince of Wales. Virgil. Ostendent terris hunc tantum fata. By John Webster. London, Printed by N. O. for William Welby dwelling in Pauls Church-yard at the signe of the Swan. 1613, forms a portion of a tract, the general title of which (in white letters on a black ground) runs thus :

Three Elegies on the most lamented Death of Prince Henrie,

The first			Cyril Tourneur.
The second	}	written by {	John Webster.
The third			Tho. Heywood.

London Printed for William Welbie. 1613. 4to.

Prince Henry died, to the great grief of the whole nation, on the 6th of November, 1612, in his nineteenth year.

TO THE

RIGHT HONOURABLE SIR ROBERT CARR, VISCOUNT ROCHESTER,* KNIGHT OF THE MOST NOBLE ORDER OF THE GARTER, AND ONE OF HIS MAJESTY'S MOST HONOURABLE PRIVY COUNCIL.

My right noble lord,

I present to your voidest leisure of survey these few sparks found out in our most glorious prince his ashes. I could not have thought this worthy your view, but that it aims at the preservation of his fame, than which I know not any thing (but the sacred lives of both their majesties and their sweet issue) that can be dearer unto you. Were my whole life turned into leisure, and that leisure accompanied with all the Muses, it were not able to draw a map large enough of him; for his praise is an high-going sea that wants both shore and bottom. Neither do I, my noble lord, present you with this ·night-piece to make his death-bed still float in those compassionate rivers of your eyes: you have already, with much lead upon your heart, sounded both the sorrow royal and your own. O, that care should ever attain to so ambitious a title! Only, here though I dare not say you shall find him live, for that assurance were worth many kingdoms, yet you shall perceive him draw a little breath, such as gives us comfort his critical day is past, and the glory of a new life risen, neither subject to physic nor fortune. For my defects in this undertaking, my wish presents itself with that of Martial's; †

> O utinam mores animumque offingere possem !
> Pulchrior in terris nulla tabella foret.

Howsoever, your protection is able to give it noble lustre, and bind me by that honourable courtesy to be ever

Your honour's truly devoted servant,

JOHN WEBSTER.

---

* *Sir Robert Carr, Viscount Rochester, &c.*] The minion of a weak prince, created Earl of Somerset, in the year during which the present tract was printed. He died in 1645. The connection of this infamous man with the still more infamous Countess of Essex, and the murder of Sir Thomas Overbury, are circumstances too notorious to require repetition here.

† x. 32,—" *Ars* utinam mores animumque effingere *posset* !" &c.

A MONUMENTAL COLUMN.

A FUNERAL ELEGY.

THE greatest of the kingly race is gone,
Yet with so great a reputation
Laid in the earth, we cannot say he's dead,
But as a perfect diamond set in lead,
Scorning our foil, his glories do break forth,
Worn by his maker, who best knew his worth.
Yet to our fleshy eyes there does belong
That which we think helps grief, a passionate
      tongue :
Methinks I see men's hearts pant in their lips ;
We should not grieve at the bright sun's eclipse,
But that we love his light : so travellers stray,
Wanting both guide and conduct of the day.
Nor let us strive to make this sorrow old ;
For wounds smart most when that the blood
      grows cold.
If princes think that ceremony meet,
To have their corpse embalm'd to keep them
      sweet,
Much more they ought to have their fame exprest
In Homer, though it want Darius' chest :
To adorn which in her deservèd throne,
I bring those colours which Truth calls her own.
Nor gain nor praise by my weak lines are sought :
Love that's born free cannot be hir'd nor bought.
Some great inquisitors in nature say,
Royal and generous forms sweetly display
Much of the heavenly virtue, as proceeding
From a pure essence and elected breeding :
Howe'er, truth for him thus much doth impórtune,
His form and virtue both deserv'd his fortune ;
For 'tis a question not decided yet,
Whether his mind or fortune were more great.
Methought I saw him in his right hand wield
A caduceus, in th' other Pallas' shield :
His mind quite void of ostentation,
His high-erected thoughts look'd down upon

The smiling valley of his fruitful heart :
Honour and courtesy in every part
Proclaim'd him, and grew lovely in each limb :
He well became those virtues which grac'd him.
He spread his bounty with a provident hand,
And not like those that sow th' ingrateful sand :
His rewards follow'd reason, ne'er were plac'd
For ostentation ; and to make them last,
He was not like the mad and thriftless vine .
That spendeth all her blushes at one time,
But like the orange-tree his fruits he bore,—
Some gather'd, he had green, and blossoms store.
We hop'd much of him, till death made hope err :
We stood as in some spacious theatre,
Musing what would become of him, his flight
Reach'd such a noble pitch above our sight ;
Whilst he discreetly-wise this rule had won,
Not to let fame know his intents till done.
Men came to his court as to bright academies
Of virtue and of valour : all the eyes,
That feasted at his princely exercise,
Thought that by day Mars held his lance, by night
Minerva bore a torch to give him light.
As once on Rhodes, Pindar reports, of old
Soldiers expected 't would have rain'd down gold,
Old husbandmen i'the country gan to plant
Laurel instead of elm, and made their vaunt
Their sons and daughters should such trophies
      wear
Whenas the prince return'd a conqueror
From foreign nations ; for men thought his star
Had mark'd him for a just and glorious war.
And, sure, his thoughts were ours : he could not
      read
Edward the Black Prince's life but it must breed
A virtuous emulation to have his name
So lag behind him both in time and fame ;

He that like lightning did his force advance,
And shook to th' centre the whole realm of France,
That of warm blood open'd so many sluices
To gather and bring thence six flower-de-luces;
Who ne'er saw fear but in his enemies' flight;
Who found weak numbers conquer, arm'd with
　　right;
Who knew his humble shadow spread no more
After a victory than it did before;
Who had his breast instated with the choice
Of virtues, though they made no ambitious noise;
Whose resolution was so fiery-still
It seem'd he knew better to die than kill,
And yet drew Fortune, as the adamant steel,
Seeming t' have fix'd a stay upon her wheel;
Who jestingly would say, it was his trade
To fashion death-beds, and hath often made
Horror look lovely, when i'the fields there lay
Arms and legs so distracted, one would say
That the dead bodies had no bodies left;
He that of working pulse sick France bereft;
Who knew that battles, not the gaudy show
Of ceremonies, do on kings bestow
Best theatres; t'whom naught so tedious as court-
　　sport;
That thought all fans and ventoys of the court
Ridiculous and loathsome to the shade
Which, in a march, his waving ensign made.
Him did he strive to imitate, and was sorry
He did not live before him, that his glory
Might have been his example: to these ends,
Those men that follow'd him were not by friends
Or letters preferr'd to him; he made choice
In action, not in complimental voice.
And as Marcellus did two temples rear
To Honour and to Virtue, plac'd so near
They kiss'd, yet none to Honour's got access
But they that pass'd through Virtue's; so, to express
His worthiness, none got his countenance
But those whom actual merit did advance.
Yet, alas, all his goodness lies full low!
O greatness, what shall we compare thee to?
To giants, beasts, or towers fram'd out of snow,
Or like wax gilded tapers, more for show
Than durance? thy foundation doth betray
Thy frailty, being builded on such clay.
This shows the all-controlling power of fate,
That all our sceptres and our chairs of state
Are but glass-metal, that we are full of spots,
And that, like new-writ copies, t'avoid blots,
Dust must be thrown upon us; for in him
Our comfort sunk and drown'd, learning to swim.
And though he died so late, he's no more near
To us than they that died three thousand year

Before him; only memory doth keep
Their fame as fresh as his from death or sleep.
Why should the stag or raven live so long,
And that their age rather should not belong
Unto a righteous prince, whose lengthen'd years
Might assist men's necessities and fears?
Let beasts live long, and wild, and still in fear;
The turtle-dove never outlives nine year.
Both life and death have equally exprest,
Of all the shortest madness is the best.
We ought not think that his great triumphs need
Our wither'd laurels.* Can our weak praise feed
His memory, which worthily contemns
Marble, and gold, and oriental gems?
His merits pass our dull invention.
And now, methinks, I see him smile upon
Our fruitless tears; bids us disperse these showers,
And says his thoughts are far refin'd from ours:
As Rome of her belovèd Titus said,
That from the body the bright soul was fled
For his own good and their affliction:
On such a broken column we lean on;
And for ourselves, not him, let us lament,
Whose happiness is grown our punishment.
But, surely, God gave this as an allay
To the blest union of that nuptial day
We hop'd; for fear of surfeit, thought it meet
To mitigate, since we swell with what is sweet.
And, for sad tales suit grief, 'tis not amiss,
To keep us waking, I remember this.
Jupiter, on some business, once sent down
Pleasure unto the world, that she might crown
Mortals with her bright beams; but her long stay
Exceeding far the limit of her day,—
Such feasts and gifts were number'd to present her,
That she forgot heaven and the god that sent her,—
He calls her thence in thunder: at whose lure
She spreads her wings, and to return more pure,
Leaves her eye-seeded robe wherein she's suited,
Fearing that mortal breath had it polluted.
Sorrow, that long had liv'd in banishment,
Tugg'd at the oar in galleys, and had spent
Both money and herself in court-delays,
And sadly number'd many of her days
By a prison-calendar, though once she bragg'd
She had been in great men's bosoms, now all ragg'd,
Crawl'd with a tortoise pace, or somewhat slower,
Nor found she any that desir'd to know her,
Till by good chance, ill hap for us, she found
Where Pleasure laid her garment: from the ground
She takes it, dons it; and, to add a grace
To the deformity of her wrinkled face,

---

* laurels] The old ed. "taunts."

An old court-lady, out of mere compassion,
Now paints it o'er, or puts it into fashion.
When straight from country, city, and from court,
Both without wit or number, there resort
Many to this impostor: all adore
Her haggish false-hood; usurers from their store
Supply her, and are cozen'd; citizens buy
Her forgèd titles; riot and ruin fly,
Spreading their poison universally.
Nor are the bosoms of great statesmen free
From her intelligence, who lets them see
Themselves and fortunes in false pérspectives;
Some landed heirs consort her with their wives,
Who, being a bawd, corrupts their all-spent oaths;
They have entertain'd the devil in Pleasure's
    clothes.
And since this cursèd mask, which, to our cost,
Lasts day and night, we have entirely lost
Pleasure, who from heaven wills us be advis'd
That our false Pleasure is but Care disguis'd.
Thus is our hope made frustrate, O sad ruth!
Death lay in ambush for his glorious youth;
And, finding him prepar'd, was sternly bent
To change his love into fell ravishment.
O cruel tyrant, how canst thou repair
This ruin, though hereafter thou shouldst spare
All mankind, break thy dart and ebon spade!
Thou canst not cure this wound which thou
    hast made.
Now view his death-bed, and from thence let's meet,
In his example, our own winding-sheet.
There his humility, setting apart
All titles, did retire into his heart.
O blessèd solitariness, that brings
The best content to mean men and to kings!
Manna there falls* from heaven: the dove there flies
With olive to the ark, a sacrifice
Of God's appeasement; ravens in their beaks
Bring food from heaven: God's preservation
    speaks
Comfort to Daniel in the lions' den;
Where contemplation loads us, happy men,
To see God face to face: and such sweet peace
Did he enjoy amongst the various preace †
Of weeping visitants, it seem'd he lay
As kings at revels sit, wish'd the crowd away,

The tedious sports done, and himself asleep;
And in such joy did all his senses steep,
As great accountants, troubled much in mind,
When they hear news of their quietus sign'd.
Never found prayers, since they convers'd with
    death,
A sweeter air to fly in than his breath: *
They left in's eyes nothing but glory shining;
And though that sickness with her over-pining
Look ghastly, yet in him it did not so;
He knew the place to which he was to go
Had larger titles, more triumphant wreaths
To instate him with; and forth his soul he
    breathes,
Without a sigh, fixing his constant eye
Upon his triumph, immortality.
He was rain'd down to us out of heaven, and
    drew
Life to the spring; yet, like a little dew,
Quickly drawn thence: so many times miscarries
A crystal glass, whilst that the workman varies
The shape i'the furnace, fix'd too much upon
The curiousness of the proportion,
Yet breaks it ere't be finish'd, and yet then
Moulds it anew, and blows it up agen,
Exceeds his workmanship, and sends it thence
To kiss the hand and lip of some great prince;
Or like a dial, broke in wheel or screw,
That's ta'en in pieces to be made go true:
So to eternity he now shall stand,
New-form'd and gloried by the all-working hand.
Slander, which hath a large and spacious tongue,
Far bigger than her mouth, to publish wrong,
And yet doth utter't with so ill a grace,
Whilst she's a-speaking no man sees her face;
That like dogs lick foul ulcers, not to draw
Infection from them, but to keep them raw;
Though she oft scrape up earth from good men's
    graves,
And waste it in the standishes of slaves,
To throw upon their ink, shall never dare
To approach his tomb: be she confin'd † as far
From his sweet reliques as is heaven from hell!
Not witchcraft shall instruct her how to spell
That barbarous language which shall sound him
    ill.
Fame's lips shall bleed, yet ne'er her trumpet fill
With breath enough; but not in such sick air
As make waste elogies to his tomb repair,

---

* there falls] The old ed. "their fates;" which I should
have supposed to be a misprint for "their fare," if "food
from heaven" had not followed in the sentence. As to
"fates" of the old copy,—the compositor seems here to
have mistaken t for t, as he did previously (see note p. 374)
in the word "laurels."

† preace] The old ed. has "presse": but Webster doubtless wrote "preace," a form of the word common in his
day.

* A sweeter air to fly in than his breath] So in The Devil's
Law-case:

        "It could never have got
    A sweeter air to fly in than your breath."
            See p. 109 and note there.

† confin'd] See note ‡, p. 179.

With scraps of commendation more base
Than are the rags they are writ on. O disgrace
To nobler poesy ! this brings to light,
Not that they can, but that they cannot write.
Better they had ne'er troubled his sweet trance ;
So silence should have hid their ignorance ;
For he's a reverend subject to be penn'd
Only by his sweet Homer and my friend.*
Most savage nations should his death deplore,
Wishing he had set his foot upon their shore,
Only to have made them civil. This black night
Hath fall'n upon's by † nature's oversight;
Or while the fatal sister sought to twine
His thread and keep it even, she drew it so fine
It burst. O all-compos'd of excellent parts,
Young, grave Mecœnas of the noble arts,
Whose beams shall break forth from thy hollow
          tomb,
Stain the time past, and light the time to come !‡
O thou that in thy own praise still wert mute,
Resembling trees, the more they are ta'en with
          fruit,
The more they strive and bow to kiss the ground!
Thou that in quest of man hast truly found,
That while men rotten vapours do pursue,
They could not be thy friends and flatterers too;
That, despite all injustice, wouldst have prov'd
So just a steward for this land, and lov'd
Right for its own sake,—now, O woe the while,
Fleet'st§ dead in tears, like to a moving isle!
Time was when churches in the land were thought
Rich jewel-houses; and this age hath bought
That time again : think not I feign; go view
Henry the Seventh's Chapel, and you'll find it
          true :
The dust of a rich diamond's there inshrin'd ;
To buy which thence would beggar the West-Inde.
What a dark night-piece of tempestuous weather
Have the enragèd clouds summon'd together!

As if our loftiest palaces should grow
To ruin, since such highness fell so low;
And angry Neptune makes his palace groan,
That the deaf rocks may echo the land's moan.
Even senseless things seem to have lost their
          pride,
And look like that dead month wherein he died:
To clear which, soon arise that glorious day *
Which, in her sacred union, shall display
Infinite blessings, that we all may see
The like to that of Virgil's golden tree,
A branch of which being slipt, there freshly grew
Another that did boast like form and hue.
And for these worthless lines, let it be said,
I hasted till I had this tribute paid
Unto his grave : so let the speed excuse
The zealous error of my passionate Muse.
Yet, though his praise here bear so short a wing,
Thames hath more swans that will his praises sing
In sweeter tunes, be-pluming his sad hearse
And his three feathers, while men live or verse.
And by these signs of love let great men know,
That sweet and generous favour they bestow
Upon the Muses never can be lost ;
For they shall live by them, when all the cost
Of gilded monuments shall fall to dust :
They grave in metal that sustains no rust;
Their wood yields honey and industrious bees,
Kills spiders and their webs, like Irish trees.†
A poet's pen, like a bright sceptre, sways
And keeps in awe dead men's dispraise or praise.
Thus took he acquittance of all worldly strife :
The evening shows the day, and death crowns life.

My impresa to your lordship, A swan flying to
a laurel for shelter, the mot,‡ *Amor est mihi causa.*

---

* *his sweet Homer and my friend*] i. e. Chapman, who
dedicated his translation of Homer to Prince Henry.
† *by*] The old copy "*be.*"
‡ *Stain the time past, and light the time to come*] So in
The Duchess of Malfi ;
   "She *stains the time past, lights the time to come.*"
                                        See p. 61.
§ *Fleet'st*] i. e. Floatest.

* *To clear which, soon, &c.*] An allusion to the marriage
of the Princess Elizabeth to the Elector Palatine, which
took place in February, 1613.
† *Irish trees*] See note *, p. 16.—In Shirley's *St. Patrick
for Ireland* (*Works* iv. 441), the saint, on banishing the
serpents, &c., from that island, says ;
   "The very earth and *wood* shall have this blessing
   (Above what other Christian nations boast),
   Although transported where these serpents live
   And multiply, *one touch shall soon destroy them.*"
‡ *mot*] i. e. motto.

TO MY KIND FRIEND, MASTER ANTHONY MUNDAY.*

THE sighs of ladies, and the spleen of knights,
  Tho force of magic, and the map of fate,
Strange pigmy-singleness in giant fights,
  Thy true translation swootly doth relate:
Nor for the fiction is the work less fine;
Fables have pith and moral discipline.

Now Palmerin in his own language sings,
  That, till thy study, mask'd in unkuown fashion,
Liko a fantastic Briton; and hence springs
  The map of his fair life to his own nation:
Translation is a traffic of high price;
It brings all learning in one paradise.

ODE.†

TRIUMPHS wore wont with sweat and blood be
    crown'd:
        To every brow
        They did allow
The living laurer,‡ which begirted round
Their rusty helmets, and had power to make
The soldier smile while mortal wound did ache.

But our more civil passages of state
        (Like happy feast
        Of inur'd rest,
Which bells and woundless cannons did relate)
Stand high in joy, since warlike triumphs bring
Remembrance of our former sorrowing.

The memory of theso should quickly fade,
        (For pleasure's stream
        Is like a dream,
Passant and fleet as is a shade),
Unless thyself, which these fair models bred,
Had given them a now life when they wore dead.

Take, then, good countryman and friend, that
        Which folly lends,   [merit,
        Not judgment sends,
To foreign shores for strangers to inherit:
Porfection must be bold with front upright,
Though Envy gnash her teeth whilst she would
    bite.

JOH. WEBSTER.

---

* To my kind friend, &c.] Profixed to the Third Part of Munday's translation of Palmerin of England, 1602, 4to.
† Ode] Profixed to The Arch's of Trivmph, Erected in honour of the high and mighty prince James, the First of that name King of England, and the Sixt of Scotland, at his Maiesties entrance and passage through his Honorable Citty and Chamber of London, upon the 15th Day of March, 1603. Invented and published by Stephen Harrison Joyner and Architect, and graven by William Kip. 1604, folio.
‡ laurer] Fr. So Chaucer in The Marchantes Tale:

    "As laurer thurgh the yere is for to sene."

TO HIS BELOVED FRIEND, MASTER THOMAS HEYWOOD.*

Sume superbiam quæsitam meritis.†

I CANNOT, though you write in your own cause,
　Say you deal partially, but must confess
(What most men will) you merit due applause ;
　So worthily your work becomes the press.

And well our actors may approve your pains,
　For you give them authority to play,
Even whilst the hottest plague of envy reigns ;
　Nor for this warrant shall they dearly pay.

What a full state of poets have you cited
　To judge your cause ! and to our equal view
Fair monumental theatres recited,
　Whose ruins had been ruin'd but for you !

Such men who can in tune both rail and sing,
　Shall, viewing this, either confess 'tis good,
Or let their ignorance condemn the spring,
　Because 'tis merry and renews our blood.

Be therefore your own judgment your defence,
　Which shall approve you better than my praise ;
Whilst I, in right of sacred innocence,
　Durst o'er each gilded tomb this known truth
　　raise,—
Who dead would not be acted by their will,
It seems such men have acted their lives ill.

　　　　　By your friend,
　　　　　　JOHN WEBSTER.

TO HIS INDUSTRIOUS FRIEND, MASTER HENRY COCKERAM.‡

To over-praise thy book in a smooth line,
(If any error's in't,) would make it mine :
Only, while words for payment pass at court,
And whilst loud talk and wrangling make resort,

I' the term, to Westminster, I do not dread
Thy leaves shall scape the scombri, and be read ;
And I will add this as thy friend, no poet,—
Thou hast toil'd to purpose, and the event will
　show it.

　　　　　JOHN WEBSTER.

---

* *To his beloved friend, &c.*] Prefixed to Heywood's
Apology for Actors, 1612.
† *Sume, &c.*] Horace.—*Carm.* iii. 30.

‡ *To his industrious friend, &c.*] Prefixed to *The English
Dictionarie, or, an Interpreter of hard English words,* by
H. C., Gent. 1623.

INDEX TO THE NOTES.

THE END.

BRADBURY, AGNEW, & CO., PRINTERS, WHITEFRIARS.

www.ingramcontent.com/pod-product-compliance
Lightning Source LLC
Chambersburg PA
CBHW030821110726
47900CB00006B/1692